P9-CMW-013

CALL THE DARKNESS LIGHT

Also by Nancy Zaroulis

THE POE PAPERS

CALL THE DARKNESS LIGHT

Nancy Zaroulis

DOUBLEDAY & COMPANY, INC.
GARDEN CITY, NEW YORK
1979

ACKNOWLEDGMENTS

Many people responded generously when I called on them for help in researching this book.

Therefore, my grateful thanks to Sally Alcorn, Carole A. Bolan, Allen Gerson, Ralf Hoehn, Donald Mattheisen, Frederick Montague, Anne Panas, and Juliet Sanger;

to the staff of the Adams Library, Chelmsford, and particularly to Joan Allard, Shirley Fletcher, Susan Schleigh Foote, Linda Robinson, and Lillian Storey;

to Martha Mayo, Special Collections Librarian, University of Lowell;

to the staff of the Lowell City Library;

to Michael Kamins and Susan Stromei of the International Museum of Photography, Rochester;

to the staff of the Merrimack Valley Textile Museum, and particularly to Helena Wright;

to the staff of the Fruitlands Museum, Harvard, Massachusetts, and particularly to Edee Ryanen;

to Lewis Karabatsos, Director of the Lowell Museum, for favors large and small;

to Edward Larter, for explaining nineteenth-century looms and spindles;

to Elmer Rynne, for expounding on Lowell's Irish;

to Mary and Peter Blewett, Department of History, University of Lowell, for reading the manuscript;

and to Arthur L. Eno, Jr., who read the manuscript; who put his extensive Lowell collection at my disposal; whose knowledge of Lowell's history is unsurpassed; whose kindness in sharing it with me has never failed; and whose enthusiasm and encouragement sustained me through the writing of this book.

Library of Congress Catalog Card Number 78-74714

ISBN: 0-385-15219-1

PRINTED IN THE UNITED STATES OF AMERICA

For Alexandra and Katherine

Every web which falls from these restless looms has a history more or less connected with sin and suffering, beginning with slavery and ending with over-work and premature death.

John Greenleaf Whittier
"The City of a Day"
in *A Stranger in Lowell*

I think that, generally speaking, the manufacturing aristocracy which we see rising before our eyes is one of the hardest that have appeared on earth.

Alexis de Tocqueville
Democracy in America

Americans, you have Jesuits among you, and Jesuits are not idle. The wolf does not come as a wolf, but as one of the fold. Watch them. They will yet give you trouble.

"An American"
[Samuel F. B. Morse]
Imminent Dangers to the Free Institutions of the United States through Foreign Immigration . . .

I was given to understand that whatever was unintelligible would be certainly transcendental.

Charles Dickens
American Notes for General Circulation

Art is the Handmaid of Human Good

Lowell City Motto

All our civilization resides in these [mechanic] arts.

Edward Everett, 1837

The Church is a dumb dog, that can not bark, sleeping, lying down, loving to slumber. It is a church without woman, believing in a male and jealous God, and rejoicing in a boundless, endless hell!

Theodore Parker
"The Public Function of Woman"
Address given at the Music Hall,
Boston, March 1853

The emergence of urban industrialism in America begins with Francis Cabot Lowell.

Thomas Bender
Toward an Urban Vision, 1975

There is in this city an Association called the Female Labor Reform Association, having for its professed object, the amelioration of the condition of the operative . . . we will soon show these *drivelling* cotton lords, this mushroom aristocracy of New England, who so arrogantly aspire to lord it over God's heritage, that our rights cannot be trampled upon with impunity; that we WILL not longer submit to that arbitrary power which has for the last ten years been so abundantly exercised over us.

Sarah Bagley
Factory Tract #1, October 1845
Some of the Beauties of
our Factory System—
Otherwise, Lowell Slavery

PART I

1

There was a lighted candle in the attic room, and a pewter pap-boat half filled with gruel. Its dull gray finish reflected the flame which died and came to life again as the draught blew through the ill-joined boards around the window.

The solitary watcher kept her vigil in a rush-bottomed chair beside the narrow bed. As the night drew on, her head nodded, her eyes drooped shut. She dozed, oblivious to the lash of the autumn gale against the house. And yet some part of her remained alert, for the man lying before her was her father, and she his only kin. She must try to stay awake and hold off Death, who hovered just there, shuffling and stinking in the corner, waiting to claim his own.

She shivered and came to. The room was very cold. She was alarmed to see how low the candle had burned: had she slept so long? She reached out and put her small work-worn hand on her father's. He was colder than she. She came out of her chair, stiff and awkward, and felt for his heart. Nothing: Death had come and gone.

Now she was alone in the world.

2

The villagers buried him in the cemetery next to their plain white meeting house. They stood silent and respectful in the cold bright day as the Reverend Mr. Greene committed the departed soul to God; a few of them—women, mostly—glanced at the pale girl-child standing apart, staring at the pine coffin sunk in the newly dug grave. A strand of her curly brown hair had blown loose, whipping across her thin face. She seemed not to notice. She stood immobile, not joining in the prayer. They would have comforted her, for they were kindly people well acquainted with Death. But they were shy of her; they did not know her well.

She was not one of them. She and her father had arrived in late August, near harvest time, wandering down the mountain to this small settlement like two lost lambs. And so, in a sense, they were.

The Reverend Isaac Palfrey had been a man of God: a man whose way to the next world was paved with sermons and prayers delivered in this; a man who paid no heed to the conditions of life on earth, so intent was he upon depicting the splendors of Heaven, the terrifying particulars of Hell; a man who ate when he was given food, who starved when he was denied it, and hardly knew the difference; who gratefully accepted shelter when given a roof, but did not care if that roof covered house or stable; a man, in short, who attended to the Lord's business while neglecting his own. His daughter shared his life. She grew; she learned her letters and numbers in snatches at schools in the towns and villages through which they passed; for the sake of her mother's memory she cared for her father as best she could. She helped in the kitchen to earn their keep in houses where they stayed; she mended their clothing, and washed them from time to time; she learned—very young—to know the moment in each place when they had outstayed their welcome and so must move on, eternal wanderers in the service of the Reverend's endless mission. They were never close, the father and daughter, for the Reverend Palfrey was close only to God; but he was all she had, and so, when he died, she wept for a little time. Still, it was her mother whom she mourned.

She stood now beside the open grave and watched the sexton shovel heavy clumps of earth upon the coffin. The wind blew faded leaves in thick swirling patterns across the rows of slate and granite tombstones. A month ago, the trees had been brilliant red and gold: God's yearly gift before the long white winter. She was glad that her father had lived to see the autumn color one last time. She said a small, private prayer for him then, and as she prayed she envisioned him entering the gates of Heaven. She was certain that he would be warmly welcomed by the Lord.

3

The brief service done, the villagers straggled home. There would be no funeral feast at the Reverend Mr. Greene's. He and his wife had already extended hospitality far beyond the call of God or man. Like his parishioners he was a New Hampshireman, as hard as granite, as tough and unyielding as the tall oaks, the rock maples so laboriously cleared to make farms.

And yet, like them, he was not unkind; and he had a shrewd eye for a bargain, a canny knowledge of how always to see a way to profit. The child was small for her years—about fifteen, he thought—but she was quiet and dutiful and she had a certain cleverness. She could perhaps be useful about the house; she could at least help with the spinning. (The Reverend Mr. Greene and his wife had seven children; there were never enough clothing, it seemed.) And in the spring—who could tell? Perhaps, he thought, someone else would want her.

"Do not grieve, Sabra," he said. It was an order, not a consolation. "Your father was a mighty worker for the Lord. He is with the Lord now, safe in His bosom. Do not weep for him."

In fact Sabra's eyes were quite dry. She sat in the chilly parlor and suffered the unfriendly gaze of her hostess. No doubt they disapproved her lack of visible grief. She felt no grief: only a dull, empty place in a corner of her mind. He was dead. For her, he had hardly been alive. She had followed him on his God-inspired wanderings through the mountain villages, occasionally venturing as far south as Massachusetts, or west beyond Vermont to New York State, because she had had no choice. She had never known another life. Now, it seemed, she must find one—or make it.

She murmured an assent; she avoided their eyes. Already they had asked her to stay on, and because she did not know if they could force her to remain against her will she did not refuse their offer. But she would not stay; she knew what such a life was. She had seen other girls captive in households like this. Their lives were endless drudgery, unpaid domestic service in return for meals and a place to sleep, like as not under a leaking roof. All New England was overrun with surplus females as the young men continued to leave the rocky, thin-soiled farms which could hardly support the fathers, let alone withstand division among the sons. They went west, the young men, into the Western Reserve; the women were left behind, as barren as the landscape they inhabited.

She did not sleep in a bed that night; she sat in the same chair, in the same room where her father had died. She dozed, waiting for the dawn. In snatches of a dream she saw a female figure moving freely through the world. She could not see its face, but she knew that it was her own. When the first pale light showed at the window she took her small hair trunk and crept downstairs. Stopping at the pantry, she wrapped a loaf of bread and a piece of cheese in her kerchief; quietly she unlatched the door and walked out of the house.

Mist filled the valley so that she could not see the end of the narrow street which bisected the village. The encircling mountains, too, were shrouded. But she knew these peaks and valleys, these isolated settlements: she had walked this country all her life. There were bears and wolves in the forests, and poisonous snakes underfoot, but she was not afraid. There were spirits who stalked the unwary traveler: the ghosts of Indians, of early settlers who died battling over the land; there were the tales of old women living in remote hamlets, who warned of mysterious vanishings, of certain paths and streams, certain hills and lowlands haunted by the restless souls who once had lived there. She feared none of these. Without hesitation she walked out of the village, up the mountain road past the scattered farms. The mist cleared rapidly. When she reached the top she paused to gaze at the panorama spread below: a valley, a few more houses, another mountain and yet another, taller, wilder, visible now in the first light of the sun.

She picked up her trunk and began to walk again.

4

"Please, sir, how many miles to Lowell?"

Perhaps it was the unaccustomed "sir," or perhaps it was the sight of her pale, thin face and her rain-soaked shawl; at any rate, the peddler pulled up his horse and looked down at her from his seat in his empty wagon. His hand relaxed its grip on his pistol. She was not, after all, a brigand come to rob him. His money belt hugged his middle as he took a deep breath and felt its comforting weight.

They stood on the crest of a hill in the darkening afternoon. Beyond more hills, to the south, lay Nashua; beyond that, Massachusetts. It was late October: time to come down from a summer's travels in the north country. A peddler and his wagon did not belong in the mountains when the snows came.

"Fifty. Fifty-five."

It seemed the saddest news she had ever heard. She wiped a droplet from her cheek, but whether it was rain or tears he could not tell.

"Thank you."

She bent to pick up her small trunk and without a further glance at him began to walk. It was a far way to go. Too far—

"Wait!"

He clucked at his horse. In a moment he was at her side.

"Get in. You can take the stage at Amoskeag."

She hesitated. He would not have harmed her, but she did not know that. Besides: "I have no money for the stage."

Despite her woeful appearance her voice was clear and sweet, not like the jarring twang of so many upcountry Yankees. Her eyes—he could not tell their color—were large, and her features well-formed, if a trifle small. She was a familiar type; he had sold thimbles and buttons, tinware and brooms and snuff to hundreds of her sisters over the years, improving his English and his fortune at the same time.

"Get in anyway." He had had a profitable summer; he could afford to offer a kindness. Besides, if it had been his sister— His mouth, hidden in his thick black beard, twisted at the sudden memory. "In back. Plenty of room."

The girl hesitated a moment longer and then obeyed. God helps those . . . but this man was not God, he was a Jew peddler. Sent by God? Perhaps. She was too exhausted to care. She climbed up; on the floor of the wagon she found a neatly folded tarpaulin. She pulled it over her sodden skirts. The peddler clucked to his horse; slowly they made their way down along the muddy road.

For three days they traveled south, hardly speaking, the girl riding in the wagon like the peddler's goods. At night he rigged the tarpaulin into a small tent over the body of the wagon and they shared its shelter, such as it was, side by side. After the first night, when she understood that he would not harm her in whatever way that men did (she was not sure exactly how), she came to trust him enough to smile at him and tell him her name. She told him, too, that she was eighteen (she looked younger, he thought, not more than sixteen) and that she came from Darby, some miles north.

He neither believed nor disbelieved her; he accepted the information merely as evidence of friendship, however temporary. That she was running away was obvious; from what, she did not say. If she had committed a crime, and if one constable or another accused him of helping her to escape, he would simply tell the truth. He was well-known; he did not fear the authorities here as he had in Frankfurt.

He in turn introduced himself as Jacob Goldschmidt (his real name) and laughed when she was pert enough to ask his age, which, as he told her, was thirty-one. And so they formed an easy bond although they spoke so little, each absorbed in private thought.

Late in the afternoon of the third day the peddler stopped on a rise overlooking a wide river. Beyond it, she saw a red-brick town; the far bank was lined with long, many-storied brick buildings larger than any buildings she had ever seen. A train whistle wailed through the sparkling air; a puff of white steam showed its route. A faint sound trembled like a swarm of countless bees. Sunlight glinted on white belfries; church spires rose like stalagmites. Here and there a smokestack spewed a black stain upon the clear blue sky. The scene enchanted her. No mountain village had ever looked so new to her, so fresh from the hand of the Creator. It seemed a fairy-tale town—a glistening toy town thrown down beside the river by some happy giant of a child-god.

The peddler, who had been there many times, was less enthralled. He pointed to the road ahead of them; it led to a bridge which crossed the river just below a high broad waterfall.

"I'll take you across. What will you do then?"

"I have a letter." She did not look at him; her eyes clung to the vision before her.

"To someone who can help you?"

"Yes."

"Good."

He flicked the reins and the horse moved on. The faint, trembling sound grew louder. In God's good time it would grow to cacophony. It would obliterate the memory of all the long, slow, peaceful time before: the long years, nearly two hundred years, when people in that land lived in time with the seasons, the slow passing of winter sleep to spring planting, summer growth to autumn harvest and so once more to winter. No one, hearing it, would ever be tranquil again. It was the sound of the onrushing future: the new age.

5

The horse balked at the bridge; she showed the whites of her eyes and pulled her lips back over her teeth. Poor dumb creature, thought Sabra. How could they explain to her? She herself was not afraid at all. She had her letter, and her life ahead of her; she had made her escape to the new town, and so she knew nothing of fear. She was excited, she was happy, she urged the horse to go on as Goldschmidt climbed down and took the reins and led her slowly onto the flimsy walkway. It had been an autumn of heavy, relentless rain, and so now the river ran as high as it did in spring flood. Spray from the Falls wet them; the boards trembled under them; the water surged and thundered below as if it would tear the bridge from its foundations and send them all tumbling down to the sea.

When they were half across, Sabra turned to look at what they had left behind. She saw the encircling hills, and the road threading its way north. She saw the orange-red sun hanging low, and the thin red line of clouds above it; and the clear pale sky arching over the river valley, and the evening star bright to be wished on. And so she made her wish, and she turned her face away from the past, from the forests and farms, the quiet, secluded old north country; she looked ahead to the rumble and bustle of the new.

They came across and into the streets of the town. Goldschmidt climbed back into the wagon, while the horse, recovered from her fright, walked steadily on.

At the end of the bridge they passed a large tavern built of stone, and a few houses along the road which ran by the river; then they turned down another street and soon they came to the center of things. They passed shops and houses and more and more shops—everything in the world was for sale here, thought Sabra. She had never seen the like, not in all her travels upcountry, for she and her father had gone by the small roads, and the small villages, and not once a year had they come to anything near a good-sized town. But here was everything all around: milliners' shops, and tobacconists', and apothecaries and dry goods and shoes, all with their signs and gold lettering: Seth E. Clapp, Draper & Tailor; Albert F. Dyer, Looking Glass & Picture Frames; Francis B. Cobb, Boots & Shoes; Hutchinson's Umbrellas, Musical Instruments & Trunks; Miss Harriet Sanborn, Millinery & Dressmaking.

It was fast growing dark, and soon lights flared up in all the windows. She saw solitary clerks but no customers, and she wondered why they kept open so late when there were so few to buy. Goldschmidt explained: "They are waiting for the closing bell. Then they'll do business enough."

They moved slowly, caught in thick traffic, carriages and carts and wagons all together, all fighting to get through. She did not mind: she wanted to go slowly, she wanted to look and look about her to see it all, she thought that she could never see enough of all this newness.

And then she saw a stocky, determined-looking man dressed all in black striding fast along the boardwalk under the shop awnings. Someone hailed him, and he cheerfully replied—but in a language whose very sounds were unlike anything she had ever heard: guttural, half-articulated, strangely elided sounds, carrying with them a sense of foreign places, wild, uncivilized places.

Goldschmidt spoke to her just then, and when he saw where she was staring, he laughed. She knew that she must look silly, all dumbfounded.

"Like a zoo, here," he said. "You'll see everything here. Even a papist priest."

She felt her heart twist inside her. She thought that after all she might have done a wrong to come here. The man walked so close beside them that for all the noise she could have spoken his name if she had known it and surely he would have heard. But she would have been afraid; she never would have done it. Were there so many papists here that they needed a priest?

She laughed then, too. But still she watched the priest out of sight around the corner, and was glad to see him gone. Rome was the great whore, her father had said. Evil and wicked and corrupt, the mother of harlots.

But she laughed, and she put her fear away inside her, and she went on looking. The noise all this time had got louder and louder, not just the noise of the wheels and horses' hooves on the hard-packed dirt of the street, but the other noise that they had heard first across the river, like the sound of swarming, humming insects.

Down side streets they could see the enormous red brick factory buildings. Beside them, an ordinary house would have been a toy house, a baby-house. The sight of them frightened her. Was she to go there? Every window was alight. They might have been palaces—huge castles. Their belfries might have been spires or turrets. The walls surrounding them might have marked the line of moats—canals, here. And in one of those buildings was a man who ruled.

What would he think of her? She wondered how she must look after her journey. She was suddenly filled with doubt. What if she looked so poor that he wouldn't think her worthy of help? She put up her hands to smooth her hair; she tied her shawl more neatly around her shoulders. She was glad that she did not have a glass to see herself.

Goldschmidt smiled at her when he saw what she did. "Commonwealth Corporation, is it?"

"Yes."

"Just up ahead."

They turned a corner by a hotel and headed down one of the streets toward the river. Along one side of it was a row of connected brick houses, all alike. Along the other ran a tree-lined canal. And at the end, like a fortress, stood the mill buildings. They should have had a through way to the factory, but then, too late, they saw that the street was blocked. A crowd of people—women—filled the way from side to side and all down to the factory gate. And now they were trapped, for others had pulled up behind and they could not turn around.

The horse reared up, just then, to avoid a small boy who ran across in front, and as she reared another boy threw a stone which hit her flank. She thrashed and plunged, and Goldschmidt scrambled quickly down again to hold her fast. The wagon swayed and tipped; Sabra heard her trunk in the back thumping from side to side, but she could not turn to see if it had fallen out, she could not look away from what was before them.

Suddenly a woman jumped up onto a higher place—a stump, perhaps, or a crate—so that she was well above the heads of the crowd. Someone handed her a torch. In the gathering darkness she made a little island of flaring light. Sabra had heard talk of Amazons once or twice: unnatural, strong-minded females not content to stay in woman's sphere. This woman was one, she supposed. She was a big, raw-boned woman—a country-looking woman, and not very old: about twenty. She held the torch high, showing her strength. Its light spread to touch all the faces around her; it even reached Sabra and Goldschmidt beyond. She looked all over the crowd; then she began.

"Sisters! Will we let the Corporation cut us down?"

A few voices answered her: "No!"

"Will we let them cheat us?"

"No!" Many more.

"Will we go back until they restore our full wages?"

"NO!" They were in full cry now. She had whipped them up to it.

O God, thought Sabra, take me away. She was frightened—horrified. What had she come to—this place of papist priests, where women jumped up and yelled at crowds? She had seen women at camp meetings who in the ecstasy of their communion with the Lord leaped up and cried out for all to hear. But never anyplace else. A woman! She knew that her father would have wept to see it.

In the flickering light of the torch the woman's face looked like an imp's—a demon's face in Hell. Her eyes flashed, her teeth glistened, her features strained; saliva dribbled down her chin as she spat out her rage.

"Sisters!" she cried. "We have rights of our own, God-given, which transcend the paltry laws of men!"

A man stood at the side of the wagon, trapped as they were trapped, appalled as they were appalled at the spectacle before them. Goldschmidt, looking around for a way to escape, caught his eye.

"Horsewhip 'er," muttered the man. He was very angry. "Give 'em a dollar o' their own, they spit in yer face. A good whippin's what that un needs." He grinned; he did not seem to notice Sabra. "Or somethin' more, if yew follow."

The crowd had gone very quiet. Only a few small boys darted in and out, throwing rocks, catcalling. Their elders shushed them. Everyone waited to hear. The crowd of women thronging in the street, listening to the Amazon, had hard faces, tired, work-worn faces; they looked expectantly to the speaker, as if she held some secret which they needed to know.

"Sisters! Will we turn out?"

"Yes!"

"Screamin' whore," muttered the man. "Never seed the like. Let 'em get away from home, this is what happens."

There was a movement of the crowd behind, just then, and for a moment Sabra thought that they would surge ahead and carry them all down to the factory gate and crush them against the high wall. But then she saw that the throng had moved to give way to new arrivals: three big men holding truncheons high above their heads. They shouted orders to everyone to disperse. Their faces were hard and mean—harder even than the women's—and yet they were grinning as they plowed through, hitting right and left with their big sticks, making straight for the Amazon. Eager, they looked, and enjoying themselves.

"There," said the man beside them. He looked around, pleased as the women began to move away under the assault, the presence of authority. "That's Eben Crummet. He'll settle her, soon enough. He's a hard man, and a fair enough man for a constable. But he and his men don't like trouble." He nodded at Goldschmidt. "Them women'll think twice before they try a trick like this ever again."

The men had reached the speaker now. Roughly they put their hands up to her. One of them grabbed for her torch but she kept it away from him and tried to beat him on the head with it, but then another one got it from her. They began to laugh. Then they had her; they pulled her down hard. Sabra saw one man's hand grabbing her hair. They began to drag her away. Sabra was alarmed at what they might do to her; she knew that she would have screamed had anyone hurt her so. But the Amazon didn't. Not a single cry. Sabra felt a small glow of admiration for her courage. Not that she approved of women haranguing a crowd—but still, those men were hurting her, they were dragging her away, and she just went limp and gave them no satisfaction. Good for you, thought Sabra, admiring despite her disapproval. She saw their heads high above the crowd as they went. No one tried to stop them; no one tried to help the Amazon. Such friends as you have, sister, are no friends at all, she thought.

The crowd dispersed. Goldschmidt turned to her. She realized that she must have looked very frightened, for he left the horse and came back to stand beside her. He looked up at her; he put his hand on her arm. He was a sharp man, but kind.

"All right, Sabra?"

"Yes," she said. Her voice was unsteady, but she was right enough.

"You still want to stay here? I'll take you to Boston if you like."

"No. Here is fine."

"All right. Now we'll find him."

Their companion had stayed by; now he perked up his ears. "Lookin' for someone, are you?"

"Yes." Goldschmidt told him the name. Sabra had never seen a man's face change so quick as that man's did then. He looked back and forth from Goldschmidt to Sabra as if to make sure he had heard correctly.

"You know him?" he said.

"She has a letter."

"Do she? And you're just deliverin' her, y' might say?"

"I want to make sure—"

"Oh, I'll make sure, mister. Just you go along. You stayin' at th' American House? You got to get in there b'fore six, they fill up fast with the stages. He's just down there, see—" He gestured toward the huge complex blocking the far end of the street. "I know the watch. He don't let just anyone in, but if I tell him she's got a letter—c'mon, missy."

Sabra could see then the look of relief on Goldschmidt's face. She was mortified because she had caused him so much trouble and delay. She could see that he was glad to be rid of her, that he had begun to be sorry he had helped her, now that she was causing him to be late and miss his supper. She did not blame him. She was hungry herself. Before he could say yes or no she scrambled down. She ran around to the back of the wagon to pull out her trunk; she held out her hand to him as he came to help her. "Thank you," she said; no more.

"Good luck," he said, and no more either.

And then she had to hurry to keep up with the other one and so she couldn't turn to wave—didn't want to; then wanted to, and it was too late —and then she was trotting along, lugging her little trunk, and the street was dark and empty now, and they were coming to it.

The gates were closed tight. The man pulled a bell-rope; someone called from within.

"Who?"

"Is that you, Miller? Sam Fiske here."

The wicket slid open, a man peered out. "Fiske! Thought you was one o' them."

"Not likely, lad. Here's a lady to see his nibs."

The guard shook his head. "Can't."

"Is he there?"

"Course." A sudden grin. "But he's busy. Had a little excitement here."

"We saw it."

"He won't see no one. Come back tomorrow."

Be dutiful and obedient, her father had said. Always obey, never argue, never speak with impertinence. She could hear him saying it, even as she spoke up.

"I have a letter," she said.

The guard put out his hand. "I'll take it."

Obey. "No," she said. "I want to see him, please."

He hesitated; finally, grudgingly: "Come inside, then, and I'll see."

They heard the rasp of the bolt; the gate swung open. Her guide touched her arm. "If he asks how you found him, tell him it was Samuel Fiske who helped you. He'll know the name."

He stepped back, and she walked through into the racket of the mill yard. The heavy gate slammed shut behind her.

6

The Agent of the Commonwealth Mill—the General Manager, the Supreme Overlord, the Grand Panjandrum—stood in his office looking out through small-paned windows into the darkened courtyard of his domain. This office was a small room just inside the gate; it was adjoined by the counting-room, both of them dwarfed by the bulk of the mill buildings themselves which formed the largest part of the complex. These were, in fact, such very small rooms—one story, cramped—that the uninformed visitor might have supposed that they were accidental structures, roofed and walled into cubicles upon the discovery, say, that the builder had made mistaken calculations and had found himself with thirty feet extra of space, which he then used up as best he could so as not to look incompetent.

Not at all: the Agent's office and the counting-room were the very heart, the nerve center of this enormous enterprise. Into these rooms came the directives of the Corporation's officers in Boston; from these rooms were given the commands which made the operation run: store one thousand bales in the sheds and take the remainder to the carding rooms; call a loomfixer to Number Two; fire Dunster, she has been insolent to her overseer; check the order for indigo: the last shipment was impure. Ceaselessly, endlessly, the Agent of the Commonwealth Mill received his orders and transmitted new ones. He was at the very pinnacle of this huge complexity, and yet he had his superiors, too, and, like his hundreds of employees, he needed to keep up to the mark lest he himself be discharged. He was supreme only in Lowell; in Boston he was entirely dispensable.

Everyone admired him: he was an excessively admirable man. He was so accustomed to universal acclaim that he hardly noticed it, and yet, had it been withdrawn, he would have felt its absence very much. It was a kind of psychic corset which strengthened his nerve and stiffened his back and enabled him to withstand the pressures of his life.

He was well above six feet in height, and his long lean Yankee frame was clothed always in dark colors; a touch of white linen showed at his neck. He wore a dark gray surtout in winter, or sometimes a cloak; his high black beaver hat accentuated his height and made him seem endlessly, impossibly tall to his youngest child, and often to others as well. His face, like his body, was long and narrow; it was a face whose features were said by some to be handsome, but the prevailing fashion was for a more delicate, more romantic appearance, and so he did not quite fit the popular notion of masculine beauty. However, he was universally admired all the same; men did not succeed, by and large, by their looks. His hair was pale yellow, thick and straight, and that, too, was against the prevailing fashion, which called for darker tones. His eyes were gray in some lights, blue in others; his wide, thin mouth was generally settled into an expression of severe and pious duty, but he had the Yankee humor, after all, and so he could laugh with the best of them when something struck him funny.

Little did. He was an extremely serious, hard-working man, busy from dawn till long past dark, and he expected the same diligence from those around him—beneath him, rather, for no one in Lowell was his equal. And in all the business of production—so many bales in, so many yards out, so many hundreds of souls to be shepherded through the long and complicated process (and then to be shepherded after working hours as well, for not even so much as one operative could be allowed to lose her good name lest she soil the reputation of all the others; they needed to be constantly guarded, these women, against their natural tendencies toward flightiness and dissipation)—in all that business, then, there was not much to laugh at. Nothing to joke about, where stockholders' profits were concerned; nothing to take lightly, no chance to relax and smile, when Boston breathed constantly down one's neck, peered over one's shoulder, called one to account for the yearly profit. Profit! Dividends! A return of twelve—no, fourteen per cent! It was no wonder that this man, for all his grave and authoritative presence, had an occasional habit of gnawing the flesh inside his cheek and lip on the left side of his face. He did it unconsciously whenever anything made him anxious. And many things did, in both of the kingdoms which he ruled: the factory kingdom by the river, and the domestic, high on a hill overlooking it.

There were many cotton textile factories in Lowell, each with its resident Agent; but not one of them was equal to him. The social hierarchy in the new town was as rigid, as inviolate as that of mandarin China, the protocol equally as strict. He was the premier Agent because he Agented the oldest mill. The Commonwealth had been erected in 1822; from it had come the first piece of coarse cotton sheeting woven by the power of the Pawtucket Falls; from it now, sixteen years later, came thousands of yards of cotton cloth, coarse stuff, jeans and sheets and calico, to furnish the demands of the growing population, to clothe the tens of thousands settling into the West, to dress the millions of black slaves in the South who grew the raw cotton and picked and ginned and baled it. And so despite the fact that twenty-two other factories had come into being since the Commonwealth started up (all built by Irish gangs; all directed by—

owned by—stockholders in Boston), none of their Agents would ever be quite his equal. He was the grandest of them all, and you could see from the careful way in which he conducted himself that he knew it. The knowledge was both burden and satisfaction; he tired of his duties, his position, sometimes, but he could not have endured to be anonymous. Everyone knew him here, everyone acknowledged him, corporate hireling though he was. But the Corporation was far away; and in its absence, in its name, he reigned.

His subjects—his employees—were human beings like himself: Yankees all, native Americans, products of the upcountry villages and the coastal towns, whose Puritan ancestors, fleeing persecution, had no doubt slept peacefully in their graves to see the Congregationalist Orthodoxy in which their descendants continued. He himself attended the Episcopal Church, but no matter; he did it for reasons of business—of maintaining his position—and he remained a Congregationalist at heart. Those of his employees who wanted to keep in his good favor attended the Episcopal Church also.

This house of worship, St. Anne's, was the first church built in the city. It happened to be an Episcopal Church because Kirk Boott, the man whom the Corporations hired to oversee the building of the city, was a rabid Anglophile and, naturally, an Episcopalian. It was designed in the bastard Norman style of an English country church, and it was constructed of stone dug from the bed of the canal beside it. At first, when there were no other churches in the city, every operative was required to attend St. Anne's, no matter what her preferred denomination. Each was assessed pew rent of thirty-seven and a half cents a quarter, docked from her pay. Later, other less alien denominations formed congregations and built their own churches: Methodists, Baptists, Presbyterians, Universalists—and of course the Orthodox, the Congregationalists. Even the Catholics had a church, built on land donated by the Corporations. The presence of a priest, it seemed, had been the only way to keep the wild Gaelic laborers in line—and even with their priest and their church, they were likely to riot at any moment. But in the opinion of the several Agents, the Irish undoubtedly would have behaved much more badly without the steadying influence of their religion; and so, despite their unanimous distrust of the dictates of the Pope, the Corporations welcomed his minions and prayed for peace.

A small number of those who worked for the Agent were men: overseers, second overseers, carders, dyers. Most were women: weavers, spinners, dressers, folders. The men were docile enough, for they knew that if they worked sufficiently hard they could rise, through promotion, to as much as twenty dollars a week and an overseer's slot. Some of the women, however, were troublesome, and since they outnumbered the men so very greatly, they were much more difficult to manage. It was not the Agent's fault that their wages were cut from time to time: the stockholders must have their profits, through good times and bad. Nor was it his fault that the women were paid half and less of the men's wages, nor that the women could never aspire to twenty dollars a week or an overseer's job. He had not, after all, designed the steeply slanting social pyramid; he simply perched at its top, and looked down at those toiling beneath, and tried to keep order.

He stood now in his office and told himself grimly (he had the Puritan conscience) that he had signally failed to keep order this day. Two hundred out, at least! All the weavers from Number Three, most of the spinners from Numbers Three and Four, dressers from all the buildings. He had stood here, on this very spot, and watched them stream out at four o'clock and throng in the yard until he had given the signal, down the chain of command, to have the gates unlocked. They had marched out, then, and the gates had been locked again behind them. Ungrateful hussies! The cut in wages had been announced to them that morning; undoubtedly they had conspired the turnout during the noon recess. He thought about retribution: he knew their names because his overseers had given him lists. A check beside a name meant that the woman was an instigator; these would be dismissed and the names sent around to all other mills in Lowell and thence to all mills everywhere in New England. Those women would be blacklisted; they would never work again in a textile factory north of New-York. A line beside other names meant that the woman was on probation; she was a good enough worker to make her valuable, and not so dangerous or outspoken as the instigators. Those women would be warned by their respective overseers: no more trouble! The women whose names had neither checks nor lines would be allowed to return without prejudice tomorrow morning; they would suffer only the loss of half a day's pay. The knowledge of their bolder sisters' fate would be sufficient, if past experience was any guide, to keep them in line hereafter. The places made vacant by those dismissed would quickly be filled. The factory towns had an excellent reputation; there were always two or three women for each job.

He gazed out into the darkened mill yard. The tall buildings surrounding it were brightly illuminated; the steady rumble and thump of the machinery had become so much a part of his existence that he hardly noticed it. He thought of the yard as a quiet, peaceful place just then. Soon it would throng again with life as the closing bell rang and the operatives flocked back to their boarding houses, but just now it was empty. He stood at the window and looked out, waiting for Mr. Lyford, his subagent, to come back to him and report that those operatives who remained—the majority—were working as usual.

He saw a figure approaching from the gate: the watch. Followed by—yes—a woman. He was suddenly irritated. He did not want to see any of the women now. They had caused him enough trouble this day. A thought occurred to him: perhaps this one brought the white flag, so to speak. Perhaps she had come to plead for mercy for her sisters. His wide mouth settled into a hard line. No mercy could be allowed. They would become even more unruly if he took back the ringleaders.

The watch saw him through the unshuttered window. He knocked. The Agent bestirred himself and opened the door.

7

The watch had overstepped himself: he should have taken her first to the sub-agent. But on that night, when everything had gone awry, the normal routine had been disrupted also, and so she was allowed to see the Agent at once.

He seemed the tallest man she had ever seen, and his face as he looked down at her was very stern. The dreadful noise pounding down on her as she crossed the yard—thumping, clattering, a ceaseless, maddening din—had driven every thought out of her head; she felt witless, unable even to begin to explain herself. She stood tongue-tied before him, her trunk in one hand, her letter in the other. The watch mumbled something that she could not hear, and then he left them, closing the door behind him. She made a great effort.

"Mr. Bradshaw?"

He gave a sharp little nod, and so right away instead of trying to speak she gave her letter to him. He looked a little surprised, she thought, but he took it politely and broke the seal (the Reverend Greene's wax, and reluctant enough he'd been to let her use it). He began to read. He bent over near the lamp to make it out. She had written it in her best script, of course, since it was such an important letter; she had made this copy after she had taken down the draft as her father spoke it. It had been a long business; all one afternoon she had sat beside her father and wiped his face and spooned a little blackberry wine into his mouth and taken up the quill again to write a few words more. He had been very weak. She could see that he was preparing to die; he seemed happy, sick as he was, to be leaving this world and getting on to the next. He was sure—he told her this—he was sure that he would meet Our Savior. He had smiled a little when he said it. She had hated to drag him back, to ask him to think about her when it was the Lord who occupied his thoughts; but all the same, she wanted him to tell her what to do.

"God will care for you, Sabra," he had said. "Trust in the Lord and you will have no need of earthly help."

He had dozed, then, and she had said a prayer. But still she felt anxious, and so when after a while he came awake again she had asked him where she should go, what she should do.

"Someone will take you in," he had said.

She had not wanted to be taken in. But how would she do alone? Not very well, she thought, and so she had asked him again: did he know of anyone who could help her make her way, earn some kind of living for herself? She could not think what it might be; she was a clumsy seamstress, and she had not enough education even to teach dame school.

He could hardly talk. He shook and sweated with fever and he was very pale except for two bright red splotches on his cheeks. Bloody flux, he had, and he stank of it, and the sheets were all soiled although she had put on clean ones only that morning. The Reverend Mrs. Greene had been angry because she changed the linen every day, but she had not cared.

Finally he had told her to get pen and paper and she had had to run down and interrupt Mrs. Greene as she was getting supper and beg them of her. When she returned to her father he was asleep again, but then he came awake and he began to speak.

She had discovered then what many knew already: that it is on the deathbeds of others that we learn about our own lives. She had never forgotten her mother, for all she had been gone so long, but in the weeks just past, tending to her father's sickness, she had not thought of her as often as she had formerly. But now here she was all over again.

He dictated:

Josiah Bradshaw, Esq.
Agent, Commonwealth Corporation
Lowell, Msschts

Sir:
The young woman who brings you this letter is the daughter of myself and Charity Ainsworth, Deceased, of Newburyport. I understand that once you held some affection for Miss Ainsworth, who later became my wife. She has been dead these past ten years. I would ask you, in her memory, to do what you can for her daughter and mine, Sabra Palfrey.

With thanks in God,
Yr. Ob't servant,

She had been amazed that her mother—and her father, too, apparently—had known such a grand person as this Bradshaw. She longed to learn more of the story, but she saw with rising apprehension that her father was weakening fast. She had no time for questions.

She had copied over the letter with a firm hand and helped him to sit up while he signed it, leaning it against his knee, so that what with the wracking fever and the unsteady paper, his signature looked like that of a very old man. He was only forty-three. Was God unhappy with him, she wondered, taking him in the midst of all his work, all his service and harvesting in of souls?

She realized that Bradshaw had been silent for a very long time—much longer, surely, than he needed to read the letter. He was turned away a little toward the lamp on his desk; she could not see his face, and so she had no way to know if he were still angry with her as he had seemed before.

Finally, holding the letter, he swung around to look at her again. Still he said nothing. He looked and looked until she became even more uncomfortable than before. She could not look back; she stared down at the polished wood floor where she saw the toes of her badly scuffed and split boots peeping from beneath her skirts.

"Look at me," he said suddenly. She did so. He glanced again at the letter, and then back at her.

The expression in his eyes made her uneasy, and so, after a moment, she looked away from him again, out into the mill yard. Someone was walking across it carrying a lantern; the light bobbed up and down across the darkness like the will-o'-the-wisp flickering over a marsh.

"Where did you meet this man—this Isaac Palfrey?"

"He was my father, sir."

"No." He stared at her harder than before; his eyes withered her small store of courage. "This letter is false. Who put you up to it?"

"No one, sir." The injustice of the thing had begun to stir in her; she searched for words to defend herself. "That letter was spoken by him because he was so weak. You can see by his name how ill he was. I wrote it out for him."

"It is a forgery—signature and all. Tell me who hired you and I will excuse your part."

"No one hired me. He was my father."

"And she your mother? And on the strength of that I am to help you?" She saw that he had begun to flex his fingers. He made a fist with his left hand. She stepped back. She had seen women beaten for less than a forged letter.

He understood her fear of him. All at once his face softened a little. He was not, after all, an unChristian man.

"Tell me about her," he said.

"She died when I was a child."

"And you are all grown up now, are you?" She heard the smile in his words; she did not see it on his face.

"Sixteen."

"I met your father once, long ago. Did he tell you that?"

"No, sir."

"What did he tell you?"

"Nothing. I asked him what I should do when he—when he died. And he told me to write what he said, and take the letter myself."

She was growing tired of talking against the rumble and clatter of the machines. She wished that he would decide what to do with her—give her a place on the Corporation, she supposed—and send her someplace to get her supper. But he had not done with her yet.

"You don't resemble your mother."

"No, sir."

"She was very pretty. High-spirited, vivacious, always laughing—"

She remembered differently: a sad, sick woman who lay in agony on some stranger's cot because her husband had never had money for a house of his own. Not that he would have been content to stay in it.

"And so now you must make your own way," he continued. "No doubt your father thought you would be safe enough here."

And now all of a sudden as he spoke she felt, for the first time, a terrible desolation come over her. She wished that she had stayed with the Reverend Greene; she wished that she had never come down from the mountains; she wished that she were anywhere but here in this small room with the tall stranger who kept on with his questions, in the midst of all the strange town, and the noise, and the angry women, and the cramped, frantic feeling that comes when one is young and raw and altogether without resource, when one acts as an animal acts in danger, blindly, instinctively, without judgment or perspective. To her shame, she began to cry.

The sight of her tears alarmed him; quickly he bent to look at her. She turned her face away. He put out his hand as if to touch her and then pulled it back; he muttered something which she did not hear, for she was sobbing aloud now.

The door opened just then, and a man came in. He must have knocked, but she did not hear. When he saw her he made as if to withdraw, but Bradshaw said no, it was all right, and what was the situation in the rooms?

All was well, the man said. Everyone working. Some seemed sullen, but they'd come around. Production would not suffer. Better to work for fifteen per cent less than not to work at all. He was a small man, thin and worried-looking, and as he spoke he bobbed his head up and down in a curious way as if he thought to make a full bow and yet hadn't quite the heart for it. His dark hair was plastered down in a way that even a country girl like Sabra knew to be unfashionable. His mouth, as he spoke, opened barely enough to let out the words. His eyes flicked around the room, over Bradshaw and away again, over Sabra and the desk and the rows of cubbyholes on the back wall and back to Bradshaw again, as if he were looking for an enemy somewhere set to pounce on him.

She felt his small eyes slide over her and she looked away. Did he think that she was one of the turnout come to beg forgiveness? (He did not. He knew every operative by name, as she learned later, and he would never think that such a ragamuffin belonged to the Commonwealth Mill.)

Bradshaw dismissed him, then, and turned back to her. She had recovered herself somewhat, and she saw that he, too, seemed impersonal and even brusque again, and somehow settled in his mind, as if he had at last got used to the idea of her, and had decided what to do with her.

"So you want a place here, do you?" he said.

Something made her hesitate just then. She sometimes wondered, later, how different her life would have been if she had answered promptly. Such little things decide our fate; such small actions—or reactions—point our way. If she had answered promptly, either yes or no; if she had showed him some decisive wish—but she hesitated. She had been frightened by what she had seen of the factory and its operatives; she hated the noise, the huge forbidding buildings; she wanted very much, at that moment, to go back—where? She did not know.

Of course he understood: he was not in charge of all those souls in vain, he understood very well how people think. He picked up the letter which he had put by on the desk; he studied her for a moment longer. And then he said something that surprised her very much—more than anything that had gone before.

"Well, then," he said. "Perhaps you don't. In that case—" He turned down the lamp, he reached for his hat and cloak hanging by the door. "Come along. I know someone who will be glad to see you."

She followed him because she had no choice, but she was mystified. What did he mean? Her trunk seemed much heavier now, and she realized that she was very tired. And hungry—her stomach rumbled, demanding its daily portion. As they went out across the yard she saw that torches had been set, so that she could see now how big a place it was, trees and shrubs all around, and then the bells began to toll and suddenly the other noise—the rumble and clatter of the machines—stopped, and for a moment they heard only the bells pealing from the white belfry high above, and then the bells stopped, too. Suddenly they were engulfed: from every building, streaming down and out across the yard, came tens and scores of them—hundreds: all the women hurrying past. The Agent stopped in the middle of the yard; the swarm of women broke around him and his companion and then closed ranks again, as if the two of them were an island in a cresting river. The brims of their coal-scuttle bonnets hid their features; faceless, nameless, they hurried on. One or two nodded and spoke quickly to Bradshaw in passing, but no one seemed to notice Sabra. On and on they came, an endless progression.

At last they stopped. Bradshaw and the girl stood alone. The torches flickered in the night wind, casting shadows on the high brick walls. From somewhere came the sound of a slamming door.

"Come along," he said. He bade good night to the watch; they passed through the gate. A boy held a horse harnessed to a tilbury. Bradshaw helped her up and handed up her trunk. For a moment she remembered her friend the peddler. Then Bradshaw was beside her and they drove off.

They passed down the street which an hour earlier had been filled with angry females and their audience. Now all was quiet, deserted; the water of the canal which paralleled the street was black and still. Bradshaw said nothing. They passed the long row of attached brick houses—the Corporation boarding houses; through unshuttered windows in the bright glow of the lamps within, Sabra could see women sitting at table. She imagined sitting with them. Why was she not? Where were they going?

They turned into the main street: the long expanse of lighted shops, each with its sign. As before, there were few customers in and out. She remembered Goldschmidt's explanation: after supper, she thought, they will all come out to buy. It seemed a wonderful thing to do. She had never been in a store of any kind except the general stores in the villages. They turned down another street: more and more shops!

Still he did not speak. She glanced at his stern, pale face. He was very grand in his tall beaver and full cape; why was he troubling himself to drive her anywhere, she wondered. If he had no place for me in his mill, why did he not simply direct me to another?

On they went, turning again, over a bridge above a small river—much smaller than the other. The road led up a hill.

"Soon, now," he said. His voice was not unkind.

She remembered what her father had said of him, after signing the letter: "He is a worldly man, Sabra. Like all his kind, he is entirely devoted to getting money. These manufacturers will turn all God's green countryside into a factory before they are done, and they will not be one step closer to the wisdom of the Lord." The words had come out painfully. "Remember that you are my daughter. And the Lord's daughter, too. Be obedient in all things, but do not allow yourself to be corrupted in that place. They think of nothing but money there. They forget their salvation."

She shivered. The night was cold. Higher and higher they went. She turned to look back. The city spread out below, the dark buildings picked out with points of light. Overhead arched the starry sky: she saw bright Orion, and Cassiopeia, and the thick cluster of the Milky Way.

And somewhere, unseen, was God.

They passed no more buildings now; the way was dark, the road bordered by alternating fields and trees. And then, ahead on the left, she saw lights.

"There," he said. To her surprise, he pulled up the horse and they stopped. He turned to look at her. His face was dim; she could not make out his expression.

"You did not want to go on the Corporation," he said.

"I need to earn my way, sir." Her teeth were chattering so that she could hardly talk.

"So do many others. That is why they work in the factory. But listen to me, Sabra Palfrey. Are you prepared to take a gamble, as I am?"

Gambling was sinful. Everyone knew it. "Yes, sir," she said.

"Very well. Now here it is. I live just ahead, where you see the lights. My family waits for me there. I have a wife, three daughters—two about your age—and my wife's sister, who lives with us. I am proposing that you stay with us also, for a time. Stay for a week. See how you do. If you are happy you may stay on. If not, you may go on the Corporation."

Although she had not had much experience of the world—of fine folk in the towns—she knew the country people very well. She thought of the Reverend Croone's grudging invitation to remain with his family, and of the dreary life she would have led if she had accepted. Did this man, too, want an unpaid servant—a maidservant for his daughters?

Had she been older she would have questioned him: why? on what terms? with what conditions? But the young did not question; they were trained up to comply to the wishes of their elders. She had expended her small store of independence; now she was tired, she was hungry, she longed for a place in the world. Any place.

"Well?" he said.

She hunched her shoulders against the wind. The lights of the house twinkled brighter than the stars. It is God's will, she thought.

"Yes, sir," she said. "If you wish it."

He made no reply; he flicked the reins and they went on. They turned into the drive and pulled up before the columned portico. The house was square, white, very large. Lights streamed from the windows. She heard the sound of a piano, someone singing, a shriek of laughter. Then the music stopped; in the sudden silence she heard the sound of rushing water. The river, she thought, somewhere near. A man came out. With a brief greeting to Bradshaw he held the horse while they climbed down, and then he put down Sabra's trunk.

"Come along," said Bradshaw. "They will be happy to see you."

She picked up the trunk; she followed him up the steps. Suddenly the door flew open.

"Father! I've been watching—"

She stood silhouetted against the light within; Sabra could not make out her face.

"Well, Rachel," he said.

She stood back to let them in. An astral lamp of ruby glass stood glowing on a marble-topped table in the center of the wide hall. Sabra glanced shyly at the girl who had greeted them; then she looked away to Bradshaw, to the polished squares of the parquet floor.

He introduced them. Sabra looked at her again: the first fashionable young lady she had ever seen. Her pale, perfect face was framed by loops of dark shining hair; her dress—deep blue—fell in graceful folds over her slim figure; her eyes were gray with heavy dark lashes, her mouth very red, laughing now as she greeted her father's unexpected guest.

She could have been cold; she could have been haughty, as befitted her station. But as Sabra would learn, she never thought about such things. She took the stranger's rough hands in her own fine soft white ones; she declared that Sabra was her salvation. Her father watched them. Sabra could see that he was pleased to have made his daughter happy. Then, excusing himself, he proceeded upstairs. "I will inform your aunt," he called back over his shoulder.

At once Miss Bradshaw took charge: she summoned the housekeeper from the kitchen and ordered hot water—in her own bedroom, she said, and a pot of fresh tea as well. She was like a general ordering troops. Her eyes flashed, her slim shoulders straightened to give emphasis to her words. Her voice was low and sweet, but underneath Sabra heard the hard note of iron will. Like—what? Like another voice that she had recently heard. She could not at once remember. Later—several days later—she placed it: Miss Bradshaw's voice, as unlikely as the comparison seemed, had sounded for an instant—no more—like the voice of the harpy on the stump, the malcontent haranguing the Corporation.

She was sure that she was not mistaken. This one is angry too, she thought. But with whom? And why?

8

To the good citizens of the new manufacturing town it was a matter of some curiosity, and no little speculation, how Josiah Bradshaw, Agent of the Commonwealth Mill, managed to keep himself and his family in a fashion more nearly that of one of his employers in Boston, than of a businessman, exalted though he was, who worked in their midst every day. "How does he afford it?" they said. "He must have money of his own." (He did: a little.) "The Corporation must pay him an extraordinary salary." (Not so much, but more than other Agents: about three thousand a year.) "His wife must have brought considerable property to him when they married." (No: hardly anything.)

It was on the subject of his wife, in fact, that the good people engaged in their most fanciful—and therefore most enjoyable—speculations. She was not, they thought, a very—uh—democratic person. (They spoke not in terms of Old Hickory, for this was a Whig town; they used the term nonpolitically, to express their essential Yankee spirit.) "Look at the way she shuts herself up in that Greek temple up on Belvidere Hill," they said. "She hardly ever comes into town except for church, and even then not very often." They were right. She seldom appeared, and when she did it was a brief visit on a mild day, a hurried trip to the dry-goods shops for a few yards of ribbon, or a moment at the bookseller's to purchase a novel or two: nothing heavy. Almost invariably she stopped at Boyden's Apothecary, where her constant patronage had made her a valued customer. Some of those who discussed her so frequently had never seen her; others, luckier, had caught a glimpse of a pale face in the carriage window, a graceful form clothed in gray velvet passing from carriage to shop. The report was that she was a handsome woman, but cold: she had an air of remoteness which chilled even the most persistent of those who would make her acquaintance.

Formerly she was more accessible. The Bradshaws had lived near the mill, in a fine stone house across from the red-brick Congregational Church on Merrimack Street. But when the Belvidere land was annexed to the town, in 1834, Bradshaw built his new house. "The Parthenon," people called it, with more than a little contempt. They were puzzled: why would she not live among them? "Her health," some said; "she needs the good fresh air on the hill." "Her pride," said others; "she will bankrupt him before she is done."

In fact neither answer was correct. It had not been her decision to remove. Her husband had decreed it; and, like the good wife she was, she obeyed. Every law, every custom, every preacher's sermon said that she must obey. And she did: he could not complain of her.

Bradshaw built his grand new house because as jealous as he was of his position, he felt a need to escape it. The cares of his employment weighed very heavily upon him; he liked to absent himself, each night, from the congestion of shops and boarding houses and hotels and schools and—yes—rumsellers; he liked to escape to his hill. (He thought of it as his hill, although in fact he owned only a couple of acres of it; all the other acres belonged to the brothers Nesmith, who would one day make a fortune selling them off piece by piece.) Up there, on a Sunday afternoon, he could stroll out across his small garden to the stone wall overlooking the steep drop down to the river. At night, as he tried to sleep, he could hear the soughing wind in the trees; only when it was strong from the west could he hear the bells ringing the hours of the night in the town. And when he was down in his office, in the midst of the racket of production, he could keep in a quiet corner of his mind the image of his family passing their days well removed from the hurly-burly of town life. He was thankful to have been able to protect them: females all, they were flighty and easily led, like all their kind. He had had, within the past few months, a very vivid—a very frightening—example of just how easily the female heart could be traduced, how swiftly the delicate female brain could be misled. He had had a bad time of it: a great deal of worry. Fortunately the good people of the town knew nothing of his difficulty; if they had, their tongues, always loose and wagging where the Bradshaws were concerned, might very likely have dropped off altogether.

He had not yet puzzled out the way in which the trouble began. He was certain that his wife had not plotted it. She had her faults: she was withdrawn, she was too quiet, very probably she was lazy; undoubtedly she took advantage of her sister's presence in the household. But she was not to his knowledge deceitful. She spent her life daydreaming, and playing the piano, and cosseting herself with a stupendous array of medicines, but she was not a bad woman. She was weak, but she was true. She would not knowingly cause him distress.

In his sister-in-law, too, he had the most complete confidence. It was she who supervised his household; it was she who had come, years ago, to stay when Rachel was born and who swiftly became such a necessary part of their lives that she could never get away again. Not that she had any place to get away to: she was the elder daughter of a failed merchant of Boston, ruined by Mr. Madison's War. Once she had been affianced to a likely young man. But he had made one last voyage as supercargo; the ship had gone down (at a severe loss) in a storm off the African coast. And so Miss Amalia had seen her younger sister married instead, to Josiah, and upon her father's death and Rachel's birth she had become, in a way, a Bradshaw too.

Miss Amalia had always adored her sister, five years younger than herself, despite the fact that Sophia's birth had caused their mother's death. Miss Amalia had reared the baby sister, had helped her to learn to walk and talk and make neat stitches in her sampler; had said (when the money stopped coming in, when the ships could not sail) that if there were only one shilling to spend then Sophia must spend it; if there were only one good dress to wear, then Sophia must wear it. And, at last, if only one of them were to marry, let it be Sophia—for Miss Amalia's heart was at the bottom of the Atlantic in the wreckage of the *Victory*.

Marriage and birth, birth and death: these were women's way—but not, it seemed, Miss Amalia's. She stayed on at her father's house until he died, shortly after the marriage; and then, summoned by Sophia, she joined the Bradshaws, first at Newburyport and then in the new town. Josiah had had a good offer to Agent a mill, and Sophia wanted the company of her elder sister in the lonely years that followed their move. The babies, too, demanded more attention than Sophia could give; and servants did not run a household by themselves. They needed direction which Sophia, weakened by repeated efforts to produce a son, could not give. And so Miss Amalia had come, at first for a few months, and then for a year, and then, finally, forever.

She had been glad to go. She loved the babies—first Rachel and Eliza and then, in succession, two weak little ones, girls also, who came before their time and lived only a few hours; and then a boy—a boy!—who lived for three agonizing months; and then Lydia. The last birth had caused Dr. Knight to shake his head and say (not to her, of course, but to Josiah): "I'd not like Mrs. Bradshaw to suffer such a confinement again, Josiah, although the next one, God knows, might slip out easy as a greased pig. But she's not strong. She suffers from a weakened constitution. She'd best not conceive again—or at least not for a good while." And, having bled her, he had gone about his ministrations.

Miss Amalia had been terrified. To be with child or to have just delivered a child was, it seemed, the natural condition of the married woman, although there were some who went for years without a pregnancy, she did not know why. And certainly Death, in all his forms, called as frequently at childbed as anywhere. His presence hovered over every birth; many men outlived two and three wives and more. As the elder sister who in fact if not in name saw to it that the household continued to function, Miss Amalia had always felt quite competent to speak her mind to her brother-in-law about the slightest detail of their lives: "We will need to buy a piano, Josiah, Rachel and Eliza are quite old enough to learn to play"; or: "Lydia's rash has gotten considerably worse, Josiah. I am going to send for Dr. Knight again"; or: "If you plan to bring Mr. Bellingham and Mr. Deane to dinner, Josiah, please let me know so that I can tell Mrs. Gumm in time."

But on this subject—the question of whether or not her sister Sophia would live or die in the effort to bear still more children—a son! Above all, a son!—Miss Amalia did not have the courage to speak. She understood, of course, that all men wanted a son; she understood that it was her sister's duty to provide that son. And Sophia had tried: had come near to death in the attempt. Surely, Miss Amalia thought, surely she should not be required to risk her life again. Miss Amalia had not the faintest idea what it was that began the dreaded process inside her sister's body; had not the slightest clue what passed between the married couple behind the closed door of their bedroom which resulted in such illness, such pain, such very real danger to the wife. (She knew, of course, that women who were not married underwent such illness, also, such agony and danger: but such women were not to be considered. They did not, for Miss Amalia, exist.)

She had seen the look of disappointment—bitter, painful loss—on Josiah's face when Lydia was born; and had seen, too, how manfully he accepted the fact of yet another daughter; and how quickly, how dutifully, he had inquired after the health of the wife who had produced her. But —he wanted a son. It was not after all a crime to have such a desire; was it, Miss Amalia wondered, a crime to act upon it, knowing that his wish might cause his wife's death?

There had been no more babies after Lydia; no stillbirths, no miscarriages. And gradually Sophia's health had improved—her physical health, at least—and Josiah had seemed content enough, and Miss Amalia had begun to believe, gratefully, that the danger had passed. There would be no more children, and she and Sophia—and Josiah, too—would live to be old (barring Death in his other personae) and, living, could enjoy the three girls, who surely were happiness enough for any man.

Miss Amalia loved her nieces as if they were her own children. That warm maternal instinct commonly believed to be smoldering in every female heart had been fired up anew with each succeeding birth, and it had burned all the more brightly upon the living for having been banked at the dead. She hardly ever thought of the babies who had succumbed; she had been far too busy caring for the three who had survived. She often thought, with warm and loving pride, that she had done very well by them. They were charming girls. Everyone said so. The two older ones had acquired all the accomplishments necessary to the well-bred young lady: a smattering of music, a little drawing, a little light French conversation, enough skill with the needle to embroider, say, a handsome trousseau. And Lydia, at seven, promised to do as well; she was a pretty, lively little thing, the pet of the household and yet not spoiled, always willing to submit to further instruction from her primer, or to learn another question and answer from her catechism. In a few years' time she too would attend Miss Dexter's School for Young Ladies in Bradford, or some institution equally suitable.

The question of what was suitable, and what was not, was in fact a major difficulty for Miss Amalia. She was extremely conscious of the Bradshaws' position, both literally and figuratively, above everyone else in the new town; and if the air at the top of Belvidere Hill was exhilarating, it was also brilliantly clear. She saw quite well that although the factory town offered Josiah good employment, it offered his daughters somewhat less in companionship and amusement. Paradoxically, she had been relieved when Josiah had announced that he was building a new house. Life in the center of town had begun to press upon Miss Amalia; she had begun to fear that Rachel and Eliza would become friendly with the operatives, or ask to attend Lyceum lectures, or take to running about the streets in and out of the multitude of shops. At least in their new home they were more confined; Mr. Gumm, who drove the carriage, was a reliable informant, and even though Rachel was fond of saddling the brown mare and riding where she would, she was considerably less free to come and go than she had been when they lived near the factory.

The problem of suitable social contact remained: at whose homes could the Bradshaw daughters appear? Or, to put it more bluntly: at whose homes might Rachel and Eliza—and, in time, Lydia—meet properly eligible young men? Where, in Lowell, might they get husbands? The population of the town was perhaps 19,000. The Bradshaws were socially acquainted with about fifty—and even a dozen or so of these were, in Miss Amalia's opinion, insufficiently well-bred. Dr. and Mrs. Knight were of course eminently respectable, as were Mr. and Mrs. Peabody; the several other Agents, always suitably deferential to Josiah; the lawyers Blood and Hopkins; Mr. Munson, who published the Whig paper; a few others. Of all of these, there were perhaps three families who had marriageable sons—say six young men in all, and only five if one discounted Silas Blood, who, aimless and dithering at twenty-four, seemed never likely to settle down to anything despite the position awaiting him in his father's law office.

Miss Amalia's thin pink face was apt to take on a gloomy expression under the abundant white ruffles of her cap when she thought of those young men. Not one of them had shown any meaningful interest in her girls (although Silas was always very sweet, very polite); and in truth her girls had not shown any interest in them either. "Boring," they had pronounced; "insufficiently graceful." There had been, during the past summer, a promising evening at Mrs. Dr. Knight's; her son, a student at Yale College, had brought home for a visit a fellow student who had stayed north to escape the heat of his native South Carolina. The visitor had been most attentive to Eliza, and there had been a letter or two since. Miss Amalia had discreetly inquired of Mrs. Dr. Knight whether the young man would return, but without satisfaction: Mrs. Dr. Knight, having no unmarried daughters, was unable to tell Miss Amalia if he would ever come back.

Despite the fact that she was a gentlewoman, well aware of all the niceties of feminine conduct, Miss Amalia was capable of admitting unpleasant truths to herself, if not to others. One of these was that, although Eliza was perfectly willing to look out for a husband, she was hampered in her efforts because she was an undeniably plain young woman with a personality to match. Another was that, although Rachel was an undeniably beautiful young woman, with a merry, lively, captivating disposition, she was not at all interested in snaring a young man and became positively irritated whenever Miss Amalia—with great tact, with delicate restraint—brought up the subject.

"I am only eighteen, Aunt," she would say with an unbecoming grimace; "let me be free awhile longer. There is no one here for me in any case. Would you have me marry that dolt of Mr. Peabody's, who managed to graduate from Colby College without ever hearing of Edward Gibbon? Or George Abbott, who can tell good raw cotton from bad in an instant, but who cannot carry on a conversation about any other subject whatever for more than three minutes' time?"

Thus Rachel, the first-born, the beautiful, the accomplished one, the learned one; the one who, in the face of her father's displeasure, had continued her study of Latin and Greek with Mr. Hale, the one who read history and philosophy late into the night until her eyes threatened to give out. Graceful and accomplished, yes—living witness to Miss Amalia's careful tutelage; but something, somewhere, had gone wrong. (So Miss Amalia confessed to herself; never to anyone else.) Too much study was unwise for females; too little attention to getting a husband was even more so. For months past Miss Amalia had watched the girl, and worried secretly, and then, six weeks previous, had seen the undeniable, irrefutable proof that all her suspicions had been correct, and that Rachel, if not severely admonished, would not only be condemned to spinsterhood, even as Miss Amalia, but would ruin herself and all the family with her.

Eliza, searching in Rachel's sewing cabinet for embroidery thread, had come upon a copy of a certain newspaper.

Had run to Miss Amalia with it; had dropped it upon her aunt's lap as if it were a live thing; had demanded instantly (and rather vindictively) that Aunt Amalia inform Father; had stood eavesdropping, discovered by her aunt, during the dreadful shouting scene between Rachel and Josiah in the latter's study; had refused to speak to her elder sister for days afterward, declaring that she, Rachel, was a traitor to them all and particularly to Eliza, who had so recently discovered a promising matrimonial prospect in the person of a young gentleman from South Carolina—a young man who most assuredly would not choose to marry into a Yankee family if he knew that that family nurtured in its bosom a viper who read the obscene propaganda put out by the fanatical abolitionist Garrison.

Sophia knew nothing. Eliza had threatened to tell her, but Miss Amalia, supported by her brother-in-law, had forbidden it absolutely. Sophia's health would not suffer the shock. Sophia's health, always paramount in Miss Amalia's mind, was not to be jeopardized even by so serious a matter as this. She had slept through the confrontation of father and daughter, her senses numbed by laudanum, and had not, in her vague and dreamlike way, seemed to notice the strained atmosphere of the household in the days following. Rachel had been restricted: no more trips to town in the carriage with Mr. Gumm, no more rides to Mr. Hale's house for her lessons. Miss Amalia herself had burned the offending newspaper without reading so much as a word; she had not wanted to contaminate her mind. She had, however, been unable to avoid seeing the silhouette on the masthead: a crude woodcut of a Negro slave at auction.

In recent days the incident, although not forgotten, seemed to be safely past. Josiah and Rachel had spoken kindly to each other again; Eliza and Rachel, for want of other company, had become friends as before; and Miss Amalia, ever watchful, had begun to believe that their lives would run placidly again, that no further unpleasantness would intrude upon them, that the girls would find husbands, her sister's health improve, her brother-in-law's position remain secure. She strengthened these beliefs by itemizing them, as requests, every night in her prayers. And, because there had been no new trouble, she was confident that God had heard her.

And then one cold evening in early November, her brother-in-law arrived home with a stranger, and Miss Amalia, the Lord's supplicant, was cast down into confusion and doubt, and was forced to question whether all her prayers had fallen upon deaf ears.

As she listened to his hurried explanation, thinking quickly of the way in which their domestic arrangements would need to be juggled in order to accommodate the new arrival, she allowed herself one swift, bitter verdict. She observed to herself that if Josiah were determined to take in another child, he might have made it a boy. Then at last he would have had his son. But of course he had not chosen her: she had come to him. And, like his wife, he could hardly be held responsible for the sex of the child whom he produced.

9

Up the curving staircase, then, Miss Bradshaw in the lead. "Come!" she said; she herself carried Sabra's trunk. As Sabra followed, she saw that a girl had come part way down to meet them: a girl a little younger than Miss Bradshaw, and not nearly so beautiful. In fact she was quite plain—a condition not belied by the ornate flowered pattern of her green dress, her carefully arranged hair in fat finger curls on either side of her sallow cheeks.

Miss Bradshaw hardly paused to introduce her: "My sister Eliza—Sabra Palfrey." No explanation, no invitation to join the welcome. Sabra saw quite plainly that the sister's smile was slow, her greeting distinctly cool; and so, she thought, Miss Bradshaw does not want to embarrass me by giving her sister the opportunity to refuse to join us. She passed the girl, murmuring hello, and went on.

At the top of the staircase stood a small lady in brown bombazine; her head was crowned by a white cap, extravagantly ribboned and ruffled and frilled, such as Sabra had never seen on the country women she had known. That cap dazzled her; she stared at it so that she almost forgot her manners. She hardly dared meet the sharp blue eyes underneath.

"Aunt, this is Sabra Palfrey," said Rachel. "Father has brought her home and put her in my charge."

The lady's eyebrows rose to meet her ruffles. She extended a thin hand to the bedraggled newcomer.

"How do you do, Sabra Palfrey?"

Sabra did not dare to presume upon her good will by telling her how she did; she thanked her, and sought refuge in her boot toes.

"We are going to have a wash, Aunt, and a cup of tea. Perhaps you would rather not wait supper for us. We will be down in half an hour."

Once again her tone of absolute command struck Sabra as odd, for she had been brought up always to defer to every adult. But Miss Amalia did not seem to mind; she smiled a little at her imperious niece—but not at Sabra—and said that, yes, they would proceed with supper, and not to disturb Mama.

Miss Bradshaw led the way down the broad upper hall to her room; she threw open the door and hurried Sabra in and pushed the door firmly shut behind them.

"There!" she said, putting down the trunk. Her face was radiant; her laughter bubbled up irrepressibly. "Now—let's have a look at you! You are half frozen; come to the fire, sit close and tell me everything!"

Sabra, somewhat dazed, sank down into a crimson velvet chair and held her hands to the blaze. She was not yet ready to tell very much, for if she had learned little from books in her life, she had learned something of human nature; and she knew that to tell everything was often to put oneself at a disadvantage, especially when one knew so little of one's interrogator. Confession was an intimate thing; she was not accustomed to intimacy. Still, she felt her shyness begin to thaw under the intensity of Miss Bradshaw's interest, even as her cold hands warmed at the hearth, and so, after a moment, she began to talk. It is always pleasing to be liked, even for the wrong reasons. Miss Bradshaw liked her, she understood, not for herself—for Miss Bradshaw did not know her—but for the interest she provided. I am an Event, thought Sabra—a curiosity, a thing produced for her gratification. Still, it was good to be fussed over, to be petted and exclaimed upon. They smiled at each other; Sabra began to feel somewhat less exhausted. She saw that Miss Bradshaw was an extraordinarily appreciative listener.

"Walk?" she exclaimed. "And call me Rachel—I insist upon it. You will be like a—like a cousin to us, although we have none. You walked all that way? And a peddler—!" She paused to consider. "I would never have had your pluck."

Sabra remarked that pluck is often only desperation.

"Yes, but if you had waited until spring you might have saved a little money—"

"There is no way to earn money in the country. If you are a farmer's wife you can travel to the towns to sell butter and eggs, but there is nothing for a solitary female to do but earn her board, and count herself lucky at that. There is no money to be had."

"And so you came to be an operative—oh, but this will be better! You can live with us! We are so dull here, you will make all the difference! You are exactly like a girl in a story I once read. She set out, just as you did, and she found her long-lost uncle, who was a duke, and he trained her up to be a great lady—"

Sabra smiled a little at the comparison; she asked how the story ended. Rachel laughed.

"I don't remember all of it. But it was a happy ending—oh, very happy. She managed to inherit all his money, and she spent her life doing good works."

"Didn't she marry? That is the usual happy ending."

Rachel's smile faded. "I don't recall." She gazed silently for a moment at her companion. "But it doesn't matter. The good works were the important thing."

Sabra was saved from making a reply by the appearance of the housekeeper bearing cans of hot water and, a moment later, the promised tea. She gave the newcomer a hard look, and a grunt instead of a word of greeting; she closed the door unnecessarily hard as she went out. It was obvious that she had no need, as Rachel did, for an interesting visitor to enliven her life.

While Sabra washed, Rachel rummaged through her clothing to find something that might fit, for she was two or three inches taller than her guest, and a good deal fuller in the body. Sabra wore only a shift under her homespun dress; in her trunk was her father's Bible, and a copybook or two, and two cotton handkerchiefs. Nothing more.

Rachel produced, at last, a pretty lace-trimmed shift, two petticoats, and a dress of plain blue-gray broadcloth which, she declared, would do well enough until she could find something else, something of Eliza's perhaps; and of course they could begin sewing the very next day and give Sabra's measurements to the dressmaker as well. And they must find a corset; Miss Amalia would insist on that.

Modestly, Rachel turned aside while Sabra slipped on the undergarments. Never had she worn such fine cloth, so soft that it was almost slippery. Then, before the exertion of putting on the dress, Rachel poured out their tea into small flowered cups so thin that they were translucent; then she settled Sabra again in the velvet chair, her shawl over her shoulders, her feet comfortably propped on an embroidered cricket. Rachel herself seemed too excited to sit, and so, eager for more conversation, she perched on the endrail of the narrow, four-poster bed.

"Nothing ever happens to us here," she said. Her fingers played nervously with the lace at the edge of her wide white bertha. "There is absolutely nothing to do except look forward to the next party at Mrs. Dr. Knight's, or the next picnic or the next sleigh-ride, depending on the season." She grimaced. "When we lived in town it wasn't quite so bad. We saw the activity around us, at any rate. We saw the railway cars on the day they started up; all the little Irish children ran behind, trying to catch a ride, and one of them fell off and was nearly run over. But then Aunt made us come in, Eliza and me, and so we did, and we wrote it down in our day-books. We learned at Miss Dexter's School to keep a journal, but I have let mine go because there is never anything to put into it. But you shall have a page all to yourself. I will write you up and decorate the entry with a garland of leaves and flowers."

Sabra had never known anyone who had nothing to do. All the women upcountry, the women in the villages and on the farms, worked from dawn until long past dark, and few of them ever had the time—or the energy—to keep a journal, much less to rest, to read a story or sew a pretty bit of trimming. Help was scarce: thus her invitation to stay on at the Reverend Greene's. It did not occur to her that Rachel's isolation, her boredom, might be as difficult to endure as the grinding drudgery of the country women. She could think of no reply that would not be dishonest, and so she finished her tea and stood up to put on the dress. It smelled of sweet herbs; it felt quite heavy as she settled it over her shoulders. She pulled the wide belt tightly around her waist and turned up the narrow cuffs; she saw that although the hem might have been an inch or two higher, she could, by remembering to lift the skirt, avoid tripping as she walked.

They stood before the glass while Rachel helped to comb her hair. It was a wonderfully decorated thing, that glass, framed by carved wood turnings, and bearing across the top a painted scene of skaters in a winter landscape: made to reflect beauty, it was a beautiful thing itself. The wall on which it hung was papered in a blue figure of tiny fleurs-de-lis on a white background; the floor was carpeted in a darker blue. A small cherrywood writing table, a matching chair before it, a painting upon the wall over the bed of a ruined building, square and white like the Bradshaw house, with columns equally imposing. This seemed a surprisingly simple chamber for the elder daughter of such a grand house, but it was a far more elegant one than any she had ever lived in.

Rachel stepped back, pleased with her efforts, and yet determined on further improvements.

"There," she said. "How pretty you look! Your hair falls naturally along your face, and you see how easily I made ringlets. Tomorrow we will wash it with a vinegar rinse, and Eliza shall attack you with her curling-iron to make the side-curls hold."

Sabra turned her head slowly, fearful of disarranging herself. Rachel pulled here and there at the dress, trying to get it to hang properly; she repinned the small silver brooch which she had produced to hold the edges of the wide collar close together at the neck. She suddenly remembered Sabra's feet, shod now in a pair of her own thin black cotton hose. What for shoes? She had nothing to fit, for her foot was much longer and narrower than Sabra's. She was genuinely distressed. "The effect will be ruined—and you do look so handsome, Sabra, you look a completely new person! But Eliza's feet are the same size as mine, and Aunt Amalia's far too small." And so Sabra pulled on her old boots again and followed Rachel down to supper.

The entrance hall was in darkness now, for someone had turned down the lamp and extinguished the candles. A rectangle of light spilled out from the front parlor; from behind the closed door opposite they could hear the faint sounds of the family at their meal. Halfway down, Rachel paused and held up her hand for silence. Sabra hesitated behind. She stared at the lighted place. She saw a shadow pass: a woman's form. She heard Rachel take a deep breath; then they proceeded. Rachel led the way, not to the others, but to the open door of the parlor. She went in; Sabra followed.

They were so alike, the two women, mother and daughter, that for a moment Sabra was confused. She thought that her fatigue and hunger had played tricks on her vision—that she was about to succumb to a faint, and that before she did, she was seeing two where only one should be.

Dark hair, pale skin, tall, queenly form, perfect delicate features—but then she met Mrs. Bradshaw's wide eyes. They were gray, like her daughter's; Sabra saw the vacant, dead look, the dull expression, and it seemed that there were not two women more different in all the world.

Rachel at last had found her misplaced deference. She presented Sabra to her mother; her voice was gentle and soothing as she drew them together, her attitude entirely submissive.

Sabra made her awkward curtsey. Mrs. Bradshaw stood with her hands loosely clasped at her waist, a puzzled expression upon her beautiful face. No, thought Sabra, it was not beautiful. It had no spark of life to animate it. There seemed to be no brain behind those staring eyes, no soul alive within that lovely form.

"It was kind of you to come down, Mama," said Rachel. "Do you feel well enough to have supper with us?"

Mrs. Bradshaw seemed not to have heard. She made a brief movement of her head, as if to clear it, and then she said, in a voice as lifeless as her eyes: "Where is your mother, child?"

"Dead, ma'am."

"I am . . . I am sorry to hear it. I knew her once, long ago."

"Yes, ma'am."

"I wanted to see you."

"Mama—"

"I wanted to see you because I knew your mother." She smiled a faint smile. "You will be good company for my daughter."

"Will you come to supper, Mama?"

Mrs. Bradshaw turned her gaze upon her daughter. "I will sit by the fire for a while," she said. "Then I will go upstairs. But you must eat—you and—what is your name again, child?"

"Sabra, ma'am."

"Yes." She turned away. "I will sit by the fire for a while, and I will think about your mother, Sabra. Then I will go upstairs." Sabra saw Rachel's expression: love compounded by concern. She settled her mother on a delicate carved chair by the fire and then they went out, leaving Mrs. Bradshaw alone.

The family, excepting small Lydia, who was already asleep, sat sparsely arranged around the table, faces gently illuminated by the twin candelabra. They had almost finished eating, but they had kindly saved a good portion of everything: vegetable soup, oysters, potted beef, peas and onions, three breads, jellies and pickles, apple pie and plum cake. In the interest of meeting Mrs. Bradshaw, Sabra had almost forgotten her hunger; but now, confronted with the repast, she fell upon it like a starveling.

They watched her as she ate. No one spoke as she devoured her food; Rachel only picked at hers. Mr. Bradshaw leaned comfortably back in his chair at the head of the table, a quizzical expression on his face—not unkind, not disapproving, but contemplative, as if only now was he considering the consequences of his impulsive act. Miss Amalia sat at his left, a little anxious-looking but not unkind, either, and prompt to pass along another helping whenever Sabra's plate grew empty. Eliza, sitting next to her aunt, looked unfriendly still; she held herself very straight in her chair, her hands folded in her lap, and stared coolly at them all.

At last Sabra could eat no more. Miss Amalia offered another slice of cake, Rachel passed a dish of sweetmeats, and her refusal of both gave Miss Amalia the signal to rise and leave the table. Mr. Bradshaw took his leave, then, and, wishing Sabra good night with the others, retired to his library at the rear of the house. Sabra followed the women into the parlor, deserted now, and Eliza seated herself at the piano while Miss Amalia took up her knitting and Rachel produced an album of verse for Sabra's amusement. But her fatigue had finally overpowered her, and shortly they took mercy on her and bade her go to bed. Rachel led her up to the little room on the third floor where she was to sleep; she helped her to take off the new clothing, she produced a nightshift of warm soft flannel. She saw Sabra into bed as if she were a little child; she kissed her good night and tucked her up in the warmth of the soft feather mattress and thick filled comforters. Then she tiptoed out and left the door ajar.

Sabra heard the rushing sound of the river below; she heard the wind rising in the trees, the howl of a dog far distant. The myriad events of the day, all jumbled together in her mind, slowly receded. In the final moment before she passed over into sleep, she realized that the family had not said evening prayers. But she was too far gone to rise and kneel beside her bed, and so as she lay she murmured a word of thanks to God for her deliverance; and then she slept.

10

It was the custom of Josiah Bradshaw to entertain at his home certain of his employees, both male and female, each year on the Saturday evening after Thanksgiving. Nowhere in his terms of employment with his superiors in Boston was it stipulated that he must do so. He acted, in this annual instance, entirely upon his own shrewd judgment of human nature. It was a singular honor for an overseer or an operative to be asked to join Mr. Bradshaw and his family at home; everyone knew that it was, despite the polite fiction, universally mouthed, that no one in the new town was better than anyone else; that all were equal in their labor; that here in the new town, the new country, labor was the great leveler. Bradshaw, honest man that he was, ignored all such democratic nonsense; he summoned his employees, certain troublemakers excepted, as a feudal lord might have summoned his vassals, sure in the knowledge that they would appear.

This year there was an added inducement to go: word had spread, here and there, that Mr. Bradshaw had taken into his home a poor girl who presented herself to him on the night of the turnout. Some people denied it: Bradshaw was not known for his generosity, he was not perceived to be a warm-hearted man, and obviously only a soft-headed, warm-hearted fool would take in a stranger. Hadn't he trouble enough with that wife—?

"Ah," replied the cognoscenti, "the girl is connected to him in some way! She is a long-lost niece, or some connection equally compelling."

People could not believe it. They saw the stranger in the carriage with Miss Amalia and Rachel, and still they could not. Some of them saw her at closer range in the Bradshaw pew at St. Anne's, and were well convinced of her presence, but astonished at her unfamiliarity with the arcana of Anglican ritual. "She is visiting," they said; "surely she will go soon." They appealed to Codwell the grocer, whose delivery boy drove up to the Bradshaws' twice weekly and was therefore a source of undoubted authenticity, despite the fact that he was Irish. Codwell swore by him—there's not a better boy in all New England, he said—and so young Patrick's intelligence, filtered through Codwell, was relied upon and elaborated upon until the stranger had become, briefly, a topic of conversation more interesting even than Mrs. Bradshaw herself, and Patrick was besieged with questions from maidservants and matrons alike.

He answered as well as he could, for he was indeed an honest lad, bright and quick, hard-working, anxious to please. He understood that his future success lay with the good people whom he served, and he did not want to offend anyone. She is as pleasant as may be, he said. He had seen her several times, hard at work in the kitchen under the housekeeper's eye, but he could not say whether she was entirely a servant. He might have added that she had a particularly sweet smile which did not quite hide an air of uncertainty, of not yet having settled in. But he kept that observation to himself; he knew what was forward and what was not, and since he labored very heavily under the knowledge that he was an alien himself, he hesitated to ascribe that condition to anyone else, particularly to an American.

Mrs. Dr. Knight, who had spoken with the new girl on somewhat different terms than Patrick's, was of the opinion—very loud—that you cannot make a silk purse from a sow's ear. People interpreted this variously: some said that Mrs. Dr. Knight had given the newcomer three pairs of doeskin gloves and a warm welcome to her home, while others had heard that she refused to receive the Bradshaw women now that they had the new encumbrance constantly in tow.

And so, on this night, those few of the favored operatives who had been invited, and who had also heard of the stranger's presence, were in a state of pleasant anticipation as they drove up to the Bradshaw portico and alighted, genteel young ladies from head to toe, exhilarated by the unaccustomed sensation of a carriage ride. What they observed this night would be reported at length to their less fortunate companions; even the plainest, the shyest of them would be popular for at least a week with her fellow boarders as they elicited from her every jot and tittle of the evening's events. Such were the benefits arising from this invitation—intangible, nontransferable, but benefits all the same. One cynical young woman remarked, after last year's evening, that she would as soon have had the time to rest her feet, and, further, that at her wage she couldn't afford to share the hire of a carriage. It was a foolish remark; she had not been invited back. Bradshaw knew her name; she was a competent drawer-in, but she had a wayward tongue, and sooner or later she would say too much and receive, for her pains, a bad-conduct discharge.

He stood now in the foyer of his elegant home, flanked by his two eldest daughters, his new protégée, his sister-in-law, and even his famous wife. As each young lady came in, she passed down the family line, shaking hands, murmuring amenities, and then proceeded upstairs to deposit her cloak and bonnet in the appointed chamber. Then she descended to the festivities: music and conversation in the parlor—the drawing room, rather—and the pleasant fantasy that for this night, at least, she was equal in status to her employer, and that such a home was in fact her permanent place of residence.

Soon the Bradshaw house was filled with the most genteel folk imaginable. Candles gleamed on brown ringlets and gold, on dark chignons and—yes—graying side-curls; the shining floors and figured carpets were graced with well-shod feet tapping to the rhythm of the music. (No one danced: dancing would not have become so well-bred an affair, and besides, there was no room.) Laughing faces, belying their fatigue, greeted as long-lost friends those with whom they lived and worked every day; work-hardened hands, one or two stained with blue-dye, were encased in the finest quality gloves, some new, some neatly mended. Gold pendant watches and fine lace collars were much in evidence; gold ear-knobs and silk dresses as common as calico. To the uninitiated, this would have seemed a social level so high that the air was certifiably thin; only the most practiced, most discriminating nose could smell the robust tang of ordinary working folk.

Such a nose, long and rather crooked, belonged to the young man standing near the piano. From time to time, when the young lady seated at the keyboard attacked a song which he knew, he joined the group to sing; otherwise he stood quietly by, a pleasant, rather wistful expression on his homely face. Although he was not one of Josiah Bradshaw's employees, he was there legitimately, for he was a friend of all the family—as was his father, who did not attend. He always enjoyed himself on occasions such as this, where he could meet a more varied group of people than that offered by his own circle. He was a tall young man of four-and-twenty, big-boned, loose and awkward under his ill-fitting brown frock coat; his straight black hair was rather longer than the current style, but his dark, deep-set eyes were fashionably melancholy. His gray cravat was crooked, his boots not as highly polished as his host's. So deceiving are appearances that the uninitiated might have mistaken this young man for an interloper from some country hamlet; in fact he was quite near the top of the new town's heap, for his father was an attorney at law, very friendly with the Corporations, very well paid for his services to them. Enoch Blood, Esq., had always assumed that his only offspring—the young man in question—would join him in his practice. But Silas had shown no aptitude for the law—no aptitude for anything much, and certainly not for the general rush to make a deal of money. Not many weeks past, the senior Blood had had a quiet, well-chosen word with Bradshaw in the hope that his friend could influence the young man to settle down to some kind of at least potentially remunerative employment. Bradshaw did not like young Silas. Surrounded as he was by men scrambling to rise in the world—scrambling for his own position, in fact, although they would never have it, for they lacked the proper social connections in

Boston—he had little use for one so lacking in gumption as old Blood's son. On the other hand, Silas was a pleasant, helpful fellow, much admired by Amalia for his gentle manners and kindly disposition; Bradshaw did not mind having him around the house. It was even possible that Rachel would look upon him one day with more than sisterly affection, and in such an event Bradshaw would gladly have secured him a good position at once, in Lowell or elsewhere, in gratitude for lightening the burdens of a worried father's heart.

By nine o'clock all of the guests had arrived: weavers, carders, drawers-in, spinners, overseers (some with wives), a second hand or two. They had, all of them, worked upward of a twelve-hour day, a seventy-two-hour week, hard by the dangerous, clattering machinery, breathing in the lint-filled air, sweating and freezing and sweating again as they passed from their workrooms to their houses to get their dinners, and back to the factory again; they had, with their uninvited fellow workers, produced upward of one million yards of cotton cloth this week, consuming in the process half a million pounds and more of ginned raw cotton, and for their labors the women had received a dollar or two or occasionally three, the men four dollars and up. No matter: they looked as fresh and lively, here in this elegant setting, as if they had never worked a day in their lives.

One of these paragons caught Silas' eye across the crowd from where she stood near the fireplace. They smiled and nodded; he remembered, just in time, to attempt a bow. The young woman who acknowledged it was a plump and pretty little creature with bright brown eyes and a head of heavy dark gold hair. They knew each other, these two, from meeting at church—they were both Unitarians, very modern in their thinking—and from occasional attendance at the Lyceum lectures. She looked away; she resumed her observation of the crowded room. She seemed strangely isolated for so merry-looking a girl, but she preferred to watch silently rather than join in the conversation swirling around her head. Occasions such as this were special to her, not for the opportunity to pretend to social position, but for the chance to watch her friends and acquaintances from the mill in a different setting. She was unfailingly amused by the pretensions of her equals; for her they were like actors and actresses in a play. Of course there was no theater permitted in the new manufacturing town, since the proprietors insisted upon the highest moral tone to their enterprise, but Minerva Swan imagined it all the same; she watched everyone, she saw everything, and every night before retiring, no matter how exhausted she was, how deadened her brain from the noise in which she worked, she wrote in her notebook a bit of description or a scrap of dialogue gleaned from some event of the day. That night she would have more material than usual from which to select.

She saw now that the Bradshaw family, including the new one, who looked shy and slightly ill at ease, had begun to move around the room to mingle with their guests. Miss Swan watched closely; she observed the details of everyone's costume, the way in which the guests responded to the pleasantries tossed out at them. She watched Mrs. Bradshaw approach Mr. Blood. She saw the young man's rather dark complexion suddenly stained by a dull red flush. Mrs. Bradshaw offered him her hand; he took it. They said a few words. She paused—a moment too long?—and then she moved on. He followed her with his eyes. The incident was not lost upon Miss Swan; she observed it well. She tucked it away into an accessible corner of her mind, but she was unable as yet to understand its significance.

The music stopped. The piano player, a young woman from the folding room, acknowledged the applause. Miss Amalia began to direct the guests into the dining room, where the table held a large carved ham, trays of cakes and cookies, small dishes of ice cream, plates of pickles, and various other examples of Mrs. Gumm's culinary ingenuity. A bowl of lemon punch stood to one side; many of those present were Temperance, and would have been deeply offended to be in the presence of strong drink. In the general flow toward the repast, Miss Swan, waylaid by the Corporation's paymaster (a notorious bore, and vastly irritating in his self-importance; rumored also to have a free-searching hand), missed what was perhaps the most interesting vignette of the evening: a swift transaction from Miss Mary Russell of the spinning room to Miss Rachel Bradshaw of Belvidere Hill. Something had furtively passed hands; Miss Russell was a little nervous, but Miss Bradshaw carried off the moment with perfect calm. No one had seen anything. Together, chatting amiably, they proceeded to the crowded table.

It had always seemed to Miss Amalia that these annual receptions for her brother-in-law's employees were at once the most difficult and the most enjoyable of all the social events of her calendar. Difficult, because they occurred two days after Thanksgiving, itself a major effort of preparation, and a time, too, for the inconvenience of the annual visit of Mrs. Julia Bradshaw Wethertbee and her husband. Mrs. Wethertbee and her brother, Josiah Bradshaw, were not close; he disapproved of the sentimental verse which she manufactured for the newspapers, and she envied his large salary which he had never offered to share with her and her less fortunate husband. Their presence was always a source of annoyance and strain for Miss Amalia, who managed the logistics of the household, and she was always shamelessly relieved when they departed on the Friday after the holiday for whatever town in which they happened to live that year.

But Miss Amalia enjoyed the annual party for the operatives, too, because she thought that it was a splendid, visible instance of Josiah's very real concern for his employees. She knew that he regarded them always with a concerned, parental eye: they were like so many school children under the stern management of the master. These evenings on which he received them into his home allowed him to show the warmer side of his feelings for them. He was a good man; she was happy that occasionally he could show his goodness.

The company drifted back and forth between the rooms, across the wide hall. Their spirits had been enlivened by the food, the refreshing lemon punch. Another musician sat down to the piano; a group gathered round and tore into "The Lass of Richmond Hill." The pompous paymaster discovered that he could croak out a few notes after all, and soon his voice boomed out over everyone else's; a shy lady whose cough seemed to have disappeared found that she could sing a little, too; Miss Swan observed that her friend Mary Russell seemed to have warmed up considerably from her initial nervousness; even Eliza Bradshaw, whose saucer of tea this evening most definitely was not, lacking as it did any promise in a matrimonial way—even she had begun to smile, to exchange more than minimal civilities with her father's employees, to join the singers.

As the tall clock struck eleven the guests began to take their leave. The Bradshaws regrouped to say good night. Even Mrs. Bradshaw, whose lovely features were taut with fatigue, stood with the others ushering out her guests. The candles had burned low in their sconces and candelabra; someone had spilled punch on the dining room carpet; someone else left a half eaten fruit tart on the marble mantelpiece; the shining hardwood floor of the hall had been badly scuffed and would need to be waxed and polished first thing on Monday morning. No matter: it had been a successful evening, and Miss Amalia was very pleased.

Soon everyone had retired. They lay in their beds, warm and comfortable, gently breathing. Lydia slept the heavy sleep of childhood, her dark curls escaped from her nightcap, her thin arms clasping a favorite doll. Eliza lay stretched on her stomach; even in sleep her face bore an unhappy expression. Perhaps she dreamed of a wedding that was not hers. Rachel rested easily on her side, one hand under her pillow, an arm thrown out above the comforter despite the cold. Miss Amalia snored slightly, but no one heard her; her sleep was as untroubled as the child's. Mr. and Mrs. Gumm lay comfortably together in their small room on the third floor; they worked hard, their lives were uncomplicated, they rested easily at night. In the room next to theirs, Sabra was curled up tight, her head under the comforter; she smiled in her sleep and murmured a word or two. Mr. and Mrs. Bradshaw lay separately side by side in their large bed, his body tense and rigid even in his restless sleep, hers drugged into limp and dreamless slumber.

Below their promontory the river rushed on. The town was dark and quiet save for an occasional prowling cat. In the boarding houses the women lay six and more to a room, two and three in a bed. Many of them coughed away the night, or breathed so hard that they kept the others wakeful. Some had nightmares; some, miserably homesick, sobbed themselves to sleep and dreamed of country homes unthreatened by foreclosure.

And yet not everyone in the city was asleep. In the Irish shantytown—the Acre—a crash and a shouted, drunken oath briefly shattered the silence. The watch in the mills were awake and making their rounds. Silas Blood was awake. He sat at the window of his room in his father's house in Hurd Street in the center of the city. He did not move, or close his eyes; after a while a tear slid down his cheek. Tired as he was, he did not want to lie down on his bed. He feared sleep: in sleep he lost control, in sleep his body betrayed him and he awakened frightened, his heart pounding, the dreaded wetness staining his nightshirt. Lately he had tried a remedy for his affliction: "Dr. Delaney's Celebrated Curative Instrument for the dread disease known as Spermatorrhea, or Involuntary Nocturnal Emissions." It had not helped. He knew the reason for his condition, but he would sooner have died than tell it to a doctor. Often he was desperate; he feared the madness which would inexorably result if he did not find a cure, and yet no cure seemed possible.

In a house to the north, on the moonlit road by the river which led to New Hampshire and thence, ultimately, to Canada, two adults and a child lay huddled together on an attic floor, wrapped in a heavy blanket, newly warm in their woolen clothing which only that night had been given to them. They could not have said exactly where they were, nor could they have told, no matter how severely they were whipped, the names of those who concealed them. The child slept; his father fought to stay awake and failed; the woman lay alert, listening for the sound of their discovery.

11

The next morning Sabra awakened at dawn. She lay quiet for a time, comfortable in the knowledge that the person who must rise and dress and go downstairs to start the fires was Mrs. Gumm, not she. She heard her now moving about in the bedroom next door. In the several weeks since Sabra's arrival, Mrs. Gumm had become more friendly, although not so warm as Rachel and Miss Amalia, and Sabra offered the housekeeper a brief thought of sympathy as she went heavily down the stairs to start the day.

Sabra had been deeply shocked, on her first Sabbath with the Bradshaws, to learn that they did not observe the Lord's Day strictly: Mrs. Gumm cooked as usual, instead of preparing the food the day before; the girls were allowed to read anything they liked, even novels—even the *Awful Disclosures* of Maria Monk, whose salacious revelations of the sins supposedly committed in a Montreal convent were titillating one and all, including Eliza Bradshaw; playing was not forbidden to Lydia, or to anyone who wanted to join her in a game of hide-and-seek or battledore and shuttlecock. Sabra had seen Eliza paint a water color on a Sunday, and she had heard Rachel play a song—not a hymn—on the piano. She had been troubled in her conscience as to how to behave, since her father and all the people they had known had been very firm on the question of keeping the Sabbath, and so she took out her father's Bible and read the twenty-first chapter of Job; she said a prayer, and then she told herself once again that she was in this house through God's will, after all; and so, somewhat relieved, she went downstairs to join the others just setting out for evening services.

Lying warm and cozy now in her bed, she stretched out her cramped legs, but when her feet touched the cold place at the end she pulled them back quickly. In the pale light showing at the window she could see the plain, comfortable furnishings of the little room which had been given to her, and she wondered, as she had wondered every day since she arrived, at the enormity of her good fortune in having been taken in. Sometimes, just coming awake, she did not remember for a moment where she was; she thought, many days, that she must be still upcountry, but she could not remember with whom, or where, or why; and then as she awakened fully she remembered everything, and always she felt a little wave of relief and gratitude overtake her.

She turned over carefully so as not to lose her warm place, and her hand touched something which had slipped down under the covers: a little rag doll which Lydia, with all the love and care that a seven-year-old can give, had made and presented to her during her first week with the family. It was a nicely made doll, better than Sabra could have made herself, with black yarn hair and a pink dress and finely detailed eyes and mouth. For a moment, upon receiving it, Sabra had been reminded of another, older doll, one which she had had since early childhood, stolen from her the year before, a bitter loss even though she was nearly grown. Lydia had said that she loved Sabra very much; she proved it by following Sabra like a puppy, and chattering to her for hours at a time, and frequently irritating Rachel with her determination always to be as close to Sabra as possible; for Rachel had taken the new arrival in charge, and she did not welcome intrusion from anyone, even her baby sister.

Sabra had been glad to be taken in charge. New as she was, awkward and untutored as she was in the ways of town life, of life as it was lived in the homes of the wealthier classes, she was an eager pupil for all their tutelage. She watched them, day after day, as they went about their lives, so different from any life she had known. The country women with whom she had lived had worked harder than their men. They picked and cleaned the wool from their sheep, and spun and wove it; they cut and sewed the family's clothing from that weaving; they washed and mended, scrubbed and cooked; they nursed and birthed and buried; they tended the family vegetable plot and put by all its harvest; they milked and churned and sold butter and eggs in the village markets; they fed the small stock; they picked apples and cherries and blueberries and raspberries; and in their free time, they took in a bit of sewing or extra spinning to help fill the family purse.

Here the very basis of life was different: Mr. Bradshaw earned a salary, and from that salary he gave them money to buy what they needed: food, clothing, furnishings—everything. The women of the household had no share in the earning. It seemed to Sabra a remarkable thing that these women lived largely without labor—without labor, that is, beyond the ordinary cares of housekeeping. Of course, housekeeping in so large and elegant an establishment was more of a task than keeping a small house of four rooms in an upcountry village; but still, it was not the life of a farmer's woman. These Bradshaw females seemed almost a different species, and so she watched them as if she were a sojourner in a strange new world, she paid strict attention to their manners, and very quickly she came to do as they did, and to lose the rough edges of her difference.

She had had a hard time, at first, in the matter of drinking her tea. When ladies came to call in the afternoon, they conducted their conversations between lacings of hot, strong tea, the best of the China trade. From the cup-fuls which Miss Amalia poured for them, each poured some into her special tea saucer and drank from that; then she poured a bit more, and so on. It was a skill not easily acquired, this pouring neatly and swiftly so as not to let any liquid dribble off the cup and stain one's dress; but unless one had it, one was not a proper lady, and so Sabra practiced it diligently in secret in the pantry until she felt sufficiently adept to attempt it with the others. Rachel discovered her one day; for a wonder, she did not laugh.

"Right your cup a little more quickly," she said; "here, let me show you." And she smiled so kindly, and seemed to understand Sabra's little troubles so well, that Sabra felt even more devoted to her than before.

Lacking as she did a mother, or a sister, or any relation at all, she was a willing victim for all Rachel's attentions. She did not deceive herself:

Rachel would have undertaken anyone who fell into her hands. It was not Sabra upon whom she seized, it was the Homeless Waif—a ready subject for her energies, no matter who it happened to be. Still, Sabra allowed herself to think that Rachel might not have been quite so warm to someone else, that she might not have been quite so determined to refashion a less promising subject.

Sabra blossomed in the warmth of the older girl's attention. She felt as if she had lived all her brief life until now as a kind of shadow—an appendage to her father. No one had ever said, as Rachel did: "We will buy Bullard's ointment for your skin, and Goldsmith's *Essays* for your mind, and Aunt will teach you her special technique for beading. I haven't the patience for it, but you should learn it if you can. And tomorrow I will ask Eliza to start you at the piano; she plays very nicely. Would you like that?"

Of course she would: she liked everything, and Rachel most of all. In fact, and very naturally, she came to love Rachel as she had never loved anyone. She became devoted to her—this elegant, beautiful young woman of eighteen years who seemed just now to have no greater object in life than to shower attention on a poor country girl.

It occurred to her that she would willingly leave the comfort of her bed, this morning, for a chance to visit with Rachel before the rest of the household arose. The week just past had been a rush of preparations for Thanksgiving and the reception for the operatives, and she had been pressed into service full time by both Mrs. Gumm and Miss Amalia. She had had no more than a word with Rachel; their daily routine of lessons (for Rachel was tutoring her remorselessly in half a dozen subjects, including French) had been abandoned for the labors of hospitality. Sabra had missed their hours together; she wanted to see her now.

Sabra got up from her bed and pulled on her wrapper. She tiptoed out of her room and down the darkened staircase. Far below, in the kitchen, she heard the faint sounds of Mrs. Gumm's industry. She came to Rachel's door; feeling delightfully adventurous, she silently turned the knob and peered in through the crack.

Rachel sat propped up in her bed. By the light of a candle on the night table she was reading what seemed to be a folded newspaper. She had been concentrating so intently that she did not see Sabra at once; when finally she did, she uttered a startled exclamation and thrust the paper quickly under the covers. She looked angry as well as startled; then, relenting, she put a finger to her lips and motioned Sabra in.

Sabra shut the door behind her; she obeyed Rachel's silent command to sit beside her on the bed.

"I'm sorry if I disturbed you," she said. Rachel's nightcap had fallen off so that her dark hair fell down around her shoulders; she looked, at first glance, much younger than she did ordinarily; and yet, looking closer, Sabra saw that the older girl's face was hard and drawn this morning, and her fingers seemed like individual bands of iron on Sabra's arm.

"Speak softly. Is anyone else awake?"

"Only Mrs. Gumm, I think."

"Couldn't you sleep?"

"No. I wanted to talk—"

"I know. Did you enjoy yourself last evening?"

"Yes. They seemed very pleasant, very well behaved—" She had meant to say, "well-bred."

Rachel grimaced. "Only the most ladylike, the most gentlemanly, receive Father's invitations. None of the turnout would ever see the inside of this house."

Sabra had told her of the commotion she had witnessed when she arrived in the city with Goldschmidt. Rachel had been interested to hear of it. Her father had reported nothing of it to her, she said, and she was glad to learn what little Sabra could tell. She would have liked to see the Amazon, she said; she had never seen a woman speak—or shout—in public. She told Sabra then about the infamous Grimké sisters from South Carolina, who had in the past year so deeply offended public opinion by addressing the gentlemen of the legislature in Boston on the subject of slavery, and who had been violently condemned for their pains by the Orthodox clergy, whose Congregationalist tenets were very strictly those of St. Paul.

As Rachel moved her legs under the heavy coverlet, they touched the newspaper. She released Sabra's arm; she sat up a little and impatiently pushed back her hair. She pressed her lips firmly together and studied Sabra for a moment as if her new charge were a candidate for some great reward, and Rachel alone the one to say whether or not she should have it.

Finally she said: "You are my friend, are you not, Sabra?"

"Yes."

"And we have been very good to you since you came to us?"

"Yes. Very kind."

"Well, then." Rachel moved over; she held up the covers. "Come in with me, you will catch cold sitting there."

Sabra obeyed her; she stretched out beside her. She felt her warmth. Rachel smelled of lavender and of her monthly discharge, too, but Sabra did not mind. It was a warm and familiar odor, a woman's odor. Like many young girls she felt more at ease with women; men were always apart. Despite her life with her father, she felt that she could never be close to one of them as to one of her own sex. She knew that young girls grew out of that feeling as they matured and joined their lives to their husbands'; but even so she had often seen very little closeness between husbands and wives. She had seen that men never troubled themselves about women's affairs, nor women about men's, and that a woman married for twenty years and more was apt to be closer to her sister, or her daughters, or even to a special woman friend, than to the man who had been her master all that time. So she lay happily now, and suffered Rachel to hold her close with one arm while she raised herself upon the other to watch Sabra's face as she talked. Rachel pulled out the newspaper; she dropped it on the coverlet, she held Sabra close again and began to whisper her secrets.

"Do you know what that is, Sabra?" she said, meaning the newspaper.

"No."

"It is Mr. Garrison's newspaper. Do you know what that is?"

"No." Sabra felt uneasy, although the name meant nothing to her; she heard the undertone of excitement in Rachel's voice, and she began to feel that she did not want to hear what Rachel had to say—and yet, of course, she did, since it was Rachel who said it.

"Mr. Garrison is an anti-slavery man, Sabra—an abolitionist. Do you know what *that* is?"

Sabra had seen an abolitionist once; he had been shouted down while he spoke, and when she had asked her father why the people hated him, he had explained that they were Godly folk who knew that abolitionism was a spawn of Satan, contrary to the Bible and all its prophets.

"Yes," she said, although the expression on Rachel's face made her unsure.

Rachel gave her a little hug. "*Do* you, Sabra?"

"Yes. They are working against God's will—and against the law, too"—for the constable had seized the man whom she had seen and hustled him away.

"Ah, Sabra! You have been misinformed. Listen!" And Rachel began to tell the story of a poor little boy, beloved of his parents, who was sold away from them, never to see them again, and of their cries and lamentations, begging their master to relent, but he did not; and then she told of the martyred Lovejoy, lynched by a mob in Illinois for publishing the truth; and of a mob of gentlemen in Boston who almost killed this same Garrison who had, like Lovejoy, published the facts of chattel slavery in an issue of the paper lying before them now—a man with a price on his head, who lived with the daily threat of murder because he would be heard.

It was all a revelation to Sabra, but she could see that it was the stuff of life to Rachel. She came alive as she whispered, her eyes lighted up, her body shook and trembled with the force of her pent-up emotions, her anguish on behalf of all those poor people—"Yes. they are people, Sabra, like you, like me!" And Sabra could not dispute her, for she did not know. She had never thought about it. But she could see that Rachel was relieved to talk; she needed someone in whom to confide, and Sabra was that one—for, Rachel said, her father had forbidden the subject, had chastised her severely for reading Garrison's paper.

"How did you get this copy, then?"

Rachel smiled grimly. "One of Father's invited guests, last evening, was kind enough to bring it to me—entirely in secret, of course. Whenever I go into town now I am closely watched. I am not allowed to go alone, lest I might slip away and buy a copy for myself."

Sabra stared at the lovely face not six inches from her own: the eyes were hard, the voice bitter. It suddenly came to her that Rachel Bradshaw was a very great sinner. For it was a sin to disobey one's parents, especially one's father, and Rachel was incurring untold danger to her immortal soul by continuing, willfully, knowingly, to disobey him. Sabra was frightened; at the thought of Rachel's damnation, she began to cry.

Rachel understood. Gently, tenderly, she wiped away Sabra's tears. "You must remember that there is a higher law," she said.

"Than God's? O, Rachel—!"

"No—than man's, silly. There are ministers of God who do this work, and the anti-slavery men speak in churches, often enough. It is a matter of interpretation."

Rachel tucked the newspaper under the covers again; she sat up, leaving a cold place where her warm body had been. "I mean to do more than simply read of what others do," she said suddenly. She looked at Sabra very hard, as if the younger girl were a whip-wielding slave driver instead of her own miserable, doubting self.

Just then they heard footsteps in the hall: undoubtedly Miss Amalia's, for she was always first up after Mrs. Gumm. The sound of her loose, embroidered slippers went on past Rachel's door and down the stairs.

"And if you tell anyone—"

But she knew that Sabra would never tell. She knew exactly the extent of Sabra's devotion to her. She put her hand on her new friend's cheek; she pulled her close and held her tightly for a moment.

"There may come a time," she said, "when I need more than a—more than someone to listen to me when I am so full that I must speak, even like this, in secret. No one else will hear me, so you must do so. And if I need a different kind of help—"

Sabra trembled; she stopped her tears. As ignorant as she was, she knew that she had no argument to offer to this headstrong, determined young woman who seemed so fatally careless of the conventions in which she had been reared. And so she promised to help in whatever way that Rachel asked—how could she not?—and she slipped from Rachel's embrace and escaped back to her room, her mind confused, her heart sorely troubled. She dressed herself in Rachel's castoff clothes, she put on Miss Amalia's paisley shawl, she made her bed and put Lydia's doll carefully on the center of the pillow, she went downstairs to eat Josiah Bradshaw's food, in Josiah Bradshaw's house, never to confess to any one of them who had all been so kind and generous to her that she had agreed to sabotage their will and succor the traitor in their midst.

Later, in church, her mind wandered; she said a sort of continuous silent prayer throughout the service so that she almost missed standing for the final hymn, causing Miss Amalia to glance at her sharply, and still her mind was troubled. For although she prayed to God so diligently that day, she never knew that He heard, for she received no answer from Him, and she had no idea what she was to do.

For it was as plain as anything could be, that if she helped Rachel in whatever way she demanded, and if that help were discovered, she would lose her place in the Bradshaw house and be sent away, never to see Rachel again; and yet if she refused Rachel, the older girl would turn against her, and probably hate her; and she had become so dependent on Rachel's warm and sisterly affection that she did not think that she could live without it. And so she pondered her dilemma, and fretted and worried about it, and the winter drew on, and every day she awakened wondering if that would be the day on which Rachel would betray them. And she prayed to God, over and over again; but He did not speak to her, and so she grew accustomed to her fear, and she began to think that it was God's will, and that He had a reason for making her suffer it.

12

Christmas came and went. It was not a holiday in Orthodox New England. The factories ran as usual; the blue laws did not apply; not a lighted tree or a sprig of mistletoe was to be seen.

At New Year's the Bradshaw family had a quiet celebration. Small presents were exchanged: a cameo brooch, a tortoise-shell box, albums of verse both secular and religious. Mr. Bradshaw distributed two silver half-dollars to everyone, even the Gumms. In the afternoon, acquaintances came to toast the New Year with hot milk punch; it would be a good year, they said, a prosperous year. Trade had picked up everywhere. People came and went, a constant flow of well-wishers until long past dark.

Enoch Blood, Esq., and his son were the last to leave. Sabra had seen the younger man several times since the night of the party, for he was a frequent visitor and had, it seemed, the status of a favorite cousin or even a brother. He often came to call for tea, and once or twice Miss Amalia had invited him to stay for supper; usually he drove his trap or his small sleigh up the hill, but sometimes (as he said to Sabra with a kind smile) he preferred to walk, since walking gave him more opportunity to think. What he thought about he did not say, and Sabra was far too shy to ask. He seemed very intelligent, for all his slow-spoken way, and she was sure that he had more than enough to occupy his mind. He was the only young man in the city with whom she had had any contact thus far; she had met several of them two weeks previous at a social evening given by Mrs. Peabody, but she had been too shy to acquaint herself. She had never known any town-bred bachelors; they were very different from the country lads she had encountered. And since she had no pedigree to reassure them, they were shy of her as well.

Silas Blood stood now in the Bradshaw parlor, leaning against the mantel, looking somewhat untidy as he always did, his dark hair less carefully combed than it might have been; as he leaned down from his height, he smiled in his melancholy way. He, Sabra, and Mrs. Bradshaw were alone. Rachel and Eliza said good-bys in the hall; Lawyer Blood had taken his friend Bradshaw's arm and guided him to the dining room for a private word on a pending Corporation case; Miss Amalia had gone to assist Mrs. Gumm. Near the hearth, Mrs. Bradshaw reclined on a Grecian sofa, as fragile a thing as she; Sabra perched on a lyre-backed chair halfway across the room.

No one spoke; after a few moments, Sabra became uncomfortable in the silence, and she thought that she must say something to keep up the festive spirit of the day. She looked up from her hands clasped in her lap. What else, she wondered, did one do with one's hands? Graceful gestures were beyond her. She saw that the other two seemed not to notice her. Mrs. Bradshaw stared into the fire; Silas Blood stared at Mrs. Bradshaw. His face was somber, his smile disappeared; he seemed to have forgotten that they celebrated the birth of 1839.

Suddenly Mrs. Bradshaw put out her hand in a graceful gesture and commanded Sabra to her side.

"Come here, child. Sit beside me. We must think of some conversation to amuse our friend Mr. Blood, or he will desert us for livelier company. Will you not, Silas?"

She ignored his startled gesture of denial; she adjusted the flowing skirts of her mauve shot-silk gown to make room for Sabra beside her. All of a sudden, in that moment, she had showed more animation than at any time since Sabra's arrival in the house nearly two months ago. Her full mouth curved into a smile which might have captured the late Lord

Byron himself; her pale skin glowed, not with good health but with the heat of the fire; her large gray eyes, no longer dulled, no longer vacant, seemed windows to a strange new world of feminine enchantment.

She took Sabra's hand; she pretended to read its palm. "We must make a prediction for you, for the New Year, Sabra. You have been happy with us? Yes. Now: how can we make you happier still? What would you like to have? I know—yes, of course. You would like to have a—what shall we call him? A suitor? An admirer? Yes. We will call him an admirer. No, don't pull away. This is important. Women are put on earth for one reason only: to have admirers. But you cannot take just anyone. He must have certain qualities to make him eligible to steal your heart. Yes, that is what they do: they steal your heart. So you must be careful whom you allow to come close."

Until that moment she had looked only at Sabra. Now she turned up her face to the young man looking down at her; her body gave a slight, involuntary shudder, so slight that Sabra would not have noticed it had their hands not touched.

"This young man—your admirer," continued Mrs. Bradshaw, still watching Silas, "must be a gentleman. Of course he must. But not all gentlemen are gentle, Sabra; some of them are very cruel. You must understand that. He must be kind, that is the first thing. And he must be devoted entirely to you. And of course he must not be too extravagantly handsome or he will admire no one but himself."

She dropped Sabra's hand; she extended her delicate, drooping fingertips to the young man before them. From the tips of her pumiced fingernails to the full curve of her heavy, dark chignon, her pose made a line as graceful, as imperious as that of a prima ballerina. The long extent of the arm draped with a shawl of tatted lace, the angle of the head, the eyelids not fully opened—thus increasing the eyes' authority, their mystery—all of this would have seduced a stage director into an ecstasy of admiration. But Mrs. Bradshaw had never seen a ballet, nor would she: such things were indecent.

Silas stepped toward her. He took the proffered hand; he raised it to his lips. Again a shudder passed through Mrs. Bradshaw's half-recumbent form, much greater this time, a movement sufficiently acute to jar her careful pose so that she needed to cling to him for a moment to recover herself. Silas remained immobile, bowed over her hand.

Sabra looked down. She was a country girl, inexperienced in the way of worldly folk, but the most awkward country girl in all New England would have sensed, at that moment, that she was superfluous to the ongoing drama between her two companions.

She stood up; she murmured something about helping Miss Amalia. They did not respond; they paid no attention to her. When she reached the sliding doors which gave onto the entrance hall, closed this day to protect the delicate health of Mrs. Bradshaw from the constant draught of people coming and going, she turned to glance back at them before she slipped out.

Silas Blood had sunk onto one knee. Mrs. Bradshaw sat up straight, her head bowed toward his, her imperious gesture forgotten, her face as sorrowing as the face before her. Their foreheads almost touched. The pose might have been entitled "Mother Comforting Grieving Son"—and yet that was not it, that was not the right thing to call it.

What, then? Sabra did not know. She felt ashamed—embarrassed, as if she had accidentally caught sight of someone's unclothed body. It was not her fault that she had seen, and yet it was she who cringed and turned away. She felt as she had felt so often in her travels with her father: unwelcome, intrusive, a hindrance to other people's happiness.

She slid shut the doors behind her and went to make herself useful to Miss Amalia.

13

Unquestionably the most hated man in New England, and perhaps in all America, was the fanatic, Garrison. As 1838 passed into 1839, and the anti-slavery societies agonized over the question of whether to admit women to an active role in their deliberations, Garrison shouted defiance to the established order with his every breath; with his ceaseless attacks upon the slaveholders, he fanned the smoldering embers of the New England conscience into a faint, flickering flame of righteousness. By all but the most far-seeing humanitarians he was regarded as a dangerous instigator, a threat to the Union and—worse—to the sacred right of property. No one hated Mr. Garrison more than the slaveowners, unless it was the Northern mercantile and manufacturing gentlemen. His name was anathema, North and South; his doctrines, those of a traitor. And of all the Northern gentlemen who so hated and feared him, those who engaged in the manufacture of cotton cloth hated him the most. If he succeeds in his insane schemes, they said, there will be no cotton, for whites will not work the fields. Only blacks are suited for such work. And if you free the blacks you will have no labor, no cotton—no factories! The tens of thousands of Northern hands who earn their wages in our mills will be thrown out of work, the factories will shut down, the shareholders will go bankrupt—impossible! Silence that fool, they said; arrest him, lynch him if you will—but silence him once for all so that we may return our full attention to bidding for next year's crop.

So the interests of North and South were heavily intermingled; and it was no wonder that passions ran so high, that invective ran so low, that abolitionist tracts were banned from the South, that abolitionist speakers were stoned in the North.

And so, too, it was inevitable that Rachel Bradshaw's determination to help Mr. Garrison in his work would have roused her father's fury; that Bradshaw would instantly have been dismissed had the shareholders in Boston discovered her activity; that she endangered not only herself but all the family by her obstinate allegiance to Garrison's hated cause.

But as the days passed, Rachel did not mention Mr. Garrison again; and so, for a while, Sabra began to feel somewhat more at ease, and there were many days when her fears did not trouble her at all.

And then one evening as the family finished their supper, Mr. Bradshaw made an announcement which for a time drove all thought of Mr. Garrison from even Rachel's mind.

"We are to have a visitor," he said, "in about two weeks." He addressed himself primarily to Miss Amalia. "She can have Eliza's room, perhaps. Arrange things as you see best. She will be here for several days."

All of them seized upon the relevant word, but since it was Miss Amalia to whom he had spoken, it was she who must reply.

" 'She,' Josiah? Who is it?"

A look of distaste soured his fine features. "I had it from Boston this morning. They want her to have the fullest consideration. She is a Frenchwoman who has taken it into her head to examine the former British colonies. To see how we do, I suppose, and report back to her readers the curiosities which she encountered on her excursion through the wilderness."

"Mercy!" exclaimed Eliza, forgetting for the moment that it was she who might be inconvenienced by the arrival of the guest. "Does she travel alone?"

"I certainly hope so, since I have been requested to house and feed her. Most unsuitable."

"Why does she not stay at a hotel?" asked Rachel. "Then she could walk where she wanted and not need to depend on the carriage."

"It is the general opinion that she will be better off under our care. I am to accompany her on her tours of inspection."

"Of course," said Miss Amalia. She looked slightly preoccupied, already preparing for the disruption. "We must do everything we can to make her comfortable. We must have a dinner in her honor—and a social afternoon for ladies, do you think, Josiah? Yes—absolutely. Who knows what she will say about us if she is unhappy with her visit?" Her agitated glance fell on Sabra. "When you have finished your supper you may go to help Mrs. Gumm with the dishes—take that tray, there's a good girl. Tell her I will be along to see her in a few moments. We will organize a thorough program for—what is her name, Josiah?"

He fished in an inner pocket and extracted a letter, which he consulted. "Henriette Fallières," he said. Pronounced in his flat Yankee voice, the name sounded ridiculous: later, when they heard Mlle. introduce herself, they thought it the most beautiful name that they ever heard.

In the days before the guest arrived, the three older girls engaged in delicious, hurried speculations about her: how would she look? how would she speak? would she, in fact, speak English at all, or would they be reduced to Rachel and Eliza's primitive French augmented by sign language? what would she wear? and, most important, what would she think of them?

"She will think nothing of us," said Rachel as they sat cozily in front of the nursery fire late one afternoon. "Why should she? Probably we will see very little of her. She will spend most of her time in town, at the mills."

"Whyever would she want to come to America?" muttered Eliza through clenched teeth as she bit off a length of pale blue silk thread. She was embroidering yet another tablecloth, her expectations having been raised by the arrival of a letter from New Haven the previous day.

"Whyever not?" replied Rachel mildly. "I am sure that it is very different here from France. And therefore interesting."

"Aren't you looking forward to meeting her?" asked Sabra. She let her knitting drop; it was a hopeless tangle and would have to be unraveled and started over, since no human foot existed which might fit into that grotesque shape. "I am. I've never met a French person before."

"Neither have we," smiled Rachel. She reached out to take the knitting, just as if Sabra were a child of Lydia's age; but Sabra did not mind, for she knew that Rachel would never criticize but only offer to help in the kindest possible way.

"All French people are corrupt," pronounced Eliza. "Mrs. Dr. Knight said so the other day, when Aunt and I called and Aunt told her that this woman is coming to visit. Mrs. Dr. Knight said that Aunt should have put her foot down and refused to have her in the house."

"Mrs. Dr. Knight is simply jealous," said Rachel. "She is afraid that she won't get to meet her. O, I do wonder if she speaks English!"

She did. She arrived one clear mild day during the thaw when the melting snow made rivers in the drive, and the air was soft and the sun warm and winter a thing easily forgotten. Mr. Bradshaw had gone to meet her at the depot on Merrimack Street and drive her directly to the house, so that she could refresh herself and rest from the rigors of her journey before beginning her inspections the next day.

All the girls were too excited to wait indoors, and so in a short time their boots and the hems of their skirts and petticoats were soaked from running up and down the drive every few minutes to see if the carriage had come. Twice they caught a glimpse of Miss Amalia at the parlor window; Sabra was glad to see that she was as curious as they were, if less willing to show it. Of Mrs. Bradshaw they saw nothing; she was resting in her room, preparing for the exertion of meeting her guest.

After a while, to amuse Lydia, the older girls began to build a snowman. Sabra decided that she was wet enough, and so she left them and walked around the house on the shoveled path to the back garden. Gingerly she brushed the snow off the top of the stone wall to make a seat; she settled herself and looked over the treetops on the steep slope below, down to the river shining in the sunlight, and to the west, to the crowded town, the thrusting spires of all the churches, to the red-brick factories huddled in the sharp curve of the river, their bulk spiked by smokestacks, the bright blue sky over all.

It was the third week in January. She had been with the Bradshaws for almost three months. She had, it seemed, become a part of their family. Nevertheless, during all that time she had been nagged by the thought that she was after all an outsider, present on sufferance; and if she did anything very wrong—if she helped Rachel, say—she would be cast out again. But now, at almost the moment of the visitor's arrival, she felt a new sense of pride, of belonging. The Frenchwoman would be the stranger, and Sabra would be one of those to whom she turned for help, for explanations, just as she would turn to all the others. "Tell me about this," she would say; "and about that—why do American girls do so and so, why do they dress in such a way, behave as they do?" Sabra hoped, for Mr. Bradshaw's sake, that the operatives in the mill would not take it into their heads to stage another turnout for the visitor's edification.

She heard Lydia's voice: "They are here! She's coming! Sabra, she's here!"

She ran—stumbled—in time to see the carriage turn into the drive. Rachel and Eliza had mounted the front steps to greet the guest; Lydia stood hopping between them; Miss Amalia had opened the front door and now stood waiting with ill-concealed excitement.

Gumm drew up the horses; the carriage door opened and Mr. Bradshaw stepped out. His face was impassive as always, but Sabra thought that his wide thin mouth looked more tightly drawn than usual. He stood ready to assist his passenger to alight. There was a brief pause. The family stood as if spellbound, waiting to see her.

And then a silvery voice floated out from the depths of the carriage; to their amazement and relief, the words were unmistakably English, and very loud: "One moment, Mr. Bradshaw, please! I must just collect myself. Would you be so kind as to hold my ear trumpet?"

14

It is a fact of human nature universally acknowledged that if there is anything to see, people want to see it; that if there is anything to know, people want to know it; and that, most of all, if there is anything to see, to know, someone will be ready and eager to communicate it so that all may benefit, not least the communicator.

Everybody is curious about everybody else. Gossip sells; so does more verifiable information. And when you have a brand-new country, and a brand-new town within it, a city sprung up overnight on the banks of a great river, an Experimental City devoted to manufacturing, populated by picturesque young ladies who do the work—thousands and thousands of young ladies—a City of Spindles run on philanthropic lines entirely (so it was said) for the ladies' benefit, then you have something to be seen, you have something to be known, and most assuredly you have a legion of eager scribblers ready to enlighten everyone on both sides of the Atlantic having the price of a volume or two.

No amount of Corporation dividends could have bought the favorable puffery provided gratis by these visitors. They came; they gaped and gawked; they wrote nothing but good news. Once in a while they were rude: Frederick Marryat, the English novelist, said that he had heard the most accomplished swearing in America upon the lips of a female at Lowell.

Some, thinking to flatter, committed excruciating faux pas, as when Michel Chevalier in 1836 compared the new manufacturing town to a Spanish town filled with steepled convents; the operatives reminded him of industrious nuns. Did he not know that in Protestant America, and most particularly in Orthodox New England, convents were the most hated institutions? That people feared and despised convents—"the Pope's brothels," they called them—and that upon the slightest provocation they raided them, terrified their occupants, and burned the buildings to the ground as they burned the Ursuline Convent in Charlestown in 1834?

Of course he did not know it. He was a Frenchman. Very probably he was a Catholic himself. He had intended a compliment. Convents, indeed! Was ever a man more insulting?

But most of the visitors performed as expected; grateful for such fascinating subject matter, they praised the city and its founders in thoroughly unobjectionable terms and never asked to see anything not included on the regulation tour.

15

"But that is ridiculous! You have never seen the work at the mill? You should learn something of the world around you! How can you understand what it is to live, if you do not see how people—women, just like you—get the means to do it?"

The voice was the voice that had come from the carriage: loud and clear, the words precisely enunciated, beautifully accented. And now, a few days later, they had had the face and form to go with it. They were not yet entirely accustomed to her, but at least she was somewhat less startling to their eyes and ears; they did not feel compelled to look away and then look back again, as if to reassure themselves that there really was such a creature as Mlle. Henriette Fallières living on God's green earth alongside them.

She was a small woman with a neat, graceful figure. She had a fine clear skin; close-set eyes, very black; small thin hands. Her clothing were exquisite: on this day she wore a slate blue coat-dress trimmed in black braid, with an attached, matching pelisse. A collar of black lace ringed her smooth white throat; a wide black morocco belt accented her tiny waist. But none of this, attractive as it was, disguised what in another woman would have been three disastrous liabilities:

First, her hair was that most unfortunate color: red. Not brown-red, or golden red, but a bright carrot-red that not even her smooth center part and plain Grecian knot could offset.

Second, she was monstrously ugly. Seen from a distance, or from an angle, her appearance, despite the color of her hair, was not unpleasant. But when she faced you, when she looked directly at you, the first shock of her ugliness was almost more than composure could bear—your composure, not hers. Her face was dominated by a large and bulbous nose. Sabra did not understand how a person could have been born with such a nose; it must have developed, she thought, as the result of some horrible illness about which none of them had the courage to question her. The nose was all the more pronounced because she almost completely lacked a chin; her profile receded sharply from her mouth to her neck like a badly cut silhouette. As if to compensate for this deformity, the upper portion of her face was markedly larger than normal; a high, knobbed, domed brow dominated the whole, and, because of the under-development of the lower portion, gave her face the impression of lunging at one, led by the forehead.

Her third disadvantage was her deafness. In order to hear anything at all she had to employ an ear trumpet which she needed to point directly at the speaker. At first Sabra was quite shy of it; she found that when it was pointed at her she suddenly forgot whatever she had been about to say. But gradually it ceased to bother her, and by the end of Mlle.'s visit she hardly noticed it.

These dreadful personal liabilities, which would have turned some women into angry and bitter viragoes, or forced them to become reclusive, retired from a world which had little place for unattractive females, had in Mlle.'s case encouraged her to perfect the arts of charm and conversation and so by sheer force of her personality distract her companions from the initial shock of her appearance. One needed only five minutes in her company to swear that Mlle. Henriette Fallières was the most beautiful creature in the world. They all fell captive to her, even, apparently, Mr. Bradshaw, who ordinarily seemed to disregard women as much as any man did.

At the breakfast table that morning he attempted to explain to her why his daughters, his wife, his sister-in-law, and his new charge had never been to see the place where he so assiduously earned his living.

"It is not fitting," he said. "Ladies should not visit factories. Certainly children should not." As he spoke he cut his beefsteak with what seemed unusual ferocity.

Mlle. allowed herself a brief exclamation of surprise. "How many people did you tell me were employed in your factory, Mr. Bradshaw?"

He chewed; he cut; he chewed again. Sabra wondered about his digestion. They were not accustomed to much conversation at meals, and certainly not to interrogations of the master of the house. "About eighteen hundred," he said.

"And how many of those are female?"

Would he speak sharply to her, Sabra wondered, and thus risk the wrath of her pen? Miss Amalia's face was blank, Rachel's and Eliza's sharply attentive. Lydia was not yet capable of understanding the dangers of Mlle.'s questions, but she, too, watched the visitor closely, captivated as they all were by the charm, the intensity of this bright butterfly caught for the moment in their chilly net.

Mr. Bradshaw swallowed the last of his meat; he took several gulps of coffee. He did not seem to be annoyed; he seemed, in fact, willing to tolerate her questions, if not to welcome them. He smiled at her in a conciliatory way, but there was something else in that smile, a kind of response to her challenge which only later was Sabra to learn to recognize. A man and a woman may speak of anything—the weather, the price of tea, the condition of heathen souls—but if that challenge and response were there, they were really speaking of one thing only: the endless dance, the eternal attraction between the sexes.

"About twelve hundred are female, Mademoiselle."

"And how many children?"

"Very few. We do not employ large numbers of children in Lowell."

She smiled at him demurely; she poured more coffee for herself and sipped at it delicately. "At least not very young children, I believe. Not children of six or seven such as work in Rhode Island. But children of ten, eleven—I saw them myself yesterday."

"With time out—three months a year for school, remember. We will not hire them otherwise. And they are only doffers, at that. They do not work hard."

"But long, *non?* Thirteen, fourteen hours a day?"

"Mademoiselle—" He understood the criticism, but he did not lose patience with her.

"And surely, if the women and children can bear to work for you so long, then your own women and children—yes, even the little one—can bear to see them do it."

She smiled at him; and he, more pleasant and gracious now in defeat than Sabra had ever seen him when he had his way, gazed at her thoughtfully for a moment, his cool eyes considering that improbable face.

"Very well," he said at last. "We will go this morning." He glanced swiftly around the table. "Be ready in half an hour. I will tell Gumm to bring around the carriage."

And so it was settled. They went to fetch their cloaks and bonnets, Eliza grumbling at the interruption of her morning's sewing. Miss Amalia, warning them not to forget their India rubbers, went to tell her sister of the expedition, for Mrs. Bradshaw always breakfasted in her room.

It was a cold, gray morning, just starting to snow. They jolted out of the graveled drive and onto the icy, rutted road. Although Sabra had seen the Commonwealth factory and all the others from a distance on her excursions to the shops and to St. Anne's, she had not returned to it since the night she arrived in the city. Even then she had not been inside the factory itself. Mlle. Henriette, who had been just three days in Lowell, knew far more than she, or Miss Amalia or any of the Bradshaw women, about what went on behind the high red-brick walls of a cotton manufactory. That it was a veritable humming, throbbing beehive was obvious; but what precisely was done to produce the honey was a mystery to them all.

They were soon enlightened.

They left the carriage at the gate and walked into the mill yard, where Mr. Lyford came running out to greet them and to be presented to Mlle. To the other women he gave only the most perfunctory greeting. In a moment he had turned back to Mlle., and, with Mr. Bradshaw at her other side, they entered a door in one of the buildings. Rachel shepherded the others behind.

Instantly they were caught up in a Hellish noise so great, so overpowering, that human speech was impossible. Here they heard only the shrieking, pounding, thudding, clattering voices of the machines, and they were struck dumb by the cacophony, the maddening, mind-shattering din.

For a moment, just inside the door, they halted, watching Mlle. and her guides make their way through the nightmare of machinery. They were, it seemed, in the presence of a row of insatiable monsters, devouring the endless supply of fluffy gray-white stuff fed into them. Mlle. and the men had stopped beside one of them, and as she reached out her hand in a tentative way, as if to touch the web of carded cotton emerging, Mr. Bradshaw seized it and held it, shaking his head, admonishing her. In another moment, having seen enough of the monster, they moved toward the far end of the room where a narrow, circular staircase led to the second floor.

Lydia clung to Sabra's skirts as they attempted to follow. Reaching down to free herself, Sabra saw that the child was terrified, crying hard. She bent down to shout into her ear.

"Come, pet, it will be quieter upstairs. We must stay with your papa."

Lydia shook her head, tears running freely down her face. "I want to go home!" she screamed. "I hate it here!"

Rachel and Eliza had reached the stairwell; Miss Amalia had stayed behind, torn between her duties of chaperonage and her concern for Lydia's terror. Finally she leaned toward Sabra so that her mouth almost touched the girl's ear. "I will take her outside to wait!"

They reversed positions, Sabra's mouth to Miss Amalia's ear, both impeded by their bonnets. Sabra was conscious that they were being closely observed by the ostensibly busy operatives tending the machines.

"Don't you want to see the rest of it?" she shouted.

"No, I will take her into Josiah's office—or into the yard!"

Without waiting for a reply, she and Lydia fled down the aisle to the outside door, leaving Sabra to find her companions in the upper rooms.

They stood before a row of perhaps a hundred spindles, watching the thread being drawn out. Mr. Lyford was explaining the process, gesticulating (less danger here of amputation), glancing at Mlle.'s face to see the effect of his revelations. She seemed entranced, giving him her entire attention; Rachel and Eliza seemed less interested. Eliza, in particular, looked bored and unhappy. The noise here was not so oppressive, although from the floor above came a rhythmic thud-thud which in a few moments made Sabra's head begin to throb in tempo. Her nose and throat were growing uncomfortable, too, from the stale, heavy air which was permeated with lint and foul smoke from the oil lamps; the room was hot and oppressive, although through the tall windows which faced the river she could see the snow swirling down. She wondered why no one thought to open them to the cold fresh air outside.

Again they moved on, to the next floor, where she saw the source of the thudding, throbbing noise: the great looms, fifty or more, whose brass-tipped shuttles flew back and forth like deadly arrows. She saw perhaps twenty women standing throughout the room tending the machines, watching closely the long white webs of emerging cloth, glancing constantly back and forth to see that the warp threads did not snap, that the shuttles continued smoothly on their courses—lithe Arachnes dancing attendance on their mechanized masters.

Mlle. stood with the men halfway down the center aisle. Their little group had been joined by a third man, the overseer of this department. They communicated in a sign language, animated on her part, more restrained on theirs; seen from a distance they looked like a group of marionettes caught in the wrong play. From where Sabra stood near the entrance, she was able to see Bradshaw's expression: never had he looked upon any of his children with the mixture of pride and affection which he bestowed upon these lifeless, yet frighteningly active pieces of machinery.

Eliza touched her arm; she leaned in close. "I am going down," Eliza shouted; giving Sabra no chance to reply, she turned away. Sabra watched her descend the steep narrow stairway until the top of her blue bonnet had disappeared. Then she turned back to the confusion of the weaving room, and, following the example of Mlle., tried to understand something of what she saw.

The operatives did not seem to notice the visitors, although Sabra was sure that their presence did not go unremarked. She recognized several girls who had attended Mr. Bradshaw's reception: one, a fair, plump young woman whose name was (she thought) Miss Swan, caught her eye and smiled. Sabra did not mind. She knew that Eliza would have called Miss Swan bold and forward, but Sabra felt reassured at the slightest evidence of human feeling in this world of roaring machines. She smiled back, and nodded; she walked to Miss Swan's place between the looms and watched her as she tended first one and then another, unerringly pacing her movements to match theirs. The operative's face was shiny with perspiration; dark patches of damp stained her brown bodice. Sabra would have liked to speak to her, but since the deafening clatter all around made speech impossible, she continued to smile, feeling rather foolish now, and very much in the way. She turned her attention to the shuttle's swift tracery across the strands of the warp, but after a few moments, when she had seen it travel back and forth perhaps a hundred times, she felt that she had seen all there was to see of the operation of the power loom, and so she looked around her to see what else she could. The room was long, high-ceilinged, pillared by support columns, with a row of tall windows on either long side. She made her way to the nearest window and looked out. She stood above the river. Through the snow she saw the opposite shore; as she glanced down she was startled to see how high they were. Black water foamed over the rocky bed; torrents of spume shot out from spillways underneath the factory building. She rested her forehead against the cold glass; she felt the vibrations from the hundreds of pounding machines. Quickly she stepped back. Would the building collapse one day from that incessant strain? Would frantic operatives throw themselves from this very window onto the rocks below, rather than be caught in the wreck of splintered timber and disintegrating brickwork? Had the gangs who built this monstrous place done their work well—well enough, at least, to protect the lives of those who labored here? She glanced out again, but the height made her dizzy and so she turned back to the machines. Mlle. and her party stood some distance away, half obscured by the giant looms; Sabra looked around for Rachel. She stepped between two looms and made her way out into the center aisle. Rachel stood perhaps fifteen feet away, beyond several machines, standing close to a girl whom Sabra recognized as another of Mr. Bradshaw's guests. Standing very close—were they shaking hands? Just then Rachel turned away, she came out to the center aisle and walked toward Sabra although she did not see her. Rachel's head was lowered; the brim of her bonnet obscured her face.

She passed quickly and joined her father and his guest. They were, it seemed, done with their tour and ready to descend. Mlle. flashed a quick bright smile to everyone; she seemed fascinated by what she saw, although to Sabra it was unpleasant beyond words. How could they stand it, these operatives—twelve hours a day and more, six days a week? It was by their labor that the Bradshaws lived; but for a whim of Mr. Bradshaw's, she would have been among them.

Slowly, carefully, holding tightly to the railing, they made their way down the treacherous circular stairs whose treads narrowed at the turning to no more than three inches.

They crossed the snowy mill yard evading the railway cars which steamed directly up to the doors of the sheds to unload the bales of raw cotton. In Bradshaw's office, they discovered that some small difficulty in the day's business had arisen which would require his presence at the factory for another half-hour. He looked up from his consultation with Mr. Lyford and regarded the women—a cluster of nonproductive females —with some puzzlement. What were they to do while he attended to his business?

"I suggest that you extend your researches by going to Mrs. Glidden's boarding house, Mademoiselle," he said, and because he addressed the stranger, his tone was light and pleasant. "There is a half-hour before the dinner bell rings. She will feed you well, as she has the dinner prepared for the girls, and you will be able to sample for yourself the nourishment which we provide our employees."

"You are very kind," said Mlle. "I would be most interested to go. But will we not be in the way? She is a busy woman, is she not?"

His mouth twitched: hardly a smile. "She will be happy to do it—at my request," he said.

Sabra glanced at Eliza. That young lady was undoubtedly suffering, since she had wanted to spend some time that day trimming a new silk shawl to wear to Mrs. Peabody's the next evening. Now, it seemed, she might need to stay up half the night to finish it, for Eliza's vanity was considerably stronger than her need for sleep.

Bradshaw scribbled a note and gave it to Miss Amalia. "Tell her to feed you well, Amalia, and introduce Mademoiselle. Tell Mrs. Glidden that she is free to answer any questions that Mademoiselle may wish to put to her, and please to do so at my request. I will join you presently."

Mrs. Glidden's establishment was halfway down the row of brick houses set at right angles to the mill gates. She proved to be a cheerful, red-faced woman of about forty-five, who, as she revealed at seemingly endless length, had been in Lowell for five years and never happier in her life, caring for "my girls," as she called them. While places were being set at the long table covered with oilcloth, she proudly showed her visitors the amenities of her house.

The front room on the first floor was her own apartment, from where she could keep a vigilant eye on the comings and goings of her boarders and where, as she said proudly, the door was always open for any girl who felt the need to confide in the mother-away-from-home that Mrs. Glidden so clearly felt herself to be. A framed copy of the Corporation's rules for its employees hung over the fireplace, silent assistant in the task of keeping good order. Beyond the landlady's quarters, occupying the greater part of the downstairs, was a long room which served as the dining room and, in the evening, as the girls' parlor. Upstairs—for she was thorough, was Mrs. Glidden, and she showed all—were the bedrooms; they were mostly of a decent size, except for the small chambers at the front and back of the house, but so crammed with beds and bureaus and boxes and clothing that it hardly seemed possible that four or six girls could squeeze themselves in and perform in relative peace all the necessary tasks of their toilettes. However, Mrs. Glidden averred that her girls were a fine group, exceedingly genteel. "Good honest girls, mind you, from good honest country stock. Most of 'em read and write better than I do myself." Curfew was never a problem at her house, she said, although she had heard last week that a girl in a neighboring house had been dismissed for being late twice in three nights. "They don't know what's best for them, sometimes," she said. "Ten o'clock's plenty late, when you're called awake at five in the morning—and besides, late hours ruin a girl's reputation and spoil her chances for a husband."

As they returned to the dining room to find their meal awaiting them, Sabra thought that to live so close-packed under Mrs. Glidden's watchful eye would be more than enough reason to be willing to spend twelve or thirteen hours a day at the mill. Although the boarding house was not more than half the size of Mr. Bradshaw's home, some forty people lived there. Sabra thought of her small room next to the Gumms', which, although hardly luxurious, was at least her own; she thought of Rachel's and Eliza's spacious chambers, of Miss Amalia's—how did they bear it, these close-packed girls who worked and lived constantly in each other's presence?

The commencement of the meal diverted her thoughts. It seemed at first that in order to impress them, Mrs. Glidden had ordered an especially bounteous feast; but she assured them that the girls who would soon arrive, summoned by the noon bell, would be given exactly the same meal. "They work hard, indeed they do, and we feed 'em well, and keep up their strength there's talk of starting a hospital at Mr. Boott's house, but no need to fill it up right away, is there? This is all on Corporation orders, miss Here, just try this mutton, none better anywhere the way I bake it. They tell me what to feed the girls and I do it, just as they say—oh, they're careful of their help, very careful, just like fathers to their children."

She smiled and nodded at them as they sampled the Corporation's menu; and, indeed, it was as good a meal as Sabra had had anywhere before she tasted Mrs. Gumm's cooking.

Lydia soon had had enough. She sat dozing in her chair, unaccustomed to the morning's wearisome routine. Soon after, Eliza and Miss Amalia pushed back their plates; then Rachel gave up, firmly protesting Mrs. Glidden's attempt to give her just one more slice of dried-apple pie. Finally Sabra paused, unable to put down another mouthful. Mrs. Glidden looked at her accusingly.

Mlle., for a wonder, continued to eat, although ordinarily she seldom took much more than Lydia. And all the while, through mouthfuls, she kept up her conversation with her hostess: what was the most pleasant aspect of her job? did she have favorites among the girls? what was the funniest thing ever to have happened in the house? the saddest? what were the weekly expenses for food? wood? soap? And so on, until Mrs. Glidden had become so enchanted with the attention showered upon her that she forgot her chagrin at the others' poor appetites and bloomed forth happily under the sun of Mlle.'s interest.

That it was a genuine interest none of them doubted. Mlle. really did want to know all those details. No one, not even one so clever and charming as Mlle., could have manufactured such a curiosity. Whether or not every item which she unearthed on her tour would eventually find its way into her manuscript they did not know; probably Mlle. did not know herself. But she seemed to need to saturate herself in her subject, to discover more about the objects of her attention than perhaps they knew about themselves. They were all fair game for her net, and, once caught, they were taken up and scrutinized and seduced into revealing all; and then, ever so gently, set down again, feeling (because of her great tact) not exploited but positively useful, as if they had performed some great service (as perhaps they had) in the furtherance of some important work. She would tell all France about them; they could not but believe that France would be better for it.

"How long do the girls stay with you, Mrs. Glidden?" (Finishing her potato; turning to a dish of sauce; expertly managing her ear trumpet all the while.)

"And what do they do after they have finished their time here? Do they return home?" (Eating the last of the vegetables; accepting a slice of pie.)

"And how do they amuse themselves in the evenings?" (Cutting a piece of cheese; stirring sugar into her coffee.)

Sabra was so engrossed in watching and listening to Mlle. that she was startled when the door opened and Bradshaw came in. Snow clung to his greatcoat and to the tall gray beaver hat which he held. His face was oddly flushed, and at the instant of coming in he wore an angry look, almost distraught, as if he were about to accuse one of the females before him of the most outrageous behavior. Both Mrs. Glidden and Mlle. rose to greet him. Their attention seemed to soothe him. Rapidly his face cleared; he returned their welcoming smiles, and with hardly a glance at his daughters or Sabra, and only the barest greeting to his sister-in-law, he positioned himself beside Mlle. and proceeded to inquire whether she had had a profitable morning's discovery. Mrs. Glidden, meanwhile, went to the kitchen for more hot food; as she disappeared they heard the clanging of the bell in the mill tower.

"There," said Miss Amalia, "we should have hurried. Now we'll be caught in the crush. The girls will be running in for their dinner and positively trample us."

"No, Aunt," said Eliza with a sour look. "You forget how genteel they are. Such ladies will never trample anyone."

No sooner had she spoken than they heard the front door burst open, feet pounding through the hall. Instantly, it seemed, they were inundated by a horde of operatives, some chattering, a few laughing, but most seeming simply intent upon getting to their places and bolting down their food, rushed to them on steaming platters by Mrs. Glidden and her kitchen help. Indeed, most of them hardly noticed the little group of visitors, even though it contained a man. Sabra noticed that here was no polite conversation, no relaxation which surely they must have desired after their morning's labor. It was a grim and necessary business, this meal, to be got through as fast as possible only to rush back again to the machines.

At a nod from Bradshaw, the party of onlookers filed out. When they reached the street they saw that the snow had stopped; the air was milder, and already the cover of white had begun to soften into dark watery patches on the frozen mud, encouraged by a warming sun now appearing through the clouds. A few stragglers to the noon meal brushed past, their faces pale and tense.

At the end of the row of houses near the mill gate, Sabra saw a small crowd gathered around a tall, hatless man who stood on a wagon. He was haranguing his listeners in a perturbed and even violent way, waving his long thin arms, pointing first at one person and then another, turning and twisting his body as if he were in the grip of some consuming ague. Most of his audience seemed unimpressed; they stood with blank expressions and that tentative stance which indicates flight, but here and there Sabra saw a truly affected one, or two, who heard the man's message, whatever it was, and took it genuinely to heart.

"Abijah!"

Bradshaw's outraged voice turned every head. He had been walking at the back of his little group, in conversation with Mlle., but now he strode forward. The preacher—for he was that, and not an agitator as Sabra first had supposed—swung violently around to face him. His face was convulsed, his eyes burning, his hair wild; he raised his hand as if in benediction.

"Come, brother! Join me in God's work!"

"Get off the property, Abijah! I warned you, I'll have you arrested—"

The preacher thrust out his arms in a gesture of supplication. The sun formed an aureole of his shiny, tousled golden hair, so that he seemed a radiant angel come unexpectedly among them.

"Brother! Brother! The Lord is coming! Help to prepare His way! Leave your money-grubbing and welcome the Lord!"

Lydia tugged at Sabra's skirts. "Who is that man?"

"I don't know, sweet."

"Why is Papa so angry with him?"

"I don't know that, either. It will be all right. Don't worry."

"How distressing," murmured Mlle. soothingly, craning her neck and pointing her trumpet toward the preacher. "The world is filled with madmen, is it not? Who is this one?"

"He is—"

"Eliza!" Miss Amalia's voice was strangled, fearful; her hand shot out to grasp Eliza's arm.

Eliza glanced at her aunt; a silent message passed between them. Then Eliza turned again to Mlle.

"He is my father's brother," she said. She ignored Miss Amalia's restraining hand. "And you are right, he is insane. He comes here purposely to embarrass us—do you remember, Rachel, the last time?"

"Yes," said Rachel. Her eyes followed her father, who, ignoring the preacher's outstretched hands, had disappeared through the gate. The crowd, on his appearance, had begun to drift away, and now the preacher stood quiet, his face turned up to the sun, his eyes closed in some private communion with his deity. "And he has broken his promise. I am not sure, it was some years ago, but I think then he promised to stay away. And Papa may have given him money to do so, I don't know."

"And he promised to go south and never come here again," said Eliza. "Not here, not even to Massachusetts. Dreadful man, frightening people—" She broke off as three men appeared from the mill yard. Swiftly and efficiently they seized the preacher and threw him down onto the ground. He offered no resistance; he lay for a moment and then slowly and calmly he got to his knees, and then to his feet. Heedless of the snow and mud on his shabby clothing, he turned and walked away from the mill, toward the little group of watching women. They drew back as he approached, but they need not have feared an unwanted greeting, for he walked unseeing, his eyes fixed on some inner vision. Sabra saw that he was, indeed, very like Mr. Bradshaw, the features slightly coarser, the head slightly larger. It was an uncomfortable thought, that two such similar bodies could house such disparate souls.

What had he been trying to tell them? He had been shouting the same warning that her father, dying, had whispered to her: "Do not allow yourself to be corrupted. They forget their salvation." But why had he chosen this place? She knew the spirit that moved these holy men, the commands from God which they struggled to obey—but why here, why now? Her father had never spoken but in a church. Street preaching was undignified, he had said; the Lord's word should be given in the Lord's house. A man who shouted promiscuously in the street was no better than an agitator like the abolitionist whom they had seen. She felt a sudden rush of sympathy for Mr. Bradshaw: she did not wonder that he was angered and embarrassed by this eccentric relative.

They watched him go. He passed down the length of the boardinghouse block and turned onto Merrimack Street and was gone.

Suddenly Miss Amalia bent down to peer at Lydia, still clinging to Sabra's skirts. "Lydia, mind what I say. You are not to mention this to your mama when we are home. Do you understand? She would be distressed—most upset. She must not know."

The child nodded soberly. She might not understand what had just occurred—her elders did not fully understand it themselves—but she did know about her mama and the importance of not upsetting her.

"Ah," said Mlle. "We are rescued."

The carriage pulled up beside them. Mr. Gumm looked more sour-faced than usual, but Bradshaw's composure seemed restored. He got down to help them in; they set off for Belvidere Hill. None of them mentioned what had just occurred; even Mlle., with her insatiable curiosity, did not have the courage to assault her host's grimly placid demeanor with unwelcome questions. Instead, after a while, as they jolted across the Concord River Bridge and up the steep Andover Road, they spoke of the morning's tour: of the comeliness of the operatives, of the difficulties of rethreading a broken warp, the excellent boarding houses provided by the Corporations.

And so when they arrived home, they were able to report quite truthfully to Mrs. Bradshaw that it had been a most interesting expedition, and that they were glad finally to have seen the exact way in which cotton cloth—the source of all their support—was produced in the Commonwealth Mill.

She received this information with her usual vague interest. Sabra wondered, not for the first time, what intelligence, what urgent news, might animate that lovely face, those large, mild eyes. She was seized with a sudden, wicked urge to tell Mrs. Bradshaw about the preacher, but of course she stifled it. It is not her fault, she thought. Mrs. Bradshaw consumed a great many medicines; a visit to the apothecary was almost always among their errands when they went shopping in the town. No doubt the medicines (for what illness, wondered Sabra) had weakened her, sapped her strength.

It occurred to Sabra that Mrs. Bradshaw and Mlle. were about the same age. As they all gathered in the parlor for their tea, that afternoon, she glanced from one woman to the other: one single and childless, one married and a mother; one homely, one beautiful; one busy and very much a part of the world, one indolent and removed from the world almost entirely. One alive, she thought: and one dead.

Later, as she helped Mrs. Gumm in the kitchen, she asked the housekeeper if she had ever been to see the mill.

"No, child, why'd I want to do that?"

"It's interesting. Very noisy and dusty, but interesting all the same." This brought no response more than a grunt, so she ventured further. "Has Mrs. Bradshaw ever been to the mill, Mrs. Gumm?"

"What'd she want to go there for?" said the housekeeper contemptuously. "No place for a lady, is it? And besides, it's as well she stayed home this morning, and I don't mean just on account of the snow, neither."

Sabra paused in her task of wiping tea cups. "Why?"

"She had a visitor, that's why, and so pleased after his visit, I hardly recognized the look on her."

"Oh? Who?" Mrs. Bradshaw had had some good news, then, some pleasant project of good works laid before her, perhaps, to occupy her time—

"I don't care what Mr. Bradshaw says about him," said Mrs. Gumm (for like all her kind she knew the secrets of the household which she served). "He's a real likely young man, for all he don't take to the law like his pa. If he'd just settle down they say he'd make a fortune—"

"Who, Mrs. Gumm?"

"Ain't you listenin' to me when I talk, child? Silas Blood, that's who."

16

They came at last to the final day of Mlle.'s visit. That evening, the Bradshaws were to entertain her at a dinner; the next morning she was to leave on the railway cars for Boston. Her itinerary in America was a combination of places and people which she herself wanted to see—Lowell, Boston and New-York, the Congress at the national capital, a colony of Shakers at New Lebanon, a plantation in the South; and, on the other hand, places and people in which she was not particularly interested, but which had been visited by previous travelers and therefore made mandatory for her investigations.

"Believe me," she exclaimed, "I would not give *that*"—a snap of her fingers—"to see Sing Sing! But M. de Tocqueville saw it, commented upon it, brought it to the attention of the public—and so now everyone will think that I—what is the word? That I shirked—yes—shirked my duty, if I do not see it as well." She shuddered. "Convicts—horrible! And all that *politics*—yes, I am interested in politics to a degree—a very small degree, since I am as powerless in France as you are here to influence the course of events." She smiled brilliantly; her high, knobbed forehead lunged at each of them in turn. "The revolutionists forgot us, did they not? In both countries, France and America. I have read your Declaration—oh, yes, many times. And once I met the wonderful Général Lafayette—although he was not then, poor man, what he was when he fought here. But they were all very busy with the rights of man, *non?* And as for the rights of women—" She stopped; she shrugged, aware that she had indulged in private opinions which were of no interest to her audience.

They did not dream of questioning her. Her eccentric thoughts were of a piece with all the rest of her: odd, foreign, so alien that one simply gaped at her. They would no more have thought of trying to refute her than to change the course of the sun across the sky, or shift the river from its banks.

Besides, they had no idea what she meant. "The rights of women?" The phrase was meaningless. Some new fad in Paris, they thought; some new heresy from the decadent French.

On the morning of the dinner party, Sabra was alone in the kitchen, plucking a fowl, when a peremptory knock on the back door announced the arrival of Patrick O'Haran, the delivery boy from Codwell's West India Goods. Hastily she wiped her hands on her apron and went to admit him. He staggered in under the weight of a heavy box of provisions and carefully set it down.

"Good morning, Patrick," she said, trying not to look too pleased at his presence; he was after all only a grocer's boy, and Irish at that, and certainly therefore not a suitable object for her friendship. She knew that she must look higher than Patrick if she were to better herself. And yet she had come to anticipate his visits: he was always cheerful, always friendly, always ready to entertain her with some tid-bit of town gossip which even she, a newcomer, enjoyed because he delivered it with so great a show of secrecy and extractions of promises never to breathe a word of it that she had to laugh at his performance. "Now don't tell no one," he would say, his thin, chapped face a caricature of conspiracy, "but I hear that Mrs. Peabody's cook's givin' in her notice 'cause they let the dog—a big old black Lab—into the house, an' he runs off with the food all th' time, an' last week they didn't have no dinner on Sunday 'cause the dog got up on his hind legs and pulled the cold roast off the table just when the cook turned her back for a minute. An' Mrs. Peabody told the cook to go right ahead an' leave. You can always hire a cook, she said, but a good dog is hard to find."

And Sabra would swear eternal silence, and giggle with him, and go on about her work greatly heartened at the thought of having a gentleman friend to amuse her, even if he were only Patrick. Often she slipped him a stray apple dumpling or a surplus piece of cake—a gesture which undoubtedly had something to do with his gregariousness—but she thought that he liked her for herself, too, and so inevitably she became fond of him.

This day he looked especially thin, especially harried. "Mornin'," he said, panting a little. "Can't stay, everybody wants extra today, got to get back—how's everything here? How's the Frenchie?"

She had discovered during her first meeting with Patrick that, poor and lowly as he was, he had a hearty disdain for anyone else's claim to position. Mr. Bradshaw was always "the Boss," to Patrick; Dr. Knight was "Sawbones"; the mayor, "His Mightiness," and so on. She did not mind his flippancy; it gave her some small secret amusement, and some perspective on the realities of the world—reasons which she was sure motivated Patrick, too, even if he could not have phrased them. Probably he could have, had he cared to.

"She's fine." She looked around for some small bit of food for him. He lived with his mother and an impossibly large number of brothers and sisters in a squalid cabin, so she inferred from what he said, in that area of the town known both as the "Acre" and as the "Paddy Camp Lands." She was certain that none of them ever had enough to eat. His father was dead, crushed by a falling block of granite while working on the gang that cut the Hamilton Canal. "You just wait, Patrick, she will write us up and we will all be famous. Perhaps I should introduce you so you can be famous too." She put half a dozen sugar cookies into his hands; instantly he began to devour them.

"Never mind," he said through a mouthful of crumbs. "What'd I want to be famous for? Just livin'—that's all I want. Yer havin' a party for her here tonight, then?"

"Yes. Who told—" But she had forgotten: in some mysterious way, he knew everything. She took two apples from the bowl on the sideboard and handed them to him. He did not begin to eat them; he stuffed them into the pockets of his ragged blue jacket, and she thought that at least two of his family, and possibly more, would have a treat that evening when Patrick returned home. He grinned his thanks. "Well, I'm off. Mr. Codwell'll take it into his head to thrash me if I'm not back on time." He turned to go, but then, his hand on the door, he paused and looked back. He considered her for a moment.

"Did y' have a good time at Haggett's Pond last Saturday?"

The question was unexpected; she had to stop and think before she could answer. "Oh—yes. Yes, we did. Were you there? I didn't see you." They had taken Lydia to ice-skate the previous Saturday afternoon. To Sabra's surprise, Mrs. Bradshaw had accompanied them, and even Mlle. had ventured, briefly, onto the ice.

Patrick's face flushed deeply. "If you should be goin' again—" He hesitated. Never before had she seen him at a loss for words; she could not imagine what he was getting at.

"Let me know when you're all goin' again, and I'll make it worth your while. I promise!" And before she could reply he had bolted out the door.

She returned, puzzled, to her fowl, for Mrs. Gumm liked to unpack the groceries herself. Why would Patrick want to know when they were to go skating again? She knew that he could have no dishonest purpose in mind: to wait until everyone save perhaps Mrs. Gumm and Mrs. Bradshaw was out of the house, and then possibly to make some attempt at burglary. No. Patrick was sharp, he was flippant—arrogant, even—and he wanted very much to get ahead at something or other; but she was sure that he was not a thief. It was very odd; whatever could he want?

Her ruminations were interrupted by the return of Mrs. Gumm, grimy from her morning's preparation of the fires. She cast a critical eye to see whether Sabra had done with the fowl. "Good," she said. "Now go and set the table—for sixteen, mind—while I start the soup." And so in the rush of preparations for Mlle.'s entertainment Sabra forgot, for a time, Patrick's request, and abandoned herself to the pleasures of counting out the silver, folding napkins, handling the delicate plates and bowls, decorated with blue Chinese landscapes, which gave off a tiny chime if she flicked them, just so, with her fingernail. Accustomed as she was to coarser country ware, she reveled in the luxury of this rich man's things; she felt privileged to touch them, to imagine them as her own.

The guests were to arrive shortly after seven. It was a raw, dark day, threatening snow, and Sabra was glad to be warm in the house; she did not envy Mlle. as she traveled from place to place in the town making her tireless inquiries. Mlle. had planned a full schedule in an attempt to omit nothing, to learn everything before she went away, and so they did not expect to see her again until five o'clock at the earliest. Thus they were surprised when, shortly after three, they heard the wheels of a carriage in the drive—a hired hack, as they saw when they looked out. Mlle. had gone to town with Mr. Bradshaw that morning and had planned to return with him. What had happened?

"Sick," muttered Miss Amalia, as she left the girls and hurried to the door. "Sick, like as not, and all our plans spoiled."

They heard her exclamations and Mlle.'s muted reply; just as they had gotten to their feet to see what was wrong, Mlle., with Miss Amalia supporting her, appeared in the doorway.

She looked as though she had been through a battle—as, indeed, in a way, she had. Her pale gray gown was splattered with a dark stain which might have been paint, or mud, or even dye (she had gone to visit the printworks that morning), but they saw a long red smear across her cheek, and they knew that so fastidious a woman as Mlle. would not have been so careless as to stain herself in that way. Then, too, her behavior was not that of a person who has merely got in the way of a pot of paint. Her easy charm, her bright welcoming smile, were absent now;

she stood where Miss Amalia led her, before the fire, and stared not at her companions but into the flames with eyes that had seen some horror of which they knew nothing.

They brought up a chair and she sat in it. Miss Amalia sent Sabra to the kitchen to fetch a basin of warm water and a cloth to wash Mlle.'s face and begin to sponge her dress; later Mrs. Gumm could take it and give it a thorough cleaning. When Sabra returned to the parlor Mlle. seemed to have revived somewhat; she was eating a piece of lemon cake and talking in a low, strained voice. "I was at the Appleton Corporation," she said slowly. "Mr. Talcott is the Agent there—most kind, most helpful. We had toured three floors. We were at the roving frames watching the drawn sliver being twisted down. I was standing next to a girl, very young, not more than fifteen, a lovely little girl, they told me later that she had only just come, that she had been on the Corporation less than a month. I feel that somehow it was my fault, that had I not been there, she would not have— Well. I stood beside her, watching—I could not speak to her, of course, because of the noise—and I must have distracted her, because she turned to me. She turned to me—"

Her voice broke; her strength failed her so that she could not hold her trumpet, but needed to rest it in her lap while she struggled to regain her composure.

"Dear Mademoiselle," exclaimed Rachel, "let us take you upstairs—"

But of course Mlle. could not hear her. After a moment she lifted her trumpet again, as if, in order to speak, she needed to be able to listen. She continued: "Her hair came undone. They told me that she had been warned to wear a net. But she was young, careless—the young" (here she looked meaningfully at the young women listening to her) "never think that a calamity will happen to them. Always to someone else, they say—and so they endanger themselves, they do not take the most elementary precautions— Ah, that poor child!"

She closed her eyes. "The machinery—the belts and wheels—caught her hair. Not more than a single strand, but it was enough. Caught her hair and pulled her down, caught her arm—" She opened her eyes; she peered at them to see whether they understood. "The wheels tore off her scalp," she said. "Caught her hair and tore off her scalp, caught her arm and crushed it—"

Her words echoed in their ears. *Tore off her scalp*—but how could such a thing happen? *Crushed her arm*—but this was the model city, so it was said: the workers' paradise. Such dreadful accidents happened only in England. Not here, not in this raw new red-brick Eden, not two miles distant from where they sat, warm and comfortable and safe from the rigors of the world. *Tore off*—

"They could not stop it," said Mlle. Her voice was more intense now, as if this fact was the most important of all. "They could not stop the machine for—I don't know, a minute, two minutes—it seemed an hour. We held her, we reached to pull her back, but the teeth of the wheels were imbedded in her flesh, we could not get her free." She shuddered; violently she shook her head. "As deaf as I am, I can still hear her screams. I hear them now, in this room. And her face—I saw her face, I have never seen a face like it—"

Suddenly, with great firmness, Miss Amalia interrupted her. "You must understand that such a thing has never happened before," she said. "It was a terrible accident, yes, but it was indeed an accident, and you must not blame yourself. And you must not think that such accidents are everyday occurrences. Nothing of the kind has ever happened before—"

"To your knowledge."

"To my—but I tell you that it has not! Everyone would know of it—"

"The overseer was annoyed that the machinery needed to be stopped. He was more than annoyed. He was angry. Can you believe that? And one of the women there, one of the operatives spoke to me, when the wheels were finally still, when the room was quiet and they were working to get her out, this woman told me that it was not the first time someone had been caught. Not the first time, she said, and then she saw that the overseer was watching us, and she moved away from me. Would he dismiss her, do you think, for talking to me?"

"I am sure—" began Miss Amalia; and then she hesitated, making it clear that she was sure of nothing at all. "They are fair men, the overseers. Of course I do not know this particular one, but I am sure—I *know* —that they dismiss only for good cause. I cannot imagine that talking to you—"

"In such circumstances," said Mlle., with something of her former spirit.

"In any circumstances. You are an honored guest, at liberty to see what you will."

"Not this," said Mlle. grimly. "I understood very well that they were sorry that I was there to see this. Do you know, when I announced to my friends at home that I was going to America, many people told me that I must come here, to this very city. But of course you know how famous you are. Everyone has heard about you. 'You must go there,' they said, 'it is something new, it is a miracle, a new life for thousands, it is nothing like Manchester or Lyons, the people at Lowell are as fine as you will see anywhere, they work, yes, but they are not factory slaves, they are not poor beasts chained forever to their machines—' No, child, no more cake. My stomach is still uneasy. But give me more tea. I am very cold, I cannot seem to warm myself."

She laid by her trumpet again; she leaned in toward the fire. Rachel handed her her cup; absently, her thoughts far away from the Bradshaws, she drank from it. They sat silent around her, not wanting to speak among themselves, not daring to speak to her.

Miss Amalia's admonishments had made them aware of the larger implications of the tragedy which Mlle. had witnessed. Many visitors had come to see the new city; most of them had been sufficiently well guided, sufficiently impressed, to write favorably of what they saw. And so they made it possible, through their glowing reports, for the manufacturers to hire more young women to replace those who went home. It needed only one bad report—one warning of the management's carelessness, of its callousness—to undo the good of all the praise before.

Now, watching the visitor as she sat silent before the fire, they realized that they had no idea what she would say about them, about their proud little city, the showplace of the Yankee capitalists. Undoubtedly Mr. Bradshaw would be most distressed; he had been so carefully instructed to oversee her visit. Sabra wondered if he had been with her at the Appleton Mill. No, she thought, or he would have brought her home himself. All his care and trouble for her had vanished in a moment, for what remained in her memory would be the image of the mortally wounded girl, the callous overseer, the whispered report of the operative. . . .

At last Mlle. raised her trumpet again; she managed to smile at their worried faces.

"Ah, well," she said. "They called the amiable Dr. Knight, at whose home I was so pleasantly entertained. He is to be with us here tonight, is he not? We will hope that he has good news. And now I will go to change from this—" She glanced down at her ruined dress, which had been, it seemed, only further stained by their efforts to clean it.

She went upstairs then, while her listeners dispersed to help Mrs. Gumm with the final preparations for the dinner. As it happened, Dr. Knight worked with sufficient speed over the victim to attend the party. Afterward, when it was too late, they wished that he had not.

17

Nine o'clock of a raw January night. Down in the town the mills stood quiet, the great water wheels immobile, the flow stopped in the power canals. The shops were just closing. Here and there a tardy operative lingered over a display; money came hard here, and the women needed to guard against seductions on all sides. Bonnets, shawls, gloves, shoes, jewelry, books, umbrellas, capes—the shopkeepers had a cunning eye for what would part a young miss from her pay, they had a talent for showing all the riches of the town to these poor country girls starved for show of any kind. And of course the shopkeepers had a captive clientele: how could a man help but grow rich, when he had seven thousand customers with two hours every evening free to browse? They lived off this army of operatives; they were parasites, some said, suckling on this endless flow of steady wages, swollen and grown fat on the operatives' life-blood.

Up on Belvidere Hill sat an assortment of their betters. Parasites also? Perhaps. It would have been an excessively harsh judgment, and yet they seemed even fatter, more swollen than the tradesmen. Several of the ladies, in fact, seemed ready to burst from their tight lacings; they picked delicately at the fourth—or was it the fifth?—course of the meal, so as not to seem impolite, but it was apparent that they could consume very little else without some adjustments somewhere, preferably in the region of their corsets. The gentlemen, too, seemed replete: their talk had become desultory with the appearance of the roasted quail, and now their eyes darted back and forth less restlessly, less anxiously, than they had done an hour or so before.

The host and his sister-in-law labored under the shadow of the day's events. They knew, although most of their guests did not, that Mlle. Fallières' opinion of the city and its famous enterprise had been badly prejudiced by the accident at the Appleton Mill. She was not herself this evening: her vivacity, her charm, her interest in all their lives had been muted; she seemed removed from the conversation, she propounded no stimulating topics for discussion. Her thoughts were elsewhere, with the injured girl, perhaps. When Dr. Knight arrived, freshly washed and shaved, showing no trace of the bloody mess attendant on his duties, she questioned him about the girl's condition. He answered cautiously. She was resting, he said, under the mercies of an opium draught. Her condition was extremely grave, of course, but not as much of her scalp had been lost as they had feared at first, and so even though the arm was gone, she was a strong, healthy girl, fresh from the country, her constitution had not yet been weakened by the rigors—

But here Mr. Bradshaw had provided a timely interruption, and Mlle.'s brief burst of curiosity on this single topic had been cut short. She watched Dr. Knight now as he meticulously cut his meat. Each small bite disappeared quickly between his full, red lips; occasionally, between swallows, those lips issued words of amiable response to the fragments of conversation provided by the rest of the company. Dr. Knight, in the way of many of his brethren, had an uncanny knack of shutting off his powers of memory, so that the distasteful practices in which he engaged to earn his living did not spoil his infrequent moments of leisure. He labored tirelessly to sustain the health of the population; to the best of his knowledge (acquired through his attendance at the rounds of old Dr. Mercer of Andover) he soothed, and healed, and occasionally resurrected them—snatched them from the very jaws of Death, if not from the belts and wheels of the cotton machines. And he was to be rewarded for his labors: the Corporations had announced, not a month since, that they would buy for a hospital the handsome Georgian palace built by the man who had overseen the beginnings of the new town, the late Boott. Dr. Knight was to be in charge. And surely there, surrounded by the best equipment, by sober, decent men to nurse, by a staff of doctors as hard-working as he—surely he would do some great work. He had already begun to plan. There were diseases peculiar to factory labor which until now he had been unable thoroughly to investigate; *prolapsus uter*, for instance, might well respond to a new operation which he had imagined. Until now, he had had no opportunity to attempt it. But with the new hospital, with every instrument to hand, with ample room to house the numbers of patients he would need to perfect his technique, with countless subjects waiting for his skilled knife—yes. He would succeed. No doctor this side of the Atlantic had a more fertile field to plough. Hundreds—thousands—of women awaited his attentions. He would succeed; he would publish his discoveries. Fame and riches awaited him.

So ran his thoughts under the current of amiable talk around the table. From time to time he glanced at his host, aware of Bradshaw's restraint. A bad day; unfortunate that the Frenchwoman saw the mishap. The operatives could be warned—threatened—easily enough to mind their tongues, but this annoyingly curious traveler was a more difficult case. He looked at her, sitting across from him beyond the candelabra, between Peabody, Agent at the Hamilton, and old Lawyer Blood. Dr. Knight's fleshy mouth lost its smile as he suffered once again the small spasm of distaste aroused in his manly bosom by the sight of a homely woman. Mlle.'s charming personality—the armor in which she encased herself to confront the hostile world—had had no effect on him; he could not for a moment forget that she was that affront to all right-thinking men, a homely female. And a forward one as well: several evenings previous, at an entertainment for her in his own home, given at the insistence of his wife, he had found her ceaseless questions most offensive. A pretty face, a good shape and a dull brain were the female qualities most valued by Dr. Knight; in his opinion (he was accustomed to having his opinion well received), this foreign inquisitor could not decamp too soon.

The quail was removed; the beef appeared. Several of the guests moved uneasily in their seats, longing for digestive powders. A phrase innocently dropped by Mrs. Long, wife of one of the Aldermen, caught Dr. Knight's ear. He belched; he hastened to respond.

"Lyceum lectures, ma'am?" His heavy face peered around two intervening bodies to confront her. "A longer season, you say?"

Mrs. Long, braver than she looked, replied that the girls seemed to enjoy the Lyceum evenings; since the lectures always dealt with the most informative topics, they undoubtedly profited from them as well.

"Profit? How do they profit?"

"Why—they learn, Dr. Knight. They expand their knowledge of the world."

He withdrew his gaze; he looked around the table. As it happened, no one else was speaking. He had all their attention.

"Better they should contract it, madam! Cancel the lectures, I say. Women have no business knowing anything about the world! The world is men's affair!" There was no immediate response, and so he added, more loudly: "The business of women is babies, madam! Babies! New souls to populate this great country! New native-born American souls, madam! Have you seen the latest figures from the ports? Do you know that last year alone—in one year, madam!—over five thousand people landed at Boston? Over five thousand, and the majority of them papists! And that is only the figure at Boston, it does not include New-York or any of the Southern ports. Do you know that, madam?"

Mrs. Long did not know it. She had never thought about it. Unlike the factory women, she was removed from the world, she was entirely preoccupied with her domestic duties. She bit her lip; she blushed; she looked down at her untouched portion of meat.

Lawyer Blood offered the opinion that the gentlemen in the legislature might be—ah—persuaded to enact restrictions.

"Restrictions—yes! An excellent idea. But even now it may be too late, sir. They breed like the salmon in the river, these people. Do you know that there is a woman in the Acre who has just borne her twentieth child? Her twentieth! Now how can we compete with that? No, madam—" He peered again at Mrs. Long, whose eyes remained downcast in mortification at having begun, however innocently, so indelicate a discussion. "These operatives should not be gadding about in the night air! They should be in their rooms, asleep, conserving their strength so that when their time here is done, and they return to their homes to marry—as so many of them do—their constitutions will be as strong as the day they came to us, and they will be able to bear their husbands fine troops of healthy sons to maintain the native American position at the ballot-box!"

He looked triumphantly at his host, perhaps in hope of a nod of agreement. But the good doctor had ridden his hobby-horse too far; he had ridden it, in fact, into the land of the gauche, where people say what they think, and frequently live to regret it.

Bradshaw returned the stare. He was visibly angry. The papist across the table was angry, too, although she was not so quick to show it. There was a silence around the table. Several of the ladies picked at the sweet custard which had replaced the beef. Several of the gentlemen cleared their throats. Mrs. Dr. Knight, shimmering in yellow silk, searched desperately in the well-stocked cupboards of her mind for a way to rescue her husband from his self-indulgent flight.

At last, to their mingled relief and alarm, Mlle. Fallières replied. She smiled at Dr. Knight; she uttered a charming laugh before she spoke.

"Do not mistake what you have here, Doctor. It is precisely because the operatives here attend Lyceum lectures, while the operatives in England, in Europe, do not, that your Experiment is so successful."

She had been seated with a little space to her left, so that she could easily, skillfully, raise her trumpet to hear his reply.

"They come for the money, Mademoiselle."

"Ah, but for the experience of the world, too, do they not? There are books here, libraries, newspapers—even though, as you say, they will retire to marry, still they are bright girls, many of them, who would attend colleges with their brothers if they were allowed."

This new heresy seemed momentarily to stun Dr. Knight into silence. In the next instant, Mrs. Gumm and Sabra had appeared with urns of fragrant coffee. It was that moment in every promiscuous evening—every evening, that is, of men and women together—when the women rose and departed, leaving the men to relax in comfortable brotherhood. The women exerted themselves to the effort; they rose as one, following their hostesses' lead, and in not more than half an hour the gentlemen proceeded to the parlor to join them, their cigars safely extinguished, their profanity neatly tucked away, their sharp and active brains turned off once again so that they might more easily endure the company of their women.

A short time later, after the last guests had driven away and the sound of the carriages creaking down the drive could no longer be heard, Josiah Bradshaw turned to his sister-in-law. Her face was tired and pale under the ruffles of her cap; he understood her devotion to the household, her ceaseless labor to undertake her sister's burden. And yet he did not feel grateful, for he was her benefactor, after all, and not the other way around. Still, she was a help to him. Although he never acknowledged this fact to her, he admitted it to himself from time to time.

"A pleasant evening, Amalia," he said. His eyes left her, passed briefly over the listless face of his wife, and came to rest on Mlle.

"Pleasant indeed, M'sieu Bradshaw," she said. She looked as fresh and animated as she had that morning when she had set off on her journey of inspection. Amalia had told him, privately, before the guests arrived, of Mlle.'s distraught condition when she had returned from the mill. She seemed completely recovered now. She smiled at him.

"Mademoiselle, if I might have a word with you—"

Still she smiled. He thought that probably she knew what he wanted—needed to say. He felt a spasm of annoyance; he began to chew at the inside of his cheek. Damned clever female—!

He said good night to the others and ushered Mlle. along the back hall to the room that he called his library. In fact there were a hundred books, at least, arranged on the tall narrow shelves flanking the windows. But he never read them; he was not a reading man. He knew that Rachel often came here to read; several times he had thought to forbid her, but—after all—he loved her, and he continued to tell himself that the unsuitable activity of her brain would not harm her body's health.

He shut the door behind them; from the low-burning fire he took a light to light the pressed-glass oil lamp. He was annoyed to see that his hands trembled. He had had long experience at controlling his anger; why did it threaten to escape him now?

Mlle. Fallières stood easily by the pedestal table in the center of the room. She seemed perfectly at ease, her ear trumpet poised to catch his words. He would have liked to see her distraught, weeping as Amalia had described her earlier; such a sight would have given him a comfortable sense of superior control. He remembered their conversation at the breakfast table some days since: the unacknowledged challenge and response between man and woman—

"I hope you do not write about that girl," he said abruptly; and instantly damned himself for a fool. That was not the way to persuade her!

She surveyed him. "I must write about the most interesting, the most dramatic things I see. And the most—what is the word? Significant? Yes."

"There was nothing significant about that. It was merely an accident. You will only shock and pain your readers by describing it."

"And the men who own the mills, I will shock and pain them, too? No one writes unflattering reports about the Lowell cotton mills, isn't that right? And you do not want me to be the first?"

"It was an extraordinary thing. It will not enlighten anyone except to show that accidents happen here as elsewhere."

"It would be extraordinary if they did not."

"But we do not need—"

"'We,' M'sieu Bradshaw?" She looked at him as if she were his equal. He felt another emotion rise to supplant his anger: for the first time in memory, he felt fear. If this woman wrote a sufficiently unflattering account of the factories, Boston would hold him responsible. A bad report, made all the worse because it came from a foreign pen, would reflect badly on everyone, not just the one factory where the accident occurred. People would say that Lowell was a bad place where bad things happened; fathers would not let their daughters come down to work in the mills if they read of things such as belts and wheels that tore a girl to pieces.

Graciously she held out her hand to him; she smiled at him as he took it.

"I will try to be fair, M'sieu Bradshaw. I will try to be objective. I have been happy here. I will not repay you badly."

She said a hurried good night, then, and left him alone. He was appalled to see how quickly, how completely, she had understood him. He felt ashamed: humiliated. Begging a visitor—a female visitor!—for a good notice! Needing her good will, because her spite could jeopardize his position!

He flung himself full length onto the brocaded chaise. He closed his eyes, but he felt no peace, no rest. Images of the evening's party flashed through his mind; snatches of conversation still buzzed in his ears. He knew very well that his duties to the Corporation were not ended, each day, with the closing bell; he was expected to maintain his position at all times. Social evenings, church attendance, meetings at the Mechanics' Hall—always he was not simply himself, but the embodiment of the Commonwealth Corporation. An ordinary man could perhaps unbend and enjoy a party in his own home, but not the Agent of the Commonwealth Mill. Of course he could give it up: he could resign, he could return to Newburyport or go to Boston, he could try to make a living in one of the great trading houses. But such a living, for a man with no capital to invest, was a highly doubtful one. He would have to begin all over again, like a boy fresh out of pantaloons: clerking perhaps, or secretary to some rich merchant— No. Nathan Appleton, only the year before, had cleared two hundred thousand dollars from a China ship, but Appleton had had capital to invest. He, Josiah Bradshaw, had not. He had instead an annual salary from the directors of the Commonwealth Corporation; and the woman who had just left this room had the power to endanger even that.

He loosened his cravat; he moved restlessly on the chaise, which was too short for his long body. If only he had a son! Then he would work at anything, he would know no fear, he would devote himself in whatever way necessary to succeed—to grow rich. For a son, any sacrifice would be worthwhile! But Dr. Knight had said, "Never again."

A small bright flame of resentment—anger—had begun to flicker at the back of his brain. Knight was an ass. What did he know? What did any of them know, those medicine men with their mysterious phrases and their air of insufferable superiority? Was there not a higher Providence which determined whether one lived or died, regardless of the doctors' ministrations? Knight had four sons. How dare he tell another man not to try to get even one?

Suddenly he sat up. He felt an unfamiliar sensation in the private regions of his body. He was not a concupiscent man. Some men, he knew, were constantly troubled by their uncontrollable urges. He had never been so. For him, the release of his seminal fluid had been solely into his wife's body, solely to get her with child. Thus he had avoided the dangers of insanity and death brought on by self-abuse.

He thought of his wife in their bed. He felt just then that he would perish under the weight of his terrible longing. Why was he being punished so? Why could he not have what was every man's right? He tortured himself with thoughts of the boy: a tall, strong child, with his mother's eyes, perhaps, but with a firm, intelligent face like his father's. A boy who liked to ride, to run—a boy quick to learn, easy to teach. A son: a reason to live!

Swiftly he extinguished the lamp. He left the room. He hurried up the staircase, pausing at the last curve to listen, to hear if anyone still were awake. But he heard nothing, and so he hurried on, possessed by his vision.

I will have him, he thought. He pushed open his bedroom door; silently he closed it behind him.

She understood. She roused from her half-dream and took him into her soft white arms as if she were welcoming a lover instead of the instrument of her own destruction.

Both of them understood this: his need, and her obedience to it, even at the cost of her life.

Shortly afterward, just past midnight, the wounded operative died. The news did not reach Bradshaw until after Mlle. Fallières had departed on the Boston cars at nine o'clock the next morning.

18

After breakfast all thc Bradshaw household gathered to bid farewell to their guest. Her trunk stood ready in the hallway; Mr. Bradshaw awaited her at the door. She embraced them; she bestowed upon them her brilliant smile. "How kind you have been—how generous! I will never forget you!"

They followed her out to the pillared porch. They watched Mr. Bradshaw hand her into the carriage. As it lumbered down the drive, they saw a white handkerchief flutter from its window. Then she was gone. Sabra thought of her journey: by the cars to Boston, by packet boat to New-York and the South. She tried to imagine such places. What would Mlle. see? Whom would she meet?

Only three months ago, Sabra had thought herself fortunate to be taken into this house. Now, as she returned to the warm, elegantly furnished rooms, seeing the placid routine of the family's life stretching before her, she felt that she was in a place of confinement. The shining paneled doors seemed the doors of a prison; the kind inhabitants, her guards.

I am ungrateful, she thought. He might have put me into the mill, and yet he brought me here. I am luckier than most.

To make a private atonement, she offered that morning to clean the fireplaces for Mrs. Gumm. In the afternoon she played with Lydia, and heard her lessons, so that Miss Amalia could rest from the rigors of the week just past. She read to the child a story about a pilgrim who journeyed to the Holy Land. She tried to imagine Jerusalem: what did the pilgrim see there? The words of the story meant nothing to her. She wanted to go to Jerusalem herself.

The next day, looking for Rachel, she found her reading in her father's library. Sabra glanced over Rachel's shoulder: *Ferdinand and Isabella.* Those words meant nothing to her, either, although certainly Rachel found some interest in them. But why that, thought Sabra. Why anything? What possible use will Rachel have for all the information she collects, all that she learns?

She struggled to subdue her restlessness. Something will happen, she thought. I will not spend all my life in this house, reading to Lydia, polishing silver with Mrs. Gumm, waiting for Mr. Bradshaw to return home at night to give us some news.

One day in the first week of February, Rachel asked her to go into town. "Just the two of us in the small sleigh," she said. She smiled, but there was a hard note to her voice. "I am given special permission to go, to make calls—with you as my chaperone."

And Sabra wondered at this, too, for Rachel had often expressed her contempt for ladies who spent their afternoons gossiping in one another's parlors. But she did not argue; she was glad to escape the house for even so short a time. As they descended the hill, she took deep breaths of the cold air and burrowed her hands more deeply into her muff and tried to imagine that she and Rachel had set off on some grand adventure. What that might be, she could not imagine: anything, she thought. Rachel will surprise me when we arrive.

But Rachel merely drove to Mrs. Whitney's house, where several ladies had already gathered. Hotly, vociferously, they discussed the news from Paris: the fashionable length for cloaks, the number of puffs in sleeves, the depth of flounces, the prettiest trimming for pelisses and pelerines. These things were already out of date in France, but in America they were of the greatest moment. Then someone mentioned the Reverend John Franklin, who had recently assumed the pastorate of the Second

Universalist Church. The Reverend Mr. Franklin was a bachelor. Several of the ladies present, including Rachel Bradshaw, were spinsters. Endless, simpering conversation was expended on this point, for there was no man in the world more fascinating than a bachelor minister.

Sabra could not understand why Rachel had gone to Mrs. Whitney's, nor why, when they had returned home in the cold, rosy sunset, she had reported the excursion in such enthusiastic detail to Miss Amalia. But she did not question. The afternoon had seemed to make Rachel happy; Sabra, in her devotion, needed no further explanation.

After that day, they went out together two or three times a week. Sometimes Miss Amalia or Eliza joined them, but on those occasions they needed the larger sleigh or the carriage, and the services of Mr. Gumm, and so more often they went alone. All the household seemed to understand that Rachel was now to be indulged as if she were a convalescent recovering from a nearly fatal illness. "Go and enjoy yourselves," Miss Amalia would smile. "Remember me to Mrs. Blodgett"—or Mrs. Hathaway, or Mrs. Trask, or any other of a dozen acquaintances.

Eliza showed little interest in paying calls. She had, it seemed, a satisfactory understanding with the young Southern gentleman; at any moment she expected that he would approach her father and ask the crucial question. Eliza, these days, needed nothing but her thoughts to entertain her. She declined to expose herself to the cold; she chose instead to sit mooning by the fire, dreaming happy Southern dreams.

One day toward the end of the month Rachel drove them to pay a call, not upon a lady, but upon a gentleman—an old man, the oldest man Sabra had ever seen, whose long white hair tumbled down over the high collar of his dark coat, whose smiling face was a wrinkled map of pleasure as he greeted his two young visitors. He sat in a high-backed chair, a rug across his legs. He and Rachel were old friends, it seemed, although she had not visited him for months, not since she had been confined to the house.

At once the two of them began an earnest conversation, leaving Sabra free to examine the cheerful, sunny parlor. The walls were lined with shelves of books; the table in the center of the room was piled high with pamphlets and newspapers. Sabra read a masthead: *The Anti-Slavery Standard.* She looked sharply at Mr. Hale. He was talking to Rachel of matters that Sabra did not understand: political matters.

"The Congress will not stand for it, you see," he said. "They will continue to gag him. And of course that is precisely what he wants."

"Why?" said Rachel. She sat leaning forward in her chair, her hands tightly clasped together; her eyes searched his ancient face as if she could read there the answer to the riddle of the universe—or, at least, to her own dilemma. "Why does he want that? I thought he wanted to be allowed to present the abolitionist petitions."

"Ah, but he does!" Mr. Hale's eyes twinkled; his white-maned head shook to emphasize his opinion. "But he wants even more to force the constitutional issue. We must continue to gather signatures, to deliver hundreds—thousands!—of petitions, to increase the pressure. We must never for an instant let up!"

For what seemed an endless time, Sabra watched and listened as Rachel asked and Mr. Hale explained. Sabra understood none of it. She watched the hands of the grandmother clock in the corner. Never had time passed so slowly. And all the while, as they talked oblivious to her presence, she felt a growing sense of unease—an awareness that even though their conversation was unintelligible, it was dangerous all the same. Rachel has tricked me, she thought; she brought me here only because she could not come alone. The clock struck three, but they did not notice. Then the quarter hour, then three and a half. Sabra moved restlessly in her chair. Her ribs ached from the pressure of her corset. She wanted very much to go home. The old man's face was kind, his smile was sweet—and yet he spoke madness, he spoke calmly, patiently, explaining to Rachel the tactics of disobedience, of treason.

At last Rachel drew back. Her eyes were suddenly dull, her face discouraged. "And what can I do?" she said. "Mr. Hale, I must help them. Please tell me how."

"When I had your note last fall," he said, "I thought that I would refuse you if you came to me again. For your own good I would refuse you. If your father forbids it, I thought, how can I in good conscience encourage you to continue?"

"And what of my conscience?" said Rachel.

"Ah. There you are. What, indeed?"

"I must do something more. Even something more than collecting signatures."

"Yes." He contemplated her: so young, so beautiful. She might make an excellent marriage, he thought. She might give birth to a fine brood of children as beautiful, as intelligent as herself. And yet she chooses to risk it all—to risk her father's wrath, the censure of the community. He gazed at her with compassion. Why were some souls so tormented? He was a very old man. He had lived through the Revolution, had known Sam Adams and poor Paine. The firebrands. Their voices had been silenced soon enough. The excesses of the French had frightened everyone. The propertied classes had swiftly seized control. And now this new firebrand had flared up, the abolitionist Garrison vowing to smite the consciences of the comfortable, to break the chains of the slave at any cost.

The old man wished passionately that he were young again. How he longed to leap up with Garrison and flail the mob with blasphemous words! Freedom! Yes—that was blasphemy to these sanctimonious manufacturers, these blind servants in the thrall of Mammon! They were slaves themselves, he thought, as helpless to remove themselves from their ceaseless quest for profit as was the black slave to throw off his shackles. And in their insatiable need for raw cotton—millions and millions of bales of cotton, year in, year out—they strengthened that unholy system of chattel slavery which Garrison sought to destroy.

And here was the daughter of one of those manufacturers, seeking to right the wrongs of her father and all his class. The old man was not an Orthodox man, but he did not deny the occasional hand of Providence in men's affairs. This young woman, he thought, has been sent to me to do the work that I can no longer do myself, invalid and immobile as I am.

"I cannot tell you anything definite," he said. "You know of course that warm clothing are always in demand. Collect them if you can and leave them here. A few of the women on the Corporations have been most generous; I had several large parcels of woolens in the past month, but more are always welcome. As for more direct assistance—Deacon Varnum tells me that they are searching for a new route. The ports are closely watched now, and certain stations on the inland routes are becoming too well-known. There is a farmer in Chelmsford who passed along a dozen people last year, but I understand that he has been subjected to unpleasant pressures from his church, and he is unwilling to continue."

"I must do something more," said Rachel again. She reached out and took his gnarled blue-veined hands in hers. "Do you understand me when I say that I believe that God intends me to do this? That I believe that He will punish me if I do not?"

He returned the pressure of her hands. "Poor child," he said. "Then you risk retribution either way, from your father or from God."

After a long moment she said: "Then I know which I must choose."

They said good-by. Rachel drove home in silence, brooding over her visit. Sabra sat stiffly beside her. The red sun sank behind the western hills as they climbed the road to the Bradshaw house. On either side lay snow-covered fields and woods; from the chimneys of an occasional house came plumes of smoke; the warming glow of lamps and candles shone from unshuttered windows.

Sabra thought of the first time she had traveled this road, on a cold November night, seated beside her benefactor—the kind, good man who had taken her into his family. Now one of his family was prepared, not for the first time, to disobey him. And she, Sabra Palfrey, had a clear and pressing obligation to inform him—

"Of course you will not mention this visit at home, Sabra." Rachel's hands did not waver as they held the reins; her eyes did not turn from the road.

"I don't—"

"If they ask you, say that we went through the shops."

"We have bought nothing." Sabra heard her voice ring oddly high inside her head.

And now Rachel permitted herself a sidelong glance at her unhappy companion. "Of course not," she smiled. "We are thrifty. We went only to look—only to amuse ourselves."

On they went through the frozen twilight, two young ladies home from an afternoon's outing. Miss Amalia caught sight of them from the parlor window as they turned into the drive; she smiled as she watched them approach.

"There, Sophia," she said to her sister. "You see? They are not late after all. I am glad that Sabra came to us, I am glad that Josiah took her in. She is a good influence on Rachel."

19

Sabra did not forget her promise to Patrick. One Friday morning not long after the visit to Mr. Hale, she told him that he could probably expect to find them at Haggett's Pond the following afternoon.

He received her information with an irritating show of indifference.

"You did ask," she said, annoyed.

"Sure I did," he said. "And I thank you for tellin' me."

He did not mention the reward which he had implied, and Sabra felt that she could not ask for it without a severe loss of dignity. He was only a poor Irish boy, after all. He had nothing to give to anyone.

The next afternoon the party set out: Rachel, Eliza, Sabra, Lydia, and Mrs. Bradshaw. For all her poor health, for all her fatigue and chosen indolence, Mrs. Bradshaw enjoyed ice skating. Silas Blood came by in his father's swan-necked sleigh to collect them.

It was a bright, bitter day, glittering expanses of snow alternating with dark stands of pine and bare-branched oak and maple, here and there a birch tree as startlingly white as the snow. Haggett's Pond lay several miles down the Andover Road away from the city. Traveling through this country scene, you might never know that the factories had come: this landscape of low-lying farmhouses and gently rolling woods and meadows had stayed unchanged since the first coming of the white man almost two centuries before.

The girls chattered happily as they went, while Silas told riddles to amuse the child. Mrs. Bradshaw sat quietly, as was her custom, seeming oblivious to the talk around her and yet, every now and then, interjecting a word or two to show that she heard it after all. The horses' breath steamed up into the cold air; their harness bells jingled; the iron runners of the sleigh sang on the hard-packed snow of the road. Mrs. Bradshaw had a sudden, painful sense of herself—of all of them speeding happily through the winter landscape on a sunny afternoon, her children beautiful and healthy around her, her husband's waif well settled in, her friend —her dear friend—Silas Blood comfortably shepherding them on their expedition. She felt that the moment was too precious to let pass. She wanted to hold it, to keep it—to stop time's passage. She could not have explained this wish, for she was not an articulate woman. Her mind had atrophied years ago; she had no vocabulary, no analytical skill. She was dimly aware of her deficiencies, but she had never had a reason to correct them. She experienced these rare moments of self-awareness as a blind woman experiences memories of vision: tangentially, obliquely, fleetingly—and then they vanished, leaving her as sightless as before. She bit her red lip and felt the pain; she turned her face to the wind and felt the cold; she laughed. She felt tears sting her eyes.

Sabra had not enjoyed her first attempt at skating, several weeks previous, but this day she determined to do better. She buckled the leather straps over her boots; she moved her feet cautiously, trying to get used to the weight of the elaborately curved runners that curled up and back toward her toes. Despite the warmth of her flannel petticoats and drawers, she was cold; she wanted to begin, to warm herself.

Skaters thronged over the ice. It was a large expanse; the trees on the opposite shore were only a narrow dark fringe between ice and sky. In the center of the pond was a danger spot: dark, thin ice not solidly frozen. No one needed to approach it, for there was more than enough room on the safe part. Back and forth, around and around, went the skaters: mostly children, their cheeks bright with wind-whipped color, some staggering, some gliding with great skill, some solo, some clustering together like flocks of winter birds. Shrieks of laughter, cries of fright echoed through the air, mingling with the scrape and clash of iron blades ringing on the ice.

Lydia wore her new scarlet cape and hood, so everyone could easily keep an eye on her. She set off wobbling, but soon she had her balance. Eliza and Rachel were both excellent skaters, although Rachel was slightly more daring; soon she had gone some distance down the shoreline, her dark skirts billowing with the speed of her graceful progress, the blades of her skates tracing a solitary pattern as she glided back and forth.

Mrs. Bradshaw skated well, too, although not so well as her elder daughters. She accepted Silas' proffered arm as she had accepted his help with the straps of her skates, and together they set off slowly, weaving their way through the ebb and flow of children around them. Sabra tried to keep up but she could not. She managed to stay upright for a time, however, and once or twice she glided almost smoothly.

After a while Lydia found playmates. They stretched themselves out, hand in hand, to form a chain. Screaming and laughing, they began to play snap-the-whip. Their thin, shrill voices filled the air as, faster and faster, they raced strung out in a line held fast by a boy in the center. To add to their delight, a large brown dog, seeing the fun, ran out from the shore and back and forth among them, barking in ecstasy, providing his wriggling body to be tripped over.

Sabra stood still, balancing herself, to watch the game. She glanced down beyond the children to see if Rachel still skated alone. A movement in the woods just there caught her eye and she looked again. Someone stood half hidden by the trees which lined the shore near the spot where Rachel skated. So, she thought: I told him and he came.

At that moment she lost her balance, slipped, caught herself, and slipped again. She fell hard, landing on her side. She was not hurt, but she was tired and so she pulled herself up to a sitting position and cheerfully waved away a boy's offer to help. She looked back to the children. They had discovered a new game: someone's cap thrown out, a race each time to see who would reach it first, the dog or the children. The dog won each time, and each time he dutifully brought it back so as to continue the game; but then, tiring, he caught it one last time and ran away with it toward the dark center of the pond.

A few of the children started after him and then stopped, mindful of the danger. Pleadingly they called to him to return, but he ignored them and went on, happy to be alone with his prize.

Just then a sound cracked like a gunshot through the children's voices. As Sabra looked she saw the break in the ice just by the dog, and then another, and another, as his weight broke through.

Instantly the children's pleadings turned to anguished cries as they realized his peril. But for the moment they held; none ventured out. As quickly as she could, Sabra heaved herself up; her body was numb from her brief, cold rest. And as she looked again she felt her warning cry stick in her throat until, painfully, she got it out.

"Lydia!"

The child ignored her. The dog by now was aware of his danger; he stood, whimpering, on a rapidly sinking fragment of ice.

"Lydia! No! Stop!" Mrs. Bradshaw and Silas, suddenly aware of what had happened, added their cries to Sabra's, as now did the children.

Lydia ignored them all. Slowly, steadily, stepping rather than skating, she made her way toward the dog. Suddenly Eliza dashed out toward her only to be pulled back by the others.

Silas turned to the throng of children. "Lie down!" he commanded.

Roughly he began to push them flat onto the ice. "Get a branch! A stick!"

Clumsily Sabra and a few others scrambled up onto the bank to search the snow-covered ground for a strong bough. Hurry! She tripped and staggered; with slow numb fingers she tried to unbuckle the straps which held her skates to her boots.

Lydia had stopped. The dog, crying pitifully now, had got onto another piece of ice, which, like the first, would not support him. Lydia held out her hands; she was perhaps twenty feet away from him.

"Come, doggy! Come to me!" she called.

Someone found a branch, a long, twigged thing, and sped with it to Silas. He had by now formed the children into a chain stretching from the safe solid ice out toward the dangerous middle; he himself had to stay well back because of his weight. He took the branch and skidded it out to the first child in the chain, a boy of perhaps ten.

"Now hold it, and start moving out—stay flat!" he commanded. They began to inch their way toward Lydia.

Mrs. Bradshaw stood near the shore. Her eyes were wide; her lips moved in some private anguished prayer. Rachel, who had by now skated back from her solitary spot, stood with her arm around her mother. Sabra saw no sign of Patrick, nor did she think to look for him.

The dog, floundering, had managed to heave himself part way onto a solid piece of ice, his hindquarters half submerged. Behind Lydia, all around her, the expanse showed breaks which would soon split wide.

"Lydia! Listen to me!" called Silas. Even as he spoke they heard another sharp *crack*. "Lie down flat! *Lie down!*"

She seemed not so much terrified as confused. She stood still facing the dog, a small scarlet figure terrifyingly far away. She glanced around as if to assure herself that she was safe. She was not safe. The crack had become a fissure. At Silas' command she sank to her knees: no further. She called again to the dog, which still struggled half in, half out of the water.

"Lydia, we will get the dog if we can! First we must get you!" called Silas. "Lie down flat!" And, to the children: "Move out slowly! That's right! Stay flat, keep the branch out front—good!" But again the ice split, and the children stopped.

"Doggy!" shrieked Lydia.

His strength exhausted, the dog had fallen back into the water. He paddled valiantly for a moment and then, overcome by the cold, he began to sink.

At the same instant the ice on which Lydia knelt split away from the main. Now, finally, she was afraid; now, finally, she scrambled to save herself, but she was too late. The ice under her feet was gone, and she was going too, pulled down by her heavy, wet clothing. Her voluminous little skirt billowed up around her for a moment as she clutched frantically for a hold on the firm edge. She got it; she held.

Sabra was aware of a movement down the shore, but she could not look away from Lydia. In a moment Patrick had come into view, moving rapidly across her field of vision, first on foot, then on hands and knees, then flat on his stomach. In front of him he pushed a straight branch about an inch thick. He approached Lydia at an angle to the chain of children and rapidly came nearer to her than the first boy. He stopped. He called to her softly but in the silence everyone could hear.

"Hold, now. Don't move."

Sabra was aware that Mrs. Bradshaw was crying, but she could not turn her eyes away from the child. It was as if she needed to keep her sight on Lydia; to look away would be to abandon her to certain death.

Patrick inched closer. Silence. Then a sharp new *crack*.

"Hold, now. Don't thrash about." Soft, reassuring.

Lydia was sinking. Only her head and the upper part of her torso were above the water now.

Patrick held out the branch. "One hand—*one* hand—that's it. Good. Now the other."

She reached for the branch, caught it; held fast. Slowly, gripping the branch with one hand and balancing himself with the other, he began to squirm back to safety.

He called softly to the children. "Come up behind me. Try to grab onto me."

They obeyed; they began to squirm across the ice, a long wriggling line. Hurry! thought Sabra. Please, please hurry! There is nothing I can do, she thought. I am helpless.

Cautiously Patrick rose to his knees. The ice cracked. He pulled Lydia in fast and seized her hand. The ice split beneath them. But the first boy had caught Patrick's jacket and held fast, and at Silas' cry they all pulled, Silas pulling at the end. Patrick was half in the water now but he had Lydia firmly in his grip. They pulled again and hauled back. She was out.

Half frozen, sobbing—and just then a man leading a horse appeared on a path through the trees. He called out that a girl had run to fetch him at his house and a good thing she had, by the looks of it.

They bundled Lydia in Silas' cloak, and the man, who owned the pond, it turned out, held her close on his horse as he sped down the road to home. Rachel, handing her mother unceremoniously to Silas, wrapped her own cape around the shivering Patrick. Some of the children, released from the tension of the ordeal, began to cry; others hung around Patrick in a shy, admiring circle.

Silas drove them home. Rachel insisted that Patrick accompany them. He sat up front beside Silas. No one said anything on the return journey.

They were all conscious of the dreadful fate which had almost overtaken them. They feared to talk about it. *What if she had drowned–?* No. They could not even think about it. No one thought, either, to question Patrick's providential appearance at the pond; and certainly, thought Sabra, this is not the time or place for me to tell them how and why he came.

When they arrived they found Lydia in her bed, well tucked up in blankets and hot bottles, and Mr. Gumm already gone for Dr. Knight. The man who had brought her back was being given hot flip in the kitchen; no, said Miss Amalia, Josiah had not been sent for, it had not seemed necessary, and he would be home soon in any case–

Mrs. Gumm frowned at the sight of Patrick standing shivering in the front hall, but at Rachel's insistence–and Miss Amalia's, too, once she heard their tale–he was taken into the back parlor to sit wrapped in a blanket before the fire while Mrs. Gumm dried his clothes as best she could in the kitchen. "Throw 'em out is more like it," she muttered to herself. "Filthy rags."

The farmer looked in to see him. "Good job, boy," he said. "Child who fetched me said a dog was the cause of it."

"Yes," said Rachel quickly, before Patrick could answer. "A brown dog. Was he yours?"

"White nose and feet?" said the farmer. "No, he wasn't mine. But I tried to shoot him three times last week. He's been runnin' with a pack, killin' chickens. Even went after a goat two days ago. They're like that, y' know. Friendly as a pup one minute, and then the next minute they've turned killer. Good thing he's dead."

He held out his hand to Patrick, who with some difficulty managed to take it and still keep the blanket wrapped around.

"What's yer name, boy?"

"Patrick O'Haran, sir."

"Well, Patrick O'Haran, if ever I need a smart quick boy I know where to find him. Where d' you live?"

"Acre, sir. I work for Mr. Codwell."

"You can tell him he's got a good lad." And, with a friendly nod, he departed. Miss Amalia brought in a mug of steaming oyster soup and Patrick again manipulated himself so that he could hold it.

Rachel and Miss Amalia sat with him; Eliza and her mother had gone to tend to Lydia. He did not look at the women. He held the mug to his lips, sipping as fast as he could, eyes downcast, shivering still despite the heat of the fire. Sabra watched him anxiously. She could see that he was not himself. This was a new Patrick: quiet, shy, ill at ease. Did he regret his heroism, she thought. But of course not. He had done a great deed–something to be congratulated upon, something to remember when he grew old. He had stored up a treasure in Heaven for himself that day. Did good deeds count for Catholics, she wondered.

Suddenly she shuddered, overcome once again by the terror which had held her as she watched the small scarlet figure struggling in the expanse of breaking ice. *What if he had not come?* People said that the Irish—that mysterious, difficult race—had the gift of second sight. Did Patrick have it? Had he known, somehow, that he should be at Haggett's Pond that afternoon? Why had he asked her to tell him when they would go skating again?

He swallowed the last of the soup and instantly Rachel jumped up and took the mug from his small, chapped hand. She set the mug on a side table; she turned again to Patrick and leaned down to him. She put her hands on his shoulders; she looked intently into his face before she spoke.

"We can never repay you for what you have done for us today, Patrick."

He made no reply. Sabra wondered at this.

"You have saved our precious little girl." Rachel's voice trembled. "And if ever—ever—we can do anything for you—"

Miss Amalia, who had been nodding sympathetically, suddenly interrupted: "I am sure that your father, Rachel dear, will make the proper gesture—"

Rachel ignored her. "You must tell us, at once, if we can help you in any way. We are forever in your debt."

Still he said nothing. Sabra could not believe that this was the same boy who so enlivened her days by his chatter, his irrepressible comments on everyone, everything—why does he look like that, she thought. He looks as if he'd lost his wits.

He had asked her to tell him. And she had; and she had seen a figure in the trees just by the place where Rachel skated. Patrick, watching.

She felt a small kernel of annoyance begin to harden inside her heart. You are my friend, she thought, not Rachel's. You can never hope to be hers. Say something, she thought. Don't sit there mooning at someone so far above you. Say something bright and funny, be Patrick again!

Eliza looked in just then to announce that Lydia wanted to see Rachel. The moment passed; Patrick got out a word of thanks, Rachel went upstairs, Miss Amalia went to the kitchen to see if Patrick's clothing had dried.

And now that they were alone, Patrick seemed to relax, to become himself once more. He grinned at her; he rearranged himself in the wrapped blanket and offered her an exaggerated wink. She was glad to see her friend again; at once she forgot her annoyance.

"You really were very brave, Patrick."

"Yep." He grinned at her more broadly, cocky, pleased with himself.

"Really. You might both have drowned." For the first time, she realized what that might have meant: if Lydia had died, it would have been a tragedy for the Bradshaws. But if Patrick had died in his attempt to save her, his entire family might have perished as well, for Patrick was their breadwinner.

"I'm hard to drown," he said. "I float easy."

She smiled at his familiar bravado; then her smile faded as the scene flashed through her mind again: the frozen pond with its murderous, open center; the small scarlet figure of the child; the fruitless attempts at rescue; and then finally, after endless moments, Patrick's appearance. Finally.

They heard footsteps descending the front stairs.

"Patrick—" Suddenly she knew what was wrong with the sequence. "Why didn't you come right away when you saw that Lydia had gone in?"

He looked into the fire. Someone came hurrying along the back hall. His face suddenly was sober, suddenly hard: closed up tight.

"If it had been someone else," he said, "I wouldn't have bothered." He looked up at her defiantly, as if challenging her to remonstrate. "I only came when I saw it was her."

20

Josiah Bradshaw was an honorable man, fair and just, always prompt to pay his few debts. He was quite prepared, therefore, to present himself at Codwell's West India Goods store on the Monday morning following his little daughter's rescue, to ask Codwell for a moment's conversation with the delivery boy.

Mr. Codwell, a small, dry man accustomed to dealing with boarding house matrons and the housekeepers of the middle classes, was somewhat taken aback at Bradshaw's presence. He seldom saw gentlemen in his store, and certainly not gentlemen so distinguished, so rich, who carried with them like strong eau de cologne the scent of money and power.

At once, alarmed, he sent the clerk to the back of the store to fetch Patrick, who had returned from his morning's deliveries and was now sweeping out the storeroom. Mr. Codwell hoped, very sincerely, that there was no problem, that Patrick had done nothing wrong, that Mr. Bradshaw had no complaint—?

No complaint, said Bradshaw. He looked away from the storekeeper's nervous glance; he surveyed the dim, crowded interior of the shop. Shelves of spices, sugar, coffee, tea, chocolate, barrels of molasses dark and light, boxes of fragrant herbs, rose leaves, snuff, tobacoo, raisins, sacks of flour and rice, great wheels of cheese. Some men, in some secret place buried deep within their layers of starched linen and well-cut broadcloth, might have been amused by Codwell's apprehensions, but Bradshaw was not such a man. He had little imagination; he seldom concerned himself with other people's feelings. Like a well-made piece of machinery, he simply, dutifully did what he was designed to do. It was his duty to perform this errand; he was in fact performing it; when it was completed he would return to the larger, more pressing duties of his factory.

Patrick was not half so nervous as his employer. Although he had never seen Bradshaw, he knew at once the identity of this distinguished gentleman. He ducked his head and said good morning in an easy way, not fawning or cringing as some would have done. Bradshaw was tall, and Patrick was short, so he needed to tilt his head back to look into Bradshaw's face; and he did so with such confidence that his employer was at once relieved of his worry. The lad had committed no misdeed, then.

To his credit, Bradshaw spoke directly to the boy: he knew where his debt lay.

"You were a brave boy on Saturday afternoon, Patrick. My family told me what you did, and I have come here to thank you."

"Yes, sir."

Codwell gaped; the clerk gaped; Patrick suppressed his ready grin.

"More than that. You took a great risk, and you deserve a proper reward."

He reached for his small pocket purse and withdrew a coin. He held it up for all to see: a large, heavy, golden coin embossed on one side with a woman's coroneted head—a Liberty head—and on the other with the proud eagle, shield on its breast, talons clutching the laurel and arrows.

Even Patrick's self-assurance was shaken then. A half eagle—five dollars! He was aware of the clerk's envious sniffle, of Mr. Codwell's clucking tongue and ready, obsequious gabble.

"This is indeed a magnificent gesture, most generous, Mr. Bradshaw. Well, Patrick, what do you have to say for yourself? Perhaps you can tell us what you did to earn this great sum of money?"

"He saved my daughter's life," interjected Bradshaw smoothly. "We are eternally grateful to him." He handed the gold-piece to Patrick; the boy took it with a murmured thanks. He let it lie for a moment in the palm of his hand while he stared at it. He had, in truth, expected some reward, but not all this money. Another glimpse of—another meeting with—Bradshaw's eldest daughter would have pleased him equally as well.

"I have no doubt," continued Bradshaw, "that you will earn many more of these before you are done, Patrick—not by such means, of course. But you are a fine boy, and I am pleased to have Mr. Codwell know it."

His errand completed, he made a graceful exit. Codwell turned at once upon his young employee, demanding to know why, and how, and where—but even as he demanded, Patrick heard a new note in the familiar, nasal voice: a note of grudging respect, perhaps. A note of envy.

Patrick told him enough to silence him. He put the heavy coin into the pocket of his ragged jacket—the pocket, for a wonder, had no hole—and returned to his sweeping. At five-minute intervals throughout the day he felt to make sure that the coin was still there; and in the evening, when he returned to his mother's cabin, he had the joy of showing it to her, and listening to her cries of happiness and pride in her dearest boy, and seeing the awed faces of his brothers and sisters as he allowed them, just once, to pass it around among themselves, and feel the weight of it, and the ridges of its design, and see its wonderful shine, glinting and golden in the light of the Betty lamp. And late that night, when everyone else was asleep, he rose from his pallet and in the darkness he took the coin from his pocket and put it into a small tobacco tin found only last week in Codwell's refuse. Then he moved to one side a battered wooden chest which stood against the tarpapered wall; he dug a hole in the earthen floor beneath, and buried the box and filled the hole and put the chest in place again. And the next day and the day after that, when the children asked him what he had done with the coin, he grinned and shook his head and wouldn't tell them, but said he was saving it for a rainy day, and not to pester, for he was the man of the house and he would have them obey him.

It occurred to him that none of them thought to ask what would have happened if he had drowned while performing his great deed. Would Bradshaw have made his way through the muck and rubble of the Acre, knocking on lean-to doors until he found the grieving family, presenting that same golden coin to the widowed mother as some small recompense for the loss of her eldest son?

Never, thought Patrick. He'd never have done that. They'd have been left to live or die as they would. He thought of Bradshaw and his family and their fine house and their carriages and all their money, and always plenty of food. He pictured Rachel, and his heart fluttered painfully in his skinny chest. He thought of his own family, and the hovel in which they lived, and the constant struggle to feed themselves, to put a bit by for hard times. And it came to him then, in the weeks after Bradshaw's visit to the store, that perhaps the debt had not been fully settled, after all.

He owes me yet, he thought. He hasn't paid up full. The knowledge comforted him; it worked in him like a mother yeast in vinegar. Bradshaw's a fair man, he thought. When the time comes, he'll see that he owes more.

21

February slipped into March; March blew and stormed for a time and then suddenly vanished, giving way to April. People shed their heavy winter cloaks, their flannel underthings; they lifted their faces to the sun and smiled; they lingered in the streets, along the shop windows, stopping to talk, enjoying the warmth: unfolding, thawing out. They knew that April was treacherous and sometimes snowy, but this year seemed different. Look, they said, how early everything is coming into bud; we are done with winter, we have survived it once again. They grew reckless: housewives gave orders to their servants to stop the fires; they packed away the winter underwear; they canceled orders for coal and wood.

In the mills the workers celebrated the "blowing-out": that time, early in every spring, when the operatives no longer toiled by lamplight at the beginning and end of the day. They hated to work by the glow of the smoky, rancid whale-oil lamps, even though the lighted work-days of winter were shorter than the long, fourteen-hour shifts in high summer. But it never seemed right, to many people, that you worked by artificial light in the factories; the ceremony of "lighting-up" in the fall was a hated reminder of the extent of their bondage. The children—the little bobbin-doffers—could find no shadowed corners now in which to huddle and frighten each other with tales of ghosts and witches while they waited for the long wooden bobbins to fill; the women coming out of their houses in the mornings could run to their workrooms now, for they had the pale warning light that announced the coming of the sun, they no longer stumbled in the darkness; the overseers, at closing bell, had that much less to worry about when they locked up, for as well constructed as the buildings were, the hundreds of flaming oil lamps always meant the danger of fire. Each one needed to be carefully extinguished at night; the overseers were responsible. The mills were tinder boxes—

hot, lint-filled air, thousands of pounds of cotton, six stories of wooden walls and floors inside the red-brick facades. Everyone agreed: "blowing-out" was a happy time.

Sabra ran outdoors a dozen times a day to breathe in the soft warm wind which carried spring back from the south. She felt intoxicated by the weather; she felt that she would blossom, too, with the trees and flowers; never, in the mountains, in the north country, had she seen such an extravagant spring, such lavish bloom of willow and maple, crocus and tulip and forsythia, flowering crabapple and lily of the valley. She lingered in the garden and on the porch, forgetting the tasks awaiting her within; she contracted so acute a case of the season's well-known fever that Mrs. Gumm was moved to mutter darkly about sulphur and molasses and all the spring cleaning yet to be done. "You and Eliza both," she said; "I don't know which one's worse"—for the young Southern gentleman had visited again, had spoken to Josiah, and Eliza, giddy with joy and relief, thought of nothing but the day when she would achieve every woman's greatest goal: the getting of a husband, the true beginning of life.

Sabra smiled with the others at Eliza's carrying-on, and yet she acknowledged, to herself at least, that Eliza was right to be so happy. What else was there, for a woman, but to marry? A spinster—even a happy, busy spinster like Miss Amalia—was no one. People laughed at unmarried women; they were objects of ridicule, the butts of salacious jokes. Sabra did not always understand the jokes, but she knew their intent. Spinsterhood was shameful—degrading. And yet, thought Sabra, we cannot escape it by ourselves; we must wait for them to rescue us. And if they do not, then they turn on us and mock us for something beyond our control. No wonder Eliza was so happy. It was Rachel, so totally unconcerned about marriage, who was the deviant.

"What will you do there?" she said to Eliza one day.

Eliza looked up from her needlework; her face wore a puzzled expression. "What do you mean?"

"I mean, how will you live when you go south? What will you do all day?"

"Why—I'll do as I please!" laughed Eliza. "What a silly question. I will have any number of things to do, I suppose. Running the house, and —ah—seeing to the children when they come—" Her face flushed slightly. She looked annoyed. "You needn't worry about me," she said. "I'm marrying well. His father owns more than a hundred slaves. Do you know how much that property is worth? Unless cotton fails completely—which it never will, as Father can tell you—we'll be safe for the rest of our lives. Nothing will ever bankrupt us. And if it does, we can always sell the blacks. Even if every factory in New England closed down tomorrow, cotton could still be shipped to the British even more than it is now. No:

look after yourself, that's my advice to you, or you'll end up like Aunt. And perhaps not half so well off, either. No one wants an unmarried female hanging on. What if you don't marry? Do you want to spend the last years of your life working in a mill to support yourself? Or in the poorhouse?"

Sabra could think of no reply; she realized that she had never approached the subject of her future with anything like Eliza's practicality.

"If you were to ask me," continued Eliza, "I would say that you should begin to apply yourself." She had picked up her embroidery again: pale blue flowers on white silk. It seemed to be a nightgown. Her needle flashed expertly in and out as she spoke. "You've been gadding around with Rachel for weeks, now. And where do you go? To Mrs. Peabody's? To Mrs. Trask's? You'll never find a husband there. Some of them have sons, or brothers, true enough, but they all want their men to marry money, and you haven't got any. So you have to look elsewhere. And don't forget: this is a city where women outnumber men five to one. Lots of girls come down to the factories in hopes of finding a husband—smart, pretty girls who work here a year or two and save up a nice dowry and make a fine catch for any man. This isn't England, after all. Factory girls here are as respectable as we are. So you have a lot of competition." She smiled encouragingly; now that her own future was assured, she felt that she could afford to be generous to everyone, even to Sabra. "I'll speak to Father," she said. "Perhaps he'll be able to think of some likely young man."

They were interrupted just then by Mrs. Gumm, looking for help with the starching. But in the days following, Sabra thought increasingly of what Eliza had said. What will become of me, she wondered; what will happen to me? She wished that she could tell her worries to someone. Eliza was too self-absorbed; Rachel would scold her, would thrust a book at her and tell her to read, to improve her mind; and neither Miss Amalia nor Mrs. Bradshaw, these days, had time or patience to listen to her.

For Mrs. Bradshaw was not well, and Miss Amalia, who had prayed and worried and worked and hoped, all the years, so that her beloved sister might continue to live, was struck down with the knowledge that all that effort might come to nothing now; all that hope and prayer might have been in vain.

Mrs. Bradshaw lay in her bed and suffered her sister to attend her. She had dismissed Dr. Knight with a wave of her hand, a despairing glance. They had had a private conversation. She had informed him of her condition; he had struggled to find some words of cheer, of hope, although privately he believed that he faced a dying woman. He admired her enormously. She was the highest, purest, most admirable type: the woman who sacrificed her life for the sake of others. Another Bradshaw child, he thought. How good, how noble she is! How well she understands her purpose in the world!

As he went out, saying good-by to the distraught Miss Amalia, he met Rachel coming in. Her bonnet hung down her back, her dark hair flew in wind-blown tendrils about her face, she chattered excitedly to Sabra following behind. She seemed to bring with her into the house the very essence of the season: warm and free, blooming with promise. She and Sabra greeted Dr. Knight cheerfully and hurried upstairs, bent on some business clearly more pressing than polite conversation with the good doctor.

He paused; he stared after them disapprovingly. He was familiar enough with the household to know that Rachel was not a model young lady: she was altogether too fond of having her own way, of neglecting her womanly duties. She was very strong-minded. Dr. Knight pressed his full lips together in sudden irritation. It was not impossible, he thought, that Rachel's obstinacy, her eccentricity, were in part responsible for her mother's weakened constitution, and thus in part for her inability to safely bear another child. Worry over such a daughter could debilitate even the strongest woman. He turned upon Miss Amalia.

"You should curb that girl," he said sharply. "She will destroy herself—and her mother, too, perhaps—if you let her continue so free. And she reads far too much. Josiah told me so himself. She will overtax her brain."

Humbly, Miss Amalia bowed her head and murmured an assent.

"You should put a stop to it," he said. "She will make herself unfit—she will destroy her ability to—ah—" He hesitated; he reminded himself that he addressed a maiden lady. He cleared his throat. He felt that it was his duty to speak as forcefully as possible. "I will not be responsible for the consequences," he said. "Females cannot undertake strenuous mental activity. It destroys their internal—ah—balance. Forgive me, but I must speak plainly. If she continues as she is now, she will discover one day that she cannot bear children. All the best medical authorities agree on this point. An independent spirit and an active mind destroy a female's reproductive organs. It is no wonder that Mrs. Bradshaw's health is so delicate. I am positive that she is overwrought and worrying herself into the grave over the behavior of that girl."

Miss Amalia, who did not know the precise reason for her sister's sudden, rapid failing, twisted her hands together and tried to think of a reply that might elicit a more hopeful prediction. She did not like this blunt, bluff man, but he was a friend of Josiah's. Therefore her own feelings toward him did not matter. Fortunately, she thought, he does not know the worst of it; he does not know about that dreadful newspaper.

"We all love Rachel very much," she said at last. "We do not like to see her unhappy."

"Unhappy!" His hand was on the door knob. He had already overstayed his time. "I warn you, miss, that her unhappiness now will be nothing compared to her unhappiness when she discovers—too late!—that she has made herself unfit to fulfill a woman's highest obligation. Good day to you. I will see Mrs. Bradshaw tomorrow."

When he had gone, Miss Amalia stood for a moment in the hall, trying to regain her composure. I must speak to Josiah, she thought. She knew that he did not like to bother with domestic affairs, but this was, she thought, near enough to a crisis that he might not mind. He must speak to Rachel again, she thought; we were wrong to allow her to go out again so frequently. And he must get a lock for his library door.

But Bradshaw, that evening, was engaged to attend a meeting at the Middlesex Mechanics' Association. A demonstration of a new carding process was presented. He did not arrive home until nearly midnight. As he drove up Belvidere Hill he allowed himself to relax for a time, to savor the cool, sweet night air. Already the mill rooms had become uncomfortably hot; if the weather continued so mild, they would be unbearable by June. To the soothing accompaniment of the horse's hooves thudding on the dusty road, he pondered the question of the coming summer's heat. Last year, the overseers had requested permission to have water buckets in the rooms. Each operative, they said, could be allowed one drink every hour. Many of the women had taken to fainting at their machines; and in truth the temperature in the upper floors was well over one hundred degrees. The women's dresses had been soaked with perspiration; as far as Bradshaw knew, no operative yet had devised a way to simulate sweat, and so he had agreed that their discomfort—their dehydration—had been genuine enough. But one trip to the water bucket every hour! He had calculated that to be at least forty-two minutes out of every woman's working day. Multiplied by the number of operatives—impossible. Their production would suffer enormously. Boston would not stand for it. Brusquely he had denied the request. Water buckets might be put near the overseer's desk in each room, he said, but no operative was to be permitted more than two drinks a day, and production must not suffer. Each woman who went to the bucket was responsible for getting her neighbor to watch her machines—and no one was to take a drink without permission.

He slept well that night, unmindful of the slow, drugged breathing of his wife beside him, and in the morning he awakened and dressed as the faint sound of the rising bells from the mill towers drifted up the hill. This day, Mayor Luther Lawrence (newly elected: a good, safe Corporation man, brother to the energetic Amos and Abbott Lawrence) was to shepherd a party of visiting dignitaries through certain mills, the Commonwealth among them. Bradshaw wanted to go over the account books with his paymaster before the delegation arrived. Thus he was gone well before Miss Amalia awakened at seven-thirty. At the moment she became conscious, when the cares of her life settled like a heavy weight upon her shoulders, she was struck once again by Dr. Knight's warning. When she realized that Josiah had gone, she was both relieved and further worried. But—"I will keep quiet for a day or two," she told herself. "I will not take any drastic action. Perhaps Sophia will be better today. Perhaps I will not need to say anything unpleasant to Josiah—or to Rachel either, for that matter. Perhaps Dr. Knight was mistaken."

She had gone to see Sophia then. Afterward, her perception sharpened by the terror of that visit, she contemplated her eldest niece at the breakfast table. The girl looked overwrought. A hectic flush lighted up her cheeks, her eyes sparkled with what was surely mischief—ah, Rachel! thought Miss Amalia. Find a husband! Marry before it is too late, before even you, as beautiful as you are, lose your chance! How like Sophia she looks, thought Miss Amalia; and how differently she behaves! Sophia has always been obedient, docile, unassuming—and yet it is she who suffers now. For what crime? What has she done? And Rachel flouts our chastisements, she behaves as she will, and she suffers nothing. She remembered Dr. Knight's warning: "She will be unable to bear children."

After breakfast Miss Amalia looked in on her sister again and found her sleeping. She gave instructions to the girls and Mrs. Gumm not to disturb her, and after conferring with Mrs. Gumm about the day's schedule of cleaning she settled with Lydia for an hour's lessons. She could not concentrate. The child was drilling in subtraction, and Miss Amalia discovered that seventeen less eleven was a monumentally difficult question. Round and round went her thoughts, always concentrated on the image of her sister's face: pale, sweet, almost maddeningly serene. Why does she not cry out, wondered Miss Amalia. Why does she not protest?

Miss Amalia gave it up; she admitted defeat, she put away the copybook, the slate, the arithmetic text. "Go find Eliza, sweet," she said; and the child, happy to be dismissed from her drudgery, scampered quickly away. Miss Amalia sat for a moment in the sunny nursery. The cradle had long since been stored away, empty, unused, almost forgotten in the attic. No, she thought. No! Not again!

Sudden panic seized her. She felt that she could no longer bear to sit in this room, to follow the familiar routine of her day. She wanted some demanding task—some work that would absorb her thoughts and relieve her of the torment of her fear.

But there was no such work for her to do, and so she got up from her chair and went downstairs and stepped outside into the back garden. She stood at the low stone wall which marked the steep drop to the water below; she looked up the valley to the distant hills encircling the majestic sweep and curve of the river, in high flood now as it carried down to the sea all the melting snow of the north country. She gazed unseeing at the landscape. What am I to do, she thought. I am helpless; I can do nothing. She felt the sun warm on the shoulders and back of her dark dress; the ruffles of her cap fluttered around her thin, anxious face. The trees on the slope below, and on the opposite shore, were bursting with new leaves, new life. All the world was coming into bloom. Springtime: the time of birth.

And birth was often the time of death.

And Death was with her now. Miss Amalia could feel his presence all above, all around this shimmering, burgeoning landscape.

He had been in Sophia's bedroom that morning. He had left his mark upon her face. Miss Amalia, pouring the steaming tea into the saucer as she had a hundred—a thousand—times before, had suddenly looked up at Sophia and had seen not the familiar beloved features but the grinning, triumphant image so long feared, so long combated.

Just for a moment she had seen him, all in a flash, looking out at her from Sophia's tired, beautiful eyes. Then he was gone. But she knew. He had threatened them each time that a child was on the way. Sometimes he had taken away with him a little victim; sometimes he had let the newcomers stay—Rachel, Eliza, Lydia. But always he had come, as if his proper place was at Sophia's side during those times when she suffered and struggled to bring new life—new Bradshaw life—into the world.

Only a moment: and Sophia had known what her face showed. She had smiled wanly at her sister; she had tried in her gentle way to relieve Miss Amalia's fears.

"What is it, Amalia? You look as if you'd seen a ghost."

"No." She had been able, a little, to smile.

"Amalia."

"Yes, dear."

"Did Dr. Knight tell you what was wrong with me?"

"He said—" She caught herself in time. "No."

"But you have guessed, just now." She put her saucer on the tray; she lay back, exhausted. Her dead-white skin had no more color than the lace-trimmed pillow behind her head; only under her eyes was her pallor relieved, stained by dark smudges.

Miss Amalia, choking back her sudden tears, had been unable to reply. She had sunk onto her knees beside the bed and gathered Sophia into her arms and held her close. It had been Sophia, then, who had been the comforter. "Don't, Amalia," she murmured. "Please don't. You'll break my heart, dearest. There. Hush. Hush, now."

Miss Amalia, standing now in the sunlight, confronted with the beauty of the day, the promise of the season, considered the question which she had been, that morning, unable to ask—had been unable to phrase until this moment.

Had Josiah forced himself upon her?

Or had she, for some inexplicable reason, chosen to try, one last time, to give him the son he so desperately wanted?

Miss Amalia was of the opinion that women did not choose. They were mere vessels, chosen by God—or their husbands. And always they must submit to that authority. Even though they risked their lives. Even though, submitting, they journeyed through the valley of the shadow of Death.

Tears blurred her sight. She turned back to the house. She felt heavily weighted with the knowledge that somehow, somehow, she must calmly continue in her daily routine. To delay going indoors for a moment longer, she walked around to the front. She heard hoofbeats, the rattle of a carriage. She blinked to clear her eyes.

Just turning in at the gate, driving his father's light trap, was Silas Blood. She had never begrudged his visits. Let him come, she had thought; he cheers her, he comforts her. As Gumm tended to the horse, she greeted Silas almost gladly and led him into the house. He had brought the mail, as he often did: one of his thoughtful kindnesses. A letter for Miss Amalia from Mrs. Clapp, who was visiting in Saratoga Springs; a letter for Josiah; a note for Rachel. Miss Amalia hesitated at this last. Should Rachel be allowed to receive it?

But her thought came too late, for Rachel emerged into the second-floor hall and came downstairs to greet Silas, and happily took her note before Miss Amalia had a chance to consider further its confiscation.

At once, Rachel ran back upstairs to her room, where Sabra was struggling with *vocabulaire* at a table by the window. She broke the seal; in a moment she had skimmed the brief message. She read it again to make sure that she understood it. She realized that her face must show some trace of her thoughts, for Sabra had stopped her work, she was sitting open-mouthed, visibly alarmed.

Sabra felt her heart beating painfully against her ribs, which were crushed into her tight-laced stays. "Just another quarter-inch every week," Eliza had said. "It's terribly important. Men hate thick-waisted women." If only I could take a deep breath, she thought. If only she would speak—

"Put away that stupid work," said Rachel abruptly. She folded the note into a tiny square and slipped it between the buttons of her bodice. "And get your bonnet and shawl."

"I promised Mrs. Gumm—" Sabra was surprised at her own words, for never had she hesitated when Rachel gave a command. But now she had a sudden sense of caution, of a delaying hand, a warning voice.

"Never mind Mrs. Gumm. Come on. If Aunt or Eliza ask you, say that we've gone to the stationer's for a new grammar."

Slowly Sabra stood up. Her impulse to obey was very strong, but still she hesitated. "And where will we go instead?"

Rachel's face was alight; she looked triumphant, possessed all of a sudden with high purpose. Only the week before, Sabra had read to Lydia a story of a young woman in France, centuries ago, who had heard the voices of angels. So might that girl have looked, the way Rachel looked now: a being set apart, given to see where others were blind—

"It is Mr. Hale," said Rachel. "He wants to see me at once. And of course you must come with me. He says—"

At that moment, through the open window, they heard the bells begin to toll in the city far below: not rising bells, or dismiss bells, or bells to mark the hour, but a random tolling, individual voices sending forth their warnings of alarum.

Rachel's control gave way. In a spasm of excitement she embraced her protégée. "Oh, Sabra! He says that he needs my help! It is very urgent! At last—at last, I am to be allowed to serve! I am to be allowed to do something!"

22

Black night and a bitter wind, a wild, blowing darkness in which the lumbering, creaking carriage seemed a ship tossed on a stormy sea, the heavy gusts thudding against it like the blows of great waves, sending it lurching onward, a frail vessel doomed to founder.

Sabra sat inside, alone, while Rachel struggled to guide the horses. Sabra did not know where they went, for Rachel and Mr. Hale had told her nothing. She steadied herself against the door; she clung to the seat, terrified, her body bruised by the bone-crushing ride, her mind numb with worry and fear.

Rachel wore boy's clothing. That fact alone was sufficient cause for Sabra's alarm, but there was, she knew, far worse to come. Locke's farm in Chelmsford, Mr. Hale had said. He had spoken rapidly, intently, hardly noticing Sabra. Go by the river road, through Middlesex Village. It seemed impossible that the interview had taken place only yesterday morning. It seemed a week ago—a year. Rachel had been mad with joy. An adventure such as she had never imagined had suddenly come to her because a man in Chelmsford had lost his nerve. As well he might, thought Sabra. Who in full possession of his senses would undertake a journey such as this?

They had had good luck: the city was in turmoil. The bells, the previous day, had tolled the news that Mayor Lawrence had been killed. As a result, all Lowell was distracted in mourning, Josiah Bradshaw suddenly more preoccupied even than usual. He had no time, now, to notice the comings and goings of his family. He was closeted this night with the Aldermen. They needed his guidance, as foremost representative of the industry which supported the city, to pick the right man to succeed to the mayor's office.

"Who killed him?" Eliza had said, voicing Sabra's thoughts. She remembered the mob of angry operatives, the ranting woman whom she had seen on the night when she and the peddler had come down into the city. She remembered Rachel's story of the crowd that had tried to lynch Mr. Garrison.

But Mayor Lawrence had met a kinder fate. While conducting visitors through the Middlesex Mill, he had fallen into the wheelpit and crushed his skull. They had needed to stop production for the entire morning until they got him out. The week's balance sheet would show a heavy loss. The delegation, appalled, had left the city as quickly as possible. A special train had taken them away; the resident Agents of the several Corporations had hastily agreed, on behalf of their directors in Boston, to share its cost. The Board of Aldermen, quickly assembled that afternoon, had requested a public funeral. The Lawrence family had refused. The Aldermen, rebuffed, had proceeded with their pressing business: the choice of a successor. That night they had met, and all this day, and into the night again. Josiah Bradshaw, *ex officio*, had met with them. The rest of the Bradshaw household had retired early. By ten o'clock everyone was asleep. Rachel had gone around to the bedrooms to make sure. Then she and Sabra had crept downstairs; they left the kitchen door unlatched. Their transgression was so severe that Rachel had forbidden Sabra even to mention it. "We will not be caught," she said. "They will never miss us. Do you want these poor people to be sent back?"

They had walked down the hill to Mr. Hale's, where a carriage awaited them. When they arrived, they went inside while Rachel changed her clothing in the back parlor. The housekeeper helped her. Rachel's hands trembled so that she could hardly unbutton her bodice. She had never worn boy's clothes. She felt odd—intoxicatingly free.

Sabra was aware that the horses had slowed. She looked out. They were turning off, coming into the yard of a large farmhouse. A solitary dog howled; a light shone at a darkened window and then the door opened slightly and a man's voice called to them.

"Who is it?"

"Delivery service," replied Rachel promptly. "You have your shipment ready?"

"Right," said the man. He disappeared into the house, shutting the door behind him. Rachel climbed down and came around to the side of the carriage to speak to Sabra.

"All right?" she said. Her face was solemn, but her eyes betrayed her: they were sharp and bright, glittering with the excitement of what she did, what she was about to do. Her hair was pulled back into a cap, but even so, thought Sabra, no one seeing her close would be deceived for a minute.

"Yes. I'm all right."

"Good. Now listen: Mr. Hale said that often they are terrified. You must speak to them soothingly, sing to them if you must—anything to quiet them. I will get some food from this man. You may give it to them if you think it necessary."

"Where are we taking them?" said Sabra. Her apprehension had given way somewhat to curiosity. She had never seen a black person before.

"We go up the road by the river to Tyngsborough. It will take an hour, perhaps, if all goes well."

What could go wrong, thought Sabra. Anything—everything. A broken wheel, a bolting horse, an hysterical passenger. She closed her eyes and said a quick prayer. She heard the door of the farmhouse open again, and she looked to see their passengers.

The farmer came first, followed by two figures whose crouched and cautious walk at once identified them as aliens. He opened the carriage door and motioned them inside.

In the dim light of the carriage lamps, he saw Sabra. He had seemed almost as apprehensive as the fugitives, and now a look of irritation crossed his face.

"Who's this?" he said to Rachel. "I told Hale I wanted no one else. Bad enough you had to come."

"She is my cousin," said Rachel. "Without her to help me I could not manage. Mr. Hale approved."

The blacks climbed into the carriage and settled themselves opposite Sabra: a woman and a young girl of perhaps twelve or thirteen. Their heads were wrapped in turbans; although each wore a shawl, they were shivering. They did not look at Sabra. The woman put her arm around the girl. They whispered to each other for a moment, and then the girl put her head on the woman's shoulder and settled herself as comfortably as she could.

"I don't like it," said the farmer.

"Then tell Mr. Temple to be more reliable," said Rachel. Her voice was hard, although quiet as befitted the stealth of the occasion. Sabra watched her in some surprise. She saw the farmer's hand tighten on the edge of the door; then he spat a great flood of tobacco juice, barely missing Rachel's trousered legs.

"Be off, then," he said. He glanced at them once more; his long, equine face had not a hint of the elation which had suffused Rachel's face when she had learned of her night's work. Sabra wondered why the man involved himself in such an effort if he had no satisfaction from it. Perhaps he does, she thought; perhaps he simply cannot show it.

"We'd like some food—and a bottle of cider," said Rachel.

"They've been fed. Twice."

"All the same."

He grumbled, but he went into the house, returning a few moments later with the cider and a small pack of food wrapped in oiled paper. He thrust them in at Sabra; she took them; Rachel sprang to her seat; and so they began their journey once again.

As Rachel turned the carriage out onto the road, Sabra stared at the two females opposite. Their skins seemed part of the darkness, but then the child, not moving her head or shifting from the woman's embrace, suddenly raised her eyes to Sabra's. So clear a gaze, so direct, caught in the faint light—and so quick, for suddenly she looked down again, as if she had been warned not to examine her benefactors too closely.

Poor creature, thought Sabra. For a moment she forgot her own fears. What must their terror be? Upon what reserves of strength had they drawn these last weeks as they made their way north? What horrors had made them risk the journey? A brutal whipping from an enraged overseer? A threat to sell them apart?

On they went. Was ever a stranger cargo trundled through the fields and forests, down the pleasant country ways of northern Middlesex as went that black night in Ephraim Hale's carriage, north to the Merrimack and thence north along the river road to Tyngsborough? Two fugitive slaves worth a good deal on the auction block, a foundling white girl worth very little, and the daughter of the most prominent man in Lowell, worth a fine price in a marriage settlement until her intended discovered her fondness for adventure, at which time, probably, she would be worth nothing at all.

She drove at great speed. The carriage made an unholy racket as it creaked and lumbered through the night—hardly a secret means of transport—and Sabra was grateful that her companions were so calm, for surely, she thought, if I needed to reassure them I should have to do so at the top of my lungs.

As they came out onto the river road they heard a warning shout, and for a moment Sabra thought that they had been discovered. But it was only someone in an even greater hurry. Rachel pulled sharply over without slackening their pace. As the other driver passed, Sabra caught a glimpse of an angry face turned to stare at them. He will remember us, she thought. If anyone asks him, he will remember us. Hurry! She thought to give her companions the food, the bottle of cider. She leaned forward; gently, so as not to startle her, she touched the woman's arm.

The woman jumped and let out a strangled cry instantly cut off by some instinct of preservation. Her eyes were wide with terror; she clung tightly to the girl as if Sabra had reached to snatch her away.

"Please," said Sabra, handing over the provisions. "I didn't mean to frighten you. Take this—it is food and drink."

The woman did not move to acknowledge Sabra's words. After a moment a hand reached out and the child took the proffered gifts. Her eyes met Sabra's, and Sabra saw in them not fear, not even gratitude, but only a calm acknowledgment of what she took.

The carriage turned off the road just then, and pulled up in front of a large white house facing the river. Rachel climbed down; cautioning her passengers to wait, she stood silently for a moment as if she looked for a signal. None came at first, but then from the darkened porch a man's figure emerged and hurried down the steps.

"Must you drive with lights?" he said abruptly.

"I was told to," said Rachel. At the sound of her voice he looked at her sharply.

"Is Mr. Temple here?"

"No. He—he could not come."

"Then the delivery should not have been made."

"We had no choice. It had to be done tonight. They could not stay where they were."

"Weak links," muttered the man. "Weak links—they will destroy us all. Very well. Let us see what we have."

He opened the carriage door and beckoned out the two fugitives. When he saw Sabra he frowned, but he made no comment. With a curt good night he shepherded his charges toward the house. Rachel looked in at Sabra.

"Was it all right?" she said softly.

"Yes. They didn't say a word."

"Good. They usually don't, Mr. Hale said, but once in a while one of them gets frightened. It is such a dreadful journey, and they are so terrified of being caught."

As we should be, thought Sabra grimly; but she kept silent.

Rachel reached in through the open door; she clasped Sabra's hand. Her face was alive with joy. "We did it, Sabra! We did it! Now back to Mr. Hale's and then home to bed."

Sabra made no reply, for the words which came to her were bitter words of stern reproach for Rachel's foolhardiness—and, worse, for her own. "If I never do anything else until I die, Sabra, I will not have lived in vain! I am happier, this moment, than I have ever been." Then Rachel disappeared; nimbly she climbed back to the driver's seat.

More fool you, thought Sabra; but still she said nothing. She steadied herself as the carriage moved off again. This was not the time for recriminations. And perhaps, after all, they would get back safely. What madness, what dreadful lapse of duty had led her to accompany Rachel tonight? To follow along so quietly, to assist in this action which could only lead to unimaginable retribution? We will be discovered after all, she thought; we will be severely punished. She braced herself against the shuddering interior of the carriage; she prayed, hoping that God would hear.

At last they came to the environs of the city. Sabra heard a bell strike one. A short while later they pulled up to Mr. Hale's door. From the blackness of the side garden stepped the figure of a man. With a murmured word of greeting he climbed up and took the reins as Rachel clambered down.

Inside, the housekeeper had hot tea waiting. Mr. Hale sat in the parlor. Although the room was dim, illuminated only by the fire, they could see his eager expression, his eyes shining with anticipation as he waited impatiently to hear their news.

"Well?" he said. "All safe?"

"All safe," said Rachel. She pulled off her cap, she stood before him in her jacket and trousers as stalwart as any boy. Her dark hair fell over her shoulders, her excited laughter bubbled up. She knelt before him and took his hands. "They are one step further along the way."

"I was afraid for a while that we would need to send them back. No one but you would consent to take them. We are grateful to you—to both of you—beyond words."

"No. It is I who must be grateful." Her face glowed. Neither of them looked at Sabra. She stood just inside the door, not wanting to intrude upon their happy exchange. She was cold, she was tired, she could not begin to comprehend the excitement—the exaltation—which bound these two.

Rachel stood up, then, and both girls gratefully drank the proffered tea. Mr. Hale extended a hand to Sabra; he beckoned her close.

"I have not thanked you. Rachel says that you are her faithful friend. You have done good work this night. Even though the world will never hear of it—cannot, for we must be secret—I want you to know that there are those who thank you."

"Yes, sir." She could think of nothing else to say; she had not the courage to tell him that she cared nothing for escaped slaves, that she had gone only because Rachel had told her to go, that she would have gone wherever Rachel told her, but that now, badly frightened, she would never go again.

He released her. Rachel went to put on her dress, and then they set out for home.

To their surprise the Bradshaw house showed a light in the hall. "Someone is ill, no doubt," muttered Rachel. "Never mind—come on."

They crept around to the back and silently let themselves in at the kitchen. They climbed the back stairs in the darkness, feeling their way. They heard no sound but the faint noise of their stealthy footsteps. At the second-floor hall Rachel stopped and turned to Sabra; she put out her arms to the younger girl and held her in a wordless embrace, as if to say "Thank you." Or perhaps: "Courage." They stood for a moment together, each drawing comfort from the other. Sabra felt the tension in Rachel's body, her lithe, quick strength; she smelled the rosewater scent, overlaid now with the lingering odor of the boy's clothing. Sabra was very tired. She leaned against Rachel's shoulder. She was unable to believe that they had come back safely undiscovered. Never again, she thought. Never again.

They heard a footstep on the front stair. In the reflected light from the hall below they saw Josiah Bradshaw ascending behind the balustrade.

He paused when he reached the top. He looked down the hall to where they stood in darkness. Sabra felt his anger as surely as if he had reached out and struck her. Her knees weakened; she almost fell as Rachel quickly pulled away. Never in her life had she been so afraid as she was now, confronted by this man whom they had so radically disobeyed. Did he know? Did he guess? Would he berate them, beat them perhaps?

The most frightening thing of all was that he said nothing. He simply waited, staring at the place where they stood. Rachel stepped out first; automatically Sabra followed. As they came into the dim light, he held up his hand to caution them to speak softly.

"Well?"

His eyes burned down on them like the eyes of the Recording Angel. Rachel stood firm; Sabra wished that she herself might die on the spot.

"A message came from Dr. Edson, Father, a sick woman needed food—"

"Do not tell me stupid lies."

Their voices were barely audible: not like his previous discovery of her wrongdoing, when Eliza had run to him with the forbidden newspaper. Rachel met his eyes in an attitude of defiance; she squared her shoulders and drew down her mouth into a hard straight line exactly like his own.

He made a swift decision then; he sent them to bed directly. In his position at the mill he was accustomed to dealing with offenses: tardiness, insolence, light behavior, theft. He knew that the solitary meditation of a guilty heart often produced a more complete confession than impulsive phrases blurted out on the spot. Therefore, until the morning, he would not question them more. Be quiet, he said; do not wake the others. I wanted only to make sure that you were safe. Now go to bed.

And so they parted: Rachel to her spacious, comfortable room, Sabra to her smaller, humbler chamber one flight up. Sabra would have given a good deal, just then, for a word of comfort from either of those two implacable Bradshaws, father and daughter. But it was not forthcoming. She slipped on her nightshift and crawled into bed. She closed her eyes. Scenes from the night's events flashed before her: scenes all in darkness, as she was now. She was too tired, too desolate to cry. She lay rigid on her small narrow bed and listened to the night wind buffeting the house; she heard the river, far below, rushing to the sea. After a while, comforted by the familiar sounds, she fell into a restless sleep.

23

The eastern sky was gray when she awakened. She heard Mrs. Gumm move about in the next room and then go quietly downstairs to start the day's work. She meant to get up, then, and prepare to deal with whatever fate awaited her, but instead she slipped back into sleep again.

She awakened to full daylight: a gloomy day of wind-blown rain spattering against the glass. For a moment she could not remember why it was important to get up quickly, to make herself ready. For what? But then she saw the dress which she had taken off the night before and thrown aside. It hung half off the back of the small Windsor chair. Its hem was soiled with mud; its soft gray plaid skirt showed a blot of grease where the food had leaked through the oiled paper. She saw once again the faces of the fugitives. She felt no compassion for them, no pride that she had helped them, only a sense of stunned astonishment that she had been foolish enough to do so. Bravery was for those who could afford it; for most people—for her, for Rachel—it was madness.

She did not want to cry. Crying will weaken me, she thought. She got up and splashed water into the basin and bathed her face. The floor was cold on the soles of her feet; the water was cold on her skin. She shivered in her thin shift. She was glad for her discomfort. Although she suffered it every morning, it seemed especially acute today: a special punishment. She put on her plainest dress, a dark blue broadcloth; she pulled her hair into a knot at her neck. No fussing with curls and loops and braids today, she thought. He will see me unadorned, as plain as I was when I came to him.

She heard someone climbing the stairs outside her door. Without knocking, Miss Amalia came in. Her face was the face of a stranger: blank and staring, no warmth, no recognition. She stood just inside the doorway as if to step into the room might contaminate her. She knows, thought Sabra; he has told her.

"Josiah—Mr. Bradshaw—will see you now in his library," said Miss Amalia. "You are to go to him at once." She did not meet Sabra's eyes. She spoke rapidly, as if she had learned her words by heart and needed to say them before she forgot what they were. Plainly, she did not want a reply.

Sabra walked past the small, neat, familiar figure. Her eyes were dry; she felt her heart beginning to harden. As she descended the stairs she saw no one; all the doors to the second-floor rooms were closed. She proceeded down to the library. She knocked; at Bradshaw's command she went in.

He stood by the window looking out at the streaming rain. When he turned to Sabra, she saw that his face, like the day, was harsh and bleak. He looks much older, she thought, than the man who had found her worthy, five months previous, to join his household.

"Well?" he said. His voice was hard: as hard as Rachel's voice had been the night before, remonstrating with the truculent farmer.

She stood before him, her eyes downcast, her hands folded against her blue skirt.

"Look at me, Sabra."

She obeyed him.

"I have spoken to Rachel this morning."

She struggled for control. Do not cry, do not beg—

"She is not well. She has a fever."

A month or so ago, Eliza had given her a romance to read. The heroine had repeatedly escaped from her predicaments by fainting at the crucial moment.

"She has imagined some fantastic story which she told to me as if it were the truth. But of course she is ill—delirious—and so we must not believe what she says."

The heroine had been mesmerized by an evil old man.

"I must warn you not to repeat anything that you think may have happened."

She looked down; the strain of watching him was too great. The carpet under their feet was patterned in brown and gold. A rich man's carpet. In the end, the heroine had eloped with a wealthy nobleman.

"Such gossip can have unfortunate consequences. Do you understand me?"

To her surprise she found that she could speak. "Yes, sir."

"Look at me, Sabra."

His eyes were cold and bleak as before. And yet now she thought she saw something else in them: a baffled, questioning look, an expression of bewilderment. Of pain, she thought. He is hurting very badly. All these books, and none to give him words of consolation.

He turned away from her. From the shining surface of the table desk he picked up a note, folded and sealed.

"This is for Mrs. Clapham. Her boarding house is Number Five. She will give you a bed. There is a place for you at Number Two mill, in the spinning room. Ask Mrs. Gumm for a bite of breakfast before you go."

She put out her hand to take the note. But he did not relinquish it at once, and so they stood for a moment linked by the small folded paper. For her, the gesture was more telling than if they had touched.

She thought he had done with her. But still he held on, and then all in a rush he said: "You should have come to me. You should have refused her, you should not have gone along. She is ill—indeed she is ill, Sabra. Somewhere, somehow, her mind has been warped—twisted—she is not what she should be." His voice had gone hoarse. She stared at him, fascinated. She had never seen a man cry. "I thought—I thought, when I brought you here, that you could help her, provide companionship for her, a new interest, someone whom she could train up—" He paused to collect himself. "I did not imagine that you would encourage her in her wrongdoing. Your father was a good Christian man, after all. And your mother— Well. It is too late now. Go—and mind your tongue."

It was not until she had left him that she realized that he had given her no chance to plead her case, no chance to defend herself. He wanted no explanation from me, she thought. He heard it all—too much—from Rachel. And I am to suffer the consequences.

She pushed the unfairness of it out of her mind. She had expected to go on the Corporations when she came down to the city with Goldschmidt. Her employment had simply been delayed for a while. Now she would begin. A little time, she thought: a year, two years—no more. I will work, I will save as so many do, and then I will see what opportunity presents itself. It cannot be so very bad, after all, since so many do it so willingly. I am strong, I have my health. I will survive.

She ascended the stairs. She saw no one. The house was as silent as a house of mourning. She paused at the second-floor hall. She wanted very much to go to Rachel. She looked at the closed bedroom door. Is she weeping, she thought. Defiant? Does she know that I am to go away? And what will happen to her?

She stared at the smooth white panels of the door. No, she thought. She should come to me. She turned away; she continued upstairs to her room. Quickly, decisively, she surveyed its contents. I came with very little, she thought; I will leave in the same way. The clothing that she had worn on the night of her arrival had long since been torn into polishing cloths, and so she had no choice but to wear the dress she had put on that morning. And a shawl, she thought, a bonnet, a nightshift, perhaps the mesh purse—no more. She knelt to retrieve her small battered trunk from its hiding place under the bed. She took her father's old Bible which had had a place of honor on the night table; she held it for a moment, trying to recapture the memory of the child of the itinerant preacher. Often, in those days, she had opened the pages at random and, closing her eyes, put her finger on a place on the page. Then she had read the verse, and had taken from it some direction, some solace which had been so lacking in her isolated, wandering life.

Now she knelt on the floor beside the bed and closed her eyes. She opened the book. Her finger came to rest on a page. She read:

> And after thee shall arise another Kingdom inferior to thee, and another third Kingdom of brass, which shall bear rule over all the earth.

Daniel interpreting the dream of Nebuchadnezzar. And who would prophesy for her? What had kingdoms to do with Sabra Palfrey?

She put the Bible in the trunk, and then the nightshift. There was nothing else. Every other thing that she had acquired since her arrival—the tortoise-shell brush, the locket and chain, cologne water, lace collars and cuffs, the silk dress and the gray plaid, the sketch books and pencils, the water colors, the French grammar—all those she left, for she was no longer Sabra Palfrey, Mr. Bradshaw's—what? What had she been here? She did not know. She knew only that she was once again alone to make her way in the world, and that she would have small need of such expensive baubles in the Corporation boarding house. And, moreover, she wanted no debt to the Bradshaws. They will not say of me that I took as much as I could when I was sent away, she thought.

She put on her paisley shawl; she adjusted the blue bonnet on her smooth hair and tied the ribbons under her chin. She thought that perhaps she should go to Lydia, or to Mrs. Bradshaw, to say good-by. No, she thought. He will tell them what he pleases, it does not matter what, and I must think now only of what is to come. I am a pariah here. And perhaps, after all, I am better off. At least, now, I will have some money of my own. I am free; I am none the worse for my sojourn here.

And so, lecturing herself into a state approaching optimism, she took up her trunk and went down and out of the house. She did not stop for breakfast. She walked steadily down the drive and so on down the hill. She did not look back. The cold rain fell steadily, so that her bonnet and shawl and shoes were soon soaked through, her shoes and her skirt soon filthy with mud. The crowded little city lay before her. She thought of it as a way station. Not long, she thought.

As she crossed the bridge over the Concord River, which flowed smooth and high to meet the turbulence of the Merrimack beyond, she felt as though she passed from one world into another. The town closed in around her as she made her way. Soon she was absorbed into the maze of streets, her small, resolute figure lost in the hurrying crowd.

PART II

1

In the early days some said it was the noise that plagued them most, although others complained about the long hours of standing, while still others resented the close confinement of their rooms at night, vermin in the beds and no air.

But still they came, and most came gladly, finding in their new servitude a freedom lacking in their former lives.

Freedom? Call it money.

They earned it well: a dollar, sometimes two or three, every week. And in those early days it seemed a miracle.

They were only females, after all: God's afterthought.

As with all miracles, repetition dimmed it down to a thing to be expected. The sun rose every day in the east; the river flowed endlessly down from the north to feed the canals which turned the wheels which powered the looms which wove the cloth; the money came in return for work.

The money was saved, or sent home to the farms where again it seemed a miracle: these creatures who heretofore had been useful only to breed new generations of men now proved to be the salvation of the mortgaged land. The news spread: a girl need feel useless no longer, ashamed no longer at being deserted, unclaimed by one of the favored sex. She could exist independently. And decently: the factory towns, it was said, were models of propriety. No girl need fear to go there; no father need fear that his virgin would come home deflowered, spoiled for the prospect of marriage.

And so more women came to work, more mills and factories were built, the towns grew, burgeoned, bore shops and churches and schools and fine homes for the resident Agents. All New England sprouted manufactories; every freshet spawned a water wheel. It was, some said, the true millennium: God's grace to His chosen people, the descendants of those Puritan Saints who had settled this land in His name two hundred years before. And now here was their reward: profits undreamed of, earned by the honest labor of honest farm girls come down from the hills to seek their fortunes.

The fortunes, of course, remained with the proprietors. And the women found—independence? Dignity? The means to educate themselves, to gain an unaccustomed self-respect?

Most assuredly. At least in the beginning.

Of all the manufacturing towns in New England, Lowell, Massachusetts, was the first. It was there on the banks of the Merrimack, ancestral home of the great Passaconaway and his people, that the merchants of Boston undertook a speculation that for a time exceeded their wildest hopes. The town seemed to have sprung full-grown from the peaceful countryside. It soon became the eighth wonder of the civilized world. Important people like Davy Crockett came to see it. President Jackson came too. The proprietors of the mills paraded their female operatives for Old Hickory and he marveled to see them, a mile and more of lovely women, all in white, each carrying a green parasol, preceded by a banner bearing the motto: "Protection to American Industry." He enjoyed himself immensely, so it was said. Never had he imagined such a spectacle. They walk! They talk! And they spin and weave twelve hours a day for the greater profit of the Corporations! And glory to God, hardly a one has lost her virtue.

No one wanted another Manchester. The names of Britain's manufacturing cities stank in the nostrils of the prudent Yankee capitalists: "No Birminghams here in the new land." In America, they said, and most especially in Lowell, we will have our industry pure, thank you, and we will offer our females a dignified life free of old world degradations. Factory work can be decent work; we will prove it, and make our profit as well.

How gallant they were; how solicitous of the moral welfare of their employees. They were somewhat harder on themselves; they stretched their own consciences to the breaking point, and perhaps beyond. Before they manufactured so much as a yard of cloth they manufactured a pleasant fantasy for the credulous farmers of Chelmsford who owned the prime land near the waterfall which was to power their mills. They went to inspect it in November of 1821: a drop of thirty feet. We will buy the land, they said, for a hunting preserve. We are wealthy merchants of Boston and Newburyport, they said, and we want a place to shoot waterfowl. The farmers were amused, disdainful: such were the prerogatives of rich men. And they pocketed their money and then they watched with indignation that grew to fury as Hugh Cummiskey and his gang of Hibernian canal-cutters, having walked the twenty miles from Charlestown, set to work to dig the canals and lay the foundations of the mills, thus increasing the value of the land a thousand-fold.

So much for the sporting interests of the gentlemen entrepreneurs.

There had been one of their number, not long deceased, who had played an even less gentlemanly game. But perhaps the British forced him to it; certainly no money could have bought what he so earnestly desired and what the British refused to sell. And so he memorized it, without a note or a sketch to help him, and brought it safely home in his head, and reconstructed it: the power loom. He built it first at Waltham, on the Charles, and saw that it worked, and saw too that more water-power was needed; and died never knowing of that thirty-foot drop. But when the new town had begun, and they needed to baptize it so that it would have a place on the map of Massachusetts, they gave it his name; and the name was known throughout the land, and was for some the same name as Utopia; and, for a while, his spirit lived and his memory was honored; and the new town prospered and became a city; and the entrepreneurs grew rich.

It was Lowell cloth made by Lowell girls: and the Lord smiled deceivingly upon them, and held back His wrath.

2

Mrs. Zenobia Clapham received Sabra with all the enthusiasm of a mother hen presented with a stray gosling: instinctively she tried to perform her maternal duty to the new arrival, but she could not refrain from a certain irrepressible clucking while she examined her person.

Sabra found her in her small room at the front of the house, working at her account books. Without any preliminary explanation, she gave the landlady Bradshaw's note; Mrs. Clapham glanced at it and then examined her new charge rather more closely.

"Well, now," she said, "aren't you the one they took in?"

"Yes, ma'am."

Mrs. Clapham's eyes traveled down Sabra's bedraggled self to the polished floor, onto which the girl had dripped a muddy puddle.

"And now you're coming here?"

"Yes, ma'am."

Sabra did not mind the woman's questions—a certain natural curiosity was to be expected, after all—but the sharp and penetrating eyes, traveling up and down her figure, made her feel exposed in a most uncomfortable way.

She was altogether a sharp woman, was Mrs. Clapham: sharp eyes, sharp nose, sharp chin, a tall, ungainly frame covered by clothes which hardly concealed the sharp and fleshless bones beneath. Her brain was sharp, too, for she was a woman of business, and she needed ever to be alert to those who would take advantage of her position and so expose her to the calamity of dismissal from her post. She was as much an employee of the Corporation as any spinner or weaver, for the boarding houses belonged to the mill owners, and Mrs. Clapham, like all the other matrons, was merely hired to run hers on an allowance. She needed to be careful with her account books to see that not too much food was prepared, not too much soap or firewood consumed; and yet on the other hand she needed to satisfy her boarders' hungry stomachs, and keep them strictly to the Corporation's rules lest all their reputations be soiled by the behavior of one or two flighty ones. Should any one of them stray from the regulations, the bolder girls would denounce Mrs. Clapham for her lax standards and pick up and board elsewhere, to be followed by the more docile, and so leave Mrs. Clapham's house bereft of boarders and therefore no longer a profitable enterprise for the Corporation. So Mrs. Clapham and her fellow boarding-house keepers had two masters, both equally demanding, and it was no wonder that she was so sharp and curious and always on the watch lest something—or someone—slip past her and ruin her for life.

"Well," she said, getting to her feet, unfolding her bony length, "I'll see where I can put you. Lucky for you I lost a girl three days ago. She had th' lung, poor thing, she cried when she went and said she loved me more than her own mother, and said she'd be back as soon as ever she could, but she's gone home to stay. Once they get th' lung they can't ever work here again."

She led Sabra out into the hall, where she paused to summon—sharply —a servant girl to wipe up the muddy trail, and then she led the way upstairs, alternately questioning and enlightening as they went.

"You have to be healthy, y' know, to work on the Corporation. Have you ever been sick?"

"No, ma'am."

"No problems with your lungs?"

"No, ma'am."

"Well"—on to the third floor; the air grew staler and more fetid with every step—"you have to be healthy to stay. You can't do it otherwise. Girls come in, think they're goin' on a lark, an' they get pretty tired after a week or two and want to go home again, but of course they can't, seein' they've signed the one-year term. You ever worked in a factory?"

"No, ma'am."

"Well, it isn't all bad. The Commonwealth's got pretty fair overseers, and of course they keep their houses decent, paint 'em every year, plenty of food, they see that you're well cared for, that's a fact. Here we are— middle bed, share with Betsey Rudd, she's clean and neat and she don't snore, there's a blessing." She turned to fix Sabra again with her sharp eye. "D' you snore? The others won't like it if you do."

"No, ma'am. I don't snore."

Sabra put down her trunk and looked about. It was a small square room with a fireplace on the inner wall, one window tightly shut, three beds crammed into a space meant for two at the most. Around the walls were rows of pegs at eye level on which hung bonnets, shawls, dresses; trunks and bandboxes were ranged around underneath. Two small chests of drawers stood side by side under the window, a basin and ewer on top of each. The air in the room was even fouler than in the hallway; suddenly conscious of her empty stomach, Sabra sat down on the nearest bed and loosened the top buttons of her bodice. Mrs. Clapham, who had been straightening a crooked bedcover, glanced at her with some concern.

"You all right? You sure you ain't sick? I don't think for a minute Mr. Bradshaw would send me a sick one, but maybe he didn't know—"

"No—no, I'm just a bit tired." It seemed an effort to speak; the bad air had made her dizzy. "Do you—could I open the window for a moment?"

Mrs. Clapham's face settled into sharp lines of disapproval. "Windows open on May first, not before," she said. "The girls don't like a cold room." She hesitated; then: "Land, child, don't you have any dry clothes to change into? Well, rest for a minute and wash your face and hands and come downstairs to my room. A good hot cup of tea'll do you wonders, and then you can get on over to Number Two and see Mr. Weldon, while I see about dinner. The bell will ring before you know it, and then they have to be fed fast." And, throwing another sharp glance at Sabra's sodden form, she made her way downstairs.

Sabra sat for a few moments, breathing through her mouth in short, shallow breaths until the air no longer seemed so foul. Then she stood up, ignoring the suggestion to wash, and peered out the streaming window. The room gave onto the back; she saw a patch of muddy yard, an outbuilding attached to the rear of the house, and, beyond a strip of alley, the rear walls of another row of boarding houses. She heard noise which might have been the rain on the roof, or a steadier, deeper sound from the mill. For an instant she allowed panic to overcome her. She wanted to bolt, to escape—where? She would have smiled at herself had she not been so tired. She reminded herself of her promise: two years at most. And at the end of that time—yes. She saw herself free, made independent by her saved-up wages. The image of herself flashed through her mind. Yes. There were many far worse off—many who would never be free. She put her trunk along the wall beside the others and went downstairs.

Mrs. Clapham gave her a cup of tea, weak and lukewarm, reviving nevertheless.

"You don't want to ruin that good dress," she said. "Do you have an apron? No? You'll need to get one. The lint'll get on that broadcloth and you'll never be able to brush it off. For the matter of that, you'd best use your first pay for a piece of cheap calico and make yourself a proper workdress."

"Yes, ma'am." These practical things had not occurred to her; what else, she wondered, would she need to know to survive in this place?

Mrs. Clapham's sharp glance traveled to her feet. "You'll need some pattens," she continued. "Your shoes won't last a week, runnin' back and forth in the mud, and you might as well keep them for best. There, now —be off with you. Say you're new at my house, and they'll let you in at the gate."

3

The red-brick fortress loomed across the canal, dreary like everything else in the rain; it seemed a gigantic prison whose gates shut off forever from the world those who were sentenced to go there.

To the accompaniment of the persistent throbbing and humming, Sabra rang the call-bell at the gate; when the watch had admitted her she inquired for Mr. Weldon. "See Mr. Lyford first," said the watch; and so, after all, she found herself in the Agent's office. To her relief, Bradshaw was not there. His subordinate showed a brief flash of recognition, overlaid by—what? triumph? malicious amusement?—but he asked no questions. She realized that Bradshaw must have warned him of her arrival. He handed her a paper to sign, a year's term agreement, and then he led the way out across the mill yard, dodging the carts of baled cotton and the railway tracks which bisected the space. They entered one of the buildings, and in the deafening noise climbed the narrow, winding stairs to the third floor.

The huge room was filled with machines whose function was to spin out the thick white ropes of cotton onto tall bobbins. Perhaps forty young women tended them. Lyford led Sabra to a man who stood bent over a stopped machine at the end of a row. He straightened as they approached; he ducked his head at Lyford, but he hardly glanced at his new operative.

"Sabra Palfrey!" shouted Lyford close by the overseer's ear; and, turning to Sabra: "Mr. Weldon!"

She nodded and smiled. She felt very sick again. The room was hot and humid, the air thick with lint. There was a foul odor here, too—a moldy, musty stench combined with machine oil and the smell of unwashed bodies. Lyford went away, then, and she was left standing awkwardly in the way. Weldon seemed to have forgotten her; he returned to his examination of the stopped spinning frame. At length he lifted his head to pronounce his verdict into the ear of the operative standing by:

"It needs a new roller! Get the boy to fetch a mechanic from the machine shop!"

The more important matter attended to, he turned his attention to Sabra. He beckoned her to follow; he led her halfway down the long aisle of whirling bobbins to a girl about her own age.

"Stand here! Watch what she does! Those are your frames next to hers!" And he left her to return to the more pressing matter of the malfunctioning frame.

The girl nodded at Sabra in a friendly way. "Handle here! Just turn it on! Watch the roving doesn't foul! If it breaks, tie it!" Having made sure that her bobbins were filling smoothly, she led Sabra to the next row of frames and turned the handle. At once the machine came to life: whirling, clacking, throbbing, a little iron monster with a pulse stronger than any human's.

Sabra nodded and mouthed a thank you. She confronted the machine before her. She watched closely the twenty-five or so strands of thick roving spinning out onto the tall bobbins. Everything seemed to be working properly. Throughout the workroom, women were standing as she was standing, watching their frames. The noise was overwhelming. Her nose and throat had begun to itch and tickle. Her heavy dress was uncomfortably warm in the hot, humid air. She had a sudden sense of unreality; she thought that she must be in a dream, that she would soon awake and let the memory of it fade away. Yesterday at this hour, she had been helping Mrs. Gumm to prepare the noon meal; Lydia had been at her lessons, Rachel— No. She must not think of Rachel.

Her acquaintance at the next frame caught her eye and smiled. Conversation was impossible over the noise, but she ventured to shout a few words: "Better mind that roving, it'll get snarled!"

Sabra nodded her thanks and leaned over to examine the thick white ropes feeding onto the bobbins. She misjudged the distance; the whirling quills buzzed at her dress. She stepped back quickly. To catch one's hair on that—!

The girl left her frame and came to Sabra's side. "Like this!" she shouted, holding herself well away from the bobbins and reaching back into the frame to straighten the roving. "There," she shouted, "you'll be all right now!" With a friendly nod she returned to her station. Sabra observed her frame with new respect: it was a tedious master, but a demanding one.

She stood for what seemed hours but was probably no more than an hour and a half. She fell into a kind of stupor, mesmerized by the movement of the parts, and so she was startled by the sudden cessation of the noise when it occurred. Only her frame continued to run; all the others had stopped, and now, faintly, she heard the sound of the bell. All around her the operatives were rushing from their frames and crowding to the stairway door. She recalled the noontime rush into Mrs. Glidden's dining room: now she was a part of it. Her neighbor touched her arm as she passed.

"Come on—we haven't much time. You need your dinner!"

Hastily Sabra turned off her machine as she had been shown and followed after, joining the throng on the stairway. Before the bell had ceased, they were down and streaming out in a great wave across the mill yard. The rain had lessened to a cold drizzle. The gates stood open; they hurried through and across the canal and down the block of boarding houses. Clusters of girls trooped into each one. Sabra's acquaintance from the spinning room, a few yards and many girls ahead of her, ran into Mrs. Clapham's. Sabra followed, propelled by the crowd, and found herself in the warm and aromatic dining room where the long table was already three-quarters full. Her acquaintance, who sat across from her, finished filling her plate and began to eat rapidly. She spoke to Sabra through her food.

"What's your name? I'm Rosa Cummings. Did you just get here today? Where did she put you to sleep? Better take some of that meat, we've only twenty minutes."

Sabra answered as best she could, helping herself to what food was nearest: baked mutton, boiled turnips, pickles, hot bread. As she glanced down the length of the table she saw the plump, jolly Miss Swan and, beside her, another girl who had attended Bradshaw's evening. They did not notice her, nor did they speak to each other; like the others, they ate with a curious and single-minded ferocity, as if they would never eat again; they conveyed their food from their plates to their mouths with all the relentless, repetitive movement of the power loom. It was as if for this brief time they had been transformed into eating machines, and eat they did, efficiently and thoroughly, so that at the end of the brief meal the serving platters, which had been so full, were entirely empty. In the background, shuttling to and fro from the kitchen, was Mrs. Clapham; she did not appear to see Sabra, and Sabra made no attempt to speak to her.

Before Sabra had finished her meal the bells began to ring again. Immediately the girls rose and dashed for the door. Sabra followed them as quickly as she could. Outside, as she saw that she was being left behind, she began to run. She arrived back at the spinning room with a painful stitch in her side, her heart beating fast, the uncomfortable sensation of undigested food lying heavily in her stomach.

The morning had seemed very long; the afternoon was an eternity. Her back ached, her feet ached, her arms and neck ached and then became so stiff that she could hardly move them. Mindful of her earlier mistake, she tended her frame carefully; but even so it demanded only a small part of her thought, and soon her mind was running back and forth like a frantic animal seeking escape from its cage. Once—just once—she allowed herself to remember that she had signed a year's promise; but the thought was too painful to endure and she willed her brain to think of something else. Whirling and pounding, whirling and pounding: she became numb, the noise beat in her head, her lungs constricted, she thought that she must sit down or at least walk a few paces back and forth, but she could not leave the frame for fear the roving would tangle again. At some point in the afternoon Mr. Weldon stopped by to see how she did; he did not ask about her, but inquired if the frame ran smoothly and if the bobbins filled to an even depth.

She lost all track of time. She might have been in this cavernous room a week, a month—it seemed that she had always stood by the frame, tending its rackety movement; and the memory of that other girl, Sabra Palfrey come down from the mountains, living with the Bradshaw family, faded far back in her mind like the memory of the heroine of a story read long ago.

At last the bells rang again, signaling the turning off of the machines for the night. The operatives, hungry for their supper, made their way to the stairs, less frantically now for they would not return until dawn. Sabra followed slowly. As she passed through the mill yard, shivering in the cold air after the heat of the spinning room, she glanced inside the windows of the Agent's office to see if Bradshaw were there. She saw only Mr. Lyford, working at a ledger.

Supper at Mrs. Clapham's was not quite so bountiful as the noon meal, but still far more than Sabra wanted to eat. Relaxed now and looking forward to their few hours of leisure, the girls chatted to each other in a friendly way. After the meal, Rosa Cummings retired to a corner with several friends to gossip and sew; others, putting on their bonnets, extended to the group at large an invitation to tour the shops. Some announced that they were going to that evening's Lyceum lecture. Sabra saw nothing of Miss Swan, who had left the dining room directly after supper.

She remained sitting at the table as Mrs. Clapham and her servant, a thin, harassed-looking girl, cleared away the dishes. She watched them dully through the haze of her fatigue. At last Mrs. Clapham bent to look at her anxiously. The landlady's face seemed to loom up uncomfortably close; Sabra smelled the snuff on her breath as she spoke.

"It's hard, the first day or two," she said. "Go on up to bed. Take a candle from the sideboard, but be sure to put it out before you go to sleep. I don't want the house burned down around our heads."

Sabra did as she was told; with great effort, holding the candle carefully, she climbed the two flights of stairs and opened the door to the bedroom.

It was empty. The stale air, although still unpleasant, was not so offensive as it had been that morning. By the dim light of the candle she saw that her trunk still sat on the floor next to the others. She set the candle on one of the bureaus, blew it out, and, overcome by weariness, fell onto the bed which had been assigned to her. All the noise of the mill seemed concentrated inside her head: her ears buzzed, her brain buzzed, her eyelids would not stay closed but twitched and fluttered with the memory of the din. I cannot bear it, she thought; and then mercifully she was asleep.

At some time in the night, she was aware of her bed-mate crawling in beside her. Sounds of heavy, labored breathing filled the room; she heard an occasional cough. Suddenly it came to her all over again where she was, and where she had formerly been, and what, so cruelly, she had lost. Too tired and wretched to hold back her sobs, she began to cry.

The girl lying next to her said nothing, but after a moment Sabra was aware of a hand resting lightly on her shoulder and then seeking and finding her own. She held tight; gradually her tears ceased and she was comforted, glad of the darkness, glad that her bed-mate could not see her blotched and tear-stained face. Fatigue overcame her again; holding to the stranger's hand as a child clings to its mother, she fell asleep once more.

4

Sabra adjusted herself to the pattern of her new life: bells to rise, bells for work and dinner, work and supper, bells again for curfew. Exhaustion dogged her. Every night she thought that her body would collapse before she could return to her bed at Mrs. Clapham's. Her back and legs and feet ached and stiffened into separate parts as hard as the iron machinery; her arms numbed into two jerking, recalcitrant automata no longer responsive to the directions of her brain. At night she crept back to the boarding house and, often too exhausted to pick at her supper, pulled herself up the stairs to sink down upon the thin feather mattress until the morning bell jerked her into consciousness again.

She lost track of time. She was oblivious to the ripening spring, the first lush weeks of May. Her life had narrowed down to a series of separate moments. Survive this day, she told herself. One more day—one more hour. Keep at it until the dinner bell; and then: until supper. She no longer thought of the future; she had forgotten the past. She lived entirely in the present moment. The dreadful noise of the machinery in the mill acted as a kind of battering ram on her imagination, on her spirit, killing them as surely as if someone had taken a club to her head and beaten her unconscious. One girl among many hundreds, many thousands, she endured because she was determined to endure, she labored through the days like a cog in a giant wheel. At night she slept the sleep of the dead. If the others snored, or cried out, or tossed restlessly in their sleep, she never heard them. Her face lost the pretty fullness, the healthy glow that had come to her at the Bradshaws'; once again she was the pale, thin girl-child who had walked into the mill yard on a night in November, six months ago and more.

But then one morning toward the end of May, when she had been on the Corporation for a little more than a month, she awakened before the rising bell. She moved a little, cautiously, so as not to disturb Betsey Rudd. She turned her head and watched the pale rectangle where dawn showed at the window. In the dim light she was aware of the quiet forms of the other girls. None of them snored; but Jessie Pratt, a small pale girl from Maine, had a thick, painful way of drawing breath that signaled, to the practiced ear, certain illness to come. She had refused to go to the Dispensary, or to allow Mrs. Clapham to call Dr. Knight to the house. She was perfectly all right, she said shortly; but every now and then one of the others would catch her resting mid-way up a staircase, or lagging behind as they dashed from breakfast table to workroom, from workroom to dinner. They knew little about her except that she worked to help support a widowed mother and a brother at Bowdoin. She needed every penny, and so they had given up asking her to buy a Lyceum subscription, or to tour the shops of an evening. They felt no hostility in her refusal: it was a comfortable understanding among them that some could spend their pay, while others needed to save. No one lost status, either way.

Sabra lay quiet now, and watched the day come on, and listened to that one pair of hurting, lint-filled lungs. Soon they would all go down to their breakfast; they would begin another day. She found, this morning, that she was able to think of the spinning room calmly, without trepidation. She had become accustomed to it: had come to terms with it. She understood the machinery a little better now. She was no longer afraid of it. She had passed through and survived her term of initiation;

now all that remained was to live on until she could get away. I am fortunate, after all, she thought; I have only myself. Others must stay for years—they must work for their parents, for brothers and sisters. Some even had children to support: they were widows themselves, and the children stayed with relatives or friends while the mothers came down to the factories to earn a living. And then there were some poor women who could not tell their stories; and, for a time, it seemed that Sabra was one of them. These women—some, God help them, with children—had been driven to run away from husbands who beat them, who would not support them. They came to the factories with new names, made-up names to conceal themselves from discovery. For if their husbands found them, these women had no more recourse in the law than had the fugitive slaves. Every cent of their pay belonged legally to their husbands: the law said so. The law said further that the children belonged to the father: he could come and take them away and the mother had no right to have them back. Occasionally these men came searching for their runaway wives. Only the week before, Sabra had watched a thick-set, angry-looking man who had bullied Mr. Weldon into letting him walk through the spinning room, peering at every woman there. He had gone away, much to all their relief, without finding whom he sought. Some of the women had protested, later, to Weldon: we ought not to be subjected to such indignities, they said. What right had you to let this man come through? It is bad enough that we are on display for every delegation of visitors; we ought not to be alarmed by angry husbands seeking revenge.

And so it was that some of the women were open and friendly, while others were more reserved. As it happened, several of the women at Mrs. Clapham's had attended Bradshaw's reception the previous Thanksgiving, among them Minerva Swan and Mary Russell. They had seen Sabra there; they had remembered her. When she came to board, they had naturally been curious to know why. Had she quarreled with her benefactor? Had she chosen to come to the factory of her own free will? What exactly had been her arrangement with Mr. Bradshaw?

They had asked a few tentative, friendly questions during her first days among them; and then, seeing her reluctance to answer, understanding her exhaustion, her bewilderment, her difficulties of adjustment, they had let her be. Some in fact confided to each other that she was better off among them, instead of being immured with the rest of the Bradshaw women in that Grecian temple on top of Belvidere Hill. Here she is independent, they said, and free to advance herself as far as any woman can. Others disagreed: it seemed to them the height of their feminine dreams to be taken in by the grandest folk in town. She was foolish to leave, if she did so of her own accord, they said. But either way, they were willing to allow her to tell what she chose, and in her own time.

They were decent, good-hearted girls; they could wait a few weeks more to hear her story.

When she had been on the Corporation for a week, it seemed a month; now at the end of May, the month seemed a year. And yet each day was easier, each night less painful. She was settling in.

One day she looked up from her filling bobbins to see a party of visitors strolling down the center aisle. At their head was Josiah Bradshaw. Her heart gave a great, wrenching leap; she felt her legs go weak. She had not seen him since she left his house; she could not look away from him now. He was gesturing to the gentlemen whom he had in tow. He did not look in her direction: purposely, it seemed to her. She wanted him to look at her, and yet she was grateful that he did not. He had hurt her very deeply, he and his daughter both, and she was not sure that she had sufficiently recovered to withstand a glance between them. In five minutes he was gone. She looked back to her frame and found the little bobbin-girl standing beside it, waiting to doff the thick spools of white thread.

The next day but one was pay day. Instead of rushing back to their houses at closing bell, the women formed a long line snaking across the mill yard and doubling back on itself. An hour before, attended by two guards, the paymaster had brought to his office the heavy canvas sacks of coins from the bank. Now he stood behind his high desk, checking names in his ledger, calling out the proper amount for each woman as she came through and gave her name; his assistant handed out the pay. The women waited patiently, chatting back and forth, smiling, cheerful. This was the high point of their lives: getting their money. In other factory towns in Attleboro and Taunton, in Pawtucket and Whitinsville the owners paid in scrip good only at company stores. No one, man or woman, could be independent there: no father's farm paid off, no brother sent to college. Here it was better: you got little enough, but you could spend or save it as you pleased.

Sabra stood with the others from her workroom. It was after seven o'clock but still daylight. The sun had sunk behind the factory buildings; overhead the sky was clear and pale. The yard was shadowed; a light had come on in the paymaster's office. Sabra felt a pleasant sense of anticipation. She had not been included in the first pay after she arrived, since new hands had to work two weeks before being added to the payroll. So now she would be paid more than a month's wages: more than eight dollars, as she calculated. She would buy a length of calico for a workdress; her blue broadcloth, which she had had to wear every day, was stained with perspiration and covered with lint. She had not had money even to buy a yard or two of unbleached muslin for an apron, and of course, as a newcomer—a stranger—she could not ask to borrow. Now, she thought, I will buy calico and a plain bonnet and a pair of clogs—for her shoes, too, had been ruined by the mud. And perhaps a subscription to the circulating library. And next month—yes, next month I will rent a pew at the Second Congregational. And I will open an account at the bank.

The line moved, and moved again. They were close to the office door now. Sabra heard the comforting clink of coins from within; she saw the happy, satisfied expressions on the faces of the women as they emerged. The paymaster's voice droned on: "Hibbard, nine dollars twenty-four cents. Barber, seven dollars eighty-six cents. Rudd, eight dollars seventy-two cents."

At last it was her turn. "Palfrey, eight dollars twelve cents." She was aware of the hot, cramped room, the polished brass and wood, the long ledgers of names. She held out her hand. The coins fell into it: sixteen half-dollar pieces with their star-wreathed Liberty heads, a dime, two large copper pennies. She started to say thank you, but she checked herself. None of the other women had said it. And why should they? By their labor they piled up profits for the owners, and if they themselves got some small gain, why need they be grateful for it?

She caught up with Betsey Rudd. Together they passed out of the yard, through the gates. The tree-lined street along the canal swarmed with laughing, chattering women. A spirit of celebration seemed alive in the deepening twilight: everyone was happy on pay day. Sabra felt a surge of hope; she felt the heavy coins in her fist. I will survive, she thought. I will get away.

5

One evening early in June, Sabra met Minerva Swan on the second-floor landing at Mrs. Clapham's. It was the first time that they had met alone. Miss Swan was an amiable young woman, always surrounded by friends in the parlor; but most evenings she broke away early to retire to her notebooks. To be even privately literary, even without publication, was, in New England, to be respected and admired. Miss Swan cared nothing for respect, for admiration: she would have scribbled in her notebooks if scribbling had been a passport to damnation. As it was, she tolerated her friends' approbation as she would have tolerated their deference to a deformity: a crippled leg, a withered arm, a brain insufficiently quick. Modest, self-effacing, but quietly determined and altogether conscious of the human frailties which bound them all, asking no special privilege, Miss Swan was a paragon of industrious femininity. Every night, and for long hours on Sundays, she devoted herself to her work: to her real work. She allowed nothing—no one—to deter her. She paused, now, when she saw Sabra coming down from the floor above. It was past eight o'clock: time to be at her writing table. Still, this was an opportunity which her lively curiosity could not ignore.

"How are you getting on?" she said.

"I'm all right, thanks."

"Spinning's not a bad place to start. And Mr. Weldon's not a bad sort, either. You could do worse."

Mr. Weldon, in fact, had hardly spoken to Sabra beyond the minimal instructions which he had given to her. He showed far greater concern for the machines than for those who tended them. More than once, Sabra had seen him bend over a recalcitrant frame and speak encouragingly to it, while ignoring its operative.

"Yes," she said. "I suppose I could."

Miss Swan put her hand on the door of her room, mindful of the passing time. But then she hesitated. From the parlor below came loud laughter, catcalls, a few chords strummed on a guitar.

"We have parties here, too, you see," she said, "although not so grand as Mr. Bradshaw's."

The name sounded strange to Sabra: curiously historical. She recognized the remark for the invitation that it was, but she could not yet accept it.

"No," she said. She nodded a pleasant good night; she continued downstairs to sit at the edge of the lively group in the parlor, to take comfort from their casual, careless sociability. Miss Swan watched her go. She did not feel rebuffed. It was her consuming interest to understand people. She felt that she understood Sabra. She would make a note of their conversation, and after it she would leave a page or two blank. She was certain that in good time she would have more to add. She went into her room and closed the door behind her.

Sabra liked to sing, although she had no voice; but at Mrs. Clapham's, enthusiasm counted as much as ability, and so she spent a pleasant evening singing what she knew and learning what she did not. She forgot her encounter with Miss Swan. At nine-thirty, humming "Auld Robin Grey" as she climbed the stairs with the others, she went contentedly to bed and fell asleep at once.

She dreamed of the Bradshaws, and dreamed so vividly that when she awakened she was afraid, for she did not know where she was. She thought to call Mrs. Gumm and ask who were these strangers crowded into her little room. When she was fully awake, and knew where she was, she felt a spasm of passing regret: a memory of sorrow rather than sorrow itself. But the tears, the bitter homesickness of her first weeks had gone.

She felt as though she had won a small but significant battle. She closed her eyes to the darkness and fell asleep again until the morning bell.

Spring advanced and greened into summer. The operatives saw little of it. As they dashed back and forth to their noon meal they were briefly aware of the hotter sun on their shoulders; they rose to full daylight now, and went to bed not long after dark. On Sundays they walked by the river.

Some of them (but not Miss Swan) were fond of composing little verses to the wonders of the natural world:

> There's beauty in the smallest flower
> That lifts its head to drink the dew. . . .

No one would have thought so to rhapsodize upon the spinning jenny, or the power loom. Caught in a raw new urban world of burgeoning technological wizardry—a world of men's inventions—they reverted always to the life they had left behind. The rural, the bucolic, were their ideal. No man would want a girl who professed to admire a nail-cutting machine or a self-top card stripper.

Most evenings, despite the longer light and the pleasant weather, Sabra was content to stay at the boarding house after supper. When the evening meal had been cleared away, the long table was pushed against the wall, chairs were arranged in convenient clusters, a pot of tea kept ready, and Mrs. Clapham stationed herself in her room, available for help or consultation but not intrusive. These evenings were important to the newer girls, or to those who had no family, no fiancé waiting in a country village. The women gathered like sisters; they achieved a sense of community, of shared purpose. They felt that they all ventured together as pioneers into the future—into the new world where women worked for wages. They were very conscious of their unique status, and despite the difficulties of their lives, their evenings together reminded them of their good fortune. Every one of them could tell a story of abandoned, penniless females with no means of support, women helpless to survive who would have been happy to exchange places with even the lowest-paid factory girl. And so they assembled, of an evening, and gossiped and sewed and sang and passed the pleasant hours until curfew. Often, at pay time, they would be visited by peddlers of shoes and newspapers, sweetmeats and books. Then they would laugh, they would buy or not, as they pleased, and send the peddlers away, and feel themselves fortunate indeed to be able to have the choice.

Some preferred to go out at night. Betsey Rudd preferred it, and almost always she invited someone to accompany her. She attended every

Lyceum lecture; she visited the circulating library once a week; she knew the contents of every shop by heart. She felt restless, she said, after her long day at her frames; she wanted to get her money's worth from the town while she was there. She planned to go home eventually to a village in the Berkshires: one church, one schoolhouse, one general store. Often, in the long winters, she had seen no one except her family from one Sunday to the next. So she enjoyed the busy life in the town, and kept delaying her return home, and sometimes thought that if her good health continued she might never go back at all.

One night she invited Sabra to go walking. "I don't need to buy anything, do you?" And Sabra, who did not, said that she would go, because she liked Betsey and was happy to have the chance to perform an act of friendship for her. She ran upstairs to get her bonnet.

The shops on Merrimack Street were busy with the evening trade. No one hurried; no one laughed out loud; no one stank of gin: all were restrained and refined, a nightly parade of the flower of American womanhood, a slap in the eye to the British.

Betsey Rudd had been on the Corporation for five years, since she was fifteen. She knew a lot of people in Lowell. Always, kindly, she introduced her acquaintances to Sabra; but then, naturally enough, she would have some item of gossip to pass along, or to receive, about which Sabra knew nothing; and so Sabra would stand patiently and wait. Once she moved to the edge of the boardwalk and looked up beyond the awning to the night sky. Just then the evening railway cars from Boston came steaming into the depot across from St. Anne's. Had she been alone, she would have walked to see the cars. As it was, she promised herself the adventure of a ride in them some day, just like Milo.

Since the night was fine, and the hour just past eight-thirty, Betsey wanted to stroll a little farther. They crossed the dusty thoroughfare, empty of traffic now that the day's rush was done, and climbed once again onto the relative cleanliness of the canopied boardwalk running along the shop-fronts. Approaching this spot by way of Merrimack Street from the boarding house had thrown off Sabra's sense of direction, and it was a moment or two before she realized where she was. Then, looking into the window of the store, she saw Patrick. He stood behind the counter, measuring out a weight of flour; he looked very different from the boy she had known. Instead of the ragged clothes which he had formerly worn, he now wore a neat gray jacket like Mr. Codwell's. His hair was smoothly cut and combed, and even in the two months or so since she had last seen him he seemed to have grown several inches.

She wanted very much to speak to him. Here at last, she thought, among all the crowd of strangers was a friend for her. With a murmured word to Betsey, Sabra stepped inside the shop. She watched Patrick as he finished with his customer; his smile was bright and assured as he wished her good evening, and Sabra noticed that the woman smiled at him in return, unmistakably Irish though he was.

Cautiously she approached the counter. He turned to serve her with that same smooth and deferential smile; it lingered on his face for some seconds after his eyes had gone wary with recognition.

"Hello, Patrick." She felt strangely shy; his name sounded awkward as she spoke it.

He nodded at her. His smile had vanished. "Evenin', Sabra."

"I didn't know you were working in the store now."

"That's right. Since the first of the month."

"Do you like it?" What she meant was: "Do you earn more money?", for she remembered his constant hunger and his care for his mother and his brothers and sisters. But his manner put her off, and she hadn't the nerve to question his well-being so bluntly.

"O yes, I like it all right." His eyes flicked away, surveying the store for possible customers. There were none; she saw no sign of Mr. Codwell.

She felt uncomfortable—an embarrassment to him. She thought of what she might say to remove them to their former terms of easy banter. Before she could check herself, she said: "Do you—do you still make deliveries? Or are you here all the time now?"

Again, it was not the question she wanted to ask, but he understood her meaning. "Haven't you seen them, then?" he said. "Mrs. Gumm told me you was gone, but she didn't say where and wouldn't stand for no questions. What'r' y' doin'? On the Corporation?"

"Yes." She did not want to talk about herself. Someone might come in at any moment, and now, with the mention of Mrs. Gumm reminding her painfully of the times they had shared in the Bradshaw kitchen, she was suddenly overcome with the desire to hear what news he had.

"How are they, Patrick? Have you seen them?" She remembered how he had looked at Rachel. Just this once, she thought, and then I will put all of them away forever. "Nothing—of Rachel?"

His face was blank; his eyes hard. She remembered, too, that he could be exasperating when he chose.

"Naw."

"O, Patrick, please! Please tell me! I've heard nothing since I—since I left."

He leaned toward her and spoke in a low voice. It occurred to her that Mr. Codwell might be overhearing them behind the door to the back room.

"She's gone, too," he said. "I don't know where, and I don't know why. I figured you two got yerselves into some kind o' trouble. Course no one told me anythin'—I just put it all together, I hear this an' I hear that." Suddenly he seemed as anxious to unburden himself as she was to listen.

"The way I figure it, you done a stupid thing to get yerself throwed out. An' you done a worse thing to Miss Rachel, after they was so good t' you. So now yer on the Corporation, workin' like the rest of us. Some folks would've give their eyes to live with th' high muckety-mucks, but you felt different, I guess. I ain't surprised you've not heard from Miss Rachel, or any o' them. Well, I've not heard, neither. Miss Rachel's gone, and Mrs. Gumm's as mad as a hit bee, and Mrs. Bradshaw's taken very sick, an' I don't know nothin' else. Yes, ma'am?" He straightened and smiled at a woman who had come in, and turned away from Sabra to wait on her.

Sabra felt as stunned as if he had reached out and slapped her. To utter a word of protest was beyond her; she stood mute, still trying to understand the fact of his condemnation. Suddenly she turned and walked quickly out of the shop. Betsey still gossiped with her friends; silently Sabra stood by, waiting for her to finish, but she did not hear the low and amiable chatter. She heard Patrick's hoarse and painful words: "Some folks would've give their eyes." So he was angry with her, he blamed her, it seemed, for Rachel's absence. He had looked at Rachel as he had never looked at her, Sabra; and now Rachel was gone.

And, too, she thought, Patrick is gone for me. Now that I am no longer a Bradshaw, I need not delude myself that he is my friend. She stood at the edge of the little group of women. The Bradshaws were gone and done with: for her, these females were now her family and home, her only bond with her fellow creatures. She looked at their smiling, animated faces. Not one of them had anything like Rachel's beauty, her spirit, her captivating warmth. They were honest workingwomen unacquainted with the luxury of taking the world's sorrows on their shoulders. They wanted nothing more than to earn their wages and marry some man as plain, as honest as themselves. They were not Miss Rachel Bradshaw, true enough; but they were decent, friendly people, each girl with her pay in her pocket, her modest hopes and dreams for an ordinary life unruffled by mad, impractical schemes and reckless adventure.

She moved in closer, and they made way for her, and Betsey introduced her all around. She was one of them; it seemed not such a terrible thing to be, after all.

6

Sabra began to go out more frequently in the evenings; sometimes, showing new-found independence, she went alone.

The wound which Patrick had opened began to heal. She was careful to avoid that part of Lowell where Mr. Codwell's store was situated; on the few occasions that she had to pass it she kept her eyes straight and never once looked inside. She did not fear that Patrick would recognize her: in their long-brimmed calashes, which resembled nothing so much as upturned coal scuttles, the thousands of factory girls were virtually indistinguishable one from another.

On a night in July, an unseasonable night of heavy rain and lashing wind, having stayed too long browsing at the stationer's, longing to buy a copy of *Ivanhoe* and finally deciding against it, she hurried back to Mrs. Clapham's barely in time for curfew. The long muddy street was deserted; here and there, light from a window gleamed in the water of the canal. She shivered as she went, soaked and chilly, berating herself for her tardiness, glad of the thought of a cup of hot tea and her warm bed.

She ran up the steps, her hand outstretched to the door. Something tripped her; she fell against the panel and steadied herself while she looked to see what it was that she had stumbled on.

A light shone from Mrs. Clapham's room at the front of the house. In its dim illumination she saw at her feet a small pale shape against a slightly larger, darker mass. The mass moved; a sob escaped it.

She bit her lips to still her instinctive outcry. Evil spirits or ghosts did not whimper on the steps of a boarding house in the middle of Lowell. She leaned down toward the thing and quickly drew back: ghosts did not have such a smell, either.

From the mill she heard the curfew ring. The clanging of the bells seemed startlingly close. On the last peal the door flew open and Mrs. Clapham peered out, searching for her last, late charge. The light from the hall showed Sabra plain; Mrs. Clapham let out a sharp exclamation.

"Mercy, Sabra, you gave me a fright! What are you doing standing there in the rain? Come in, child. Law! What's that?"

It was—just barely—a recognizable human being. It sobbed again; it turned its face up, flinching in the light.

"Get away with you!" snapped Mrs. Clapham. "Come in, Sabra, you'll catch your death—get away, or I'll call the watch on you!"

She stood aside to allow her boarder to go in. Sabra hesitated. Homeless beggars were not commonly seen, at least not on the main streets of the city. What went on in the Acre no one knew. What impoverished and homeless there were, were soon dispatched to the city poor farm, where they were put to some honest work to keep them from embarrassing their more fortunate fellow citizens. Presumably a place could be found there for this waif, too.

It bestirred itself. It stood up. It was very small.

"Please, mum. Don't do that. Can I sleep in the back shed, mum? Just the night?"

The accent was unmistakably Irish: hardly surprising.

Sabra glanced at Mrs. Clapham, who seemed irritated rather than angry. A cold wet claw grabbed at her hand; instinctively she pulled away, but then, looking down at the little face, she allowed herself to be held. She saw dirt, and several running sores, and an ugly bruise under the left eye: an emaciated face, a sunken look such as one sees in the very old, but this was hardly more than a baby. A long strand of wet black hair escaped from the rag that covered its head: a girl, then. The child sensed her weakening and clung harder.

"Mrs. Clapham, if you'll feed her I'll pay you for it. Couldn't we let her stay in the kitchen? Just the night? And tomorrow I'll see about her. Perhaps the Reverend Burnap could help, or perhaps even the priest. . . ." Her voice trailed off. She was afraid of priests. She had no wish to speak to one, even on so pressing a matter.

"Come in at once, Sabra, or I'll lock you out and you'll lose your place," snapped Mrs. Clapham. "The idea—and have her rob me blind and be gone before the morning bell with as much as she could carry back to her folks?"

The child shook her head; she was shivering violently. Both she and Sabra were dripping wet. We cannot stand on the steps all night, thought Sabra; and so, acting on an impulse of her heart, she took the child's hand and walked past Mrs. Clapham into the hall before the landlady could arouse herself to shut the door.

"Sabra! That child is not to come into this house!"

Sabra looked around for help. The parlor was dark and empty, but at the head of the stairs, having overheard the confrontation, a little group of curious onlookers had gathered. Most of them were in their nightclothes, modestly clutching shawls around their shoulders. Sabra saw Rosa Cummings, her neighbor in the spinning room, among them. Their eyes met; Sabra's must have held some special plea, for at once Rosa took the warm woolen shawl from her shoulders and threw it down. Sabra seized it gratefully and set to rubbing the child's face and hair and sopping up the water from her tattered clothing.

"Who is it?" called a voice.

"A beggar child," called another. "She's got a sickness, for sure. Put her out."

"Feed her first—she's only a baby."

"Let her stay the night. Is she sick, Sabra?"

Someone threw down a blanket; wrapping it around the child's shoulders, Sabra slid off the rags underneath. Her feet were bare, and bruised and filthy like the rest of her; she tolerated the handling well enough, but when Sabra had done, and stood up and looked around, trying to determine how to proceed with the rescue, she felt the cold little claw seek out her hand again as they stood together against Mrs. Clapham's indignation.

But Mrs. Clapham was outnumbered now, and so for the moment she held her tongue. The girls had begun to come down the stairs to have a look at the child; almost unanimously they seemed to want to keep her, at least for the night.

Mrs. Clapham went down fighting. "I shall be dismissed," she said. "I'm not allowed to take in strangers—I'm not allowed to take in anyone who isn't on the Corporation. You girls are going against regulations, it's strictly forbidden, you'll be the ruin of me, I tell you. What if she's sick, like Abby said? What then? If she's got ship fever—"

But they overbore her. Someone ran out to the kitchen to put water on to boil, and they roused Huldah, the kitchen help, to get out the big laundry tub, and someone else fetched some bread and meat and the last of the pie and sat the child down at a corner of the worktable.

She ate what was put in front of her with a voraciousness and intensity which was different from the operatives' hurried mastication at breakfast and dinner; they ate quickly because they were rushed, but she ate like a starving little animal. Like Patrick, thought Sabra.

The girls hovered around, intrigued by this sudden little drama; Mrs. Clapham continued to protest to another group in the hall. Rosa Cummings smiled at Sabra.

"Poor Mrs. Clapham. Charity isn't on her list of regulations."

"Will she really be dismissed if they find out?" said Sabra. "Why should they care, if I pay for her food?"

"I suppose they couldn't advertise homes for the homeless," said Rosa, "but this seems to be a special case, and just for the night. Mrs. Clapham knows perfectly well that we can blacklist her, and refuse to board here if she doesn't do as we want. She's caught between them and us, poor woman."

Sabra glanced at the child, who had devoured every morsel in front of her and was looking for more. What on earth am I to do with her tomorrow, she thought. What possessed me to bring her in?

The tub was filled. A look of alarm crossed the child's face, but she allowed herself to be led to it. Several girls stood around holding the blanket as a screen while Sabra washed and shampooed her. Sabra repressed her shudders at touching the tangled, matted hair harboring Heaven knew what; the child, too, winced and flinched as she was handled, even so gently, for she was covered with bruises and welts and her skin was chafed and raw. But she stood fast, and after half an hour or so she was at least a creature fit to have in the house.

Most of the girls had by that time drifted back to bed, and Mrs. Clapham, with stern warnings of Sabra's entire responsibility for the contents of the house, had retired to sulk in her room. Sabra took the child on her lap; the dark head fell against her shoulder, and suddenly the waif was asleep.

"Poor thing," said Betsey softly. "Shall we leave her here?"

"She might come awake in the night and be afraid," said Sabra. She looked down at the damp, black curls, the head heavy against her body. "Let's carry her upstairs. She's so small, she'll fit in with us. Do you mind?"

"No, she's clean enough now. Come on."

They put the child between them in the bed. She never awakened, and Betsey, too, was soon asleep like the others. But Sabra lay awake for a time, and remembered how, not so long ago, a girl hardly more than a child herself had been helped along the way by a peddler driving his cart.

In the morning Rosa offered to ask another girl to help her tend to Sabra's frames while Sabra took the child to the priest to see if he knew her family (although, having seen the bruised little body and the hunger with which she ate, Sabra was not sure that the family, if one existed, deserved to have her back). The child slept through breakfast, and so Sabra sat by the window sewing until she should awake. It was past nine when she opened her eyes. She sat up at once.

"Well," said Sabra. "Do you feel better?"

The child nodded.

"Here. I saved you some pie from breakfast. Are you hungry?"

The child reached out and took the food and gobbled it down. Sabra thought that her face seemed already to have lost the pinched, starved look of the night before. Her black hair gleamed in the morning sun; her eyes, Sabra saw now, were not black but dark blue. Her skin, where it was not discolored, was very white.

"Now," said Sabra, seating herself on the bed beside the child. "What is your name, and where do you live?"

"My name's Biddy," said the child promptly.

"Biddy what?"

She shrugged. "Just Biddy."

"Well, Biddy, where do you live?"

"Don't live no place."
"Well, where do you stay?"
"Any place I find."
Her voice rose and fell in that lovely lilting way; her eyes met Sabra's as she spoke, so calm that she might have been answering questions from a catechism which she knew by heart.
"Don't you have any family?"
"Just my ma."
"And where is she?"
Biddy hesitated for the first time. "Don't know."
"And there is no one else?"
"No. They're all dead."
No sign of grief—and yet she seemed a normal child, with the usual quantity of wits.
"All of them?"
"Yes. I came over last year with my ma and my little brothers. My pa was here already. But they all took sick in th' winter an' died. All except Ma. The priest said it was the mercy o' God. So since then I've not seen Ma much. I bin livin' where I can. Folks lets me stay awhile, an' I gets some money in handouts."
"Who beat you, Biddy? When did you get that bruise on your face?"
The child looked away; she did not answer. From behind the fall of hair which nearly covered her face, Sabra saw her lip begin to tremble and curve down. Poor thing, thought Sabra. She did not want to sorrow her further, and so she stopped her questions.
"Well, Biddy, you must get up now. We are going to see what to do with you."
The child whipped around toward Sabra again.
"Can I stay?"
"Well—certainly, until we find you a place. I was going to speak to the priest—"
"No!"
It was as if Sabra had said that she would talk to the Devil. Biddy grabbed her hand so tightly that she cried out in pain. "Not him. Please—can I stay here? I can work, I can scrub and cook, I'll earn my keep, sure I will."
Sabra reminded herself, somewhat bitterly, that a moment's impulsive kindness could turn into a cruelty to the object of one's charity. She herself had suggested that the child be allowed to stay; but now, faced with Biddy's plea, she hesitated. Best not to give her hope until I know for sure, she thought. Mrs. Clapham's anger had been undiminished at the breakfast table. Undoubtedly her answer still would be an unqualified no.
In the hope of softening the inevitable refusal, Sabra attempted to ex-

plain to the child something of the regulations of the boarding house, but Biddy only shook her head and clung all the more tightly. At last Sabra gave up, and promised to do her best.

She went downstairs and spoke to Mrs. Clapham. She told her that the girls wanted to keep the little newcomer: she could work in the kitchen and sleep on a pallet beside Sabra's bed. When she was a little older she could doff bobbins at the mill, or pick waste if they would not let an Irish girl work as a doffer.

Mrs. Clapham gave in. She knew she could not oppose all her boarders when they had set their hearts on something, and after all, she said to herself, who will know? The child will not eat much, and certainly I can use the extra hands in the kitchen. I will tell Mr. Bradshaw that I have hired her.

When Sabra told Biddy that she could stay, the child said nothing, but threw her arms around Sabra and held her tight as if she would never let go.

And Sabra, a little surprised at her own show of feeling, put her arms around the child and kissed her hair. She has been given to us for a purpose, she thought. We cannot send her away.

The waif became part of their lives. Within a week she was everyone's pet, and even Mrs. Clapham could find no fault with her. She was very useful, not only in the kitchen, but throughout the house; she greatly lightened Mrs. Clapham's burden. She had only once to be shown how to do something and she knew it perfectly: laying a fire, setting the table, beating the wash. In the evenings she settled in a corner of the parlor; she loved to hear the music, although she never sang. She slept on a pallet on the narrow strip of floor between beds in Sabra's room.

She was, she thought, ten years old. She knew neither letters nor numbers, but she was bright and quick and soon the girls had taught her all of Colburn's *Arithmetic* and a good deal of the *Primer*. They made two calico dresses for her, and petticoats and drawers and half a dozen white aprons; they combed and braided her hair and soothed her skin with ointment. Because she was so thin they saved extra desserts for her, and bought her sweets in the shops. She never went out with them. She stayed in the house, doing what Mrs. Clapham bade her; when she was done she went out to the back and sat in the little strip of yard, under a grapevine, content like a cat in the sun. She asked for nothing; everyone gave her everything.

She said nothing about her life. She answered their questions with a shrug or a few muttered words; when they saw that she was troubled by their interrogations, they stopped.

One morning when the girls had gone to the factory, a boy came to Mrs. Clapham with a note. Unable to contain her curiosity, she stood at her open front door to read the message.

Mrs. Clapham:

It has come to my attention that you have hired an Irish girl to help you in your domestic duties. Please understand that while it is permissible for you to do this if your budget allows, her name must be entered at my office as an employee of the Commonwealth Corporation.

J. W. Bradshaw, Agent

Standing in the glare of the hot sun, Mrs. Clapham felt a cold fear pass over her. Who had told him? It unnerved her to think that she sheltered a spy among her flock, and yet someone must have informed on her. He could not have known otherwise. Biddy had not been out of doors except to sit in the back yard. Had someone seen her from the houses opposite in the rear?

Still, the note could have contained worse news. She might have been dismissed, just as she had warned her girls. She knew perfectly well that she should have registered Biddy at the Agent's office. She would have done so eventually. She had wanted to be sure that Biddy would stay; more, she had dreaded the chance that the Agent would not allow her to have two hired helpers—although certainly Huldah, slow and clumsy, was often more hindrance than help, especially at the busy times.

Mrs. Clapham folded the note and withdrew into her house. She felt as exposed as if a thousand eyes watched her.

With her next pay, Sabra bought some adornment for herself: a bonnet of gray moire with ecru ruching and a satin band; a pair of gray doeskin gloves; a cheap cameo brooch. She promised herself a woolen cape in the autumn. She felt different: a new person. She liked herself better.

7

"I had some news today," said Mrs. Clapham. "I thought you might want to hear it." Supper was done; she and Sabra spoke in the landlady's room. Mrs. Clapham paused. Sabra waited, anxious to get back to the friendly conversation in the parlor. "Mr. Bradshaw's wife has died," said Mrs. Clapham. "She'll be buried tomorrow. I thought you might want to know."

Sabra saw in Mrs. Clapham's face, not sympathy, not sorrow, but a stolid, matter-of-fact expression betrayed only by the avid curiosity in the eyes.

"Thank you," she said. Unable to say more, she left the landlady's room then and stood for a moment, irresolute, in the hall. She heard the voices of her companions. She did not want their company now. I must go there, she thought.

She slipped out of the house and hesitated for a moment on the front steps. Although it had been dark for an hour and more, the streets and buildings of the town still radiated the sun's heat. The stench from the canals hung over the city like a shroud, making each breath an exercise in holding back one's nausea. It was just past eight o'clock: she would miss curfew. No matter. It was a long walk to Belvidere Hill, and she was tired from her long day. No matter.

She began to walk toward Merrimack Street. She hurried past the shops, not so busy tonight, perhaps because the heat had so exhausted everyone. Up East Merrimack Street, over High Street to the Andover Road. The air was cooler here, away from the crowded city below; she could see the stars clearly now. They gleamed softly in the night sky. Somewhere beyond them, presumably, had gone Mrs. Bradshaw's spirit. Where? And how swiftly? Did the spirit long to remain on earth, or did God make the journey easy, reserving all grief for the bereaved?

A sudden weakness overcame her; she stopped by a stretch of trees to catch her breath. She must not think of Mrs. Bradshaw. She forced herself to think of the living: of Miss Amalia, Rachel, Lydia, even Eliza and her father. Should she try to see them? She did not know what she would do when she arrived; she was compelled to go, she did not know why.

She walked on. When she reached the driveway she saw the house alight as it had been on the evening when she first arrived. Several carriages stood in front of the portico. She walked toward the house. Through the tall windows she could see people standing in the parlor. She hesitated. Should she present herself? She could not bear to be turned away. Would they understand that she had come not to beg to return, but only to mourn? She felt that she had, after all, the right to mourn this woman, too—publicly, not merely in the privacy of her heart.

She realized that she could not climb the steps. She wanted to be present, but unseen. She did not want to speak to any of them. What could she say?

She walked to the side of the house. From below the cliff she heard the rush and murmur of the river. She looked in the window.

Perhaps a dozen people stood in the room. On a low bier rested the mahogany coffin. A single wreath of white lilies lay on its lid. The mourners stood silent, or spoke in low tones without gesture or expression. The window was open. She could hear their voices but she could not distinguish the words. She saw the bereaved: Josiah Bradshaw, Miss Amalia, Eliza. The Knights, too, were there, and the Peabodys. She recognized few of the others. Bradshaw looked as he had on the morning when he sent her away: diminished, robbed, desolated. Eliza held a handkerchief to her face; her father put his arm around her shoulders. It was an awkward, unaccustomed gesture. They remained so for a moment, figures in a tableau: "Grief."

One person—one dear, familiar face—was missing. Rachel. Sabra looked again to make sure. Rachel was hidden in a corner, perhaps, her face turned away— No. She was not there. Patrick had been right, then. But why, wherever she was sent, had she not been allowed to return for her mother's funeral?

And then she realized that someone else was absent, also: Silas Blood. She recognized his father, an elderly man, a stern, forbidding figure standing by the mantel.

Suddenly a woman appeared at the hall door. She was dressed all in black, with a shawl covering her head and drawn down over her face. A look of horror passed over Mrs. Dr. Knight's face. Without pausing to say a word of greeting the newcomer crossed the room to the coffin. She flung back her shawl. Her hair was white, her face withered and contorted. She knelt before the coffin; she was oblivious to the others in the room. She bowed her head. With her hands outstretched, touching the lid, she began to speak, rapidly, harshly, her voice torn from her throat. The company had drawn back. No one wanted to be near her. Eliza made one brief gesture of protest and then desisted, as if she too had fallen under the woman's spell.

Sabra felt a long-hidden memory stir at the back of her mind: a farmer's family gathered around a comfortable fire of an evening, sharing their home with the itinerant man of God and his little daughter; the old tales told, the curious upcountry beliefs and superstitions, the cures and curses, the tales of witches' spells—all part of the heritage of the country people, folk tales already old when the break with England came. And here it was now, before her eyes in this brave new town, the cradle of the country's future, which had turned its back on all the old ways and faced determinedly forward, abandoning the past.

The Sin-Eater. Taking onto herself Mrs. Bradshaw's transgressions. Freeing Mrs. Bradshaw's soul so that she might enter Heaven, so that she would not burn in Hell forever.

Mrs. Gumm came in bearing a tray: bread, salt, and wine. She put it on the lid of the coffin.

The Sin-Eater ate and drank. She spoke again, her eyes uplifted. She clasped her hands in prayer.

A long sigh shivered through the room. Someone sobbed. The watchers stirred; the spell was broken.

The Sin-Eater stood up. She turned from the coffin. She passed by Bradshaw, who handed her a small purse. She left the room.

Sabra shuddered. Her face was wet with tears. *Why?* What was Mrs. Bradshaw's crime, that she needed so public an expiation? Who had summoned the old woman? Who feared so for Mrs. Bradshaw's soul?

Sabra remained standing by the window but she no longer saw the scene within. She saw Mrs. Bradshaw as she had seen her the night in November, when she had welcomed the stranger to her house, had kindly smiled upon her, trying to bridge the great distance which had seemed to separate her from her fellow creatures. And now she was dead. How? What had killed her?

At length she roused herself. Go now. Her soul is at rest.

She stumbled down the drive to the road, down the road, down the hill to the town, down across the Concord Bridge, down into the living world. Once again she passed the shops, empty now, curfew rung. She walked unseeing past the hotels, where people still came in and out. A few stray dogs ran; they barked at her as she passed, but she did not hear them. A few stray men still lingered on street corners; they watched her, one or two called to her; she did not see them. She came near Merrimack Street; she walked past Codwell's grocery; she did not know it. Automatically, at the corner, she turned down Merrimack toward Dutton Street.

The boys had watched her go. Silently they signaled to themselves. Instantly, like a swarm of hungry rats, they were upon her. She awoke to the horror: filthy animal faces, tearing hands, unintelligible Camp Lands gibberish spat out from ravenous mouths. They pulled her down; she drew in her breath to scream and choked on their foul smell.

She heard the shout, but it was not her own: angry words in a foreign tongue. Slowly, reluctantly, their hands released her. She knelt on the dusty boardwalk, conscious that the predators had abandoned her. Someone came running; a hand reached out, pulled her to her feet.

As he recognized her his look of concern changed to anger. "You bin up there."

She steadied herself against him; his height equaled hers now, he stood firm to support her. "Yes."

"You feel better for it? Yer past curfew, you'll be sacked."

"No. Mrs. Clapham told me about it. She'll let me in."

Her hair fell about her shoulders; she was conscious of a painful throb in her left knee, and her shoulder had been scratched where someone tore her dress. They stood alone on the deserted street. Her attackers had vanished back into their warren to stalk new prey.

"Come on. I'll walk with you. I was just closin' the store when I saw them run an' I knew what they was up to. Can you walk?"

She stepped back from him. Despite her knee, she thought that she could. "Yes."

"Come on, then."

She had forgotten their last, painful meeting; this was her friend once more. "Patrick—thank you. Who—who were they? Did you know them?"

"I know 'em," he said grimly. "Damned bogtrotters. They get in trouble and folks blame all of us. O, I know 'em, all right. I licked one o' them not a week ago, when I caught him tryin' to steal a box o' tea. Danny McCormack—the biggest one—lives just by us with his old dad, an' the two o' them's drunk a river o' rum just this last month. Damned if Mr. Codwell didn't sniff my breath when he hired me, 'cause of trash like them."

The cheerful little delivery boy, stuffing into his pocket the hot roll which she saved for him from Mrs. Gumm's baking, telling her the gossip of the town—

"How did she die, Patrick?"

"Childbed."

Of course. *In sorrow thou shalt bring forth children . . .*

"And the child?"

"I heard it was a girl. But it was too soon. My mum cleans house for Mrs. Talbot up on Water Street, an' she heard 'em talkin'. They said—well, they said the baby never had no chance an' she didn't neither."

They walked in silence, then. She was comforted by his willingness to tell her what he knew. Perhaps, she thought, he has forgiven me. She did not recollect, just then, that he had been wrong: that there was nothing to forgive.

They came to the canal. At its end loomed the bulk of the mill, its white cupola glistening in the starlight. The town was quiet, the guests at the big hotel on the corner retired for the night. Her friends at the boarding house were asleep, renewing themselves for the morning bell; up on the hill the mourners wept; and surely somewhere, separately, Rachel and Silas mourned too.

8

The heat of the summer passed away; the golden autumn came and went, unseen by the workers in the mills. The first snow fell a week after Thanksgiving. A few of the operatives on the Commonwealth Corporation were disgruntled because the Agent did not entertain at his annual evening, but most were glad of an extra few hours' rest. With the onset of cold weather came even more sickness than in summer. The operatives hurried from the cold air of the street to the overheated workrooms, back and forth, back and forth. Their breath came hard as they climbed the stairs; their cheeks grew unnaturally red, their eyes fever-bright. Dr. Knight worked tirelessly at the new Corporation Hospital, ceaselessly attending: too many ill!

The *Advertiser*, a Democratic paper, printed an obituary which began: "Died, In this City of Consumption . . ." The mill management were outraged. Such epithets were as contagious as cholera.

In Boston the stockholders grew restive: the price per yard of cotton cloth had dropped by five cents. Their profits would suffer. Their dividends were threatened. When a man invests thousands, they said, he deserves a good return on his money. Another wage cut was considered and rejected: they wanted no trouble with turnouts. A solution was agreed upon: speed-up.

9

On the first Monday after the New Year the operatives went to work in a snowstorm. It was still dark when they left their boarding houses; they walked as quickly as they could over the slippery ground, their feet poorly protected by their clogs, heavy shawls pulled over their bowed heads, fighting for breath in the cold wind which drove the snow into their faces. They did not speak to one another as they hurried through the gates of the factory into the yard. Many were only half awake. They began to stream into the mill, into their separate workrooms.

At once they began to perspire, for the mill was hot and humid—the best atmosphere for the thread. The girls in the spinning room, like all the others, hung up their shawls and shook the snow off their skirts. When they turned to their frames, they found Mr. Weldon waiting for them.

Although this room was his domain, his little kingdom, Mr. Weldon was ill at ease. He hoped that there would be no unpleasantness. The solar lamps threw a harsh illumination on the neat and docile figures arrayed before him. These were good girls, he thought; they will not protest. Nevertheless he avoided their eyes as he spoke. He read his announcement in a loud voice pitched too high: hereafter, each operative in the spinning room of Commonwealth Number Two would be responsible for three frames instead of two.

The girls were angry, but they remembered that they were ladies. They held their anger in. The braver ones asked politely: By whose order? For how long—a month? A year?

Mr. Weldon held up his hand. He would answer no questions. They could leave if they wished (if they had served their year's time), although he could not guarantee a good conduct discharge. The order stood: three frames each. The newest girls would have first pick of vacant places.

Grumbling, the operatives went to their machines. At precisely six o'clock the locks were opened, the water came rushing through the canal to turn the great wheel in the basement, and the machinery rumbled into life.

10

Rosa Cummings showed Biddy how to embroider, and gave her a piece of cloth to work a sampler. The child was proud of her new skill. She spent all her evenings now bent over her work: slowly the motifs appeared. A border of red and blue flowers linked by a trailing green vine; a rising sun, golden-rayed; an alphabet within; a motto: "A penny saved is a penny earned." Although some of the leaves and flowers were imperfectly executed, the sun and the motto were a credit to both teacher and student.

Mrs. Clapham approved. For all her sharpness she was not an unkind woman. In the months since Biddy's unwelcome arrival she had grown to accept her and even to admit to some fondness for her. "She's a good little thing, I don't deny it," she said. "She's smarter than Huldah if it comes to that"—although given poor Huldah's limited intelligence, this was hardly a compliment—"and she bakes as good a loaf as I do myself."

For all the attention given her by everyone else, Biddy remained Sabra's special pet. Of an evening in the parlor, when she was especially tired, she would climb onto Sabra's lap just as if she were a tot of two or three, and nestle somewhat uncomfortably against Sabra's shoulder as they listened to one or another of the girls play at the guitar, or read aloud from the *Pickwick Papers*, or some more edifying text such as Edward Gibbon, or less, such as *The Last Days of Pompeii.* The child had not forgotten who rescued her; nor had Sabra forgotten the image of the half-starved little creature huddled in the rain. With that special feeling of responsibility which the rescuer feels toward the rescued, she checked every night to make sure that the child's coverlet was pulled up over her shoulders; always, waking, she put down her hand to make sure that Biddy was safe beside her on the pallet, that she had not vanished as suddenly as she had come. Sabra shuddered to think what would have happened to Biddy had she been turned away. She would rest her hand on the child's thick black hair and think: one less piece of flotsam tossed to and fro. So many homeless, so many hungry—one, at least, is safe.

11

Despite the speed-up, women still flocked to the city in search of work. Many of those who succumbed to "Lowell Fever" were brought by Agents sent out to the countryside by the Corporations. "Slavers," some called them. These men spun fantasies of the excitements of life in the town: of the riches to be had, the intellectual stimulation, the cosmopolitan atmosphere, the new horizons. Women—and some men, too—came by the thousands: the merchants could hardly keep goods in stock, the laborers hardly build housing quickly enough. The town spread like a stain on the green bosom of the countryside. The former campground of fifty thousand Pawtucket Indians, who had gathered each spring to catch the running salmon, had become a buzzing hive for twenty thousand industrious bees, not a drone among them. Work or die!

A new girl came to the weaving room. Her looms were next to Minerva Swan's. Although Minerva spent much of her free time alone, writing in her notebooks, she was a friendly soul who liked a good gossip as much as anyone. She introduced herself to the new arrival. She offered to help her if she had any problems with her looms. She herself boarded at Mrs. Clapham's, she said; she was pleased that the new girl lived next door at Mrs. Silsbee's.

The newcomer's name was Margaret Lowe. She did not expect to need any help with her looms; she had worked at Nashua for three years, and at Chicopee for two years before that; she was thoroughly familiar with the job. Abruptly she turned her back and took down the bag of powdered French chalk hanging from the arch of her loom. After thoroughly coating her fingers, she began swiftly and expertly to tie her weaver's knot on a broken warp thread.

Minerva felt slightly put out. She was unaccustomed to having her friendliness thrown back in her face. However, after a moment, she smiled to herself: this girl presented a variation on the usual reticences of those new girls who chose not to confide. There was nothing secret or sorrowful about her; she was simply, carelessly rude—and so she might be useful after all. She was a new type, and therefore worthy of a place in Minerva's notebooks.

She was a tall, brown-haired girl, well past first youth but retaining a certain sprightliness. Her features were not beautiful, but they were pleasant enough: a broad brow, a small straight nose, a mouth that smiled perhaps a trifle too tightly.

It was the movement of her body that set her apart from the others, and made her a focal point of whatever group she happened to be with. When she stood alone, as she did at her loom, she moved as if she were performing a dance instead of merely attending the movements of a machine: arms up, arms down, step forward, step back. Other operatives seemed marionettes beside her: awkward figures, stiff and wooden. This one moved with the grace of a cat; she walked conscious of the movement of her muscles, aware of every part of herself, even of those parts of which all decent females were ignorant.

Minerva observed this quality about the newcomer within a few minutes of meeting her. That night, in her notebook, she tried to describe it and found herself blushing, her hands unwilling to obey her brain. For a long time she stared at the blank page before she could write a few sentences. They were unsatisfactory; she crossed them out and tried again, with little better success. Since she did not know the reason—or could not admit it—for the fascination of Margaret Lowe's presence, she had no way adequately to describe it.

She resolved to have another, closer look at Miss Lowe. All the next day, trying not to seem to stare, she observed the newcomer's attentions to her loom. Late in the afternoon, as darkness fell and the whale-oil lamps were lit around the workroom, Minerva saw Miss Lowe turn her head away from her work and look in the direction of the staircase. Minerva followed her glance.

Josiah Bradshaw stood at the door. Like Minerva Swan, he observed the newcomer. He seemed aware of no one, nothing else.

That night, Minerva had two difficult descriptions to attempt: Miss Lowe's presence, and the expression she had seen on the Agent's face.

12

"It's none of my business," said Mrs. Clapham. "I don't know anything about it, and I'd advise you girls not to pry. It's none of your business either."

But their curiosity raged, fed almost daily now by bits and fragments, speculation and rumor. Even Mrs. Clapham herself was not above visiting her counterpart in the next house to see what that good woman had to report. But Mrs. Silsbee, like Mrs. Clapham, had been hired by Josiah Bradshaw to manage a Corporation boarding house; she would not jeopardize her livelihood by careless tattle about her employer. She knew nothing, she said in a chilly, dismissive tone; had seen nothing, heard nothing—nothing at all.

The denial said very little for Mrs. Silsbee's powers of observation, since every girl in every house on Dutton Street had by this time seen the closed carriage draw up at Mrs. Silsbee's door, and Margaret Lowe either get in or get out—of an evening, say, or a Sunday afternoon. Some lucky few had caught a glimpse of the gentleman accompanying her: not many men had hair of just that shade of yellow.

The girls hung on the affair; they traded tantalizing snippets of information back and forth like Lord Byron's verses. One had seen them say good morning in the mill yard; another had seen him examining her loom and accidentally brush her shoulder; still another—lucky soul!—had seen the carriage stopped beside Reed's Tavern far out on the Mammoth Road—it was the very same, she said, she would not mistake it for any other. No one asked her how she herself had come to such an unlikely place.

Sabra heard it all. They did not try to question her. She was one of them now; they understood that she knew as little as they, and had no source of information closed to them.

She could of course have gone to Patrick. He would know more than anyone; he always did. But she dreaded meeting him. She had not seen him since the night he had rescued her from the Paddies. For a brief time after that she had half hoped to see him appear at the boarding house to call on her, not as a beau, of course, but simply as one friend inquiring after the well-being of another. But he never came, and so she was shy of seeking him out. She did not do so now, when a few words from him would have made her the center of attraction for an entire evening, at least. Let them be, she thought. It is no affair of mine. Mrs. Bradshaw is dead.

13

One evening in March two gentlemen alighted from the railway cars at the Dutton Street Depot and crossed to the Merrimack House to have their supper.

The older man was clean-shaven, although his gray hair was unfashionably long. It straggled untidily from under the brim of his gray beaver hat and flowed over the wide collar of his dark gray coat. His cravat was clumsily tied; his boots were cracked and smeared with mud. He looked about as he walked, but his eyes were not focused on the crowded street. He might have been extremely short-sighted, or walking in a dream. The younger man, whose black surtout hung awkwardly on his tall, gaunt frame, guided his older companion as they went. The young man seemed purposeful and efficient; he seemed to know exactly where he was going, as if he had been there many times before; were it not for the thick black beard and moustache which covered the greater part of his face, he might have been one of the gentlemen connected with the management of the Corporations. But of course no Corporation would have employed a man with such a growth upon his face.

The hotel dining room was nearly full. They took a table in a far corner; the younger man sat with his back to the room. They ate methodically, saying very little, each preoccupied with his thoughts. Indeed, had it not been for the fact that the older gentleman had been so very particular with the waiter about his order, an observer might have thought that he hardly noticed what he ate. But he did notice: he examined the contents of his plate very carefully. He had ordered a mess of vegetables, a loaf of bread, an apple pie, and a pitcher of water. He cast a mildly censorious eye upon the younger man's supper, which was the same as his own except for a piece of roast beef. The younger man was aware of his companion's disapproval; nevertheless he ate heartily, sipping his water as if it had been wine.

Their supper quickly finished, the two men paid and left. They had not come to Lowell for the cuisine.

In the Lyceum hall the audience—mostly females—chatted quietly, or read some book or magazine, while they waited for the lecture to begin. It was a pleasant, spacious room with white-painted walls and wide windows overlooking the street. A speaker's platform rose at one end; upon it stood a lectern made of oak, a small side table, and several straight-backed chairs.

Sabra sat between Rosa Cummings and Samantha Trowbridge, a new girl. She stifled a yawn. She had slept badly the night before, waking several times from haunting, unpleasant dreams whose details she could not remember. Each time she woke she had reached down in an instant of panic to make sure that Biddy still slept beside her. The bedroom had been unusually stuffy and malodorous; she had risen at five with a headache which had lingered all day and which now pulsated painfully at the base of her skull. But she had come out this evening all the same; having paid in advance for the series of lectures, she did not want to miss even one.

Two men entered the hall from a side door near the speaker's platform. The younger one sat in the first row of the audience; the older ascended and stood behind the lectern. His eyes were clear and calm as he looked out over the crowd. At once they quieted expectantly. In a high clear voice he began to speak.

He told them first about himself. He said that he had been born the third son of a wealthy man in Boston. His youth had been passed in a setting of the greatest luxury. It was not until he had reached his majority that he realized the injustice of the world: how men—and how women, too—were forced to scramble all their days after the great god Mammon, merely to get enough to live. How in the course of their struggle they came to ignore the call of their higher natures. How they lived all their lives never hearing the sweet voice of the spirit, which needed only one single recognition to be heard, and which, once heard, transformed the listener's life from struggle to an enactment of the love of God. God, he said, was all around, waiting—not in the churches only, but in each man's heart.

Assiduously the audience took notes, not stopping to think about what they heard. The speaker spoke slowly, pausing from time to time to collect his thoughts; they had no difficulty recording them. In words of two and three syllables—easy words, nothing obscure—he made his explication of the mysteries of human existence.

And then he spoke of a better way to live: a way more closely in harmony with Nature, less destructive to the spirit than the life of a factory town. He spoke of a Community—a carefully selected group who would live independent of the world, self-sustaining, each person sharing all tasks so that no one would become deadened by monotonous repetition. Then he paused a somewhat longer time to give emphasis to what he would say to them next. Women, he said, would have an equal place in this Community: an equal voice in its management. All policy would be decided by vote, and each female would have the franchise. Several of the women in his audience looked up expectantly at this, but most sat unmoved, staring down at their notes. After a moment he continued: the various work that would need to be done, the financial obligation of each member, the search for the right location. For more than a year, now, he had been making in his lectures this proposal about the equal place of women in his Community, for it was a principle in which he devoutly believed; but always, without exception, the response was as cool as it had been tonight. He could not understand: why did an audience largely composed of females ignore a chance for freedom which they could find nowhere else?

The acolyte in black sat motionless. He had listened to this speech and its variations many times before. He could have given it himself, if necessary—although it never was, for the speaker was a healthy man, never sick for so much as a day.

The women filled the pages of their notebooks: the meaning of life, the transcendence of the human spirit, the small still voice within, the organization of a more perfect life. They got it all, just as they had got the lectures on the classifications of plants, the French Revolution, the lives of great men. Each talk was like a little window opening onto a wider, unknown, undreamed-of world: this, then, was what the recruiting agents had meant when they spoke of the richness of city life. And, indeed, this evening's lecture was well worthwhile: some of them had taken as many as six pages of notes. On some evenings they felt cheated, not being able to get more than one or two.

The speaker's voice trailed off. Apparently he had finished. A low buzz of conversation arose. The gentleman in black sat up; he turned to survey the audience. At the sight of so much assembled femininity a spasm shook him and then passed swiftly; they were too many, there was not one definable object on which to focus. His eyes passed over their faces: pretty girls, plain girls, old, young, laughing, solemn—

Sabra's eyes met his. He recognized her first; she, for a long moment, was not sure. When finally she saw who he was, she wanted instantly to look away but she could not. She blushed; her face burned. Samantha spoke to her. She did not reply. She stood with her companions as they rose to go and felt her knees weaken, but she could not sit down again, for everyone was standing now and she would lose sight of him behind their backs.

Silas.

He stood in the aisle next to the wall. Ignoring her companions, she pushed through the crowd to reach him. He did not smile at her as once he had done. His dark eyes were filled with pain; now that she stood next to him it was as if he could hardly bear to look at her. She thought that perhaps she should simply have turned and gone out; perhaps it would be too difficult for him to speak to her, unavoidably conjuring up memories of times past, times best forgotten, dead. But she could not turn away. She stood close enough to touch him; under her voluminous clothing she felt her self.

She experienced a familiar emotion then: the same which had caused her to rescue Biddy. Now it welled up in her heart again. How thin, she thought, how bereaved he is.

"Well, Sabra," he said. He did not smile. He bent down to her, giving an impression of intimacy to their pose. He was glad that he had remembered her name.

Her lower lip trembled. He saw it and shifted his body uneasily. Here, then, was that one object, plucked from the crowd–

"I did not recognize you," she said, and fell silent, embarrassed. It was the wrong thing, a reminder of the past–and yet she did not know what else to say, and she must speak of something to hold him for a moment.

He shifted again. He was very uncomfortable. *The sweet voice of the spirit–*

"How are you?" As soon as he had spoken he found that he was interested to know the answer.

"Well enough. I'm on the Corporation."

"I didn't know." He did not know anything recent of the city; this was his first visit since he left nearly a year ago. "And do you like it, being an independent female?"

The Waltham clock on the wall lacked twenty minutes to curfew; the hall was nearly empty. Rosa and Samantha had gone.

"Yes. I was tired at first, but I've gotten used to it."

"And you live–"

"At Mrs. Clapham's. Number Five, Commonwealth."

"Yes."

She had to go. Mrs. Clapham would lock the door and she would be dismissed.

"I must go–the curfew–"

"Ah, yes, I had forgotten about that." He saw that his mentor was still deep in conversation; presumably those females to whom he spoke lived with their families, not so watchful of their virtue as the Corporation. He hesitated and then made up his mind. "Just let me speak to him and then I'll walk with you."

She had not expected such a gift. She accepted it gratefully. They did not speak as they crossed Merrimack Street; then, taking her elbow, he said abruptly: "I was sorry to hear about your leaving the Bradshaws."

The dark bulk of the mill blocked the end of the street. Here and there a latecomer hurried to her house. Sabra did not want to speak of the Bradshaws; she did not want his pity.

"Perhaps it is for the best," she said.

"Perhaps. Rachel was—"

She thought for a moment that she had willed him to stop; but then she realized that he was merely searching for a consoling phrase. Had he heard from Rachel? Unlikely, she thought. Speak of something else. She was acutely aware of the pressure of his hand through the calico sleeve of her dress, the thick wool of her shawl. Speak of something else, learn something about him—

"Are you—will you stay here now?"

"No. We are here only for the evening. We go back to Boston on the late cars. Then to Mr. Winfield's home in Concord tomorrow, to Worcester the day after, then to Springfield and on into New York State."

She envisioned him: traveling, seeing the world. To conceal her disappointment, she said, "It sounds an interesting life."

"Yes. Very interesting. Tiring, but a worthy cause."

They came to Number Five. Sabra glanced up; a head peered from the second-floor window, silhouetted against the light within. She felt a nervous giggle rise: just so were Margaret Lowe and Josiah Bradshaw seen, by heads at windows, casual glances around a door ajar.

He took her hand. "I am happy that you are well," he said. She felt that he spoke sincerely. "Perhaps we will return here, in a month or two. I don't know."

She wanted to end their meeting on some more definite note, but she could think of nothing sufficiently modest. She allowed her hand to remain in his; she smiled up at him.

"I am glad to have seen you," she said. "Have a pleasant journey." Surely, she thought, those were not words too bold.

He watched her as she went in; then he turned and retraced his steps. A pretty little thing. Unfortunate that she called up memories best forgotten. He walked quickly. By the time he reached the Lyceum hall, where his companion awaited him, his head was filled with thoughts of their coming journey. He hoped that their schedule would be filled: both of them needed new boots.

Sabra said good night to Mrs. Clapham, ever watchful, and went up to her room. The house was filled with the odors of its inhabitants and the food they ate. The familiar stairway and hall looked drab and much smaller than usual, stiflingly narrow. From the bedrooms came tired, desultory chatter; once or twice someone laughed.

So it had been last night, so it would be tomorrow. Day following regimented day, each ending with a few moments' gossip before sleep overtook. Day after day: and meanwhile Silas saw the world, and never thought twice about his freedom.

In June, Miss Margaret Lowe and Mr. Josiah Bradshaw were joined together in holy matrimony at the bridegroom's residence on Belvidere Hill. Spectators at the ceremony noticed that the groom, usually a self-contained man, seemed agitated and even openly distraught. The bride, on the other hand, played her part with perfect composure. She seemed to be an extraordinarily refined young lady. A stranger, looking in, would never have known that she had worked a day in her life.

14

The water ran low again that summer; most of the mills, including the Commonwealth, shut down for two weeks. Those operatives fortunate enough to have homes and families upcountry gladly took leave of the stifling city. They would not be paid in any case; better to go home and fill their lungs with fresh country air. Those who remained were allowed to stay at their boarding houses, but in order to pay their keep they were forced to draw on their savings.

Rosa Cummings went to visit her sister in Amherst. She invited Sabra to come along. "It will do you good," she said. "They have a farm. You can lie about all day and help with chores when you want. You need the air, and my sister is a wonderful cook. You're too thin, Sabra. You need fattening, and a chance to rest."

But Sabra did not want to go. Although she dreaded the long empty days at the boarding house—and, worse, the depletion of her small savings—she did not want to leave for even a few days. He will be sure to come just when I've gone, she thought. And if he does not find me he might not come again.

It was a fragile hope blossoming out of a tiny seed. They had, after all, spent barely a quarter of an hour together; but she cherished it, and brooded over it, and after a while she came to live on it. Every day she allowed herself, just once, to think: tomorrow. And so she stayed; nothing could have induced her to go away.

What did she want from him? Only what every woman in the world wanted from every man: acknowledgment of her existence. Courtship? Marriage? She did not think in such definite terms. But there was not a single woman on the whole of the Corporations who could afford to overlook an eligible man: not a woman among all those thousands who did not see her spinsterhood as a thing to be abandoned at the earliest possible moment. Men were scarce. Women were nothing without them. The girls on the Corporations spun endless fantasies: when I am engaged, when I marry. . . . The laws giving men absolute control over their wives were not thought of. The husband and wife are one, said the law, and that one is the husband. No matter. No woman wanted to say: I am not chosen; I am passed by, ignored, rejected. And so Sabra waited, and hoped, and passed the time as best she could; and any one of her thousands of sisters would have done the same.

In the evenings, after early supper, she walked by the river. Often she lingered until dark. I must stay in the city, she thought; I must be here if he comes to find me.

Minerva Swan stayed, too. She had family in Vermont but she seldom mentioned them: a father, Sabra thought, and a brother and sister. Minerva put her enforced vacation to good use. Every day she stayed in her room, writing, writing, to emerge late in the afternoon, tired but peaceful, ready to spend a few sociable hours with the half-dozen girls who remained.

The child Biddy had grown; Sabra wondered that she had not seen it before. They had been wrong about her age, she thought; the girl was blossoming, she was at least twelve or thirteen. It was her wretchedness which had made her seem so young. But now, after a year of good food and decent care, she was suddenly on the verge of womanhood. Sabra, only eighteen herself, felt years older when she looked at Biddy; she felt like a mother reckoning up the astonishing number of birthdays of her child.

Biddy often consented to go out with them now, having lost somewhat her fears of discovery. No one would recognize her, thought Sabra; she has changed so much. If they did not walk by the river in the evenings, they walked across the Central Bridge to the Dracut shore, sometimes as far as Christian Hill, sometimes back again to stroll down Merrimack Street. Despite the shutdown, most of the shops remained open; the girls amused themselves by strolling slowly past the windows, choosing what they would buy when they had their pay again.

They never went near the Acre—naturally not, no operative had business there. When they passed an Irishman on the street, Biddy averted her head. In her blue calash and neat, clean calico dress she looked as much a factory girl as her companions; no one looking for a Camp Lands waif would have given her a second glance.

Late one afternoon Minerva, emerging from her room, found Sabra and Biddy fanning themselves in the parlor, reading by turns from the latest issue of *The Literary Souvenir*. Minerva asked them to walk with her to the post office. Ordinarily Sabra would have declined; the heat had enervated her, she never went out now until after supper; but this day, not knowing why, she agreed. Biddy declined to go with them, remaining to help Mrs. Clapham prepare the much diminished meal.

At the post office Minerva was rewarded with a letter. Her hands trembled slightly as she opened it. The bored clerk, fretting away his time until closing, winked at Sabra.

"You, too, miss? What's the name?"

"No," she said. "There's nothing for me."

"You never know," said the clerk. "Let's just see. What name?"

His insistence annoyed her; she did not like to be reminded of her isolation in the world. To prove him wrong she grudgingly told him.

He disappeared to check his cubbyholes and returned in a moment, triumphant.

"There you are, miss. Like I said, you never know. Ten cents an' it's yours."

She took the envelope reluctantly, sure that there had been some mistake. Her name was not uncommon, after all. But no, there it was, undeniably for her: "Miss Sabra Palfrey, No. 5, Commonwealth." The return address was unfamiliar: "Three Elms, Concord." She did not recognize the large, flamboyant handwriting: who made elaborate capitals like that? She turned away from the prying eyes of the clerk and held the letter for a moment before she broke the seal. At last it has come, she thought; only he would write to me, there is no one else.

Minerva, mindful of the clerk, touched her arm. They walked out into the heat.

"Aren't you going to open it?" said Minerva.

"Yes." But she was afraid. It could only be bad news: "We leave tomorrow for the West," or "We leave tonight for England." She felt that she could not bear it; she must have a moment to strengthen herself.

"What is yours?" she said. "You look like the cat with cream. Is it good news?"

Minerva beamed; her round, rosy face laughed out from beneath her coal-scuttle brim. "Yes. The editors of *The Ladies' Hour* want to see some other samples of my work."

For a moment Sabra forgot her own letter. "But that's wonderful! Are they going to publish one of your stories? What is it, a romance?"

Minerva beamed at her. "Yes. And they say they like it very much. I can hardly believe it, after all this time."

Sabra stood on the boardwalk and stared at her companion. Already Minerva looked different, no longer just a fellow worker.

Minerva was embarrassed. "Open yours," she said.

Sabra broke the seal and read what was, after all, an innocuous, even curt, communication:

Dear Sabra:

We will be in Lowell the 25th and 26th August. Can you meet me at the Merrimack House at 2:00 p.m. the 25th?

S.

The heat was like a furnace, and she a live coal.

"Come on," said Minerva. "You look faint. Let's get back to the house." Surely, she thought, it must be bad news. She hurried along. She bent to look again at Sabra's face and was puzzled. Strange calamity, to produce such a look of joy.

15

Beyond the treetops the deep blue sky; at their feet the broad and placid river moving sluggishly toward the Falls. Solitude: they alone intruded on the island's wilderness. Somewhere in a thicket of fir trees, perhaps, lingered the unhappy ghosts of Wannalancit and his father, the great chief Passaconaway, but they did not alarm the two who reposed on the shore. This was white man's territory now: the tribes who had come by the thousands each spring to catch the run of salmon had long since been dispersed, their miserable descendants a public curiosity now in the forests of Dracut.

Silence: they heard nothing but the beating of their hearts. The sun warmed them, glinting on the water, making patterns of light through the trees; but the air was cool, a premonition of autumn. The leaves of a blasted oak had turned already: scarlet against the surrounding green. In the distance, at the great bend, the red-brick city glittered in the bright day, but they did not see it. They were far away from that world—much farther than a mile or so upriver.

They sat side by side. Their borrowed skiff bobbed in the water a few yards down the shore. Near the spread of her skirts lay the bonnet which she had discarded. He lifted his hand and with his finger traced the line of her cheek: it was a gesture of experiment rather than affection. She submitted. She did not look at him. She could not see his face, which bore a curious expression for a young man engaged in so pleasant a pastime.

He began to speak. He told her of the history of the island. Once it had belonged to Jonathan Tyng, a man of parts in Colonial times. He had had a son. The son had got a servant girl with child, and had murdered her rather than face the fruit of his sinning. And so now the island, and the surrounding shore, were haunted by her ghost as well as Wannalancit's; she appeared at the dark of the moon, so it was said, mourning her unborn child, cursing her betrayer.

The sound of his voice mesmerized her so that she was startled when the story ended. She saw that his eyes were filled with tears. He withdrew his hand. Her skin was soft, but not soft enough. Her body was well-formed, but not the Venus which once he loved. Her hands were somewhat rough; her bosom—he had never seen her bosom, but he could not imagine that it equaled that other which he worshiped not so long ago. She was a fair young woman. No more.

And yet—he was in agony, he must have relief. He turned away. He felt cheated. The excursion had been a mistake. Her face reminded him too vividly of the one he had lost.

He forced himself to think of his work in the months ahead. His labor, and that of his companion, was beginning to succeed: they were making converts. Soon—in five years, perhaps, or ten—they would have laid the foundation for their New World; then the human misery all around them would be gone, and the Light would come to thousands—millions—who labored now in spiritual darkness. Their Community would be the working model; hundreds more would spring up in imitation.

His rebellious member quieted and lay flaccid. As always, contemplation of his mentor's dreams had soothed his body's torments. Like the girl beside him, he watched the river flowing by.

She turned to him and offered him a smile. She sensed his unhappiness (but not the agony from which he had just emerged; she had not the worldly experience to know that). She was a little puzzled, too: she had thought to feel some pleasant sensation of romance, like a heroine in a story, but instead her heart had felt only pity. Perhaps in time, she thought: it is too soon.

Nevertheless she was disappointed. She would have liked just one kiss, preferably on the hand.

16

In October *The Lowell Offering* appeared. It was a phenomenon: who would have thought that factory females could write and edit a magazine? Stories, essays, poems, songs—even an editorial defending their virtue against the slanders of Orestes Brownson, a notorious gadfly who had written (they thought) that the mere association with machinery made a girl unchaste, as if the flying shuttle could somehow fly inside her and deflower her. Actually they mis-read him, as he said in his reply to their reply to his original essay. He had said only that he wished workers to share in the profits of their labor; he had wished to show how the capitalists oppressed those who came as hands to their factories.

They did not understand him; they heard only the supposed slur on their good name, and that slur they would not—could not—tolerate. If public opinion believed that any girl who went on the Corporation was damned to infamy, as Brownson said she was, then they must all lose their chance to earn money—for who would marry the infamous? And what girl in full possession of her senses would willingly throw away her chance to marry?

Minerva Swan beamed, proud to have been one of the contributors. Although two of her stories had been accepted by *The Ladies' Hour*, it was sweet triumph indeed to be known locally, even if only by the initials with which she signed the piece.

Sabra thought—and said—that the contributors should have signed their names. "Are you ashamed of your name?" she said. "I think it's pretty—much prettier than mine."

"They all use *noms de plume*," said Minerva. "They don't want to seem forward or vain. Even to use one's own initials is considered a bit proud. I should have called myself Nymphea, or some such."

Her story was a romantic tale of a young woman who, seeking her fortune, came to Lowell to work in the mills, met an eligible, upstanding young man, married him, and lived happily ever after. Sabra knew of only one instance where an operative had met her husband while working in the mills, and that, being Margaret Lowe, was hardly typical. Still, everyone adored the story; Minerva had many compliments.

A week before the New Year, Sabra had a letter from Silas. He and Winfield had lectured through New York State and Pennsylvania and into the Western Reserve. They had had great success. People saw the wisdom of what they said; their Community, dedicated to the uplift of man's spirit, might begin as soon as the following spring.

She read the letter in the parlor after supper; Minerva had brought it to her. She closed her eyes, picturing Silas and his companion traveling through the winter, stopping at taverns or at the homes of believers, speaking wherever they could find an audience. She remembered her childhood, traveling from town to town with her father, seeking souls to be saved. It had been a hard life: they had lived, literally, on faith, on their certainty of being right. Now Silas was doing the same.

Sitting near her were several girls including Betsey Rudd and Rosa Cummings. Their faces were weary, their voices hoarse from the cotton dust caught in their throats and lungs. The speed-up had exhausted everyone, but there was little hope for a protest. Turnouts were easily got rid of, and there were many women, ready and eager to earn a bit of money, waiting to take the places of those who were dismissed.

From somewhere—from some other boarding house on some other Corporation, perhaps the Hamilton, perhaps the Appleton—had come a new phrase: "Ten Hours." It was, to those who whispered it, a phrase of hope, an incantation of deliverance. To those against whom it was directed—the entrepreneurs in Boston, their Agents in Lowell—it reeked of revolution: open warfare. Ten Hours! Impossible! Profits would fall—would become nonexistent. Ten Hours! It was an affront, a bold incitement to stir up the operatives and make them discontent. Fourteen hours a day was not too long: they worked it, didn't they? And hadn't they worked it for twenty years? Why, now, the demand for shorter time? The speed-up? Nonsense. The human body was an inexhaustibly adaptable mechanism. They would adjust to the speed-up. Let no female—or male, either—on any Corporation in Lowell mention Ten Hours: it was a plot of idle dreamers, a scheme of fuzzy-brained Utopians, of foreign trouble-makers and their dupes.

In the parlor at Mrs. Clapham's, there was a brief lull in the conversation of the women gathered there. Sabra glanced at Betsey and Rosa; they seemed to be talking more animatedly. She heard Betsey's words: "Ten Hours." And then: "petition." And then the general talk buzzed up again and she heard nothing more. She looked away. She wanted nothing to do with petitions. She thought of Silas' Community. Would women like these be happier there? Healthier? Or would "Community" turn out to be yet another way to work everyone to death, particularly females? How long would be the work-day in Mr. Winfield's New Society?

With Silas' letter, Minerva had given her a copy of the second issue of the *Offering*. Most people thought it even better than the first. Minerva had had another story printed: again, a happy ending by marriage. What other happy ending was possible? Some new girls arriving at the factories said that their families had allowed them to come because they had seen—or at least heard of—the *Offering*: coming to the mills where such paragons of cultivation also worked, they felt as if they had enrolled in some exclusive finishing school.

The first issue had earned a small surplus of money. A little heap of gold coins was distributed to the writers. Many of them demurred. They did not want to seem greedy. Woman's sphere was to serve, not to profit. They had so enjoyed the exercise of composition, they said, that it seemed most unladylike to sully the enterprise with talk of dollars and cents. Eventually, each of them took what was given. Minerva Swan was pleased to take it: for years, now, she had robbed herself of sleep, of recreation, to work at her notebooks. The *Offering* would bring large praise to the manufacturers whose benevolent stewardship, so it would be said, fostered such literary enterprises. The manufacturers would point with paternalistic pride to the *Offering*, to the young women who wrote it, to the enlightened factory system which permitted it. Why, then, thought Minerva, should we not have our small dividend, too—a tangible dividend, in hard cash? She put her share—two dollars—into the bank, and returned to her room, to her notebooks. Her next contribution would be fact, not fiction: she wanted to write about herself, about all their lives as factory girls. She could not have said exactly why, but she felt that it was important that someone do this: there has never been a class of women like us, she thought. And she felt, too, that Time hurried her along. I must write quickly, she thought. She could not have explained that, either. I must make a record of our experience, she thought; I must not let it pass untold.

17

Sabra became ill. A sore throat developed into a cold; her lungs began to hurt, to fill with fluid. She lay in a fever. Mrs. Clapham was distressed—as she would have been for any of her girls, but especially for Sabra. She did not want any trouble. She wanted no accusation from the Agent that she ran her boarding house inefficiently, without proper sanitation or adequate meals for the operatives in her charge. Further, she was still unsure about the degree of the Agent's concern for this girl: true, he had sent her to work in the mill, but all the same he might still cherish some special interest in her.

She moved Sabra to the small sick-room at the back of the second floor and nursed her for two days. Then she sent to the mill for permission to call Dr. Knight.

Sabra did not recognize him. He examined her and shook his head. Phthisis had spread virulently that winter; many women, their lungs irreparably damaged, had left the city to go home to die. He gave Mrs. Clapham two packets of powders with instructions for their use and promised to call again the following day to bleed the patient. He would move her to the Corporation Hospital when he could, he said; at the moment there was not a single empty bed and besides they were short-staffed.

When he arrived home later that night he mentioned to his wife that the Palfrey child—surely Mrs. Knight remembered her?—was ill at Mrs. Clapham's. Mrs. Dr. Knight expressed surprise that Sabra was still in the city; not seeing the girl at St. Anne's, she had thought that she had long since moved on.

When Mrs. Dr. Knight called on Mrs. Bradshaw the following afternoon she mentioned the news in an aside to Miss Amalia. Miss Amalia did not now sit in the parlor with the mistress of the house; she lurked in the dining room across the hall, playing at a piece of embroidery. She had long passed caring that the callers whom she had formerly received in the parlor with her sister saw her now in a less exalted state. She was so hungry for companionship—a word of greeting—that she would have risked her brother-in-law's wrath to stand on the porch, if necessary, to catch the ladies going in and out.

For many months now Miss Amalia had labored under the new Mrs. Bradshaw's tyranny. She had been removed to Sabra's former bedroom on the third floor, denied the use of the parlor, discharged from her position as instructress to Lydia. Undoubtedly her recent afflictions had quickened her sense of Christian charity; or perhaps she was simply, unbearably lonely. At any rate, two days later, after much plotting as to the use of the carriage, the number of errands to be run, etc., she appeared at Mrs. Clapham's boarding house with a jar of calves'-foot jelly and a bottle of mustard plaster. She was delighted to find Sabra past the crisis. Heedless of infection, she kissed her and cried a sentimental tear.

"Sabra, dear!" she said fervently. "Are you all right? I came as soon as I could. Mrs. Dr. Knight said you were quite ill."

Sabra lay in a daze of convalescence. "Yes," she said. "I was." Had she been stronger, she would not have wished to see Miss Amalia. As it was, she suffered her presence.

"But you are better now! The fever has gone, Mrs. Clapham said. I was so worried, we had no idea you were still here. Mrs. Dr. Knight said she was sure you had left. But never mind. I'm glad to see you, even under these circumstances. I've brought you some jelly, and a plaster—I'll put it on before I go, it will draw the poison out and warm your lungs."

She settled herself on a straight-backed chair beside the bed and twitched at the bedcovers and patted the slight mound which was Sabra's leg. She felt all her maternal affections rise again in her bosom.

"Now," she said. "I won't tire you by staying long, but tell me how you've been—up until this illness, of course. Do you like your work? Is it pleasant living here with all the girls? Mrs. Clapham seems quite competent. Does she feed you well? Do you remember how we ate the day we visited Mrs. Glidden's with Mademoiselle?"

She realized her error at once: a reminder of past days when her life flowed pleasantly down well-defined channels, when she felt that she had a useful place in the world. She wanted to hurry on to safer topics, but a horrid stubborn lump formed suddenly in her throat and she could say nothing.

Sabra looked away. Through the window she saw the sky: squares of brilliant blue. The cold March wind thudded against the panes. Almost two years, now: the time she had allowed herself. And yet she had no plans to go, nor any means to do so.

Miss Amalia's silent struggle to recover her powers of speech had betrayed her. All her plans to cheer the invalid evaporated; she felt that she must speak to someone about her life or she would no longer be able to live it.

"Oh, Sabra. I know it hasn't been easy for you here. But now that I see you I think you were well out of it—out of *us*. Yes—for all you must be so tired, and have little enough money to save out of your pay, and no family to care for you but Mrs. Clapham and the girls you live with here."

The lump rose painfully again but she forced it down. She took Sabra's hand. Sabra turned from her contemplation of the sky and looked at the unhappy little woman sitting so tensely beside her. She wished that she were not still so weak. She wanted very much, in that moment, to say to Miss Amalia: "Tell me about it, tell me anything you like—but first tell me of Rachel. Where has she gone? What is she doing? Why did she abandon me?" Go away, she thought. And: stay, and tell me even though I do not ask.

"You know of course how she died." Miss Amalia's voice was as rough as any cotton operative's. Her mouth trembled; under her eyes were deep shadows, evidence of sleepless, anguished nights.

For an instant Sabra was confused by the pronoun. Not Rachel; surely not Rachel—

"You know that it was another child that killed her."

Her sudden terror receded. Somewhere, somehow, Rachel lived.

"Yes," she said.

"After you went away—and I have thought many times how unjust, how cruel it was of us—of Josiah—to send you, and I was cruel, I was unjust even as he was, Sabra, and I beg your forgiveness now. I was wrong. We were all wrong to blame you, to think that you had any responsibility for Rachel's madness—"

She wept, then, while Sabra lay quiet and watched her. She heard the noon bell begin. Soon hordes of hungry women would rush in to their dinner, and then rush out again to work until dark and after. Meanwhile she would lie here, a different kind of captive, listening to the sad recital which now she knew must come.

"Rachel is in New-York," choked Miss Amalia. "Josiah put her with distant family—second cousins of his father's, whom I have not seen once in my life. They must have been surprised indeed at Josiah's request that they take Rachel in. She does not communicate with us, but we understand that she is well. We never speak of her at home. We never speak of anything. They hardly talk to me. I know that Josiah wishes that I would go away, but I have nowhere, no one—" She succumbed again to her tears.

New-York, thought Sabra. She had no idea of New-York, she could not imagine what it was. She allowed herself a sudden rush of bitter thought. Does she work in a factory there? Does she drag herself home after fourteen hours of tending spinning frames?

Miss Amalia, still weeping, continued her recitation: "You cannot imagine what my life has been since Josiah married that woman," she said. "She is a perfect shrew—oh, not to him, to him she is milk and honey—but to me, and to Lydia, and Miss MacIver—you don't know her, she is new, she came to governess Lydia—and the Gumms—oh, we could tell Josiah a thing or two, if he'd listen, which he will not, being so thoroughly ensnared—bewitched—that he cannot tell day from night nor good from bad, and I wonder that his bones don't positively snap from his being wrapped so tightly around her little finger. It is disgusting!"

From below, they heard the noise of the women running in. The bedroom door was slightly open; the smell of roasted mutton drifted up, overlaid by the subtler odors of spiced sauces and fresh-brewed coffee. Sabra recognized a new sensation: for the first time in many days, she was hungry.

"You know she is quite common," said Miss Amalia. "Much more so than many girls here, I should say, and certainly not fit to—to—" she struggled with it "to bear the children of a Bradshaw, much less to sit at his table as mistress of his house and be presented to the world as a proper successor to Sophia." She sobbed; she wept uncontrollably. "O poor Sophia. Poor dead girl." For a moment Miss Amalia bowed her head and gave way to her tears. Then gradually she became calm again. "I thought I would die, myself, that night," she said slowly. "It was very hot—so hot, and even up on the hill we had no air. She couldn't breathe. She burned with fever. I sponged her, I gave her water, I tended her day and night, from Sunday, when it began, until Wednesday, when she—when she finally—died. She suffered—I cannot tell you how much. It is not right that any human being should suffer so. The baby, when she came, was long dead by the looks of her. Dr. Knight gave us no hope. He bled her twice, he administered opium. Then he said that he could do nothing more. 'She is in the hands of God,' he said. The heat in the house was so intense that the candles bent in their holders. It was impossible for the rest of us even to draw an easy breath. On the last day, thinking to give her some relief, I—I cut off her hair. It was so heavy, it gave her great discomfort. She thanked me. Even in the midst of dying, she smiled at me, at the last, and said she knew all I had done for her, all our lives. She knew how I loved her. At least I have that to remember. And then—and then—" She buried her face in her hands.

Sabra thought of the mourning scene which she had witnessed. Why had the Sin-Eater come? And at whose request? But she did not ask. Poor Miss Amalia, she thought: in your own way you suffer as much as she did. What words of consolation could soothe her?

"She and the child are both at peace—"

"Yes," sobbed Miss Amalia. "At peace. Their souls are at rest. It is all that comforts me now. For I know—I see it every day—that he is tormented, he will never rest easy, it is a judgment on him and I rejoice in it! His three girls were not enough for him—no! He must have a son! A son! All well and good for him, he didn't have the agony of it, the risk of death! Well enough for him to cast it up to her! 'You've given me only daughters,' he said, 'but I must have a son, I want my name to continue!' His name, mind you! At the risk of her life! I will never forgive him. Let him suffer with this new wife whom he has inflicted on us. He bought her for a brood mare, he might as well have hung a sign around her neck: 'For purposes of reproduction!' But he was mistaken. Yes! The Lord avengeth, Sabra, and that is my sweet joy, no matter how miserable they try to make me!"

She leaned forward; her kind, anxious face was suffused with hate. Sabra shuddered; she felt her little strength ebb, but she could not turn away from such intensity.

"*She cannot conceive!*" hissed Miss Amalia. "It is disgusting—I hear them, we all hear them, night after night, like animals, making noises that should never be heard in a decent house, crying out for all to hear—even in the daytime he has taken her, simply ordered her away from the dinner table! I cannot tell you the revolting atmosphere of that house now. It is like a—like a barnyard! I cannot describe it. But all in vain. In vain, thanks be to God! He cannot get a child on her, try as he will. God is just, God is merciful, He has stretched forth His hand against Josiah and He will smite him! Josiah will never get his son now. He is condemned to spend the rest of his life with her—barren as she is, he is condemned to her. 'Justice is mine, saith the Lord'—and it is true, Sabra, it is true!"

Quieted by her paroxysm, Miss Amalia leaned back in her chair and closed her eyes. Shortly she roused herself and in a normal tone announced that it was time for her to go. She seemed to have forgotten her promise to apply the plaster. Sabra was relieved: she did not want it. She wanted only quiet, solitude; she wanted to recover in peace, both from her illness and from the ordeal of listening to her visitor's recitation.

Miss Amalia left with a promise soon to return. But as the days passed and she did not, Sabra assumed that she regretted her revelations and was too embarrassed to come back.

This was not so. Miss Amalia would gladly have visited Sabra another time, many times. But she did an unwise thing: humiliated, downtrodden as she now was in the Bradshaw household, she could not resist one small flare of defiance toward her oppressor. When Mrs. Bradshaw inquired where she had been, she replied truthfully. After that, Miss Amalia was not allowed the carriage again.

18

Within a week Sabra was well enough to return to work. Not long afterward, a letter arrived from Silas:

April 15, 1841

Dear Sabra:

We are in New-York for a few days, having completed a successful tour of the Western Territories. We will come briefly to Concord, and then from Boston we go to England for some months. People there have begged Mr. Winfield to visit them, both to instruct them and to receive the latest intelligence from England and the Continent. They have also promised to raise a good sum of money for our work—a promise which cheers us indeed.

While I am in Concord I will try to get to see you. But if I do not, please remember that our visit together last summer was more gladdening to me in retrospect than it may have seemed at the time. I am often shy of showing what I feel, and my friendships suffer for it.

We had a good reception all during our trip. People are eager to find a new style of life which will be a union of physical and spiritual and mental effort, each complementing the other. They are tired of scrabbling to survive.

Mr. W. still feels that his teaching applies to factory workers as much as to the poor farmers, the dispossessed ruined by the late Panic, to whom we have mostly been speaking. So no doubt you and your friends will see us again in Lowell when we return.

I hope you are well. If I do not see you within the next week or two I will surely be there in the fall.

Your friend,
Silas Blood

For two weeks after that—for three—she waited. She relived their excursion on the river: the hot, silent day, his hesitant touch. Short of walking the streets of Concord, she did not know how to find him. She stayed at Mrs. Clapham's every night on the chance that he would come. She made up pretty speeches and promptly discarded them in favor of others. She tried a new way of arranging her hair. She closed her ears as some of the other girls spoke of their husbands-to-be waiting for them in their native villages.

By the middle of May she gave up. He was on his way to England to talk to important people and collect a sum of money. It was a noble work. How did it feel, she wondered, to lead people to a new life? To try to change the world?

19

"There is a place upstairs if you want it," said Mr. Lyford. "Three and a quarter a week."

She took it: weaving. She tended two looms. The work was less tedious than spinning, but it was also more difficult. And dangerous: she had to contend with the flying shuttle now, a brass-tipped piece of hollowed-out wood, the hollow filled with the long wooden bobbin wound thick with the filling thread. The shuttle was shot back and forth between the warp yarn strung through the heddle-eyes of the harness. Occasionally a shuttle mis-fired; more than one weaver had been injured or even killed by a flying shuttle.

"Clean looms Saturday nights before you go!" yelled the weaving room overseer, Mr. Critchlow. He left the details of instruction to the neighboring girl, a tall, sallow girl who seemed enormously put out at being disturbed.

"Knot your thread like this!" she shouted, demonstrating so rapidly that Sabra could not follow. "And thread your shuttle like this!" She put a filled bobbin into an empty shuttle; pointing to a small hole near the shuttle's tip, she lifted it to her mouth. "Suck in! You have to suck the yarn through the hole, you can't thread it otherwise!"

The operatives called it "the kiss of death": the swift intake of lint-filled air deep down into the lungs—more lint breathed in that threading than in a hundred ordinary breaths. Shuttles were manufactured so that they could be threaded in no other way. You had to perform that murderous operation to keep your looms running. Someone in the management of the Corporations had figured that sucking the yarn through the shuttle hole saved at least ten seconds. Multiplied by the number of shuttles that needed to be re-threaded every hour, every day, those ten seconds became an important factor in a company's profit.

As a weaver, Sabra cleared two dollars a week above the cost of her board. She put the extra money in the bank. She no longer felt the desire to buy adornment, or books, or candy, or any other luxury. Perhaps, she thought, in the fall I will have a new dress. But nothing before then. She did not put it plainly to herself that Silas might need her money. But it pleased her to think that she might offer it to him, that in some small way she might contribute to his work. She felt more important for it, more purposeful. She applied herself diligently to her new position. Soon she was producing above quota: forty yards a day.

20

Summer came; the heat descended. The weaving room, five stories up, was hotter even than the spinning room. The windows were not allowed to be opened. They were in fact nailed shut in an effort to maintain a constant humidity so that the threads would not break. The girls tucked handkerchiefs in their sleeves to mop their faces and necks; they undid the top buttons of their bodices as far as decency would permit; they sluiced themselves with water from the bucket by the stairs.

At night Sabra lay in the stifling bedroom and thought of January: snow and ice. Like everyone else she slept naked. Mrs. Clapham disapproved, but she was powerless to enforce an order of nightclothes on so obviously suffering a population. Sabra grew accustomed to the sight of unclothed flesh: it did not matter, there was no question of modesty, nothing mattered except relief from the suffocating heat. She could not swallow her food; she grew paler, thinner, shadows under her eyes, the eyes themselves taking on the glazed look of a dumb tormented creature unable to understand or escape its pain.

On Sundays the women sprawled along the river's bank like casualties after a battle. Sabra longed for those hours by the water as a thirsty traveler longs for drink; and, having drunk, returns again to her journey.

One day she fainted at her looms. Mr. Critchlow and his second hand straightened her cumpled body on the floor and fanned her and revived her with wet cloths on her face. She was too weak to walk, and so they carried her down the four flights of stairs and across the yard and settled her on the sofa in the Agent's office. They decided against sending for Dr. Knight. It is only a brief collapse, they said; she will be back to work in half an hour. They left her with a wet cloth on her forehead, promising to look in at her shortly.

She was frightened. Was she going to be ill again? Typhus, perhaps, or cholera? She could not get sick now. Silas was coming back, she wanted very much to see him. If I die, she thought, it will all have been for nothing. What have I done in this life? Nothing. Seen nothing, been nothing. No, Lord, she thought, not yet. Do not take me now.

The door to the office, which had been left ajar, was suddenly pushed open. Josiah Bradshaw came in.

For a moment they did not recognize each other. Then: "They told me they'd put a girl from Mr. Critchlow's room into my office," he said. "I did not know it was you."

His voice was as she remembered it: a dry flat nasal sound. How odd that such a voice could so twist her heart.

But she was appalled at his appearance. That had changed very much. He looked ten years older—twenty. His eyes had sunk back into his head, his cheeks were hollow, deep lines had formed from the corners of his nose down past his wide thin mouth to his chin. His pale hair was turning silver. He looked driven, haunted: his eyes stared at her as if she were a ghost—as indeed she was, for him, since he thought he had buried her among all his hundreds of operatives.

I should hate him, she thought, for what he has done to us all; but I cannot, he is too wounded. Why?

"It was the heat," she said. "I have not been sleeping well." She attempted to sit. The room tilted; she lay back again.

He had remained standing by the door. Now he came in; she saw that his pale gray coat was stained with perspiration, and that he, like his operatives, mopped his face with a handkerchief.

"You have stayed," he said.

"Yes."

"I did not think that you would."

He had thought nothing; he had not cared. "I had no place else to go."

A wagon laden with baled cotton rumbled across the yard outside the office window. A fly, seeking escape, buzzed against the glass. How odd, she thought, that I have a private audience with him. There are some who would be glad of such a chance.

"No," he said. "I suppose you did not. You are well, then, and reasonably happy? We treat you fairly enough, do we not, at the Commonwealth Corporation?"

Some would say not; some would say, "Ten Hours."

"Yes," she said.

"Mrs. Clapham runs a clean house?"

"Yes."

"The girls are decent enough?"

"Yes." He knows all this, she thought. Why does he ask?

"And you have lately been promoted, since Mr. Critchlow is your overseer. You earn top wages now, and you are not yet twenty-one."

"Yes."

A faint smile crossed his face. "Save like some of them do and you will be able to buy a boarding house of your own."

Or help to underwrite a New Society. . . . "Yes."

He seemed to have forgotten whatever business it was that had brought him to his office. He took a straight chair and sat near her, leaning forward, elbows on knees. His eyes were like the winter sky.

"When you lived in my house," he said, "you were led by your friendship into a dangerous and scandalous action. Perhaps I should not have blamed you as severely as I did. Perhaps—but it is done, we cannot go back."

She realized that it was an apology. Again she tried to sit up, and this time she succeeded; the room stayed level. Tell it to Miss Amalia, she thought; I do not want to hear.

"You have worked well," he went on. "And I am glad of it—for you, and for us. We value our good operatives. As you see, we promote them. So I am going to warn you, now, of another danger into which a friendship might lead you. There is, as you may have heard, a treasonous element at work here, and at every mill. They are radicals, stirred up by outside agitators. They seek to destroy our profits. They cannot—or will not—understand that if our profits fail, then the mills will fail. No one will have work. Everyone, including themselves, will starve. It is not good enough for them that we have provided the most decent working conditions in all history—that here, for the first time, to be a factory operative is still to be a human being, not a degraded brute. They want to destroy this system by forcing Ten Hours on us. We cannot stand it—we will not. Any operative caught agitating will be instantly dismissed. She will be blacklisted, she will never work again in any mill in New England. That is why your present place in the weaving room was free. The girl who worked there was foolish enough openly to circulate a petition against us. She will work in no mill in Lowell again—nor in Nashua nor Chicopee nor anywhere else."

Far above the mill yard in the gleaming white cupola the noon bell began to toll. Before its sound had ceased the yard was flooded with operatives streaming out through the gate. Sabra's thoughts went with them: across the canal to the boarding houses, into the dining rooms, hurry, eat, hurry. . . . And where was her predecessor at the looms?

Had she a home—a poor farm somewhere, a widowed mother perhaps? Work or die. Work or die.

"Do not involve yourself with these trouble-makers," he said. "You have redeemed yourself, and I am glad of it. You have a good position here. In five years' time you can save as much as a hundred dollars if you are careful. Do not endanger yourself by associating with our enemies."

"No," she said. She was surprised at his solicitude: why was he warning her? He continued as if he had read her mind.

"And if you should hear any gossip—any plan to stir up trouble—any talk of a turnout, agitation—" He looked away. "I can make it worth your while to tell me what you hear." He met her eyes again.

"I have heard nothing," she said. She thought of Betsey Rudd and Rosa Cummings whispering together in the parlor; she thought of poor Jessie Pratt, who had died only a month ago. "Nothing at all," she said. He nodded; he seemed to believe her.

A man came in then: Mr. Critchlow, back to see how she did. His dour face betrayed no surprise at their tête-à-tête. She could get her dinner now, he said, and come back on a late slip. And—just this once—he would not dock her pay.

21

In October, Silas Blood and Henry Winfield returned from their sojourn in England. They had been warmly received everywhere; they had raised a little money—about fifty pounds; they had come away convinced that the British understood far better than their American cousins the importance of working to correct the evils of the factory system. And so they came back to the new country buoyed by the good will of the old, and began once again the weary round of lectures and meetings and begging for money that would in the end enable them to realize their dream.

Silas had gone to England disheartened by their failure to found the Community before they left. He returned more sure than ever of the importance of their task. Against Winfield's wishes, he had insisted upon visiting Manchester—that infamous symbol of all things foul in the British system. He had spent three days there, Winfield reluctantly in tow, walking the streets, calling upon factory owners, conferring with ministers who had as their lives' work the comforting of the human refuse of the city's industrial enterprise. At the side of those Reverend gentlemen, he had visited the homes of the operatives; he had attempted to speak with some of them. He had come away shaken, horrified, filled with new doubts and yet strengthened in his conviction that his work, his and Winfield's, was more important even than he had believed. Manchester—dear God! Was this what Lowell would be?

He remembered particularly a visit one afternoon to the room of a family living in a courtyard off Long Millgate Street, hard by the foul, stinking stream known as the River Irk.

When they arrived, they found that the woman had given birth two days previous to her tenth child. In two days more, she said, she would be back at the factory. The family consisted of a mother, father, and the five children who had survived—six, now, with the new one. The children ranged in age from ten to two. Only the two-year-old was unemployed; all the others ran bobbins in the mill. The mother seldom saw them because they slept at the factory, tucked away in a corner, five nights out of seven. This was a particularly fortunate family, the Reverend gentlemen explained, because, first, the father had not deserted; and, second, all of its employable members had jobs. The recent cotton famine had caused much hardship. Thousands of hands had been thrown out of work. Many hundreds had starved; many more had died of typhus and cholera and pneumonia and tuberculosis, their poor wasted bodies weakened by the loss of even the few ounces of bread that had formerly, in a manner of speaking, kept them alive.

The woman had lain on her filthy cot, her baby suckling weakly at her breast, and answered Silas' questions in lifeless monosyllables. She looked like a woman of sixty; she thought that she was about twenty-seven. No, she had never been to school, nor had any of her children. Her husband had attended a charity school for about two years; he could write his name. She had lived in Manchester all her life; she had gone into the factories when she was old enough to carry bobbins—about five or six. Her parents had been cotton operatives also. She had never seen the countryside. She knew no life other than the one she had lived—endured, rather, thought Silas—although she was aware that there were people in Manchester who drove about in fine carriages and who regularly had enough to eat. Somewhere, she knew, was the young Queen who lived in great splendor. She was not sure exactly what America was, or where—but she had heard of it, she said.

Silas had stood uncomfortably, breathing through his handkerchief the foul odor of the room, listening to the hoarse voice of the subject of his investigations, and he had thought of the cotton operatives he knew, the women he had seen all his life working in the factories at Lowell. They hardly seemed members of the same species. Would they, one day, be like this woman before him? Would they come to stay in the factory town, and their daughters and granddaughters after them, condemned to a lifetime of slavery on the Corporations?

He was filled with hatred for the men who had brought to America even the threat of such horrors—and, too, for all the men who had come to make their livings off the new town. His own father had got rich currying to the Corporations. Would the Corporations fail when they had driven their operatives to the level of the wretch lying before him? What mattered all the riches in the world when they were gained at such expense—such terrible suffering?

He had traveled to London, afterward, fired with a determination to combat the industrialists with every means at his command. He thought bitterly of his father, who had opposed his association with Winfield—had said, in a voice hard with outrage, that Silas was a fool, a humbug, a damned sniveling milk-sop afraid to plunge into the rough and tumble world of making money. The elder Blood, heavily hung about with the Latinate trappings of his vocation, had been unable to express in plain English his deeply wounded feelings. His tough, ruthless mind, which could always see a profitable path for his Corporate clients through the maze of precedents and loopholes, had been unable to comprehend the urgency of his son's mission.

Silas had met Henry Winfield during the autumn after Sophia Bradshaw's death. He had been desolated, unable to understand that he would never see her again. He had never thought clearly about his devotion to her. He had known her for as long as he could remember. When he was a boy she had seemed a surrogate mother—an impossibly beautiful, kind, gentle paragon of womanhood. His own mother had died when he was born. He had been brought up by hired help: dutiful and good, but hardly inspiring of that great love which welled up in him, demanding a suitable object. As he grew older, his devotion to Mrs. Bradshaw began to change; he saw her differently, less as mother, more as—what? He had never allowed himself to put a name to it. Had she lived a few more years, had he been less shy, there might have come a time when he felt compelled to make a declaration to her. But that, he knew, would have been a calamity—for she was a good and honorable woman, and she would no longer have tolerated his visits, his dumb, persistent presence, if she had known the emotions which inspired him. Or perhaps she had understood, after all; he didn't know. Somehow he endured his loss, and then he found Winfield and a new focus for his ardor: the challenge of building the Community. He had been glad to leave Lowell. When Winfield's lecturing took them there, he went along as a stranger. He felt nothing but revulsion now for the city and all its pretensions to grandeur. The ruling interests proclaimed that they had founded a new Eden—an industrial Eden. Silas knew better.

When the two men returned home to Massachusetts, they began at once a new series of lectures. Few people in Lowell came to hear. Most were in the city through necessity, not choice, and they declined to pay for the privilege of hearing their lives condemned. True, their work was hard, their wages low—but how do we know, they said, that what you offer is anything better? Will we be paid wages in your Community? Will your moral standards be sufficiently strict so that our reputations will not be ruined? Will young men want to marry a girl who has participated in Winfield's Experiment?

The lecture was given to an audience of thirty-two. Five dollars were donated. The next evening Silas went to Mrs. Clapham's to call on Sabra. They walked out into the cold, November night. She could see that he was unhappy—disappointed at their failure; she listened unbelievingly as he told her of his investigations in Manchester. She felt suddenly humbled. Here was a man who—she was sure of it—would change the course of the world. What was she, compared to him? Nothing, she thought; I am nothing. Why does he even bother to visit me? She longed to be of help to him, but she could only offer her small donation: fourteen dollars, saved and put into a purse whose design she had embroidered herself.

They stood in front of Mrs. Clapham's, chilled from their walk; he must leave quickly if he were to catch the last stage back to Concord. He took her hand; in the manner of many of his countrymen, he tried to pass off his deeply touched feelings with a jocular remark.

"All this, Sabra? Fourteen dollars would buy three new bonnets, at least. Wouldn't you rather have them?"

"No," she said. She wanted very much to ask when she might see him again, but she knew the dangers of seeming too forward. "I want to give it to you. Bonnets aren't important."

Swiftly he bent and kissed her chin—her cheek, under the protective brim of her calash, was inaccessible—and then he was gone.

Wearily she turned and went inside. One kiss, she thought, for fourteen dollars: and what would be the price of a wedding ring?

22

The citizens of Lowell did not want to hear ill of themselves. Certainly they did not hear it from Charles Dickens, who took the "mad dragon of an engine with its train of cars" up from Boston one January day and toured the town under the guidance of Samuel Lawrence. He saw—well, not everything, but at least everything that his mentor wished to show.

Mr. Lyford hurried from floor to floor with his announcement: "Look sharp now, a delegation is coming through!" The girls were puzzled. Visitors descended upon them all the time without warning: they were accustomed to being on display. Besides, he had no need to tell them to look sharp; they looked sharp every minute, their jobs depended on it. They were quick and smart as a matter of course; they felt slightly insulted at Mr. Lyford's admonishment. This must be a very special person indeed, whose visit demanded such precaution.

The delegation appeared and strolled down the aisle. The visitor was enchanted. He had never seen anything like this; it put England to shame. Bright pretty faces, carefully arranged hair—even ringlets! Slender forms bent gracefully to their work, here and there a well-turned ankle—delightful!

When he wrote it up, he mentioned three things particularly. First, the boarding houses of the women operatives very often contained a joint-stock piano. Second, many of the women patronized a circulating library. Third, and most extraordinary, the operatives had got up among themselves a periodical, *The Lowell Offering:* "A Repository of Original Articles, Written Exclusively by Females Actively Employed in the Mills." He had taken away with him "four hundred good solid pages, which I have read from beginning to end." Of course he was concerned that his English readers would not believe him, that they would think that he was writing fiction again. Factory slaves reading and writing? Incredible.

Minerva Swan glanced at the retreating backs of the little group. She was pleased to have seen, even so briefly, the famous man himself. He will write about us, she thought; he will think us worthy of some mention. And if he can do it, so can I; but I can do it better, for I know what it is really. She felt a slight contempt for the visitor—for all visitors who came to look and who, having looked for an hour or two, went away again to give their ill-informed opinion of the grand Experiment so briefly seen. Minerva thought that if they really wanted to know about the town, they should come incognito and work on the Corporation for a while. Since most visitors were men, they would of course have difficulty in getting the flavor of boarding-house life—and the female boarding houses were a prime attraction, a central theme in the picture—but that obstacle could be overcome. And certainly, as workers, as machinists, say, or in the dye houses or the carding rooms, these gentlemen would learn a few things that Minerva was sure the Corporation hierarchy did not whisper into Mr. Dickens' ear as he strode smiling through the mill.

The thought that she knew more than he did about this subject which seemed to interest him so much made her smile a little to herself. It was the sly smile of the servant who has outwitted her master, the secret promise of the slavey to herself that, when the time was right, she would turn the tables on her oppressor.

That night she worked late at her notebook, sitting alone in the parlor long after the other girls had gone to bed. Mrs. Clapham, peering in at her, saw the golden head bent, the plump hand holding the quill moving rapidly back and forth over the paper. Stuff and nonsense, thought Mrs. Clapham. That new magazine of theirs is taking up time that could be put to better use—sleeping, for instance. But she respected Minerva's concentration; she did not interrupt.

The *Offering* was not at all in Minerva's mind. She had done with the *Offering*. It was not her plan to spend her precious free time scribbling for what had become—everyone said so—a Corporation mouthpiece. Its novelty had worn off; fewer copies were sold, less money given to the contributors. Minerva's last story had earned her seventy-five cents. Let others sacrifice their sleep to play the Corporations' tune, she thought; she worked now for herself, for a larger reward.

23

"I don't know who it was," said Mrs. Clapham tartly. She was put out. It was Saturday night—pay day, generally the pleasantest evening of the month, and now had come this intrusion. "He didn't have a calling card, the dirty little bogtrotter. He just said to tell Biddy that she was wanted at Mrs. McCormic's." She turned on the girl. "Do you know where that is?"

They stood in the kitchen, an unhappy little group: Mrs. Clapham, Biddy, Sabra, and Betsey Rudd. In the background stood the servant Huldah, moaning softly and stroking her cheek at this trouble which she could not understand but which made Mrs. Clapham so upset and therefore doubly irritable.

Biddy looked down. "Yes, ma'am."

"After all this time. I can't understand it," said Mrs. Clapham. "Somebody's known all along where you were." She was as much alarmed as irritated: she had become fond of Biddy, and had trained her up well; certainly she did not know how she would manage now if the child were to leave. And surely somebody—the same who had beaten and starved her? —wanted her back, else why the summons? She had sent the bogtrotter packing, not even admitting that she knew such a person as Biddy. But he had known; she had seen it on his dirty face. (And smelled the rum on his breath as he spoke. Savages! She wondered that the Corporations didn't tear down the whole miserable Acre and send all its inhabitants packing back to Ireland.)

"Should you go, Biddy?" said Sabra. "You don't have to, you know. They can't make you go."

"O yes. I'll go." Biddy looked up; her face was calm. Of them all she was the least alarmed.

"Not alone," said Mrs. Clapham. "I won't have it. It's not safe for a decent woman in the Acre."

"We'll go with her," Sabra said, "Betsey and I."

"All right," said Mrs. Clapham, somewhat relieved. "Mind you're back by curfew or they'll have my job."

"Don't lock us out," said Betsey. "We'll come back as quick as we can."

A blowing April night, but the wind was warm, carrying spring. They hurried down Dutton Street, their cloaks billowing out behind them. Despite her fears for Biddy—why did they want her?—Sabra was not unhappy at their destination. Ever since she first met Patrick she had wondered about the Paddy Camp Lands and the people who lived there. A wild, alien race, feared and despised—and yet Biddy was one of them, and Patrick, too.

They crossed Merrimack Street, turned and passed the busy, bright hotel, turned left into an alley, instantly into stinking darkness. Biddy stopped and held out her hand. "Don't say anything," she said. "Let me talk. It'll be all right, they won't hurt you, only they don't like strangers. Some are very angry, and if they're drinking they're nasty. So let me talk. I know the woman."

She led the way down the alley. On either side were heaps of tin and scrap lumber which might have been mistaken for the remains of a village razed by enemy troops, were it not for the fact that through makeshift doorways they could see the gleam of a hearth, a space close-packed with people, an occasional figure passing in and out. There were no windows. The hovels stood close on each other; free-standing, they might have collapsed. Muck pulled at the women's clogs; stray pigs and chickens tripped them. Sabra clutched at her skirts, lifting them to mid-calf, all modesty gone. She was terrified lest she stumble and fall. All around she heard the miserable evidence of the inhabitants: a baby's wail, a shouted curse, a drunken argument, and then, even worse, a sudden silence interrupted only by the snorts of the rooting hogs.

"Not so fast!" she hissed at Biddy. "I'll fall!"

"Or we'll lose you," muttered Betsey behind her. "Merciful Lord, what a place! How do they live?"

Biddy slowed; she was a dark shape ahead of them. She seemed to melt into the general blackness. Dear God, thought Sabra, what if she has to stay here and we are left to find our way back alone? The alley turned and twisted; twice Biddy had led them off onto a branch, even narrower and more foul than the main way.

Sabra saw lights gleaming on water: a canal. Biddy turned down an alley which paralleled it. She stopped at a heap of wood and metal indistinguishable from any other and rapped on the door.

It opened at once. They went in—or, rather, stopped just inside the door, for a half-dozen people filled the tiny, low-ceilinged room and they had no way to advance.

The man who had opened the door and quickly shut it behind them pushed his way to a pallet in the corner. A figure knelt beside it, murmuring to the woman who lay there. The man bent and spoke; the watcher looked up sharply at the three who had come in.

"Come on, child," she said. "She may know you, she may not, but you've done well to come."

The others made way, glancing curiously at Biddy as she passed through. The light was dim: a small fire in the crude stone hearth, two or three Betty lamps around the walls. No one spoke, but several people looked with some suspicion at the strangers. One of the women held a suckling infant, but she paid no attention to it; her eyes were on the figure on the pallet.

Biddy knelt opposite the woman who had spoken: Mrs. McCormic, wondered Sabra. The woman on the bed lay motionless, her eyes closed. Every few seconds she uttered a low, strangled sound. Biddy stared at her; her lips moved silently.

Mrs. McCormic nodded in a satisfied way. "There, Kathleen," she said, glancing up at the woman with the baby, "I told you she'd come."

"Well she should, after all this time," said the woman addressed. "High and mighty now, Mrs. McCormic, one o' them now, I'd say." She cast a glance half curious, half hostile, toward the intruders. "They'll cause trouble for us, see if they don't."

Mrs. McCormic sniffed, but she made no reply. Sabra wondered if she agreed.

A knock at the door and again the man—a guard?—opened it. Two men; Sabra stared at the first, for she had seen him—where? Yes. The man whom Goldschmidt had identified as the priest—the man who had called out in the strange tongue, frightening her as she rode into the city. Behind him now, a younger man whose cap was pulled down over his forehead. Sabra did not at first recognize him; then as he turned toward her she saw Patrick.

A sudden tension came into the room at the appearance of the priest. The women bobbed a curtsey to him; the men ducked their heads. He was a short, solid man whose expression was, surprisingly, angry. Surely he cannot be annoyed at being called to a deathbed, thought Sabra. Although she wanted to speak to Patrick, she watched with fascination as the priest knelt quickly beside the dying woman and without a word to Mrs. McCormic, moistened his fingers from the contents of a small bottle, touched the woman's forehead, and then began rapidly to recite: "Per istam sanctam unctionem . . ."

As they heard the familiar words the watchers in the room bowed their heads; but, Sabra noted, not Biddy, not Mrs. McCormic. Their eyes remained stubbornly open, their heads up. Sabra did not want to move, she did not want to draw any further attention or hostility to herself or to Betsey. But she did want to speak to Patrick. It was unfair that in a city peopled by strangers, she should be denied a friend—especially a friend so comforting, so enlivening, as Patrick once had been.

". . . misericordiam indulgeat tibi Dominus quidquid deliquisti. Amen."

She put out her hand; she touched his arm. She was afraid that she might startle him, but he turned calmly, he showed no surprise. He raised his eyebrows in a matter-of-fact question: What brings you here? But he must know, she thought; he knows everything. He had known—she was sure of it—where to send for Biddy.

The priest's voice had stopped. He reached out and rested his hand across the woman's eyes. Then he began as rapidly as before to recite in that strange, wild Irish tongue.

The company sighed: another soul sent on its way.

Sabra pulled lightly at Patrick's sleeve and nodded toward the door. At once he turned and led the way out. She motioned to Betsey to stay, and then she followed Patrick into the alley.

Before she left the room she caught a glimpse of Biddy's face over the priest's shoulder. Her eyes were wide; tears ran down her cheeks, but she was not sorrowing. She looked joyful, a witness to a glad event.

Outside, Patrick loomed beside her in the darkness.

"Who is that woman dying?" Sabra whispered. "And how did you know where to find Biddy? Oh, Patrick—this horrible place! Are you all right?"

Be my friend again, she wanted to say. It seemed incredible to her to be standing in the midst of the Camp Lands, inquiring of the health of an Irishman—but he was not that, he was simply Patrick; once her friend. She remembered the thin little face, the cheerful words, the hungry eyes on Rachel.

He laughed softly. "Brave, aren't you, to come here? At night, too—no place for a decent Yankee girl."

"We didn't want her to come alone. She hasn't been back since—since she came to Mrs. Clapham's."

"We thought she should be sent for. We wouldn't have blamed her if she'd stayed away."

"But she didn't know why. The boy didn't say why she was wanted. It could have been anything."

"O no. She knew. There'd be no other reason. Nothing but to say good-by. That's when folks are sent for."

"Is that—is the woman her mother?"

"She is. Same as sent the child away for you to find. God rest her soul."

She saw the movement of his hand as he crossed himself, white against his dark coat. After a moment she understood his meaning. "Sent—I thought Biddy ran of her own accord?"

"No. Bridget sent her. She was afraid she'd kill her one day. She knew her own trouble—drink, and ten children to feed, and this."

His hand made a motion to encompass the alley, the hovels, all the squalid life around them.

"But—" Surely he was mistaken. "She was badly beaten. Bruised and cut—starving, Patrick. We thought her father—"

"No. It was her mother who beat her. And sent her away. She was a good woman once, they say. Kind and good. And in the end she saved Biddy's life. She cried for her after she left, she wanted her back. Then after a while, when she heard the child was well, she gave up. The drink helped her forget. She always used to go for Biddy. I don't know why and I don't think she did."

The sounds of life rose and fell around them in the darkness. Better dead, thought Sabra, better dead and never have a mother at all. She brought up her own memory again: cool soft hands on her forehead, a loving face, sad but loving, looking down at her. Better only that, she thought, than the memory of being beaten—

The door opened; the priest came out, followed by one of the men.

"I'll not come here again," said the priest. "This is the last time. The woman's not fit to have a prayer said in her house."

"Yes, Father," said the man. "We tried to tell Bridget, but she would come. 'Mary can help me,' she said, 'get me to Mary.' She'd have crawled if we hadn't brought her."

"She's a changeling," said the priest. "She deals with the Devil. Don't tell me she doesn't. I'll say it again tomorrow at Mass. No one is to come here."

"It's the want of a doctor, Father." The man's voice was low, humble. "If we could get a medical man—"

"Don't tell me what it's the want of," said the priest, more sharply. "It's the want of faith in Our Lord to bargain with the Devil. No one comes to Mary McCormic. Is that clear? Not if they want me to come at the end."

"Yes, Father."

The priest turned to Patrick. "You'll see about the digging?"

"Tomorrow."

"All right." He turned and walked away down the alley. Patrick touched Sabra's arm lightly. "Tell Biddy I'll be along to see her in a day or two. You were good to bring her."

He followed the priest. In a moment he was gone. The mourners had begun to emerge from the deathwatch; they filed out and made their way home, vanishing into the darkness.

Sabra went inside again. Mrs. McCormic and Biddy stood talking together beside what was now the corpse of Biddy's mother. The woman's arm was around Biddy's shoulders, her head bent in earnest conversation. Betsey Rudd stood waiting.

"Let's go," she whispered. "It must be very late."

Sabra nodded. "In a minute."

She did not want to interrupt Biddy, but she was curious to know Mrs. McCormic. She stepped toward them; the Irishwoman looked up and smiled at her.

"I hear you take good care of this child," she said. Her angular face was not unattractive, thought Sabra; it contained a certain spark, a vitality rare enough in anyone, let alone a resident of this place. Her eyes were pale; her hair was dark, a white streak at the side. She took Sabra's hand and held it tight; Sabra felt the life in it, the strength flowing up.

"Michael Dineen might have a place for her now," continued Mrs. McCormic. "He's married now, Biddy, got a room above the tavern on Salem Street. He'd take you in if you wanted."

"No," said Biddy. "I'll stay where I am."

"Goin' on the Corporation, then?"

"I don't know." She glanced at Sabra. "I'd like to. I'd like the money."

"Next year, perhaps," said Sabra. She hated the thought of Biddy's imprisonment; she thought her far better off at the house, but of course the girl would want money, she could not continue forever dependent. And sooner or later, she thought, the Corporation will hire an Irish weaver. Biddy might as well be the first.

"Yes," said Mrs. McCormic. "You have a chance there, Biddy. Best keep it." She smiled at Sabra. Despite several gaps in her teeth, her smile was bright and engaging. "Let her come back, though. She don't have to fear anything now. Let her come back and visit if she wants. We'll be glad to see her." She patted Biddy's arm. "You take care of yourself. And don't grieve. Your ma's at rest now. It's us left here who have to worry, not her."

24

In the City of Spindles there were many voices, drowned by day by the cacophony of the machines. But in the evenings in the boarding-house parlors, in conversations in the street, in gatherings of the Church Improvement Circles, a few brave women spoke the forbidden words: Ten Hours. A magical phrase, a charm to be invoked when weary legs ached and lungs filled with lint, when letters home were unwritten and uplifting books unread because fourteen hours a day were too many, too long to give of one's life. Ten Hours, they said, we are not machines; Ten Hours and let your dividends come down. We sell our labor, not our lives. You are killing us.

Some heard; some did not.

The words were spoken more loudly: Ten Hours! Four thousand names on petitions sent to the legislature—safer to sign now, they believed, because the Corporations could never discharge so many experienced hands. Their stockholders would not stand the loss of profit. Ten Hours: and let us go away as healthy as we came. Ten Hours: and let us keep this means of earning money. Do not hire us for two dollars and then cut us down, do not put your heels at our throats and squeeze the life from us and then call us strong-minded—unladylike!—when we protest.

Some heard; some began to agitate, to demand reform.

Most did not. They were afraid. The danger was too great. Not the danger of being discharged and blacklisted: that they could face, that they could survive. No: the danger they feared was that men would shun them, that no man would ask a trouble-maker—even one who worked in a good cause—to be his wife. That fate—spinsterhood—was too high a price to pay for even Ten Hours.

25

In the darkened bedroom the women were quiet. They might have been asleep. Then Sabra heard Betsey Rudd's voice.

"I put a petition on the bureau. Anyone who wants to sign can sign tomorrow morning. I'll put it out again tomorrow night."

Sabra came fully awake. Betsey—but surely she knew the risk, one word to Mr. Lyford and she would be discharged and blacklisted.

No one replied for a moment; then Susanna Burns said: "That's a foolish thing to do, Betsey." Susanna Burns was new, a spinner; she had been on the Corporation for only three months.

"All right. Shall I tell the girls in Number Four?" (Rhoda Clark, a weaver.)

"No. Don't mention it at the mill. We're passing the petitions at the houses."

"I daren't sign, Betsey." (Martha Friend: a sweet, quiet girl who hadn't bought so much as a piece of ribbon for herself in a year and a half. She had, she said, a brother at Colby College: all her money went to him.)

Sabra said nothing. She wished that she could see Betsey's face. To take an action—any action—seemed to her a wonderful thing. And surely the person who behaved so was a different person; to remain an ordinary operative and yet to circulate a petition—a ticket to dismissal—seemed impossible. Surely Betsey must look very different, instantly she had made her announcement. Her skin had gone green, perhaps, or her hair turned red. One did not behave so and remain what one had been before.

Cautiously she put out her hand and touched Betsey's face. Dry: no tears. She smelled the sharp, bitter smell of Betsey's hair. For this small, familiar friend to be so brave seemed a wonderful thing. Sabra was filled with admiration for this new David whose arsenal of stones must surely be very small.

She thought of Bradshaw's words: "If you should hear of any plan to stir up trouble . . ." No. Not even to add to Silas' fund for the Community will I tell you of this.

But neither will I sign. Silas might not approve.

In the morning when first bell rang at five, Sabra was instantly awake and out of bed. She dressed rapidly, not looking at the paper which Betsey had left. She is a brave girl, thought Sabra, but I dare not: I have nowhere to go if I am dismissed, it is all very well for the others, they have family. She said nothing to Betsey.

As she hurried down Dutton Street in the lightening darkness, she pulled a piece of bread from the pocket of her apron and nibbled at it. An hour and more at the looms until they trooped back for breakfast. Then five hours until dinner; five hours after that until the supper bell; an hour more until dismissal. An endless day. Work or die.

26

If Patrick came to visit the child he came when Sabra was not there, for she never saw him. But Biddy went out now quite often, and where else but to the Acre? Then, too, she began to attend Mass regularly, and often at odd times during the week she would slip out with a word of explanation about some Feast Day, some special service in the church. Her new piety would have been admirable, thought Mrs. Clapham, if it had been directed toward, say, Congregationalism; Rome she feared. Having become accustomed to—fond of—the child, she was now annoyed to think that Biddy was slipping away, back to the mud and filth from which she had come.

"All very well," muttered Mrs. Clapham, "but just when I need her she's off there, picking up dirt to track into my house, coming back talking that talk again that a decent American can't understand, clattering those ju-ju beads in my face—" For Biddy had acquired a rosary, she did not say where, and often now she was to be found telling her beads instead of practicing the fine sewing which had formerly been her leisure occupation.

Sabra, too, missed the girl's friendship.

"Out today, Biddy?"

"Just awhile."

"And whom did you see?"

"O, Mrs. McCormic. And her neighbor, and her neighbor's new babby."

"Is it a pretty girl, the baby?"

"No. A boy. They're very glad of it, too. And not pretty at all. Ugly. But very loud. He'll live, sure enough, with those lungs."

She smiled; a vacant expression came over her face. Everyone knew that look: when I have my own . . .

For some reason that she could not understand, Sabra was suddenly irritated. The child was not yet fourteen.

"Have you seen Patrick O'Haran?"

"Now and then. He's very busy."

Remember me to him, thought Sabra grimly. She felt a pain in the region of her heart and put it down to dyspepsia. I knew him before you did—but perhaps she had not. Patrick had always known everyone, it seemed.

She saw with some surprise that Biddy had flushed quite pink.

"He's found me a place," she said suddenly.

"A place—on the Corporation? Surely not. How could he?"

"No. In service. In a fine big house. He says I should go, he says I'll learn things I'm not learning here. And the Corporations don't hire Irish except for cleaning. I might not get a good place there for a long time."

She would be missed. By everyone. "Where?"

"At Mr. Munson's. On Pawtucket Street." The name meant nothing to Sabra. "I'm to get a dollar a month. And my keep, of course. Patrick says I am lucky to go there. They can have their pick of girls."

Patrick says, Patrick says—Sabra looked at the girl, tried to see her as Patrick might have done. Blue eyes behind the thick black lashes, a pale narrow face, cheeks blushed pink, thick black hair drawn neatly into a chignon, a small body, delicate—many girls were showier, better-looking. But Biddy had charm, she insinuated herself into one's heart, she aroused instantly all the compassion and protective instinct of both sexes. An unlikely domestic, thought Sabra; no doubt Mr. or Mrs. Munson would soon be waiting on her, or at least cautioning her not to overtire herself.

"And when do you go?" She saw the child as she had first seen her: the miserable bundle of rags huddled on the steps. One life salvaged.

"Next Monday I start." Biddy's eyes filled with tears. "O, Sabra, don't think I'm not grateful. Don't ever think that. But Patrick says—"

"I know, Biddy." In a rush Sabra put her arms around the girl and held her close. The small neat head rested for a moment on her shoulder. Biddy smelled of soap and yeast and, faintly, of attar of rose. Sabra's throat ached so that for a moment she could not speak. You are mine, let Patrick say what he will.

She remembered then who Munson was. He had the Whig paper, the *Courier*, in whose columns he labored ceaselessly for the welfare of the Corporations. They had rewarded him with a seat in the legislature, where he continued his work for their benefit. In his editorials he waxed particularly virulent against the Ten-Hour movement, which was, he said, an invention of the Owenites and other such limbs of Satan. An odd friend, surely, for Patrick?

27

Across the land the prophets of God thundered doom: Armageddon. In country churches, in the cathedrals of the cities, on busy street corners, and in lonely mountain villages their warning was heard: prepare for the coming of the Lord! Thousands watched the heavens for a sign. He will come in a great flame, the preachers cried; He will call to His bosom the born-again, He will abandon to the fire the damned sinning sheep. Repent! A great awakening stirred the people. Everyone was on the alert. When would He appear? It seemed a wonderful thing to be alive in such a time, the time of the Second Coming: make haste, make ready, purify your soul so that you will not be left behind, for behold, the Bridegroom cometh!

A hot, sunny Lord's Day in July. The dusty roads clogged with carriages, traps, stages; hundreds of people on foot. The green countryside was luminous, shimmering in the heat; little clumps of stragglers gathered by the banks of nearby streams to drink, to bathe their tired feet—but quickly, quickly, do not linger, hurry on to the designated place where you will hear the message of the Lord: Repent!

Sabra perched uncomfortably on the burning leather seat of the trap and fanned her perspiring face. They moved slowly in the long line of traffic. As far as she could see in either direction the road to the campground was thronged with a slow-moving procession. Men selling stronger drink than water had good business from the impatient travelers.

She glanced at Silas. The reins hung loosely in his hands. His eyes, shaded by his wide-brimmed straw hat, looked unfocused on the crowd ahead. He had spoken earlier, with enthusiasm, of the day ahead; but for some time now, lost in thought, he had said nothing. She respected his silence—he had, after all, important things to think of—but she was beginning to be slightly bored, and faintly sick from the heat. She wished that they could stop by a stream as the foot travelers did; lacking that refreshment, she was glad that Silas showed no interest in the rumsellers.

She had been surprised when he had invited her to come out. She had not seen him for some time; he had been lecturing alone in New-York and had returned to Concord only the week before. When he had proposed the excursion to hear Father Miller, she had not at first wanted to go. She was aware of Father Miller's message, she had seen his tracts, and she had not forgotten the unpleasant day when she had heard the Reverend Abijah. They were all the same; her father, had he lived, would have joined them here today, caught up in the Great Awakening, abandoning indoor preaching for the larger audiences of the camp meetings. She was frightened when she thought of the blazing Hell awaiting her—the Hell her father had preached. She said her prayers; she went to church; she did not know what else she could do to save herself. Certainly she could not claim to be born again when her conscientious brain told her clearly that she was not.

Silas, it seemed, was curious: he had heard of the growing fashion for the prophets of the Second Coming, and he wanted to investigate for himself the secret of their hold on their listeners. "They know how to grab tight on a person," he said, "in a way that I can't. I want to see how they do it. Besides, you'll enjoy seeing all the crowd. Everyone turns out: Dunkards, Baptists, Come-outers, Methodists—and the Adventists themselves, of course."

And so, rather than spend a long Sunday at Mrs. Clapham's, mourning Betsey Rudd's recent, sudden dismissal, she had put aside her distaste and come with him.

She allowed her thoughts to linger briefly on her departed friend. Betsey had been with them in the morning and gone at noon: as sudden as that. Mrs. Clapham, tight-lipped and more sharply spoken than usual, had said only that Betsey had taken her trunk, half an hour before dinner, and had asked to be remembered to her friends. But they had known, all the same: she had been discharged for circulating Ten-Hour petitions. Two girls on the Hamilton Corporation had met the same fate only the day before. The Corporation management was growing ever more watchful, more quick to dismiss for causes real or imagined. Sabra felt a choking sensation in her throat not caused by heat, or dust from the road, or lint from the mill. Betsey had been her first friend on the Corporation; she had not yet become accustomed to her absence. Probably, she thought, I never will.

Slowly they rounded a bend in the road and saw their destination. To their right a narrow dirt track branched off; it led past a meadow to the fringes of a great woods. In front of a tall stand of pine trees had been erected an enormous tent; before it was a jerry-built speaker's platform, or pulpit, faced by rows of rude log benches. From the front of the pulpit hung two lengths of canvas. Upon one was painted the dream of Nebuchadnezzar; on the other, the wonders of the Apocalypse: dragons, the scarlet woman, mystical beasts and symbols.

Smaller tents formed a semi-circle around the benches. The place was thronged with people, the seats well filled, the crowd passing back and forth between the tents. The preaching had not yet begun; an old man with long white hair led a spirited discussion in front of one of the small tents but even from a distance Sabra could see that he cast no spell upon his audience. They wandered back and forth, paying little attention. They were restless for the main event.

Silas tethered the horse in a shady place and slowly they made their way through the crowd to a seat. The camp meeting had been in progress for a week; this was the last day. Sabra stared curiously at the people all around her: wild-eyed women with children hanging at their skirts, old folks gossiping among themselves, vendors of food and drink, tired-looking men hawking pamphlets and tracts, the young of both sexes performing a kind of tentative mating dance.

They found a place near the front with a clear view of the platform. The sun was very hot, the tangy smell of the pines intoxicating. Sabra breathed deeply, filling her lungs; she was so accustomed to the heavy, lint-filled atmosphere of the mill and the stale air of Mrs. Clapham's that she felt a little giddy now in this clear country air. Silas sat quietly beside her, the wicker basket containing their lunch tucked under his legs, his long thin hands resting easily on his knees. He smiled down at her. He was glad that she had come out today. She was a pleasant companion, always happy to listen when he wanted to speak, always happy to respect his increasingly frequent desire for silence. Although he was to all appearances a young man with a purpose, he had come in the last six months to question the worth of what he had chosen to do with his life. The ceaseless travel, the endless speeches, the hunt for money, the trips back to Concord to renew his faith at its source—to what purpose? It was a question which would not have occurred to him a year ago; only recently had he formed the thought to ask it. Was not this camp meeting the better way, perhaps, to ease the burden of people's lives? Was it not better to promise them salvation in the hereafter—a promise to which one could never be held—than to urge, cajole, persuade them to try to find their happiness here, on earth, in a Community?

His mentor, Henry Winfield, would have been puzzled had he known of Silas' doubts, for in the winter and spring just past Winfield had become very sure that soon their dream would be realized. And in Massachusetts, not off in the wilderness of the Western Territories where, among other dangers, they would have had to contend with the still savage and hostile Indian tribes whose lands were being inexorably sacrificed to the white man. A wealthy manufacturer in Springfield whose eccentricity was deplored by his family had made a tentative offer of fifty acres of land—hardly a kingdom, but at least a beginning. Selected families, carefully chosen for their qualities of industry, sobriety, and dedication to the Community ideal, would make the first settlement; after some thought, Winfield had decided that a carpenter and a farmer might be useful additions to the group. Above all, he wanted unity. The dissensions which had plagued the Owenites at New Harmony, which already had become evident at Brook Farm, were to have no place at his colony. He stood firm in that. Anyone who objected to the regime would be instantly dismissed, without reimbursement of his investment. Winfield would tolerate no questioning of his wisdom; anyone with an open mind could see that he offered the true way.

He was not a dictator; he had never tried to force anyone to follow him. Any disciple—and he had many—could leave at any time. But to stay with Winfield was to agree with him; his gentle nature could not bear an argument. His disciples fitted their varying frames into armor of his design; he made no alterations.

The flap of the great tent was pushed aside; the crowd sighed and stirred like a field of wheat responding to the wind. Sabra, touched by the excitement, craned her neck to see. Three men emerged from the tent; the two younger supported the third on either side and with some difficulty got him up onto the platform. He was an old man whose broad body, sturdy as it must once have been, seemed hardly strong enough now to support his big square head. His mouth moved as if in silent prayer; his eyes surveyed the crowd as if it were an antagonist, and he alone to combat it.

"I didn't realize he was so old," whispered Silas.

Father Miller stood safely on the platform now. One of his assistants held a tin cup to his lips; drops ran down his chin as he drank.

A hush fell over the crowd. People leaned forward, waiting: Come, Father, come, tell us what we long to hear.

The preacher stood quiet, looking out at his audience spread before him. He seemed stronger now, as if he had taken life from them, as if their yearning, their need for him, had flowed into his body and revived him.

The silence became unbearable: a thousand souls struck dumb in the still, hot noon; the breeze soughing in the pines; the world stopped and hushed and silent, hardly breathing, for no one dared to move, the spell dare not be broken. Ah, Father—

"Repent!"

A woman screamed. A sigh went out from the crowd, a mass expulsion of their breath, their fear, their joy. They were as one, waiting to be ravished.

"Repent, I say, for the Lord cometh!"

Sabra felt her beating heart. No, she thought, I have nothing to repent of.

"The time is come! Let us all rejoice!"

Yes: yes—

"The Lord is with you! His trumpet shall sound! And He shall judge ye from the book of life, and cast ye down into the lake of fire!"

Yes: yes—

"Make haste to prepare! His day is at hand! His chariot descends! Repent!"

Yes: yes—

"For, lo! In the midst of our days we shall be caught up into His bosom! Hear it! Hear it! And repent!"

Yes: yes—

The crowd rocked and swayed; Father Miller fed on it, he gathered up his strength from it.

"Believe it! The Heavens shall part, the Lord shall come down among us!"

Yes: yes—

"He shall raise the dead!"

Yes: yes—

"He shall damn the sinner!"

Yes: yes—

"He shall consign him to eternal fire!"

Yes: yes—

"Damnation and everlasting Hell! Repent, before it is too late! Repent and come to the Lord!"

Yes o yes—

The crowd was ecstatic, moaning, rocking back and forth.

Sabra trembled violently; she gave herself up to her terror. *Dear God—!* Silas took her hand and leaned close to speak.

"The Unitarians would not approve!"

She managed to turn and smile at him. She held tight to his hand; it was large and strong, an anchor in this turbulent sea of rioting emotion.

"Repent!" O yes— "The world will end!" O yes— "Burned to a cinder in the realm of Satan!" O yes yes— "Repent and ye shall be saved!" O save us, Father, take us, take us— "Come to the Lord! Sinners all—come unto Him and He shall snatch you up!" O yes O yes—

A cloud passed over the sun: a sign from God.

"Repent! The Day of Judgment is at hand!"

On their feet, stamping and swaying, delirious with joy, sobbing, screaming—

"Repent!"

She clung to Silas' hand until she thought his bones must crack, but still she held. Madness—

"Repent!" The voice was a shriek, answered by the cries of his inflamed followers.

"He is a master," said Silas, raising his voice against the din. "Look how he has them, they would follow him anywhere, he has them helpless—"

Sabra could not take her eyes from the flailing, writhing figure on the platform. Was the man possessed? Surely he was right, the world was wicked, it would end in the thunderclap of doom. The cloud passed, the sun blazed down again: she felt the flames of Hell.

Father Miller fell to his knees. The mass of gyrating flesh before him crumpled in imitation. Automatically Sabra moved to follow, but she felt Silas grip her arm, hold her back.

"No," he said. He held her very tight, she felt his strong hand through the thin stuff of her sleeve. She looked at him and felt her terror subside. His dark eyes smiled at her; his familiar bearded face was calm and strong. "You have nothing to repent of, Sabra. Pray if you must, but do not kneel. You will stain your dress."

He smiled; with enormous relief she smiled back. The crowd groveled, waiting. The sky darkened again; a few drops of rain began to fall. Father Miller prayed: "O Lord we beseech Thee . . ."

"Come on," whispered Silas. He let go her arm and seized the basket and took her hand as they pushed their way through the crowd. "Any minute now," he said, glancing up at the thick-piled clouds. He pulled her along. "In here." They ducked quickly into one of the small tents at the edge of the encampment. It was crammed with crude beds, straw pallets, hand trunks, a snoring mongrel dog in one corner, a makeshift table littered with dirty dishes and Adventist tracts.

Sabra was dizzy: the heat, the excitement, had reduced her to a condition of trance. She was aware that she was trembling again; she was aware that outside this dim and noisome canvas the sudden summer rain had become a downpour; she was aware that had she not now leaned against Silas she would have fallen.

From far away she heard the preacher's voice: "For we are all lost sheep, O Lord, and we beseech Thee . . ."; closer, the drum of rain on the canvas roof; closer still, the resonant beat of Silas' heart through his stiff shirt front. She became aware of the contours of his chest. Stand up, she thought. She felt his hands on her arms: pushing her away? No: supporting her. He was trembling also. Stand straight, she thought, and move away. He smelled of sweat and starch. She wanted to lean against him forever. ". . . for we are all damned, O Lord, all lost to Thee if Thee will not save us . . ."

She lifted her head and saw his face. Why so sad, why despairing?

His arms went tight around her. Fainting, falling. He revived her. Save me O Lord.

28

Josiah Bradshaw put out his hand. When his fingers touched the cut-glass decanter he grasped it firmly, not wanting to spill the expensive liquid which it contained; then he poured briefly into his glass. Carefully he replaced the decanter on the table beside him. Carefully he lifted the glass to his lips and drank.

Thunder rolled down the river valley. Through the tall windows he could see the flicker of lightning. The day had been unbearably hot; sitting in his pew that morning he had wondered how Dr. Edson had managed to deliver his sermon without fainting. Margaret, sitting beside him, had mopped her face quite openly—an unladylike thing to do, an unsuitable example for the other women in the pews behind them.

An exceptionally bright flash illuminated the room: his room, his library, his private place. He sat there often now, late into the night, not to read or work, for he seldom lit a lamp: but to hold that decanter and lift it to fill his glass and drink and fill the glass again. It had become a ritual: home for supper after last bell, a hurried silent meal with Margaret and Lydia, Amalia and Miss MacIver, and then retreat. Since today was Sunday he had come here early; the sun had not yet sunk behind the western hills when he had closed the door behind him and entered into what had become his refuge. In a little while—later, later—he would go upstairs and lie down beside his wife and sink into unconsciousness. He never tried to see if she were awake.

He heard the bells down in the city strike eleven, a faint peal, far away. For a moment his mind pictured the sleeping town: streets and streets lined with houses, rooms and rooms filled with bodies, all sleeping. Thousands of females, who before dawn tomorrow would arise and go out into the mills and begin another day's work to increase the profits of the Corporations. And of all those thousands, he thought bitterly, he had chosen the one who was flawed. Any one of them—the poorest, the most humble—could have accomplished what Margaret could not; any one of them could have given him his son. And he—he choked on the last swallow from his glass—he had chosen wrongly, had allowed himself, driven by his passions, to take that one who had so enchanted him that he had never dreamed that for all her promise she would be barren. As barren as his heart; as empty as his life.

Divorce was impossible: unthinkable. The Associates who had brought him here sixteen—no, seventeen—years ago had been very firm about the conditions. They had taken him on as Agent because he was the son of an old friend of theirs, but they would keep him, they said, only if he behaved himself and caused no scandal. It had been a near thing with Rachel, but the disruption caused by Mayor Lawrence's death had diverted everyone's attention and no one had discovered—or gossiped about—her misbehavior. Old Hale, the instigator, had mercifully died not long after. And whatever business there had been between Sophia and that weak reed of Blood's had been safely aborted by her death. And now, married again, he must keep up his respectable facade. A divorce—and on what grounds, after all?—would so seriously impair his authority that he would be powerless to control the increasingly restless operatives. And he must keep control; there must be no turnouts, no slowdowns. The price of cotton goods had dropped alarmingly in the past year: a yard of calico which twelve months ago had sold for twenty cents now went at fifteen, and the price was falling still. Unless more cloth was produced and sold, the shareholders' profits would drop. They would not stand for it. They would dismiss him and find someone who could extract the work from the girls. The new system of premium payments to overseers whose workers produced extra yardage was working tolerably well, but if the demands from Boston continued, he doubted if even premiums would suffice. Already Ten Hours had become a byword in the town; just this past week he had dismissed three operatives for circulating petitions. One girl—Rudd was her name, he recalled—had become quite frantic; she had not protested her dismissal, but she had begged him not to blacklist her. In the end he had had to call on two second hands to put her forcibly out of his office; the scene had given him a migraine which had lasted until he had had two glasses of whiskey that night.

He lifted his head. A sound had intruded—not the distant explosions of the thunder, but something more immediate, something here in the house.

Surely not a Camp Lander—although they grew bolder by the day, preying on citizens who lived within striking distance in town, making their quick haul and scurrying back to their dens in the Acre before the constable could be summoned. But Belvidere Hill was too far; they would not venture across the Concord River Bridge.

He told himself once again to hire another couple to replace the Gumms. When they had died of fever within a week of each other at the New Year, Margaret had been reluctant to take on new servants. We can manage, she had said; Miss MacIver is willing to help, we don't need anyone else. Somehow the house had been kept in order, the floors swept, the meals prepared. He had been aware that the burden of the work had fallen to Amalia; she even waited on table now, sitting down only after the meal had been served. But she had not complained, and so, thankful to be spared the extra expense, he had deferred to Margaret's wishes. He had not thought to wonder why she wanted no hired help.

But now, alarmed, he wished that there were another man in the house. He tensed, listening; he heard a soft chord, and then another; an off-key voice attempting to sing:

O that I saw her just once 'ere she died. . . .

Annoyed, he stood up, steadied himself, and walked out of his library and down the hall to the parlor.

In the glow of a candle he saw his sister-in-law at the piano. She was wearing her night-dress; her gray hair hung untidily down around her face. Although he had walked quietly she sensed his presence and turned to face him. Her eyes were vacant; she did not seem to recognize him.

"Now, Amalia," he said, "go upstairs. You'll wake Lydia and Margaret if you play the piano now. You can sing tomorrow." His words were surprisingly clear; often when he had drunk a good amount he could not enunciate at all.

Miss Amalia shook her head. "No," she said, quite loud. "She doesn't let me."

It was true; he knew it, but he did not wish to think about it. He did not wish to be bothered with domestic difficulties.

"I will speak to her," he said soothingly. "Now come to bed. It is very late."

"No," she said, as loudly as before. "I cannot sleep. The thunder woke me. Josiah—" Her eyes slid over him, then caught his and held. He looked away. She was a plain woman, but she had her sister's eyes. "Josiah—did you hear it?"

"Hear what?" He heard his voice: still clear. But he was terribly tired. He wanted only to go upstairs and lie down and sleep.

"The piano."

"I heard you, yes."

"No. No. I mean before."

He saw a tear slide down her cheek. How old she is, he thought suddenly. An old woman. Yet once she had been only five years older than Sophia; how had she come to this?

"No, Amalia, I heard nothing before. You were dreaming, perhaps."

"No. I was not." Her voice cracked with the urgency of her thought. "I heard it. The thunder awakened me and then I heard it. Someone playing, someone singing—"

"There was no one, Amalia."

"Yes. I heard her. I came down to find her."

"Who?" He leaned against the carved back of a small brocade sofa. If only he could rest—

"*Her.* She was singing, just as she used to do. I heard her. She was here. O, Josiah—we had the woman come to put her to rest. Why did she come back?"

He shook his head. He felt quite ill, he must get up to bed. "No."

"Yes. *Yes.* She is not at peace, Josiah. *I heard her.* She wanted something. She is here now, but we cannot see her. She is watching us, I feel her eyes—Sophia!" She rose unsteadily from the piano bench and peered into the dark corners of the room. Slowly, haltingly, she began to walk, her hands outstretched. "Sophia! What is it, dearest? What do you want?"

I am dreaming now myself, thought Bradshaw. This cannot be. She is mad, the work is too much for her, we must get Dr. Knight to see her.

Miss Amalia crept around the room like a frightened animal—frightened of what she would find, yet longing for it: "Sophia! I am here! Please come!" She stumbled against a chair, righted herself, and resumed her journey. Her tear-stained face was all expectant, her eyes wide to catch a glimpse of her heart's desire. "Sophia?"

With an effort Bradshaw steadied himself and reached out and caught her arm as she came toward him.

"Amalia! Stop it! She is gone, she cannot come back!"

For a moment, still caught up in her search, she did not seem to hear him. Then she looked anxiously into his eyes. "What?"

"She is gone, Amalia. You were dreaming. She is dead. She cannot come back." Bitter words—bitter truth. She heard him; she understood. The hope faded from her face; her body slumped. Slowly she shook her head.

"I thought I heard—"

"A dream, Amalia."

"A dream."

He let go her arm; automatically she began to massage the place where his fingers had hurt her.

"Come, now. Upstairs. It is very late."

She stood quite still beside him. "A dream."

"Yes. Now come." He touched her shoulder lightly, as if to reassure her. She started; she turned her ravaged face up to him.

"She is dead, Josiah."

"Yes."

"She is dead three years."

"Yes."

"Dead and buried."

"Yes."

"In the cold ground. The worms eat her flesh, her bones laid bare—"

"Stop it, Amalia."

"Dead!" She stepped back quickly, recoiling from him as if he were Beelzebub. "You killed her, Josiah. She is dead—and you killed her!"

He felt his heart lurch. The woman was mad—

"Yes! As surely as if you put a knife through her heart!"

Outrage battled with his grief and won. He struck her and watched the dark place stain her cheek where his hand had hit.

She began to laugh.

"Never. Never. You will never have it. Never. God is good, God is just, you are paid for your crime. You will never have it. You will grow old and die and your name will die with you. You are fit to breed only women—women! Never will you have a son, Josiah!" Her breath came in hard spasms; her body trembled as if a demon engine had started up inside her.

He turned and left the room. Either that, he thought, or strike her again. Silence behind him, silence upstairs: it seemed impossible that they had not been overheard. He was sorry for Lydia: this was not what he had wanted for her.

The door to his bedroom was shut. Softly he opened it; as he stepped inside, a bright flash illuminated the room. He saw the figure of his wife upon the bed, covered by a sheet. Her eyes were open.

He stood beside the bed. He remembered how, once, even a brief glimpse of her body bending over her loom had aroused him. Now he felt nothing. Her failure to conceive, even though he knew that the fault was hers, had deadened all his natural impulses. He could hardly remember even the feeling of desire.

I will have him, he thought. Beside him his wife turned away, presenting her back. Damn them all, he thought; I will have him. From some other woman, if necessary: but I will have him.

29

In matters of intimate relations between himself and members of the gentle sex, Silas Blood was, in practice, a celibate. In theory, he very warmly espoused the sexual doctrines of Robert Dale Owen: limiting the birth rate was the solution to all the world's ills, and the way to limit it was by the withdrawal of the male organ prior to ejaculation. Silas thought it a wonderful idea; he had read Owen's tract on the subject,

"Moral Physiology; or, a Brief and Plain Treatise on the Population Question," and had been comforted to know that wiser heads than his had wrestled with this problem and found a solution to it. To have allowed himself to be so weak as to permit even one drop of the critical fluid to enter into a female would have been, to him, an unforgivable lapse. Mr. Owen, in his wisdom, preached this way to all who would hear: self-denial was unnecessary, consideration for the opposite sex all-important. Chivalry, to Mr. Owen, was the key; chivalry, and stern vigilance. For females so unlucky as to encounter selfish or undisciplined men, Mr. Owen had only reproach: consort with true gentlemen, he said, and you will be safe. Although you are the vessels of reproduction, you must consign to us the power over your lives. Rest assured that no gentleman would even dream of so inconveniencing a lady, so endangering her life in return for her favors, unless he absolutely lost control—and then, fair one, you may ascribe that loss to the intoxication of your innumerable charms and so salvage some comfort from the debacle of an unwanted pregnancy.

Silas was a great admirer of Mr. Owen's father: an industrialist who had tried in his native Scotland to improve the lives of his operatives, who had seen and attempted to ameliorate the evils of the factory system, who had expended his fortune in an attempt to establish his vision of the good life at New Harmony—that ill-starred enterprise in Indiana whose failure surely was no fault of Robert Owen's. His experience was a valuable lesson to all who would imitate him: be certain of your followers, trust none but the proven hearts.

In September, Silas and Winfield began a long tour: through Worcester and Springfield (with a visit to the generous manufacturer), through Troy and Albany and down the Hudson to Poughkeepsie, to New-York and thence through the Middle Atlantic states. By stage and railway car and packet boat they traveled; on hope and promise they lived. They had several hundred dollars in contributions; they had fifty-seven applications to join the Community when it began. They were encouraged; they were optimistic. Weary travelers slogging toward the Promised Land, they saw all about them the first tantalizing landmarks of their destination: the hard cash underpinning, the firm promises of support so necessary to their success.

Silas saw many pretty women on the way. Some of them spoke to him in the evenings after Winfield's lecture, or as members of welcoming committees when the speech had had sufficient advance publicity. He understood his attraction for them. They were lonely in their native towns, they were unmarried, without hope of marriage. He understood that to them he seemed a figure of enormous interest; after a while he came to expect the attention which they gave to him, the sweet smiles, the fluttering lashes, the eager questions intended to draw him out, to make of him a special friend.

But he never allowed himself to be caught. In a quiet corner of his mind, he kept the memory of the sweetest smile, the brightest eye of all, laboring as he labored, waiting and hoping as he did for the day when the Community would begin. Had he analyzed his feelings for her, he might yet have proved to be the son of Enoch Blood, Esq.—for she had no money but her small wages, she had no position, no help to offer him save her devotion and her honest heart. But he thought of none of that: he thought only that he loved her, and that once, in a cluttered tent at an Adventist campground, he had kissed her, and that that one embrace had bound them for all time, each to the other. For she was no less a lady because she worked in a factory, and he no less a gentleman because he espoused the Communal life. And so for her sake as well as his own—how he loved to chain himself to an ideal!—he resisted the charms of other women; he wrote to her twice a month; he looked forward to the day when he could settle down with her in Winfield's Eden, and practice on her to his honorable heart's content the prudent sexual teachings of Robert Dale Owen.

Sabra lived through the autumn in a haze of anticipatory daydreams. No longer was she one of the unchosen. In the weeks of late summer, before he left on his travels with Winfield, Silas had come regularly from Concord to see her. He became a familiar face to the denizens of Mrs. Clapham's boarding house; that good lady herself, in the joy of seeing yet another of her girls make good—that is, snare a man—had taken, as she coyly declared, to setting her clock by him, so punctually did he appear every Sunday.

Had she known of the exact nature of Silas' plans for himself and Sabra, Mrs. Clapham would have been somewhat less enthusiastic about his visits. For if Silas followed Robert Dale Owen on birth control, he followed Henry Winfield on marriage—and marriage, said Winfield, was the old way: the enslavement of women, the thwarting of a natural human desire to experiment, to move on, to form new partnerships when the old had grown stale. In Winfield's Community there would be no traditional marriages; each couple wishing to unite would sign a contract which could be torn up—dissolved—at the wish of either. Winfield would say a few words at a Community ceremony, and a couple would be united. They could part with equal ease.

Silas had explained Winfield's philosophy—but not Owen's—to Sabra on his last visit before his departure. In the face of his eloquence, his devotion to Winfield's way, she had thought it an admirably sensible plan; but she had thought, too, that her fellow boarders, not to mention Mrs. Clapham, would doubtless think it foolish at the least, and wicked at worst. So she was noncommittal when they asked her about her plans to marry: when we can, she said. When the Community is begun. She saw herself there, free of the burden of factory labor, working at Silas' side. How happy they would be!

His letters gave her infinite consolation. She often thought, reading them, of her terror on the day of Father Miller's exhibition. She had been very foolish—misguided, to tremble with fear at his warning of the Apocalypse.

Surely this world would end—this world of endless drudging work, of wage slavery, of dictatorship by a few rich men. Father Miller had been right about that. But the end would come, not in a consummation of fire, but in the gift of new sight given to all men and women by the labors of Silas Blood, among others. Father Miller and his acolytes, exhorting in their error, served only to distract people's minds from the truth: that the salvation would come here, on earth, for everyone; not in that select Heaven whose doors were open only to those terrorized enough to confess their sins.

And so she saw now with Silas' eyes: and she saw the evils of the factory system. She heard with his ears: and she heard the unholy noise of the machinery, the impotent, discontented grumblings of her sister operatives, powerless to prevent their own exploitation. His mind, his thought became her own; and so, fortified with new perception, she thought that she understood the error of life as it was generally lived. With the zeal of the convert, she embraced the need for a new way.

She saw that the malcontents who were exhorting Ten Hours labored in darkness. Ten Hours was meaningless—an irrelevance. Ten Hours assumed that the factory system must continue, when in fact the only hope for them all was the return to the land, the growth of true community, the self-sufficient enclave fashioned on the principles of true equality—men and women, rich and poor, Christian and nonbeliever.

In her new enlightenment, she saw that Betsey Rudd, discharged and blacklisted for her Ten-Hour agitation, had sacrificed her job for nothing. Where was she now? How did she live? Sabra remembered that Betsey had come from Goshen, a village in the Berkshires. She wrote a letter to her there, asking her to think about joining the Community. She was sure that Silas would not object, for Betsey was the very best type of girl: hard-working, honest, bright and kind. After some days she had an answer.

Nov. 15, '42

Dear Sabra,

Thanks for your letter, and for asking me to join Mr. Winfield's Community. It sounds too good to be true, and you are lucky to be going there.

My mother has been ill, and my sister also. So I will need to stay here for a while—I don't know how long. I'll let you know if I can get away next spring, but I can't leave now.

I miss you all, and I certainly miss my pay. I couldn't earn a dollar here to save my soul. I don't see many people. It's hard to get into the village because Father sold our trap last month. But I read when I can, and hope my brain doesn't wither away.

I'm *not* sorry for what I did. Let me have news of you and everyone again soon. Your letter cheered me very much.

Your friend,
Betsey

For two weeks after Betsey left, Sabra had the bed to herself. It was the longest time that anyone in the house could remember a place being vacant; usually a new girl appeared within a day or two to take the place of the one who had gone. But they had heard, with increasing frequency, of the Corporations' difficulty in finding new help. The recruiters—the slavers—journeyed to the far north country now to fill their long black wagons with new hands, and they were given a bonus of a dollar a head for every girl whose home was more than a hundred miles distant from the factories. But, of late, girls were not so eager to snatch at the chance for life away from the lonely drudgery of the farms. There was drudgery, too, on the Corporation, they had heard; the overseers and Agents were as tyrannical as any father or brother. If you come here, they heard, you have a new master, but a master all the same; and you risk your health, even your life, to earn your pittance. Even though it is more than you or any woman ever earned before, you must understand the difficulties you face in getting it.

"Have you talked to her?" said Minerva, several days after a new girl had finally arrived to take Betsey's place.

"No more than to say good night. What of her?"

Minerva had lingered unusually long that evening at the supper table. She sat now with Sabra, picking at the last of her plum tart; she seemed tired—discouraged. She had just received a manuscript returned from the third publisher to whom she had sent it. A book, not a story—three hundred pages of laboriously written plot, each page representing the loss of at least half an hour's sleep. For all her work, all her fatigue, Minerva remained plump and jolly-looking; a stranger, gazing on, would never have guessed that she was as fiercely intent on her purpose as, say, the Ten-Hour agitators were on theirs.

"Ask her where she comes from," said Minerva. "She will not tell you at first. She may not tell you at all, but I gather that she is not what she pretends to be."

"Why?" said Sabra. "What has she to conceal?"

"I'm not sure." Minerva's round face settled into an expression of gloom. "But I think—and it's only a suspicion, mind you—I think that she has—uh—lived a life that most of us would rather die than live. I think that her reputation was in some way compromised—"

"Does Mrs. Clapham know?"

"Of course not. Do you think she'd let her stay on if there were the slightest question about her character?"

"What will you do?" she said. "Will you tell Mrs. Clapham?"

"Not just yet," said Minerva. "In fact I probably won't need to tell her at all. The girl will show herself for what she is, sooner or later. She has not adjusted well; I am sure that she will not stay. The discipline is too confining for her. She will go back to what she came from." She shuddered; her fertile imagination allowed her fully to imagine the horrors of which she spoke. "She will be ground up in the wheels of the world," she said; and, liking the phrase, she repeated it to herself. An idea had just come to her: why not a story about such a girl?—if she could write it in a sufficiently genteel way, of course, for the public would not stand for any salacious material from the pen of a woman.

Filled with new purpose, she pushed back her chair and stood up. "I'm going to work now," she said. "What are you doing tonight?"

"O—nothing," said Sabra. She wished that she could say: "I am writing to Silas," but his itinerary was unplanned, she had no idea of his address on any given day. "I'm tired," she said. "Perhaps I'll go to bed. I'll say one thing for that new girl: she's a quiet sleeper."

30

Mr. A. P. Critchlow, the overseer in the weaving room of the Commonwealth Number Two, had had a difficult day. In the morning he had been summoned to Bradshaw's office, where, to his dismay, he had been informed of the new premium system which was to go into effect immediately: a dollar a head for him for each girl who produced ten yards a week more.

The extra money would be helpful, Mrs. Critchlow having recently given birth to their sixth child, but he dreaded the means by which he must obtain it. The girls had been quiet these last months, since winter was always a quiet time. Spring and summer brought restlessness, journeys home, vacant places, new hands to train. They might not remain docile with this new announcement. And if they took it into their heads to protest—to turn out—he, A. P. Critchlow, would be blamed for not being able to keep his girls in line. Their conduct, both within and without the mill, reflected on him as well as on the Agent; he was always alert for news of them, he always asked around at the houses. He felt it his duty to know what they did with themselves at all times; he was very conscious of the need to maintain a high moral tone.

He had delayed his announcement of the order until after the noon bell which brought the girls back from their dinners; then, weakening, he delayed again. How he hated himself at such times! They were only women, after all. He earned six or seven times as much as the best of them. They could never advance, no matter how able they were: the best weaver in the mill would never be more than that, while, he, Amasa Prout Critchlow, could aspire to—well, not to an Agent's post, he had not the proper family connections for that—but at least to sub-agent, the Agent's surrogate with a dozen men under him.

Knowing all this, confident of his superior place in the God-ordained hierarchy, he hesitated still. He shuddered to think what would happen if they ever came together strongly enough to turn out all at once; certainly his position would be taken from him, at the very least. At worst he would be blacklisted like any operative. No mill in New England would hire him as an overseer if it were put about that he could not control his girls.

It was the girls whom everyone came to see. He thought it a bad thing, this celebration of female weavers and spinners. It went to their heads; he could see the secret look of pride on their faces when a delegation came through. No one ever looked at A. P. Critchlow on such occasions; all the attention was for them. If he were Agent, he would never allow a single visitor into the building.

In the afternoon a harness strap had broken on one of the looms. Worse, no mechanic was immediately available to repair it; not before tomorrow, came word from the machine shop. Critchlow chafed and fumed. Since the beginning of the railroad, seven years ago, the machine shop had become increasingly less useful to the factories. As hundreds of new miles of track were added every year, hundreds of new locomotives and cars had to be built to traverse them. Thus the mechanics at the machine shop were less frequently available to repair a broken loom or spinning frame. In some of the mills, he knew, the condition of the machinery had become a scandal; one girl in the Hamilton Number Three, tired of waiting for her loom to be repaired, had attempted to become something of a mechanic herself, to the vast amusement of her overseer.

And now, just before the evening supper bell, two warp threads—improperly dressed, no doubt—on Palfrey's loom had broken and she had spent a good ten minutes trying to re-tie them. At the first peal of the bell the operatives threw the handles to stop their looms and raced for the stairway; Sabra Palfrey, he saw with some surprise, remained behind, still drawing up the thread in an attempt to get a full warp.

He approached her softly in the sudden quiet. He was pleased to see that she started when he appeared at her side. What was it someone had said about her? "Dangerous company, Mr. Critchlow, the girl kept dangerous company last summer—and unchaperoned, too." He was not sure exactly what dangerous company was, but it bore looking into.

"Trouble, Sabra? Here, let me see."

As he leaned over the tautly strung yarn he brushed her shoulder. Instinctively she drew back. He felt a warning excitement begin to stir somewhere in the depths of his small torso.

Since she made no reply he continued in a friendly way as he pulled out the thread.

"Yes, see, this warp is weak all the way along, spun out badly, this kind of thread'll break no matter how you dress it, you just have to pull it out until you see it's even all along—"

He glanced at her as he worked; she stood impassive, watching his hands.

"There. That'll do, it's strong from this point. Now you can tie it on."

He straightened, automatically running his hand over his head to smooth his thinning hair.

Obediently Sabra chalked her fingers and leaned to tie the thread. She was aware that he was standing close—too close—but she ignored him. She did not like him; she had stayed, not to please him, but to save herself from staying late to finish. Better to miss supper than to stay after last bell; besides, she was not hungry. It was a bad night. Wind-driven snow beat against the tall windows facing the river; she did not miss having to battle her way to Mrs. Clapham's and back. She thought that after she repaired the broken threads she would sit for a while on the stairs and rest her back until the bell sounded for the girls to return.

Critchlow stood between her and the aisle. As she finished tying she muttered a word of thanks and stepped to one side to get out. He stepped, too, as if he were her partner in a dance. His movement blocking her way was as eloquent as any improper word: instantly they understood each other.

"Sabra—"

"Excuse me."

She refused to meet his eyes. She stood quite still. The whale-oil lamps ringing the walls threw harsh shadows across the floor, angular black patterns. The snow melted on the windows. The room was very warm; Sabra felt the perspiration on her face, but she did not try to wipe it off.

Any movement now seemed an admission of defeat, or at least of weakness. She must stand her ground.

But no. There was an escape, after all.

She turned and started down the narrow space between the looms toward the windows. She could get out that way. Surely he would not follow her.

She felt his hand on her arm. A lifetime of instruction—to be obedient, docile, ladylike, gentle—inhibited her instinctive reaction.

He was surprised at her submissiveness; he was surprised at his own temerity. The fact that she did not shake him off emboldened him; the feel of her arm beneath his hand, thin, firm, yet soft, sent an imperious signal to his brain. What they said was true: she was a loose one. Any decent girl would have put him off immediately.

He retained his grip and backed her into the frame of the loom behind her. He put his free hand on her neck, not to strangle, but to press against the life-throbbing pulse. He crowded her, felt the outline of her body beneath her uncrinolined skirts. He felt his own body respond. His wife would not be available for weeks. It was not right for him to be so deprived.

Now, too late, she reacted. His breath smelled of tobacco and onions, his mouth was an obscene opening in his tight little face.

"Stop it—" Her spine was crushed against the metal frame. She pulled at his hand on her neck. He tightened his grip and pushed himself harder against her.

"Now, miss." He grimaced. His teeth were pale brown. A drop of spittle hit her cheek. "I've been hearing about you. People say you're a sly thing. What does that mean, eh?"

"Get away—" No use; he had her fast.

"You know we can't keep no one who don't behave herself. Corporation can't have a bad name, can it? Now why don't you tell me what it is you did with that fella—"

His stinking mouth came close. Violently she wrenched her head away. Her struggle excited him unbearably.

"Little minx, ain't you? Now if you'll just quiet down perhaps you and me can fix it so's I don't have to discharge you. I always had a liking for you, Sabra—"

Scream, she thought. She fought down her rising nausea. *Get away—*

"Mr. Critchlow!"

She felt him freeze. In a second he had released her and stepped back, looking for the source of that voice which, so providential had it been, might have been the voice of God Himself but which was only Josiah Bradshaw come to confer with his overseer.

The Agent stood in the aisle, disgust and disbelief struggling on his face. Critchlow, with the air of a small boy who has been caught with his hand in the candy jar—not a grave offense, surely?—turned to face his employer.

"What is the matter here?" Bradshaw glanced at Sabra but did not acknowledge her presence.

"Ah—a little trouble with the threads, sir, but it's all fixed now." He attempted a smile.

Bradshaw's eyes traveled down him and up again. Stupid, stupid— Surely she could not have enticed him, she was a decent girl, after all.

"Sabra?"

"The warp threads broke, and I stayed to tie them."

Sabra's friendship with Silas Blood had not yet come to Bradshaw's attention: what was common knowledge in the town did not always reach the ears of those who purportedly controlled that town. Had he known of it, he might have been less willing to assume her innocence in this case; but since he knew nothing, his outrage was all for Critchlow.

They heard the bell calling the operatives back to work. With an abrupt movement of his head, Bradshaw beckoned the overseer to follow him downstairs.

Left alone for a moment until the other girls returned, Sabra moved her body cautiously. Nothing seemed broken. She rubbed the sore place on her back where Critchlow had pressed her against the loom. Were it not for that pain, she might have thought the past minutes nothing but a brief hallucination brought on by fatigue, hunger, loneliness—o, Silas! She leaned against the metal bar, trembling. To go away, to leave this endless labor, to live at peace in some quiet country home soon, she thought. Soon the Community will begin, and I can go away and have my life.

She heard footsteps on the stairs, the sound of voices rising. She turned and went to her place.

31

By seven-thirty that evening, when the operatives were dismissed for the day, the snow had stopped and here and there a star shone in the cloudy night sky. Bradshaw shrugged on his greatcoat, picked up his tall black beaver hat, and, stepping out into the mill yard, locked his office and called good night to the watch. As he passed through the gate and climbed into his waiting cutter, he saw the last of the operatives scurrying into their boarding houses. He felt a brief sympathy for the hapless Critchlow. Driving past the boarding houses and seeing the shapeless forms hurrying inside, he admitted to himself that Critchlow's misconduct—and certainly it was misconduct—was, all the same, understandable. To be surrounded every day by such numbers of females, to work with them, talk to them, smell their scent as they passed, see their pleasing forms bent to their tasks—the strange thing was that incidents such as today's did not happen more frequently. A man was only human, after all, no matter how hard he might try to deny it. Bradshaw thought of his own infatuation with his present wife. Did Critchlow have such a desire for Sabra, he wondered? Or, starved as he was because of his wife's frequent confinements, would he have behaved so with any girl?

He turned the horse down Merrimack Street toward the great bend in the river, away from the direction of his own house. He was expected this evening at the home of Matthew Munson, whose devotion to the cause of the Corporations had frequently to be rewarded, among other ways, by the presence of the manufacturing hierarchy at his table. Tonight would be a gathering of gentlemen whom Munson would enlighten on the prospects for several pieces of important legislation in the coming session of the Great and General Court, where he so faithfully warmed his seat in the interests of his benefactors.

To Bradshaw's left lay the Acre: alien ground. He reminded himself to mention to his host the possibility of restricting immigration, say, by a legislative decree. Probably such a thing was not possible—but certainly it seemed desirable, with new arrivals flooding the port of Boston daily, making their wretched way to other cities of the Commonwealth. Only last week two Irishwomen had applied for positions in the spinning room, when everyone knew that Irish were fit only to pick waste. The recruiters in the north country had not sent down enough hands in the last six months, and Bradshaw had been momentarily tempted to hire the applicants. The overseer had appealed to the Agent to make the decision: "They seem decent enough, sir, but I don't know. The girls won't like it." Finally he had refused them. They could hardly speak English, and could neither read nor write; they would not be operatives of whom he could boast that they were as genteel as any lady—like the *Offering* girls, for instance. He had been rewarded for his prudence the next day by the delivery of ten new American girls from whom to choose. It would be a bad day indeed, he thought grimly, when he was forced to hire foreign help because no native girls would apply.

He turned left onto Pawtucket Street, which ran parallel to the river above the bend. Munson's house was a gaudy new yellow affair of pointed gables and elaborately carved, white-painted trim; it looked like nothing so much as a setting for one of the stories in Lydia's book of

German fairy tales. Bradshaw's aesthetic sensibilities were offended by that house: he was a plain man, heart and soul.

The housekeeper admitted him and showed him into the parlor, where Munson entertained two earlier arrivals: Bright, of the Hamilton, and Trask, of the Massachusetts. He exchanged greetings and stood by the fire to warm himself, accepting from his host a cup of hot flip. It was badly flavored; it lacked sufficient rum. He sighed and resigned himself to the evening, thinking longingly of his quiet room on Belvidere Hill.

The discussion at dinner centered on the question of a bill before the legislature to end imprisonment for debt. What line, Munson wanted to know, did the Corporations wish him to take? He could make a speech in favor of the bill if they wished; then again, he could oppose it. They had only to tell him what to do.

The conversation droned on through the meal. At last, after they had done, Bradshaw sat back to enjoy his cigar. But it did not taste good, neither it nor his glass of port. Nothing had, he realized, for a long time. He ate, he slept, he went through his days like a well-tended machine, powered by—what? He had been staring at his glass while the others pursued the discussion. Now he raised his eyes, merely to restore focus, and by accident met the eyes of one of the servants who was clearing the dishes from the opposite side of the table. He realized that she had been staring at him; now, when he met her glance, her pale face colored a little and after a moment she looked down, attentive once more to her work.

A frank stare is a personal, intimate thing. Bradshaw was accustomed to a more obsequious manner, especially from females, most especially from female servants. He had felt curiously exposed, for an instant, under those eyes (very blue, black-lashed; a pretty face, too). There had been nothing impertinent about her look; it was simply a recognition, as if she had said—would have said, had she had the chance—"I know you."

She did, in fact, know him. He had once given Patrick O'Haran a five-dollar gold-piece. Patrick had it still; he had let her see it once, although he had not told her why Bradshaw had given it to him. That he had done so at all was enough to place him forever in her own private hierarchy of persons to be admired, along with Mrs. Clapham and Sabra Palfrey and Mary McCormic and, of course, Patrick himself. She wished that she could speak to this tall, impressive, powerful man who sat at Mr. Munson's table and ate and talked and yet seemed curiously detached from the company, not paying attention. But of course to speak to him would have been unthinkable unless he spoke first. She wished that he would; she was sure that she would have been brave enough to answer. But he did not: he simply met her gaze, and for an instant, no more, some wordless message had passed between them; and then she had bent her head again and continued with her work and the gentlemen had retired to the parlor to continue their political discussion.

For all its brevity the moment stayed with Bradshaw through the rest of the evening at Munson's and all during his long journey home. He had felt those eyes upon him—he felt them now, still—and yet he had not minded, had not taken offense. It was an odd moment to take away, but not an unpleasant one. He turned into his driveway; after stabling his horse he made his way around to the front door of his house.

And opened it, and staggered again under the burden of his life.

A low, wailing voice—like the chant of some savage, he thought—assaulted his ears. It appeared to come from the second floor. The rooms downstairs were dark, unoccupied. After listening for a moment to make sure that the voice did in fact come from within the house, he ran up the stairs and then, following the sound, down the hall to Miss MacIver's room—formerly his sister-in-law's.

A sliver of light fell onto the hall carpet. He pushed open the door.

"Amalia?"

He saw a tableau: three figures. Sitting at one side of the bed, his wife Margaret. Bending over on the other side, the governess, Miss MacIver. In between, the object of their attentions: Amalia. Several lamps gave a pitiless illumination to the scene; a fire burned high in the small fireplace. A nauseous smell filled the air.

He stepped inside the room. The wailing had stopped at the sound of his voice; he guessed that it had come from Miss MacIver.

"What is it? What happened?"

As he stepped closer to the bed he saw that a dribble of dark fluid ran down Amalia's chin; her face was as white as the pillowcase, her eyes sunken, half closed. She lay as still as Death.

It was his wife who answered his question. "She took something, we think. We don't know what. She's been vomiting, unconscious—"

Swiftly he brushed her aside and took Amalia's wrist. He felt a faint pulse.

"What have you given her? Where is Dr. Knight?"

"We tried to get her to swallow an infusion of lobelia," said Miss MacIver. Her voice broke; she was trembling. "We found her in the kitchen. It was all we could do to get her up the stairs. The doctor—"

"The doctor is at home, I assume," snapped Margaret. "We discovered her only an hour ago, and since it is such a bitter night, and only the two of us here aside from the child, we thought you would be home at any moment and could go to fetch him and thus prevent one of us from freezing to death on the road." She had gotten to her feet; with very little effort he could have seized her and shaken her and forced from her some more respectful speech—but not now, not here.

"Very well," he said. He laid Amalia's hand back on the coverlet and felt her forehead. She was very cold, even to his hand still cold from the long ride home. He straightened and looked at them. "I will go. Keep her warm, try to get her to drink again—"

An exclamation from Miss MacIver cut off his further instructions. "Look—she is trying to speak! What is it, Miss Thayer? Tell us what you swallowed!"

She bent over the bed, but Amalia, struggling to focus her eyes, looked not at her but at Bradshaw. Her face worked with the effort to speak; a fresh eruption of dark fluid spilled from her mouth. For a moment the room was very still. Bradshaw waited. After this, he knew, there would be no need to fetch Dr. Knight.

The words for which Amalia struggled finally came. "Murderer," she whispered. "Murderer." She paused; she made a great effort. "When lust hath conceived, it bringeth forth sin: and sin, when it is finished, bringeth forth death."

And then a flood from her twisted lips, and a shower of sparks from the fire, and Miss MacIver's wailing began again.

32

On the night of February 17–18, 1843, a great comet came blazing up from the southern sky. Many people saw it. Many feared it. Some—not so many—made use of it. A few took notes and drew sketches so that its appearance would be well documented. It was later calculated that this was one of the largest comets ever seen: its tail was two hundred million miles long. Almost everyone who saw it received it as a sign from God; even unbelievers were given pause as they watched the fiery wanderer hurtling across the heavens.

Josiah Bradshaw saw it from the window of his library: a brilliant streak arching through the night high above the river valley. He was not a superstitious man—he was not even, any longer, a very religious man—but as he watched its luminous progress his heart rose and his soul came free from the deadweight which had burdened it for long months past. He felt a tear come to his eye, and, unashamed (for who could see except an increasingly distant God?), he wiped the tear away and took courage and made his resolve once again.

Sabra Palfrey was aroused from sleep by the cries of her companions. As she watched at the window, she felt the return of the terror which she had experienced at Father Miller's camp meeting. Ah, God—! But the fears of the other girls kept her from fully experiencing her own. They were terrified, badly shaken: what did it mean? The Apocalypse? In vain Elizabeth Parker, who wrote of scientific subjects for the *Offering*, attempted to calm them; it was a natural phenomenon, she said, it had nothing to do with the end of the world. Sabra fastened herself to this knowledge, this calm voice explaining what they saw; she echoed Elizabeth's words as she soothed the quaking, awestruck females around her.

The house was in an uproar. Everyone was awake. Mrs. Clapham, angry that she had been called too late to see the spectacle, strode up the stairs, nightcap askew, to scold her charges and shoo them back to bed. Comets, Ten-Hour, ruined reputations, weak lungs—all were trouble, all were conspiracies (of whom, she did not stop to think) to keep her constantly in agitation, constantly fearful of losing her place. In calmer moments, in the privacy of her room, Mrs. Clapham prayed quietly for an uneventful life; now, afraid of mass panic, she spoke sharply to her girls and ordered them, all distracted as they were, back to bed.

Minerva Swan went willingly enough, although even after her roommates quieted she remained awake, seeing again in her mind's eye that awesome trajectory of light. How to describe it? More—how to use it? For surely such a thing must be used. It was a gift from God: she must not refuse it. She wished that she were a painter. How easy, to brush pale color against a field of black and call it "Comet."

Silas Blood, itemizing supplies for the Community, saw the comet from Henry Winfield's house in Concord. Winfield himself was not at home; he had gone to lecture in Boston and had not yet returned. Silas watched the display in the sky with interest, sorry that Winfield was not with him. Winfield's comments on such an extravaganza, so meaningless apart from its own ephemeral beauty, would have been words to treasure as they forged on together in their great work. Comets, signs from God, spiritual revelation—all were irrelevant, all distractions from the true task, which was to make Heaven, or a reasonable imitation of it, here on earth. When the light had faded, and the sky was dark once more, pinpricked by stars that seemed unaccustomedly faint, Silas returned with new diligence to his work: fifty shovels, twenty axes, fifteen saws. How dull a list for so daring a venture! But he must hurry, Winfield must hurry, their time was growing short. The new religious mania sweeping the land—the Millerites at their camp meetings, the Mormons, the Shakers—all were potential enemies, diverting souls and, more important, cash from their own venture. This comet tonight would be the spur to new recruitments by the preachers of Armageddon; new enthusiasm would spring up for the Second Coming, people would increasingly neglect their earthly lives to prepare to meet the Lord. And the Lord would keep them waiting; and their lives would disintegrate; and finally, disheartened, they would come to the end of their days without ever having known the best that the world could offer: the New Way, Winfield's dream.

Father William Miller, who had given his name to those who would be saved on the Day of Judgment, saw the terrible glowing thing in the sky as he was being driven home from an evening's preaching at a small country church near Portsmouth. Instantly, in his hoarse, quavering voice, he ordered the driver to stop. Fighting off assistance, he scrambled down from the carriage and stumbled into the snow-covered meadow at the side of the road. He was dressed in an expensive cloak fashioned of the finest camel's hair; on his head rested a shaggy, white, broad-brimmed beaver hat. He lifted his face to the heavens. His hat fell off, exposing his head to the cold, but he did not notice. He sank onto his knees. For him, this was the final warning—the last magnificent omen from the Lord. Surely, now, it would come: the end of the old, the beginning of the new, the burning of the damned, the salvation of the born-again—the Apocalypse! He had waited for it all his life; he had warned others of what was to happen. He had been mocked and scorned and ridiculed; people had reviled him, had persecuted his followers. He had remained firm in his faith. And now God had rewarded him, had sent this blazing messenger for all to see. Repent! Now he could make his calculations. He would fill sheet after sheet of foolscap with a maze of numbers—he had his formulae, and now from this date he would be able to figure precisely the date of the final hour, the general conflagration. People had grown impatient with him in recent months. "When?" they said. "Tell us exactly when, Father, so that we may make our preparations. Should we plant our crops next spring, or will next spring never come? Should we make our harvest, add a room to the house, send our children to school?" Now he could tell them. He was overwhelmed with joy. His legs froze in the snow; the night wind whipped about his ears. At last the driver came to fetch him, afraid for the old man's health. With some difficulty he got the preacher back into the carriage. Neither of them noticed the beaver hat lying in the snow; the farmer who found it, the next day, considered it a gift from God.

In New-York, Rachel Bradshaw saw the comet as she performed an errand of mercy in the company of a female friend. Together they had attended a meeting at which certain agitators had fulminated against the President, the Congress, the several governors, the state legislators, the churches—against all the established order which allowed the institution of chattel slavery to continue. Refreshed and filled with new purpose, they had stopped to visit a poor woman who, deserted by her husband, had attempted to support herself and her three young children by sewing shirts. She had worked eighteen hours a day for the past year, earning between twenty and twenty-five cents a day. Now she had fallen ill. Her children were hungry, her landlord threatening to evict her from her miserable room. The indignation stirred up in the two young women by the agitators at the meeting now found immediate focus in the sad spectacle before them. Horrified, deflected momentarily from their larger, general purpose, they concentrated now upon the specific: was not this poor woman a slave also? They promised to return in an hour with food and clothing. They hurried out into the street again sobered and shocked by what they had seen. Just then they saw the comet, and to them, as much as to Father Miller, it seemed to be a sign; and as they gazed at it, mesmerized by its brilliant path, they made new resolves as firm, as dedicated as his. Chattel slavery had its growing number of enemies; but who would speak for the poor slaves in the Northern cities, living out their lives by the slavery of their needle?

Certain Boston capitalists saw the comet, but they were mostly practical, hard-headed men little given to open-mouthed wonder. The only natural phenomenon that had ever struck them dumb was the thirty-foot drop of the Merrimack River at the Pawtucket Falls. For them, a sign from God—the supreme overseer—was not a comet but a drought; the end of the world was not the Apocalypse but a rise in the price of raw cotton.

In the Paddy Camp Lands, the huts and hovels in which the people lived had no windows, and the refuse-clogged alleyways were hardly fit for nighttime strolling; and so only a few inebriates staggering home from the rumseller's saw the comet, but they put it down to hallucination and thought no more about it. But the priest and his sexton saw it, and thought that indeed it might be a sign: of a brighter day for their people, perhaps, or at least of a new church building. The sexton, who had been a Whiteboy in County Clare, allowed himself to hope that the comet might even be a sign of God's favor to the Liberator—O'Connell, in this case, since the sexton had never heard of Garrison. But he kept his thoughts to himself; the priest frowned upon all nationalist sentiment, and had explicitly forbidden all criticism of England, of landlords, of the Union Bill, and all such historic entrapments.

In the small hours the comet burned away, leaving the night sky black and empty, the stars hardly worthy of notice. Why had it come? Where had it gone? What had it signified?

33

Midsummer: the time of low water. Many of the mills shut down. The girls dispersed. The city baked in the sun. The slow time: the time of sickness. Cholera and typhus came fast again in indiscriminate slaughter. The water in the canals lay stagnant and foul, poison for all who drank it. The inhabitants of the city drank it. Many died.

Death came to the countryside, too, but there he had a smaller harvest, at least in summer. But if he could not straightaway take people's bodies, he could attack obliquely at their minds. Death stalked the spirit, even in the green and peaceful country.

On the Prospect Hill Road, twelve miles west of Lowell, a horse and trap carried two young people to the summit of the rise. They had been traveling since early morning in the hot sun, which now, by noon, had dried the road to powder. The way ran the length of the hill. Spread below them to their right was the broad Nashoba Valley. Mount Wachusett rose blue in the distance. The countryside was very still. The few isolated farms which they passed seemed uninhabited, although here and there they caught sight of a figure weeding a garden or hanging out a wash.

Sabra was dizzy from the heat, or perhaps from her delight in her companion; she was thirsty and hungry; she wanted only to alight from the jolting trap and lie down in the shade to rest. She had not seen Silas for months—not since late March. He had been away again, busy, occupied with his and Winfield's affairs. She glanced at him from beneath the brim of her palm-leaf bonnet. He had shaved his beard; once again he looked as he had when she met him at the Bradshaws', except that now, of course, his face had matured, had lost the baffled, hungering look it had worn when she first knew him. Decidedly, he was a homely young man. But men did not need beauty as a woman did; they needed only the willingness to marry, to support a wife. Any man, even the ugliest, could have his pick of women in New England.

He felt her scrutiny. With his free hand he patted her arm. "Almost there. Do you see that big oak up ahead? The way to the house is just beyond it. We will have to lead the horse down through the meadow—there is no road."

They came to the place and climbed down. Sabra stretched her legs gratefully. She took a deep breath. The air was sweet with the smell of clover. They stood at the edge of the road and looked down across a broad expanse of meadow to a dark red farmhouse shaded by tall trees. In the past several months the "Consociate Family," as they called themselves, had gathered here at this place which they called "Bountiful" to show the world how to live the perfect life. They were guided by their mentor, Moses Trueworthy. Now, seeing it for herself, Sabra felt a small shock of disappointment. It was distinguished from any ordinary farm only by the beauty of its setting. She had thought to see something quite different, she did not know what. To one side of the house was a cluster of conical shapes: beehives. She saw a peak-roofed well, a grape arbor, and, beyond, an expanse of apple trees. As they began to lead the horse across the meadow, she saw emerge from the orchard two figures, two men, the shorter one attired in a long, flapping brown smock and broad-brimmed straw hat, the taller dressed more conventionally in coat and trousers. They were deep in conversation, heads wagging, hands alive; the smocked one tripped over something but caught himself before he fell.

"Ah!" said Silas. "There he is. I was not absolutely sure he would be here, and I wanted you to meet him. He often goes off at short notice."

"Which is he?" said Sabra cautiously; but she knew before he spoke, and her heart sank.

"The shorter one," said Silas. "Wait until you meet him. He is a genius, Sabra, he could reform the world if only he would consent to dress properly. But you must not mind the way he looks. Listen to what he says."

"And the other?"

"Jasper Pike, I believe. I haven't met him. They say that when Trueworthy visited England two years ago, Pike talked to him for an hour and sold his business at once and swore that his life's work lay with the Consociates. But the English have always appreciated Trueworthy's teachings more than people here have done." Like Winfield, he might have added: they had enormously admired Winfield, too. And by his countrymen he was ignored— No. Today was a special day; he would allow himself no bitter thoughts, no premonitions of failure. He had come here at Winfield's request to see how Trueworthy fared in his experiment; he would do that, and add, if he could, a special request of his own. No more.

They led the horse down across the meadow to the farmhouse; during these few minutes the two conversationalists, seemingly oblivious to their surroundings, circled the house three times, as if the expression of their thoughts depended on the quick propulsion of their legs. They had begun their fourth circumnavigation as Sabra and Silas came up; catching sight of the newcomers, the smocked figure gave them a cheerful wave without breaking stride.

"Halloo! Glad to see you! Water the horse in back—go right in and sit down—make yourselves at home!" The last words were uttered as he rounded the corner of the house and disappeared once again from view.

Silas laughed. "There, isn't he pleasant? I'm sure he didn't recognize me, although we've met. But when he gets to thinking and talking, he forgets."

In the house they were confronted by a harassed-looking woman whose pale face and straggling gray hair contrasted with her lively, intelligent eyes.

"Ah—Mrs. Trueworthy!" exclaimed Silas. "How good to see you again! Do you remember, we met at Mr. Winfield's last year—Silas Blood—and this is Miss Sabra Palfrey."

She rewarded them with a brief, somewhat pained smile.

"Yes, of course, Mr. Blood. How good of you to call. We were just about to sit down to dinner. Please join us."

Looking behind Mrs. Trueworthy, Sabra saw a room which was no more than a wide extension of the entrance hall. A fireplace filled one wall; a long table set with many places took up most of the rest of the space.

"That's very good of you, thanks," said Silas.

"I'll just call the others," said Mrs. Trueworthy in a tired voice. She disappeared through a back door and in a moment they heard the sharp clang of a bell. Through a doorway on her left Sabra saw two scraggly men poring over a pile of books. Beyond them, high on top of an overflowing bookcase, she saw a large marble bust of a snub-nosed, bald-headed man who bore a startling resemblance to their host. At the sound of the bell they came to attention and bolted out to the table, almost colliding with the newcomers in their rush. Sabra heard the thunder of feet overhead; in a moment three more men came careening down the narrow stairs and took their places. No one spoke to Sabra or Silas, although they did receive some curious glances and a friendly nod or two. Three of the five now at table wore linen smocks like Mr. Trueworthy's. Now, from outdoors, came a scramble of children—three little girls, it seemed, all dressed in identical smocks with similar short-cropped hair. The largest girl lugged a baby perhaps eight months old. They were followed by a tall, luxuriously bearded man and by Mrs. Trueworthy, who took her place at the head of the table, settled the baby on her lap, and waved a distracted hand at the newcomers.

"Sit where you will—take a plate—Mr. Trueworthy and Mr. Pike seem to have disappeared again, so perhaps you will say the words, Mr. Brown."

There was a general shuffle as everyone moved to give Sabra and Silas a narrow place on one of the long benches. Then a silence fell as they looked expectantly at the tall man with the beard. After a moment came his low, rumbling voice:

"Live in peace; work in health; love thy neighbor; harm no living creature; renounce the lusts of the flesh; hear the dictates of the spirit; obey God's will. Amen."

At once there was a scramble for the bowls of fruits and vegetables both cooked and raw—peas, beans, carrots, cherries, peaches—and the plates of large brown rocks which seemed to be bread baked in knobby, fantastic shapes. Silas had said that the Trueworthys were followers of Sylvester Graham—but surely Graham did not prescribe such odd dimensions for his loaves? Everyone devoured the food as if half-starved. They would put the girls at the boarding houses to shame, thought Sabra, so fast do they eat. But then there was so little here, compared to the abundant table set by Mrs. Clapham, that to attempt to eat slowly, to hold back from grabbing a dish, was not to eat at all. With Silas' help she secured a portion of vegetables; with some effort he managed to divide a loaf of bread between them. She was glad enough to drink the cold water set out in pitchers, but, having quenched her thirst, she would have been happier still for a glass of lemonade or a cup of tea. Neither, it seemed, was on the menu at Bountiful.

Given the rapidity of mastication, and the paucity of the repast, in ten minutes or less most of the men had finished their meal and, without a word to Mrs. Trueworthy or to the guests, had risen from the table and returned to whatever they had been doing when the dinner bell had rung. The children vanished, too, taking the baby with them; finally only Mrs. Trueworthy and Mr. Brown remained with Sabra and Silas.

"Delicious, Mrs. Trueworthy," said Silas heartily, draining his mug of water. "Good plain food, pure cold water. A meal fit for a—not a king, no. For a philosopher!"

Brown eyed him warily. "You folks from Concord?"

"Ah—I am, yes, and this young lady is one of the celebrated mill girls from Lowell. Allow me—I am Silas Blood, and this is Miss Sabra Palfrey."

Brown nodded agreeably enough, but did not introduce himself to them in turn; after an awkward moment Mrs. Trueworthy murmured, "Amos Brown."

He stood up, not to shake Silas' hand but to return to his work. He was a big man, well over six feet, as broad as a bull; his shoulders bulged under the thin, coarse stuff of his gray shirt, his heavily muscled forearms protruded from his rolled sleeves. His hair and his beard were lightly flecked with white; he was perhaps forty years old. He paused for a moment before he went out; then he spoke to Mrs. Trueworthy as if they were alone.

"Did you ask him?"

"Yes."

"And what—"

"No. He said no, he said he won't have it. It's against his principles."

"Principles," snorted Brown. "Let him eat his principles. I'm goin' to Harvard Village tomorrow and I'm bringin' back an ox. If he don't like it, he don't have to eat what I plant."

A look very like terror passed across Mrs. Trueworthy's thin, careworn face. "You mustn't—"

"O yes," said Brown. "I must. But don't you worry about it. I should've spoke to him myself. I'll tell him tonight. Don't you mention it." He hesitated for a moment, but said nothing more. Then he turned and went outside.

Mrs. Trueworthy made no move to rise and clear the table. Sabra, who was quite willing to help, thought that she should wait for a signal from her hostess before she began to pick up the plates.

Silas cleared his throat. "You prosper here, ma'am? The children seem well—"

"Yes," she said abruptly.

"Ah—it seems that Mr. Trueworthy engages in such fruitful discussion that he nourishes his mind to the detriment of his body. That was Jasper Pike walking with him, was it not?"

"Yes."

Sabra thought somewhat irreverently that long years of marriage to a renowned conversationalist seemed to have atrophied Mrs. Trueworthy's own powers of speech.

"Well—" Silas looked around, somewhat at a loss; he smiled encouragingly at Sabra. "If you ladies don't mind, I think I'll go outside and find Mr. Trueworthy. I have some messages for him from Concord and Boston. Thanks again for the dinner, ma'am. Sabra, will you be all right for an hour or so? I believe there's a very good collection of books in the library, and perhaps you can help Mrs. Trueworthy?"

"Of course," said Sabra. "Anything I can do—" She glanced at Mrs. Trueworthy, who sat quite still.

Silas left by the front door. After he had gone the two women sat silent for a long moment; then suddenly Mrs. Trueworthy leaned forward, her elbows on the table, and stared at her guest, her eyes alive with curiosity.

"You work in a mill?" she said.

"That's right."

"A cotton factory?"

"Yes."

"Mr. Trueworthy was in England two years ago. He went to Manchester. He said that it was dreadful—Hell on earth. Lowell is not like that?"

"No. I have heard of the English towns. Lowell is quite—well, not Heaven, perhaps, but certainly quite decent."

"And you are independent? You support yourself with no help from anyone?" It was as if Mrs. Trueworthy allowed herself to express her thoughts only with the removal of the last male. She has not been silenced after all, thought Sabra; she is merely cautious.

"We do, yes."

Mrs. Trueworthy's eyes shone. "What do you earn? Excuse me for asking such personal questions, but I see so few people, everyone comes to talk to my husband, not to me—and I am interested. I would like to see Lowell some day. It is a splendid idea, to give women a chance at a decent living, independent—so many have no hope. The owners are regular philanthropists, they are so kind, are they not, to have started up the manufactories in order to provide women with an occupation. We all should be grateful to them."

Sabra thought of Betsey Rudd, of Ten-Hour, of Jessie Pratt's damaged, lint-filled lungs. "I earn two dollars and twelve cents a week above board," she said.

"Two dollars and twelve cents," breathed Mrs. Trueworthy. "Every week?"

"Well—every week that I work. Of course I do not get paid if I am sick, and I am not paid now, for the next two weeks, because the mills are shut because of low water."

"Still—two dollars and twelve cents," repeated Mrs. Trueworthy. "Do you know, never in my life have I had that much money. Not for my own. What little comes in from Mr. Trueworthy's admirers—and he does have admirers by the score, but most of them are as poor as we—that little always goes again immediately. We barter for much, but some things only cash can buy. Two dollars and twelve cents! Why, in a lifetime—in ten or twenty years, even—you could save a fortune out of that! You could be wealthy! Even if you worked for only a few years—!"

"Of course most of the girls do just that," said Sabra. "Very few stay a lifetime. It's been only twenty years since the mills started up, and I know of no one who has been there that long. Mostly they work for a while and then get married. Some work after they have married, of course—"

"Ah, but then their wages belong to their husbands," said Mrs. Trueworthy with the air of one offering a final, irrefutable argument. "Married women don't count. Do you mind—I am just curious—but may I ask you how much you have saved? You have worked for how long?"

"Four years and a little more." Four years! "And as for my savings, I'm afraid I've saved very little."

"You should. You will need it. You should not waste that precious money on clothes, or jewelry, or whatever—"

"O, but I haven't wasted it, Mrs. Trueworthy. I am sure that you have heard of the Community which Mr. Blood is planning together with Henry Winfield. They constantly need funds to carry on their work—even as Mr. Trueworthy does. I have given most of my money to them."

Mrs. Trueworthy looked down at the table; she made no reply. Her face, which had been alive with curiosity and the enjoyment of their talk, became once again the tired and—what? defeated?—countenance with which she had met them. She nodded, her eyes still downcast. "That is very generous of you."

"Generous it may be," replied Sabra, "but then I expect to be rewarded, too, with a place in their Community. I am looking forward to it with great happiness."

Mrs. Trueworthy met her eyes again. "When do they expect to begin?"

"Why—they had hoped to start this summer, but there was some difficulty about the property title. Next spring now is the time they have fixed."

"Next spring." Mrs. Trueworthy's mouth twisted into a small, tight smile. "Next spring. Well. I wish you good luck. You will need it."

Resting her red, rawboned hands on the table she pushed herself into a standing position. She began to pick up the dishes, scraping and stacking them at the table; even Huldah at Mrs. Clapham's did not do that, thought Sabra, and the Trueworthys were after all supposed to be gentlefolk. She began to help, carrying unscraped platters—there was very little left in them—out to the scullery.

After the meal had been cleared away Mrs. Trueworthy began to measure out the flour for a baking. She worked steadily, silently, her face set; it was as if she, like any cotton operative, was mindful of the overseer, for all that he was not actually in the room. Sabra, watching her, wondered about that face: was this the happy member of that Communal life about which she had heard so much from Silas? Sabra forgot Mr. Trueworthy's library; this woman before her seemed a source of much more pertinent information. But like many libraries, Mrs. Trueworthy was locked. And the key—?

"You are quite famous, you know," she said. "Everyone in Concord is talking about you, Silas says."

"They talk about my husband. Not me."

"No, but I believe that you are mentioned quite frequently."

Mrs. Trueworthy's mouth seemed to set more grimly. "I am merely an instrument to be used in Mr. Trueworthy's work. Do not forget that. I do not. Besides, I thought they talked about the Ripleys at West Roxbury."

"O, yes, but this is a much more interesting experiment, they say."

"Interesting," said Mrs. Trueworthy. "Yes. I am sure we are that."

Sabra heard the faint note of sarcasm.

"I wonder if you could tell me, since I plan to go into a Community myself—do you miss the world? I often worry that I will miss it, for all that I will be glad to leave the factory. But one has to be so—dedicated—for this." She looked around the sparsely furnished room—Mrs. Trueworthy worked at the dining table for lack of other space—and thought that the boarding-house parlor seemed luxurious by comparison.

Mrs. Trueworthy paused. She did not look at Sabra as she spoke, as if her eyes would contradict her words.

"Yes. One must be dedicated."

"And are you? Forgive me, but I am as curious about this as you are about my life, the wages I earn."

After a moment Mrs. Trueworthy replied. Her voice was low, expressionless, speaking words that she had memorized long ago and repeated many times.

"Moses Trueworthy is a very great man, Miss Palfrey. I am privileged to share his life, wherever that life may lead. My children, too, will realize when they grow up how fortunate they were to have such a man as their father."

"Because he seeks the New Life?"

"Because he seeks God."

"And so the things of this world—"

"Are to be renounced, insofar as we have the strength to do so."

"And you never have doubts about the wisdom of this way?"

Mrs. Trueworthy's eyes met Sabra's. "Mr. Trueworthy says, 'When in doubt—about anything—abstain.'"

"But one must live, all the same. One must eat, have clothing—"

Mrs. Trueworthy's lips twitched. "You have not met Mr. Bowers. He meditates all day. He does not believe in clothing. He walks at night, naked, through the meadow and up into the hills. He believes that clothing are an impediment to spiritual growth. He is closer to God, he says, when he perambulates in the state of Nature. I told him I wanted to see him close to God in January."

They laughed together, then; Mrs. Trueworthy, for a moment, looked as young as a girl. "Word got about in Harvard Village that a mysterious white figure was flitting across the countryside. People thought it was a ghost. They were very frightened. One night, several weeks ago, an armed posse rode out from the village and nearly captured him. Fortunately he was able to run back to us in time. Mr. Trueworthy went out to speak to them. Somehow he was able to make them understand that Mr. Bowers was merely practicing his religion. But of course he is very eloquent." Her face lost its light; she paused, seized by some private thought of which she could not speak.

"What about your children?" said Sabra. "They do not miss having playmates, a regular school—"

"They have a school here, Miss Palfrey." Again Mrs. Trueworthy's face was closed, the words spoken by rote. "Mr. Pike has them for three hours each morning. They keep journals, their grammar and penmanship are excellent, they know Greek and Latin and the Ancient and Modern Histories. . . ." Her voice broke; she grimaced as she attempted to regain her place in her recitation. "Mr. Trueworthy, of course, has charge of their spiritual development."

"Of course," echoed Sabra. "To have their consciences formed by such a renowned philosopher makes them fortunate indeed—"

"We are all fortunate," said Mrs. Trueworthy flatly. "If the world remembers us at all it will be because of our association with him."

Their conversation was interrupted just then by the appearance of Moses Trueworthy himself, with Jasper Pike and Silas Blood in tow. He came in quite like any ordinary human being, stepping over the threshold and mopping his high, broad brow with a large white handkerchief. Perhaps his mind was still on the subject of his conversation, or perhaps he was simply blinded by the passage from the brilliant world outdoors to the more subdued light of the kitchen; but at any rate, for a moment he seemed oblivious to the presence of the two women. It was not until Mrs. Trueworthy made an introduction—"Miss Palfrey from Lowell"—that he was aware of Sabra; then he turned to her, extending his hand, and murmured a greeting.

"Ah—yes—Miss—ah—pleased, pleased—"

Sabra, who had risen to her feet, was left with an impression of mild blue eyes, an average-sized man, curiously weak-looking despite his majestic brow. He shambled around the room, muttering snatches of his thought as he went. He had hardly looked at her; certainly he had not seen her. After a moment he allowed Mrs. Trueworthy to sit him down at the table, Silas and Jasper Pike across from him, and place before him a loaf of bread, thickly sliced, and a mug of water. He ate in silence, his thoughts elsewhere. His two companions, having been served nothing, watched him, seeming to draw sufficient refreshment from that alone. Mrs. Trueworthy concentrated on her work; Sabra was left free to observe the men.

Her gaze rested briefly on Silas. She knew his face as well as she knew her own—better, in fact, for she seldom looked into a mirror. And although she never tired of looking at him, she did not do so now for long, with these two new figures of such interest before her. Moses Trueworthy chewed steadily; he was clearly alone with his thoughts. His massive head, sparsely covered with graying brown hair, nodded slightly on his heavily seamed neck. He looked like a ruminating cow. She settled on Jasper Pike: lean, hungry, intent on his chosen prey. A long narrow head crowned by long auburn hair slicked down flat over his collar; a long pointed nose, a long swath of jaw, small eyes of unknown color: a curiously discontent, untranquil face for one so totally engaged in the pursuit of human happiness. Only once did he remove his eyes from Trueworthy's visage to cast a swift and angry glance at Trueworthy's wife. Sabra saw with some dismay that she returned it: they glared at each other for a moment, openly hostile.

In fact they were at war, these two, although neither admitted it. They battled over the man breaking bread before them: the renowned philosopher, the man whose visions of Utopia had led him to live according to his ideals, much to the consternation of ordinary folk. After a long winter of discussion and planning, Pike had taken the mortgage on the farm; since he had assumed the financial burden of the Consociate Family, he had thought that he could assume also the direction of its development. He had thought that at least he could dictate the elementary rules by which, in good time, they would reform not a dozen souls on an isolated farm, but the entire world, north and south, east and west—even the heathen Chinese, he thought, would come around to his way in time.

Annihilation of the self was his most ardent wish: to stifle in every bosom that natural, human tendency to act in animal self-interest. "Harmonic being," he called this ideal state: the triumph of the spirit over the flesh.

The sex act was anathema. He knew: he had tried it once, and had got a son for his pains. The boy lived now with the mother in Liverpool. Pike did not care if he ever saw them again, particularly the boy. Every time he looked at the child he was reminded—revolted—by this living evidence of his own animal nature. No! The base self which demanded release must be crushed—rooted out and destroyed. That fact had come to be the nub of his problem with the Trueworthys. Mrs. Trueworthy did not want to surrender her husband to Pike's scheme; she wanted to live a "normal" life. Normal! He was overcome with revulsion every time he thought what such a word implied: gross, degrading coupling like soulless animals. Every day he preached his doctrine of celibacy to Moses Trueworthy, and every day the philosopher wrestled with the problem, agonized over it until his broad brow was as furrowed as Brown's fields. Come with me to see the Shakers, Pike had said. They had gone: had seen the busy workshops, the bursting storerooms, the thriving trade in herbs and baskets and well-turned chairs. Pike had labored with his friend as they walked home: you see where they get their energy, he said, they store it up within themselves to do God's work, they do not expend it wastefully on sexual indulgence. Trueworthy had nodded thoughtfully, seeing the logic of Pike's arguments—but then he had confronted his wife again, and weakened because he thought he loved her. That very night he had coupled with her: Pike was sure of it. Fools!

Mrs. Trueworthy was a thorn in his fleshless side in other ways as well. Obedient as she was, devoted to her husband and his beliefs, still she had rebelled on the matter of a lamp. She was so busy during the day, she said, that she needed light after dark to sew. Pike had forbidden it. Lamps burned whale oil: a treasure taken from the bodies of helpless beasts hunted down and cruelly slaughtered. No whale had ever harmed a man; it was sinful to kill them, doubly sinful to enrich their murderers by buying the products of the kill. Mrs. Trueworthy had understood very well the logic of his argument, but still she had persisted: she needed a lamp at night. Bayberry candles would do as well, but they were too dear. No one at Bountiful had any ready cash. Finally her husband had given in to her, and now she had her lamp. Pike cringed every time he saw it; he had not forgiven her her victory, her successful challenge to his authority.

In other matters of conscience, Mrs. Trueworthy had been more cooperative—although always, when she spoke to him, she wore that look of indefinable antagonism. She had agreed that no animal product could be used at Bountiful, nor any product which had caused harm to any living creature, man or beast. Neither cotton, harvested by slaves, nor wool, stolen from sheep; neither leather taken from dead animals nor silk taken from live ones; not milk or butter, not cheese, eggs, fish, or any kind of flesh; not tea, coffee, or molasses, all shipped in by slave traders; not sugar or rice; not even manure on the fields was permitted, for was not manure the product of animals as much as skin or meat?

"Aspiring" crops were the best: apples and pears, cherries and peaches and plums, peas and beans, wheat, rye, oats, buckwheat, corn. After some discussion, Pike and Trueworthy had agreed that "base" crops must be grown as well, despite the fact that they grew downward into the earth instead of up into the air. And so their diet included potatoes and beets and carrots and radishes; it had been a hard compromise but a necessary one. Potatoes, in particular, were wonderfully filling; in some happier future time, Pike thought, some genius—some other genius, a botanical rather than a philosophical one—would perfect a substitute for potatoes which would grow above ground, thus enabling the conscientious both to fill their stomachs and quiet their nagging minds.

Some other genius: and how was he to be born? The lusts of the flesh were the root of all evil; renunciation was the cross on which they were to be sacrificed. In that, the Shakers were correct. Increasingly as the summer passed, Pike had thought longingly of the busy, self-contained community not three miles distant. Why was he staying on at Bountiful, when there, so close by, lived those who practiced his beliefs?

He watched Trueworthy finish the last of his bread. The philosopher closed his eyes for a moment of meditation. There was now on Pike's long, sour face an expression very close to contempt, for he had come to know this man better, perhaps, than he had anticipated. Trueworthy was brilliant, but he was weak in the matter of his wife. Another month; two at the most, thought Pike. Then, if he still wavers, if he still cannot give her up, I will leave him.

34

In the late afternoon Sabra walked with Silas through the meadow to the orchard. The sun sank toward the distant mountains, casting long shadows on the grass. In the adjoining field they could see the tall figure of Amos Brown as he walked a rough furrow sowing a late crop.

Silas took her hand. "Peaceful, is it not? A place to restore the soul."

Sabra caught herself from replying that death was peaceful, too. She shut out from her memory the image of Mrs. Trueworthy's exhausted face. Instead she murmured "yes"; she held Silas' hand, she breathed in the sweet country air and tried to ignore the warning, hungry rumblings in her stomach. Supper, it seemed, was served late, so that the Community's inhabitants could take full advantage of the day's light for their work.

"Did you enjoy your conversation with Mrs. Trueworthy?" said Silas.

"Yes, I suppose I did. But it is curious—I came here to learn something from this place, from her. And yet I think she learned as much as I." And she told him—feeling slightly as though she were betraying a confidence—of Mrs. Trueworthy's questions about her earnings.

Silas, although he tried to hide it, was sincerely shocked; and she saw this.

"Everyone says that she is such a selfless paragon—such a perfectly attuned helpmeet," he said. "Was she really so curious about such a worldly thing as your money?"

"She thought that I spent it on clothing—bonnets and such."

"And when you told her where it went, she approved, I suppose."

Sabra hesitated. "Yes."

Silas frowned. "I have been surprised, too, today," he said. "Apparently Mr. Pike is unhappy with things as they are here. He did not say so to me directly, of course, I hardly know him—but from the direction of his discourse and questions to Mr. Trueworthy I am positive that Mr. Trueworthy has been a disappointment to him in some way."

They came among the trees, which were laden with tiny green apples.

"How?" said Sabra. He had released her hand to put his arm around her shoulder; his tall thin body jostled hers as they walked.

"I don't know. Pike wants something, I think, that Mr. Trueworthy is not prepared to give."

"Is it important?"

"I don't know that, either. What seems important to me is the fact of their disagreement. If these two men, renowned far more than Henry Winfield for their philosophical solutions to the problems of living in this world—if these two, situated in what would seem to be truly a Paradise, cannot agree, cannot make it work, cannot find the way to show the rest of us—" He shook his head; caught at a low-hanging branch to hold it out of their way; stopped as they reached a stone wall bordering a meadow beyond. Gently he took her shoulders and turned her to face him.

"But never mind that. Listen. I have something—some good news."

He smiled down at her. She felt the familiar sensation: because he saw her, she existed.

"I have asked Moses Trueworthy for his blessing. On us. I have asked —Sabra, he will join us."

She did not understand; and when, after a moment, she did, she saw at once that her slow reaction had hurt him.

"Join us!" She searched his face: no, he was not joking. "When?"

"Now—tonight—after supper. He likes you, you know. He spoke most highly of you."

She was annoyed at this last, although she could not have said exactly why. Was it so important to Silas that Moses Trueworthy approved of her? What if he had not?

"He didn't speak to me once, nor I to him. How can he like me?"

"A man of his wisdom doesn't need to hear you speak to understand. He read your face. He knows the pure in spirit."

Although she would have liked to pursue the question of the philosopher's sensitivity, she returned her thoughts to the more pressing question. Tonight! They sat on the stone wall facing the meadow. Beyond lay the broad Nashoba Valley, and then the distant mountains, the tallest, Mount Wachusett, towering over all. They heard no sound louder than the crickets' thrum. A peaceful, golden afternoon; a refuge from the busy world, tranquil and unspoiled, a haven for those souls who would live according to the spirit's dictates. And yet did not this place, too, have its unrest, its stubborn passions running close beneath the surface? Tonight! Suddenly she turned away from him; she began to walk back through the orchard.

"Sabra?"

He hurried to catch up with her. His homely face was alive with concern. He reproached himself: he had been too abrupt, he should have broken his news to her more gently. He took her hand again and held it for a moment; then, softly, he kissed it and laid her palm against his cheek. She stood quietly before him, head down, his reproachful words sounding in her ears.

"If you do not wish it, Sabra, I will tell Mr. Trueworthy that we—that we have decided to wait."

She withdrew her hand. "It is what you want," she said.

He felt a rush of feeling for her. How small and thin she was, how hard she worked, and always for him! He loved her very much, more than he had realized. He put his arms around her, glad that she could not see his face.

"I want his blessing on us, Sabra."

She felt his heart beating through his shirt, his thin gray coat. Last summer they had stood like this in the tent at Father Miller's campground. Then he had gone away all the winter; and returned; and surely would go again, working for his dream.

She wished that she could be alone for half an hour. She wished that she had someone—some female close to her, a sister, a mother—with whom she could discuss her situation. Mrs. Clapham, delighted as she was whenever one of her girls married, would have been horrified at the thought of a "joining" at Bountiful. Minerva Swan, perhaps? She tried to summon Minerva's plump, pretty face to her mind's eye, but it would not come. She shook her head. Just there, at the edge of her vision, she had seen—what? The familiar phantom, the figure which she had tried and failed so often to see; now it skittered away once more. She wanted to grasp that image, confront her—for it was female, unquestionably—demand of her: "Who are you? And what? Why do you come?" No: it was gone, fled into a field of light, its familiar retreat.

He turned her face to his. She saw in his dark, deep-set eyes an expression which she was sure she understood. O, to be loved, to be cherished—!

"How will we live? When we go away from here, where do we go? To Concord?"

"No. We will return to our separate lives. I must go west again in September. We must raise more money. And next spring—next summer at the latest—we will go into the Community together, as man and wife."

"Then why this—ceremony—now, tonight? Why not wait until then to marry?" Even as she spoke she felt guilty; she had never questioned his judgment.

"Because we are here, and he is here, and—to put it quite frankly—I want to take advantage of his presence. I do not believe that he is well." He dropped his hand, looked away from her across the valley; his face was troubled. "When I saw him today I realized that we should not wait. Not if we want his blessing, which most certainly I do. If we wait until next spring, he may not be here. He may not be anywhere. Perhaps Jasper Pike will take him back to England, perhaps he will fall ill—I do not know. I want to accept his offer now, while we have him. I feel that our life together will be blessed if we do this thing here and now. We do not need civil or religious ceremony. We need a spiritual blessing which only he can give. Mr. Winfield could join us at any time, of course, but I want Trueworthy. Winfield is a more practical man, and his Community will succeed where this one may fail. But Trueworthy is closer to the Ultimate. I want to hear him say the words over us. Can you understand that?" He returned to her, clasping both her hands.

She smothered her annoyance at his question; she was not a child, of course she understood. If only he had given her some warning—

"Yes," she said. "Of course." She looked down; she saw the blue-and-white flowered gingham of her dress. To be married in this! To return to the factory as if nothing had happened!

In accordance with what Silas had told her about Winfield's views on marriage, she had not planned for her wedding as so many girls did, had not laid up a dowry, had not embroidered sheets and pillowcases, had not sewed a trousseau or bought furnishings, china, silver. It had been more important—was, still—to give what money she had to Silas' work. And yet—was it to be, finally, an impromptu affair at this poor farm, an opportunity grasped rather than an event, no matter how modest, planned ahead?

Apparently.

And, with that, she felt a transformation. Her separate self suddenly disappeared; she felt a new person in her place. A very different person, as yet faintly discerned, but even now welcome, for it was not herself but her reflection of him. She no longer need be concerned about what she was. Only about him: and she would reflect his being. Her new identity would be his. Sabra Palfrey would exist as a name for a while longer, perhaps, but now—this minute—that person had gone. Instead, Silas Blood had taken on a new dimension. She would disappear in him: in his life's work.

She gave him her answer; she reached up to him, she put her arms around his neck and felt the sweet pressure of his mouth on hers. In her new-found joy, she had forgotten entirely the image of Mrs. Trueworthy's face: she saw only her own golden life ahead, safely sheltered against the world.

35

Moonlight flooded the orchard. The little band of celebrants stood ringed around the bridal couple. All were still; it was a moment of meditation. Crickets sang their song; one of the children yawned loudly. Up on the hillside near the road the white ghost of a figure flitted to and fro, but he, communing closely with his God, knew better than to intrude his naked body like some pagan wood-nymph on the ceremony beneath the trees.

The guiding spirit of them all cleared his throat and stretched out his hand to the two young people before him.

"We are gathered here tonight to consecrate the union of—ah—Sabra Palfrey and Silas Blood. This is a union of mind as well as body; of spirit as well as flesh; of life purpose as well as mutual love."

He turned his face to the sky; his eyes were open, his features contorted into an expression of longing.

"O God, whose teachings guide us to seek a life close to Thee, take these two young people to Thy heart and cherish them. Show them Thy Light, the True Way, the life to live on earth to prepare them for Thy Heaven."

The voice trembled. A night wind rustled the leaves. Someone hiccoughed.

"O God, remove from these two souls all earthly desires, all fleshly wants. Catch them up into the clear light of Thy Heavenly love and illuminate their hearts with Thy wisdom. Save them from this world. Protect them from its passions. Give to them the strength to live their earthly lives in accordance with Thy teaching, and let them know—"

A loud sneeze came from the ranks of the spectators. The speaker, thrown off his thought, returned his gaze to his subjects.

A silence. Then: "Do you, Silas, take Sabra to be your wife?"

"I do."

"And do you, Sabra, take Silas to be your husband?"

"I do."

"I pronounce you one in the eyes of God."

Silence again. Then, awkwardly, Silas kissed her, pushing askew the crown of meadow daisies braided for her by the children. A general relaxation; a small surge forward to congratulate the happy pair.

Sabra watched it all; most especially she watched herself—strange, new, adorned with Nature's tokens. It was as if the spirit of her former self hovered close above the treetops, not yet quite daring to depart, needing to make sure that this new person—this shadow of Silas Blood—would survive before she might safely take her leave.

She smiled and nodded at the gaunt, hopeful faces around her. One figure stood apart; he turned, seemingly impatient, and she saw his lowering stare: Jasper Pike, poorly concealing his outrage at the profaning of his domain by such a ceremony.

They stayed at Bountiful for three days. All the beds in the house were taken, and so at night they slept in a tent in the orchard. Silas was pleased that Mr. Owen's sexual theories worked so well in practice. He had tried to explain them to Sabra on their first night as man and wife, but he had stuttered and stumbled, for once in his life at a loss for words, and so finally he had given up trying to tell her and had simply gone ahead and acted. She had, he thought, behaved remarkably well; he knew that many men suffered with hysterical wives on their wedding nights—women who refused to perform the marriage act, who fainted in horror when they learned what was expected of them.

On their last day with the Consociate Family, Mrs. Trueworthy sat with Sabra under the grape arbor while Silas settled some final important question with her husband and Jasper Pike. As she spoke, she idly watched the baby, Conscience, crawling through the weedy grass at her feet.

"I'm glad you came to see us," she said. "I've enjoyed having another—having a woman to talk to. Perhaps you can come again."

"Yes," said Sabra. "Yes, perhaps I—we—can." She had not yet become accustomed to the plural; she reminded herself once again that she was no longer alone.

"And if we can ever help you in any way, Sabra, please let us know. Mr. Trueworthy thinks the world and all of Mr. Blood, I can see that he does, for all they disagree on certain questions of procedure. So if there is ever anything we can do—"

Sabra smiled in a deprecating way. As much as she had come to like this plain, tired, earnestly good-willed woman, she could not avoid a small spasm of contempt: help from this poor creature? The Trueworthys themselves, come winter, would need all the help they could find; their harvest, if indeed they had a harvest, would be little enough to see them through until next year. Still, Mrs. Trueworthy had meant the offer as a kindness, and she must accept it in the same spirit.

"Thank you," she said.

"Just let us know," said Mrs. Trueworthy. She reached out and patted Sabra's hand. "Anything at all. Oh, *Conscience*—"

The baby had vomited grass, and so their peaceful moment came to an end as Mrs. Trueworthy scooped her up and rushed her into the house.

Shortly afterward, Silas came leading the horse, and they said good-by to Bountiful.

36

The great wheel of the year turned, began the downslide into autumn. Operatives came, operatives left: some of their own accord, some dismissed.

"Why, Miss Swan," said Mr. Lyford when Minerva handed in her notice, "I thought you were happy here."

She knew what he meant: experienced weavers were hard to find now, and of course he was sorry to see her go.

Before the summer shutdown, she had sent a manuscript to Hutchins & Ross in Boston. And so when Mr. Hutchins wrote and asked her to go to see him, the factory was closed and she was free to go. She took the cars. She had never ridden them before, she had never been to Boston before. The streets were more crowded than the streets in Lowell on pay day. Twice she was lost and had to stop to ask directions, and both times they were kindly given. But when she found the offices of Hutchins & Ross it all became easy like a dream. In a dream, very often, you can do what never seemed possible in life.

"Minerva Swan," she said.

"Erastus Hutchins," said he. He made a little bow. He should have looked comical, a little fat man trying to bow gracefully, but he looked gallant enough to her. "Charmed," he said. "Indeed. Sit down, sit down. Have you ever written a book before, Miss Swan?"

"Yes, sir, but not published. But I've had my stories printed in *The Ladies' Treasure* and *The Ladies' Casket* and *The Jewel*. And of course in *The Lowell Offering*."

"Ah—of course, *The Lowell Offering*. I have seen it. Amazing." He shook his head.

"Why is it amazing, sir?" Of course she knew why, but she wanted to hear it from him.

He gleamed at her. His eyes were very dark, piercing; they seemed to say that he knew everything, although of course he did not and he quite openly admitted it. She found that trait most admirable and refreshing.

He laughed. "Never mind. You know as well as I, as well as the high muckety-mucks who employ the young ladies who—ah—write it. But I warn you"—and he shook a fat finger at her—"I want no *Offering* stories here. No *Ladies' Treasure* for me, miss. We're not that type of house. We want punch at Hutchins and Ross—we want punch, and zip, and turn-the-page." He patted her thick manuscript, which lay on the desk before him: *The Web of Life; or, Three Years in a Cotton Factory.* It was at page four that the heroine, Chastina Farnsworth, made her fatal decision to run away from a life in domestic service to work in a cotton mill. For the first time, Minerva wondered whether she should have put that incident on page one.

"How long have you been at Lowell?" he said.

"Eight years, sir."

"That is a long time."

"Long enough, yes, sir."

"You know the place well."

"Yes, sir."

He flipped quickly through the pages, stopping now and again to read some passage more slowly, as if to reassure himself of the page-turning qualities of Chastina's story. Minerva looked around his office. It was a small room with two windows overlooking the busy street. The desk was piled high with manuscripts and printers' proofs; the bookshelf crammed, books overflowing onto the floor. A single picture hung on the wall: an etching of the poet Shakespeare. Well, thought Minerva, his stories have punch enough even for Hutchins & Ross.

After a few moments he looked up and contemplated her. He reached behind him and took a new volume from a cluttered table. He handed it to her.

"Have you seen this? It's just out."

It was *American Notes for General Circulation* by Charles Dickens.

"No, sir."

"He visited your city."

"Yes, sir. I saw him as he toured the mill."

"Indeed." He grinned at her. "Then as you may know he was quite enthusiastic about it. He said that you all had pianos in your boarding-house parlors, circulating libraries, Lyceum lectures. He said that you were all ladies of high culture."

Minerva shrugged. "Many people have visited the cotton factories. Many are impressed by what they see. They come through on tour. Some of them spend as long as a day, even two days. Then they go back where they came from and write us up."

He laughed. "Very good, Miss Swan. 'Even two days.' That's very good. And I take your point." He tapped his fingers on her manuscript. "From what I see here, you do well to write under a pseudonym—ah—"

He turned back to the title page. "Matthias Simmons. Yes. A man's name is much more suitable for this kind of—ah—writing. The public would not stand for a lady's name—a female name—on such a book." He smiled at her, very jolly. "Obviously you are tired of working in a cotton factory."

She had not put it quite so bluntly to herself until that moment, but as he spoke she realized the truth of what he said. She was tired; and, tired or not, if her book were published, pseudonym or not, the identity of its author would no doubt soon be discovered and she would be dismissed at once. Better to leave on her own, with the honorable discharge; certainly she would be blacklisted if she tried to stay on.

"I am tired of it, yes, sir. But I must live. And so until now I have earned my living there."

"And from now on—?"

"I would like to think that I could live—even as Mr. Dickens does—from the proceeds of my pen."

Mr. Hutchins surveyed her up and down, and suddenly she remembered Mr. Dickens' well-published complaint during his American tour. American publishers pirated him, he said; he received no payment from copies of his books printed and sold in the United States. She blushed, overcome by her tactlessness.

"It is a highly uncertain income, my dear Miss Swan. The public is fickle in the extreme. It clasps an author to its bosom one season, and the next it will not buy his work, no, not if he were Shakespeare resurrected, climbing down from his place there on the wall."

In her confusion she could think of no reply except some foolish optimism. She knew well enough that the female public adored stupid tales of romance, but she had done with that kind of story. She could no longer bear to write what seemed so false an account of women's lives. If Mr. Hutchins advised her to cater to that public, she thought, she would reclaim her unwanted manuscript—she thought of it as her child, her poor unwanted orphan—and retire again to Mrs. Clapham's and live out her days in silence. Her soul rebelled at the idea, and yet—

". . . fifty dollars," Mr. Hutchins was saying. And, when he saw that she had not heard his previous statement, he repeated it: "I will pay you fifty dollars for the copyright to this manuscript. I will publish it. Perhaps I will lose money, perhaps not. It is impossible to tell. But I think that the appropriate time to bring out a book like this would be in the next six months, after the public has had its chance to digest Mr. Dickens' observations. Your tale will make an—ah—interesting contrast to his. Timing is everything. A year from now would be too late."

She glanced at the clock on the wall. Three forty-five. When the factories started up again, this time would be only halfway through the long afternoon in the weaving room.

"One thing more," he said. He tilted so far back in his chair that instinctively she moved to help him when he crashed to the floor. But of course he did not crash; he knew just how far he could go. He looked suddenly thoughtful, very grave. "She lives in the end," he said.

"Yes."

"It is not the convention. She should more properly die. They always do, these heroines who—ah—do not conform to Woman's proper role. Either die or marry. I prefer a good death scene, myself, with about a two-page speech of remorse from the young lady."

"This one must live, I think, and without a husband. She is not a bad person."

"Hm. No. Well. I trust your instincts, Miss Swan—or should I say, Mr. Simmons? Yes. Now: what are you going to do? You agree to my offer?"

"Yes."

"Good. You will have ten copies complimentary. Some publishers give only five. But"—again he waved his finger at her—"you must immediately begin another. At once. Today. Do you have a subject? A sequel, perhaps?"

"No. Well—not exactly a sequel. Another view, possibly."

"Again the young lady, her trials, her struggles, et cetera?"

"Yes."

"Good. It always sells. Try to have her die this time. Now you listen to me. You go back to your boarding house and you take up your pen and you write the first chapter tonight. Tomorrow you hand in your notice. More important, tomorrow you write the second chapter, and so on. Do you have a place to live when you leave the factory?"

"No, sir."

"Come to Boston, then." He reached into the drawer of his desk, shuffled among the clutter, and took out a slip of paper upon which he scribbled a few words. He handed it to her.

"This will introduce you to Mrs. Hathaway. She keeps a respectable boarding house in Bowdoin Street. You will be quite comfortable there, and she will bring you good luck. She has boarded several of my most successful authors."

She took the paper. He stood up, held out his hand. "My clerk will give you your money. Lysander!"

A spry youth poked his head around the door.

"Fifty dollars for Miss Swan. Have her sign the receipt."

The head withdrew.

Mr. Hutchins gave her a stern look. "Remember, Mr. Simmons, you must work! No idling! I don't deal with geniuses here, I deal with workers. Genius starves unless it works. They'll tell you when you die that you're a genius, but while you live, you live on work."

She heard the click of the money box in the outer room. As she went out the clerk handed her a small heavy pouch. She felt its weight; her heart lifted.

* * *

Hail Mary, full of grace, the Lord is with thee; blessed art thou among women, blessed is the fruit of thy womb, Jesus. . . .

Patrick said, why, Biddy? What happened?

But Biddy couldn't bear to tell him. She wrapped the ring in a bit of cloth and put it into his hand. She saw his look: as if she had put a knife into him.

Why, he said. Come outside, he said, and we'll talk a minute. The store was crowded, only one clerk there besides himself. No, she said, I can't talk. And it was God's truth: she couldn't.

Then he understood. There's someone else, he said. Well, he said, and haven't you done well for yourself up there with the Munsons. It was me that got you the place, he said. And this is how you repay me? Walkin' out? Who is it, he said. Tell me who it is.

She could not. She remembered the time he showed her the gold-piece, how happy and proud he was. That gentleman's my friend, he said. Look what he gave me—all this money. How could she tell him it was that same one, and he gave her money, too?

Get out of the store, he said then. That woman's got to you—Mary McCormic. Father Mahoney said not to go there, but you've been all along, haven't you? She put you up to this.

She shook her head, unable to speak. This was none of Mary McCormic's doing.

Get out, he said, or I'll call the constable an' say you were stealin'. His voice sounded like tears.

She went away, then, she went back to Munson's and took her things, her notice already given, and went to the place where the gentleman said he'd fetch her.

And he did, he came and lifted her into the carriage and took her to the place he had ready and put her down all gentle and held her close and told her that she was his salvation, his only hope. And she was, she knew it, had known it from the first. Something in his eyes when he looked at her. O God: was it a sin to save someone? She had kept him alive. But for her, he would have left it all, the mill, the house, everything. That wife of his.

At night Biddy could see the lights of the city across the river, and she thought of him working there, making it all go, and coming to her after.

Five months, and now the snow fell. And she had felt the first life in her.

Holy Mary, mother of God, pray for us sinners, now and at the hour of our death. . . .

* * *

Listen, said Mrs. Clapham. They're talking turnout again.

Sabra hardly heard. She sat alone at the long table as Mrs. Clapham cleared away the remains of supper. In the hall a group of women huddled, whispering.

Troublemakers, said Mrs. Clapham. Agitators! Have you seen the *Advertiser?* Rivers of blood in the streets, they say. The English weavers at Fall River are petitioning for Ten-Hour, they say. The English are foreigners, they have no right to petition. Nor have our American girls. They will all be dismissed and who will take their places? The Irish?

Sabra did not reply. Her back ached badly; she concentrated on gathering her strength to stand. She was dizzy, exhausted. I must get upstairs, she thought. I must sleep so that I can work tomorrow. In the morning she would vomit again, as she had for weeks past.

She must not miss time now, for she could not work past the New Year and she needed to earn as much as she could until then. O Silas, she thought: what am I to do?

You look flat out, said Mrs. Clapham. Get upstairs. That young man, she thought. Where's he got to?

Even Winfield didn't know. Sabra, desperate, had written to Concord to inquire. Somewhere in the Western Reserve, Winfield had answered; sooner or later he'll come back.

But not soon enough, thought Sabra. Whenever he comes, it will be too late. And when I must leave, where will I go? Who will take me in?

I hope it's not Minerva Swan you're worrying over, said Mrs. Clapham. Matthias Simmons indeed! I won't have that book in my house. I understand that the girl lives in the end. Disgraceful. No decent girl will come to the city to work after reading a book like that, all suffering and gloom and then in spite of everything she lives.

With a last worried glance at her boarder, she departed to her kitchen chores. And after a while, Sabra found the strength to rise and go upstairs to bed.

Not much time now: every day, every hour brought her closer to departure.

When she handed in her notice, Mr. Critchlow said that he was sorry to see her go. But he could not meet her eyes: his wife had just borne him another child.

On Christmas Day, after the other girls had gone to work, Sabra packed her small trunk, said a brief good-by to Mrs. Clapham, and walked to the American House to meet the unemployed teamster whom she had hired to take her to her destination. In her reticule she had ten dollars and seventy-five cents.

PART III

1

Deep winter. The small red farmhouse lay half buried in the drifted snow. In the barn the solitary ox waited out the shortened days until the return of spring, when he would work again. From the chimney of the house rose a thin spire of aromatic, applewood smoke, the sole evidence, most days, that the farm was inhabited. No one came or went; no neighbors called from the villages of Harvard or Still River. Through the white days and long silver nights the three inhabitants endured. They heard the bitter wind roar down from the north; they listened as it buffeted the house, thudding against the windows and whistling and moaning around the corners and down the chimney as if it would vengefully batter down the walls and whirl away those safe and snug within. It might have been the voice of all the hostile world outside, mocking them, trying to destroy them. Survivors of a lost campaign, they were reluctant to come forth to surrender.

They sat by the fire: a man and two women. The man, Amos Brown, had stayed at the farm because it was a refuge from those who persecuted him because he would not shave his beard. "The old Jew," they called him. On his rare visits to the surrounding settlements, small boys pelted him with stones. Once, before he ever heard of Bountiful, he was arrested on a warrant of complaint by a neighbor who had been offended by his beard. Brown was ordered to shave the beard or to pay a fine. He refused to do either; goaded beyond endurance by the neighbor's taunts, he had at last struck a blow. He was jailed for more than a year. The experience strengthened Brown's determination. He liked his beard. He would keep it. When he heard of the colony assembled by Pike and Trueworthy, he had walked to the farm and presented himself. They had gladly taken him in despite his agnosticism, his lack of fervor for their holy cause. They had not realized that running a farm would be so much work. They had anticipated long days free from the distractions of city life during which they could discuss and contemplate and refine the articles of their faith. They had not imagined themselves scrabbling in the fields. And then, just when they had begun to grapple with this new issue—the working of the farm—Brown had appeared and offered his labor. They had welcomed him, if not with open arms, then at least with quieted consciences. The beard was of no consequence; what mattered were his strong arms and back, his knowledge of how to plant a seed and nurture it to fruition. Even his insistence on the ox came, in time, to be forgiven, when they saw how fast their meager supply of food was being consumed.

All through the golden autumn, through the harvest of the small crop of oats and rye, apples and pears, Brown had stayed and worked: silent amid the eternal conversation, steadfast when, with the first chill of winter, the faithful had begun to drift away like the cheated remnants of an audience at the end of a disappointing entertainment. And when finally he was left alone, he resolved to stay on and work the farm and open the door to wayfarers, to the world's dispossessed, even as it had been opened to him.

He was not alone for long. In mid-December, before the first heavy snow, he was working one afternoon in the barn, repairing a piece of harness, when he heard a loud knock at the kitchen door of the house. Emerging to greet the caller, he saw a woman of perhaps thirty-five or -six, fashionably dressed in a blue, fur-trimmed pelisse with a matching blue bonnet and fur muff.

"Sorry, ma'am," he said. "No one's t' home."

She started at his first words, her hand dramatically flown to her bosom; then she relaxed a little and surveyed him.

"You are at home, I see," she said. Her voice was high and sweetly challenging: the voice of the determined charmer. "Where is Mr. Trueworthy?"

"Gone, ma'am."

"Gone?" She took a few tentative steps across the yard toward him; as she came nearer he could see that she wore—yes, certainly—a spot of color on each cheek. Her brown front curled improbably from beneath the brim of her bonnet: surely it did not quite match the heavy chignon behind? "But—that's impossible. How can he be gone? He knew I was coming. I wrote to him. Where is he?"

Brown lifted his broad shoulders and dropped them again. "He went to Harvard Village for a few days. He may be back in Concord now."

The woman glanced around the deserted farmyard. Her bright, expectant look had hardened into an expression of calculation. She seemed to debate with herself for a moment; then she smiled at Brown engagingly and held out her hand.

"I am Lizzie Crabbe," she said. "I am one of Mr. Trueworthy's most devoted admirers. I knew him in Boston, years ago. You are—ah—?"

Brown introduced himself and even took her hand, releasing it at once. In the moment that he met her glance he saw that her eyes were blue, very bright, illuminating her heart-shaped face.

"How do you do, Mr. Brown," she said. She laughed. "I seem to have come too late. I have missed all the excitement."

"Yes, ma'am," he said. "Though the excitement was pretty well over by the end of the summer. The last couple of months were pretty grim."

She gazed up at him with a gratifying show of interest. "Is that so? But how very sad—I thought it was all going so well, I thought it would go on forever."

"No, ma'am. They wasn't up to it."

"But you must tell me all about it, Mr. Brown." She turned and walked toward the house; automatically he accompanied her. "Did they quarrel?" she said. "Did they find an error in their system?"

"They did." They came to the kitchen door. Swiftly she caught up the small valise which she had deposited on the doorstep and allowed him to usher her, the first of his wayfarers, across the threshold.

In the days immediately following Lizzie Crabbe's arrival, as Brown gave to her to the best of his understanding the reasons for the failure of Moses Trueworthy's dream, there came a moment when both of them accepted the fact that she would stay awhile. One evening after supper, as they sat by the hearth, Brown was attempting yet again to explain the collapse of the Consociate Family. He sighed deeply, staring at the fire, loath to live again the last unpleasant weeks of Trueworthy's presence, and yet feeling that he owed at least some account of the debacle to this tardy devotee.

"He didn't bargain on Jasper Pike, you see," he said. "And Pike—Lord, what a man!—Pike didn't bargain on *her*. Those two hated each other. Maybe they always did, I don't know, I never knew either of 'em before this past summer, but they hated each other then, sure enough, and both of 'em was ready to fight to the death, if need be."

"Fight?" said Lizzie. "I thought everyone here was in harmony. What would they fight over?"

"Him."

Their eyes met and held, even as their faces flushed.

"Yes," she said at last. "I see. I had not realized—but then, one cannot always know these things. I met Mr. Pike only a few times. I sensed in him some disquiet, some desire—but not that," she added quickly. She laughed a little to conceal her embarrassment. "Where did he go? Back to England?"

"Not so far. There's Shakers not five miles distant. He went to them."

"Ah. Yes. The celibate life." She looked down. "God's chosen."

"So they say."

"And Mr. Trueworthy was deeply grieved at his departure?"

"Deeply grieved—at something. The failure, more likely. He tried to die. He failed at that, too."

"How dreadful. To try to die, I mean, not to fail at it. How—?"

"In the barn. No, not a rope. He just climbed up into the hayloft and wouldn't come down."

She shook her head in disbelief. "Poor, poor man. And yet, such will, such self-control—how did he come out, finally?"

"They talked him down. Mrs. Trueworthy and the children. Just stood there and called up to him. Took turns. When one got tired, another one'd come. Told him they needed him, and the world needed him more —although it was the other way around, if you ask me. In time he gave in. Came down. Ate something. Told me they was leaving—everyone else'd gone by then, this was just after Thanksgiving. Told me I could stay on if I liked. I said I would, for the winter at least."

She nodded sympathetically. "It was very good of you to stay and watch the property, guard the house—"

"One place is as good as another to me. It's peaceful here. The land'll give good harvest if it's tended proper." He gave her a sudden grin. "And the ox don't mind my old beard."

A log broke, fell, showered sparks. The wind rose and thumped against the house. They heard the tap-tap of the dry tendrils of the Dutchman's-pipe scratching at the porch window.

It occurred to him to inquire about her plans, now that her mentor had fled. He looked at her. She sat opposite him quietly enough, her face averted, the brown front, which had been genuine after all, carefully arranged on her forehead. Only her hands belied her serenity. They lay tightly clenched in her lap, white-knuckled, betraying.

And so he did not ask her anything. Instead he leaned forward; she turned to face him.

"I could use some help come spring," he said, "if you'd care to stay. Plenty of room now. No one'll bother you. Surely I won't. I been bothered enough in my time not to want to plague anybody else. So you're welcome, if you like."

He knew nothing about her, this small, cheerful woman whose happy exterior only just failed to conceal a loneliness equal to his own.

"You are very kind," she said slowly. "Actually—no, that is not true. I was going to say"—again the embarrassed laugh—"I was going to say that I have many invitations to pass the winter, many friends who want me to visit. But it is not true. I have no one. No place."

He nodded, satisfied that his judgment had been correct.

"You are very kind," she said again. It was (and he understood this) her highest praise.

A week later they celebrated Christmas. Earlier in the fall, after their own small harvest, Brown had hired himself out to neighboring farmers. Now he collected payment from one of them: a slaughtered pig. They dined on it, and on apple and berry pies, and on nuts and apples and cider and a very creditable plum pudding. Afterward they sat, as had become their custom, beside the fire. Lizzie Crabbe worked at some half-finished knitting of Mrs. Trueworthy's that she had discovered in her bedroom bureau. It seemed to be a child's muffler; she could sell it, she thought. Amos Brown whittled a piece of birchwood into a fantastical creature which he thought he might try to sell also. It had snowed the night before, stopped during the morning, and was snowing now again as darkness fell. They felt snug and secure, sitting by the fire; the haven which Lizzie Crabbe had anticipated had not materialized, but this very different refuge was not unwelcome. The travails of her existence had not prepared her for kindness unencumbered by favors expected—demanded—in return. She could not quite believe her good fortune in finding Amos Brown in place of the philosopher whom she had come at last, weeks late, to join. She had thought to save her soul by casting it at Trueworthy's sandaled feet; instead, her soul was tending itself while her body took shelter and sustenance under Amos Brown's kindly wing. She put down her needles for a moment and watched him as the wooden figure emerged under his skillful hands. She had often envied the serenity—real or contrived—which she had seen in other women; now, unexpectedly, she had come upon it herself. She smiled at him, about to speak, when she heard a knock at the front door.

At first she did not recognize the sound. She thought it was a loose board, an unclasped shutter banging in the wind. But Amos got to his feet at once and went to answer. Was it one of the village folk, perhaps, come to harass them? She heard Amos' voice, and then a reply. Hastily she rose and went to see for herself.

On the narrow porch, indistinct in the fading light, stood a woman—a shawled figure white with snow. As Lizzie came up behind Brown, he stood aside to let the stranger in. She stepped across the threshold while Brown snatched in her trunk and slammed shut the door against the winter night.

"Quick," said Brown, "get her some coffee. She's half froze. Never mind—I know her—here, girl, have this"—and he took Lizzie's shawl from a peg by the door; unwrapping the stranger's own, he put the dry one around her shoulders and led her into the parlor.

Lizzie hurried to fetch the coffee warming at the kitchen hearth. She returned to find Amos settling the new arrival by the fire, clucking anxiously as he rubbed her frozen hands.

Lizzie was aflame with curiosity: who was this person? Why had she come? But she held back her questions, and went to fill a plate with leftover pork and apple pie.

The girl's first words had been an inquiry for Adelaide Trueworthy. When Brown told her that Mrs. Trueworthy had gone, that everyone had gone, she said no more. She sat quietly, her face expressionless, allowing them to tend to her. Somewhat embarrassed, Brown confessed to her that while he remembered her face, he could not recall her name.

"Sabra—Mrs. Blood," she said.

"Right. You came one day with that young fellow to visit. And you was–" He stopped when he saw the expression on her face. He avoided Lizzie Crabbe's avid eyes. Later he would tell her, when they were alone.

She would not say why she had come. Her pale face took color, her numbed hands warmed and held her cup; her eyes focused. At last she allowed Lizzie to take her upstairs and help her into bed. Before they had reached the top of the stairs Lizzie knew everything important about this girl, although she said nothing, merely watching with a newly sharpened eye as Sabra climbed heavily, unsteadily before her.

Lizzie opened the door to a small back bedroom. At once they heard a scurry of tiny clawed feet. Lizzie held her candle steady, but they could see nothing. This had been Rufus Larned's room, Brown had said; he had lived entirely on crackers, some of which, apparently, still remained to give sustenance to the nonhuman population of the farmhouse.

Sabra made no reaction to the sound. After a moment she took the candle from Lizzie's hand and walked into the room. It was a desolate place: a small bed, a chest of drawers, a framed quotation on the wall, and both it and the wall stained from leaks in the sharply sloping roof. "Temperance is the Harald of Holiness," it read.

Sabra put the candle on the chest and sat down on the bed. The room was very cold, its air musty and stale. In one corner was a small open box: the container for the mice's feast.

"I'll fetch you another blanket and a hot brick," said Lizzie. "You just sit. Tonight you'll have a good rest, and tomorrow–"

"Tomorrow I'll go," said Sabra. She looked around the room as if she had forgotten for a moment where she was.

"Go! Whyever go? We've plenty of room here. You can stay until–" Involuntarily her glance traveled to Sabra's waistline. "Until you're fit to get about," she finished lamely.

Sabra sat quite still, her head bowed. "That won't be for some months," she said. "I came because Mrs. Trueworthy said if ever I needed help–"

"Mrs. Trueworthy needs help herself, now, if you ask me," said Lizzie. "A fine mess they made of it here. Mr. Brown's the one to manage this place. Come spring he'll have it all planted proper, and a good harvest in the fall. So think about staying on, at least for a while." She went then to fetch the blanket and the brick. When she returned she found Sabra asleep, curled up like a child against the cold. Lizzie covered the still form and slipped the brick under the blanket and took the candle with her as she left. Poor creature, she thought; and she went downstairs to confer with Brown about their new charge.

She found him clearing away Sabra's meal. She watched him for a moment and then said: "She must stay, Mr. Brown. You know–*do* you know her condition?"

He had not, until that moment. He paused, holding the coffeepot and looking at her with an expression of such dismay that she could hardly refrain from laughing.

"You mustn't worry, Mr. Brown. We'll manage."

He shook his head; as they settled themselves again before the fire, he told her of the wedding in the orchard, and the daisy crown, and Trueworthy's blessing.

Lizzie was briefly enchanted, but she promptly forgot her delight in the scene as she considered the missing bridegroom.

"Where is he, then? It's ridiculous—to marry someone and go off—"

"He's preachin' somewhere, no doubt," said Brown. "That's what they do, those folks—preach and preach and preach. The world'll fall down around them and still they'll go on preachin'. He'll turn up, still yappin'. I wonder what he'll have to say to her."

Snow fell heavily during the night. By morning it had drifted halfway up the windows. Even if Sabra had continued in her resolve to leave she could not have done so; but after her long sleep, and a hearty breakfast, she allowed herself to be persuaded to stay. It was not as if she were imposing, Lizzie said: "We're glad of the company, and since you've no place—"

No place: no refuge but this. Her breath fogged the window; she rubbed a spot clear and looked out across the endless white wasteland. They might have been on the moon. Somewhere, beyond their imprisonment, was Silas. He did not know where she was; she had left no word. But, finding her gone from Mrs. Clapham's, surely he would guess. He would come. She closed her eyes and said a brief prayer—not so much to God, but to herself, willing herself to be strong. To live however she must. To see him again. She turned to find Lizzie and Brown watching her with some concern. She managed a smile.

"Yes," she said, "very well. You are very kind—"

"There," said Lizzie, reaching out to pat Sabra's arm. "It will be all right—there!"

2

The winter passed. Snow fell, and fell again, followed by days of brilliant sun, blinding light on the white landscape; by clear bitter nights when the stars glittering in the black sky seemed close enough to shower down. Sabra wondered occasionally what it would matter if they did. If the Apocalypse came now, she thought; if our lives ended, if we went to sleep forever—surely not burning in Hell, simply an endless sleep, the world stood still, the millwheel stopped—?

She felt sleepy most of the time. She felt bewildered: lost. She had been transformed into a drowsy, heavy stranger whose body had contracted some monstrous disease, who struggled powerless to control its growth. She had against her will embarked upon a perilous voyage whose destination was bloody pain; she knew nothing, thought nothing of the prize for making that journey. She could not envision the future; her mind was clouded. She lived each day not looking beyond the next. She waited.

It was a hard winter, the worst in memory. The annual thaw never came. February was colder than January. March brought more snow. It seemed that spring was lost forever. Brown spent many hours in the barn, companion to his ox. Once in a while he wrapped himself in his old greatcoat and his long muffler and broad-brimmed leather hat and walked the three miles to Harvard Village to the general store and the post office. He had a small supply of his own money which he had kept back from the Consociate Family; now, through the winter, he expended it for coffee and tea for all three of them and a little tobacco for himself. The villagers despised his beard still, but since his fellow eccentrics had gone away they did not regard this single man as a threat. They knew nothing of the two women with whom he had so kindly shared the shelter of the farmhouse. Had news of this new arrangement, this miniature experiment, reached their ears, they would undoubtedly have found another charge on which to arrest him, a charge far more serious than wearing a beard.

Every day, now, Sabra felt the life turning and kicking inside her. As the weeks passed, she began to wonder about it; she became ever more curious to see it. To get it out. To be herself again: a separate person. To hold it; to see its face. She no longer thought of Silas. She thought of the child, whose birth would bring back her own life.

"In the summer, Sabra, you must go to find your husband," said Lizzie Crabbe. "You can leave the baby here with me. You must find him and bring him back." She was a practical person who had learned well the ways in which a woman survived in this world. The preferred way—but not her own—was to have a husband.

Sabra sat staring at the fire, drowsy and contentedly full after the midday meal. Brown, for lack of any better occupation, had gone upstairs to lie on his bed and contemplate his existence; in fact, as they all knew, he would soon be asleep. Outside, a light fall of snow had turned into a blizzard. Sabra had become so accustomed to their being held prisoner by the winter's storms that she hardly noticed new snow. Sometimes she thought that she must have been there always, and would be there forever; for the rest of her life, she thought, she would live in the small rooms of this farmhouse, listening to the snow beating against the windows, the wind pounding at the walls.

"Sabra? Are you sleeping?"

"No." She roused herself to glance at her companion. In the weeks since she had come, Lizzie had been as a mother to her, or a kind older sister. I am lucky, she thought, to have found her in Mrs. Trueworthy's place; Mrs. Trueworthy, for all her good will, would never have had the time, the strength to care for me as Lizzie has.

"Well, then," said Lizzie. She peered at the neatly numbered calendar which Brown had made and hung on the wall. "This is February twenty-fifth. By June you'll be well on your feet. The baby can live on the bottle for a few days. You must go to Concord. You must demand to see him."

"He will come to me here. He will know that there is nowhere else I could be."

"Men do not like unpleasant surprises."

Sabra heard the warning. "You mean the baby," she said.

"I do. He thinks that he is coming back to a wife who will have been at work all this time. How will he feel when he sees his wife dependent, with a dependent child?"

"I don't know. We never talked about—about a family."

Lizzie contemplated the girl seated across from her, the heavily burdened body, the bright, pretty face framed in irrepressibly curling brown hair. Sabra looked very young, and quite helpless as women always looked when they approached their time.

"So he may be displeased."

Sabra returned the older woman's stare. "He is a good man, Lizzie. How can he be displeased? It is not our choice. It is God's will when a child comes. He must accept it."

Lizzie allowed herself an unladylike snort. "He must do nothing of the kind. You aren't even legally married, from what Mr. Brown told me. O, I know—in your own way you are. According to the dictates of your conscience. And his. But in a court of law it wouldn't hold for a minute. These men are fond of setting up all kinds of grand schemes to lead folks to a better life, and I'm in agreement with them as far as that goes. I came here myself to join Mr. Trueworthy. But sometimes they forget that they're dealing with real human beings, not a set of chessmen on a squared-off board who can be moved around any way they please and nobody the worse for it. From what I understand, Mrs. Trueworthy had a hard time of it here, for all her husband and Mr. Pike thought they'd planned everything so carefully. And it's the same with you. It's all very well to marry, either the way you married, or in a church or what, it's the intention that counts. But dealing with the consequences, that's another thing. They don't always take the consequences into account, these philosophers. I can't say I blame him. You're a real pretty girl, and he was going away again—no need to take on, Sabra, these things need to be talked out sometimes. Now listen: he's bound to come back sometime soon, unless he's had some sickness or injury out there. We'll worry about that when we know for sure. But for now we'll assume he's coming home in the spring. What are you going to do then? Go into that Community he's been working for?"

"Yes." Sabra stared down at her hands clasped together on her swollen belly. The baby gave a sudden lurch; she felt it against her hands, she watched the rippling movement under her calico smock.

"I'll vow he's an Owenite," said Lizzie contemptuously. "They all are, nowadays, all these Community-minded men. Mr. Owen is in great fashion with them, and his son as well. If they were the ones who suffered the consequences, they'd drop that blathering old Scotch fool like a hot iron. Do you know what I'm talking about?"

"I—yes." Sabra felt her burning cheeks, far too hot to have been warmed by the fire.

"Of course you do. And don't tell me it's God's will that you're with child. It's Robert Dale Owen's stupidity, that's what it is. Now when your man comes back, he'll try to practice that way on you again—listen to me, Sabra, don't turn away from me. If you plan to spend the rest of your life in Mr. Winfield's Community, that's all well and good. It'll be better than the factory for you if they go at it the proper way. But you'll have your work cut out, too, and you don't need to weaken yourself in the bargain by dropping a baby every year. That's right—you don't need to."

Although Sabra's face was still uncomfortably warm, her instinct for self-preservation had overcome her modesty. She listened now with unfeigned interest as Lizzie went on.

"There are ways to protect yourself, Sabra. Do you know that? Of course you don't. No one ever does, until it's too late. Now you take my advice. I know what I'm talking about, never mind how. While you are at Concord, or better yet, perhaps you should take the stage to Boston—it's that important, Sabra—you visit an apothecary and you buy a female syringe and some white vitriol. You dissolve a lump of vitriol about the size of a chestnut into a pint of water. *Immediately* after your husband has—ah—performed the act, you fill the syringe with the solution and you douche yourself. Yes—down there. Not once but three times. You must clean yourself thoroughly. Do you understand?"

Sabra nodded, still unable to meet Lizzie's eyes. "Yes," she murmured. She had never heard of such a thing. She could not imagine— Struck by a sudden thought, she looked up quickly. "Is it not wrong, Lizzie, to interfere so with Nature—?"

"Interfere!" Lizzie's voice cracked with indignation. "Mr. Owen's way interferes, too, doesn't it? The only difference is that his way does not work. No woman is safe with an Owenite in her bed. Have you ever heard of a Dr. Knowlton, Sabra?"

"No."

"He is a Boston man. He wrote a little book on checks, some years ago —on the means by which women themselves may prevent conception. He wrote it all out very plainly—the syringe, the white vitriol, everything. The authorities were very angry with him. They put him into prison for his trouble. They might better have given him some public reward. He is a far greater benefactor than all the philanthropists in the city put together."

"Many doctors say that women should have as many children as they can. They even recommend childbirth as a cure for consumption."

"Doctors don't die of childbed fever," said Lizzie, "and they don't bleed to death when one of their theories goes wrong." She laughed shortly, looking slightly embarrassed now herself. "Well—now you see why I am not received in polite society. Moses Trueworthy was my only hope, when I came here. I am so outspoken that no one else would have me. I was staying with the transcendentalists at West Roxbury for a time, but even they, as open-minded as they are—or think they are—drew the line at Dr. Knowlton. The moment I mentioned his name, I was politely asked to leave. They are trying very hard to be respectable."

For all her proselytizing, she did not dislike babies. She had often wanted one herself. But the means to care for it—to bring it up free from hunger and want, to live without the nagging worry of where the next meal was to come from—yes, that was the problem with babies. One needed a man's sure support when one had a child, and nothing in the world, it seemed, was less sure than that.

Several weeks later, as they sat together one evening, Sabra tried to rise and could not; and then the weakness, the feeling that her abdomen was falling apart, transformed itself into a long, slow pain, not great, but an intimation of the struggle to come. She moaned in surprise; she sat back.

"There," said Lizzie. "It's begun. It may be false but we can't know, so let's get you up to bed while we can."

Gently, firmly, she helped Sabra to her feet. Together she and Brown got her up the narrow stairs, Lizzie all the while keeping up a soothing quiet chatter—not so much for Sabra's sake, for she thought that Sabra would do well, but for the easing of Brown's worry. Much to Lizzie's annoyance, he looked very frightened. Why were men such fools about giving birth, she thought, when they never had to endure it?

"That'll be all right, now, Mr. Brown," she said when they reached the door of Sabra's room. "Go down now and make some coffee and I'll call you if I need you. Everything will go as it should."

And, having dismissed him as tactfully as possible, she helped Sabra into the room and set about the business of the night's work.

3

Pain enveloped her. Pain caught her up and shook her and smothered her and threw her back, exhausted, only to seize her again, too soon, before she had time to summon up her strength to withstand him. All the long night she gave herself up to him. In the dim and flickering light of the candle she was aware of Lizzie's face hovering over her, Lizzie's voice speaking soothingly to her, Lizzie's hands holding hers giving her the power to endure yet another onslaught. Once, twice, she saw Amos Brown's face loom anxiously, peering down at her, muttering words of comfort which she did not understand. Once, during a respite, she thought of her mother, who had suffered this to bring her into the world, whose own mother had suffered, and her mother and all women back into time: and who had died, birthing a little corpse. Please, she cried. Please.

The baby was born with the first light of the sun. Sabra saw it through a mist of fading consciousness: a tiny wet pink snorting thing, dark hair plastered across a miniature skull. Lizzie was enchanted. Expertly she tied off the cord and cut it. She wrapped the baby in a scrap of worn flannel which she had carefully washed several weeks ago; she held it for Sabra to see.

"A girl, Sabra. Look, how perfect she is! Can you hold her? Ah—there! See how she knows you."

The baby did, indeed, seem to know that body from which so recently she had been separated. She ceased the tentative cries with which she had met Lizzie's ministrations; she lay quiet in Sabra's arms and then found the breast and suckled. And lived.

Sabra lay back and watched her child. She had not yet emerged from her long dream; she was not yet herself. But she had, now, this charge, this treasure; she would be separate again, but never again alone; she would be herself, but more than she was, vastly enriched. In that cold little room, in that lonely farmhouse, refuge for outcasts, she felt as if she had, after a long journey, come home at last. And against all teaching, all reason, all knowledge of the world, she was glad of a girl.

"You need to drink now," said Lizzie. "Mr. Brown is making some gruel, but just take this first. Careful, don't spill on her—o, Sabra, isn't she precious!"

Lizzie beamed as she held the hot tea to Sabra's mouth. "What will you call her? I hope you haven't thought only of boys' names; she's as sweet as a little rosebud. Would you call her Rose? That's right—drink it all."

Sabra thought for a moment; the tea had greatly revived her. Although she felt very tired and knew that she must sleep, her brain had begun to clear.

"Clara," she said, trying it; and instantly she heard it, she knew that it was right.

Clara closed her eyes and went to sleep. With infinite care Lizzie took her from Sabra's arms and nested her in a blanket-lined drawer. Sabra slept.

For a week and more the baby thrived while Sabra regained her strength. On the tenth day she sat on the edge of the bed and then stood and took a tentative walk, a few steps to the window and back. She longed to see the outdoors again, although snow still covered the ground. When she returned to her bed and lay back she felt as if she had gone a great distance. And then, for the first time in many days, she thought of Silas.

She called him up to the front of her mind: she saw his tall, lanky form, his thin face, heard his flat sardonic voice whose tone changed drastically only when he was in the presence of those few whom he considered his superiors: Trueworthy, Winfield. Suddenly she longed to see him. Ah, where was he? He must be told of his child: he must see her. A week or two more, she thought, and I will ask Mr. Brown to take a letter to Harvard Village, to the post office. I will write to Mr. Winfield again. Surely by that time he will have news. She closed her eyes, comforted by her resolve. We are safe here for a while, she thought; and come spring, come summer, the Community will begin and we will have our home.

One afternoon several days later she was awakened from a half-dream, half-drowse, by Lizzie's anxious voice.

"Sabra—Sabra, wake up! The baby—"

At once she was alert, sitting up. Lizzie had lifted Clara from the drawer; now she gave her to Sabra.

"She can't seem to open her eyes, Sabra. And look, she's gone so pale. Her little hands are stone cold—"

The baby did not awaken; she could not nurse. But they felt a heartbeat—faint, fluttering, but still discernible.

"Mr. Brown!" Lizzie's voice was harsh; she fought down her panic.

He came upstairs in a rush, hearing the urgency in her call. He looked at Clara, lying still in her mother's arms; he looked at the two women who seemed to think that he could help. He could not help: he knew nothing of babies, nothing of doctoring. But—yes. He knew where they could go.

"Bundle up," he said sharply.

They stared at him as if he had uttered a profanity.

"That's right—we're all goin'," he said. "The snow's hard-packed an' it's not too cold today—about freezin', maybe. Quick, now! We still have a good four hours of light." He remembered Sabra's condition. "If you can't walk it, missus, I can carry you and Miss Crabbe can carry the baby."

Somehow, despite her weakness, her trembling fear for Clara's life, Sabra managed to put on her clothing; they wrapped the baby deep in a blanket and somehow they got out of the house and across the meadow to the road, where the snow was packed down hard and they could walk with some ease. After a time Brown lifted Sabra and carried her; Lizzie panted on beside, cherishing her precious burden. At last a farmer driving a sled came upon them. Because he did not know them, he volunteered to take them on; and when he heard of their need, he drove them to their destination.

4

Dutton Street was quiet as a tall young man dressed in plain dark clothing picked his way through its slushy mud. His face, had anyone passed to see it, was pale and drawn beneath his high, dark beaver; it wore a determined expression, as if he had an important errand to perform (as indeed he had), as if he were unmindful of his wet and muddy boots, his spattered trousers. Then, too, his face showed the effects of a lingering fever which had severely weakened him and from which he had only recently recovered.

He climbed the three wooden steps of Number Five. After pausing for a moment, he firmly, resolutely, pulled the bell handle. He heard the echoing tinkle inside the house; then the footstep of the respondent.

The door opened a few inches. Mrs. Clapham peered out at him. "No salesmen excepting Saturday nights."

"Excuse me—Mrs. Clapham—you may remember me—"

Her hand went quickly to her mouth, whether in joy or fear it was at first impossible to tell; then the light in her sharp eye betrayed her. She threw open the door.

"Why—it's Mr. Blood, isn't it? Come in, do come in—my, it's been a while since we've seen you! It's nasty cold still, but we'll be warm soon enough—"

She talked him into the house; without actually touching him, she steered him into her private parlor. Despite the imminence of the noon bell she could not abandon him. She was too eager to hear what she thought he had to say.

"Now just sit down. I must know all about Sabra. How is she? We miss her terribly, she was such a good, sensible—" Her voice wound down like a machine which had lost its power. "What is it, Mr. Blood? Don't tell me she's ill? Where is she?"

He was too surprised to lie. "I assumed that she was here, Mrs. Clapham."

"But—no. No. She left us on Christmas Day. She said she was going to a new life."

They stared helplessly at each other, bound for an instant in their common dilemma.

"I thought she was with you," Mrs. Clapham finished lamely.

Silas shook his head. "No. I have just returned from the West. I have not seen her—I did not know—she said nothing more? No address, no hint of where she might have gone?"

"Nothing," said Mrs. Clapham. "I've been hoping for a letter from her these past two months and more. It's not like her, not to write. She'd know I was thinking of her."

Images flooded his mind, memory consumed him so that although he heard her voice he did not understand the words she spoke. The meadow in the hot July sun, the orchard in the moonlight; Sabra in her crown of flowers; the happy faces wishing them well. . . . But no, Trueworthy had gone, the experiment had failed, Bountiful was no more. He saw it in his mind's eye: deserted, blanketed by snow, the silent, empty rooms which only last summer had heard such confident, hopeful voices. All gone now; except—perhaps—

"Excuse me, Mrs. Clapham, I am sorry to have troubled you. It was a pleasure—no, don't see me out—"

Mrs. Clapham's curiosity, aroused so quickly and now frustrated so cruelly, made her more bold than ordinarily she would have dared to be. She followed him into the hall; she plucked at his sleeve.

"If you stay to dinner, Mr. Blood, I'll ask the girls. Someone may have heard and just forgot to tell me—"

"No. You have been very kind. Good day to you—"

He escaped. As he hurried down the steps he heard the noon bell. He quickened his pace; he did not want to get caught up in a mob of hungry operatives. Bountiful: that ill-begotten child of Trueworthy's fancy, of Pike's obsessions—abandoned now, testament to their folly. Bountiful!

Where else could she have gone? And why had she gone at all? Why had she left her employment with no word, no message for him when he came? She had no one in the world to whom to turn—certainly she no longer had the Bradshaws. That very isolation, that loneliness, had been part of her attraction, had made her seem more vulnerable and therefore more desirable. For the ones whom we can most easily hurt are the ones to whom we are most often drawn; the well-defended fortress, strongly set about with guards, does not invite invasion. He felt something brush against his cheek. He looked up and saw the first soft white flakes falling gently, inexorably, from the iron-gray sky.

5

The Elder's hands were large and strong, hardened by long years of work; and yet he handled Clara so tenderly, so kindly, that she did not cry when he took her, nor when he unwrapped her and felt carefully her tiny limbs, touched her painful abdomen, opened her mouth to see her tongue. Perhaps she is beyond feeling, thought Sabra. Perhaps she has already passed the line between life and death. She does not feel anything; Death has called her and she goes now to him and leaves us here behind to suffer her loss, to mourn her little life.

They stood in the Dispensary, an anxious audience to Elder James' ministration. The afternoon light had brightened for a moment as the sun made a last brief appearance following the shower of snow. Now as the golden disc descended behind the mountains the light faded fast. Sabra was aware of Lizzie Crabbe's heavy breathing beside her as she tried, with remarkable success, Sabra thought, to wait patiently for the diagnosis, the blessed herbs which would lessen Clara's travail. Amos Brown stood stolidly, his eyes like theirs fastened on the tiny patient whom he had entrusted to the wisdom of this colony of Mother Ann's disciples. He did not know, nor did he care, if Harvard Village held a doctor. He had no time for doctors: sawbones all, cut off your leg as quick as look at you, too anxious to get on to the next patient to attend properly to the one at hand. And never—and this was the worst of it, to Brown—never admit that the illness passed their understanding.

These people were different. For all their arrogance, for all their maddening insistence that they must renounce God's world in order to survive it, they were honest—or perhaps self-confident—enough to admit that sometimes God sickened a body beyond their ability to heal. What was more, their very other-worldliness, their spirituality, seemed to give them a kind of insight into material things, thus enabling them to diagnose what a gentile doctor could not see.

"Take her, please." Carefully Elder gave the baby to Sabra and turned to the shelves of labeled bottles filled with dried herbs which lined the wall beside him. He hunted for a moment and then selected one and poured a small amount of its contents into a porcelain mortar. He ground it vigorously, not looking at them as he worked.

Clara lay wrapped in her blankets: still, white, cold, hardly breathing. Lizzie Crabbe leaned over to look at her.

"She's not in pain, Sabra," she whispered. "Be thankful for that."

Sabra nodded. Her throat hurt too much to speak. In her mind she heard a voice: her own. Dear God. Please let her live. Dear God. Please. She felt a sudden guilt at thinking the prayer. This was God's will. Everything was God's will. What right had she to challenge it? She must accept, she must resign herself. God had a reason for making Clara die. That reason might never be made clear to her, but she must accept it, humbly, as His wish.

No.

She started as Lizzie touched her arm. Elder James was speaking to her.

"Bring the little one here. Now. This will be a surprise to her, but we will help—so—just hold her close."

He had made a solution of the ground powder—Sabra saw the label now, it was "Dittany: *Cunila mariana*"—and now he held a spoonful to Clara's pale lips. Gently he eased it between them, some of the liquid dribbled out, but some—enough?—went in. Clara choked. Sabra held her up, patted her back, put her down again for another spoonful. Clara swallowed automatically, coughed, and lay still.

"Now," said Elder James, "we will put her to rest and you shall eat supper with us. Then we will look at her again."

He took Clara and laid her on a small cot in a corner. Expertly he rewrapped her blanket, stretched another over her, and tucked it in tightly at the sides. As he straightened to his full height, Sabra noticed that he was almost as tall as Amos Brown. And—she had not seen it before—a handsome, well-made man. He was kind, intelligent, capable: a good catch for any woman, she thought. She was aware of Lizzie Crabbe beside her. But no—she had forgotten. These were God's elect, they did not couple. As they followed him out of the room it occurred to her to wonder how a celibate had such knowledge of handling babies.

6

The horse was badly winded. He had ridden her too hard, but his anxiety, his sure knowledge of Sabra's whereabouts, had made him careless of the animal's welfare and, indeed, of his own. He thought only of Sabra: why had she left the factory? Had she had some problem with her health—a nervous collapse, a weakened lung? No: Mrs. Clapham would have known of it, she would have told him. His concern was overlaid by annoyance. He needed every penny, now; he had returned confident of her thrift, sure that again she would have saved a purse for him. Over the winter, as he talked his way from town to town, from city to isolated frontier settlement, he had had a stunning, wrenching revelation about himself, about his work; like all such new awakenings, it would die aborning if he had not the money to give it life. He had counted on her to help him. It seemed impossible that she might not.

By the time he reached the Harvard Road, the sun had set; as he urged the horse up Prospect Hill through snow-covered woods and meadows he saw the rising moon, a flat, battered silver disc in the ultramarine sky. Had he not been on so urgent a mission he might have stopped to admire the landscape, if not to rest the horse; but tonight he was oblivious to natural beauty, to kindness. He must get on to Bountiful.

When he reached the place where the meadow stretched down from the road to the farmhouse, he reined in and surveyed the scene below him. The house was dark; no light anywhere, no smoke from the chimney. But where was she, if not here? He looked again, and saw what he had missed before: footprints leading down across the meadow, footprints of more than one person. Intruders? Vandals come to set the place on fire? He listened: the wind whistled through the bare-branched trees along the road. He heard no other sound.

Painfully, stiff with cold, he dismounted. He walked into the meadow and bent to examine the tracks. He saw that he had been mistaken: the footprints led away from the house, not toward it. One set was very large, heavily indented; two were smaller, less distinct, partially swept over by the afternoon's snow flurries. Three people had left the farm. The tracks stopped at the hard-packed snow of the road. Impossible to tell if they had walked or ridden after they crossed the meadow. And in which direction—?

The horse snorted and shifted her hooves. He spoke softly to her as he remounted. Carefully he guided her down across the meadow, avoiding the marks in the snow. He could go no farther tonight. He would take shelter, and stable the horse, and continue his search in the morning.

He pushed open the heavy barn door. Moonlight streamed across the well-swept floor. The horse snorted softly. He needed to tend to her at once or she would founder. From the interior he heard the scraping, clumping sound of a hoof: another horse? Why had they walked when they could have ridden? His eyes searched the stalls and found a massive, bulky form: not a horse. A cow, an ox—no matter, evidence of the farm's habitation, a guarantee that someone would return. He led the horse into the next stall but one, unsaddled her, began to scrape her sweat with a scraper which he found hanging by the gate. Outside the stalls he found a bucket of water. He let her have two or three mouthfuls; then, throwing his greatcoat over her blanket, he began to walk her up and down the aisle under the indifferent gaze of the ox. At last he was able to put her back into her stall and leave the barn, pulling the door firmly shut behind him.

The snow in the yard was bisected by a shoveled path, the kitchen door unlocked. The house was cold. He felt along the mantel and found a box of lucifer matches. A whale-oil lamp stood on the table. He lit it and looked about. By the embers in the hearth stood a coffeepot. He picked it up: half full. Straightening, he held his breath for a moment, straining to hear a sound of habitation—a foot stepping on a creaking stair tread, a door opening on rusted hinges. He called a warning: "Hallo!" No answer. For a moment he felt uneasy. If he suddenly turned, would he catch Trueworthy's linen-smocked figure flitting around the door frame? If he listened carefully, would he hear Trueworthy's sandaled feet slap-slapping along the bare floorboards, counterpointed by the murmured syllables of his endless discourse?

He took a deep breath; he steadied himself. Nonsense! Best see to provisioning. He took up the lamp and carried it into the larder. He saw kegs of flour, wrapped meat, a barrel of apples, several loaves of bread, a large, half-eaten cheese. He set down the lamp, took the bread and cheese into the kitchen and returned for the light. He laid a fire and set the coffee to warm. Whoever had stayed on at Bountiful was a good housekeeper. Hungrily he bolted a slice of bread, and then another accompanied by a piece of cheese. It occurred to him that despite the silence, someone—some real person—might still be in the house. Might be waiting upstairs after hearing him come in; might be frightened enough to come down armed with a weapon—the ones who remained might have none of Trueworthy's open hospitality. He listened again: no sound. Still: best be careful. He took the lamp and climbed the stairs. He looked into each small bedroom; he saw no one. In one of the rooms the bed was rumpled, unmade, the covers thrown back; and in that room, too, a drawer lay on the floor. Odd. He went downstairs again. The wind rose, buffeting the house. He was glad of the fire. Wait, he thought. They will come back.

They arrived at mid-morning, a little caravan deposited at the top of the meadow by the Brother deputed to drive them in a wagon. Silas saw her, saw that she carried something—a blanket-wrapped bundle. He saw the alarm on their faces at the smoke from the chimney. He stepped out onto the porch to greet them.

7

The word went out from Father Miller: October 22, 1844. The world will end that day. Christ will come in His flaming chariot, He will snatch up to Heaven those souls which are saved, He will consign to endless Hell everyone else.

They had pestered him unmercifully to set the date. He was afraid: once, twice before he had announced it and nothing had happened. The sun had risen at dawn and set again in the evening; the sky had remained inviolate, unbroken by the appearance of the Lord; streams had run calmly in their beds, the oceans rose and fell with the turn of the tide, mountains and valleys remained unshaken, cities stood firm where they were built.

His humiliation had almost killed him. He had withdrawn, retreated from public view. He had beseeched his God to enlighten him. He had worn down countless pencils to tiny stubs, he had used up reams of paper, figuring, calculating, tracing out endless mathematical formulae into webs and spirals of squiggly numbers; and then, still unsure, he had figured all over again and—dear Lord!—had come out with a different answer. The poor old man was half mad with his arithmetic. Eyes glazed, hair rumpled, cravat untidily hanging loose, lips mumbling and muttering as he struggled to add and subtract, to divide and multiply—hurry! Hurry! His followers nagged at him, they questioned him every day, they hungered insatiably for the blessed numerals which fell from his dry, swollen lips.

He calculated until he could calculate no more. He could not have added two and two—no, not if the answer had meant his own salvation.

There it is, he said: that is positively the date. Mark it well; prepare for the end.

The army of the faithful had their uniform: long flowing white robes, carefully stitched to the tune of a millennial hymn, carefully folded away until the hour of judgment. Where shall we await Him, asked the believers. Hilltops and graveyards, came the answer; on village greens, in the peace of your homes—await Him where you will, but make ready, for the day is at hand! Array yourselves, alert yourselves! Dispose of all your worldly goods, make amends with your enemies, flock with us to the highest hill, seat yourselves among the tombstones—for the dead will rise, as well, and you must be prepared to welcome them.

All through the summer the agitation swelled in the hearts of the faithful. People left their work to pray; as autumn drew on, they neglected the harvest to assemble to sing hymns. Crops were left to rot while people made their peace with God; old debts were settled, quarrels made up, property given away in anticipation of the end.

In the farmhouse at Bountiful, Lizzie Crabbe sat in the light of Mrs. Trueworthy's whale-oil lamp and stitched a Millerite robe. Insects buzzed and fluttered around the narrow glass chimney; Lizzie liked them no more than anyone, but she hardly noticed them now, so intent was she on her task. Sabra sat across from her, sewing a little sacque for Clara; from the darkness of the porch, through the open windows, they inhaled the pungent odor of Amos Brown's pipe.

Sabra would have liked to ask Lizzie about her coming journey, but Lizzie, so voluble about affairs of the flesh, was strangely reticent about her recent spiritual adventure. She had gone one evening to a Millerite meeting at a nearby farm. How she had learned of it, or why she went, she never revealed. When she returned to them she had been unwontedly silent. Her eyes had looked beyond them. She had seen visions which she could hardly comprehend, let alone explain to her companions.

Sabra had missed Lizzie's friendship, for Lizzie now was caught up in a new existence, and her previous life meant little to her. She sang snatches of Millerite hymns as she performed her chores; she was to be seen at odd moments kneeling in prayer; she had taken to scribbling little lists on scraps of paper. My sins, she said when they asked her what these were. I have so many that I must write them down to keep track.

And still, for all these outward signs of piety, Sabra was not convinced that Lizzie's conversion was real. Why is she doing this, she wondered; for like all manias, the Millerite craze was incomprehensible to those unafflicted by it. Lizzie would tolerate no questions, no arguments. "I have seen the light," she said; and that was that. Sitting with her now, Sabra felt as though she sat alone, for Lizzie was not with her for all that her physical self sat calmly sewing in the lamplight. Lizzie's spirit had sprouted wings; she wandered in the vast heavens, she listened to hear the footsteps of the Lord.

The newest member of their household had claimed the departed Trueworthy's study for his own. He sat there now, as he did for long hours day and night, wrestling with his manuscript. It was a denunciation of everything he had done, every word he had spoken for the past five years in Winfield's service. To compose it was very difficult; he wracked his conscience by the hour, he held up to the cold light of objective scrutiny every idea, every value, every tenet he had proclaimed in Winfield's name. All of it had been wrong—foolish beyond description. They seldom saw him. The formulation of his arguments took every moment of his waking hours; he had little time to talk to anyone and in fact he had not spoken to Lizzie at all since he had discovered her sudden, new-found devotion to Father Miller.

He had not intended to do this work at Bountiful. He had thought to stay with Winfield until he had completed his dissection of that good man's philosophy—a traitorous act, as he admitted to himself, but no more than Winfield deserved for unashamedly taking five precious years of Silas' life in the pursuit of his phantom Community.

Winfield's dream would never be. Silas wondered that the man himself did not understand that fact. Winfield's Community was a paradise of the mind; it would never be lived. Increasingly, with each swiftly passing day, Silas felt the urgency of warning people against all such false prophets—against Winfield, against Father Miller, against the struggling transcendentalists of Brook Farm, the isolated communities of Shakers, against Graham of the unbolted bread and Fowler of the phrenological bumps, against Moses Trueworthy and his garrulous solutions to the world's ills, against the industrial Edens, so-called, of the factory towns—all of them were in error, all doomed to swift and certain failure.

The shock of Clara's existence had thrown him into two weeks of melancholy. He could not understand how so brilliant a man as Robert Dale Owen could have given wrong directions. Had he, himself, made some error, some miscalculation? He searched his memory, his conscience. He was sure that he had proceeded according to Owen's prescriptions. What had gone awry? How had Clara come to be?

He had had no choice but to stay at Bountiful. Without money, without prospects for money, he knew that he was fortunate to live on Brown's generosity. "Stay on," Brown had said. "You do your work, I'll do mine." And so Silas had retreated to the study to compose his warning, his denunciation. In his winter's travels, he had collected a fat notebook of statistics: the numbers of steel workers at Pittsburgh (and how many unemployed?); the numbers of seamstresses in Philadelphia (and how many starving?); the shoe workers at Lynn, printers and carpenters and hatters and plasterers and all the hundreds and thousands of dispossessed farmers who, mortgaged beyond any hope of redemption, had lost their land to the banks and insurance companies.

Now he addressed himself to these unfortunates, as well as to those who would help them. Be cautious, he said; be not deceived by empty promises. Beware the eloquent philosopher who approaches you with outstretched palm. He will retreat in haste, once he has had your contribution; you will not see him again this side of Heaven.

And all the while, as he was struggling with his task, all the long bright summer and through the mellow days of fall, he had struggled with the other problem, too: the question of what to do about—what to do with—his unexpected little family. As soon as he finished his manuscript, he had a further task awaiting him. Sabra and their child had no part in it. Soon, now, he must tell her. He had no idea where he would find the necessary words. All his words went onto paper now; he had few left for those with whom he shared a roof. Many days he hardly spoke to her. She did not seem to mind; or at least, she seemed to accept his taciturnity without resentment. He was aware that she was entirely preoccupied with the baby. Lizzie Crabbe gave her good company. Amos Brown bothered no one. Silas knew that he could not have asked for a more propitious place in which to work. And yet he was restless—anxious to be away again. As September drew to a close and October ate away the days before the winter's onslaught, he began to chafe and fret. He must be gone again—farther, this time, than ever before. Soon he must tell her, advise her what to do while he was away.

At least, this time, he would not leave her victim of Owen's mistakes—or his own. That fact, if nothing else, would comfort his conscience while he was gone. He had not touched her since his startled embrace upon her return from the Shakers. Had not desired to touch her: preoccupied as he was with matters of the spirit, of the mind, he wanted nothing to do with those of the flesh. Lizzie Crabbe had changed bedrooms with them so that he and Sabra occupied a larger bed, but he might have lain next to a stone for all the feeling she aroused in him. He remembered dimly his brief passion of the previous summer, but that feeling had belonged to another man, not himself as he was now. He was consumed, these weeks, by passion of a very different kind. It had nothing to do with a woman's body. His organ of regeneration was as superfluous to him now as his appendix. It never occurred to him to wonder what Sabra thought about his behavior. She left him well alone: that was all he asked.

For her part, she waited, as she had waited all the long winter before. She lived in a dream with her child. She was content to be as she was. Soon, she thought; soon he will come back to me. To us. And then we will begin. She had not followed Lizzie's advice; she had not purchased the items prescribed by Dr. Knowlton. I will ask Silas' opinion, she thought, the first chance I have.

In late September, on an uncommon day of cold rain and wind, Lizzie Crabbe left them to go to a Millerite family in Groton. When she had gone—with promises to write, with fond hopes to meet in the next world, a tearful kiss for Clara, a whispered word of encouragement to Sabra—the house seemed unbearably empty. Sabra returned to the kitchen and looked at the closed study door. And now, for the first time, she felt the small, warning tension of resentment.

8

Sabra looked down. Below her, stretched at the base of the tree, lay Silas; beside him, on a blanket, Clara. Both slept in the midday heat. She reached for an apple, plucked it, examined it. She took a bite. From her perch in the tree she could see nothing but leaves, branches, the two motionless figures below. She considered dropping an apple on Silas' head. No: he would awaken angry. She wanted no rancor to spoil the golden day. Indian summer: Nature's gift before the long cold punishment of winter. Having experienced one winter at Bountiful she had no wish to live through another. Therefore: climb down and awaken him, not with a missile but gently, sweetly, so that he will not be in bad humor.

She disengaged her skirts from the clinging branch and came down. He snored in small, soft explosions; beside him, between his body and the baby's blanket, lay his notebook. He had brought it along to work in it, consenting to leave the room where he had labored all summer only if he could bring his manuscript with him. He had worked too hard all summer, not fully recovered from his illness of the winter before. But he had been driven, insistent; he must finish it, he said. He would not tell her what it was.

She leaned over and blew a strand of hair from his forehead. He winced and turned his face toward her.

"Silas," she whispered.

He opened his eyes, looked up into hers. She had hoped that he would smile when he saw her, but he did not. After a moment he sat up.

"How long did I sleep?"

"Not more than half an hour."

He frowned. "Half an hour too long."

Eyes downcast, she accepted the reproof and tucked it away in a corner of her mind. She must not encourage argument. There were more important things to discuss—to disagree upon, if need be—than the length of his nap.

She composed her face; she smiled.

"Silas."

He looked up at her. He had taken up his notebook again and begun to read the last words he had written:

". . . and so we denounce these principles of Communality for what they are: vain, false hopes held out to desperate men and therefore seized upon not for their own worth but because of the miserable circumstances of the lives of those to whom they are presented. Any new idea will be acclaimed by one who has no hope. Such acclaim does not validate the idea; it simply confirms the hopeless situation of him to whom it is offered. . . ."

The words rang true. But he must continue, must not lose momentum, must not allow himself to be deflected. He lifted a curious eyebrow, tolerating her. She sank to her knees beside him.

"Silas, what are you going to do when you finish that?"

He contemplated her. He had hoped that her question, inevitable though it was, would be delayed for a week, a month, until he had finished his manuscript. Until that day, he did not want his mind distracted with questions, arguments, plans—

"I shall go on," he said.

"I thought you said that you were no longer sure about the Community."

"Not only am I not sure, Sabra, I am downright against it."

"Well, then—"

"By 'go on,' I mean go on with the way which I see clear before me."

She squinted slightly to show her attention. She sat before him, her skirts billowed out around her, her hair tousled, her cheeks flushed with the warmth of the sun. False warmth: each night grew colder.

"What is that?" she said at last. If only he would speak openly, freely to her as once he had done! These last weeks he had hardly talked to her of anything, let alone of his work. He seemed to have retreated to a private country; she did not know how to enter it, she did not know the language.

He glanced at the sleeping baby. He hoped that she would not awaken. How strange, to see himself in such a tiny creature! He had not yet become accustomed to her; he thought that possibly he never would.

He turned back to Sabra, girding himself for what he must say. If this had to be the moment, so be it. Sooner or later she must know.

"Sabra. I must leave soon. No—don't speak until I've finished. I want you to understand. There is a new way open, and I must follow it. I must go to France. No—please—wait. There is a system there which I must study. A new plan for living—an organization far superior to anything we have here. The disciples of a man named Fourier are organizing groups called Phalanxes. If I can master this plan, and bring it back, I will have achieved more than I ever dreamed—certainly more than I could have done at the side of Henry Winfield."

He looked away across the meadow to the dark red farmhouse. He saw Amos Brown come out of the front door and walk into the apiary. He felt Sabra's eyes upon him. If she utters one word of reproach, he thought, I will get up and walk away. I will leave now, today. I have worked too hard, suffered too much to listen to the laments of a female.

She said nothing. She waited obediently.

"I am called, Sabra. I cannot resist, it is not my choice. I am called and I must go. The work must be done. All about us the country sinks into a hell of poor workers, a hell of hungry folk whose lives are controlled by a few powerful men who grasp at the throats of their workers and squeeze the life out of them and then cast them aside like so much refuse. There must be a better way for people to live. This country was not intended to be another England, another rotten edifice where only those few at the top can breathe, and all the rest, at the bottom, must suffocate and die."

He sat up straight; his eyes glowed as he warmed to his subject. Although Sabra dreaded what was to come, she was so relieved to have him speaking to her at last that she hardly cared what he said. Say it, have it out, but tell me, tell me—

"Listen to me, Sabra. Do you know that in New-York and Boston there are women who work days as long as you worked in the factory—no, longer, sixteen, eighteen hours—women who sew shirts and who get fifteen cents a day? Do you know that in Pittsburgh the iron workers are near starvation, and that in New-York two thirds of the laboring classes live on a dollar a week? Mr. Greeley, in the *Tribune*, advises them to quit the city altogether and go West. This injustice is against Nature, Sabra, it is against God! It cannot continue. We will have bloody uprisings, we will have a revolution which will make old Sam Adams' doing look like child's play! Mr. Emerson speaks of self-reliance. Tell that to the men and women who went on strike in Boston this past summer—needleworkers, tailors and tailoresses who are paid so little for their labor that it is an insult to their human dignity. How can they be self-reliant when they cannot live by their work? You must understand how my heart bleeds for these poor people, how I long to help them. I cannot rest if I do not save them from their misery. It is my calling, and I must follow it."

She felt the slow, tentative stirring of rebellion in her heart. She thought of the closed study door. She remembered Lizzie's words: "Men do not like surprises."

"What about Clara and me?"

He seemed to flush; or perhaps it was only the warmth of the day, the warmth of his emotion for the world's oppressed.

"You must not think that I have not considered you."

"No. I do not think that." O, Silas—!

"You—ah—I will take you back to Lowell. You can board in a private home, you can find a wet-nurse, you left with an honorable discharge so surely they will be glad to have you back. . . ." His voice failed as he saw her face.

"No."

"Sabra, it is the only way. I must go, I must learn the organization of the new system, and the men who can teach it to me are in France."

"No. I will not go back to the factory."

"It is important that you earn money again. We will need it when I return. You must save every penny."

"I am your wife. I will not be separate from you."

She reached out, grasped his hands. She fought down her rising panic: months, years alone, shifting as best she could, waiting for his visits. No. No. Think: what will keep him? She had seen his involuntary recoil as she touched him. Very well: let go his hands. There is another way. Do not beg, do not cling.

"Sabra. Trueworthy is not a minister of the Gospel."

If he sees that you are determined to keep him he will flee all the faster. Therefore: draw him to you as honey draws the fly—

"And when he performed the ceremony it was a valid act—for me, for us. But it was not valid in the eyes of society. He had no right to do it."

You will suffer the consequences. But you will suffer anyway, any path open to you leads to heartbreak and pain, you cannot let him go—

"Sabra, I beg you to understand. I did what I did because I loved you. I still do. But I must go, I cannot stay here and do nothing."

Her fingers were stiff and awkward. She felt panic again, fought it down again (do not let me fail because of a button!), tore at the neck of her dress. Sleep, Clara, sleep—

"No!" He might have been gazing on all the devils of Hell instead of her white flesh. "In God's name—stop it, Sabra!"

She leaned toward him. She seemed to be watching herself. Move slowly, gently, do not alarm him—

He put her away so violently that for a month afterward she bore the marks on her shoulders. He sprang to his feet. He was appalled at her immodesty, at her display which, far from arousing him, only sickened and repelled him and made him long for the freedom of the sea, the fresh wind in his face, the comradeship of like-minded men which he was sure awaited him on the shores of France. She had revealed more to him, just now, than her woman's body; she had revealed her spirit, the workings of her brain. He felt suddenly cheated—tricked. Like all her sex, he thought, she was petty, narrow-minded, unable to grasp the larger issues. How could he have believed that she was a fit helpmeet for him? She had not understood him at all, just now. She thought only of herself. "Put back your dress! You shame me, Sabra, you shame yourself—" He took a step backward, narrowly missing Clara; he turned as they heard Brown's voice.

"Halloo! Come and see the parade!"

Brown stood in the front yard, pointing up the rising meadow to the road. A cloud of dust hung above it, raised by the feet of a white-robed throng which made its slow, shuffling way to the top of the hill. Snatches of their song drifted down:

> Now, hark! the trumpet rends the skies;
> See slumbering millions wake and rise!
> What joy, what terror and surprise!
> The last Great Day has come!

Sabra shivered. *Walk across my grave.* They moved on, pilgrims coiling upward preparing to meet their Lord. How calm they were! How confident that in less than a week, now, the Apocalypse would come! And in her desolation her heart went out to them; she felt one with them, for her world, too, was about to end, and she was as powerless as any Millerite to stay God's will, or man's.

9

"I am the Word," said Mother Ann. "It is not I that speak, it is Christ who dwells in me. I feel His blood running through my soul and body."

In England she had been a weaver in a Manchester mill. Reluctantly she had married; in agony she had borne four infants. All had died. In her grief, she had understood the wrath of God: He had punished her for the sin of concupiscence. From that time she refused her husband. The marriage act is an act of sin, she said, even as the transgression in the Garden. She joined a group of Shaking Quakers. They were strange people, obsessed with the spirit of the Lord. In their ecstasy, they came out of their poor and humble homes to disrupt the Anglican services, yelling and dancing in the aisles of the church, scandalizing the staid congregation.

The authorities put her into prison. She came out unrepentant. "I am the Second Coming of Christ," she said, "the Bride of the Lamb. Follow me for I am your Saviour."

In 1774 she had a vision of a new land across the sea, a place to build her church. She took seven believers with her. On board the *Mariah* they danced and sang their worship. The captain was angry with them; he threatened to throw them overboard. A storm blew up. It seemed that the ship might founder. Mother Ann looked up at the creaking, swaying mast and saw a golden angel. She told the captain that the ship would be saved, and so it was. From then on, he allowed them to sing and dance and shake as much as they pleased.

In America they suffered persecution and want, and it was some years before they could separate into their own Community. They were accused of being British spies; they were thrown into prison, harassed by patriotic citizens, beaten and driven from place to place by angry mobs. Mother Ann suffered frightful indignities. But their faith never faltered, and at last they began to prosper. They founded their first Society at Niskeyuna—Watervliet, New York, near Albany. After the war, people began to come to them. Villages, or "Families," were founded at Harvard Village and Shirley and Tyringham and Hancock in Massachusetts; at Canterbury and Enfield, New Hampshire; at Sabbathday Lake and Alfred, Maine; at Enfield, Connecticut; and, at New Lebanon, New York, the ruling Family. In the early years of the nineteenth century, Mother Ann's teachings spread to the south and west. Families were established at Union Village and Beulah, Ohio, and at Pleasant Hill and South Union, Kentucky. By 1844, more than six thousand souls had chosen to join. Their fame spread; people flocked constantly to see them, to observe their curious ceremonies, to sample and buy their products—woodenware, herbs, seeds, cloth, foodstuffs. The visitors from "the world" saw the neat, well-constructed buildings, the great stone barns, the well-tended gardens and livestock, the thriving industries. The onlookers were called "gentiles." Many of them could not understand how such a strange doctrine produced such obvious prosperity. Strange, indeed: celibacy was the rule, constant work and worship the way of life. Women had an authority equal to men's: Elders and Eldresses jointly ruled the Families. No one was allowed to own anything, but no one ever suffered want. It was a doctrine of apparent simplicity and good sense: from each according to his ability, to each according to his needs. Later in the century, Elder Frederick Evans would send to Leo Tolstoy some Shaker pamphlets. They were received and read with great interest by that tormented soul seeking his own way to salvation.

In 1837, as the Mormons fought their way west guided by the angel

Moroni; as the transcendentalists struggled with the problem of the Oversoul; as Father Miller spoke ever more urgently of the coming of the Apocalypse—and eleven years before the Fox sisters revealed their spiritualist rappings to a startled world—Mother Ann, who had been with Christ in Heaven since 1784, began to speak again to her children. They received her messages through chosen ones known as "instruments"; her words were written down and called "gifts." The hearts of the faithful swelled with joy at this new evidence of Mother Ann's love. It is the beginning of a great revival, they said. Soon all the world will flock to join us, and Mother's teachings will be fulfilled.

10

Eldress Hannah's eyes were brown: large, calm, peace-filled eyes, reflecting the tranquillity of her soul. Intelligent, perceptive eyes: she saw at once that this new arrival would stay only awhile and then depart. This one had come, not with a strong heart to give to God, but a heart wounded by the gentile world, a heart in need of healing. And as for the infant—

Eldress sighed. Infants were valuable. Perhaps, somehow, when the mother left (as surely she would), they could keep the child.

They sat in a small, bare office, Eldress behind the plain table, Sabra before her on a straight-backed chair. She held Clara in her lap. Cold November rain dripped down the window panes; the room was damp and chilly, lacking a fireplace and warmed only by a small box stove.

From a drawer in the table Eldress took a small record book and a quill and inkwell.

"You have visited us before, have you not?"

"Yes."

"And the baby has been well since then?"

"Yes." Sabra dipped her head to look at Clara's face; instantly she was rewarded with a joyful smile, a little scream of delight. She hugged the baby, kissed her—causing another spasm of chuckles—and met Eldress' eyes. Yes, she thought, I come to join you in your celibacy, but I am glad that I had her before I came. For I would have missed it all, had I come before; and although I will have no more, I would not have missed bearing her, having her to love. You never had a child; therefore, poor as I am, I am richer than you.

"Good. Now—your name again, please."

"Sabra—Blood."

Eldress, about to write in her register, caught the hesitation and looked up. "We must have your legal name. It will not be revealed to anyone outside this Family, but we must have it for our records."

"I understand. My name is Sabra Blood."

Eldress nodded, wrote a few words.

"Occupation?"

"Weaver."

"Place of residence?"

"Lowell."

"Do you use intoxicating liquors?"

"No."

"You have been staying with the old Jew, have you not?"

"For the summer, yes."

"Were you a member of Mr. Trueworthy's Community?"

"I visited it."

"But you did not subscribe to his beliefs?"

"I admired his goal. His means of achieving it—"

Eldress' lips twitched; her fine eyes gleamed.

"Yes. He is a most unusual man. O, yes, we knew him well here. We even entertained his disciple, Mr. Pike, about a year ago. They used to come now and then, sometimes with Mrs. Trueworthy and her children, and we would feed them." Eldress shook her head. "A fine woman. Misguided, but admirable all the same. Well." Her voice resumed its businesslike tone.

"Age?"

"Twenty-two."

"Place of birth?"

"I think it was Bennington."

"You think?" Eldress contemplated her. There was something about her—something appealing, some quality of being a kindred spirit—that Eldress Hannah, for all her intelligence, could not have defined.

"My father was an itinerant preacher. He told me several times where I was born. Once he said Bennington, once Deerfield, once Hanover. Bennington will do as well as any."

Sabra glanced down at the drooling baby on her lap, and just at that moment Clara spit up a trickle of milk. Sabra mopped it with her handkerchief. Feeling better, Clara smiled widely at her mother. She had three teeth; a fourth was just coming through. Sabra glanced at Eldress, anticipating the next question; but Eldress seemed distracted. She sat quite still behind the table, the pen held above the notebook, her gaze resting upon the young woman and child before her. Disconcerted,

Sabra looked away. The Shakers were supposed to be sensible people, not given to falling into sudden trance. What was wrong?

"Is your father still living?" The voice was somewhat unsteady, fainter than before.

"No. He died six years ago." So long: it might have been a hundred.

"And your mother?"

"She died when I was quite small."

Eldress blinked; she bent her head to see what she wrote. She took a deep breath. She met Sabra's eyes and smiled. Whatever struggle had taken place within her had passed, leaving her peaceful and efficient once again.

"You understand that you are to be taken in as a novice. If you decide to stay, we will ask that you consign to us your worldly goods. If you go, you may of course take what is yours. Do you have any money, any furniture, jewelry—"

"I have seven dollars and thirty-three cents."

"Nothing else?"

"A few clothes. Some things for the baby. They are all in my trunk."

"Yes—well, I won't put those down. You may leave your money in our strongbox. It will be perfectly safe."

Sabra held up her small pocketbook, handed it across the table. Three meals a day, work, peace, solitude—the world would go on (certainly it would, the Millerites having been confounded), but she need not suffer it. Here was her refuge, hers and Clara's; she asked nothing more. Would she, she wondered, emerge some day and discover that the world had changed, had been transformed—say, by Silas? No; never. He would make no difference.

Eldress took the pocketbook and, rising, went to a closet and took out a large metal box which she unlocked with a key selected from a ring at her waist. She put the pocketbook into it, closed and locked it, and returned it to its place on the closet shelf.

"Very well. Now I will show you to the dormitory. The baby—wait, let me make a note of her name—Clara?—yes, she can go to the nursery. I will have a Sister take her there."

"But—" Sabra remained in her chair; her arms tightened around Clara's small plump body. She had not foreseen such an abrupt separation. "She always sleeps with me."

Eldress' eyebrows lifted in gentle surprise. "In the same bed? Isn't that dangerous?"

"No, she had her own little bed, blankets in a drawer beside mine. She could do the same here until she is big enough for a trundle."

"I'm afraid that's against our regulations. The other sisters would be disturbed."

"She's very quiet, she sleeps through the night—"

Eldress paused by the door. "She must sleep with the children. It is quite safe; a Sister has charge of them, she sleeps in their dormitory. You will be able to see her—to nurse her—whenever you need. Come, we will take her ourselves."

Sabra's anxiety had communicated itself to Clara; as she stood up and lifted the baby to her shoulder she felt the baby stiffen and cling, heard the first warning protests which promptly became loud and desolate wails.

She followed Eldress out of the office building across a yard to one of two doors in a large two-story wooden structure whose plain, spare design made it seem, in the dreary rain, remarkably like an almshouse. Inside corridors led to either end of the building; they turned right and went to the end where, without knocking, Eldress opened a door and preceded Sabra into the room.

It was filled with two rows of low cots, all neatly made, all save one unoccupied. A little girl of perhaps four or five lay at the far end of one row; beside her sat a young woman sponging her face and talking to her in a soft voice.

No, thought Sabra, not in a sick-room. She patted Clara, whose cries had subsided, and stood near the door.

Eldress paused near the middle of the row and then went to the child's bedside. She spoke to the attendant in a low voice; directly she came back.

"I thought that she had recovered," she said. "Apparently she has taken worse."

She surveyed her two new charges with a worried look while Sabra wiped the baby's tear-stained face. After a moment she beckoned Sabra into the corridor and shut the door behind them.

"It is against the rule," she said. "But that child has been very ill. We are fortunate that the others have not been affected. Although of course none are so young as this."

She stood so close that Sabra could catch her scent: strong lye. They were alone in the corridor. Suddenly Eldress held out her arms; her face, encircled by her plain white cap, had a hungry look, an expression of sorrowful longing.

"Let me hold her for a moment," she whispered.

Sabra was too astonished to refuse. Carefully she handed Clara over, hoping that the baby would not resent being given to a stranger. The baby did not resent it. She turned her face to the new face before her, she reached an exploratory, clutching hand to the brim of the cap, she chuckled and gurgled and dropped her face to chew on the large white kerchief draped over the shoulders of Eldress' dress.

For a long moment Eldress held her—a moment in which she seemed to have forgotten Sabra's presence, the place where they stood. Perhaps, thought Sabra, she must revise her assessment of this woman. Who had she been before she heard Mother Ann's call? Were her arms the arms of a woman who had had babies and lost them? Or the arms of a barren wife who never held a child? No, she thought, that one is mine; you cannot have her.

They were all three startled by the sound of a bell being rung outside. With a sudden movement of alarm Eldress gave Clara back.

"Supper," she said, in not quite her normal voice. "Come along. You may bring her with you. I will take it up with the ministry."

Quickly she swept down the hall leaving Sabra to follow.

The supper which Sabra ate that night was as good as any she had ever had at Mrs. Clapham's, and far better than what she had eaten for almost the last year at Bountiful. Baked ham with raisin sauce, beans and bacon, potatoes, applesauce, tomato pie, saffron bread, pickled celery and cabbage, maple sugar cake, blackberry jam pudding—here, she thought, here truly was Bountiful, produced by folk every bit as convinced as Moses Trueworthy that they followed God's way; but in this place, God's way included strict attention to the tasks of this world, including the care of one's physical needs.

Clara drowsed on her lap while she ate. She was conscious of the stares of the other sisters at the long table; she avoided their eyes. Although talking was forbidden, she knew that in the absence of the two eldresses, Eldress Hannah and the other whose name she did not know, they would have spoken to her, questioned her. Like Mrs. Clapham's, she thought, they are glad of a newcomer from the world outside. But at Mrs. Clapham's, one had only to step into the street to be part of that world; here, one was shut away forever while the world went on, all unknowing.

11

She was assigned to packaging in the herb room. A number of sisters worked with her, all seated at long tables, all industrious and silent, all dressed alike in their small white caps and crossed kerchiefs and drab gray dresses. She, too, had been issued the regulation costume. The strings of the cap chafed under her chin, and the shapelessness of the dress, even for one so little vain as she, made her feel curiously sexless—neutered. As it was intended to do.

The work was tedious, undemanding, inexpressibly boring. Worse: it was lonely, for conversation was not allowed save at prescribed times in the evenings. Sabra found herself uncomfortably alone with her thoughts. She had not foreseen this isolation in the midst of hundreds of souls. She had thought, when she left Bountiful, to find a different kind of life: busy, gregarious, leaving her mind no chance to function.

Now she sat alone with the others in the sweet-smelling herb room, pouring ground Elecampane root into small paper packets printed with the name of the herb, its properties and uses, its origin at the Harvard Shakers. Thousands of such packets were sold to the world: Comfrey Root and Queen of the Meadow, Spikenard Root and Feverfew, Poppy Flowers and Hyssop, Wormwood and Life Everlasting.

From time to time Sabra glanced at the other women, her hands all the while continuing the motions of her task. Most of them did not notice her curiosity; they sat with eyes downcast, no expression on their faces. It seemed impossible that they would concentrate so hard on their labor; more likely, she thought, they were saying private, silent prayers, allowing their spirits to commune with the Lord. She herself was unable to do this. Try as she would to control her thoughts, she found herself reliving her last days with Silas at Bountiful; and then, after he went away, her short time with Brown, when she realized that she, too, must go.

She had once heard a girl at Mrs. Clapham's speak of a "broken heart." She had never understood the meaning of that phrase. But now, as the days shortened toward December and with each new day the full understanding of her situation came to her more clearly, she felt in her bosom, in the place where her heart had always beat, a throbbing pain which began with the rising bell before dawn, and burdened her all the day, and hardly left her in her restless sleep at night. She told herself that her heart would heal; she trusted that in time her memories would sink beneath the calm surface of the new life, the new home to which she had fled with Clara. In the meantime, she endured her aching heart as she had endured her first difficult days at the Commonwealth Mill.

It had been Brown who had suggested that she come here. He had watched her with concern after Silas' abrupt and angry departure. He had understood the reasons for Silas' bad temper: the young man wanted money, even as everyone else, and she had refused to board out her child while she earned it for him at the factory. Well and good, thought Brown; but he had seen her crying, had understood her grief, her reluctance to spend another lonely winter at the farm without even Lizzie Crabbe for female company.

Lizzie had vanished from their lives. Brown had thought that she might return when the world had continued, after all; but they saw no sign of her, heard no word.

One day about two weeks after Silas had gone away, Brown had seen

Sabra standing at the front window holding Clara and looking out over the gray November landscape. It was that dead time between the color of the leaves and the first fall of snow—the time, more than any other, when one feels that the earth will never again return to life, never again bear seed and sustenance. He had cleared his throat in a hesitant way, and then, failing to get her attention, he had spoken before his shyness could stop his tongue.

"You can stay on here, and gladly, y' know. That way, he'll find you easy enough when he comes back."

She had turned to him a face as desolate as the landscape. "He isn't coming back."

"You sure? Seemed to me he said somethin' about it—"

"Yes. But he will not. Not for years and years—too long for me to wait."

"So what will you do? Why not stay on here? You know me well enough to know I'm not hard to get on with, and the little 'un likes me." He had extended a crooked, calloused, tobacco-stained finger to Clara, who promptly set to chewing it. Brown had never had a child, nor yet a wife; but if this is the result of marrying, he thought—this small, gurgling, drooling mite—a woman might well be worth the trouble. He had no idea where he might find one.

Sabra had held tight to her child while she thought of a reply. She had said aloud just then the words which for days she had heard in her mind: "He isn't coming back." What in Heaven's name was she to do? She was fully sensible of Brown's kindness, and yet she knew that she could not spend a winter alone with him on this isolated hillside. Nor could she bear to think of boarding Clara away while she earned a wage. How were they to live?

"Thank you," she said at last. "But I think that perhaps I should go."

"Where? You've no family—"

"No. But I would like to make some kind of life for myself. I cannot just stay here and wait, and wait—I must do something." She turned again to the window, but now her eyes were filled with tears, and she saw only a blurred, dun-colored smear beyond the glass. "I had thought that by now we would be safely in the Community, Silas and I. Now it seems that Mr. Winfield will never start it, and if he does, it will be without us."

Brown cleared his throat again, this time with unnecessary violence. Women's tears unnerved him almost as much as their parturition. "You remember when the baby was sick," he said, "and we went to the Shakers?"

"Yes."

"Well. If you don't want to stay here—an' I've no hard feelin's, I understand all right why you don't—you might think of goin' to them. You can go for a trial time, to see how you get on. They're good people, if a mite strange; but it's a life."

At first she had been astonished at his proposal; then, thinking about it, she had come to see its merits. As Brown had said, she need not commit herself beyond what they called the novitiate. And even if she decided to stay on, Clara would not be bound by that choice; she could make her own determination when she came of age. And in the meantime they would have a home—a family, in fact; they could be together, fed and sheltered, removed from the cares of the world. The sticking point for most people—the ban on intimate relations—was nothing to her. Her husband had gone away. She needed nothing to do with any other man.

And so now she sat at a table in the herb room and sifted powdered root into envelopes. She looked again at her co-workers, and this time she had an answering glance from a young woman across the table and down two places. She might have been a pretty thing, if the principles of *Godey's Book* had been applied to her; as it was, attired in the Shaker garb, her skin innocent of soothing, softening lotions, her hair invisible under its covering cap, she was almost nondescript. Almost: but still her oval face held a shadow—a memory—of prettiness, and the faint smile on her rosy mouth gave life to her expression. Her eyes were brown, large, and deep-set, and they too revealed something more than the dulled, vacant look of her sisters.

At the boarding house, thought Sabra, she might have been a friend. Here she would remain unknown; for friendships were not encouraged at the Family, and all one's devotion went to God and work. Still—daringly—Sabra smiled at her, and she was gratified to see a smile in return.

A short time later the bell rang for the noon meal. In the afternoon, when Sabra had nursed Clara and tucked her up for her nap in the nursery, she saw that the almost-pretty girl was gone from her place in the herb room.

As a novice, Sabra shared a dormitory with other newcomers trying out the Shaker regimen. There were, at the moment, ten new women; the men's half of the building had a novices' room as well, but of course the women, and especially the new women, had no knowledge of the brethren's affairs. Sabra did not know how many men, this autumn, were attempting as she was to live this strange new life.

The strangeness was not so much in the communal life, for she had experienced something of that at Mrs. Clapham's; nor was it in the unrelieved, industrious routine, for she had always done her share of work wherever she lived. She puzzled about it in her hours in the herb room, her silent meals in the long dining room where all religiously cleaned their plates—"Shaker your plate!"—even as they religiously kept quiet. In the evening gatherings where new hymns were learned, or portions of

Scripture read by Eldress for their edification, she watched the faces of these women—these disciples of Mother Ann. They seemed stranger even than she had imagined. Why? They are like me, she thought. They have two arms, two legs, women's bodies, women's hearts: why are they as different from me as heathen Chinese? As Indian princesses?

At the beginning of December, work assignments were changed in the monthly custom and Sabra was sent to the kitchen. Here she worked with a dozen other women to prepare the meals for the hundreds of members of the order. Although the assignment necessitated early rising, she liked the work: Sister Ruth, in charge, was a kind and gentle woman, perhaps forty years old, perhaps sixty, whose strict discipline of her troops was ameliorated by a sweet voice and an attitude of helpful encouragement. Under Sister Ruth's supervision, even the clumsiest woman might rise to culinary heights hitherto undreamed of. From her little domain, three times a day, came dishes which would have caused any royal chef, had he tasted them, to curdle his blancmange in envy: herb soup, baked veal cutlets, chestnut pudding, mushrooms in sherry butter, saffron bread and lemon bread and pumpkin loaves, Rose Geranium rolls and butter orange fluff, chocolate cream cake, floating island, spiced cherries, pear honey. . . .

As it happened, the girl whom Sabra had noticed in the herb room had been assigned to the kitchen also. Sabra resolved to speak to her when she could. For several days she had no chance; but then one afternoon, as she was seated at the table paring vegetables for a stew, the girl sat down beside her, knife in hand, and companionably reached for a turnip which she began to peel. It was mid-afternoon; except for an elderly Sister at the sink, washing potatoes, the kitchen was deserted.

"My name is Philomena Pratt," said the girl abruptly, but in a quiet voice so as not to be overheard. "How are you getting on?"

Sabra introduced herself, and they talked for some minutes before the appearance of Sister Ruth reduced them once again to silence. But in the days that followed, they were able now and again to exchange a greeting, a few words of conversation, and so their acquaintance ripened into what passed for close friendship in that austere and self-contained Community, where only worship allowed release of human feeling, and all the heart's affection went to Mother Ann.

One evening toward Christmas, a party of visitors from Boston stayed unexpectedly to supper. Sister Ruth's placid face took on a harassed look as she calculated numbers of portions, seating arrangements, and other vital details which could not be allowed to disrupt the tranquil order of the Family. "Sabra, put some of that beef onto a separate platter," she said in a voice much sharper than usual; "and keep back some of everything else. You'll have to eat in the kitchen tonight, they've ladies with them who were put at your place at table—you, and I think Philomena, she's just taking out the tureen—yes."

They lifted down two slat chairs from the wall pegs and sat together at one end of the long worktable. From the open door of the dining hall they heard first Elder James and then Eldress Hannah saying grace; then silence broken only by the soft *clink* of knives and forks against thick stoneware.

Philomena had a brief battle with her conscience and lost it—and yet, so anxious to speak, still she hesitated. Then, whispering so that her transgression would not be overheard by the silent company without: "How is your baby, Sabra? I saw her yesterday and she smiled at me."

"She is well."

"Do you—forgive me, I do not mean to pry—but do you mind not being with her always?"

They had little time; the evening meal would be finished in a matter of minutes. Sabra had not the luxury of taking the few seconds to make a considered reply. "Yes," she said.

Some of the light went out of Philomena's eyes. "What will you do, then?" she said. "Will you stay?"

"I—I don't know. I will try."

Philomena struggled again. "And your—husband? He died—?"

"No." She was aware of her aching heart which just now, oddly enough, ached somewhat less. "He did not die. He went away. He had what you might call a—" What? She could not put a name to it. "A mission abroad," she finished lamely.

Philomena's mouth dropped slightly open in surprise. "But if he is alive—why do you not wait for him? Do you not want to live with him again?" Her face suddenly flooded with color as she realized the implication of her words; but then, as willing to be hung for a sheep as a lamb, she hurried recklessly on. "Sabra—can you tell me how it is, to live with a man? A husband? Is it—is it—" She could not, finally, bring herself to ask what she longed to know.

Sabra remembered Lizzie Crabbe, confronting her months ago with blunt advice. How would Lizzie have answered this painful inquiry?

"It depends, I suppose," she said.

From the dining hall they heard the scrape of chairs on the bare wood floor as the Family rose to pray thanks for the meal.

"On what?" hissed Philomena, leaning close. "On what does it depend, Sabra?"

"Why—on the man."

As the first of the kitchen help hurried in, carrying empty platters, the two women sprang apart like guilty lovers. No one noticed them; promptly they rose and joined the others in the work of clearing the meal.

It was not until several hours later, after the evening meeting, that Sabra realized that Philomena's oddly urgent inquiries had answered her own puzzlement about the nature of the Shaker women—that quality in them which had made them seem so alien, so different from most of the women in "the world." Of course, she thought: the nature of women has to do with men. These women are at peace, they are delivered from the search for a man—a husband—which so occupies the thoughts of worldly women. No wonder they seem so calm—dull, even; they have no need to be lively to catch some man's eye. They can live independent of a husband's support, just as the factory women can. But the work here is healthful work; no one suffers lung disease, no one collapses from standing twelve hours at the looms, no one goes mad from the noise.

And no one has a child, said the voice in her mind; and no one ever falls in love. To fall in love, to marry, to bear children—all the world's teaching pointed that way, and were not these women, separated from it, therefore terribly deprived? Therefore less? Therefore, somehow, not quite human?

She lay on her narrow cot—a single cot, for there was no sharing of beds here, no chance of accidental contact with another body—and listened to the quiet, unobstructed breathing of the other women in the room. Tomorrow, she thought, will be the same as today; and the day after the same again. She had thought that that monotony, that security, was what she had wanted: that, and time for her heart to mend. She had thought to learn from the example of the other women in the Family, to take strength and tranquillity from them while striving to find her own.

Now she had found one who was not tranquil—perhaps not even strong. The discovery unnerved her. Even these people, it seemed, had doubters and backsliders. And if others doubted, so might she; and if others backslid—

O Silas, she thought. She moaned aloud from the pain in her heart and the longing to put her arms around her child.

12

O Lord, we worship Thee, and we dance and sing and shake out our love for Thee.

For the spirit of the Lord is in us all, and the spirit of Mother Ann dwells in us, and gives us life.

For we are the children of God, and our lives we give for the salvation of our souls.

Then sing! Then dance! In square-order shuffle and marching lines; in ring dance and whirling gift, in cross and diamond and speaking in tongues, in warring gift to exorcise Old Ugly.

Strange melody filled the meeting house; the thud of stamping feet shook the well-made floor. Lines of swaying, jerking bodies met and dissolved, turning, separating, re-forming in new designs. The room smelled of sweat and damp wool. The building vibrated with the frantic rhythm of the dance. The worshipers' faces were faces in trance; their eyes were glazed, unfocused, their bodies writhed and leaped in frenzied passion.

The room had become the world: and all life was there, all love, all ecstasy in communion with God. There was nothing else. Sound and movement, movement and sound: come to us, Mother, come to us now, for we are the children of a free woman, we are chosen to mortify our flesh and crucify the demons of our lust.

On a bench along the wall, Sabra sat with the other female novices and with those sisters too old or too ill to participate in the worship. At the far end of the room sat a similar row of brethren. As she watched the dance, she felt the worshipers' ecstasy, she felt herself begin to yield; almost against her will, her feet began to tap out the rhythm of the song.

The way of God is holy,
Mark'd with Immanuel's feet;

Every Sabbath since she had arrived, she had sat and watched the service. It had been explained to her that when she felt Mother Ann's spirit enter her own, she would rise and join the dance. Until then, she was to sing the hymns which had been carefully rehearsed at evening meetings during the week, and attend the service as a spectator.

Lust cannot reach Mount Zion,
Nor stain the golden street.

Once, the Sabbath worship had been open to the public. Many had attended as a lark, as they would have gone to a circus or a theater. Often they went away sobered and repenting their mockery; they had felt the flame of devotion, the complete sincerity of these simple folk who had separated from the temptations of the world.

If you will have salvation,
You first must count the cost,
And sacrifice that nature,
In which the world is lost.

But some years previous, in 1837, a new fervor had come to Mother Ann's children: a visitation from the spirit world, messages from Christ in Heaven, from Mother Ann herself. It was the time of Mother Ann's Second Appearing. And in their ecstasy they entered into a period of wild excess in their Sabbath meetings, and they saw that the visitors from the world did not understand their new fervor. Meetings were closed; the world was welcome no longer.

The singing stopped. Everyone knelt to pray. Gradually their hard breathing came easy; their hearts returned to a normal beat. Their faces cleared. Where had they been? They could not have said. They knew only that the spirit that had sustained them through the dance had gone away. Their hearts were empty now; their eyes, which had seen visions of glory with Mother Ann, now looked once again upon each other, upon the plain blue and white interior of the meeting house, the stand of pines beyond the window, the dwelling house opposite—the everyday sights of the ordinary world.

But they had their faith to sustain them. They had seen beyond. Next Sabbath they would make that journey once again. In the interval they would put their hands to work and their hearts to God as Mother had commanded.

Later that evening the brethren and sisters visited each other in their rooms. Permission needed to be secured from the Elders and Eldresses so that each person's whereabouts was known: no one was allowed to make an unexpected call. The brethren and sisters sat in rows facing each other. Conversation was general; no two people were allowed to talk exclusively together. Nor was anyone allowed to speak of the world: the affairs of the Society, the work of the shops, the plans for spring sowing, autumn harvest, were the only approved topics.

Sister Philomena had asked permission to visit Sabra's dormitory. She sat with the sisters facing the row of brethren. Soft voices, occasional low laughter filled the room. They are genuinely fond of one another, thought Sabra; enforced separation has not stifled all their human feelings. She glanced at Philomena, two seats down; then opposite to the Brother on whom Philomena's gaze was fixed. He was a handsome man of perhaps thirty, whose broad, well-made face was ruddy and glowing with health. A cheerful smile, a pleasant word or two might have been expected from such a man, but he sat silent and sober, his eyes downcast. Sabra responded to a question from the Sister beside her—yes, she said, she was happy enough here, she didn't mind the work—and then glanced again at the Brother. He was staring at Philomena; his attractive face was clouded by melancholy.

The moment passed. He looked down again, and soon the visit was over and it was time to retire. Sabra stood with the others as they clasped their hands to their chests, bowed to each other, and stepped out in single file. The Brother followed Philomena with his eyes.

The next day Philomena did not appear for kitchen duty. Sister Ruth informed her helpers that Sister Philomena was ill and had been sent to the infirmary. Sabra asked for permission to visit her, but it was denied. One evening in the middle of the week she was returning from her time with Clara when she passed the door of the sisters' sick-room. Usually it was closed, but now it stood open. She saw that only one bed was occupied; in the glow of the single sperm-oil lamp, no nursing sisters were to be seen. She hesitated. It was against the rules to visit without permission, and a far worse misdeed to have a private conversation. Sister Philomena lay quiet, her eyes closed. She is sleeping, thought Sabra; I must not disturb her. Still she lingered. From distant rooms she heard the voices of the sisters learning a new hymn for the Sabbath worship. I must go, she thought; they will know that I did not need all this time for Clara.

Still she did not move on; and just then Sister Philomena, as if conscious that she was being observed, turned her head and looked at the figure standing in the doorway.

"Sabra?"

And now of course it was too late; she had at least to step in to say hello. As she approached the bed she saw that Philomena's face was wet with tears, and gaunt and strained—whether from physical or spiritual illness it was impossible to tell.

Sabra stood beside the bed, not daring to sit on the ladder-backed chair next to it.

"Can I help you, Philomena? Would you like me to call the Sister?"

Philomena shook her head, once, slowly, as if she could make no more effort than that. "Sit down," she whispered. "I asked to see you, but they refused me."

Fighting down her fear of discovery, Sabra pulled the chair closer to the bed and cautiously perched on its edge.

"Do you know my trouble?" said Philomena, very low. "Has anyone announced it? They said that they would tell all the Family if I did not confess."

"No—no one has said anything. Confess what?"

Philomena's tears continued to flow, but she made no move to wipe them away. Sabra took a clean white cloth from the candle-stand and gently pressed it to Philomena's cheeks. She felt the hot skin, she saw the fever-bright eyes behind the reddened, blinking lids.

"I am to die and go to Hell, Elder James said. He said that I must root out all my feelings or I will be damned. I could die from this fever, Sabra, and if I die now I will burn forever. He promised me that. They labored with me today in the ministry. I went there, sick as I am, because they had heard bad of me, and they called me to account."

Sabra saw the face of the Brother at the union meeting. Yes—and Philomena had questioned her that time in the kitchen—

"What is it, Philomena? Can you tell me?"

Philomena turned her head away; she bit her lips. Under the blue coverlet her body lay as still as a corpse. She hardly seemed to breathe. Only her work-worn hands showed her distress: they clasped each other tightly over her bosom, as if one were trying to escape and the other holding it back.

"Last summer," she said, still with her head turned away, "we went to gather huckleberries in Groton. Brother William spoke to me. It was no more than a few words, but someone saw."

Faintly they heard the sound of many feet thudding in unison on a bare wood floor: a new dance for the Sabbath. Sabra waited for Philomena to continue; when she did not, she said, "Is that all? He spoke to you just that once?"

"No. He has said a word—only a word, only good morning or good evening—several times since. And I—I have said good morning to him."

She might have been confessing murder. She might have been a woman of the streets confessing, in her death agony, the foulest sins of the flesh. Suddenly she turned her head to Sabra so violently that her body wrenched under the bed coverings.

"Sabra! I have watched for him!"

Her mouth twisted in an ugly way. She was trembling with fever and with the torments of her conscience, and she sobbed aloud now so that Sabra shushed her, afraid that someone would hear.

"Listen to me, Philomena. Have you told this to the ministry?"

The reply was strangled, barely audible. "Yes."

"Then you have obeyed the law. You have nothing to fear."

Violently Philomena whipped her head back and forth, back and forth, as if she could drive the Devil from her soul even as the Family exorcised him in their dance.

"No. No. They said that I must root it out of me. They will practice the warring gift on me, they said, to bring me back because I am drifting away to the world."

"And you are afraid that you cannot root it out—that you will still watch for him."

"Yes. O yes. I am afraid. Sabra—" She reached out and with a hot, trembling hand seized Sabra's. "I feel that I am alive only when I see him. Nothing else matters. I live only for those moments, even if I can only catch a glimpse of him as he marches at meeting. Do you understand that?"

Sabra felt her throat tighten. She nodded because she could not speak. I have waited, too, she thought, for a word, a sign—I came here because I could wait no longer. And is my heart empty and subdued? Am I longing still to see him?

"Perhaps—perhaps you should go away, into the world," she said slowly. "Have you thought of that, Philomena?" She saw the sudden terror in Philomena's eyes.

"No."

"But others have done it. It is better than suffering so."

"No. No. We would be damned forever. We would have no chance to be saved. Even if I must burn, I cannot drag him down with me. To be an apostate—no."

"What will you do, then?"

Philomena's grip slackened; she withdrew her hand.

"I will confess again. I will let them war on me. I will do penance."

"And—"

"And I will root it out of me, and he out of him." Her eyes gazed unfocused on the whitewashed wall. She lay quiet, her hands folded once again on her bosom. Automatically Sabra reached to straighten the slightly rumpled coverlet, for anything less than perfect order was an offense to Mother Ann watching over them from Heaven.

"Good night," she whispered. Swiftly, impulsively, she leaned down and kissed Philomena's burning forehead; and then, appalled at her indiscretion, she hurried out to join the dance.

13

Christmas Day dawned bright after a heavy fall of snow. The Shaker village looked new-born: pure and sparkling, a gift of God's love to the faithful. A group of brothers shoveled neat paths to the meeting house. Their cheeks reddened in the wind; their breath came in clouds. They were joyful in their work, as they were in all their tasks. Shoveling was nothing to them. Their muscles were hardened by long hours of toil in the fields, and they made fast work of the two feet and more of snow.

In each dormitory, one member read from the Book of John the parable of washing the disciples' feet; then all joined in, following the example of the Lord, and washed each other's feet. Then they proceeded to the general meeting, where Elder Harmon read from the Scriptures the story of the Savior's birth. The Lord's Prayer was sung, and special Christmas prayers said, including a remembrance for the poor.

As the words of the last prayer faded away, a breathless silence fell over the assembly. They knew that they were not yet done, for this was Christ's birthday and would they not therefore receive a special gift?

They waited in their rows of benches, the brethren at one end of the room, the sisters at the other. But one was absent: Sister Phebe, who had several times served as an instrument through whom those in the spirit world sent "gifts" to their earthly friends. Messages had come from the Lord, of course, and many from Mother Ann, but others communicated also: George Washington, and the old French prophets, and the prophets of the Egyptians and the Hebrews—Jeremiah, Ezekiel, Elijah, Deborah.

Spiritual jewels were often sent, and raiment of silk and velvet; wine and fruit, homely items such as brooms and wreaths of bright flowers. Gifts of love and humility came down, and golden chains, and trumpets, and silver swords. All of these were received through certain sisters, and so today Sister Phebe waited in the ministers' apartment next to the meeting hall, and those without waited, too, for their Christmas gift from the world beyond.

At last she appeared, holding a piece of paper cut into the shape of a heart and covered with fine script. As if she were walking in her sleep, she passed unseeing into the center of the room. In a high, clear voice she began to read.

"Beloved: I send you this day my best love and my choicest gifts: a basket of cakes of love, a silver chalice filled with the water of life, raiment of strength and comfort, a flock of white doves to bring you peace."

As she read, the Family listened with rapt attention. Like well-trained actors in a play, they followed the cues which Sister Phebe read to them: pantomiming, they passed around the basket and each took her or his portion of the love; they drank from the silver chalice; they adorned themselves with the silken shawls and golden crowns. O, how generous was Mother Ann! How deeply solicitous of their welfare! An onlooking gentile might see nothing, might mock their credulity; but they believed, they ate and drank and admired the evidence of Mother Ann's love as if it had been palpable in their hands. As perhaps it was.

Finally Sister Phebe paused as if for dramatic effect. They understood that she had something more to tell them. They waited, all expectant; muted excitement filled the room with an almost palpable tension. Tell us, they begged, although not a word was heard; what is your message, Mother Ann?

"In little more than three years' time," said Sister Phebe, "will come a revolution. It will be a political revolution, and therefore none of your affair. But mark it well, for it will be the signal for the millennium. Far away across the sea, men will fight each other. You will hear of it, for some of the defeated will find their way to you. Welcome them, and remember what I have said."

They strained to hear, to understand. What had revolution to do with them? The millennium! She had promised! Such prophecies often came:

they had learned of the death of Lafayette weeks before the news arrived from France, and they had heard of that wonderful new invention, the telegraph, long before anyone in the world save Morse himself had dreamed of such a thing. So now they listened to this latest revelation with perfect confidence that it would come true.

Sister Phebe stood silent before them, her head bowed, her hands clasping the fine-scrawled paper. Then her rigid form swayed slightly like a sapling in a gust of wind; her knees gave way and she coiled gracefully to the floor. Three brothers gently lifted her and carried her to the retiring room.

The meeting ended with a hymn of thanks to Mother Ann, and then Elder James opened a barrel of choice apples. Each took one as the company marched out to the dining hall for Christmas dinner. Sabra bit into the sweet, crisp flesh of the fruit; she felt the cold air on her face, the bright landscape hurting her eyes. These things were real. The hard-packed snow beneath her feet, the tears in her eyes, the apple which she ate—these were what she knew, what she understood. She had not understood what had passed in meeting; she had prayed with the others, but she had been unable, in good conscience, to pantomime the receiving of the spiritual gifts. She had not known that such things happened in the United Society. Messages from the spirit world had not been part of the bargain. I can accept it all, she thought—the work, the isolation from the world, the prayers and dances and hymns; but mesmerism—and the belief in spirits—no, that I cannot.

Christmas dinner was a bounteous feast. Sister Ruth and her helpers might have been accused of the sin of pride, had anyone been mean enough to carp. But all were gratefully hungry, and as each new dish appeared from the kitchen, it as quickly disappeared into the mouths of the faithful. They ate oyster cream soup and stuffed turkey and chestnut pudding, ginger beets and pumpkin bread and white bread and herb bread, applesauce and brandied peaches and pickled walnuts, tomato chutney and rose hip jam, apple pie, mincemeat pie, cranberry pie, plum jelly turnovers, fruitcake and gingerbread. Afterward they knelt and gave special thanks this day, for all their blessings.

That evening there were union meetings in the dormitories. Sabra came in late from her visit to Clara. As she slipped into her chair she felt the comfortable atmosphere in the room: the quiet talk, the easy chuckles, the warm and friendly interest of brothers and sisters, each for all. She saw Brother William, but Philomena, although she had been recovered some days since, was not among the sisters. But of course not: they would not be permitted to attend a union meeting together for a long time—months, even years. Brother William spoke easily to a Sister opposite him; Sabra did not know her name. His face was unsmiling, but he seemed calm and self-possessed. She remembered Philomena's torture, her agonized words of confession. Had Brother William undergone a similar torment? Or was he less attracted to Philomena than she to him? Words suddenly came into her mind; she could not remember where she had read them: "He for God, and she for God in him." But it was so. There was always that impediment. Even Shaker women, seeking God, had first to put men out of their hearts.

14

"Welcome the stranger," said Mother Ann, "for he will be your friend."

They obeyed her in this as in all else, and the more visitors who came to inspect them, the more they saw the wisdom of her words; for strangers who came for a day to see how they did returned to the world with accurate information, and their reports helped to dispel the falsehoods and slander which had dogged the early years of the experiment. Vicious reports had been circulated: tales of sexual orgies during worship, tales of the deliberate rupture of families to entice new members, tales of children kept against their will, of property confiscated, husbands or wives deserted. Naturally people were curious about such goings-on; but often enough, when they troubled to see for themselves, they realized that what they had heard had been in error. Their good reports helped to counteract the bad, and so always they were made welcome, no matter how busy the season; they were given a tour of inspection, and invited to dine, and invited, too, to purchase something—a packet of herbs, a palm-leaf fan, a wooden box, a jar of applesauce—and sent away with a cheerful wave and a kind word to tell their fellows in the world that these people were amazing clever, and not a laggard among them from what could be seen.

On a mild, moist day in January, Elder James was conducting a party of three gentlemen from Worcester through the shops; if they wished, he said, they had time before dinner to see the barn. They wanted to see it very much, they said; they had heard much about the ingenious design of the Shaker barns, and not for anything would they miss seeing this one. They left the chair shop, where the brethren were turning legs and caning seats with practiced skill. As they made their way along the slushy path they paused on a slight rise to look about them: they saw the hog house and the blacksmith shop, the herb house and the granary and the stable, the garden shop and the medical shop, the meeting house and two large dwellings, the saw house and the shops where palm-leaf hats and brooms were made. They pondered the peaceful scene: how had it happened here, when all the world was mad for reform and communal experiments rose and fell, it seemed, with the ebb and flow of the tides. Perhaps they would find the answer yet before they went away; certainly no one had tried to hide anything from them. They walked on, past the rear meadow, to the entrance to the large building of dressed stone—the largest by far in the village, and far bigger, of course, than any gentile barn.

The interior was dim and cavernous, filled with the sweet smell of hay and well-kept animals. Fifty cows and several oxen stood in clean-swept stalls. In the hayloft, two young men pitched down hay in a whooshing rhythm; two other young men scrubbed the floor from front to back along the broad center aisle. The visitors listened carefully as Elder James explained the system of trap doors in each stall through which the dirty straw was swept; and the barn was built with entrances at two levels, he said, to facilitate getting the animals and their feed in and out. Admirable, said the gentlemen; most ingenious and efficient.

Elder James paused. Something had caught his eye. In a corner crouched a small boy. Elder James knew him; he was Abel Thompson, an orphan from Leominster. He had lived with the Family for three years. Excusing himself, the Elder approached the child, who seemed to be murmuring to himself.

"Abel. Why are you not at work?"

After one frightened glance, the boy ducked his head and withdrew farther into his corner; and now, behind him, Elder James saw the reason: a gray mother cat nestled with her litter in a bed of straw.

Elder James was not an unkind man, but he was devoted to his faith. He felt his heart quicken, he felt a tension run through his body as it did whenever he discovered wrongdoing. For the moment, he forgot his tour of inspection. He thought only of this small sinner before him, and of how he must make the child understand his duty to Mother Ann. His hand shot out and grabbed the shoulder of the boy's gray jacket. He pulled him up to his feet; he peered at the cat.

"Answer me," he said. "Why are you not at work?"

The child hung his head; his mouth worked as he tried to hold back his tears.

"I was on my way to the shoe shop," he said at last. "I just came in to see her for a minute."

"And how often have you done this?"

No reply.

"Abel." Elder James searched his agile mind for words to make himself understood. He felt the child tremble beneath his grip. Suddenly he crouched down so that they were face to face. He put his hands on the boy's arms. "You know the rules," he said. "If you had stopped to do some necessary errand, I would not mind your being late to the shop. But I fear that you have made a pet of this creature."

Still the child would not look at him.

"Is that so, Abel?"

The boy nodded. Behind them, the kittens scrambled over each other, mewing, fighting for nourishment; in the long rows of stalls the cattle shifted from hoof to hoof; the gentlemen waited patiently by the door until Elder James would rejoin them.

"You know that it is forbidden," said Elder James. He allowed himself a moment's rueful reflection: children were valuable, indeed, but they did not always repay the time and trouble necessary to rear them—to educate them, train them to a trade, teach them the ways of the Society. Many of them went away when they reached adulthood. Better, perhaps, to get the necessary recruits from those grown enough to understand Mother Ann's laws, who would not need to be reminded over and over again of the proper way to behave.

Elder James straightened; he put his hand on Abel's neatly combed brown hair, which was cut severely all around, untapered, in the distinctive Family style.

"Go to the shoe shop, child, and do not come here again. You must not form an attachment to any beast. We do not permit it; it is against the law. Go on, now."

The boy said nothing, nor did he look at Elder James. He walked steadily out of the barn past the curious eyes of the visiting gentlemen. Elder James felt relieved; once, some years ago, he had had a boy openly defy him in the matter of a dog. Such arguments severely disturbed his tranquillity. He was perfectly willing to let the world wend its careless way to damnation, but he would not—could not—tolerate forbidden behavior in his own domain.

By the next day, despite the ban on unnecessary conversation, the story had gone all through the village: another child caught making a pet. It happened all the time; there was never a child alive, it seemed, who did not have the urge to make friends with one or another of the animal population. Each child had to be instructed anew that such friendship, while not as sinful as close attachment between humans, was nevertheless wrong and contrary to God's law as interpreted by Mother Ann.

Sabra saw the boy in the children's dormitory when she went to suckle Clara. Even for a Shaker child, she thought, he seemed unusually quiet. She bent her head so that her cheek touched Clara's dark curls. She felt the small plump body heavy in her arms. This is not my place, she thought; I did not know enough about them when I came.

At union meeting, several days later, she had a moment of private conversation with Philomena. She saw that her friend had put on a new attitude; no longer was she the suffering, sinful woman who had sweated out her fever and her confession in the infirmary.

"I have done it," said Philomena. There was an edge to her voice: pride, thought Sabra. Pride, too, was a sin.

O God—what was not?

"I have rooted it out, Sabra. I am free of all feeling for him. I made my confession to the ministry yesterday. Now"—her face fired up a little; her voice took on a harder edge—"now when I grow old, when I die, I will go to the Lord with a clear conscience. I will be saved."

When I die . . . She stared at Sabra triumphantly, as if at a stranger; and Sabra, after a moment, turned away and spoke to the Sister at her other side.

When I grow old, she thought, I will die too. And will I die, never having lived?

O Silas.

The next day she asked for a private audience with Eldress Hannah.

15

"You must understand," said Eldress, "that if you leave the child in our care, it is with the agreement that she will live with us until she comes of age, at which time she will herself decide whether to stay or go."

Once again they confronted each other across the table in the Family's office; but now, instead of November rain splattering at the windows, bright February sun shone through the sparkling panes. It seemed to Sabra a much longer time than three months since she had been in this room, speaking to the grave, kindly woman who jointly ruled this small domain.

"Yes," she said. No, she thought; I will come to get her when I can, but you do not need to know that.

"You have done very well here, Sabra. It is just three months since you came. Will you not try us for three months more before you decide?"

Eldress' face was troubled; she was disappointed at Sabra's announcement, but hardly surprised. She had known from the first that this one would not remain. What she had not known was how well Sabra would fit into the Family's routine. She was intelligent, hard-working, good-hearted—everyone liked her; there had not been one bad report from any department in which she had served. And certainly the life seemed to agree with her, thought Eldress: she had looked strained and peaked when she had arrived, but now she had taken on a little weight, the dark patches under her eyes had disappeared, her skin had lost its pallor.

She will go back into the world, thought Eldress, and she will perhaps rejoin her husband. She shuddered.

"What will you do for yourself?" she said.

"I will go back to the factory. I have an honorable discharge, and they are always glad of experienced hands."

Eldress imagined it: the crowded city, the busy, distracting life of the gentiles. Once she, too, had been in the world, and most unhappily so, for her husband had deserted her and taken their child with him. She hardly even remembered her pain now, but once it had almost killed her. She had taken sanctuary in the Society as a novice, even as Sabra had done; but unlike this young woman, Eldress had found her vocation here, and had been happy to stay on, sheltered from the world which had given her so much grief. She was a woman of more than usual intelligence; the ministry had seen this, and had elevated her to her present position of authority because of it. In the world, women were nothing; they were factory slaves or superfluous spinsters, or decorative prey to men's sinful lust. But among Mother Ann's chosen, women had virtually equal status. They could rise to authority alongside the brethren. There was no doubt in Eldress Hannah's mind that Shaker women had the better bargain, but she had seen enough of life both within and without the Society to understand the strong pull of the world's ways. Novices came and went all the time; Sabra Blood was no exception. Like so many others, she was a "Winter Shaker," coming in for shelter during the cold months, leaving again when the world beckoned in the green spring.

Eldress struggled with herself. Try to keep her, or let her go? Eldress' heart was safely God's: she seldom listened to it in temporal affairs. Why did it speak to her now in the entirely routine matter of a deflecting novice, a girl like any other?

But she was not like any other. She was different. Eldress could hardly remember a time when she had been so drawn to a fellow human being. Her own life in the world, long ago, seemed that of another woman. She was sure that she had loved her child, if not her husband, but she could not recall the feeling of that love. Now, facing the troubled young woman seated across the table, Eldress was seized by a spasm of long-dormant maternal feeling. Let me help you, she thought; let me protect you from the horrors of life in the world. Stay with us here, safe and sheltered.

Eldress was aware that Sabra was staring at her. She felt a flush rise over her face. Had the young woman read her thoughts? Many people were sensitives; one did not need to be an instrument receiving messages from Mother Ann to know what one's companions were thinking.

"Of course you are at liberty to go when you wish," she said. "But I will ask you to consider your decision one more time." She smiled, and she was relieved to see that Sabra smiled in return. No hard feelings, then. "At least stay until sugaring-off," she said, "and you can go with a sweet taste in your mouth."

When Sabra left the office, she stood for a moment on the neatly shoveled walk and looked down the little street of the village. The air was cold and clean, invigorating as winter air should be. She did not mind going out of doors here, because the rooms were comfortably cool: not like the stuffy, overheated atmosphere of the boarding houses and the workrooms at the factory. She felt her lungs expand as she took deep breaths. Another year or two in the mills, and she might ruin her health forever. But to stay on here was impossible. Only three months, and already she felt unbearably confined.

At the opposite end of the village, she saw two brothers in a sled driving away from the herb house. They were going into the world to sell their wares but they would not contaminate themselves by so much as a handshake with a gentile. If they needed to separate for any reason, each would tell the other everything he had done while he was alone; and when they returned, in two or three days, they would tell everything again to the ministry. Nothing must be allowed to intrude on their inviolate faith. And yet they could never quite escape the world. Always it was there, lying in wait outside the boundaries of the village, a threat to their chosen way.

Sabra was assigned, this month, to the weaving shop. She stepped through the wooden gate between the two granite posts and began to walk toward the small building which housed the half-dozen hand looms. The village was deserted. Everyone was within doors, working. When the noon bell rang, they would all go to their dormitories for ten minutes of prayer and contemplation; then they would proceed to the dining hall for dinner. Then back to work; then prayer and supper; then —depending on the day of the week—rehearsal for Sabbath service, or a union meeting. The routine was as inflexible as that of the factories—more, because at the factories one had an hour or two in the evenings for oneself, and all day Sunday except for church.

"But you knew that when you came," said the voice in her mind.

Ah—but to know a fact and to experience it are two very different things.

"Your life here is secure. You need never worry about hunger or want again."

She passed a dwelling house, the chair shop, another dwelling—all painted ochre, the prescribed color—and then the white-painted meeting house. All was peaceful and attractive. A landscape artist might have made a graceful canvas from the arrangement of dark yellow buildings against the snowy landscape, all tangible offerings to God, scattered under the bright blue sky as testament to the wisdom of Mother Ann's way.

"Think again," said the voice in her mind. "If you go, you cannot come back. Here you have a life. The world has not treated you kindly. Why do you want to rush back to it?"

She reached the path to the weaving shop. From where she stood, she could hear the clacking of the looms. It was a soft and pleasant sound, unlike the fearful racket of the mills.

She looked down across the main road through the village. An ancient oak tree stood at the corner by the medical shop. Her eyes had caught a flicker of movement behind the broad trunk. She hesitated. It was her duty to Eldress, she knew, to report any truant from work or school: everyone was under constant observation by everyone else. She had heard of a Shaker settlement in Ohio where the ministers had built a watchtower; from dawn to dusk a guard was assigned like a ship's lookout—not to sight a landfall, but to catch those who shirked their work or in some other way broke the order's rules.

A woman's figure appeared from behind the tree. She looked about; not seeing Sabra, she stepped confidently onto the path. She began to walk toward the weaving shop; as she drew close, Sabra saw that her face was streaked with tears. Her eyes were downcast; she walked steadily on, her drab cloak fluttering in the breeze, her shapeless dress hanging on her body like a sack. So dispirited, so hopelessly cast down, so encased in a shell of pitiless isolation was she that she looked like a prisoner walking to the scaffold. As she went past she was aware that someone stood watching her at the door of the shop. She glanced up. Her eyes met Sabra's. Her expressionless face showed no recognition. She did not miss a beat of her steady stride.

Philomena—

The name hung unspoken in the air, but Sabra heard it loudly in her mind.

She looked again at the broad, black trunk of the oak tree, and as she looked she saw Brother William's figure slip from behind it. With somewhat more stealth than Philomena, he made his cautious way in the opposite direction toward the saw house. He walks like a fugitive, she thought; like the mother and child who stole from a farmhouse one windy April night and delivered themselves up to Rachel for salvation.

"I will be saved," Philomena had said. But she had been wrong. She had not been saved.

And here at the United Society, there was no Underground Railroad to rescue sinners deflected from the way to Heaven.

16

As Eldress Hannah had requested, Sabra stayed with the Family until the sugaring-off in early March. But before the trees were tapped, the Family celebrated Mother Ann's birthday on March 1. It was a festive day, a happy day second only in importance to the birthday of the Savior Himself.

The next morning the brethren and several of the sisters went to the forest to drive the spikes into the maple trees and hang the hundreds of covered wooden buckets to gather the sap. Great bonfires were built to boil it down in sheet-iron kettles; the children were brought out to get their sugar-on-snow—freshly boiled syrup thrown onto clean snow, and chilled at once into delicious, chewy strands of candy. Abel Thompson went with the others; he ate his share of waxy, golden syrup, and like them he enjoyed the adventure of being out in the woods, the sense of holiday, the sweet taste filling his mouth and the smooth lumps of soft taffy sliding down his throat.

The children were allowed to run, to play and laugh and romp off some of their animal spirits. In their wisdom, the Elders realized that you cannot make a Shaker in a day, or in many days, and that discipline too harsh would only bring reaction—rejection, abandonment, flight to the world. So they gave the children time for freedom; the grown-ups watched, amused, as the small figures waged their snowball battles, and built a fat man in the clearing, and spread-eagled angels in every available space. The sun warmed them from a cloudless sky and melted the snow which dripped from leafless branches. The sharp smell of wood fires mingled with the odor of the boiling sap. Caps and mufflers were thrown off, jackets unbuttoned. Despite the heavy snow underfoot, children and grown-ups alike delighted in the knowledge that spring was near, that another winter had been safely survived.

Abel Thompson stood apart, watching. When another boy called to him to join in, he did not answer; he had not heard.

While the boys were at the sugaring-off, Sabra worked with the sisters to scrub their dormitory. She had been assigned, this month, to nursery duty. The children were separated as were the adults, boys on one side of the building, girls on the other, but even so Sabra felt comforted to be working in a place so near to where Clara lived. From time to time, as she passed through the hall, she glanced into the girls' room and saw her child happily pulling herself up beside a cot, or crawling around the floor under the watchful eyes of the Sister on duty.

This last month, she thought, as near to her as possible; and then I will go. She had begun to wean the child, and Clara had learned already to drink from a cup. Still Sabra worried about her; jealously she watched as one or another Sister held Clara, or played with her, knowing that it was best for the child to love and trust these other women and yet begrudging every smile, every kiss that Clara gave not to her but to someone else.

As she helped the sisters care for the Family's children, Sabra watched and listened to see how these small souls fared under the Shaker regime. All of them seemed contented, although quieter perhaps than gentile children; certainly their little bodies were healthy enough, she thought, fed on good food, breathing the clean country air, warmly dressed against the cold, and with swift and efficient medical attention close at hand should it be needed. She remembered Elder James' gentle hands holding Clara's tiny form when they had brought her for help almost a year ago.

In three days, Clara would be a year old. Sabra resolved to buy a present for her with the first wages she earned; and I will bring it to her myself, she thought, and if they forbid it to her, I will keep it and give it to her when I can afford to take her away. She does not know the difference now; but she will. She will.

One dark morning several days later, before the general rising bell, Sabra went as usual with three other women to the children's quarters to supervise their awakening. They needed help, these little ones; they were not so quick as the adults to spring out of their warm beds, they needed to be supervised at washing, at saying their morning prayers.

Sister Elizabeth, in charge of the nursery, met them at the door of the boys' room. Her usual tranquillity had vanished; she trembled as she spoke, and her voice came startlingly shrill. "Quickly!" she whispered. "As quickly as you can! Sister Caroline, to the meeting house, Sister Alice to every shop—look through the windows, they are all locked, but it is just light enough now to see. Sister Emmaline, to the kitchen. Sabra—yes—go to the barn. Try to avoid the milking if you can."

They hesitated, aware of her urgency but bewildered as to its cause.

"Hurry!" she begged. Her broad face beneath the close white cap was tense, made ugly by her fear. Then she realized that she had not explained. "Abel Thompson is not in his bed," she hissed. "He is not anywhere in the dormitory. We will all be punished for negligence if we do not find him. You know how he sometimes walks in his sleep. Even as I sleep here with them, he has got past me and into the hall before I awakened and brought him back. He cannot be very far away. Now hurry!"

The sky was gray as Sabra hastened from the building. From the kitchen she caught the scent of wood-smoke, the kitchen sisters starting up the fires for breakfast. Abel Thompson, she remembered, was the child who had made a friend of a cat. Since he had been admonished, his sleepwalking had increased. Sooner or later he would severely injure himself. She hurried down the walk and along the path toward the great barn. She saw no one; it was still too early for the milking. When she reached the door, she hesitated. A barn might be a dangerous place for a sleepwalker. She dreaded finding the child injured, or dead, perhaps, fallen through a trap door or down from the hayloft—but she must look all the same. They must find him. She pushed open the door and stepped in.

Through the high windows, the light hardly penetrated to the interior. She paused, waiting for her eyes to adjust to the near darkness. She inhaled the sweet fragrance of the hay; she heard the clump of the animals' hooves as they moved restlessly in their stalls, thinking that she had come to relieve them.

She took a step or two down the long broad aisle. "Do not frighten him," Sister Elizabeth had said; and so she tried to move without sound, searching out the deeper darkness of the corners, stepping softly into the cavernous depth of the building. She could see quite well now: the rows of cattle, the doors of the stalls, the tall supporting uprights and crossbeams forming rectilinear patterns against the whitewashed walls.

Mother Ann had said, "Put your hands to work and your hearts to God," and she had been right at least about the work, for her followers had had enviable prosperity. And more than anything else in the village, this great structure of stone and wood gave evidence of the Family's success—more than the busy shops, the thriving industries, the rich harvests every fall. This barn was like a cathedral; it inspired far more awe than the meeting house.

Sabra moved on. She peered right and left, she looked up at the edge of the hayloft.

"Abel?"

She paused to listen.

"Abel, are you here?"

No answer. She took a few more steps. Her eyes picked up an image, but in the second or two before her brain registered it, she stood tentative and confused like an intruder who has blundered upon some private ceremony.

Something hung from one of the beams.

Dear God.

As she realized what it was, she felt her legs give way. She grabbed at the gate of a stall. She made a sound: a deep guttural expulsion of her breath. *Dear God.*

It was not one thing, but two. They hung side by side, so close that they seemed a single body. And even in death, Philomena's hand clung to that of Brother William, as if, in the end, she had freely chosen the agony of eternal damnation rather than the pain of living—or dying—separate from the one whom she so helplessly, carnally loved.

The light was stronger now. It showed their blackened faces, their tongues protruding from their mouths which were like splits in pieces of rotten fruit burst open with decay.

"If I die now I will burn forever," Philomena had said; and: "I live only when I see him."

In her horror, in her great anguish, Sabra stared at the two of them, at their terrible grimaces, at their hands intertwined; she stared against her will for she could not move, she could not redirect her eyes. And then a current of air turned the body of what had been a man, and he twisted at the end of the rope as if suddenly he had been given life again: as if perhaps he knew that she watched him, and he wanted to show her one thing more, a greater horror even than the fact of his corpse or his blackened face. Her eyes did move then: traveled down the length of his body. At first she did not understand what she saw. She heard the question clearly in her mind: What is that?

And then, when she did understand—when she realized the meaning of the dark hole just there at the join of his legs, the blackening stains down the length of his homespun trousers, the gaping wound, the blood-encrusted knife still clenched in his hand, she felt her own body collapse, she tasted the bitter vomit retching up her throat, strangling the shriek that she had not the strength to utter.

A thickening puddle of blood beneath his feet, and the inexorable brightening light which revealed the wound, and the restless animals lowing for release, and the sweet barn-smell overlaid by the stench of Death, and the mystery of these two souls who had irrevocably consigned themselves to Hell; and pity them, these wretched sinners, giving up their lives, burning into all eternity, and all for the sake of Mother Ann; and pity the poor onlooker now who could never escape the sight of them, no, never again; she would live with this vision branded forever on her brain, she would die with these two monstrous shapes like dangling rag dolls swaying back and forth before her eyes.

And ah, sweet merciful Jesus, where is Thy mercy now?

PART IV

1

March 18, 1845. A man emerged from the American House on Central Street. He stood on the boardwalk watching the traffic. Hustle and bustle: the American way. It had been the same in New-York and Boston. Horses and carts, wagons, closed carriages, gigs, phaetons, huge lumbering stagecoaches. Later, at closing bell, would come the foot traffic: the operatives spending their pay at the shops. He had been surprised to learn that they were not paid in scrip, that the stores were not company-owned. The management was shrewd, to give them a pittance for their own. It gave them a false sense of independence. He squared his shoulders and turned to go into the saloon bar. He had a long day and night ahead of him; he needed fortification.

The barkeep served his customer stolidly, exchanging a few words and taking in his appearance in one glance and filing him away in the neatly ordered categories of his mind. An Englishman: middling height, heavy-boned and muscular, a face as keen as an eagle's, deep-set, angry eyes on either side of a hawkish nose. His skin was ruddy, high-colored like that of many English. He was from Manchester by the sound of him. The English had almost as many ways of talking as the Americans; the barkeep was proud of his good ear. He could place a man within fifty miles of his home, often as not, just by talking to him for five minutes. But even if this man had not said a word, the barkeep would have known that he was a foreigner. The cut of his coat, the texture of his skin, the way he carried himself—little things, but they told.

The Englishman finished his whiskey and looked around expectantly.

"Early yet," said the barkeep. "He'll be along."

The Englishman nodded. "Aye. That he will."

"Been here long?"

"Sin' last night."

"Staying?"

The Englishman hesitated. He assumed that he was known to the Corporations. This lackey might well be their spy. "May happen I will."

"It's a good place to settle, mister. Opportunity for any man who puts in an honest day's work. What's your trade?"

The Englishman hesitated again. "Weaver."

"That's mostly women's work here. But they can always use an experienced hand. You'll do all right."

The door opened; a man came in. The Englishman, having paid for his drink, got up to meet him. They shook hands and went out, leaving the bartender to his speculations. He had looked closely at the newcomer's skin, at his eyes and his teeth. He was as healthy as a prize bull. No weaver in Christendom looked in such fine condition: certainly no English weaver. The barkeep had heard all about the English mills and the poor slaves who worked there, for the Lowell entrepreneurs were quick to broadcast any evil news from across the water that made their own undertaking look even marginally superior. This man could not possibly have been a factory hand—not for many years, at any rate. Moreover, there was never a weaver in this world who spoke so clearly, whose voice rang true, unfogged by cotton dust. Why had he lied?

The two men walked slowly up Central Street toward the Freewill Baptist Church facing them on Merrimack.

"How many will attend?" said the Englishman.

"At least five hundred. They have heard of you, and they are anxious to meet you."

"And who will speak, besides me?"

"Brisbane, Evans, Mike Walsh—he's Tammany—and Ryckman, I think."

The Englishman frowned. "They're all soft-hands. I thought you said this was a workingmen's convention."

"It is. Of course. But the gentlemen in Land Reform have interested themselves in our cause—"

The Englishman spat violently onto the boardwalk. "They'll be no help. I've seen their like at home. They're like the bloody Chartists, talking their fool heads off while working folk starve."

"They are fine men, John. They speak well, they have good hearts—"

"They're soft. They'll cut and run. They want Heaven on earth. Ten-Hour's nothing to them, they won't fight for it. Print that in your paper and put my name to it if you like."

They paused at the corner of Merrimack Street. Across the busy thoroughfare, facing them, rose the spire of the Freewill Baptist Church, whose bricks and mortar, pews and altar, had been paid for not once but twice by the donations of pious, gullible mill girls, the wily minister pocketing the surplus. John Prince had not yet heard that story; but he would, and when he did, it would add fuel to his smoldering anger: one more swindle on the laboring classes, this one perpetrated by the hand-in-glove ally of the capitalists, his enemy the Church.

He looked down the long stretch of Merrimack Street. His eye was caught by a pretty girl—a very pretty girl—crossing the muddy street, lifting her skirts high.

"Your women are organized?"

"Some of them, yes."

"I understand one of them testified to the legislature about Ten-Hour."

"Miss Bagley, yes. It was she who organized the Female Labor Reform Association. Several others testified also."

Prince nodded. The girl had got across the street. She disappeared into a dry-goods shop.

"But they did no good," he said. "The Committee still gave an adverse report. What's his name? Munson?"

"Matthew Munson, yes. He—ah—was made chairman quite unexpectedly. To hear Miss Bagley's evidence, we believe."

"Naturally. Well, she's a brave lady. As they all are. She's coming tonight?"

"Yes. She's done quite well at organizing. Three hundred have joined the Female Association since January."

"Out of how many? Twelve thousand? Thirteen?"

"More or less. But it takes time. They are shy, some of them. They feel that it is unladylike to join an Association. And of course they fear dismissal and the blacklist."

Prince grinned. "Why, they're quite right to do that. That's a sensible fear. Tell her to get all thirteen thousand to join, and then let the Corporations dismiss and blacklist. That's the way to do it. They'd never find black-legs enough to run their hell-holes then."

His eyes narrowed. The girl had come out of the dry-goods store carrying a small package. She crossed Merrimack Street and walked down the opposite side of Central.

"They're a hard case, the women," he said. "A hard, hard case. But let them come. We'll find some way to use them." He grinned. "I'll see to that."

2

Sabra sat alone in the stuffy boarding-house bedroom. She had walked out in the morning, and had eaten her dinner with the girls, and now she was left with the afternoon to fill. Three more days before she could begin, the overseer at the Appleton Corporation had said. He had looked carefully at her discharge slip from the Commonwealth. It seemed in order. He had caught three forgeries in the last month, girls desperate for work. When he had checked the blacklist he had found their names, sure enough; he knew a forged discharge when he saw one. He had a weaver going at the end of the week, he said. Mrs. Pye, at Number Three Jackson Street, would have a place to board.

The cap which she had bought that morning for Clara was white, trimmed in lace, with narrow satin ribbon ties. She pictured it framing Clara's chubby, rosy face. Her heart constricted. Clara. She longed to see her. She had been gone only a day. It seemed a week. How could she bear to live apart from her? The baby would not miss her, Eldress Hannah had said. She would receive plenty of love and attention from the sisters; she would thrive. Sabra had had to admit the truth of it: in the absence of her mother, Clara loved everybody who loved her. In fact, thought Sabra bitterly, it might be best not to visit her at all. Every parting would be painful for them both; best stay away, and let her grow in peace until she had saved enough— No. By that time—two years? three? five?—Clara would have forgotten her completely. Better for them both to bear the pain than not have her own daughter know her.

Visiting would be expensive. A dollar to hire a gig—more if she had a boy to drive. She would drive herself. But only once a month. Her pay would be three dollars and ten cents a week, less one dollar thirty-seven and a half cents board. One seventy-two and a half to save. If she spent not a penny—but she must. She badly needed shoes, and a summer dress. Her old one was worn out, hardly fit for the weaving room although it would have to do. And a new bonnet, the plainest to be found, surely, but still she needed one. She could not step out of doors bare-headed, or, worse, in the little Shaker cap, and her old bonnet had been ruined by the snowstorm on the day she left Mrs. Clapham's. She would have to wear it, however, until she could afford to replace it.

Clara's cap seemed so tiny. Carefully Sabra wrapped it in its brown paper and tied the little package and laid it in her hand trunk. Sunday: two days more. She would go to celebrate Clara's first birthday. Until then she needed to fill up the time.

She forced her thoughts away from the Family at Harvard Village. Go, Eldress Hannah had said, her eyes wide with alarm at the sight of Sabra's condition; yes, you were right, I should have let you go before. It is my fault that you have suffered this—this dreadful discovery.

She shuddered now, reliving it. She pressed her hands against her eyelids as if she would press away the vision which still burned behind them, bright in the darkness: two corpses, damned for eternity, swaying at the end of their separate ropes.

Dear God: help me to forget.

She opened her eyes; she looked out the bedroom window. Across the street she saw a brick wall: the mill. The noise of its machinery hummed through the boarding house. I should rest, she thought. Soon enough I will be glad of a free day.

A newspaper lay folded on top of a bureau. She picked it up. It was the *Tri-Weekly Advertiser*—the Democratic competition to the Whig *Courier,* Munson's paper.

Biddy.

Blue eyes in a pale thin face framed by a fall of heavy black hair. And before that: the wretched bundle of rags huddled on the boarding-house steps. She, Sabra, had saved that child: she was, in a way, responsible for her as she was for Clara. (But you discharged that responsibility, said her conscience; you gave her the means to make her own way. Still.)

She put Biddy out of her mind and glanced at the newspaper. The Hutchinson Family Singers at the First Freewill Baptist Church; Santa Anna "in durance" in Mexico; Dr. Gladwin, Surgeon Dentist; Thomas Wilson Dorr imprisoned in Rhode Island in his fight for universal manhood suffrage; the new Post Office bill passed by Congress, a "glorious reform" of the present system.

On the third page, a tiny four-line announcement at the bottom right corner: an announcement of a "festival" at Wentworth's new hall that evening in aid of the Female Labor Reform Association. More trouble, she thought. She wanted none of it.

Biddy. And Patrick. She had passed Codwell's store that morning. Probably Patrick owned the place now. She did not want to see him; she did not want to see Mrs. Clapham or any of the girls whom she had known at the Commonwealth. She wanted no reminders of the past.

But Biddy was different. Like a daughter, almost, or like the sister whom Sabra had never had. In June she herself would be twenty-three. Biddy had never been sure of her age, but she was probably about eighteen now. Sabra was suddenly, overwhelmingly curious to know how Biddy was. Had she stayed at Munson's? Was she content? Was she to marry Patrick?

It was mid-afternoon: three hours until supper. She could easily walk to Munson's house on Pawtucket Street and back before the meal was served. She would not stay long. Just a few moments, a brief chat; it would not be a busy time of day for a servant, they might spare her ten or twenty minutes. She got up, took her cloak and her ruined bonnet from the peg and went downstairs.

The wind had changed. The air was colder now, raw, the sky overcast. She pulled her cloak tight around her as she walked, for the second time that day, down Central Street toward Merrimack. As she passed Codwell's she paused and looked in. She saw a clerk: not Patrick. She walked on. At the corner of Merrimack stood two young women distributing handbills. She took one. It announced the meeting which she had seen advertised in the newspaper. Nothing for her. She walked on down Merrimack Street, noting the familiar shops: Wyman and Wilson's Dry Goods, B. F. Watson's Exchange Book Store, Carver's Boots & Shoes. Some, which she remembered, were gone: Hutchinson's Musical Instruments, Dyer's Looking Glass & Picture Frames. She looked away, down to the boardwalk under her feet. She would have nothing to do with shops. She came to the depot, crossed Dutton Street, came to the Merrimack House Hotel on the corner. If she turned her head and looked down Dutton Street to her right she would see the Commonwealth boarding houses, the huge red-brick bulk of the mill at the end of the canal blocking off the view of the river. She did not look; she went on.

She crossed Worthen Street. To her left lay the Paddy Camp Lands: the Acre. A gang of ragged, shouting boys raced past her and turned the corner into the maze of alleys and narrow streets. As she looked after them she saw a rat flash across the alley behind them. She shuddered. At least she had saved Biddy from that, she thought; she might be a servant but at least she lives in a decent place. The boardwalk had ended. Her shoes and the hem of her dress were becoming covered with mud. I should not have come, she thought. What will I do if I say Hello Biddy how have you been all this time, and she looks at me and doesn't know me?

She realized that she was standing still: an odd thing to do, in a town where everyone was so busy. A woman stared at her from the window of a house. Probably she wonders if I'm coming to beg, thought Sabra. No: I don't look Irish. She thinks I'm distributing tracts.

She walked on. How could Biddy not remember? If she is there she will be glad to see me. And I her. She will not pester me with questions. She will kiss me and listen to whatever I tell her and ask for nothing more. To her, I am someone to be admired and yes loved. The thought was comforting; she longed for a few moments of companionship, of friendly gossip unthreatened by watchful sisters.

She had never seen Matthew Munson's house on Pawtucket Street, although she remembered Biddy's description of it and she knew its approximate location. When she came to the Corporation Hospital she turned left and walked down Pawtucket Street parallel to the river. Between the spacious frame houses to her right she could see the opposite shore. The northern shore: beyond it was New Hampshire. She had come from there; she had traveled down this very street in the peddler's wagon. And if some kindly gypsy fortune teller had told her then what would become of her she would not have believed.

When she reached the house—she was sure that it was the right house, gaudy and yellow—she paused for a moment, undecided. Front door or back? Surely back. She pushed open the gate. A path led through the garden to the rear of the house. She followed it.

A stern-faced, middle-aged woman answered her knock.

"Excuse me. I am looking for one of your girls named Biddy. Is she here?"

The woman looked her over. "No." She started to close the door.

"Please—do you know where I can find her? I am a friend, I have been away and I haven't seen her for some time."

"She's gone," said the woman. "Been gone for a year and more."

"Do you know where she is?"

The woman hesitated. "Dracut," she said at last.

"Is she—do you know where I could send her a letter, perhaps? Is she in service?"

The woman's mouth tightened. "You might call it that. But if you're a decent, God-fearing woman you won't go looking for her."

Again she tried to shut the door, but Sabra's need to know had made her bold and she put her hand against the frame and her foot on the sill.

"I don't understand. Is she all right? Did she—is she married?"

The woman's face filled with that implacable contempt reserved to the self-righteous.

"Her? Not likely. We think of her as dead and gone, and if you were a friend of hers I'd advise you to do the same."

With a sudden push she slammed the door, narrowly missing Sabra's hand. Sabra stood on the back porch, trying to make sense of what she had been told. Dead and gone? But only to be thought of so; not actually in the ground.

Disappointment weighted down her heart. I did not want to bother him, she thought, but now I must. He will know; he knows everything.

3

Codwell's West India Goods store was seldom busy in the late afternoon; when Sabra entered she was alone save for the clerk behind the counter.

"Is Patrick O'Haran here?"

He nodded; without a word to her he poked his head into the back room.

"Pat! Someone t' see you."

Sabra felt a little thrill of pleasure, of long-forgotten sisterly pride, as she saw Patrick step out into the front of the store. How manly he was! He had let his hair grow longer; he had filled out, become slightly taller. He looked tired, but his features had settled into a firm, hard, adult face: a face to trust, to respect. He was about twenty years old now, she calculated, but he seemed much older.

He did not at first know who she was. Then, when he did, his fleeting, pleased recognition vanished and in its place came a wary politeness.

"Hello, Patrick."

"Well, Sabra."

The clerk observed them.

"How are you?" She stifled an impulse to exclaim over his new, adult self; one reserved such expressions for children.

He studied her. She felt suddenly ugly—old and shabby. She felt what she was: impoverished, burdened with the support of the child. (No, she chided herself: Clara was not, was never a burden!) Whereas Patrick looked spruce and spry and altogether on his way up.

"O, I'm fine," he said. "I thought you'd gone away."

"Yes—well—I've come back."

Patrick became aware of the clerk's interest. "Sammy, you can go. No. Wait. We'll go."

He vanished again into the back room while the clerk unabashedly studied Sabra and she looked modestly down at the sawdust-covered floor. She was annoyed by the clerk's scrutiny. With some effort she lifted her eyes and stared back at him. An unladylike thing to do. He grinned and winked at her. If I were a customer, she thought—a wealthy customer—he would not behave so.

Patrick appeared wearing his coat and a dark cap. The cap made him look even older. She felt a little in awe of him. Telling the clerk that he would be back in half an hour, he led her out onto the street. A fine rain had begun to fall. They walked toward the American House, where the dining room had only a few customers at this hour. Patrick led her to a table along the wall, well away from the three men seated near the door, and ordered beefsteak and apple pie and beer.

Sabra thought to protest—she had, after all, paid for her board at Mrs. Pye's—but then she relaxed and let Patrick order what he would. It was all right. Obviously he could afford it, and it was an occasion for her. She would have few enough of those in the months to come. He must, she thought, be very glad to see me if he takes me to supper. She wondered if he would question her about where she had been for the past year and more. She did not want to tell him about Clara. Not yet. He had been, she remembered, capable of great anger toward her. She felt that she could not bear such anger now. Wait. See what he says.

"Now," he said in a not unfriendly way. "What is it?"

"I went to find Biddy. They said she'd been gone for a year."

"So she has." His voice was quiet and calm.

"You know where she is, then? What happened to her? Why did that woman say—"

"Say what?" Very soft.

"That she was dead. To them."

She had made an error. She should not have gone to him. He was not going to tell her. He sat quite still, his face inscrutable.

The waiter brought their food. The odor of the hot meat made her stomach turn. She pushed her plate away. Two more men had come in. They sat at the next table but one. Their voices carried; the older one had a foreign accent.

Patrick had begun to eat. She was aware that the man whom she had noticed, the man with the accent, was staring at her. She looked down at the table. She wished that she had stayed at the boarding house. It was a mistake to try to pick up the threads, to seek out those whom one had known before. Let the past die, she thought.

"When I was a little child," said Patrick suddenly, startling her so that she looked up at him again, "I can remember my father saying that it was better for a man to die here than in the old country. Because if he'd got himself here, even if he died soon after, his children would have a chance at life. He expected to die young, you see. He knew them. The Yankees. He knew what we were to them. Beasts. Animals to be used like a horse or an ox. Worse. Horses and oxen cost more than an Irishman. Use us until we drop and then go out and buy another. Never trust them, he said. Find a way to use them as they do us. Even if they say they love you like a brother, don't believe it."

He took a swallow of beer. The clock on the wall read five o'clock. More people came in: three men and two women.

"Well, I forgot what he said. And I was punished for forgetting. He was dead and gone and I thought he'd been wrong and I put his words in the back of my mind." He looked at her again. "You want to know about Biddy. I'll take you to see her if you like. It won't be pleasant, I warn you."

"Patrick—what happened to her?"

"She was bought."

Pull it out, word by word. She felt very tired. The room was warm. Voices rose, making a racket in her ears.

"By your benefactor."

I have no benefactor, she thought. No one has ever— Then she realized whom he meant.

"Mr. Bradshaw?"

"Yes."

"I don't understand."

"Of course you don't. I don't myself, but there it is. He saw her and took her away. She'd promised herself to me, but that didn't matter, nothing mattered. She went with him. He put her over in Dracut, a little place all to herself. And when her time came, and she thought she was dying, she sent for Mary McCormic. I went with her. Biddy lived, but God took His revenge. The baby died. It was a boy. That near killed

Bradshaw. He wanted a boy so bad, you see. Bad enough even to steal away another human being. She was only Irish, after all. So she wasn't as much of a human being as himself and his kind."

Long ago, standing outside Bradshaw's house, staring at the coffin. And Miss Amalia come to visit: "He cannot get a son, Sabra!" Three living children and not one a boy. Rachel's mother had died for that. And Biddy, too, sacrificed—

"And she—"

"She mourns the baby. And him. I visit her from time to time. He hired a woman to stay with her. He never visits."

"Ah—" It was not to be borne. The pale face half hidden, the small presence nestled near of an evening, so carefully tracing out the letters and numbers that they taught her. *"Please let me stay. . . ."*

She realized that she was crying. She could not hold back her tears. She pulled out her handkerchief and wiped her eyes and nose and breathed deep; and then she wept again. I must not, she thought; a lady does not cry in public. I must not embarrass him.

He observed her stolidly, offering no sympathy. He finished his meal and signaled for the waiter.

"I'm off to take the evening trade. Where are you boarding? I'll stop by to see you." When she told him her address he smiled grimly. "At least you're not on the Commonwealth, working for him."

They said good-by in front of the hotel. She watched him walk back to Codwell's, following him with her eyes. Once again she was alone: now, she thought, back to Mrs. Pye's. It was not yet six. If she wanted, she could get her supper there. During the long evening without even the solace of privacy, she would have to make talk with the girls, she would have to seem reasonably self-possessed or there would be questions, speculations, perhaps an unpleasant interview with Mrs. Pye.

She wanted only to be somewhere warm and safe and quiet. Away from everyone except Clara. And at the thought of her child—who had lived, who was loved despite her sex—her tears began again and she stood on the boardwalk, blinded, uncaring of curious stares, fumbling helplessly for the sodden handkerchief which she could not find.

She was aware of a man beside her, a clean white cotton handkerchief held out. She looked up. He was the man whom she had noticed in the dining room, the foreigner.

"Go on. You can have it."

His voice was low, strangely accented, but kind, curiously intimate. He smiled at her, proffering the square of cloth.

She took it. She wiped her eyes, blew her nose. She knew that she should feel ridiculous, humiliated; but so gentle was his manner, so kind his voice, that strangely she felt not at all ashamed.

"There," he said. "No, keep it. It's yours." He paused, appraising her. "All right now?"

"Yes. Thank you."

"It wasn't that one you were with, was it, who was forrard, makin' you cry? Tell me, and you'll be shut of him forever."

In spite of herself she laughed. "No. It wasn't his fault. Really I'm quite recovered." One did not stand talking to a strange man in the street —not unless one wanted to invite all kinds of unpleasant consequences. A lady would imply, ever so delicately, that despite her gratitude he had been, all the same, a bit forward—

"And you have a place to go now?"

"Yes." Automatically, without meaning to, she extended her hand, not realizing that she had done so until she felt his hand enclose hers in a warm, strong grasp. She looked up into his face. Even in the dim, flickering light from the lamp posts in front of the hotel she saw his eyes, brilliant blue, startlingly intense under dark brows. His hair was brown, rather long, with golden lights. She had never seen anyone whose glance was so compelling, so disquieting.

She stepped back, somewhat alarmed; she withdrew her hand. He held it just a moment too long and then let go. She looked down, glad that the brim of her bonnet concealed her face. She felt that she could not bear the scrutiny of those eyes.

She murmured as gracious a good-by as she could manage and turned away to cross the busy street. She felt light-headed—the result, no doubt, of an empty stomach—and now, after the fact, thoroughly embarrassed. To make such a display of herself in public! A warm supper and a good night's rest were what she needed; she would be better—more in control of herself—tomorrow.

Prince watched her go. Then he whistled up a boy from a group which clustered at the edge of the boardwalk by the horse trough.

"There's a penny for you if you run me an errand, boy. See that bonnet there? Now you slip across and follow her and tell me where she's gone, and I'll have another penny for you when you're back."

The boy ran off; in ten minutes he had returned. Prince nodded at the information he had to give, and paid him, and returned to his companions in the dining room.

Regardless of the success or failure of his speech that evening to the Workingmen's Association, he felt now that his time in Lowell had not been entirely wasted.

4

To her surprise Sabra slept early and well that night. She rose before dawn with the other women and ate her breakfast with them. She was aware of an undercurrent of tension around the table. Small hints, muttered, cryptic phrases, told where some of them had spent the previous evening; one girl went so far as to proclaim openly that she was a recruiter for the Female Labor Association, whose members had been so largely represented at last night's assembly. Somehow a Ten-Hour petition found its way onto the breakfast table among the pots of tea and plates of squash pie; somehow copies of a handbill announcing another meeting were pressed into every hand as the women hurried out to the mill.

Feeling still oddly adrift because there was no place where she had to be, Sabra wandered back to her bedroom. To comfort herself, to bring her child a little closer, she thought to look again at Clara's present. The room was dimly lit from the single window; the sun had not yet risen, although the sky was clear and the day promised fine. She felt, unaccountably, more cheerful than she had in weeks. Despite her interview with Patrick, despite her separation from Clara, the new day had brought new hope. She would be all right. Two more days and she would begin working; soon, somehow, Clara would be with her again. They would survive. It was even possible, this morning, to think that Silas would return. No: certainly he would. He had promised. And then they would go—somewhere, somehow they would make a life.

So her thoughts ran as she crouched to open her hand trunk. After a moment she sat back on her heels. It could not be. A mistake, surely—she had put it somewhere else. Even as she glanced around the dreary little room she knew that it was a foolish hope; she had put the cap, carefully wrapped, into her trunk, and now it was gone. Clara's white lace-trimmed bonnet, her birthday present.

Abruptly Sabra stood up, her heart thudding, and encompassed the bedroom in one glance. Surely there was no safe hiding place here for a package, no matter how small. Dresses hung on hooks around the wall; the floor beneath them was lined with small trunks and bandboxes. The single bureau was too obvious. Under a bed? Between a quilt and sheet?

She began with the clothing, feeling each garment for pockets, for some solid object concealed among the folds of calico and broadcloth.

Nothing. Next she tried the trunks and boxes, some of which were locked. In the ones which she could open she found hair brushes, bundles of letters, jewelry, books—but not Clara's bonnet. Cursorily, not expecting to discover it, she looked underneath beds; felt with her hands since the light was dim. Mrs. Pye was a poor housekeeper; her hands and skirt were filthy when she finished her search. Under someone's pillow? In a bureau drawer? No.

After half an hour she sat on her bed crying with vexation. She could not believe that one of these girls with whom she was to live for the next year and more had been cruel enough to steal the present that she had bought for her child. Perhaps the thief had not opened the package, had not known what it contained; had simply stolen it hoping for some article worth selling. Had not known that Sabra had bought it with practically the last of her money—and could not buy another. The thought that the thief might have been one even more in need than herself did not occur to her; she could not imagine anyone poorer than she.

After a while she dried her eyes and washed her hands in the scummy water in the basin and went downstairs to find Mrs. Pye. She found instead the servant: an elderly, wall-eyed woman whose cringing air and halting speech gave evidence of a miserable life and, Sabra thought, a deceitful nature. She was peeling potatoes for the noon meal when Sabra came upon her.

"When will Mrs. Pye be back?" she demanded, too distraught to try a more soothing, reassuring tone.

"Dunno. Hour, maybe."

"Is she at the market?"

"Yers." The woman did not interrupt her task as she spoke; her red, knobby hands worked quickly as she curled off the potato skins in long strips.

Sabra did not bother to reply. She turned and went into the dining room, where she sat at the table, intending to accost Mrs. Pye the moment she returned. She picked up a stray saltcellar and moved it back and forth on the scrubbed and cracked oilcloth covering on the table, following the line of a weak ray of sunlight which had found its way through the window.

Probably, she thought, that one in the kitchen took it. Yesterday afternoon while I was out. Probably she makes a handy living here, sticky-fingers, and the girls never know and think it's one of themselves. Probably Mrs. Pye gets her share. She remembered that several of the trunks had been locked. She must persuade Mrs. Pye to ask their owners to open them. Perhaps it was a fortunate thing that the landlady was gone to market: she would be calmer, better able to explain, with this time to compose herself.

She heard footsteps outside. She stood up. But instead of the landlady's key in the lock, she heard the clatter of the bell. Perhaps Mrs. Pye had forgotten her key. The potato-peeler made no appearance from the kitchen, and so, at the second ring—an impatient sound, hard and sharp, not to be denied—Sabra went to open the door.

A man stood on the step. When he saw her he grinned widely and at once removed his low-crowned, broad-brimmed black wide-awake.

"Good morning, ma'am. I thought I'd come and fetch back my handkerchief after all."

Of course. In the distraction of losing Clara's present, she had forgotten completely the events of the previous day.

"John Prince at your service, ma'am. I didn't realize you were the proprietress of the establishment."

"I'm not. I'm waiting for her to come back." She was aware, as she had been the previous evening, of the feeling that by speaking to him she was putting herself somehow beyond the bounds of ordinary, polite conversation. She had never seen a man with such a ruthless look: as if, seeing something he wanted, he would move unhesitatingly to get it and would not care who was disturbed in the process.

"Well, then," he said easily; and, hardly conscious of her movement, she stepped aside to allow him to enter. "Let me wait with you. I feared you'd be at the factory, but I thought to have a look in nevertheless."

"I have a place," she said, "but I don't start until Monday." She led him into the dining room. Now that he was inside the house, she felt totally vulnerable. Surely it was against the rules to receive a gentleman alone in a Corporation boarding house? Mrs. Pye would be angry, she would refuse to search for Clara's bonnet—

Sabra turned suddenly to face him. Only the thought of that precious scrap of batiste and lace gave her the courage to combat his overpowering presence: he seemed as out of place in this dreary abode of females as a wild stallion in the midst of a flock of sheep, and yet he stood at his ease as if he lived here.

"I am sorry, you cannot come in," she said hastily. "Please—I should not have allowed you. Mrs. Pye will be angry, I am sure it is against the rules."

He laughed. "I am sure it is. No man except the Agent gets in here before supper, I'll bet. But that's all right, Miss—ah—?"

"Palfrey."

"Miss Palfrey. And your other name?"

"Sabra."

He smiled at her as if they shared a secret, but she had no idea what it might be.

"I break rules all the time, Miss Sabra Palfrey, and generally I get away with it."

"But—no—please, you must go. I must speak to Mrs. Pye when she returns, it is very important, and if she is angry she will not listen." She heard the sharp panic in her voice; what would she do if he did not go? She could hardly put him out by force. At the edge of her sight she was aware of a slight movement at the kitchen door; surely it had been tight closed a moment ago?

"Please—" she began again. He put out a hand, caught her supplicating one, and made a small, soothing, clucking sound.

"Now. Tell me. I seem always to find you in need of help. And of course I'm glad to give it. No one's a better helper than John Prince. What's wrong? What do you have to tell this woman?"

And so she told him about the theft, and he listened quietly, patting her hand, and when she had done he nodded and surveyed her once again, the laughter gone from his face.

"Yes," he said quietly. "It's the same as bankruptcy for a high muckety-muck, for you to lose that little bonnet. And so you have light-fingers here. Not surprising, with wages what they are. I'll tell you what. Make a bargain with me. If you will do me a service today, I will pay you for it and you can buy another bonnet."

She hesitated. She had no idea how to gracefully refuse an immodest proposal.

"Good. Now here's my problem. I'm in town for only a little time, I've seen some people and I'll see more today, but while I have a space free this morning I want to take a trip to see a friend of mine who came here five years ago. I know where he is but I don't know the way. Will you come along and direct me?"

Still she hesitated; but when he told her the name of the place she went quietly to fetch her cloak and bonnet and went out with him to find his friend. On their way out they passed Mrs. Pye coming in; she looked warily at Prince, but, perhaps overwhelmed by his ostentatious greeting, made no comment other than a grudging good morning.

They walked rapidly out Gorham Street. It was a mild, sunny, springlike day. After a while, uncomfortably warm, Sabra removed her cape; she would have liked to unbutton the top button of her linsey-woolsey dress, but of course she could not.

Prince glanced at her. "Too fast?"

"No. I like to walk quickly."

He nodded approvingly. "Your lungs are good, then. The ones who've caught death from the lint can hardly walk at all sometimes. You should walk every Sunday when you start work again. Keep yourself healthy."

When they reached their destination, they found the gates closed but not locked; Prince pushed them open and they walked in.

"Now," he said briskly, as if he were considering a problem in mathematics, "where shall we find him?" He peered at the low slate headstones extending in neat rows on either side of the path. "I donnot think he'd be so far front. To the back, mayhap. I'll look on this side and you go along that."

They found the gravestone after fifteen minutes' search. It stood next to the stone wall at the rear, a little isolated, plainly carved, lacking decorative willow or urn:

Joseph Kydd
1805–1843

Prince stood for a moment studying the inscription. Sabra turned and walked a few steps away to leave him alone with his friend.

"He was a little lad," Prince said then. His voice was uneven, very low; she saw tears on his ruddy face. He had taken off his hat and he held it now at his breast with both his hands. "Little—but hard. Never sick a day. We grew up together for all that he was five years older. His ma fed me often enough when my own—well, when I needed a meal. Never sick a day. But he couldn't find work, y' see, and so when he read the advertisement he was all set to come across. He wasn't married and his folks had died, so he didn't have attachments. I didn't blame him. I'd have done the same myself in his place."

He fell silent again. Sabra, not wanting to intrude and yet feeling a need to reply, said softly: "How did he die?"

"An accident," said Prince grimly. "I had it from his friend here, he wrote to me after the funeral. O yes. I can read. I was the sharpest lad in the charity night school. A boiler exploded and scalded him to death. At the machine shop." He wiped his face with the back of his hand. "So here he lies. Better off than the rest of us."

As often as she had heard this sentiment, Sabra was moved to protest. "No," she said. "No. He is not."

Prince glanced at her as she fumbled in her reticule. As she withdrew the crumpled white cotton square they both smiled.

"I believe you called for this," she said with mock dignity.

He took it from her and dried his tears and motioned toward the gravestone. "Why isn't he, then?"

"Because—"

She had never tried to put it into words. Against her will, the image of the hanged couple at Harvard Village rose up again in her mind's eye. No—no! Keep on living; savor life, take what it could give, hope for tomorrow.

"Because we still have a chance. He doesn't."

"A chance at what?" His face showed genuine puzzlement. "At having our lungs clogged and ruined with cotton dust? At having our children crushed to death in the gears and shafting, giving up their lives to make some rich man richer than he is now?"

She looked away; she stared across the rows of tombstones, the high iron fence and the busy road beyond. Such questions made her uncomfortable. If one had no choice, then one worked as one could until better times came. Discontent was contagious; it made your life seem worse even than it was, and like a fever it sapped your strength to survive.

"Why did you come here?" she said. "To Lowell, I mean."

He grinned, easy again, his wounds covered over.

"To make trouble," he said. "To give a few rich men a bad night. And mayhap I'll succeed, if they keep on grinding down their help. They're doing me a service, but they don't know it yet. Every time they cut down wages, I'll get that many more listenin' to me."

She turned away then; she wanted no part of agitation, combining against the Corporations.

Afterward she refused to allow him to give her the payment he had promised. When he saw her determination and the distress he caused her by insisting that she take it, he put his money away.

"All right," he said. "I'm in your debt. Perhaps that's as well. Give me something to think about on my travels. How to pay you back." And with a grin he had gone.

She told herself that Clara's cap did not matter. She would not get it back, and she would only stir up hostility toward herself in the attempt. Let it go. Clara would not know the difference. And so she went out to Harvard Village that Sunday empty-handed. She spent a happy hour with her child and drank a cup of Society tea before she left, and then she returned to the city ready to go into the mill the next morning.

5

She had forgotten the noise. As she stood at her looms on her first day at the Appleton Corporation, she was jarred through every inch of her body by the clatter and pounding of the machinery, assaulting her ears, hammering at her brain, reducing her to a jerking, twitching automaton in that long high room full of machines.

She gritted her teeth and applied herself to her task: heddle-eyes of the harness correctly strung; bobbins filled, shuttle ready to fly—ah! A near miss, but she had ducked in time. She caught the eye of the girl standing across the aisle and gave a shamefaced, soundless laugh. She had lost her quickness; her fingers clumsily refused to make a proper weaver's knot. Life at the slow-paced United Society had made her forgetful of the capitalists' ruthless pace. But the Society was not to be thought of; here and now she must pay attention, she must watch as the heavy piece of coarse cotton cloth lengthened onto the take-up. From time to time the overseer passed by. He stared at her to see whether she knew how to handle the looms—three, now, instead of the two she had tended at the Commonwealth. She nodded at him each time he came to show him that she could manage, but in truth she wondered if she could. Three looms! Three great monsters to be watched, three shuttles to keep straight, three lengths of cloth to be perfectly turned out without a snag or a crooked weft row! Faster and faster she turned from one loom to the next; faster and faster the shuttles flew, the beams crashed back and forth; ever louder in her head grew the thunder of the machinery. The floor trembled beneath her feet, the windows rattled in their frames—smaller windows than the Commonwealth's, looking out at another high brick building. No river view now, no sunsets filling the valley. She thought fleetingly, bitterly, of the girl who once had written a poem about the pastoral scene spreading out below the Commonwealth Mill; the scene here was row on row of brick, a close-fettering of the mind.

When the dinner bell rang, just after noon, she paused for a moment before she followed the others down the stairs and across the street to the boarding house. She felt dizzy and a little faint. The smells of must and machine oil filled her nostrils; for a moment she thought she could not eat. But her stomach was empty; it seemed days, instead of just five hours, since she had eaten. Catching the overseer's curious glance, she took her cloak from its hook and went out after the others.

Her first week on the Appleton Corporation seemed endless, and many times during that week she asked herself whether her decision to return to the factory had been wise. She had had to leave the Society, certainly, but should she have looked for some other means of support? Domestic service, perhaps, in some kind household where she would have been allowed to keep Clara with her? Dressmaking, perhaps, with her own small establishment? Or perhaps, after all, she should have appealed to Henry Winfield for help. Surely that great and good man, that counselor to all the world, would not have turned away the wife and child of one who had been his most devoted and ardent follower?

She struggled with these thoughts at night, lying in her lumpy bed next to her sleep-mate, a stolid, four-square girl who said little enough when she was awake but who snored and snorted and muttered through the nights so that Sabra was forced to put her pillow over her head to get any rest at all.

The arguments flickered through her weary brain. Certainly she had done the right thing. No one wanted a housekeeper who was encumbered by a child—a very little child, just walking, whose every step needed to be supervised, who could not be left unattended for a moment lest she get into someone's embroidery box or fall into the fire or eat some poisonous substance. And besides, domestic service paid nothing. She would be unable to save a penny. And one did not start a dressmaking establishment with no capital: one needed a decent showroom, and samples of one's work, and a large clientele—and, besides, she hated sewing. The thought of being a slave to a needle for the rest of her life was unbearable. And as for Mr. Winfield, he was surely angry with Silas for deserting him, or saddened at the very least. He would be of no mind to help her, even if he could. He was not a wealthy man; probably he had more than enough dependents already. And she was not a beggar. She wanted to earn her own way.

On her first pay day, when she joined the throng at the paymaster's office at closing bell, she knew she had been right to come back. She forgot her aching muscles and her sore feet and her numb, buzzing ears; she forgot the noisy, noisome boarding house and Mrs. Pye's inferior food and the ache in her heart which was the absence of Clara. Six dollars and ninety cents; and next month she would have thirteen and eighty, and the month after, more than twenty—why, in a year she would have almost a hundred!

Carefully she put the coins into the pocket of her skirt and walked toward the little foot-bridge over the canal behind the towering mill complex. She wanted to put her money in the bank at once—she had an hour or more before it closed—so that it, too, would not be stolen, or (less likely, but still possible) so that she would not be tempted to spend it. She would spend not a penny, she thought grimly; she would not go near the shops. No library card, no lecture tickets, certainly no pew rent. Every cent would go into her account. And if she hurried she would get back to Mrs. Pye's before the others had finished their supper, so that she would not go hungry.

The night was cold and clear. After twelve hours in the hot and humid weaving room, she shivered as the wind penetrated the thin cover of her clothing. The black water in the canal, stilled now until Monday morning, shone in streaks of reflected light. As she came toward Shattuck Street she heard shouts and catcalls coming from Huntington Hall. Meeting, meeting! All week long handbills had been circulated, it was not known by whom, announcing meetings of the Female Labor Reform Association, of the New England Workingmen's Association. She wanted no part of them. Let me be, she thought; I'll make my own way. Nothing would change. The Corporations would never grant Ten-Hour, they would simply fire the ringleaders and replace them with new hands.

The teller at the bank was smiling and efficient, always glad, he said, to open a new account, thank you very much, miss, your money's safe with us. She came out onto the street again and was startled to hear her name spoken. A man moved toward her from the lamp post where he had been standing, and as he came near she saw that it was John Prince.

"All safe and secure?" he said. He smiled at her, and his smile was warm and kind. "You were quick enough to get away just now. I almost lost you when you came across the canal."

"Yes. All safe." She remembered that he had said something about going away. "Did you have a good journey?"

"Moderate. Just moderate. I'll tell you about it while we get some supper."

She hesitated. Plenty of time until curfew—but she was tired, she had planned to stay in bed all day tomorrow if she could, she wanted only to rest from now until the rising bell on Monday. But he had taken her arm and begun to walk with her toward Merrimack Street.

"No," she said, "I'm very tired, I think not—"

"Good. I'm tired too. We'll rest together over a nice bit of beefsteak and a plate of oysters and then I'll see you back if you like before I go on the platform."

Probably the meeting at Huntington Hall, she thought. She heard the crowd again, now, as they walked away.

"That's Jones," said Prince, "warmin' them up for me. They'll be red-hot by the time I get to them."

He steered her into the small, warm oyster saloon in the basement of the City Hall and sat her at a table toward the back of the room. "Just wait here. I'll see that fellow over there, and then I'll be right back with you."

The man to whom Prince spoke was a tall, thin, poor-looking man who lounged against the bar and did not bother to change his position as he answered Prince's questions. In a moment Prince had returned to her, and, after ordering their meal, he leaned back in his chair and smiled at her.

"Now," he said. "Tell me. How is it at work? No hair caught in the machinery, no fingers missing?"

She shrugged. Of course he was joking; accidents happened only when one was careless. Still, she did not think he was funny. "No. It was all right, except that I have three looms to tend."

"And you'll be lucky if you don't have four, by the end of the year."

"Four! No one can watch four looms."

"No?" The waiter set a glass of ale before him and he took a long drink. "Wait, m'dear. Wait. I was in Manchester this past week. I thought I'd stop at Nashua, but they told me I was needed farther north, and so I was. They're on four looms now, have been for a year and more."

She accepted his word without argument. She saw no point in discussing the matter; if they gave her four looms, then somehow she would manage. She relaxed a little, warm again after her cold walk, a little sleepy. What was she doing here with this man who was after all a stranger? She should be back in the boarding house, going to sleep.

The waiter brought their food. She took a bite and discovered that she was hungry; this was a much better meal than she would have had at Mrs. Pye's. Prince watched her, his blue eyes steady under the dark brows, a slight smile on his face.

As she ate she felt her strength return, and with it her curiosity about this man. Who was he? And why had he waited for her tonight? She had thought never to see him again. But before she could formulate a question which would sound sufficiently ladylike, not direct or bold, he began to speak again.

"No sign of the little bonnet stolen from you?"

"No."

"You never told me who it was you bought it for."

She hesitated. How much could she tell him? How much did she want to?

"My husband—"

"Went away, did he?"

She nodded, grateful that he had said the words for her.

"When I left the factory, my discharge was made out to Miss Palfrey. It seemed simpler to go on that way. I needed work, there are so many asking for each place, and I did not want them to think that I had a forged paper."

He smiled approvingly. "I'd have done the same, in your place. No need to tell them what's none of their business. And besides—" He gestured with his fork. "Soon you'll be rich, and you can buy a dozen bonnets. I heard today of a woman who saved up nine hundred dollars and bought a house in the country. Course the house came furnished with an Agent's brat." His grin flashed at her. "Folks are all so holy here, you almost forget they're human beings first off."

For one dreadful moment she thought that he would say the Agent's name, and that it would be Bradshaw; but he passed on to other topics—the quality of food at the boarding house, the sights he saw on his travels—and her anxiety faded.

When they had done eating, they walked the long way around to her boarding house. It was just nine o'clock: an hour to curfew. He had plenty of time, he said. He had planned to make only a short speech at the end to send them away in high spirits, confident of winning.

Winning what, she wondered. Two hours less a day, and a corresponding cut in wages? Weariness descended on her once again. She glanced aside into the window of a shop. It was a stationer's shop, still thronged with customers spending their pay. Through the glass she saw the display of goods: pens and paper, a box of paints, a few books.

Something caught her eye. She stopped; she looked again to see what it might have been. There it was: a fat volume bound in green, the title stamped in gold: *Love's Last Lament* by Matthias Simmons.

Minerva Swan. Sabra remembered the plump, intelligent face, the quiet determination. Minerva must be having great success. She had left Mrs. Clapham's the summer that Sabra and Silas visited Moses Trueworthy at Bountiful. There had been one letter from her to all her former friends, addressed jointly as "Dear Hearts." Sabra, preoccupied with her own problems, had briefly considered asking Minerva for help; and then, deciding against, had forgotten her.

Well: Minerva must be doing splendidly.

Sabra recognized the feeling in her heart. It was not happiness for Minerva's good fortune. It was envy: fast-flowering, stinging envy. She herself was condemned to labor in a factory like a slave for endless months, simply to get the means to survive, while Minerva had only to sit at her desk scribbling for a few hours a day to make more in a year (so Sabra imagined) than an operative could accumulate in a lifetime.

It was not fair. What had she done to be so oppressed? Why could she not have been born with some talent, some ability to make money in a less difficult way? What less difficult way was there for a woman? I will never get free, she thought. I have come back because I had no choice; and I will never get free again.

She turned away from the shop. Prince saw her distress; but let her tell me on her own, he thought. Best not to start her crying again when I haven't the time to stay and comfort her.

For her part, as they walked on quickly to Mrs. Pye's, she was glad of his silent, reassuring presence. He was a strong, solid, self-confident man —as he needed to be, in his line of work—and she felt his unspoken sympathy. She was grateful to him, and very glad that she had not seen *Love's Last Lament* when she had only herself for company.

In the weeks that followed she saw him from time to time, always without warning. She would emerge from the mill yard in the evening and see him standing at the entrance gate, or across the street. As the days lengthened and the operatives were dismissed at twilight instead of in darkness, she became adept at spotting him instantly: his stocky, slightly swaggering figure, his wide-awake perched at an angle, the movement of his body as he paced up and down, waiting for her. The first few times that she saw him, waiting, she was indifferent; she accepted him because his company offered a break in the monotony of her life. He always had some new story to tell, some interesting comment on people or events with which she was only vaguely familiar, but which, as he spoke, came alive for her and offered her brain a new cud on which to chew.

And then one raw, misty May twilight she emerged from the mill yard and stopped. She did not at first recognize the feeling which overcame her; she knew only that suddenly, for no apparent reason, she was bitterly unhappy and disappointed, and that the thought of going back to Mrs. Pye's and spending yet another dreary evening in the makeshift parlor was almost more than she could bear. Her eyes swept up and down the street, and she understood then that she was looking for him, and that he was not there.

6

Inevitably, John Prince became increasingly suspect in the eyes of the textile management. He traveled constantly back and forth spreading his message to the workers: "Organize! Organize! You can do nothing alone, but together we can fight our battle and win! We will bring the capitalist scum to its knees! We will put our hands to its throat and strangle it as we have been strangled! We will tear down the bastions of wealth and privilege which take the bread from our mouths—yes, the very lives from our bodies! We will stand fast for Ten-Hour! And before we admit defeat, we will see every factory destroyed, torn down brick by brick, we will see the sky black with the smoke from burning mills, we will dash their heads against their great wheels and drown them in their canals! Brothers! And sisters, too! Organize! Organize!"

The capitalists were not afraid of him. They were too powerful, too firmly in control, to fear the likes of John Prince. No: rather they regarded him as an annoyance—an outside agitator to be closely watched, a rabblerouser whose rantings made their lives a bit more difficult, certainly, but who presented no more real danger to them, so they thought, than a hungry flea to the dog that carried it.

Then, too, they had their weapons against such troublemakers. Silence was the first and most obvious one; and so, for some weeks, the readers of the *Courier* were unaware of Prince's existence. Other Corporation-controlled newspapers in other cities followed the same strategy: ignore him and he will go away. Or at least he will not exist, even if he stays and pursues his hopeless campaign.

This tactic failed. The magnates could control some newspapers but not all. It was regrettable but a fact all the same that anyone who could afford a press and a supply of newsprint could publish anything he liked —even Prince's nonsense. *The Voice of Industry* was particularly annoying. Having begun in Fitchburg, it soon moved to Lowell so as to be closer to its largest constituency. It appeared only once a week, but that was enough. No one could prevent its editors from printing any foolish fancies that struck them—even the demands of that infamous communist, Robert Owen, for three million dollars to start the world anew.

But if the Corporations could not prevent such rubbish from being printed, they could prevent their operatives from reading it. Any copy of the *Voice* found on Corporation property was instantly destroyed. Any operative caught reading it was reprimanded with the threat of dismissal. Copies left at the post office could not be found when the subscribers called for them. Would-be advertisers were warned that their announcements would not be accepted at the *Courier* if they bought space in the *Voice*.

Still, for a while, the *Voice* endured, broadcasting Prince's message and the speeches of like-minded men—and women, for the *Voice* had a Female Department, with editorials written by women. They printed outrageous demands for education, equal pay, marriage reform—even the vote. It struck some people as odd that while the Corporations had welcomed and praised *The Lowell Offering,* they had only the greatest scorn for the literary efforts of the women at the *Voice*.

The Corporations had another weapon in their arsenal far more powerful than the press. This weapon had many heads and hands, but only one heart: an organ which belonged exclusively to its masters. The Massachusetts legislature—the Great and General Court, which was neither great nor general nor in fact a court—stood (or rather reclined) ready to do battle for the Corporations at a moment's notice. Having been inundated with petitions from the operatives requesting that it enact a ten-hour day, the legislature bravely fought its way out from under the blizzard of paper and stood firm. No Ten-Hour law, it said. We must not abridge labor's freedom of contract; the remedy is not with us. True, we created the Corporations; but we will not regulate them. Labor must look out for its own interests; we cannot help it.

The most effective weapon of all against those who would agitate unrest was of course the power to discharge and blacklist the troublemakers. This was done with increasing frequency as Prince's words took root and the operatives looked around them and saw that there was no one to help them but themselves. And so it was understood that to become a recruit in the cause of Ten-Hour was to become a pariah—an untouchable who must find other ways to keep body and soul together than a place on the Corporations, for the Corporations (Christian gentlemen all, nurtured on Old Testament prophets) cast out whatever offended them.

Of course John Prince was aware of all of this: he knew all about the small arms and the heavy artillery and the sure and swift retribution visited upon those who aligned themselves with him. The knowledge saddened him, and angered him, and gave him a sense of the gravest responsibility. He knew that when he asked men—and women, too—to organize into Associations to fight for Ten-Hour, he asked for their livelihoods. That even a few listened and acted on his words heartened him and gave him hope, even as his knowledge of their risk weighed on his conscience.

He was a stubborn, dedicated man with right on his side; and he would keep on fighting.

7

Sabra knew little of this; had she known more still she would not have joined ranks with the agitators. She had a living to earn; it was a hard, grinding, wearing-down life, but it was the only chance she had at any life at all. On the few occasions when she gave Ten-Hour any thought, she was not enthusiastic about it. Once—only once—she spoke of it to Prince.

"If they pass Ten-Hour, our wages will go down," she said.

"They don't have to, but yes, probably they will."

"Certainly the Corporations would never keep us at the same rate for fewer hours! How can we support Ten-Hour? We can hardly survive on what we earn now."

"That is so. But once organize effectively to gain Ten-Hour, Sabra, and you will have your organization for any other reform you want—abolition of the year's contract, the blacklist, even higher wages. Anything can come, once we have that."

As the warm spring days lengthened into summer, Sabra discovered that she, as much as any organizer, had a battle to fight, and that Prince was possibly a danger to her as much as to the Corporations. Her reaction to him, and hence her problem, was different from theirs; for instead of increasingly hating this brash, bold, sturdy bear of a man, she discovered that she was beginning to be fond of him. Ever since the evening when she had looked for him and had not found him, she had been uncomfortably aware of his growing importance to her.

During the dark, close nights when she lay beside her snoring bedmate, she argued with herself about her feelings.

I enjoy being with him. Is that wrong?

No. But he is a dangerous man.

Not to me. He is always very kind to me.

He would be kinder if he left you alone. He is dangerous to all who associate with him, for he tars them with his brush.

I am not an agitator; it is known that I am not.

You are if you associate with one.

Be quiet. Let me sleep.

Restlessly she turned over and then back again, burying her head in the pillow against the tumult of her bedfellow. She was too warm; she threw off the musty coverlet. She was too cold; she pulled it back again. O, for a night—a bed—alone! Or at least for an hour's quiet!

One night as she heard the church bells toll midnight and the reassuring cry of the watch that all was well, an unbidden image flashed across her mind. Silas. For an instant she saw him. He was dressed in dark clothing, wearing a tall hat. He was walking down a street—a dark street, wet with rain, in a fashionable quarter of a foreign city. In France, perhaps, or Germany.

And then he was gone, and she lay in her bed in the stuffy, overcrowded room and listened to that faint ringing in her ears which was the echo of the machinery's roar. Where was he? What was he doing? And where had he been going, walking so steadily in the rain, alone in a faraway place?

She had not thought of him—really thought of him—for weeks. In her growing attachment for John Prince, she had forgotten the painful longing which thoughts of Silas had aroused: when will he come back? Why hasn't he written? And then Prince had appeared, and gradually filled her heart, and Silas had retreated to the back of her mind and she had no longer missed him.

She felt no guilt at seeing Prince, no sense of betraying a marriage bond. The union into which she had so readily entered had dissolved long ago; its dissolution had begun on the day Silas left Bountiful. In the long months of silence since, it had been broken completely, until now, finally, she felt quite alone. She wondered if their marriage would have been upheld in a court of law, or if, as Silas had said, it was not a legal thing after all. Was she free?

Her mouth curved into a bitter smile as she stared unseeing in the darkness. Free! Condemned to work more than seventy hours a week at an exhausting, health-destroying, mind-destroying job for an infinitesimal sum of money, faced with the task of somehow providing for her child, alone, without friends or family to help her. The question of the validity of her marriage was nothing compared to these cares. I'll worry about that, she thought, when someone proposes to me. And that's not likely.

For she had no illusions about John Prince. For whatever reason he sought her out, it was not with the idea of marrying her. She did not mind: looked at from the perspective of a husband-hunting, security-hunting female, John Prince was in any case a poor prospect. He had no money to speak of; he was hardly settled, since he traveled constantly; he was liable at any time to have to disappear completely if he angered the authorities past endurance. No: John Prince was not a prospect for marriage.

She was glad of him all the same. He cheered her, and distracted her mind. Perhaps, she thought, that is why he comes back to see me. He thinks that I am not a marriageable woman, he remembers that my husband is alive somewhere. And because he had not felt in danger of involvement with her, he had become involved after all.

Sabra's assessment of Prince's character was correct: for reasons best known to himself, he was not a courting man. That which made him dangerous—his consuming hatred of the factory owners—left very little room in his heart for any other emotion. Sabra had caught his eye as the flash of the bright wing of a redbird will catch the eye of the deerstalker in the forest: the hunter may stop to lure the bird, to see it close, to pet it, but he does not forget his original mission. Prince had been curious about her to begin with, as any man is curious about a pretty woman who crosses his path. And, indulging his curiosity, he had been pleased to discover that, for him, she possessed a most attractive quality: she was not looking for a husband.

And so he went about his business, traveling back and forth between Lowell and Nashua and Manchester, with an occasional foray south to Taunton and Fall River. But increasingly he found himself in Lowell, for there was the aligning of sides, there was the real battleground. And when he was in Lowell invariably he sought Sabra's company. She was as much a diversion for him as he was for her; when he was with her, he could forget for a time that he had a new speech to write, a new delegation to meet, a new message to give to his small, devoted band of supporters so that they might gain new strength, new heart to continue their fight. He needed to keep their spirits up; organizing, gaining new recruits, was a hard job. The women seemed to be better at it than the men. Of course there were more of them—most of the operatives were women—but even so, the few female organizers had a devotion, an allegiance to the cause, which drove them on in a way quite astonishing to John Prince. He had never seen women like these in England. There, a woman who worked in a textile mill was—yes, certainly—a human being, but so degraded, such a pathetic, filthy, ragged, gin-soaked human being that no decent woman would think of joining her at the loom or the spinning frame.

Here it was different. Here, women chose—freely chose—to work in the factories. He had been surprised to learn that. He had never before seen operatives like these—too thin, too pale certainly, for mill work was an unhealthy occupation in the best of circumstances—but dignified young ladies all the same, with pride in their work and minds that were still active and alert. Almost all of them could read and write; many of them made good use of their free time, such as it was, to educate themselves further—although of what use higher education was to a woman, Prince did not know. Still, he admired them: put them in an aristocrat's drawing room, he thought, properly dressed, and you couldn't tell the difference between them and the ladies of the manor.

Of course the Americans prided themselves on not having the aristocracy. Prince laughed at that: they fooled themselves, for they were as quick to grovel, as conscious of their so-called betters, as any class-ridden Englishman. Americans had not yet had time to establish long pedigrees: but they would, and when they did the pedigree would be based on property rather than noble blood. Not so different after all.

It was in fact a matter of social class—of preserving one's caste—which was proving to be the most formidable obstacle to organizing the operatives. And, to give her credit, Miss Bagley, the president of the Female Labor Reform Association, was well aware of the problem. Late one night, after a meeting whose attendance had been disappointingly low, she had discussed the matter with him and William Young as they sat in the office of Young's newspaper, *The Voice of Industry*. Prince did not like Miss Bagley—he did not like any outspoken woman—but he respected her; she was his best organizer.

She sat with them now, disconsolate, her worn brown dress neatly mended, a small cameo at her collar, her dark hair smoothly looped over her ears and pulled back into a heavy pug. No one could have called Miss Bagley pretty, but she tried always to look well groomed. She held in her lap a small volume, riffling its pages as she sought the passage pertinent to her argument. Prince had seen the book; it had been written by a clergyman—damn the sniveling lot of them!—and Prince would have bet his life that the man had been paid for his efforts. *Lowell: as it was, and as it is,* by the Reverend Henry A. Miles—and didn't Mr. Miles adore the Corporations, and fawn and grovel, and write his puffery as shameless as a servicing whore! But that was the way of it: if you were rich enough, you could buy anything, even men's minds. Only last night Prince had seen another lackey sniffing about, and an unpleasant surprise it had been: William Scorseby, D.D., whose face was well-known to Prince, whose parish in England, in Bradford, was near enough to the agonies of Manchester to make him familiar with Prince and his activities. Too familiar. When Prince had left England he had thought never to see any of his enemies again; and now here was Scorseby, prowling the streets of Lowell, stopping to talk with passing operatives. Investigating, no doubt; and no doubt his discoveries would be used to upbraid the women of his parish at home, factory hands who could neither read nor write, who had never had the benefits of healthy country air as these

Yankee women had. O yes: Prince knew Scorseby and his kind. The Church was a valuable ally to the factory owners, and therefore a dangerous enemy to the operatives. The Church taught obedience to authority, it taught a happier life in future, it taught hypocrisy and deceit and groveling to wealth. Why could people not understand that?

Miss Bagley had found the passage, and now she read aloud:

> Still another source of trust which a Corporation has for the good character of its operatives, is the moral control which they have over one another. A girl, *suspected* of immoralities or improprieties of conduct, at once loses caste. Her former companions will shun her everywhere. From this power of opinion there is no appeal.

Her voice was shrill with anger. Prince gritted his teeth; he hated such voices, they reminded him all too unpleasantly of times best forgotten, when he had been the recipient of such tones every night.

"You see," said Miss Bagley, "they admit it. They depend on the women to shackle themselves. No man—no Agent or overseer—need say a word. We do their work for them. We insist on being perfect ladies, we agree among ourselves that it is unsuitable conduct to complain about our wages, our long hours, our weakening lungs. No! We will die at our looms before we raise our voices in protest! We must be eternally grateful to the Corporations for allowing us to come here and work away our lives so that they may keep up their dividends!"

A melancholy smile illuminated Young's haggard face. He glanced at Prince. "She is right, John. They have—what? Three hundred in the Female Association. Those three hundred—out of twelve or thirteen thousand, mind you—are all they will get. They were the first to join, last winter, and they will be the last. The others will never sign on, not if Miss Bagley recruits for the next hundred years."

Prince shook his head. "It doesn't make sense. They are educated, they are intelligent—they can see the world around them, they know how they are exploited, it is not as if they were poor brutes like the operatives in England who can't think beyond the next bellyful of gin. Listen. All they'd have to do is write to their friends at home, warn them not to sign on with the recruiter. Then when they turn out, the next time their wages are cut, there'd be no one to replace them, no black-legs to be hired. They'd bring the Corporations down in a month—a week! If three hundred turn out they can be discharged and replaced—but *thirteen thousand!* Think of it!"

His eyes shone briefly at the imagined sight: the factories silent and still, the great water wheels immobile, the streets filled with protesting operatives.

"I spoke to a girl today," said Miss Bagley, "to ask her to join. She heard me out, at least I'll give her credit for that, she didn't shut me off the way some of them do as if I were the Devil himself. And do you know what she said? 'I've wanted to come to the mills for five years,' she said, 'ever since I was eleven years old, and Father first mortgaged the farm. Now I'm afraid it's past redemption, we've borrowed so much. But at least there's my brother. I'll be able to help him. He's only fourteen, but if I can save enough I'll see that he gets to college if it's the last thing I do. He wants so much to be a preacher, it's only right he has his chance.' 'He'll have a better chance, and you along with him, if you can earn a better wage,' I said. 'Join us and we'll all fight together.' You should have seen her face. 'O I couldn't do that,' she said. 'Father would never approve. He didn't want to let me come down in the first place. He finally consented when he heard that the girls here are perfect ladies, not forward or bold—the schoolmaster assured him of it, he said his own sister had worked here years ago and helped him through his college. The Corporations would be as watchful of me as my own father, he said, and never let me do anything unbecoming a lady. How could I protest against them, when it's them giving me the chance to help my brother?'"

The anger had gone from Miss Bagley's voice. She sat limp in her chair, just beyond the circle of lamplight; wearily she shut the offending book and laid it on Young's desk.

"You ought to print a review pointing out the error in the Reverend's logic," she said to Young. "Certainly friend Munson won't do it."

Prince had listened to Miss Bagley's recital with a growing sense of futility. What was the use of even trying, if what she said were true? And certainly it seemed to be true. They wouldn't join, they wouldn't fight—they were too glad for even a dollar a week to risk losing it. And as for that toady, Munson—

"He's up for re-election when?" he said abruptly.

"November," said Miss Bagley. "Every November he renews his contract with his masters—who see to it, of course, that his re-election is assured. Now if *we* had the vote—"

Prince smothered a smile as he thought of the noisy, reeking polling places filled with an invasion of petticoats.

"There you have it," he said. "Vote the rascal out!"

Young's face grew thoughtful. "It could be done," he said. "It might be easier to work for Munson's defeat than to recruit new members."

"With the Agents breathing down the neck of every man who marks a ballot?" said Miss Bagley scornfully. "You know that it's as much as a man's job is worth to vote Democrat in Lowell."

Young nodded slowly. "True. They see each man's envelope, they know how he votes. But it's something to work for, after all. Some specific objective. We don't seem to be able to get people to a meeting to discuss the principles of labor reform; perhaps we could organize them to work against Munson. It's still a free country, after all. A man's got a right to vote his conscience."

"Not in Lowell," replied Miss Bagley.

8

One warm Saturday night, John Prince strolled with Sabra down Merrimack Street enjoying the free entertainment, watching the crowd of operatives rushing to spend their pay before the shops closed. A billboard layered with posters and broadsides caught his eye, and he stopped to examine it. Here all the world announced itself; all the world, passing through, had something to offer—for a fee, of course, for there were more ways than one to make money in a factory town. Here was Dr. O. S. Fowler, examining cranial propensities at the Merrimack House; here was a mesmerist, or a palm-reader, or a teacher of voice, or a she-lecturer on the horrors of war and the opium trade. And, in the lower left-hand corner, a modest announcement:

Henry Winfield
"On Fourierist Community"
Sat. June 15, 1845   8.00 P.M.   Huntington Hall
Admission 25¢

Sabra stared at the name. Her heart felt strangely constricted, as if some invisible hand were wrenching it out of her body. Dear God, she thought. Fourier. That had been the name of the Frenchman whom Silas had mentioned. And if Winfield had taken him up, did that mean that Silas had returned to his mentor, had convinced Winfield of yet another New Way? She stood quietly before the billboard, her arm in Prince's, and prayed that he did not feel her trembling.

It was Winfield's poster which had caught Prince's eye. He glanced at Sabra, whose face he could not see.

"Look at this," he said. "Henry Winfield. He spoke once back home in Manchester, but I couldn't get to hear him."

"Why not?" she said. Her voice sounded strained and oddly high in her ears; my hearing, she thought, is being badly damaged by the noise in the workroom.

Prince grinned. "I was in prison," he said. "But I heard about it after.

I'd be very glad to hear him tonight and see if he's still singing the same song. Will you come?"

They moved along, propelled by the moving crowd, and Sabra waited until they had reached a freer part of the boardwalk to reply. She was glad of a moment's respite; when she spoke, her voice was calm.

"I don't much care for philosophical lectures."

He smiled comfortingly; he patted her hand.

"I'll tell you what. You can lean against me and take a little nap. You don't snore, do you? Good. I'll wake you when he's done."

"That would be unladylike. And a waste of money—"

She felt the protest rising inside her as he steered them around into the flow of bodies going in the opposite direction toward the hall.

"Come on. He won't speak long—an hour at most, and we can skip the dialogue afterward, there's nothing I want to ask him."

"No." She shook her head vehemently, although he had kept his hand on hers and she was forced therefore to keep up with him. She tried to pull her hand free, but he kept a tight hold. Why not, she thought, fighting down her rising panic. Surely I can sit for an hour, and hear it again. No. No, she could not. She could not see that face which had been the world to Silas (and so to her), she could not scan the crowd to see if Silas had come—no. No. He would not come to Lowell and neglect to search her out. But he did not know she was here. He did not know that she had gone to the Society. He did not know that she had left Clara. He did not care, he had left Clara himself.

With an effort she got her arm free, helped by a boy running through the crowd and careening into Prince as he went.

"No," she said. "You go on. You are right, I am tired, I'll go back to Mrs. Pye's and you go to hear him."

"It'll only be an hour," said Prince. "By nine o'clock we'll be out."

"No." She could not meet his eyes.

Prince was annoyed. He had thought that he had assured himself of her company for the evening, and now she was being unaccustomedly stubborn over nothing. He disliked argumentative women (except when they argued at his direction, to his benefit); he disliked standing on the crowded street begging her to do his will.

He put his hand under her chin and lifted it so that he could see her face. And then his annoyance fled, replaced by his very genuine affection which had for a moment deserted him.

"What, Sabra? No, don't cry. What is it, what's wrong?"

She shook her head. She could not speak.

Prince looked around. Damned busy town, nowhere quiet, nowhere private.

"Come on," he said. He guided her across the street and down toward the Commonwealth Canal abutting St. Anne's Church. Here was a long, tree-shaded grassy bank extending the length of the canal from Merrimack Street to the mill. Across the water stood the Commonwealth's boarding houses, the lights just coming on within. Under the trees, sitting on the grass, one had a deceptive sense of the bucolic: it was a quiet place, well away from the clamor of the shops. The soft murmur of the water lapping at the granite walls of the canal had provided a soothing accompaniment to many a lover's whispered vow.

But it was not to whisper such things that Prince came here. Sabra, feeling somewhat more composed, looked across the canal to the row of boarding houses. Mrs. Clapham's was third from the right. As she watched, the front door opened; two women came out. Their soft laughter carried across the water. They were going shopping, perhaps, or to a lecture. To hear Winfield? To listen to his concoction of dreams and half-truths, sweetened by unattainable promises, a crumb of hope held out to the starving who paid for the privilege of gathering at his table?

Suddenly she was angry. The emotion swept over her swiftly, tightening her stomach and burning her eyes and forcing her jaw to rigidity. It was not fair. Nothing was fair. Why should those women be able to spend their pay and she not? Why should Silas be able to go freely into the world and she not? Why should everyone have help, friends, money, influence—while she struggled alone, scrimping and saving, no hope, no future, a lifetime of drudgery ahead of her? She was young now, but she was losing her youth, to the weary round of rising bell and closing bell and slavery at the machines. Soon she would be old. Soon her life would be over, and what pleasure would she have had from it? She could not even enjoy her own child.

Prince waited quietly for her to speak

"Do you see those houses over there?" she said at last. "I could go now, tonight, to one of them, and the landlady would know me, would be glad to see me, I think. She would call down several of the girls whom I used to know, and we would laugh and cry and have a royal reunion."

She glanced at him. In the gathering twilight, she could see only his dark form settled comfortably beside her. She could not see his face, could not tell his reaction. No matter.

"But I will never do that," she continued. "That girl is gone, and I am in her place, and I don't want to go back. I cannot."

She told him then of her life: her travels with her father, her journey to Lowell, her time with the Bradshaws, her early days in the mill, her friendship with Silas, his devotion to Winfield. She told him of Moses Trueworthy and Bountiful, and of her marriage and Clara's birth, and Silas' desertion and her flight to the United Society, of her decision to return to Lowell. She felt as if she were speaking of a stranger. Who was that person? Her voice was low and bitter, spinning out the tale: the tale of an unknown woman. Finally she came to the end of it. "That is all," she said. "And that is why I don't want to hear Winfield."

Prince reached out and took her hand. "Do you love him—your husband?"

"I don't know. I did. She did, that girl I used to be. Or maybe not. Maybe she loved the idea of him, what he was trying to do. He was so—" So what? "It sounds foolish, but he was so noble. So good. Trying to find a New Way—not just toadying to the Corporations like his father and slipping into an ordinary life, but trying to help—"

Prince snorted. "Charity begins at home, m' dear. What'd he leave for, when he had you and the baby to look after? Why didn't he take you with him?"

"I don't know. He didn't want to be—burdened. He thought Amos Brown would look after us."

"Hah." He sat up straight, staring at her although it was by now full dark. "What about the old man?"

"His father?"

"The same. I donnot understand why you can't go to him. Tell him you need help."

"Silas wouldn't like it. He would be angry with me."

Prince's laughter echoed across the canal. "Angry! May happen you were angry, as well, when he got shut of you!" He fell silent. "You should go to see him, lass. He'd have money enough to keep you in fine style while your man goes off to see the world. Well. I can't criticize him. We all do what we must. I should be grateful to him for not taking you along. Else I wouldn't have known you. No. I won't criticize him. In a way we're alike."

"You're nothing alike. Nothing at all."

"Don't be so sure. We both want to make things better, don't we? But for different reasons. I ran across a fellow in Boston a while ago who reminds me of your man. He wanted to save the world. He had the plan in his pocket. Give everyone a slot, he said, all organized, and, lo! Universal happiness. It doesn't work so easy, but you couldn't tell him that. Now I'm different. I want to make things better, too—for the poor lad who breathes out his life in that stinking air, for the woman who—for the woman who gets up from childbed to go back to her place, because she'll lose that place if she doesn't—"

She heard his voice catch in his throat; she thought she heard him choke back a sob. She realized that she knew very little about him; for all the weeks that she had met him, talked with him, she had been so conscious of her own difficulties that she had not spared thought for his. No: that was not true. She had asked him, once or twice, about his life in England, but he had always turned aside her questions with a smile and a new question of his own, a comment on some current thing, and she had not been interested enough to persist. It had been enough that he was there; she had felt no need to inquire how. Now, however, she was startled out of her self-absorption.

"Who was she?"

She felt his hand on hers, a hard grip.

"My wife."

"And—she died?"

"It was a long time ago. She was poorly anyway, it could only have been a matter of months. Weeks, even. I've always been glad she died when she did, to save her suffering on. But I swore then, and I've sworn every day since, that I'll have back at them. Not just for her sake, although when she died it started me off. But because it's wrong. The system is wrong. When men can take other men and grind them down and use them until they're useless and then throw them aside, when they can work a man his whole life and leave him nothing to show for it but blasted lungs and a miserable death, while the man with the money sits back and draws his dividends—"

Even as her heart went out to him, her mind rejected what he said. Silas was right. You could not reform this system. You could only escape it, and leave it to die without you and all those like you who with their labor kept it alive. You could never reform the men whose money built those mills. They cared nothing for anyone: they wanted their profit, their precious dividends. They did not care how many lives were lost in the process.

She felt him move close; she felt his lips touch her hair. They sat quiet, pondering their new knowledge of each other. After a time, when she turned her face to his, it was with a sense of thanks that they had found each other, that in bearing the burden of their lives they had at least this much: each other, now.

And when at last he kissed her mouth, gently at first, and then with rising passion until her head spun and her heart overturned and she felt herself shaken with feelings she had never known—when at last these things happened to her, she forgot the difficulties of her life, forgot life itself, and clung fast to him, one human being to another, while the water in the canal rippled softly, while darkness descended over the town.

Somehow they made their way to Prince's room, a dreary third-floor cubbyhole in Market Street. Somehow they got upstairs and safely inside before they fell upon each other. Winfield delivered his address; they had forgotten him. Ten o'clock came and went; they neither knew nor cared. Some time later they heard a loud, peremptory knock on the door, and a man's voice calling Prince's name. Prince lifted his head, listening; after a moment they heard feet clumping down the stairs.

It was after midnight when Prince lit a candle beside the bed and looked at his pocket watch. "You're a little late," he grinned. His eyes gleamed like sapphires in the candlelight. "You might as well stay the night. Or shall we make up a story and go round now and see if your landlady will believe it?"

"No. She won't believe any story. I've seen girls try that before. There was a girl the other week who had a tale that would break your heart, but Mrs. Pye didn't believe a word of it."

"What, then?"

"Do you have any money?"

"Some. Ah—I see." He retrieved his trousers from the floor where they had fallen; he pulled them on and stepped to the bureau. From a small pouch he took a dollar piece. He held it up. "Will she believe this?"

"I hope so," said Sabra. She shivered, not entirely because she was afraid. The coin gleamed in Prince's fingers.

A short time later that same coin had found its way into Mrs. Dorcas Pye's palm. She was glad to have it. Times were hard, food was high. But, she warned Prince, it was not enough; she'd take it this time, and manage her girls so that no one suspected. But next time she'd want more. It was as much as her place was worth to do him such a service.

After Prince had left and Sabra crept silently upstairs, Mrs. Pye, awake in her bed, could not repress a twinge of jealousy. He was a handsome man. More than that: he had a way about him, a charm— Restlessly she turned over. He was too good for that chit with never a word to say for herself. Well. He'd pay for her. Resolutely she turned her thoughts away from the two of them. All the same, she had been surprised. She never would have thought it of Miss Palfrey. She wasn't the type. But then, no one was the type. Some were lucky, that was all.

Mrs. Pye smiled grimly in the darkness. Yes: he would pay for her.

9

She did not even know the names of the parts of her body which he aroused. Few women did. She knew only that he had become the center of her lonely world, and that hours spent with him were hours in which she did not worry about money, about surviving, about Silas and Clara and all the long years of struggle which, it seemed, lay ahead of her. His hands on her exhausted body revived it; his mouth breathed ecstatic energy into hers. Life in the mill was a brutalizing life, numbing her mind, deadening her spirit. Prince made her forget. She was grateful to him; she asked only that he remain. Often he was busy, unable to meet her; on those nights she retired early and tormented herself to uneasy sleep, imagining him, remembering him.

She became known as a solitary; somewhat reluctantly, her fellow boarders left her alone. They were friendly girls to those who seemed to be ordinary females like themselves; when they were confronted by a girl in whom they sensed a difference, they backed off, suspicious, sniffing out the reasons. Sometimes they became hostile toward a solitary; sometimes they simply ignored her. Sabra had heard of girls ostracized until they were forced to leave, but she told herself that nothing, now, could drive her out. They could silence her, for all she cared, although they had shown no inclination to do so. For whatever reason, they remained cordial but aloof, allowing her to have her private life in the few free hours left to any of them.

Mrs. Pye was another matter. She was of necessity an accomplice, and, like all paid accomplices, the weak link in their arrangement. Mrs. Pye had the power to destroy them both; but, as Prince reminded Sabra, by informing on them now, having accepted his money, she would destroy herself also. And so, for the moment at least, the landlady was not a source of worry to them.

Sabra became watchful: cunning. She noticed that she was not the only girl in Mrs. Pye's establishment to have a sick friend who required late nursing.

"Why—she takes more in bribes than she does in board money!" she said to Prince one night. "And not only for latecomers, either. There's a girl in my room who never goes out, but she bribes Mrs. Pye all the same for the privilege of keeping a bottle of whiskey in her trunk. And Mrs. Pye takes as much from her as she does from you!"

"Does she indeed," he said lightly. "That's interesting. Saving up for the day of reckoning, no doubt."

"What do you mean?"

She felt his breath on her skin. "When we are all of us called to account," he said. "You don't think we are going to be able to go on like this forever, do you?"

She touched his hair cautiously, as if it were red-hot and she afraid of being burned.

"I don't know," she said. "I hadn't thought about it."

"Don't. It won't bear thinking."

She had bought a douche-bag, as Lizzie Crabbe had instructed, and faithfully she used it. She wanted no risk of another pregnancy, for then, indeed, she and Clara would be condemned never to survive—never to have a life of their own. To her relief, her monthly flow had occurred the morning after their first intercourse; vague as she was about her anatomy and the functioning of her body, she knew that if your monthly came, you were not pregnant. The boarding houses were hotbeds of misinformation, anatomical and otherwise, but on this point, at least, she had personal experience to guide her.

Unlike most men, Prince was understanding—respectful, even—of her precaution. He did not view her douche-bag as a threat to his virility. She was a smart lass, he thought, to prevent the trouble instead of trying to get rid of it after—or even, as he knew some poor desperate women did, bearing it live into the world and then drowning it in a canal. Infanticide was an accustomed thing among the British laboring classes; he had not heard of it in America, but he assumed it existed. He was very fond of Sabra; he would not have wanted her to die or commit murder on his account. And he was grateful to her as well: she was prettier than any whore, and considerably more clean. It was she, in fact, who insisted that they visit Dr. J. V. Besse's bath-house a few doors down the street from his room at least one night a week and, as the summer drew on, two and even three times. Here, for thirteen cents, one could bathe away the accumulated sweat and lint and dirt and, for one evening at least, not be maddened by the need to scratch one's irritated skin. He smiled at her: a sweet, clean, bright American lass. And to his great relief, she didn't give a damn about politics.

10

One Saturday pay night in August, after Sabra had put her money in the bank, she returned to Mrs. Pye's the long way, down Merrimack Street and then down Central. Prince was in Nashua and would not return until Monday; she had planned to sleep through Sunday so as not to be conscious of her loss. But as eager as she was to fall asleep, she hated as she always did the return to the hot, crowded boarding house; and so she took the long way back, delaying the moment of arrival.

As she turned the corner onto Central Street she saw the open door of Codwell's store. Patrick had promised to call for her, to take her to see Biddy, but in her involvement with Prince she had forgotten that promise. She had forgotten Biddy—poor Biddy, who surely needed a friend, who had suffered beyond imagining.

Inside the store she saw Patrick and another clerk waiting on the several customers. She waited until they were done and the store empty; then she went in.

"Sure," he said. "I'm goin' out tomorrow to see her. After Mass. It's a long walk, but we have all day. Meet me here in front of the store at ten o'clock."

She felt a curious combination of dread and relief as she went on to Mrs. Pye's. Dread, because she was afraid to see what Biddy had become; relief, because her conscience told her that she should have gone to Biddy long before. Now, she thought, I will make it up to her. I will spend the day, I will go often again.

When she reached the boarding house she found all in an uproar. Every female there, so it seemed, was occupied in a frantic search, scurrying about, turning out drawers, running up and down the stairs, calling to her companions in anxious voices. Overhead Sabra could hear the clatter of bureaus being torn apart, the scrape of bedsteads pushed across the floor. In the center of the dining room at the table still littered with the remains of supper stood Mrs. Dorcas Pye, her face rigid with fury, her dark hair straggling from underneath her cap, her voice ringing out in a vituperative harangue.

"Every one of you will be reported! Every one dismissed! You will keep looking until that money's found, I don't care if it takes all night! Someone's a thief in this house, and I won't have it! You can all go, for all I care! Someone's taken my money and someone's goin' to put it back!"

Sabra caught a glimpse of the terrified servant woman hovering in the kitchen doorway. She did not enter the dining room, but went directly upstairs to her bedroom. All was in chaos. Bedding flung on the floor, trunks lying open, books scattered—someone, in her panic, had even ripped open a mattress, whose straw filling spilled out like entrails from a gaping wound.

A tall, sandy-haired girl named Olivia Eames stood helplessly by the bureau, her short-sighted eyes gazing blankly at the scene. Sabra made her way to her side, stepping gingerly across the littered floor.

"What on earth—"

"Someone stole her money—so she says," said Olivia bitterly. "Of course we've all had something taken since we've been here. I lost my silver brooch my first week, but it's different when it's something of hers. The old pig! The money's gone. We'll never find it, no one would be stupid enough to hide it here, but she swears she'll keep us looking all night and tomorrow too, if need be. Probably we'll have to take up a collection!"

Prince's money, thought Sabra; and how many others had contributed to that hoard? Ill-gotten, ill-lost—

"Come on," she said, taking Olivia's arm. "Let's go out. This is a madhouse."

"We can't. She's ordered us all to stay and search."

"We'll tell her we're going around back to look in the yard. We'll take a candle."

They sat on the back steps, which looked directly across a small patch of mud and wood-pile and privy to the back steps of another row of boarding houses. A narrow alley separated the yards; dark shapes slithered back and forth along it, and here and there was the larger shadow of a hunter cat. Sabra shuddered and drew her skirts tightly around her ankles. From inside the house they heard Mrs. Pye's voice raised again in an angry tirade, cut off suddenly by a distinctly unladylike curse from someone whose voice Sabra could not identify.

"I heard today that Mrs. Jessup, at Number Ten, has some vacancies," said Olivia. "Would you come there with me? I can't stand this woman much longer."

"Mrs. Jessup keeps a filthy house," said Sabra. "I met a girl last week whose face was raw with bites. And bed-bugs aren't the worst of it. She said she'd discovered a rat in her room one night. Ugh!" She shuddered uncontrollably. She remembered Mrs. Clapham's sharp eye for dirt, her ceaseless war on the animal kingdom.

"But she sets a good table," said Olivia. "Meat three times a day, and she bakes wonderful pies."

They heard a piercing cry from the darkness of the alley followed by small thuds as a cat made its kill.

"No," said Sabra. "I'll stay here. One place is as bad as the next." And Mrs. Jessup might not be so amenable to Prince's offerings, she thought; she would put up with a good deal more than bad food and even tonight's uproar to keep a way to be with him.

"I suppose so," said Olivia. "If anyone had told me—but there, I've only myself to blame. I would come, the recruiter painted such a rosy picture and I wouldn't stay home a moment longer. My sister and her husband were sorry to see me go. Well they should have been, for all the work I did and never a penny of my own, stuck out on the farm miles from anywhere. This is better, as bad as it is. But I'm not staying on the Corporation for the rest of my life, either. Listen: how would you like to go into business?"

"What business?"

"Dressmaking. I know a girl in Nashua who opened a shop last year and she's making—well, not a fortune, but a good living. Of course things may be different in New Hampshire."

"Yes," said Sabra. "They may be. Three places on Merrimack Street have changed hands since I came in March. It's a risky business, don't you think?"

"Only if you don't go about it right," said Olivia, her voice quickening as she spoke. "You can't just hang up a sign by yourself. You have to have partners, and contacts—you have to have a way to meet the women who will patronize you. And of course everything has to be in the best of taste, and well done. Your place has to be attractive, and you have to have a good selection of fabric—oh, I've thought it all out. As soon as I get enough saved I'm going to do it. With the proper partners, of course."

"Of course. But I don't know anything about business. Why ask me?"

"Oh, but you do. Forgive me—I don't mean to pry—but don't you save your pay every week? I've noticed that you don't buy anything, or rent a pew—and that's just good sense, Sabra. I want someone who has the backbone to save like that. And you speak well, you look like a lady, you'd deal admirably with the clientele—"

Olivia's voice caressed the word; already, Sabra thought, she saw herself as the proprietress of a flourishing establishment. And why not, if she had the gumption?

"Well," she said. "I'll think about it. But I don't know."

"If you could put in a hundred dollars," said Olivia, "and I'll have two hundred by Thanksgiving, and I'd find someone else to go in with us—"

"Wait," said Sabra, laughing at the other's enthusiasm, "I haven't said I'll do it."

"You don't have to. It's not time yet. I just mentioned it so that you can keep it in mind."

"All right," said Sabra. "I will, I promise." But she thought: how foolish! Dressmakers are as common as flies. There are a dozen on Merrimack Street alone. Every woman who needs to earn money turns to dressmaking if she can't stand the mill—although God knows the hours are as long, or longer, and even if your lungs stay healthy your eyes give out. There's no success to dressmaking unless you have a big establishment in Boston or New-York. There aren't enough fashionable women here to support two dressmakers, let alone a dozen.

The search for Mrs. Pye's stolen money proved unsuccessful, and when, after curfew, she finally permitted her charges to retire, it was with threats of discharge and blacklisting and dire mutterings about the bad end of thieves. The girls hoped that she was bluffing; most of them were too tired to care.

On Sunday morning Mrs. Pye, evidently having reconsidered during the night, made no mention of her missing money. She served breakfast as usual; she saw the church-goers off to services, and then she retired to her room. Sabra wondered, briefly, what had happened to put the landlady off the scent; but she was too apprehensive about her visit with Biddy, now that the moment was at hand, to concern herself with Mrs. Pye's trouble. Nor did she think again of Olivia Eames' proposal.

11

She met Patrick as they had arranged and they began their long walk to the cottage where Biddy lived. They did not talk at first as they went. He set a quick pace and Sabra was hard put to keep up. She discovered that although she wore no stays, her breath came hard. Soon her lungs began to hurt and she had to ask him to slow down.

He looked at her. "Too fast? We're hardly movin', Sabra."

She shook her head and spoke with some difficulty. "Please. Just stop a little."

When they had rested for a moment he set off again, but more slowly now; he glanced at her from time to time to make sure that she was able to keep up.

The cottage was on a side road that branched off where the main curved away from the river. It was scarcely visible, hidden in a grove of trees: a small white two-roomed affair, the doorway wreathed in late roses, a small vegetable patch to one side. The door was shut, the blinds drawn; smoke rose from the chimney.

Patrick rapped softly. After a moment the door was opened by a plain, elderly woman in a black dress. She had a kindly smile, and she was delighted when she recognized Patrick.

"Well, now, Patrick! A lovely day for a walk, isn't it? Come in, come in —ah—Miss—"

"This is Miss Palfrey," said Patrick. "She knew Biddy a long time ago. She's been away, she didn't know—"

"Yes, yes of course," said the woman; and, to Sabra: "I am Mrs. Shaw. Come in, she's always glad for company, poor child. Not that she gets much of it."

To Sabra's surprise, Mrs. Shaw was an American. Somehow she had thought that Bradshaw would have hired an Irishwoman to care for Biddy; but perhaps no Irishwoman, poor as she might be, would have the job.

Biddy sat rocking by the fire which, even on this summer day, burned brightly in the hearth. She did not look up when they entered, but as Patrick approached her and spoke her name she lifted her head and twisted her mouth in a grotesque imitation of a smile.

Patrick pulled a stool to her side and took her hand. Feeling like an intruder, Sabra stayed by the door; she bit her lips to keep from crying out.

For all that Patrick had warned her, she had not been prepared to meet this wreck of the girl she had known. This was not Biddy! This pale, thin, bedraggled creature whose black hair tumbled around her shoulders, whose tear-stained face was drawn into tight lines of agony, whose bare feet protruded from beneath the hem of her ragged calico dress.

Automatically she turned to Mrs. Shaw, who calmly met her gaze and motioned her to silence.

"Wait a bit," whispered Mrs. Shaw. "She isn't used to anyone else. Let him speak to her for a minute."

"Is she ill?" muttered Sabra. "What's wrong with her? I never dreamed—"

Mrs. Shaw shook her head; she tapped her forehead meaningfully. "She's ill here," she said. "She grieves, poor child. Sometimes she takes on so, and I have to give her the laudanum to soothe her—"

Biddy looked up. Her blue eyes were clouded, unfocused. As Patrick whispered encouragingly, her vision seemed to clear and she met Sabra's eyes. At once Sabra was at her side.

"O, Biddy! I'm so glad to see you! It's been so long—" Her voice broke; tears came to her eyes. Biddy refocused, saw her now close. She showed no recognition.

"Now, Biddy, here's Sabra come to see you," said Patrick soothingly. "She's walked a long way. Come and sit with us at the table while Mrs. Shaw makes us a cup of tea."

They helped her up, for she did not seem to be able to stand alone; the three of them sat at the table while Mrs. Shaw, with a cautious eye on her charge, set about preparing their refreshment.

Biddy held out her hand; Sabra took it, pressed it between her own, felt a faint answering clasp.

"He died," whispered Biddy. Her eyes were cast down, her face hidden by her hair. Suddenly she gripped Sabra's hand tightly. "He died. Did they tell you? He is dead."

"Yes, dear. I know. Don't think about it."

"Mary McCormic says he is in Heaven. But he was not baptized. He cannot be in Heaven. He will never be. I begged *him* to get the priest but he wouldn't. And now—"

The grip relaxed; the pain-filled voice ceased. A dozen phrases of condolence, of sympathy, rose to Sabra's lips; she uttered none of them. They were meaningless. There was no consolation for this poor broken creature. The figure of Bradshaw rose up in her mind: for if Biddy had sinned, so surely had he. And if Biddy was now being punished—as surely she was—what was his punishment? Did he, too, sit in a daze, mumbling tormented thoughts about the little lost soul whose death had broken Biddy? Or perhaps it was not that which had broken her. Perhaps it was his abandonment, his withdrawal of his love, such as it was.

Sabra's heart quickened as she thought of him. How cruel he was! She could not believe it, even of him who would never, she knew, be counted among the earth's benefactors. How could he have done this—and to Biddy, who had surely never harmed him, never harmed anyone?

They drank their tea while Patrick and Mrs. Shaw and Sabra made strained, falsely cheerful conversation whose pretense that Biddy joined in fooled none of them, least of all the girl herself. Sabra was grateful to Mrs. Shaw, and to Patrick, too: had the conversation been left to her she would have been unable to utter a word, but with their help she spoke of the weather, and the variety of trade at Codwell's store, and the touring Irish singers who had performed in the city the previous week.

When at last she and Patrick took their leave she felt more exhausted than after a day in the mill. And even as she forced a smile, and promised to come again (loudly, although Biddy stood not three feet away), she knew that she would not, and knew that Patrick and Mrs. Shaw understood her lie. How can he bear to come here, she wondered; once he wanted her to be his wife, and now he comes to see this wretch, this poor lost soul—what must he think? How can he bear to look at her? And how will he get his revenge?

12

By September of 1845 the Corporation owners in Boston and their resident managers in Lowell had felt the first intimation of defeat in the coming election. Their perennial Whig candidate for the legislature, their faithful servant Matthew Munson, had a visible—and vocal—Democratic opponent. His name was Frederick Procter. He was strongly supported by the Ten-Hour people. He was an articulate man with a distressingly blameless background which gave the Corporations no opportunity to discredit him and so save the election for their toady. Procter campaigned tirelessly, forcing Munson into reluctant action, but no matter how well advertised were Munson's speeches, no matter how many men were invited—no, told—to attend his rallies, Procter always seemed to draw the bigger crowd. Every copy of the weekly *Voice of Industry* sold out on the day of its appearance because it was the only newspaper that printed Procter's speeches.

Because they could not discredit Procter without discrediting themselves more, the Corporations turned their attention elsewhere. They had little success at first. None of the labor agitators who lived and worked in the city had committed any indiscretion except to criticize the factory system, and while this activity was sufficient cause for discharge and blacklist, it was not enough to discredit them and their candidate in the eyes of the men who voted. No: they needed one black sheep who would stain the whole flock. They needed to find one agitator (preferably a man, but a woman would do) whose character was so vicious, whose reputation was so foul, that anyone who associated with him—anyone like the candidate Procter, for instance—would be irrevocably fouled as well. Like hounds to the scent they sniffed over the field; very soon they picked up a trail.

One day Alphonsus Ure, the Agent of the Hamilton Corporation, was visited in his office by a small man wearing a brown checked cape and a yellow waistcoat. They conversed for perhaps half an hour, during which time the small man turned over to Ure a sheaf of papers and received in exchange a certain sum of money. By the end of the interview Ure's narrow face, which had been expressionless at the start, had broken into a large smile. He shook the stranger's hand and clapped him on the back and showed him out with all the deference which he had exhibited to the delegation from Glasgow which had toured the factory only the week before.

The next day the pages of Munson's newspaper were enlivened by an account of the personal history of one John Prince. When Prince saw the article he said nothing at first. He sat in William Young's office, the pages of the *Courier* spread before him, and read silently to the end. Then he looked up and met the eyes of his devoted followers.

"Of course you'll print a correcter version of this," he said at last. "They've got it all, damn them, but twisted—twisted! Damned clever bastards, aren't they?"

Young gnawed his lips; Miss Bagley seemed close to tears. Frederick Procter, who had just completed a successful rally at Chapel Hill, mopped his perspiring brow and waited, for once, for someone else to speak. He liked John Prince—liked him very well, admired him, was grateful to him—but if John Prince was going to throw the election—

"Of course," said Young. "I'll print whatever you say, John. But this is very bad—very damaging. Look—here—how did they know about your—ah—child by this woman? And here—this arrest—and the charge of bigamy! How could they have gotten all this?"

Prince shook his head angrily. "They have their ways to get it. I don't deny the child, I don't deny him for a moment. But it's all wrong, the way they have it here. And if it was bigamy to marry the second time, it was only because a poor man can't get a divorce in England. My wife ran away, but I couldn't get free of her. They've paid dear for this lot,

I've no doubt, but they've been glad to do it if it'll get me off their necks. I should be flattered, don't you think, that they'd be willing to spend so much time and money on me? Poor John Prince! That such mighty high muckety-mucks would think that a poor working man would be worth all that trouble!"

"I am sure they have investigated us all," said Miss Bagley. Her voice was rough with tears, with frustration, with anger at this man who, having helped their cause, now threatened to destroy it. "It is what I have been afraid of all along—that they will defeat us, not on the merits of their cause, for their cause has no merits, but on some irrelevant thing thrown up to blind everyone, to distract attention from the issue. O, John, why didn't you tell us, so that we might have been prepared? You know what they are, what they do, how they try to ruin everyone who works with us. It is my greatest difficulty to convince women that their good names will not be blackened if they join us. They treasure their reputations, their good character—and now this! No one will join us now that you are held up as a blackguard, an adulterer, a criminal—"

Young lifted a warning hand. "Enough," he said. "You do no good by taking their side."

"I am not taking their side! How can you say that! I am not, I am simply saying that if we had known we could have headed off their attack, or at least prepared a defense—"

Prince looked at her pityingly. True to her sex, she was becoming hysterical. There was only one sure way to silence a hysterical female: if she were not so homely he would do it himself. But she did not attract him. He might not be able—

". . . publish a line-by-line correction," Young was saying. He frowned as he tried to calculate in his head the number of column inches necessary. "Line-by-line, John. We'll print Munson's charge, and then our correction, and then his next charge and so on."

Young's suggestion had seemed an effective counterattack, but it did little good. Prince was snubbed openly in the street by men who had been among his most faithful followers. At an organization meeting on the evening after the rebuttal appeared, a dozen operatives, both men and women, walked out when Prince rose to speak. Word came from New Hampshire: the Nashua and Manchester branches of the Workingmen's Association wanted organizers and speakers. But not John Prince.

13

Although Sabra was not a member of the Female Labor Reform Association, it was common knowledge among her fellow boarders that she associated with Prince. Her frequent late night entrances were tacitly accepted, as were those of other girls, partly because Mrs. Pye did not object, partly because most of the women were too tired, too involved in their own survival, to concern themselves in the affairs of someone else. As long as Sabra minded her own business, and made no trouble, she was tolerated.

But now, with the appearance of Munson's exposé, the other women became wary of her. No one wanted any trouble. No one, fearing for her job, wanted to be known as an associate of a friend of the notorious John Prince. Because Sabra did not ordinarily sit and gossip in the evenings, or on Sundays, she was slow at first to realize that her presence in the house had become unwelcome, and that she, too, had become a blackened sheep.

One evening, deciding to mend her much-worn petticoat, she discovered that she had no thread. She went down to the dining room, where a dozen or so women sat sewing around the table, to ask to borrow some. The women paused briefly and then continued their talk, busily sewing as if there had been no interruption. For a moment Sabra thought that they must not have heard her, and so she spoke again, more loudly. No one answered; no one looked up. For an instant she was puzzled; then she understood.

Very well, she thought. Fools! She turned to climb the stairs when the front door opened and Olivia Eames and another girl, a new girl, came in. Olivia met Sabra's eyes. At once she turned away and made a great show of introducing the new girl to the sewing circle. Slowly Sabra went upstairs. Surely, she thought, they do not mean it. Tomorrow they will be cordial again. I have never done them any harm, I have minded my own affairs and not meddled, they will not keep it up. Perhaps, she thought, it was only that particular group which decided to shun me. Perhaps the others will speak.

She heard voices and small bursts of laughter behind the closed door of a room on the second floor. She hesitated for a moment and then knocked and opened the door. The women inside, reclining on the several beds, some seated on the floor, paused and looked up.

"Excuse me," she began, "I wondered if I could borrow some white thread?"

Every face turned away. She felt as if she had been slapped.

"Say, girls," drawled a sneering voice from within the room, "does anyone notice that bad smell? It seems to be coming from the hall."

She turned and ran upstairs. Below, she heard the door slam shut and, from behind it, a loud burst of laughter. Blinded by her tears, she reached her own bedroom. She stumbled in and sank onto her bed. Another girl had come in during her absence. She sat on her own bed, reading by the light of a candle. When she recognized Sabra she looked down again without speaking; had the light been stronger Sabra might have seen a flush rise to her cheek.

Sabra started to speak and then checked herself. Twice in one evening was enough. She had forgotten her mending. She lay on the lumpy, musty mattress and buried her face in the pillow. She had thought that she could withstand such treatment, but now that it had come at last, it was bitterly hard to bear.

When she told Prince that she had been silenced he showed no surprise.

"Naturally," he said. "You've ruined yourself, associating with me."

"But why? I'm not an agitator. I've never even signed a petition."

"Makes no matter, lass. If you're friends with the Devil then you must be from Hell. Not twenty people came to the meeting last night, and them that did told me straight out they wanted no part of me. So I'll be moving on. There's trouble in Pittsburgh, I hear. May happen I can do something there, although I can't say I know anything about iron and coal."

Sabra's heart sank. She could bear the mill, she could bear being silenced, as long as Prince was there. But if he left, she would have no one. The realization of her solitude suddenly descended on her, crushing her. She stared at him, trying to understand.

"John. Don't go. If you go, what will I—" She thought of Biddy, mourning. Biddy's male protector—protector!—had deserted her, and now she pined like a dog deserted by its master. If one attached one's heart too strongly to another, and that other was ripped away, then one was faced with a choice: either bleed to death, or, by sheer force of will, mend one's heart and survive.

He reached out to her; he stroked her cheek. "Such a pretty lass," he murmured. "Too pretty to be sent to Coventry." He willed himself to be calm. Although he had not told her so, this was their last time together. He wanted to savor it, to extract the most pleasure from every moment. He wanted no tears, no scenes, no anguished demands upon the future. He was genuinely fond of Sabra. He could not recall any woman whom he had enjoyed so much. Now, as he saw her struggle to maintain her composure, he felt a shadow of regret that he must go. His work came first. Nothing—not Sabra, not the damned capitalists—must interfere with his work; but all the same, he would be sorry to leave her.

"I'll be back," he said gently. "This will come to an end." They both knew that it would not. John Prince could never organize in Lowell again, or in any other factory town in Massachusetts or New Hampshire. That strong invisible chain forged of class and family links which bound the entrepreneurs together, whether their factories were in Fall River or Chicopee or Lowell or Nashua, would bind them together against him. No matter how many truths he spoke, no matter how just his accusations against them, his words were useless now. They had destroyed him as effectively as if they had had him assassinated, and with far less danger to themselves.

"They have not spoken to me for nine days," she said. He stroked her neck, and she concentrated on that touch, she allowed herself to think of nothing else.

"Who? The women? Fuck them. They're just jealous, they've seen what a handsome fellow I am."

They both laughed at that, for his appearance, attractive enough in a rough way, hardly met the fashionable standard for both men and women of somewhat ethereal and excessively refined elegance.

Ah, thought Sabra, how I will miss him! He is kind to me, he makes me laugh, he enjoys me as I do him—Lord, Lord, it is not fair to take him away when I have so little!

His hair was rough under her lips; the buttons on his shirt yielded easily to her fingers. His strong warm body eased gently, fiercely, into hers. There was nothing else in the world.

When the constable arrived an hour later with a warrant for Prince's arrest on the grounds of inciting to riot, he found an empty room. Although he bullied the slack-jawed landlord, the man could not tell where his late tenant had gone—"and he owes a week's rent, too—what can you do about that?" Frustrated, the constable slammed out of the tenement and into the quiet night street. He heard the bells toll midnight. Good riddance, he thought; he decided not to search further. The man had undoubtedly left town, which departure was after all the object of the issuance of the warrant.

Prince's departure left Frederick Procter free once again to campaign on the issues, and to everyone's surprise he won. His victory overjoyed the labor organizers, who had been (so everyone thought) mortally wounded by the revelations about John Prince. On the evening after the election, Miss Bagley distributed a new sheaf of Ten-Hour petitions. She was, if not jubilant, at least heartened by Munson's defeat, for with Munson absent from the Legislative Committee, they would have at least a slim chance at a favorable report on the Ten-Hour bill.

"I want five thousand signatures this time," she said to William Young. "Five thousand! O, William, bless each and every man who voted for Mr. Procter! I never thought he would win, especially after all the trouble about—"

"Yes," said Young hastily. He did not want another tirade from Miss Bagley on the iniquities of John Prince. He smiled at her encouragingly to soften his rudeness. He admired Miss Bagley immensely, but her vehemence, her intensity, her dedication occasionally overwhelmed him. "And you will get them, I am sure. Now that they see that we can elect a candidate of our own—as you say, bless those men."

"Bless them!" cried Miss Bagley. Her eyes glittered. "And Death to the Corporations!"

14

A Sabbath morning: the Lord's Day, the day of rest.

Perhaps fifteen women sat at breakfast at Mrs. Pye's. The other boarders, a dozen or so, lay slugabed. They would not go to worship. They grew insolent when Mrs. Pye chastised them for disobeying the rules. The Corporations have no right to force us to religious services, they said. Will the Corporations pay our pew rent? Will they buy us decent clothing? We cannot go to meeting in our workdresses, we must be properly attired to enter the house of the Lord. Go away and let us sleep.

But they had no rest, after all. Since shortly past dawn, the gangs hired to excavate the new canal had been laying charges of gunpowder to blast the granite bedrock in its path. With each new explosion the city shook as if from an earthquake. Windows rattled, floors shook, chandeliers swayed, dust rose and settled again. Like a war, they thought: like cannon. Waiting for each new blast was worse than enduring it. From time to time, on Sundays, they had been annoyed by the pop-pop of the militia's training exercises at the drill grounds on outer Gorham Street. That noise had been nothing compared to this. And on the Lord's Day! Were they to have no rest? The Corporations were profaning the Sabbath! Why did the ministers and the Catholic priest not protest?

The women finished their meal. Those who were going to services went to fetch their bonnets and cloaks. Sabra watched them go. Her food lay untouched on her plate. She was glad when the servant woman came to clear it away.

If I sit for a moment, she thought, I will feel better. My stomach will quiet itself. This is only a minor indigestion. Nothing more. Nothing to worry about.

She had no money. As usual, she had deposited all her wages in the bank the previous pay day, keeping only fifteen cents for some emergency. Fifteen cents was not enough for this one. How much would she need? There had been an announcement in the *Advertiser*—

She stood up. She had drunk only a little tea, but now she thought she would vomit even that. She braced herself against the table. Two missed monthly flows were a sure sign, and her nausea was the same as that with Clara. She must act to help herself. When her stomach had calmed a little, she took a copy of the *Advertiser* from a pile of magazines and newspapers on a small table near the window. Her eyes ran down the column until she found what she sought:

"Dr. F. Morrill's Italian Renovating Pills, or Female Monthly Regulator." And, in smaller type:

> Should not be taken by pregnant females, as they will in every instance cause a miscarriage.

Her hands trembled. What if she died? What if the pills failed to produce a miscarriage, but simply made her ill? She let the paper fall to the cluttered table. Lizzie Crabbe had been so very sure of her prescription for the douche. Why had it failed? She wished that she could talk to Lizzie, ask her advice. Lizzie would know what to do. But Lizzie had vanished, embarrassed no doubt by the failure of Father Miller's predictions. No, thought Sabra. I must rely now on Dr. Morrill's pills. And if they failed—

The explosion shattered the silence. She started badly, uttering a small cry of fear. Through the window giving onto the street, she saw a spooked horse rear in its traces, she heard its frantic neigh. For no reason at all, she thought of Goldschmidt's horse spooked by the bridge over the Falls.

"Sabra?"

The horse had not wanted to come down into the city. Horses were country creatures. It was cruel to work them in the towns, amid all the crowding and crushing, the dirt and the noise, never the feel of meadow grass under their hooves.

"Sabra, are you all right?"

It was the same with people. Some of them never adjusted to city life.

"Sabra, I want to talk to you."

She turned, then. She saw Olivia Eames peering at her anxiously.

"Sabra. I'm sorry for what I did the other night. It was very wrong of me."

Yes. She felt her shoulders lift and drop in a little shrug.

"And I've worried about it ever since. Silencing a girl is terrible. I couldn't bear it if they did it to me. So I was doubly wrong to do it to you. Come and sit with me for a moment. You look tired. Are you well?"

"Yes." Sabra felt oddly conspiratorial, concerned lest Miss Eames ruin herself by talking to the girl in Coventry. Olivia was a nice girl, a kind girl; Sabra would not have wanted to see her in Coventry too.

"Sabra, listen to me." Miss Eames leaned forward in a confidential way. "You remember that I asked you about opening a shop? Yes. Well, I heard yesterday that soon, now—I don't know just when—they are going to cut wages again. If they do, I'm quitting. I won't work for less than I get now, and that's fifty cents a week less than when I came. If I do quit, I'll start my own shop. Will you come with me?"

Sabra listened. "I don't know," she said at last. "I'll have to think about it."

Miss Eames nodded. "That's all right. You go ahead and think. I've found the other girl, by the way. She lives next door. She's ready to come along any time. She's an excellent seamstress, and she has a good sense of style." Miss Eames' face brightened as she spoke. "We could be independent. We wouldn't have to take orders from anyone."

Except the customers. "It's a good idea," said Sabra slowly. She was aware that her voice lacked conviction. Her stomach felt worse than before. "I just don't know if I—"

"Think about it. That's all I ask. And remember where you heard it first: they're going to cut wages soon again."

15

On the following Saturday evening, Sabra collected her pay and came out onto Jackson Street. The night was bitter cold; the throng of operatives hurrying to their boarding houses, or briefly to the shops, wrapped their cloaks firmly around their shivering bodies and walked quickly, spurred on by the wind. As cold as she was, tired, dizzy from the noisy, overheated workroom, Sabra moved slowly down Jackson Street. The crowd parted around her and hurried on, leaving her alone. The bright lights of the shops along Central Street gleamed up ahead. When she reached the corner she hesitated again. Ayer's Pharmacy was just here, at the corner of Jackson and Central. Just step inside, she told herself, ask for what you want.

Her eyes scanned the crowd. People moved more slowly here, window shopping, their passage slowed by the lure of the goods on display. Sabra examined every face, knowing as she did that she wasted her time: he was not there. He was far away. In Pittsburgh? If only she could go to someone—to anyone, to some kind friend, to Eldress, to Lizzie. If only she had someone to ask for help. If only she were not so alone. A cold tear stung her cheek. Angrily she wiped it away and went into the pharmacy.

The young man on duty took her request and reached to the shelf behind him. He wrapped the small box in a bit of brown paper, gave her her change, and winked. "Wishing you the best of health, miss," he grinned, and turned to the next customer. To Sabra's surprise, she requested the same pills.

The following Thursday was Thanksgiving: a holiday. She had decided to wait until Wednesday evening; then if she were still sick on Friday morning she would miss only two days until the Sunday. Surely that would be enough time. She clenched her fist around the tiny package and felt that she held on to her life: hers and Clara's.

When she reached the boarding house the others had begun their evening's activities: some early to bed, some gossiping in the dining room-turned-parlor, some gone out to a lecture. One girl, a new girl, had announced boldly at dinner that she was going to the theater that evening, occasioning some discussion after she left as to whether Mrs. Pye would keep her on as a boarder in view of such unsuitable conduct, so brazenly trumpeted. The theater had not been long in the city; it was still viewed as highly immoral, a sure ticket to damnation.

Sabra began to climb the stairs to her room. She wished that she might stop downstairs and gossip awhile; she wished that she had a friend waiting for her to whom she could unburden her heart. Wednesday! Four days! The waiting was worse than the act. Now, she thought. I cannot wait. I will take them now. If I miss a week's pay, so be it.

The bedroom was empty and cold. She did not light a candle, but she ignited the fresh-laid fire. She crouched down before it, watching the flames as they licked upward, throwing out a faint warmth. She wished that she could stay huddled beside the fire, but she had something that she must do. Something—for a moment it escaped her. What was it? She stood up. She was very tired; her bones ached. On the wall beside the mantel hung a small mirror. She looked at herself: a stranger. Who was this woman? Two eyes, a nose, a mouth. A resident of Mrs. Dorcas Pye's boarding house. An operative on the Appleton Corporation. The mother of a child, aged twenty months. Once the wife of—what was his name? Ah, yes. Silas Blood. He had gone away a very long time ago.

She heard footsteps on the stairs. Hurry. With shaking fingers she unwrapped the package, opened the box. Twenty small red pills. The directions printed on the lid said to take four. Eight, then, at least. She picked them out and swallowed them one by one. They tasted bitter. She choked, gasped for breath. She scooped up a handful of water from the basin and washed down the last of them. She heard voices in the next room. Hurry. She closed the box and put it in her trunk. She was shivering violently now; the fire could not warm her. She longed for a cup of tea, or even a hot toddy. She remembered the whiskey in Lotta Perkins' trunk. Was the bottle or its replacement still there, or had Mrs. Pye finally forbidden it? Lotta had paid—yes. Unlocked. Anyone could come by and take a drink. She lifted the bottle to her lips and swallowed, choked, spilled a little on her dress. Now the room smelled of liquor. She did not care. She cared for nothing except warmth, and sleep, and relief. She replaced the bottle and eased herself down onto her bed.

She lost consciousness. She did not hear the others come in; she did not hear their exclamations of dismay at the odor of strong drink which filled the room. Since they had sent her to Coventry, they could not ask her if she were responsible. They chattered to each other; they stirred the fire; they went to bed and slept.

Several hours later Sabra awoke. She thought at first that she was dreaming that someone had sliced through her abdomen with a butcher knife. She stifled a cry; the pain took away her breath. She bit her fist; in spite of her efforts to be quiet, she moaned aloud. The sound made her realize that she was not asleep. The room was dark and close. She smelled the whiskey on her dress.

Beside her in the bed a dark shape sat up. She heard a voice from another bed: "What's the matter?"

"I don't know," said her bed-mate. "She's sick, I think."

The questioner snickered. "Serves her right, sneaking whiskey. Give her a shove and tell her to be quiet."

Sabra was very cold; only her abdomen was on fire, burning, quivering with pain. Another groan escaped her. She was aware that the dark shape still sat silently beside her. She knew, too, that she would have to be far more ill than she was for anyone to speak to her, to offer to help.

She felt herself slipping back into unconsciousness; she lost track of time. After what might have been several minutes or several hours, she came awake again. As weak as she was she rolled over and hung her head over the edge of the mattress. She retched; she heard her vomit splatter onto the floor. She heard the shocked cries of her bed-mate. She heard someone get up and call the servant. She lay back, gagging on the bitter aftertaste in her mouth. Dr. Morrill's Italian Renovating Pills were a cruel hoax.

16

On Thanksgiving morning, while most of Mrs. Pye's boarders were either asleep or attending services, and that good lady herself was busy in her kitchen concocting a Thanksgiving dinner as best she could on her insufficient budget, Sabra slipped downstairs and out of the house and through the deserted streets to the Acre. It was a bright, mild day; as she crossed Dutton Street she saw the sun glinting on the surface of the canal. A woman stood at the edge emptying a slop bucket into the water; farther down, a woman holding a baby drew up a pail of that same water for her household needs.

When she reached Mechanic Street she paused. She had been here only once, at night, guided by Biddy, who had known the way. Now, in bright daylight, approaching from a different direction, she realized that she had no idea how to proceed. Before her lay the warren of turfed huts and tarpaper shanties where lived that alien and mysterious race, the Irish. Having known individual Irish, she was not afraid of the mass.

Several tough-looking men lounging outside a cabin door watched her closely. She moved on, lifting her skirts to avoid as much as possible the filth of the narrow lane. Rooting pigs narrowly missed colliding with her; bedraggled chickens pecked relentlessly at the wet ground; dogs and cats chased each other and foraged like the swine. She put her hand in her pocket to still the clink of coins and walked on.

"Please, miss—" A hand on her arm, a thin face peering out from a faded red shawl. "Could you give a penny, miss, my little ones is hungry—"

"Can you tell me where Mary McCormic lives?"

The woman's pleading expression vanished, replaced by one of calculation. "Can you give me a nickel?"

Sabra smothered the sharp retort which sprang to her lips. She was too concerned with her own problems to haggle. Nevertheless she looked at the woman with contempt. Never, she thought, never could I beg on the street! They have no pride, they would rather beg than work.

"If you tell me, yes."

"Go to the end here, turn right, then right again."

Sabra put a nickel into the thin, dirty palm and walked on. The air stank. She tried to breathe through her mouth. Small children barely clothed darted back and forth; babies crawled in the muck. An old woman puffing a pipe peered out from a doorway; she grinned when she saw Sabra, exposing raw, toothless gums.

After a while, following the woman's directions, Sabra reached what she thought was the lane—alley, more correctly—where Mary McCormic lived. Here was less activity, both animal and human. The only figure to be seen was a likely-looking boy of twelve or thirteen. For a moment, disoriented, Sabra thought that she was seeing Patrick as she had first known him. In response to her question he motioned her down the alley: "Third door, miss."

She rapped sharply on the crude boards roughly nailed together. She heard the rise and fall of many voices from within; receiving no answer, she rapped again.

A little girl pushed open the door. Behind her, in the dark, smoky, windowless room, were at least a dozen people, all talking at once; but when they realized that a stranger stood outside observing them, they fell suddenly silent and watchful.

"Is Mary McCormic here?" said Sabra. She spoke to the child, but her voice carried into the room. The child nodded, said nothing, sidled back away from the door. A figure detached itself from the group and came forward. Sabra remembered the lively, intelligent face, the impression of strength which this woman had given.

"Yes?"

"Mrs. McCormic? You don't remember me, I came here once with a girl named Biddy, when her mother died—"

"O yes. I remember you." She made no gesture of welcome.

"Could I speak to you? Privately? It's very important—"

A faint, grim smile flitted over Mary McCormic's face. She stepped outside and pulled the door shut behind her.

"I've no privacy there, as you can see. Come, we'll walk down to the canal."

Together they picked their way through the filth. The alley ended abruptly at the edge of the canal, whose steep bank was marked by several granite boulders at the top. They sat on these.

"No work today?" said Mary. "O, I forgot. It's a holiday, isn't it? Thanksgiving, they call it. For them as has something to be thankful for."

Sabra nodded. Now that the moment had come, now that she sat alone with this woman to whom she had come to ask—beg—for help, she could not speak. In a minute, she thought, I will find the words.

"An' speakin' of thankful, I heard you went to see Biddy. That was kind. And I'm grateful to you for it. But then, you were always kind to her. I haven't forgotten."

"I meant to go again, but I've only Sundays—"

"I know. It's hard. And then, I don't know that it makes any difference to her. I haven't gone myself as often as I might. Poor child."

"Do you—did she ever tell you—I still don't understand why she did so," said Sabra.

Mary McCormic turned to face her. "Don't you?" she said softly. Her eyes were luminous; her face bore a look of infinite pity.

She smiled then: a curious, crooked smile, an admission of defeat. "For sure it's a queer world," she said, "and some things in it are past understanding. We put our own heads in the noose sometimes, for all we know it's death. Somethin' inside us wills us to it. The fiddler plays for us when no one else hears the tune, and we dance—we dance—" She shook her head. Her face was somber. She stared down at the dark water of the canal. "I don't understand it," she said. "I'll never understand it. But there it is."

They sat quiet for a moment in silent mourning for the child whom they both had loved. Then, impersonal again, Mary turned and said: "Now, miss. What did you want me for?"

17

The room was dark and hot; it smelled of blood and herbs and whiskey and, faintly, of a kind of stew. From a corner the child watched, her eyes never wavering; it was, she knew, her business to watch. To learn. She was a lucky child, to have a clever mother to teach her the means to survival. "Watch!" Mary McCormic commanded her, "and jump and fetch when I say. Soon I'll let you help." And smiled fondly at the child, her youngest, her dear girl, born in America, thank God. A native-born, as good as any Yankee. The child was bright and quick, a miniature of her mother; even now, as Mary worked, she was conscious of the small person nearby, watching, remembering.

Sabra lay on a filthy quilt spread on the dirt floor. Despite the quantity of whiskey which she had drunk, she was conscious and clear-headed. She was aware of the pain; she felt the warm wet flow from her body, a flow prompted by the probing and scraping of the sharp-edged bone tool deep inside that unknown, unnamed place.

Mary McCormic knelt over her, holding a cup of steaming, pungent liquid. When she saw that Sabra was too weak to lift her head to drink, she summoned the child to hold the cup while she supported Sabra's shoulders.

"Now drink," she said. "Drink it all—it'll stop the flow. That's it." Gently she eased Sabra back again; she ran a practiced eye over her. A difficult case, for all that the passage was eased by previous stretching. At least one child had been born out of that womb. And if she was alone in the world, as she seemed to be, it was no wonder she didn't want another. A pretty one, she was; Mary was faintly surprised that she hadn't worked a marriage. Unless, of course, the man was already married—not that that stopped some of them.

A knock at the door; the child went to answer. As she opened it, she saw the crimson sunset sky beyond the roof of the hovel opposite. It was growing late; the man who had knocked, one of the several tenants of Mary's room, wanted to come in for the night.

"All right," said Mary. The child stepped aside; the man, stooping under the low entrance, came in and threw an incurious glance at the figure on the quilt before looking into the pot for his supper. Mary McCormic was a busy woman, an enterprising woman; how she earned an extra dollar was no business of his. He crouched by the fire, dipping his hand into the steaming kettle.

His figure threw a fantastic animal shape onto the rough wall. A buffalo? An attacking bear? The shadow swam in and out of focus. Sabra watched it. Death, she thought. The shadow of Death. O Clara.

She moaned. The man looked at her again with somewhat more interest. "That one all right?" he said.

"Right as rain," said Mary McCormic. "She just needs a little more time to pull herself together." She patted Sabra's thin cheek encouragingly.

"Remember last time," said the man.

Mary's mouth tightened. Last time—a month ago now, it was—had not gone well. It had been necessary to ask his help, and to pay dearly for it. Fortunately the weather had still been warm, no ice on the canal, the body had slipped in easily on a dark night with hardly a splash. The girl had been very young, hardly older than her own child: an illegal from across the Canadian border, no family, no one had missed her, no one had come looking. Mary knew that the body had been recovered from the canal, but, faced with the protective wall of silence thrown up around themselves and their own by the residents of the Acre, the authorities had conducted only the most perfunctory investigation.

This one would be different. Should anything go wrong, there would be an inquiry, the authorities would come searching—but the money had been more than Mary could refuse. Her eyes shone in the firelight. Ten dollars! She would work very hard to save this one. She would exert all her powers.

From between her breasts she withdrew a charm hanging on a leather cord: a small bone tied around with a bit of scarlet silk. She held it tight in her left hand and put her right hand on Sabra's abdomen. She closed her eyes and began the ancient incantation: a gibberish in an unknown tongue, a plea to some god—or goddess—unknown to Orthodox New England.

Toward ten o'clock Sabra struggled and sat up. She was very weak, she was dizzy, but she could not miss curfew. Mary McCormic knelt beside her, watching her anxiously, stretching out a supporting arm.

"What time is it?" said Sabra.

"Hush, dear. It's only gone dark a little while."

"I must go. I must not stay here, I cannot be late—"

"Hush, hush—can you stand?"

Sabra was aware that the room was crowded now—more crowded, even, than her dormitory at Mrs. Pye's. She gritted her teeth and swung around onto her knees. Sleeping bodies littered the dirt floor; the firelight threw erratic, rosy illumination over all. She struggled to rise. Mary's hand supported her arm.

"Now, dear, don't be in any hurry, plenty of time. There you are—"

With a great effort, Sabra stood up. Something wet and sticky fell onto the floor from between her legs: the packed cloth which had staunched the flow. It was over. She gripped Mary's shoulder.

"Is it—am I all right?"

"You are, dear, indeed you are. Everything's taken care of, you'll be fit as a fiddle in no time. Can you walk? Easy, now—"

Sabra took a tentative step. She was very sore, she felt as if her intestines would drop out, she could hardly move her legs. She was aware of the child watching from the corner of the room.

"Wait," said Mary. "You're not strong enough yet. I'll just get you a drink—"

"No. I must go." Slowly, painfully, Sabra made her way to the door, almost tripping over a somnolent body in her path.

Mary helped her, murmuring, soothing, encouraging, but all the same she was alarmed. The girl was not strong enough to walk the long way back to wherever she boarded. To be safe she should stay the night.

Sabra reached the door, but when she pushed at it, it did not open. Mary opened it for her. She must get help: a strong back.

"Frank!" she hissed. And, to her child: "Shake him up—hurry!"

The man who had first come in several hours ago was now dead asleep and reluctant to be awakened, but after the child had given a few smart tugs on his arm he groaned and sat up. He shook his head and focused on his tormentor.

"What?"

The child nodded at the two women at the door; at once he understood. He hesitated. Sometimes the living were more dangerous than the dead.

"You'll have to take her, Frank," said Mary. "She can't walk all the way." And, when he did not reply, she added with some irritation: "I'll pay. Don't I always?"

Slowly he got to his feet. "A dollar," he said.

"A *dollar*? Mother of God! For half an hour's work?"

"And what if I'm stopped? I should charge you twice that. It's not worth the risk. And I'll have it now, if you please, before I go."

Mary cursed him but she fished in her pocket and withdrew the coins and held them out. He took them; he turned to Sabra and lifted her as easily as if she were a doll. Bending, he stepped through the low door into the night.

He carried her to the corner of Jackson Street. It was past curfew; no one was abroad outside the Acre save the watch, and they did not encounter him. After he set her on her feet he disappeared without a word.

She steadied herself, holding onto a lamp post, and then slowly she walked down the row of boarding houses until she came to Mrs. Pye's.

The house was dark. As she gathered her strength to climb the three steps to the door, she heard the bells chime eleven. She dragged herself up and steadied herself against the door frame. She did not have the strength to knock. The night was cold, but her dress was damp with perspiration; her head was burning, she had begun to shiver uncontrollably. When her hand came against the door it made no sound. Desperately she clung to the frame and tried again. This time she heard a faint pounding on the wooden panel. Hear me, she thought; please hear me.

After an indeterminable time she heard footsteps in the hall. The door opened; Mrs. Pye, clutching her wrapper around her, peered out.

"You're past curfew."

"Please—"

Sabra felt her knees give way. Mrs. Pye's anger turned to alarm as she reached out to support the fainting figure on her doorstep.

"What've you done now, miss?" she hissed. "Here—stand up, what's wrong with you? Are you drunk? A fine thing! You'll have me out on the streets! What do you think I'm running here, coming in at all hours—"

Somehow she got Sabra into the house and seated on a chair in the dining room. She fetched the candle which she had set in the hall and peered anxiously into Sabra's pale, sweating face.

"Now what is this?" she said. Her voice was low and harsh. "Who is it this time?"

Sabra shook her head. "Please. I'll pay you, I can't explain—"

"Can't explain! You don't need to explain, miss! I've made plenty of allowance for you in the past, and I thought I'd have no more trouble from you." In her agitation Mrs. Pye was unable to calculate exactly how much John Prince had paid to let Sabra break curfew, but their friendship had been profitable for her and so now, as angry as she was, she was at least disposed to listen to Sabra's explanation (which would of course be a lie) and to accept the sum which would surely be offered to her. But as she waited expectantly she saw with rising alarm that Sabra was in no condition either to explain or to bargain; even as she sat propped against the table she began to slip sideways off the chair. Mrs. Pye was thoroughly frightened now. Without further questions she slung Sabra's arm around her neck and half dragged, half carried her down the hall to her own room. Explanations, money would have to wait—but not too long, thought Mrs. Pye grimly, or we'll both be discharged.

Sabra's fever rose during the night; by dawn, as Mrs. Pye was distractedly serving breakfast to the others, she had become delirious. Mrs. Pye, fearing the worst and already preparing her story for the Agent who was sure to inquire, sent her neighbor's boy running to the Corporation Hospital.

The staff doctor arrived an hour later driving a wagon and accompanied by a cadaverous orderly. After a cursory examination, and after he had ascertained from the landlady that Sabra had some money in the bank, he ordered her to be carried into the wagon.

From what he had seen and heard, he judged this to be a case for the Chief Physician, Dr. Knight, who specialized in gynecological matters. Further, he judged, it would be a case for the Agent, Mr. Ure: for surely the girl would be dismissed. If she survived.

18

The chief architect and planner for the Corporations in Lowell had been an unreconstructed Anglophile, a former engineer in Wellington's Peninsular Campaign, who may or may not have visited the Jumel Mansion in Washington Heights, New-York. In any case, shortly before Madame Jumel's ill-fated marriage to Aaron Burr, Kirk Boott built in the center of Lowell what he considered to be an appropriate residence for himself and his family: a white, porticoed, columned Georgian edifice, a twin to the older, more famous place, which did not blend well with the crowded, red-brick town all around. Such a house needed parks and gardens to surround it, and an imposing prospect to view from its tall windows. The location of Josiah Bradshaw's house would have been more appropriate, but Kirk Boott had felt very heavily his responsibility to the Corporate hierarchy in Boston, and so he had stayed, against his wishes, against his family's wishes, in the center of the city. He had built his mansion as a reminder to everyone that he was indisputably the guiding spirit of this place, the man who had planted brick and iron on the verdant river bank, who had forgone the pleasures of his beloved London to bring Industry to the former colonies. No one ever knew the depth of his homesickness, the loneliness of his labors in this wilderness.

When Boott dropped dead from his chaise in April, 1837, the Corporations bought his house to fill what had become an urgent need: an operatives' hospital. They moved it from the center of town to a site overlooking the great bend of the river; they fitted it out with a staff and supplies. The physician in charge was Bradshaw's friend, Dr. Gridley Knight. He used his position to perfect certain new gynecological operations. As the years passed, and news of his skills became common knowledge, the female operatives of the Lowell factories grew increasingly reluctant to go to the Corporation Hospital. They heard rumors of dreadful procedures: a girl with damaged, lint-filled lungs would find herself the subject of an operation on her female organs. Terrible things happened there: better to go home when you became ill. Eventually this refusal to make use of the facilities became an open scandal. Boarding-house matrons were threatened with dismissal if they did not persuade their sick tenants to go there. After all, said the Corporations, the fees are quite reasonable: three dollars a week for females, four for males. If the operatives did not have the money in the bank, they could be treated on credit and the bill would be deducted from their future earnings.

And so through the paneled rooms and up and down the graceful curving staircase came the moans and cries of the sick and injured who toiled in the mills which Boott had built; vomit crusted the polished floors, the stench of urine hung heavy in the air, blood splattered the wallpaper. Here, after his death, lived his legacy: and if in some extremity of delirium a patient saw a somber figure stalking the rooms where once Boott had lived, no record was ever made of that fact.

19

Wind-whipped snow scudded across the wide porch floor as Olivia Eames hurried up the steps and through the tall front door of the Hospital. Although her belly was still comfortably full from Mrs. Pye's Sunday dinner, she felt alarmingly weak and short of breath. The cold air hurt her lungs; she was glad to be indoors again, despite the odor which assaulted her nostrils when she came into the spacious hall. Just inside the door she set down the small trunk and the parcel which she had carried. She looked for someone to help her. Tucked beside the curving balustrade she saw a table covered with piles of papers. Behind it, tilted back in his chair, sat a stupid-looking young man in a dirty white cotton jacket. He watched her coolly; he made no offer to help. She approached him and made her inquiry.

He consulted the patients' register. Then he waved his hand toward the closed double doors of what once had been the dining room.

"She's in there. Bed number fourteen."

The ward was cold; a low fire sputtered in the hearth of the wide fireplace but its warmth did not penetrate more than a few feet into the room. Rows of numbered cots stretched down either side; fourteen was halfway down the far wall.

"Sabra?"

Sabra opened her eyes. As she recognized her visitor her lips moved as she breathed her name.

"O, Sabra, I've been here twice and they wouldn't let me see you. Are you better?"

"I don't know."

Lacking a chair, Miss Eames seated herself on the edge of the cot and peered anxiously at her friend. She reached out for Sabra's hand and held it as she smiled encouragingly, wishing that they could be more private. The space between beds was hardly more than a foot; the occupants of the cots on either side were, as she was uncomfortably aware, listening to their exchange. Miss Eames steeled herself. Eavesdroppers or no, she had to tell Sabra what had happened. But before she could find the gentlest way to break her news, Sabra pulled at her hand and began to speak, faintly, so that Miss Eames had to bend down to hear.

"Olivia, will you do something for me?"

"Of course."

"If I die—"

"O, Sabra, don't talk like that. You aren't going to die. Why, in a week you'll be up and around."

Sabra shook her head once, impatiently, and then paused for a moment to gather her strength again.

"There is a colony of Shakers. Near Harvard Village."

"Yes."

"If I die. Please. Will you go there to see a child who lives with them? Her name is Clara Blood. She is just little, not yet two. Please. I don't ask you to take her in, I know you can't do that, but if you could visit her once in a while as she grows, and speak to her—"

She paused as she saw the expression on Miss Eames' face, and then, conscious of her failing strength, she persevered.

"She is mine, Olivia. I left her there because I could not care for her here. Tell her—tell her you were my friend. And tell her that I did not want her to stay there for her lifetime. When she grows up, tell her that it was my wish that she leave. They are good people, but not what I want for her. Will you do that for me, Olivia?"

Miss Eames struggled with this information, which had so eclipsed her own.

"Yes, of course I will, Sabra. You know I will. But I will not need to do it, you are not going to die! You must not! O, Sabra—"

She held tightly to the small hand which lay in her own; and Sabra, having delivered herself of her heart's burden, now at last realized that her visitor, too, had something to say. She understood what it was.

"They have dismissed me."

Miss Eames nodded.

Sabra closed her eyes; then opened them.

"My things?"

"I brought them here."

For one terrible moment Sabra allowed herself to be overwhelmed; and then, clinging to the thought of her child, she put the horror of the past days' events out of her mind.

"Poor Olivia. They will silence you, too, for being my friend."

Miss Eames bowed her head.

"They have done so already, then."

"Yes. But that is not important. The important thing is that they have announced a wage cut. Just as I told you."

"Damn them. O, damn them." Prince had been right. No one mattered, anyone's life could be thrown away.

"Sabra, I have found a shop. I wanted to talk to you about it on Thanksgiving Day, but then I couldn't find you—Sabra, it is right on Merrimack Street, just next to Dr. Mansfield the dentist. The man who owns the building lives on the second floor, but he will let an extra room on the third to us so that we may live there. And I have spoken to Ruby Hunt, she's on the Middlesex but she'll leave any time to come with us. She has a grand sense of style and she knows everyone, she'll bring in a lot of trade—o, Sabra! We can do it if we put our minds to it, I know we can. Just think, we will be independent!"

Sabra could not help laughing, so contagious was her friend's enthusiasm. What had seemed, four months ago, a venture of the utmost folly was now her only chance to survive. For a moment she suppressed her doubts, she allowed herself to imagine their success: carpeted floor, tall-mirrored fitting rooms, shelves of the very best imported silks and bombazines and tulle, velvets and satins, trays of elegant trimmings—laces and onyx buttons and silk braid and sequins and feathers and satin ribbons. They would need to find a good milliner, for ladies liked bonnets to match their dresses; and a cutter, for there would be so much business that the three proprietresses would be far too busy fitting and selling to attend to the actual manufacture of the garments. She saw herself, in a well-fitting gray twill with a pearl brooch at her throat, writing orders for entire wardrobes for a horde of faceless, moneyed women. And Clara could come—

"Yes," she said. She lay on the cot in the cold and crowded hospital ward and luxuriated briefly in her vision.

"Palfrey?"

A nurse stood at the foot of the bed, his white smock streaked and stained.

"Yes."

"You'll have to get up. I've orders to clean your bed. A new patient's coming in."

"But—" Miss Eames rose and faced him. "She can't be moved, she's far too ill, you can see that for yourself. Where will you put her? Upstairs?"

The nurse shook his head. "I won't put her any place, miss. I've orders to clear her bed. She's dismissed."

"From the Hospital?"

The nurse stared insolently at Miss Eames. "Them as is discharged from the Corporation is discharged from the Hospital. Don't blame me, lady, I'm just on orders."

"But you can't! She will die if you put her out! Where will she go? I demand to see the doctor. Where is he? No doctor would allow this—"

"Lady, he ordered it. And I daresay he's just following orders same as me. And you can't see him. He ain't here. Now either she gets out nice and quiet, or I'll have to put her out and she can lie in the street for all I care. I have my orders."

The other patients in the ward, those who were conscious, hung on every word, relishing this unaccustomed diversion. Miss Eames hesitated for a moment; then she opened her reticule and took out a half dollar.

"Listen to me. Don't touch her. I must go and arrange for a place for her to stay, and hire a wagon to take her there. I will be back in an hour, and I want to find her right here."

The nurse took the coin. "An hour," he said. "But no more. Dr. Price'll be in later to make rounds, and if she's still here he'll have my job." He looked contemptuously at Sabra. She had not moved during their discussion; her brief strength had evaporated, leaving her weak and faint once again. She felt drowsy, very tired; it seemed that these two people by her bed were arguing about the fate of a stranger, and that the outcome of the argument could have no possible effect on her.

She was aware of Miss Eames' face bending over her, a murmured word of encouragement, and then Miss Eames went away. The nurse lingered. He scratched his private parts.

"Bitch," he said contemptuously.

She did not hear.

20

Dressmaking: the draping of lengths of cloth on the tightly corseted bodies of arrogant matrons intent on the most expensive fancy-work for the cheapest price.

The art of inventive falsehoods, shameless flattery—any distortion of the language to persuade a customer to place an order.

The strength of will to submit to the humiliation of being treated like a servant—worse, for good servants were increasingly hard to find, while dressmakers desperate for custom flocked to every inhabited settlement in New England.

The shop opened in January. By early April, the three women were bankrupt—ruined. They had not even money to buy thread. They had had many fewer customers than they had hoped, and much more competition: three new establishments had opened within a month of theirs.

The landlord, a kindly man hard-pressed himself to meet expenses, allowed them two weeks more; if they had not paid their rent by then, he said, they would have to leave.

They sat in the little showroom, a tired, discouraged trio attempting to salvage their lives. The sale of their stock—the bolts of cloth, the racks and drawers of trimmings—would not cover half their debt; and even if every customer persuaded her husband to pay what she owed, they would not have enough to carry them through. It was late afternoon: too early for the operatives to be shopping (and few mill workers patronized dressmakers in any case) and too late for the married women who, at this hour, were in their homes supervising the preparation of supper.

Olivia looked up from the account book. "We'll have to ask him for another extension," she said wearily. "We can give him ten dollars."

Without turning away from the window which gave onto the muddy street, Ruby replied: "He had a man in yesterday to look at the place. The man wanted to open a jewelry store."

"Yesterday?" said Olivia sharply. "Why didn't you tell me?"

Ruby shrugged. "Why should I? You would only worry."

It was not fair, thought Sabra. It was *not* fair! Not after they had worked so hard. And where would they go? What would they do? How would she ever get Clara back, and support them both? No mill in New England would hire her now that she had been dishonorably discharged from the Appleton. She would have to leave, to go south to New-York or Pennsylvania or even beyond. And she had not even the money for the fare.

In their consternation at Ruby's news they had not noticed that a wagon had pulled up in front of the shop. A man wearing a low-crowned, broad-brimmed hat and a plain, oddly cut suit alighted and came in. Sabra, her thoughts preoccupied, stifled a nervous laugh when she saw him. Surely this man wanted a gentleman's tailor instead of a trio of dressmakers!

And then he spoke to her, and she recognized him: Brother Elijah from the United Society. *Clara—*

"Well, Sabra, I've been hard put to find you."

Unsteadily she got to her feet, mindful that the other two were intensely curious at this apparition.

"What is it? What's wrong?"

He stood awkward and out of place in this establishment which catered to human vanity, to female desire for display and ornament.

"I was sent to fetch you."

"Is Clara sick? What is it?"

"No—no. Don't worry about her. She's fine." He coughed to gain a moment to gather his wits. Gentile women always upset him. "It's Eldress Hannah. She's failing. She asked to see you."

In her relief that Clara was well, Sabra's knees began to tremble so that she had to sit down again in the chair which Olivia hastily pushed under her.

"What's wrong with her?"

"Elder James don't know exactly. He's been doctorin' her, but he hasn't helped her any." Brother Elijah's round, earnest face peered out at her from under the brim of his hat. "You'd best come back with me if we're to be there in time."

"In time for what?" She heard her voice crack; as she spoke she had a sudden vision of the brown eyes, the tranquil face, the keen intelligence hidden behind the facade of humble service. "She can't be that sick! Why, she isn't old, she's hardly fifty! She's healthier than I am."

"She's been poorly all winter, Sabra, and a week ago she caught a fever. You'd best come. We'll be late enough as it is."

She ran upstairs to get her cloak and bonnet, all thoughts of their eviction driven from her mind by the image of Eldress Hannah lying ill. Brother Elijah had gone out to the wagon to wait for her. With a hurried good-by to her bemused partners—"I can't explain now, Olivia, but don't do anything until I get back. I'll try to come in a day or two. Don't let him force us out!"—she ran out into the cold April twilight and climbed onto the wagon seat.

For a while, as they made their way out of the city, Sabra was too preoccupied with thoughts of Eldress Hannah to speak to her companion. They came onto the road to Harvard Village. On either side lay woods and fields, snow still clinging to north slopes, the rutted road still frozen. In the sky the first stars appeared, faint in the pale west, more brilliant overhead and toward the darker east. Sabra imagined Eldress ascending to that sky, all shining and pure, to be embraced by Mother Ann and the Lord, to dwell with them in Heaven. Going home, she thought: Eldress is going home. Now, tonight: she longs to go. I have no right to wish her to stay. She has laid down her burden; she has done her work well. I should be glad—O dear Lord I am glad—to have the chance to say good-by. Hurry! she thought. She longed to seize the reins and lash the horse to a quickened pace. She shivered in the cold night wind; she choked back a sob. She turned to Brother Elijah and spoke to him to ease her grief.

"I am glad you found me."

"She told me where." He glanced at her, mildly curious. "I thought you was at the factory."

"I was."

"You didn't like it? Can't say I blame you."

"Ah—no." She did not want to be interrogated. "Tell me about the Family. Did you have a good winter?"

"Ayuh. We can't keep up with the market for herbs. We built another room for packagin'. I guess you haven't seen it. When was the last time you was out? October?"

"September."

"Ayuh. Well, the little girl's grown a lot. Course I don't see her that much. But she looks good an' healthy. An' like I said we're prospering fine. It's only Eldress as has been sick. Elder James been doctorin' her right along but she didn't get better, an' then she took a fever last week." He glanced at her again. "She always spoke well of you, y' know."

She took his meaning, heard the implied criticism.

"Yes," she said. "I'm sorry I couldn't stay."

"Some can, some can't. All the same, I know she thought high of you."

They reached the colony well after dark. Sabra hurried to the infirmary, where she found several sisters sitting in a row at the foot of Eldress' bed. By her side sat Elder James, his eyes intent on the still, pale face of the woman before him. He glanced up as Sabra approached; he motioned her to silence.

"She wanted to see you as soon as you came," he said softly, "but she was too tired to stay awake. She is very weak. Let her sleep. You may sit here so that you are with her when she wakes." He read the unspoken question in Sabra's eyes. "Yes. She will awake. It is not time yet." He stood up and beckoned the sisters to follow him, leaving Sabra to watch alone.

The room was quiet. No sound came from the other rooms of the large building: offices, stores, dormitories might have been empty, although more than a hundred people lived there. Surely they were keeping silence for Eldress Hannah; more than one Sister, thought Sabra, was crying this night, for Eldress had been widely loved, almost revered. Every novice at the Harvard Society had looked to Eldress Hannah as a model of true sanctity on which to pattern herself. Hard-working, devout, shielded by the inner glow of tranquillity, of obedience to the commands of Mother Ann, she had been an inspiration to them all.

Now her work was done. Sabra looked at the thin face, the soft, faintly wrinkled skin, the sharp line of the nose, the generous mouth which had been so often unable to repress a smile. The mouth was sunken now, lips slightly parted.

No man has ever kissed that mouth, thought Sabra suddenly; and instantly she was horrified. What had made her think such a shocking, blasphemous thing? She shut her eyes and bowed her head and whispered a hurried prayer: not to any God, but to Eldress. Forgive me: I meant no disrespect.

Eldress opened her eyes; her mouth moved in a faint smile. "Sabra," she said.

Sabra sank onto her knees beside the bed. She clasped Eldress' hand, and for a moment she felt a faint, returning pressure. Eldress' eyes glowed.

"The child is well. Are you?"

"Yes."

"I have been concerned for you. When you wrote that you had left the factory I thought that you might have had some trouble—"

"No. As I told you, I opened a shop with some friends."

"And you are doing well?"

"Yes. Splendidly."

"Good. I am glad. It was right for you to leave us, although I have missed you."

"O, Eldress—" She choked, reminded herself of the journey which lay before this woman, remembered Eldress' unswerving faith.

"Sabra. I have a special reason for wanting to see you. More than simply wanting . . . to say good-by. Here. Hold my hand and look at me so that I can see your pretty face." The wide mouth smiled, the eyes held. Death sniffed about the shadowy corners of the room, but he would not come: not yet.

"I want to ask you something, Sabra. And I want you to try very hard to answer." She paused to gather her strength, and Sabra waited, her grief momentarily overcome by curiosity. Eldress continued:

"Do you remember your fifth birthday?"

"My fifth—no. I don't. Why—?"

"You were given a little doll. She had a pink dress and shiny black hair and two petticoats—"

"And little black leather shoes," said Sabra slowly. She stared incredulous at the woman lying on the bed before her. She swallowed hard; she tried to direct her thoughts to some logical pattern. The doll had been stolen from her the year before her father fell ill; great tall girl that she was, she had cried bitterly over its loss.

Eldress' eyes filled with tears; as she blinked the tears slid down onto the pillow. Her mouth trembled. With great effort she raised her arms and embraced the young woman before her.

"I gave her to you," she said. "Yes. I gave her to you. I saved for years for that doll, a penny at a time. I lied to your father—yes, I did—and often said we had not a cent in the world, when all the time I was saving. I kept the money sewn in my clothing. He never discovered it. And when I saw your face—o, Sabra, I'd have lied to the Lord Himself for that! You were so happy. It was the only thing I was ever able to give you."

Sabra sat up, gently easing from the light pressure of Eldress' arms. She stared again at the face before her as if seeing it for the first time. A dream: she was captive in a dream. Soon she would awake. Memories swarmed up, little scenes from her earliest years: a warm summer day, wading in a cold mountain stream, laughing, held by someone with gentle hands and a soft voice, someone who loved her, who dried her frozen feet and gathered her on her lap and sang her to sleep in the shade of a pine tree; a cold winter night, staggering into a village, that same someone collapsing on the road, a door opening, warmth and kind strangers, a child crying, frightened, unattended, while grown-ups hurried back and forth caring for that same one who loved her.

"She is dead. She died a long time ago."

"No." Eldress clasped her hand, lifted it to her tear-stained cheek. "Did he tell you that?"

"Yes. I cried for her. He said she had died and gone to Heaven with my little brothers and sisters."

Eldress' face worked painfully as she struggled to speak, but Sabra hurried on. Her throat hurt; her voice was rough, unfamiliar: "He said that we had been spared to do God's work, and that when our time was done we would be with you again. Oh, *why*—?"

Eldress' words came hard, her breath labored. "I was very ill. I miscarried many times after you were born. I had no strength for the life which he chose for us. Do you remember the Wilson family in Rutland?

They were very kind. They agreed to keep me until I recovered, while your father went on. He thought I would die, you see, but he had the urgency of his mission, he could not wait. He took you, of course." She paused, searching for the words. "He said—he said it was better so, for you to be with him. I was so ill, I cried and begged him to leave you with me. But he would not listen."

"He told me you had died," repeated Sabra. "Why did he say that? Why didn't he come back for you?"

Eldress shook her head tiredly. "I had no word from him for a year. I asked every traveler passing through, not that there were many. No one had heard of him. I didn't know where he was. I was in despair. I prayed for help. And then, as if in answer to my prayer, someone showed me a pamphlet from the Society. And it seemed to me that it was the answer to my prayer. Living in the world, among the gentiles, had almost been my death. These people showed me a new life, Mother Ann's way. I thought I had lost you. And it seemed to me—perhaps I was wrong—but it seemed to me that I had been spared for a purpose, that I had had my child taken from me for a purpose. I had to believe that. Can you understand?"

Sabra nodded.

"And so I joined the Society. I changed my name, as so many do; I took on a new person, a new life. But always I hoped to find you. I used to question every visitor. I was happy here, but I could not give myself entirely. I prayed to find you. I never confessed those prayers. The Society allowed me to live. How would I have done otherwise? I had nothing, no money, no family, and so I came. I was not sorry. But sometimes I thought I would go mad, not knowing where you were."

"And then I came. Why didn't you tell me then? When did you realize—"

"Almost from the beginning. Do you remember our first interview?"

"Yes."

"I thought I recognized you. You look something like your father's mother. And then as the weeks went by, and we talked—ah, I knew. I knew then, certainly."

"But why didn't you tell me?"

"What would have happened if I had? I would have had to confess it to the ministry. Perhaps they would have put someone else as Eldress in my place. If I stayed I thought I might help you in some way. Or perhaps you would have felt pressed to join us, when in truth you might not have been suited for our life—as in fact you are not. I was wrong in being weak, in trying to persuade you so that you stayed until—until Philomena and William . . ." She paused; they passed over the memory of that horror. Eldress continued: "And then you had the child—ah, she is a darling child—and when you left, I thought, good, I can oversee her, it was against the rule, we are not allowed to form attachments, but no one ever knew. I was very careful. And she loves me best, you know, of all the women here." A pale gleam of triumph flashed in her brown eyes. "That is important, for a child to have someone to love. And it was for the best after all, because I could watch over her while you went out again into the world to make your way. It was selfish of me—sinful—but I was glad you left her with us for a little time. It was as if I had you again."

They embraced once more. Sabra kissed the pale cheek, she smoothed back the straggling hair, she murmured soft words of comfort as she glowed in the loving warmth of Eldress' gaze. All the while she felt as if a burden, carried since childhood, had been lifted from her heart. Her mother—that loved figure whose loss she had never ceased to mourn—had not deserted her, had not abandoned her by dying, had in fact been always alive, always loving her. Even when she, Sabra, had not realized it, her mother had been watching over her and protecting her as best she could. Why, she was not alone after all! Not only did she have Clara, she had her own dear mother too! She was not condemned to wander alone with no one to cherish her—

Eldress coughed, turned her head. Suddenly Sabra remembered why she was here: why she had been sent for. With a terrible cry that brought two sisters running she threw herself across the bed and clung to the still form which had begun at last the final journey to the promised embrace of Mother Ann.

"No!" she shrieked. "No! Please God, no! Save her, please save her!"

The horrified sisters attempted to lift her, to pull her away. She clung to Eldress; she would not be moved. In the agony of her loss she felt that she was dying, too. The light from the lamp grew dim; the last thing she heard was a wild, angry voice—her own—imploring the Lord for help. She heard no reply.

21

Sabra bowed her head against the cold autumn rain, clasping her shawl under her chin with one hand and holding to Clara with the other. The child trotted along as best she could on her short legs; she was very tired.

"Hurry, sweetheart, we'll be done soon," said Sabra encouragingly. She gave the tiny chilled hand a quick squeeze. "Not far now, only a few more houses, and then we'll go back and be nice and warm."

"Porridge?" said Clara hopefully.

"Yes, indeed. A big bowl just for you." Although in all truth she was not sure of it, Mary McCormic having given them a meal that morning and having, as Sabra well knew, very little left. She forced her thoughts away from the unhappy subject of food—dear God, but Clara was thin!—and led the child through a gate in the picket fence surrounding the prosperous-looking house.

At the back door she paused for a moment as she always did to gather her courage; then, hearing movement within, she knocked. A woman answered.

"No beggars."

"Please—I'm not begging," said Sabra quickly. "I'm selling—look—this beautiful lace. Only ten cents a yard, all fresh made."

She was glad of the back porch roof; although she and Clara were soaked, she could not afford to have the fat rolls of lace spoiled by the rain. From a cloth bag she had withdrawn a length of crochet-work; now she held it for the woman to see, thankful that it would not be wet.

The woman glanced at the handiwork and then, with some curiosity, at Sabra.

"You aren't Irish," she said.

"No."

"Then why are you selling Irish lace? That's no fit work for an American woman."

It was not the first time that this question had been put; by now, after weeks of hearing it, Sabra had devised what generally seemed to be a convincing answer.

"I work with a private charitable order. The Irish women are shy of venturing away from their homes. Many of them do not speak good English, and so on, so we take their handiwork and sell it for them. We keep nothing for ourselves." (How true! she thought bitterly.)

Sometimes, of course, people did not believe this explanation.

"I haven't heard of anything like that," said the woman. "Mercy! What's that? A child?"

Clara, who had been leaning into her mother's skirts so that she was practically unnoticeable, had been suddenly overcome by fatigue. She sank to the porch floor, a miserable little heap of ragged clothing, ominously silent.

"Private charitable order, indeed," snapped the woman. She retreated into the house and slammed the door. Sabra was too tired, too hungry and numbed by the cold, to feel any great disappointment. Most people refused her. She put the lace back into the strap bag which hung from her elbow and reached down to lift Clara into her arms and—somehow—walk the half-mile or so back to Mary McCormic's. Clara sniffled slightly as she lay against her mother's shoulder, but she made no other sign of consciousness. She was a quiet child—far too quiet—and so pale and thin that Sabra was often frightened. Although she always gave Clara some of her own portion, the child failed to gain weight. It seemed as if her sharp little bones would pierce her unhealthily pale skin; her small face was pinched, hollow-cheeked, shadows under her eyes.

Sabra settled the child's weight against her shoulder—so little, but still too much for her own frail strength. As she started down the porch steps she heard the door behind her open once again.

"Wait!" said the woman. Sabra stopped and looked back.

"Would you—would you care for a cup of tea?" said the woman. "It's a bad cold day and you look near worn out."

Sabra hesitated. Her normal human response to normal human kindness had been dulled by months of refusals and slammed doors. "Yes," she said after a moment. "Thank you."

The kitchen was warm and fragrant with the odor of yeast and cinnamon. The woman settled Sabra at the table, Clara on her lap, and set out a tray of fresh-baked rolls to accompany the pot of steaming tea.

"There," she said, sure now that she had been correct in her impulse to call the lace-seller back. "Have as many as you want. And I'll warm some milk for the little one. She looks real pale." As she moved around the room she threw curious glances at the pair; of course it was rude to pry, but perhaps it was her Christian duty to inquire—

"Do you sell much?" she said at last.

"Some."

"Enough to live?"

Sabra shrugged. She sipped the scalding tea.

"How old's the child?" The woman put down a cup of warmed milk. Sabra lifted it to Clara's lips. Clara, almost asleep, could hardly drink at first; dribbles ran down her dirty chin.

"Three in March."

"That young? She looks older." The woman stared, frankly curious. "There—she's coming around." She smiled at Clara, who drank greedily now, not noticing her benefactor. "Here," she said to Sabra, "have one of these." She offered a plate of cinnamon rolls. Sabra hesitated. For many months past, she had consumed enough food each day to stay alive: no more. She had learned to discipline herself: do not remember the plates of savory stew, the roast turkey, the pies and sauces and fragrant loaves of bread. Now, faced with these fresh-baked rolls, she thought, if she ate one, would it destroy her will? Would its sweetness, the soft chewy texture, make it all the harder to return as she must to Mary McCormic's lumpy porridge and tasteless potatoes? At last she could not resist. She reached out, took a roll, and, trembling slightly, broke off a piece for Clara and began to eat.

The woman continued to stare. "I'll give you credit for gumption," she said. "Peddlin's a hard thing. But then we all do as we must. Do you live in the city?"

Sabra nodded, her mouth full. Clara reached out a tiny hand; Sabra took another roll and broke it into pieces for the child.

"I don't care for the place myself," said the woman. "This is my brother's house, I've been here two years now since my father died. I wanted to go on the Corporation but my brother wouldn't have it, he said I'd be better off here helping out. They have four little ones—they're nappin' now, upstairs—and my sister-in-law's that sick with every one o' them, it's true she couldn't manage without help. She's been feelin' better this last month and so I said to her go out while you can, you'll soon enough come to bed again, so she's been out near every afternoon while the children nap. My brother has a dry-goods store on Central Street, perhaps you know it, Dearborn and Cummings. It's all very well for you, I told him, you can go out every day, but she has to stay here and deal with them, they had fever last winter and all sick at once and we thought we'd never pull them through. Of course we have an Irish girl come in to help with the heavy work, but still it's a job. Here, just let me give her some more milk, the poor little thing's half starved. Look at her drink. My nephews and the baby—that's a girl—are as fat as fat, I said to my sister-in-law, you'd better cut down on their food, we can't sew fast enough to keep them in clothing. But you know how mothers are, she thinks it's the end of the world if they don't eat till they burst, but I said, you'd save some money, cut them down a little. She's a good sweet soul, she'd cry her eyes out if she could see this one, she told me that her husband could well afford to pay the bill, he gets an enormous trade, of course, all the operatives rushin' in to spend their pay every week, I think it's a disgrace, some of them look like walking advertisements for *Godey's* and I don't think it's right, do you? They ought to know their place, some of them give themselves fearful airs. I wonder that the factories get any work out of them at all. I was glad I didn't go into the mills, although I was disappointed at first, I had counted on having my own money. But my brother was right, he said I'd hate living in a boarding house and I'm sure I would, there must be some rare ones there from what I've heard. It coarsens a woman, don't you think, to live away from home? And I hear some of the landladies are no better than they should be, my sister-in-law had company last week and they were talking about a woman on the Middlesex, I won't repeat it but it was enough to turn your stomach. My brother said he wouldn't have me on the Corporation, I could go if I wanted, he said, but I'd have to move out. And I didn't know if I could stand the work. What if I get sick, I thought. And then they needed me here, after I'd been here a week I couldn't leave, but it's hard, I can't get out, I can't meet people, I sometimes wonder if I'll ever—"

The front door slammed. A look of terror flashed across the woman's face. Instantly she snatched away their cups and the plate of cinnamon rolls and put them on the sideboard and pulled Sabra's arm, lifting her onto her feet. So sudden was her attack that Sabra almost dropped the child.

"Quick!" whispered the woman. "Out—quick! She's back early!"

They heard footsteps at the front of the house, faint thuds as objects—parcels?—dropped to the floor.

Sabra allowed herself to be pushed out the back door. She stumbled down the steps into the rain, down the back alley to a side street. Clara, replete, lay heavy on her shoulder. Well, that was a strange thing, she thought. But welcome: she felt quite revived, she would be back at Mary McCormic's in no time. What an odd woman! But kind: certainly she had been kind.

She walked steadily in the rain. It was not until she had reached the edge of the Acre that she realized that she had left behind, in the warm and fragrant kitchen, the precious bag of lace.

22

"There's no help for it, Sabra," said Mary McCormic. "You'll have to go begging or leave."

Despite the bitter January cold, the room was hot, so crowded with malodorous, lice-infested bodies that the stench drove away any appetite for food. This was as well, for there was very little food provided by the landlady. Mary McCormic insisted that all her boarders pay something; as she explained to Sabra, if she let one person stay on free, soon she would be besieged by the homeless, each with a more heart-rending tale than the last. "I couldn't bear it," she said. "I'd lose my mind if I listened to it."

Some weeks she collected as little as a dollar in all, although at all times she had no fewer than ten boarders and sometimes as many as fifteen. They gave her what they could—ten, fifteen, twenty-five cents—and she gave them a coffin-sized space on which to sleep and some kind of meal every day. She also managed, Sabra did not know how, to pay her rent to the Corporation which owned the lot of land on which her shack stood. Because she was well-known in the Acre, and was said to be honest, she never lacked for boarders despite the censure of the priest;

and she was known, too, for choosing them carefully. She would not accept anyone newly arrived in the city. Cases of ship-fever had occurred in alarming numbers, brought by the new immigrants flooding in from Boston and Montreal. After a time she became something of a legend in this regard. For many months a story made the rounds of the Acre: one cold night Mary McCormic answered a pounding on her door to find a huge, strong man, new in the city, recommended to go to her by a friend several times removed, asking for a place to stay and offering a good sum of money. She explained to him that she never accepted any boarders just arrived, that it was against her policy, that he could come back in a week and she'd make a place for him—after he visited the bath-house. The man, who was undoubtedly cold and hungry, became enraged. He threatened to hit her clear to Dublin unless she gave him a place that very night. Mary McCormic put the curse of Cromwell on him, and then, gathering her wits about her, suddenly lowered her head like a maddened bull and rushed at him and gave him a push in the belly so that he landed on his backside in the frozen mud, the wind knocked out of him, and never such a dumbstruck fellow there was in all Christendom. Afterward he held it against her; he threatened to kill her if he got the chance, and so Mary McCormic from that time kept a stout stick by her and carried it with her when she went out, and put the word about that she would kill him first. The man was a drunkard. After some weeks his body was found floating in the Suffolk Canal, and Mary put by her weapon.

Sabra lifted her hand and crushed a louse running down her neck. She was very tired. She thought that she had never been so tired, even on the worst days at the mill. For the past week she had lain on her pallet, not sick, but so drained of energy that she could hardly move even to fetch Clara's bowl of porridge. That morning, scratching her head, she had pulled away a handful of hair; she could feel the bumps of insect bites on her flesh, she could smell the odor of her filthy body. She stared dully at Mary McCormic, who crouched beside her.

"You must stir yourself, Sabra. Do you want to try the lace again? Kathleen Connolly's made some new, she said."

Sabra shook her head. "No."

She would not try peddling again, not after the disaster of losing the bag of lace. She had returned for it the moment she realized that she had left it; she had found what seemed to be the right house, but the door had been opened by a different woman who claimed not to know her, who had angrily slammed the door in her face. She had gone on then until dark, looking for the place where she had had her brief rest, lugging Clara on her shoulder. Finally she had been forced to return to the Acre, to Mary McCormic's hovel which was now her hovel, hers and Clara's, for fifty cents a week. The two women who had made the lace had taken twenty-five cents each for their trouble; Sabra had sold her Highland shawl to get the money.

"Well, then. What?" Mary surveyed her anxiously. "You don't look strong enough for housework, but if you think you can do it, I'll speak to a woman I know who knows someone—"

"No."

Sabra turned her head away. Truly, she did not know what to do. There was no possible way, it seemed, for her to survive, for her and Clara to live. A tear slipped down her cheek, leaving a trail on her grimy skin.

"Ah, now," said Mary brightly, "no need for that. Why, there's all kinds of money waitin' for you, d' y' know that? It's there for the askin', Sabra, believe me." Mary glanced down at the quiet child huddled next to her mother. There was no mercy anywhere in this world. Sabra seemed slow to realize that fact. She was fond of Sabra, for Biddy's sake if for no other reason, but she needed her board money.

"Look," she said. "Just give it a try. They can only say no. But they won't, not to such a pretty girl—why, and if you take the child with you you'll get twice as much. I know what I'm sayin', Sabra."

Well you do, thought Sabra dully. Another tear slid down her cheek, and then another. I must get up, she thought. Mary is right, I must do something to help myself. O Lord I am so tired.

Mary fetched her an unwonted offering, then: a mug of tea. Not a thing ordinarily included in Sabra's allotted ration.

"Now," said Mary. "Just drink this and let's see what you can do."

She waited while Sabra drank. Then she continued: "Now you can't go back on the Corporation, because you're on the blacklist. Not here, not anywhere, right? And you've tried the shop. Dressmakin's worse than the factory anyway, if you ask me. You don't make a penny. Lace-sellin' was a good idea, but it don't seem to have done too well. And besides, any kind of work you do will take you away from the child and who's to look after her? In two or three years she can be on her own, but she's still too young now. So you need some way to stay with her, or have her stay with you." Mary paused. The girl was holding back, she was sure of it. A spasm of irritation shook her. No one as poor as this one had the right to be so proud. She decided to speak her mind completely; if Sabra didn't like it she could leave. Neither the world nor Mary McCormic had a place for someone who refused to look sharp when she needed to.

Mary took the empty mug and put it on the damp dirt floor. Then she took Sabra's two hands and pressed them tightly between her own.

"Look at me, Sabra. And listen. You know someone who can help you. Patrick told me, long ago. I haven't forgotten. You know someone—someone with money. Someone who might be glad enough to give you some of it. He'd have his reasons, sure enough. It would be nothing to him. Five dollars, ten dollars, just enough to get you by. Just enough to keep you until the child grows a bit, and you get your strength back."

Sabra shook her head. "I couldn't. Please don't ask me to. You don't understand."

"I understand well enough," snapped Mary, her patience exhausted. She dropped Sabra's hands. "Now listen, miss. Here's your choices, as I see it. You get some money from him, damn his soul. Or you go pay a visit to the Reverend Wood, and if he likes the look of you he'll give you a ticket to the workhouse. I'd as soon have a ticket to Hell, myself, but you may think different. Or you do like many a one before you, and you go askin' them as has it to spare. With the child along you'll get somethin', I guarantee it. Enough to keep you here. I won't turn you out even if you give me only twenty-five cents a week, but I've got to have somethin'."

Sabra felt the child stir at her side. She stroked the matted hair; her heart contracted as the tiny hand reached up to touch her own. Fool, she thought. Why do you hesitate? She turned to meet Mary's eyes.

"All right," she said.

"Good for you!" exclaimed Mary. Instantly she was Sabra's friend again. "I tell you, you won't be sorry. There's nothin' to it. You'll see. Now—you don't look too spry, but still you look better'n you might. Let's just rip this skirt a little—so—and streak a little more dirt on your face—so—and be sure to walk with a limp. But don't cough. They don't like coughers. And be sure to say please, and look down, never look 'em in the eye. I'd try Fayette Street first, then you can go on up East Merrimack."

23

No one would give her any money. She quickly discovered that while people might be persuaded—or impelled by their consciences—to give a penny or two to a starving Irishman, almost no one would even listen to her once they heard her American accent. The Irish were a deplorable race, people said, but, like the native in the jungle or the heathen Chinese, they had some excuse for their miserable condition; therefore, occasionally, a good Christian might in all conscience give them some small charity. But for a Yankee woman to beg was unheard of; it was indecent, an insult to every hard-working American. They would not tolerate it.

At the end of the third day, when she still had not collected as much as a penny, she decided to knock at one more door before returning to Mary McCormic's for the night. She was on Chestnut Street, in a neighborhood of neat, well-kept homes. An occasional passer-by gave her a curious glance, for she was an outlander here; but once, when she stumbled and almost fell, two men observing her made no move to help. She seemed, to them, of a species different from their own, and while they would have rushed to help an American woman—a lady—they saw no need to exercise themselves over the plight of an Irish beggarwoman trailed by a small ghost of a child.

Sabra walked around to the back door of the house and knocked; and when the door was opened, she said, "Please, missus, could ye spare a penny for a poor woman to buy her child some milk?"

The woman hesitated; she looked down at the child. "Just a minute," she said. She withdrew, shut the door; after a moment she returned and held out a nickel. But she did not surrender it at once; she would have her say.

"You people are a pestilence," she said. "Why do you come here? No—not so quick. I'm giving you this because of the child, and I want you to promise that you will buy food for him and not drink for yourself. And I don't want to see you again, either, and don't bother telling your friends down in the Camp Lands that you've found an easy mark. Do you understand?"

Sabra never raised her eyes. "Yes, missus." She held out her hand; the woman dropped the coin into it, taking care that her fingers did not touch the supplicant's.

"Very well. Remember it," she said; and shut the door.

From that time, Sabra had a little more success. She knew that her accent was not exact, but no American knew it. She understood that she was less offensive—less threatening—as an Irishwoman; and certainly, she thought, I am one of them now in every other way. I might as well take their speech.

As the fitful spring drew on and the weather grew somewhat warmer, she went farther afield. Some days she got fifteen cents, some twenty or twenty-five, some nothing—but it was enough, week by week, to pay a little board money to Mary and have a few pennies left over to buy extra food. She even managed to save a dollar and seventeen cents, which she carried in a small cloth pouch on a string around her neck.

She and her child survived.

24

During the summer of 1847 increasing numbers of famine-ridden Irish—hundreds, thousands, tens of thousands—fled to America to try to stay alive. Any city or town in the United States with a nucleus of Irish—a town which, like the mill towns, had used Irish labor to build factories and dig canals—inevitably attracted more. Wives came to join husbands, brothers to brothers, parents to children. The Acre, already crowded beyond belief, was forced to absorb ever greater numbers. Cellars where ten people had slept now housed twenty; houses which had been built for three or four families now held ten or twelve. People slept in doorways, in alleyways, on the banks of canals. Mary McCormic and those like her, who had always tried to control the kind and condition of the tenants whom they took in, now found themselves to be the subject of muttered abuse. All very well to be careful, people said, but we've got to put these new ones somewhere. She could take four more at least, and for nothing, too, and feed them in the bargain. It was widely suspected that Mary McCormic had a secret hoard of money. She was known to be stingy with food; she was known also to charge a fine high price whenever she was called to employ her medical skill. Although she was defended by her tenants, people in the Acre began to mutter against her; and so she took to carrying a cudgel once again.

Sabra watched the newcomers pouring in, some legally, some not, many of them hardly able to speak an intelligible English sentence, most of them half dead, all of them with tales of horror which made her own condition seem well off. She shuddered when they spoke of scrabbling in the fields trying to find even one blighted, rotted potato to eat; she wept when mothers spoke of being turned out of their cottages by the landlord's agent when they could not pay the rent.

The question of how they were to survive in America was one which they had not been able to consider, so frantic were they to leave Ireland. Now that they had arrived they lived as they could. Many died; those who survived did so by any means at hand. They began to beg.

In Lowell, they begged at the same houses visited by Sabra. Often they got there first. The citizens of Lowell became angry. "Must we endure this plague of locusts?" they asked. "We cannot walk down the street without being accosted by some supplicating Hibernian, we cannot rest safe in our homes without being disturbed by the dreaded knock on the door, the tale of hunger recited by the wretched, fever-ridden interloper."

People's hearts hardened. Their Christian duty, as they saw it, was to deliver their city from this insupportable burden of surplus population. Therefore they began to refuse to give alms. "Cut off the supply," they said. "Refuse all supplicants. Let these people understand that Lowell is not a charitable institution."

Feelings ran high against England. People called for strict controls on immigration so that England might be made to feel the responsibility for what were after all her own subjects. The citizens of Lowell were no more heartless in this matter than their fellow Americans similarly inundated. They were happy to contribute to the Irish Relief Committee and did so most generously. But they wanted the relief to be applied to the Irish in Ireland—not in Lowell.

To be sure, there were some few individuals who genuinely deserved help. A Ministry at Large had been established to see to these cases. The Reverend Horatio Wood was in charge. He had his office in the Hamilton Chapel in Middlesex Street; there, from 8–9 A.M., 12–12:30 P.M., and 4–5 P.M., Monday through Saturday, he heard appeals from the needy. The remainder of his days were spent stalking the streets of the city, searching out those few souls who, in his opinion, were of that rare species, the genuinely worthy poor. His was a difficult task: he had constantly to inquire, to evaluate, to judge, to sniff out the impostor, to determine all in the space of a five-minute interview whether or not the trembling, humble supplicant was false or true, swindler or starving, consummate actor or positively about to expire. He had to be on his guard at all times. He became fanatical, both in his determination to help the genuinely helpless and to avoid being gulled. As time went by he developed exquisitely acute antennae: he could spot an impostor in a minute; in thirty seconds; in ten seconds flat.

Naturally the Reverend Wood became an expert in his field. In his Annual Report he listed, for the edification of his readers, the causes of poverty. These were:

1. Intemperance
2. Want of Employment
3. Sickness
4. Begging
5. Loss of husbands
6. Desertion of husbands
7. Large families
8. Licentiousness

And still they came; a hemorrhage from their mortally wounded homeland. At times it seemed to the city fathers that Lowell would drown in destitute Irish. The city had not been built to accommodate such enormous numbers of people who did not fit into the original design. Lowell had been built to manufacture cloth. Housing had been provided for the workers and overseers of that industry. That was all.

The men who ran the factories—the resident Agents—had other problems now, as well. Their first duty, as they knew perfectly well, was to make a profit so that the stockholders in Boston received their dividends. In order for the mills to make a profit, the operatives had to produce an ever increasing amount of cloth. Heretofore the majority of the operatives had been good docile workers: decent, thrifty, hard-working Yankee women who worked efficiently and well and made no trouble. Only a small number had succumbed to the wiles of the outside agitators who had sung the siren song of the ten-hour day and other such nonsense. But now a curious thing began to happen: the Yankee women began to go home—or to stay at home in the first place, and never set foot in Lowell at all. Slavers scoured the north country; procuring agents redoubled their efforts; handbills and recruiting posters wallpapered the landscape.

To no avail. The Corporation Agents shook their heads and deplored the softening of the native American character. It was too bad, they said, that we live in a time when people no longer want to earn an honest penny. Look what we did for these women: we gave them a chance at independence, we gave them a chance to earn money. And what do they do? They spurn us, they throw our benevolence in our faces; they go back to immure themselves in the country, far from the charms of city life. The Agents were insulted; but then, like jilted lovers, they swallowed the lump of pride in their throats and looked elsewhere.

And saw the Irish.

25

"Y' have anything to take to the gombeen man?" said Mary. She crouched before the fire, warming her chilblained hands. "What's in the little trunk?"

"Nothing," said Sabra. But there was: one thing.

"Take that, then—take the trunk. He'd gi' ye a few pennies for it. Enough to keep you for a week."

Mary glanced sideways at the young woman huddled on her pallet.

The child lay wide-eyed in her arms; she seemed to know without being told that she must be quiet, must make no trouble or disturbance. What's the matter, thought Mary. If she had the gumption to go beggin', what's so bad about this?

Billy Hogan, the gombeen man, had his place in Fenwick Street hard by St. Patrick's Church. He was a red-faced, black-haired man with a smile that could slice you sideways. When he saw what Sabra brought, he laughed out loud.

"Are y' havin' a joke on me, woman?" he said. "Y' wouldn't be tryin' to play a trick on an honest, hard-workin' man, would you now?"

"No," she said, not understanding. The open trunk, her small hair trunk that she had always had, it seemed, stood between them. She had taken out her father's Bible; she held it up for Hogan to see. His hard face broke again into a thousand lines of laughter.

"A Proddy Bible? Y' must be foolin' me. Who'd want that?"

Her father had loved his Bible; she could not remember seeing him read anything else. It was a large, heavy volume with a brass clasp and a worn tooled leather binding whose rubbed corners and scuffed surface gave evidence of devoted use.

But of course. How could she have made such an error? A money-lender in the Paddy Camp Lands would have no use for the Bible of Orthodox, Congregational New England.

Hogan grinned at her discomfiture. "I see y' understand. But the trunk's worth somethin'. Say twenty-five cents? It surely ain't new, but somebody might get use out of it. An' I thank y' kindly for thinkin' of me, an' I'll be glad t' see you back again, any time."

She took the money: a quarter. One more week of life.

And because she had not the courage to throw the Bible into the canal, she took it back with her to Mary McCormic's.

26

In the alley off Moody Street, Sabra collapsed, trembling, her breath coming in painful spasms. Clara sank down beside her. After a moment Sabra removed the loaf from her shawl and tore off a hunk and gave it to Clara. The child ripped at the soft dough with her teeth, she hardly chewed before she swallowed. In a moment she looked for more; Sabra gave it. Although she had not eaten for two days and her stomach felt as though it had shrunk to nothing, she waited until Clara had begun the second piece before she took some for herself. The joy of seeing her child eat was nourishment enough, for a moment.

The bread was a miracle. Her teeth sank into the golden crust, the soft white dough, her tongue malled it against the roof of her mouth, the chewed mouthfuls slid down her throat and filled her stomach and brought strength and life. She did not notice the sweet, yeasty taste until her third piece; then, her immediate hunger allayed, she chewed more slowly, savoring the flavor.

They were sheltered from the wind where they sat, warming themselves in the pale December sun. They finished the loaf. Sabra patted the child's cheek and smiled.

"There, sweetheart. Wasn't that good!"

Clara crawled onto her mother's lap and burrowed her head against the warm, thin, familiar body. "Want some more," she said, but without conviction. The food had made her sleepy. She closed her eyes and lay quiet in her mother's arms.

Sabra held her, feeling the soft rhythm of her breathing, the warmth of the sun, the sudden peace from the constant ache in her stomach. They could stay here awhile, she thought. The baker had apparently not missed the bread, or at any rate had not raised a hue and cry. They could stop and rest here and gather their strength; it was a far pleasanter place than Mary McCormic's.

She had given Mary the last of her carefully hoarded money three days ago. Mary had not realized that it was the last, but she would know soon enough when the next rent day came around.

Clara stirred slightly. Sabra moved to a more comfortable position. She looked down at the tangle of dark curls, the little bundle of rags that was her daughter. The daughter of a thief. Weaver, dressmaker, beggarwoman, thief. I don't care, she thought. She was very tired. I'd do it again. I will do it again. I will do it to survive. The words bobbled around her mind: *wea*ver, *dress*maker, *beg*garwoman, *thief*. She held fast to Clara. She slept.

"Hey!"

She came awake. At first she did not know where she was. The sun had gone; the darkening buildings around them were picked out with lighted windows. Her arms were numb from holding Clara.

"Get up! Who in Hell do you think you are, sleepin' on my property! Get up before I kick you up!"

He was a middle-aged man, roughly dressed. A mechanic, perhaps. He watched her closely as she staggered up, setting the protesting child on her feet. Without a word she turned and led Clara away down the alley. "God-damned bogtrotters!" yelled the man. "Go back where you came from! We don't want you here!"

His words were lost in the noise of traffic as they came out onto Merrimack Street. It was very cold, and now they were exposed to the north wind which blew down through the river valley from Canada. Shivering, they trotted toward Dutton Street.

When they reached the Merrimack House Sabra's eye was caught by a blaze of light in the lobby. People hurried in and out through the doorway: busy people, men mostly, prosperous-looking, energetic, well fed. Through the tall windows fronting the street shone something which Sabra had never seen; it seemed a magical thing, a faery thing. "Look, Clara," she whispered; she gathered all her strength and lifted the child high.

It was a Christmas tree: a German novelty urged on the hotel's proprietor as the latest fashion in New-York. On every branch glittered a tiny candle; gilded ornaments and tiny figures and sparkling crystal icicles were scattered so thick that the fir tree itself could hardly be seen.

Heedless of the jostling passers-by, the two ragged creatures gazed enchanted at the sight. Darkness came; the tree seemed to blaze more brightly. It seemed to Sabra that it was a sign: a message, a promise of hope in her hopeless world.

27

She grew very bold. She stole apples from a vendor's cart in Central Street; she stole a small box of salted cod from the fishmonger's at Tower's Corner; she stole another loaf of bread. Nor did she confine herself to food: food was the least profitable and most dangerous thing to steal. She took a gold locket from the jeweler's shop across from the former premises of the dressmakers Eames and Palfrey; she took a silver spoon from another jeweler around the corner on Central Street.

Some weeks she gave part of the food to Mary in lieu of rent; the rest was for herself and Clara. She found a man to dispose of the jewelry and other salable items: Redskin, so-called because of the color of his prominent nose. Of course he cheated her; she expected that he would.

Mary McCormic knew that this sudden upturn in Sabra's fortunes was not the result of a new generosity on the part of the city's affluent. She did not care. Sabra's enterprise helped them all to survive. At least one other of her tenants, a small pale man named John Down, was an accomplished burglar; he always paid his rent promptly and had even been known to advance her a dollar or two when she needed. All to the good, thought Mary; some steal within the law, some without. All laws were alien to her: English laws, Yankee laws—all were made by strangers, by enemies. It was the business of her life to survive in spite of them. So she applauded Sabra's new-found gumption, and she told her daughter to mind Clara whenever Sabra asked. She hoarded her rent money; she cast a spell for strength; she endured.

One evening Sabra stood near the counter just inside the door of Boyden's Pharmacy. Mr. Boyden was perhaps five feet away, assisting a woman in the choice of ointment to cure the itch. ("Dr. Brewster's is very good, ma'am, but I've had ladies tell me that nothing suits them like the Russia salve, and it'll cure ringworm and ingrowing nails and snake-bite in the bargain.") The woman hesitated. Other customers thronged around her, impatiently waiting for Mr. Boyden's attentions. At other places at the counter, which ran around the three interior sides of the shop, were clerks similarly engaged. In the past several months Sabra had come instinctively to know the moment to strike; now, swiftly, her hand darted out to the display of packets. Three were enough: to risk taking more was to risk dropping some. Concealing them in the folds of her shawl she continued to stand at the counter as if she waited for service. After a moment or two, as if she had grown impatient, she turned and made her way out.

Despite the cold, Merrimack Street was thronged with Saturday night shoppers. She walked purposefully with the crowd; no need to draw attention to herself by hurrying. She did not avert her face as once she had done; no one who knew her as an operative would look twice at the ragged, dirty figure of an Irishwoman.

She had gone perhaps fifty feet when she heard the shout.

"Hi! Stop thief!"

People on either side of her looked around but no one stopped.

"Hi! You there! Stop that Irishwoman!"

No one spoke, no one moved to touch her. She risked a glance behind. The proprietor of the pharmacy, coatless, was pushing his way through the crowd.

"You!" he yelled. "Stop thief!"

She ran. Down Merrimack to Shattuck, down Shattuck to Market. Hurry! Clutching the precious packets of Dalmeyer's Powders, she ran on: fewer people here, darkness, safety. She heard him pounding behind her but he was middle-aged and stout and less intent on catching her than she was on escaping. The cold air tore at her lungs; once she tripped and almost went head-long onto the cobblestones. Hurry! If she could reach the Acre she would be safe, he would not risk following her there. Across the railroad tracks, across Dutton Street—she could not hear him, she was safe. She looked behind. In the darkness she could see nothing, hear nothing except her own blood pounding in her ears and the harsh pull of her breath. Safe: but it had been a near thing. He had seen her, he would remember her.

"Hi! Stop thief!"

She ran. Into the Acre now, home ground, he would never find her here. Through the warren of narrow, stinking alleys and refuse-filled lanes she ran, following the twisting, turning ways with the ease of long familiarity. Never again would she be lost here; she knew it all by heart. She felt pain stabbing at her side; she leaned against a tarpaper wall to rest. Aside from the usual nighttime cries and shouts and babies' wails she heard nothing. Surely now she was safe. She listened.

Incredibly she heard him: "Stop the woman running!" It seemed to come, that voice, from at least two alleys away. Still, she had to get on. Almost there now. She reached the narrow way where Mary's shack stood. Her foot slipped into a small hole dug by a rooting pig. She heard the bone snap, felt the sickening pain as her foot twisted under her and she pitched down into the muck.

She stifled her sobs; she listened. She heard a man and a woman yelling at each other; a child crying; a drunken singer baying at the night sky. A dog slunk to her side and sniffed at her; scavenging chickens brushed her with their feathers.

Mary McCormic's was two places down. Sabra lifted herself and tried to stand. Although she bit her lips, a cry of pain escaped her. She sank down again to her knees. Slowly, dragging her injured foot, she crawled down the alley to her home.

28

Mr. Edward Boyden lost no time in communicating his outrage to his fellow shopkeepers. It was the third time in the last month, he fumed, that a thieving Irish had gotten away from his store. Other merchants matched his story with their own. The Acre had become a menace, they said; something must be done. Two weeks later they sent a delegation to the Board of Aldermen demanding increased protection, demanding that every immigrant Irish without a job be deported beyond the city limits, demanding that the Acre be razed. It was a perfect pest-hole, they said; a breeding ground for crime and disease and all manner of embarrassment to the city's good name. The Aldermen listened attentively and promised to appoint a committee to study the merchants' complaints. They agreed that the problem was a serious one; not only stores but private homes were becoming the daily victims of some Irishman's greed. It was a matter of money, they said; the city's treasury was limited, the Corporations were already taxed a substantial amount, they would be unlikely to be willing to pay more for a larger force of constables. And of course since every merchant in the city was after all doing business by the grace of the Corporations, it soon became a matter of biting the hand that fed them all. But they would see what could be done.

Sabra's ankle mended slowly. Mary McCormic had set it as best she could, and bound it up in a proper splint, but it would be a good six or eight weeks, she said, before Sabra could be up and about—and even then she would have to go slowly, carefully, no running or far walking.

For the past two months Sabra had been paying fifty cents a week board, occasionally twenty-five. Now, at the end of February, she had savings of three dollars and forty-two cents: enough to carry them for a while but what would she do when it was gone? She would not be fit to run for at least three months, and a thief who could not run when the need arose was a thief caught.

She lay on her pallet, Clara at her side, and watched Mary as she peeled potatoes and cut them into the stew-pot hanging over the fire.

"There," said Mary as she dropped in the last pieces, "I wish my Molly would hurry and get back with th' meat, or else it won't cook right." She smiled across at Clara. "Soon yours'll be big enough to help, Sabra—o, they repay all the care they take when they're little, they repay every bit of it. She's a smart little thing, yours is, she'll be worth her weight in gold to you soon enough."

"Doing what?" said Sabra bitterly. Her ankle throbbed, her empty belly ached. Mary's stew would be enough for half a dozen people, perhaps, not the fifteen or so whom it must suffice. "I suppose she can always gather kindling, that's a good living for an Acre brat."

Mary wiped her hands on her skirt and went to the door to look for her girl. Not seeing her, she stood for a moment staring out, considering. No need to worry. The child was widely known, she herself was respected, feared, even; no one would harm her or her daughter. Still, it seemed a long time. She would go out herself soon, if the child had not returned.

She came and sat beside Sabra. She pulled up the skirt which covered the splint and examined the leg which showed above it. Good: no swelling, no warning lines of red. With some affection she rumpled Clara's dark curls and patted her cheek.

"There now," she said cheerfully. "Your ma's goin' to be better soon." And, to Sabra: "Frank tells me they was lookin' last night for a fellow who took the cash box at the American House. As bold as you please, he said, and they chased him back here but then o' course they lost him." She grinned. "Frank says it was young Doyle, he was boastin' and braggin' at Cornelius Crowley's th' other night about how easy it would be. No one's seen him nor the cash box neither. But the constable's took a rare fit, says he's goin' to make an example this time. We can all expect a visit from th' law, he said, until they find the one."

Sabra shuddered. Her own escape three weeks ago was still too recent to avoid the memory of her fright. She turned uncomfortably on her pallet; her bones ached, she wanted to get up, to walk—to be free. She had been badly enough off before; how was she to live now?

"Mary."

"Yes, dear."

"What am I going to do?"

Sabra's voice was low and urgent; for a moment it distracted Mary from her concern over Molly. She contemplated the young woman who lay before her. Good skin, well-formed shape, a pretty face for all she was so thin; a good wash and she'd be a regular princess. To Mary McCormic, the answer to Sabra's question was obvious, but she hesitated to give it. This one was, after all, an American and therefore a stranger; on the other hand, they shared a bond stronger than nationality, stronger than race or religion. They were both women; and the answer to women's plight was the same worldwide.

"You need to get a man," she said. "I've wondered why you've waited so long, strugglin' on your own. You're a good-lookin' girl, Sabra, I know two or three men who'd be happy to have you. Not bad fellows, neither."

"That's impossible. I cannot marry—"

"Now who said anythin' about marryin'? They wouldn't marry you anyway, unless you turned to th' Church. No—not marryin'. Just to live, Sabra. They'd be glad of a woman, and they'd feed you better'n I can. There's Daniel Lynch, he's cuttin' on the new canal, he's got a wife and children back home an' he sends money to 'em regular, but I know he'd be glad to have you until they came over. Or Tim Quigley, if you don't mind the color of his skin. He's a blue-dyer. But he's a lovely man, and hardly drinks at all—"

At first Sabra was not sure that she had heard correctly. Then all her fears, all her frustrations, came suddenly back to her in a burst of anger.

"Thank you very much! That's a lovely prospect, isn't it? 'Just to live!' And will they take my child, too?"

"They might, if she's quiet."

"Ah, yes—if she's quiet. And if I'm quiet when their wives come over—"

"Quigley isn't married, as far as I know."

"O, splendid! He's not married! And of course he'd never marry me because I'm a heathen—"

"He might at that, come to think of it."

"He might! Dear God, Mary!" She had half risen, forgetting her broken bone; then, at the sudden pain, she fell back. To make her own way was all she asked. Did Mary still not understand that?

29

An evening early in May. Fog smothered the city, quenching the dim lights glimmering from the lamp posts, muffling the sounds of horses' hooves and metal-rimmed wheels on cobblestoned streets. Here and there an operative scurried to her boarding house; in wealthier quarters of the city late callers or early arrivals for dinner alighted from their carriages and made their way to bright drawing rooms, to dining tables laden with food.

Like a restless, vengeful spirit the Reverend Horatio Wood walked the streets, searching for those few poor wretches worthy of his help. He was very tired. He paused to wait at a crossing until a cartload of granite drawn by two oxen had passed. The new canal was almost done: more power, more mills, more operatives—and undoubtedly more poor. The everlasting poor, whom God must have put on earth for a purpose. The Reverend Wood believed most devoutly that that purpose had been to give a life's work to him and those like him in other cities throughout the great world—God's world. He was thankful to God for having done this. To be sure, his was a heavy burden. Many times he wrestled mightily with his conscience before deciding to deny a request for food or firewood or a slip to the almshouse. How cunning they were! The tales they told would have undone a lesser man. The Reverend Wood needed all his strength—strength drawn from God—to withstand the daily assaults on his naturally charitable instincts; but with God's help he persevered, and in at least nine cases out of ten, he was sure that he made the right decision in denying help. Enveloped in the armor of Charity, the Reverend Wood was able to withstand any assault.

He picked his way across the muddy cobblestones until he reached the safety of the boardwalk on the other side. He was myopic; he had to be careful how he walked lest he stumble over some unseen object in his path. Now, dimly, he saw a figure approaching through the fog. Its head was lifted, its face turned toward him. Undoubtedly a supplicant. The Reverend Wood steadied his thoughts; he felt the comforting familiar coldness enter and suffuse his heart. As the figure approached he saw that it sported a cane—or, rather, a stick—and that it had perfected, undoubtedly for his benefit, quite a respectable limp.

It was a woman: an Irishwoman. Her shawl was wrapped loosely around her head; once, he thought, that thin face under the rough cloth might have been pretty.

She came near, limping; she stopped. "Reverend Wood?"

"Yes."

"I am sorry to trouble you. I've—my little girl is ill, she is very weak, if you could give me just some bread and a little meat, and perhaps some milk—"

She leaned heavily on her stick. Standing close to her now he saw that her forehead was wet with perspiration, although the night air was cool. And her accent—!

"You are an American."

"Yes."

"You are dressed like the Irish."

"Yes."

The flickering illumination of the whale-oil streetlight made it difficult for him to see her clearly. He bent closer. An intelligent face: he was not accustomed to receiving such a steady, dignified look from his supplicants. Usually they stared at the ground, or shifted their eyes restlessly back and forth, evading his own as they told their sad tales.

"Why is that?"

"I live with them."

An involuntary revulsion twitched at the Reverend Wood's face. She saw this.

"I have no other place to live. They took me in—"

"Yes, yes. I understand." Already the woman had betrayed herself. Only the most degraded type, American or no, would live in the Acre. The Reverend Wood knew personally of several Irish families who had overcome their heritage and moved out to respectable homes in other parts of the city—poor homes, but palaces compared to the Acre.

"Have you had the doctor for the child?"

"No. I have no money, we are treating her ourselves, if she could have some milk and bread she would get back her strength—"

"Where is your husband?"

The woman did not reply. The level gaze faltered; she looked down. "Gone," she said at last.

"How long ago?" And, when she hesitated again, he added impatiently: "Never mind. Long enough, I assume, for you to be impoverished. I see that you are lame. Can you work?"

"No."

"The Corporations can very well employ a lame person in the folding rooms. I know of a vacancy at the Commonwealth—"

"No. I am—I cannot work on the Corporations."

And what did you steal from them, thought the Reverend Wood. Always the same story: knowing the rules full well, always there was one who tried to break them, without a thought of how she would live after.

He considered. Perhaps it was his fatigue, perhaps her appearing out of the fog like a spectre from his dreams—his past? his future?—but she had touched him as few supplicants had. He put his hand on her shoulder.

"If I help you, will you promise me something?"

She waited.

"You must leave the Acre. You can never make a life for yourself if you stay there."

She shook her head. "I cannot leave. I have no place to go."

The Reverend Wood felt the blood flow into his face, energizing warmth— Here was a worthy battle for a soul!

"Come back with me now to Middlesex Street, to my office, and I will give you a chit to the grocer. You can feed your child tonight—and yourself, but no one else. No one with whom you live must have a morsel. And then tomorrow at nine o'clock come to my office again and I will give you a pass to the almshouse. No—it will be all right. I promise."

She stepped back. His hand dropped to his side.

"No."

"I tell you it will be all right. I know the matron, she is a very decent woman. You can read and write—yes. And do sums? Good. She can use someone like you. Perhaps even a small salary can be arranged. I will speak to her. It is not so very bad. I go there myself once a week. If you have any complaint you need only to speak to me. Your child will do very well in the nursery there, the delinquent children are only children after all, she will not be contaminated if you are there with her—"

The Reverend Wood stood alone in the smothering fog. After a moment he walked on, searching out another victim.

30

A single light shone from a second-floor window of the handsome brick house in Hurd Street. Sabra stood on the walk looking up at it, gathering her courage. Then she took Clara's hand and they went up the granite steps. She yanked the bell-pull. From the Methodist church tower on the corner she heard the bell toll nine, its tone slightly muffled by the fog. When the last peal had faded, the door swung open. An elderly woman surveyed her for an instant and then without a word, before Sabra could speak, she slammed it shut.

"Please!" She rang again; and, when no answer came, she pounded at the gleaming white-painted panel. It opened perhaps three inches.

"Please—may I speak to Mr. Blood?"

"In his office in the morning."

"No—no, I must see him tonight."

"In his office in the morning."

"Just five minutes. I have an urgent message for him. Please."

"Mrs. Pratt?"

The woman turned to the speaker within; she did not shut the door, and so Sabra cautiously pushed it open a little farther.

"What is it, Mrs. Pratt?"

She could see a dim entrance hall, illuminated only by a light coming from the floor above. She could not see who spoke.

"A woman, sir. I told her to see you in your chambers."

"Mr. Blood!" Once upon a time, she never would have dared to be so rude—so forward. Now, rudeness was the farthest thing from her mind.

"Who—?"

He came cautiously down the narrow staircase: a dry, thin reed of a man, sparse white hair, papery skin, dark eyes like his son's but not a trace of his son's melancholy, his brooding temperament.

"Mr. Blood, may I see you just for a moment?" Shamelessly, without a thought of exploitation, she pushed the child ahead into the hall. The housekeeper turned to prevent them, but she was too late. Sabra leaned on her heavy stick; she held Clara's hand. Thank God, she thought, the child looks something like her father.

Blood confronted them. He had not the faintest idea who they were. Ordinarily, of course, he would have ordered them out at once, but something in the woman's attitude—something urgent, something honest, perhaps—prevented him. "Well?"

She had not prepared a speech. Now she simply spoke the most compelling words she could find. She put her hand on Clara's dark curls. The child stared steadily at the stranger. "This is your granddaughter. Almost four years ago, now, I married her father. Your son."

To his credit, Blood did not at once utter those hackneyed words of outraged parenthood: I have no son. Rather, he stared with instinctive attention at his new-found relation; for a moment only, he allowed himself the pleasure of contemplating her, dirty, ragged mite that she was. Unquestionably he could see her resemblance to her father. For a moment only: and then his bitterness returned, his anger at his wayward offspring who mooned after the Perfect Life. Had he stayed at home and followed his father's example, he could have been a rich man by now.

Then—yes, then, and his hard dark eyes filled with tears as he spoke, his brain raged at the boy's blindness, his stubbornness—he said: "I have no son."

"But—"

"You are mistaken. You have come to the wrong place."

"I beg you. Please. We are starving."

He stood at a distance of perhaps three feet. Long years of puffing at his meerschaum pipes had not entirely destroyed his sense of smell. She reeked of unimaginable filth. She looked like the refuse of the streets. And the child—!

He felt his heart, which his son had broken for all time, break all over again within his starched white shirt front. He thought that he would die from the pain of it. What crime, what dreadful sin had he committed, all unknowing, that now in his old age he should be so severely tried?

With a long, last, despairing look he took them in. Then, with a curt command to his housekeeper, he turned and fled upstairs.

"Put them out."

Roughly she did so; and Sabra found herself on the street again, Enoch Blood's words echoing in her ears. Then she heard Clara, clinging to her hand, begin to cry. She would have cried herself, but she had no strength. Wearily they began the long walk back to the Acre.

31

Shortly before midnight Sabra slipped into her place at Mary McCormic's. The room was dark, filled with sounds of breathing, snoring bodies. Clara lay quiet; Sabra touched her and felt rather than heard the response.

"Here, love," she whispered. "Can you sit up? Sssssh—good. Now eat this, it's good bread. And a little potato. Good."

Mary McCormic, alert even in sleep, lifted her head and listened. Satisfied at what she heard, she lay back and smiled to herself in the darkness. Sabra had acted wisely at last. Good: one less worry for herself.

In the morning Sabra said nothing. She kissed her child, who lay still asleep, and went out. Soon she returned with more food: milk, cooked beef, bread, even a bag of peppermint drops. With a grim, determined expression she arranged her purchases beside her pallet and sat back to wait for Clara to awaken.

They were, temporarily, alone in the room with the proprietress. Those of Mary's tenants who had employment had already gone to their work—canal-cutter, day laborer, domestic, a girl who peddled artificial flowers. The remainder had gone to beg, or to get food as best they might, for Mary had stopped feeding them.

"Well, now," she said. "You seem to have done all right. Who is it?" And, when Sabra did not answer: "Not the Reverend Wood, that's certain."

"No," said Sabra. "Not him."

"Did y' see him at all?"

"Yes."

"And he offered to put y' in the workhouse?"

"Yes."

"I knew it. That means he liked you, y' know. If he don't like you he just walks on, or puts you out of his office, with such a look—like you wasn't human."

Sabra made no reply; she sat with her knees hunched up, her eyes half closed.

"Ah, well," continued Mary (for she was determined to satisfy her curiosity), "Dan Lynch isn't a bad fella. He'll do y' well. I suppose y'll be movin' in with him?"

"No."

"It is him, then?"

"Yes."

"Good. He's all right. But I'm surprised he don't want y' to move into his place, for all it's so crowded. He'd want y' near by, if I know him—and to clean about, and do his wash 'n' all."

Again Sabra did not answer, and so after a moment Mary got up from her place by the fire and went to sit beside her. She cast an affectionate glance at Clara.

"I heard y' come in last night. I was glad y' had somethin' for her. You'll do all right with him, Sabra, I know y' will. He's a decent man, for all he likes his drink. Maybe you can keep him from it. Sober, there's not a better man alive than Daniel Lynch."

Their eyes met; Mary felt her heart twist inside her breast. She looked away, she looked at the food which Sabra had brought, at the sleeping child who now began to stir and open her eyes. Clara sat up. Mary watched as slowly, deliberately, with a hard and vacant expression, Sabra took the child on her lap and held her for a moment in a fierce embrace. Then she took up the food; they began to eat. Sabra did not offer to share with the landlady.

32

Mary McCormic had been correct when she had said that Daniel Lynch was a reasonable, decent man when he was sober. He worked for twelve hours a day on the canal gang; he saved his money and sent it home to his family in County Mayo. He was naturally an affectionate, sociable man who missed his wife and, more, his four children; it had been a sacrifice to him to leave them, but he hoped to bring them over soon. His wife could neither read nor write, and so his only word from her had been two hastily scribbled notes from the parish priest, reassuring him that they were well. But still he was uneasy; death stalked the land in Ireland, he wanted them safe with him.

Often—too often—he spent his money at the dram shop. Then his sorrows, his loneliness, overtook him and he became belligerent. He was a big man, a mean man in a fight, and so often he escaped with little or no harm. But he did not like to live so; he knew he was being foolish. And so he looked about him, over the grim spectacle of the Acre, and sought relief of a different kind.

He could not understand why Sabra would not come to live with him.

"I'll gi' ye that whole corner," he said, "an' th' little one comes too. I know y' love her like I love my own, I wouldn't ask y' t' leave her with Mary McCormic."

But Sabra shook her head; her mouth took on a tight, determined look. It was better that she stay with Mary, she said. Clara was fond of her, and Molly often tended the little one. The truth was that she did not want to become entirely dependent on him. She knew that this was a temporary refuge, one which would vanish the moment his family set foot on the Boston docks. Best not to disrupt ourselves, she thought. Then, too, she never knew when he would come home drunk. It was not impossible that this man, some bad night, might turn on Clara. No. Clara must stay at Mary McCormic's, and Sabra with her.

He did not press the matter. He knew that he was lucky to have her at all. Few Irishwomen, no matter how poor, would have agreed to such an arrangement: their fear of damnation was too strong. And he did not like to patronize casual whores; he wanted some affection, some warmth to the business. He liked to be able to talk a bit, to form some mutual bond. And so he contented himself with three or four visits a week.

His companions on the canal said he paid her too much, but he had noticed that she seemed healthier now, and no longer mentioned that the child was ill, and he knew that the money which he gave to her was being used to feed them both. Good, he thought. He was well paid—a dollar a day and a ration of whiskey—and he could afford to feed them all, Sabra and her child and his family, too, and save the passage money as well. He stopped patronizing the dram shop; his face lost its pink fleshiness; he felt stronger than he had done in the past year.

Sometimes on warm nights they walked out awhile. At such times, she forgot the rigors of winter. Life seemed, if not easy, at least possible. The temporary and therefore precarious security which Lynch offered seemed a stable thing, these nights. Days would come when again she must scratch for the means to survive—cold days, bitter days a year or two ahead, when his family would have arrived and she would no longer have his money to buy food. But now, this summer, she enjoyed her little respite and gathered her strength anew.

33

On the afternoon of September 3, 1847, the excavation for the Northern Canal had reached Race Street, near the new waterway's termination at the Western Canal. Ahead lay a particularly difficult stretch of granite. The explosives needed to be laid with extreme care, lest the shock of the tremor loosen the walls which had already been cut. The men worked steadily and well, fortified by their noon ration of liquor. At three o'clock, James Bicheno Francis, the Agent of the Locks and Canals Corporation, arrived for his daily inspection. At his nod, the chief engineer gave the signal to ignite the charge.

In the Acre, Sabra sat outside the door of Mary's shack, sunning herself, watching Clara as the child drew stick figures on a fragment of slate. A quiet, pleasant day, the sun soothing her ankle, a little money in her purse, her child beside her.

She heard the explosion; she felt a tremor in the ground. Blasting. Soon they would be done. Soon Daniel's family would come over. Wintertime. Best not to think of it. Do what you can now.

She drowsed for a while. A brief time later she was startled awake when Connie Crowley's boy came skidding around the corner into the alley and almost fell into her lap. He was choking with his news, frightened, excited as he told her.

Mary, overhearing, came outside.

"How many," she said.

Young Connie, panting, shook his head. "Don't know. Th' foreman told me to run and get everyone as could help. They're alive. They got to be dug out."

"Go on, then," said Mary. "Go down to Cork Street, there's men there not workin', they can help." And, to Sabra: "Go an' see about him, I'll stay here with th' child."

By the time Sabra had made her way across Merrimack Street to the site of the canal, the bells had begun to toll and she found herself surrounded by crowds of people hurrying to see. As she came near she heard the shouts of the rescuers—"Hold, now, lever it up! Hold!" Ox-drawn carts which had been standing ready to haul away the blasted granite were now being filled with injured laborers. A cloud of dust hung in the air above the deep wound in the earth; the acrid smell of gunpowder irritated her nose and brought stinging tears to her eyes.

She pushed her way through the press of bodies to the edge of the cut. Twenty feet below, where one day would run water from the river to power the giant wheels, she saw a frantic scene: the entire northern wall had collapsed from the force of the explosion, and on what was to be the canal bed now rested a huge pile of crumbled granite. Men tore desperately at the heavy fragments; from underneath came the faint, panicking cries of the wounded. Other injured men lay scattered like the remnants of a defeated army.

Three men stood on the canal bank hauling up a survivor in a rope sling. The wounded man had black hair: not Daniel. Blood dripped from an open place in his skull.

"Please," she cried to the men, "do you know Daniel Lynch? Is he safe?"

Intent on their delicate task, they did not answer. She knelt on the bank and called to the men below.

"Dan Lynch! Is Dan Lynch there?"

They did not hear her. She searched the faces of the work gang. She recognized a few of them; she did not see Lynch. Three well-dressed men arrived, running. They scrambled down the weakened scaffolding on the southern wall; separating, they bent to examine the wounded. She recognized Dr. Knight among them. But still she could not see Lynch.

Within a month, James Bicheno Francis had submitted a report to the directors of Locks and Canals: in the collapse of the holding wall on the Northern Canal cut on September 3, 1847, a total of twelve men had been killed outright; twenty had been injured. Of these, five had died, ten were still in hospital, five had recovered. The total expense to the Corporation was estimated at $1,726.35, covering repair of the damage to the canal wall and working days lost. The directors had voted not to pay compensation to the injured workmen or to the families (some of whom were in Ireland) of the men who had died. Locks and Canals had, however, assumed the cost of hospitalization for the survivors who required it; the company would deduct the payments from the men's wages when they were working again.

34

Word got about in the Acre: if you want anything—food, a place to sleep, a line to a job—go to see certain people who can help you. One of these was Patrick O'Haran. As the influx of his countrymen swelled to a flood-tide, he came to assume a position among his people somewhat analogous to the Reverend Wood's in the community at large: he seemed always to know where to find a warm blanket for a freezing child, a bundle of sticks for the fire, a measure of porridge to fill the empty bellies of a newly arrived family.

Often his work was more difficult, more delicate, for the Irish were a contentious lot, deeply attached to the separate counties of their homeland, and their spirits were chafed raw by the sorrows of their leaving, the agonies of adjustment to the new place. At home they had lived in relative peace; in America, thrown higgledy-piggledy into hideous, crowded slums, a Kerry man would take umbrage at a wink from a Corkonian, and before anyone knew how it happened, a raging brawl had begun, the Clare clappers hooting on the sidelines and looking for a chance to jump in.

Patrick O'Haran was one of the men who always stopped these fights; and when Father Mathew came to preach the Temperance crusade, Patrick rounded up men by the dozens, and women too, to take the pledge: for strong drink was the curse of all poor folk everywhere, and none more than the Irish, seducing them to fight each other instead of their common enemy, the Anglo-Saxon. Fools you are, the lot of you, Patrick would say as he strong-armed his way between two inebriates flailing at each other; break it up now, break it up. The Yanks love to see us fight among ourselves, so we're not goin' to do it any more.

Patrick's eyes grew old beyond his years; his shoulders bowed a little under the thin wool of his jacket. The cheerful delivery boy had vanished forever, replaced by a sober, serious young man who smiled on his face, not in his heart. Once he had dreamed of marrying a young girl who had seemed to love him. That dream had gone forever, and with it his chance at happiness. So he worked now to do what he could for his fellows; and every day the belief grew stronger in him that by helping his own he was vanquishing the hated English.

When Daniel Lynch and the others were killed in the Northern Canal disaster, Patrick attended every man's wake, not only in respect for the dead but in hopes of collecting a little money for the destitute widows and orphans. At Lynch's wake he saw Sabra.

He nodded at her, not friendly but not unfriendly either; after a decent time in the hot, stinking, crowded room he motioned her to follow him out into the lane for a breath of air. The night was cloudy, oppressive: humidity hung on the city like a shroud, making it hard to draw breath.

"I hear you're livin' with Mary McCormic," he said, steering her away from a stretch of excrement-fouled mud.

"Yes."

"That's a foolish thing to do. An American girl—what d' y' come here for to live?"

"I had no place else."

"You must've. Any place."

"No."

"You have a child, I hear."

"Yes."

"Who's your husband?"

"Silas Blood."

"Lawyer's son?"

"Yes."

"And where is he?"

"Away."

Patrick spat into the dirt. "An' the old man not helpin' you? Not takin' you in?"

"No."

"Y' should've stayed on the Corporation, then. O, I know you left to start dressmakin'. But when that didn't go, you should've gone back. No one'll hire you as long as you live in the Paddy Camp Lands."

"Someone hired you, didn't he? And only last week, Patrick, the Quin sisters were taken on as spinners at the Boott. And Meg O'Conor works—"

"Why hurt yourself, girl? Sure what you say is true. But listen to me: life's hard enough without adding to your burdens. I notice you're limping. What from?"

"I—tripped."

He did not reply at once. She remembered the time, long ago, when he had rescued her from the gang of attackers. He had spoken angrily, that night, of Irish who stole, giving all Irish a bad name. Finally: "Try the

Corporations again, Sabra. They're wanting American women bad these days."

The next morning she went for a place at the Boott, where the Quin sisters had been taken on. But she looked poorer, now, than some Irish; the overseer to whom she spoke was naturally suspicious. When she hesitated at the question of where she lived, and refused to promise that she would live henceforth in a Corporation house, he sent her away without a further word. He had enough problems to contend with; only the previous week, an operative with similarly unsatisfactory answers, whom he had hired in the winter against his better judgment, had committed suicide by throwing herself into the Western Canal. She was the ninth operative to have killed herself that year, the sixth by drowning. Such tragedies gave the Corporations a bad name. No vacancies, he said; you can't work here.

35

She counted her money: five dollars and sixty-seven cents. She could not feed herself and Clara for less than a dollar a week; Mary had allowed her a week's grace in the rent, but it would have to be paid sooner or later. Better now, thought Sabra, pressing the coins into Mary's hand; then she'll have no excuse to evict us.

One misty evening in October she knelt on her pallet combing her hair and pulling it back neatly. It was early, just past seven; most of the other boarders had not yet drifted in. Clara lay asleep beside her, breathing easily, her tiny hand flung across the thin blanket. Sabra looked up, aware that Mary watched her.

"Who 'r' y' meetin'?" said Mary at last.

"I don't know."

Mary watched her. An expression of concern crossed her face. "Y' want to be careful. Y' got to be able to see right away if he's honest—"

"I'll be careful," said Sabra shortly. She did not want to talk; it was difficult enough to get up her courage, without having Mary's precautions adding to her fears.

"Y' can't bring anyone here," said Mary; she sounded almost apologetic. "I've never allowed it, I can't allow it now—"

"I wouldn't anyway, with Clara here."

Slowly she stood up, wincing at the small pain in her ankle. She draped her shawl around her shoulders, leaving her head bare. Both she and Mary understood: no decent woman went out of doors without a headcovering.

Despite her admiration for Sabra's enterprise, Mary could not suppress her misgiving. True, she had encouraged Sabra to find a man to support her; but that was a very different business from nightly, casual solicitation. Streetwalkers invited trouble; many of them got it, if not from the law then from their clients. Only last week they had fished a body from the Pawtucket Canal: a young girl, horribly beaten, stabbed eleven times in the breast and stomach, strangled with her own stocking. She had been known as a thief as well as a whore; probably she had tried, once too often, to steal more than a customer was prepared to give. But no woman, taking such risks, was entirely safe. Thus Mary had encouraged Sabra to attach herself to one man, a man she knew. Soliciting strangers for an hour's time was a different game, and dangerous.

Sabra came back after midnight, grim-faced, silent, clutching her fee: a dollar. Mary heard her come in. She heard her lie down beside Clara, coughing slightly; after a long time, when she was almost asleep again, she heard a stifled sob.

Sabra fell into a routine: on Wednesday, Friday, and Saturday nights she went out. If she had no luck, she went out again the following Monday and Tuesday. Otherwise she stayed in. Her best territory was the shopping district, including the several hotels. She grew adept at spotting the transient from the native: the salesman, the cotton agent, the lecturer, the journalist passing through—all had a subtly foreign, slightly out of place look.

The barkeep at the Merrimack House was her enemy. There were several women "in residence" at the hotel; they paid him a fat percentage of their fees, and he, in turn, kept them well supplied with customers. He wanted no freelancers, as Sabra learned to her anger one night when she went in with a fresh-faced young man whom she had encountered just outside. The barkeep, espying them from his strategic place just off the lobby, bustled out and ordered her off the premises. The young man, horribly embarrassed, fled alone upstairs; Sabra found herself on the street, her arm sore where the barkeep had wrenched it, her spirit raw with self-loathing.

After that she avoided the Merrimack House; if the management set up a Christmas tree again this year, she did not see it.

A week before Christmas she became ill. She coughed incessantly, her temperature rose, every breath was like a knife in her side. Mary dosed her with Cherry Pectoral; after several days she felt better, but still weak. She did not go out. Christmas came and went. In a burst of unwonted generosity, Mary McCormic treated her tenants to a free meal of corned beef and roast potatoes. Sabra bribed Molly to go to the shops and buy an orange and a woolly lamb pull-toy for Clara. In the evening callers came crowding into the room, and Mary received them with the grace of a grand lady, offering a bottle all around and exchanging toasts to the New Year and the victory of the Young Irelanders.

On the third of January Sabra went out again. Snow had fallen during the afternoon but now the sky was clear. Cold stars glittered, a full moon rose. "It's too bitter freezin' tonight, don't go out," said Mary. "Y' have money enough, y'll catch death goin' out." She shivered and drew closer to the fire; she hated the New England winters, so different from the mild climate of home.

"I won't be long," said Sabra. "I'll just take a turn down Merrimack and down Central as far as the American House."

Mary struggled with her premonition; she had the second sight, and often it was a torment to her, watching people do what she knew they should not—or vice versa—and being powerless to convince them.

"I don't think you should go," she said again. "Stay in tonight, y're not strong enough yet—"

Sabra paused at the door; she had what she knew was an unanswerable argument. "I need the money," she said; and went out.

By the time she reached Merrimack Street she was frozen through and her determination wavered. A bitter wind cut through her shawl; her ears ached; every breath of icy air seared her lungs. She urged herself on. She had just two dollars left, she needed to buy food, she needed to pay Mary her rent. The snow was trodden into a slippery sheet. Once she almost fell; afterward she walked more slowly despite the cold.

Few people were abroad, although she assumed that she would find the usual crowd in front of the American House. She hoped that she would not have to go that far.

She saw a man approaching. She paused, watching him come on. He was tall, broad, healthy-looking, dressed in rough jacket and cap but still not poor.

She stepped into his path and touched his arm. As was her custom she looked straight up into his eyes. She had discovered that often she did not need to speak: that unwavering, self-assured stare announced her purpose better than any words. Decent women, after all, kept their eyes cast down.

For a fraction of a second the man met her look; she saw in his eyes the bright reflection of the flaring gas-jets in the shop windows. Then, hardly having broken stride, he shook off her hand and walked on.

Bitter, deadly cold: Merrimack Street almost deserted, although it was just past closing at the mills. It was a night to hurry home to a blazing fire and a full stomach and a hot-bottle underneath the bedclothes, shutters fastened against the wind.

She turned down Central Street and came to the American House.

Two men stood outside. She approached them. The taller and more prosperous-looking one took her in at a glance and turned away, but the other—shorter, older, shabbier—grinned and poked his companion in the ribs.

"Good evening, sir."

The shorter man stepped so close that despite the wind she smelled his sour whiskey breath.

"Now, missy—look, Mr. Wilson. She's got a pretty face. What d' ye say? Shall we have her?"

Several hours later, Mary McCormic lifted her head and listened. In the black, dead hours before dawn the second sight often came to her, plaguing her with waking dreams, alerting her to dangers unseen, unheard by day. What had called her from sleep and set her listening now, every nerve alive, straining—?

A scratching sound came at the door. The cat? No. The cat crouched by the hearth. Moreover, this sound was too weak, too faint to be the cat's strong claws. Instantly, silently, Mary was on her feet and across the crowded floor.

"Who is it?" she said softly. And, when there was no answer: "Who is it there?"

She heard a sound. The wind?

She opened the door. A body lay at her feet, arm outstretched. Mary caught her breath. She felt her heart painful in her breast. Dear Virgin Mother—

She bent down, touched it. In the pale light of the stars she saw the battered bloody face, she heard the low strangled sound issuing from the dark, swollen mouth.

36

In March, 1848, a woman's body was recovered from the Merrimack River below the Central Bridge. No identification was made for twenty-four hours. Then a woman who called herself Mrs. Elizabeth Shaw appeared at the morgue and claimed the body. Ordinarily, the authorities would have asked her more questions—Mrs. Shaw had not, for example, any proper identification—but an order from above had been issued and so the body was released into her custody. A hired wagon took it away to be buried. Mrs. Shaw had two companions in mourning: Mary McCormic and Patrick O'Haran. Afterward, for the first and last time in his life, Patrick drank himself into insensibility.

And when he came sober again he wept all the night, and he cursed the man responsible for his weeping, he cursed the Agent Bradshaw, the hated Yankee. And he promised revenge, then; he promised to have back at the man who had as good as murdered his sweet girl. No matter how long, he said; I will make it up. He whispered these things to himself. No one else heard.

Sabra knew nothing. She lay on her pallet in Mary's room and watched the dim daylight which filtered through the cracks in the walls and roof. She watched the light fade each day as darkness came. She swallowed what Mary spooned into her mouth; she obeyed Mary's instructions to sit up, to try to stand, to walk, finally, across the room. Slowly, beyond her will, her body mended. The bruises faded, the broken skin mended, the burns, soothed with Mary's ointment, healed and stopped hurting. Inside, too, her body recovered, the lacerations soothed by a distillation of herbs.

Mary never reproached her, never reminded her that she had been warned. For the first week she sent Clara, in Molly's charge, to the Widow Scanlan on Cork Street. No child should see its mother in such a state, said Mary; keep her for a while until the mother mends. It was a hard case, a terrible case, she said, but Sabra would survive. It was only a matter of time. She had seen worse, even, than this; she knew what must be done.

There was no question of finding the men responsible, much less of bringing them to justice. Probably they were transients, gone far away now. In any case, no authority would act without a sworn complaint, and even if Sabra had been in fit condition to proceed, she would herself have been arrested on a charge of prostitution. Only a few weeks before, Nathan Locke, the Police Court judge, had proclaimed the city's determination to rid itself of women of easy virtue whose shameless activities cast a stain upon every woman within its bounds.

No. Neither she nor Sabra would have retribution, at least not directly. And so Mary worked, and watched, and waited. She held her tongue, she mentioned nothing troubling, and gradually, day by day, she saw her patient improve.

As Sabra's body healed and her strength returned, she began to consider what she must do. She thought rationally, clearly, about her position—hers and Clara's. And when she had done thinking, and settled the matter in her mind, she turned to look hungrily at Clara and she filled her eyes with the image of the beloved little form and took it in, so it seemed to her, for all time.

You will not suffer, she thought. She felt her mind break free from the shackles of her life. You will not suffer as I have done. I will not let you. I will take you with me: we will go together, and we will never be cold or hungry again. Soon, now. When I have the strength.

37

In early April the elder Cornelius Crowley died. He was a widely known and well-respected man throughout the Acre; even certain Americans had thought well of him as a representative of a certain type which, if encouraged, might lift his fellow unfortunates to an acceptable level of existence.

He was waked in his tenement on Dublin Street. Everyone in the Acre, it seemed, was there; the keening and cursing could be heard as far as Central Street. All of Mary's people went, and of course she herself felt it her duty to go too. She knelt beside Sabra before she left.

"Will y' be all right for a little?"

"Yes. Of course. Go on, Mary."

"I don't like to leave you, but I've no choice. He was a good man, many's the time he lent me somethin' when I needed it. But I won't be long."

Sabra lay back, alone in the room cluttered with empty pallets. The firelight gave a dim illumination, softening the ugliness, the bleakness of the place. She turned her head easily. For the past several days she had had no pain or soreness anywhere. Soon she would be able to do what must be done. She turned to look at Clara, but no: she had forgotten. The child was not there. Molly had taken her to stay at the Widow Scanlan's, for Mary's tenants would return from Crowley's wake in an advanced state of intoxication, like as not, and Clara would sleep easier at the Widow's. Sabra let her thoughts drift back: she saw the child again as she first had seen her, a tiny squalling body, immeasurably precious; she heard again Lizzie Crabbe's delighted cries, felt the hungry suckling, the comfortable featherweight on her shoulder. How happy they had been, those few months with Silas at Bountiful! If she had known what lay ahead, she thought— No. One never knows. She had forgotten Silas' melancholy silences, his angry departure. That summer after Clara's birth seemed in retrospect the happiest time of her life. If only—

Something moved in the corner of the room.

And then she heard a sound: a tiny, scrabbling sound, a high shrill scream.

She sat up quickly, her reverie shattered. She stared at the place from which the sound had come. She saw a black shape, blacker than the surrounding shadows. Then another. And another.

Dear God.

She scrambled to her feet and looked about for a weapon. The heavy stick which had been her cane stood against the wall. In two steps she had seized it.

The shapes clustered in the corner, gathering for the attack. There were a dozen at least. At some point the flimsy wall must have given way, she thought, opening a crack through which the odor of food in the kettle, of live bodies on the floor, penetrated to the alley. The shapes shrilled high screams; as the mass writhed she saw the blaze of the fire reflected in small, unwavering, unblinking eyes.

She crouched by her pallet, holding the club. She threw a desperate glance around the shadowy room. No: they were only in that corner. She saw one separate itself from the mass and slither forward. It stopped to gnaw at something it found on the dirt floor. The others huddled, waiting.

Just beyond arm's reach was a low, three-legged stool. If she could throw it— No. It would only disperse them. If they broke rank and swarmed she would go mad. The adventurer, having consumed what it came upon, crouched alone, looking to advance. She hissed as she thrust the stick at it; it retreated a few inches and stopped in front of the pack.

The cat—where was Mary's cat? Always at nightfall the cat came in to sleep by the fire, often nestled beside her mistress. But not tonight. Dear God. "Here, puss! Here, puss, puss!"

The dark mass had spread. Slowly, inexorably, it oozed from the corner to reinforce its lone explorer. As it advanced it shrilled its battle cry.

On and on: she imagined sharp claws scraping her skin, sharp teeth tearing at her flesh, all their bodies swarming and slithering over hers.

She swallowed her rising vomit, she dropped the stick and sprang to the door. There was no question of fighting them; she had to escape. Without her shoes, without her shawl, she ran into the alley, pulling shut the door to contain the horror within. As she stepped away from the shack her foot came down on something furry, something dead. She screamed and stumbled on. In the darkness she could not see, but no, it was not a rat, no rat had such fur.

The alley was silent, deserted. From Dublin Street she heard the noise of Crowley's wake. They were sending him out, speeding him on to a better life. Crowley's troubles were over; he was at rest. Well, she would be at rest, too, soon enough. Now, tonight, she would do what must be done; and then she and Clara would take their leave. She needed only a little money for the stones. She had been slow to get it—too slow—but now she had had the sign. The hand of God—her father's God, Abijah Bradshaw's God—had sent it in the shape of a swarming pack of vermin to drive her into the street. Very well. Now she would act.

She caught her breath and picked her way down the alleys to Market Street. A little less dark here; more quickly she came to Worthen, and then to Merrimack. Yes. Now. Tonight. She had forgotten to think how she looked. Her appearance was a worldly thing, not to be considered this night when all her strength, all her vision were intent on escape from the world at last.

She paused in front of the busy hotel. Across the street, a late train puffed into the depot. Like the voyager to a new land who, on the eve of her departure, is suddenly impelled to visit the familiar scenes of home, she realized now where she stood and how close she was to the Commonwealth boarding houses. She had never been back. Certainly now she did not intend to visit: but just to see, to walk past, surely that could do no harm? A quick glimpse, and then on with her urgent business? She would not have another chance.

She made her way through the traffic on Merrimack Street. The noise of Crowley's wake faded; she turned down Dutton Street and saw the reflected lights in the still waters of the canal. How strange: a different world, so close upon what had become her own. The street was deserted, the women at their supper. Through the windows she could see them: how neat and clean they looked! And yet not as she remembered them, for these women's faces were unenlivened by any smile. They sat silent, separate from each other, the happy sisterhood gone. Their faces reflected nothing but blank weariness.

As she approached Mrs. Clapham's—was it Mrs. Clapham's still, she wondered—she saw a man coming down the front steps. She remembered her purpose. A solitary man, a quiet street—she might not have so favorable an encounter again tonight. Here once more, surely, was the hand of God. As he came toward her the bell in St. Anne's tower struck eight o'clock. On the last peal she confronted him.

"Good evening, sir."

Before she had finished speaking she recognized the face. Looking down upon her, incredulous, his mouth working with disgust, his hand raised as if to strike her, was the Agent of the Commonwealth Mill, her erstwhile benefactor Josiah Bradshaw.

38

For the Agent of the Commonwealth Mill, this day had been a trying, difficult day in what had come to be a seemingly endless march of difficult days, weeks, months. He had been greeted by Mr. Lyford that morning with a report of a theft in the cloth room. The senior girl had denied any knowledge of it; the folded lengths had been accounted properly the evening before, she said, offering tearfully to swear it on a Bible. Leaving Lyford to investigate further, the Agent had come into his office to find a report from the weaving room that three women had fallen ill: the early symptoms indicated typhus, but it was too soon, the Hospital message said, to make an exact diagnosis. The Agent was concerned for their health; he was more concerned for his production schedule. One did not, these days, pick skilled weavers off the street to replace those who fell ill. Worse, an hour before dinner, the spinning room overseer sent a request for permission to call a mechanic. The machines had jammed, and it was the overseer's opinion that an entire row of them had stripped their gears. The expense of repairing them would absorb nearly all that quarter's profit.

The day's troubles had not ended with the call for mechanics. In the afternoon he had had a note from the landlady at Number Five asking to see him on an urgent matter. He had called in after the closing bell; while her tenants were at supper she had received him in her private room and informed him of the growing rebellion under her roof. She was indignant: she had always kept a clean house, a decent house, she had always served the very best food that she could afford, and she took it now as a personal insult that her own girls, some of whom had been with her for years, now threatened to leave en masse. And it was not her fault: she was required to board the Corporation's employees, she was not responsible for who they were. If the Corporations hired Irish, then inevitably some Irish would come to board. Was she to be discharged, she wanted to know, because the American women refused to share quarters with the newcomers?

It had been a painful interview. Each, separately, had been aware of a shadow rising up and almost, for one difficult moment, putting an end to their discussion. There had been a time when an Irish girl slept under this roof and everyone happier for it; there had been a time when the lilt of a brogue had gladdened this man's heart, had given him hope, and had reassured him that his name would not die when he died, but would live on in a new life.

And so after a few moments' conversation he had been seized with a sorrow such as he no longer thought possible; he had been stoic for so long, denying his grief, pushing it to the back of his mind, overlaying it with the daily details of his existence, that he had been positively terrified now, tonight, to have been so overcome that he must end the interview. He promised to speak—individually—to the American women; he promised Mrs. Clapham that she would not be discharged (although she might, as they both very well knew, find herself in a short time presiding over a houseful of aliens, not a native-born woman among them). He wanted only to escape this house with its chattering inmates, its oppressive femininity. Upstairs were their beds where they retired, slept, dreamed— No! He would not think of them. Their bodies meant nothing to him.

He said good night and hurried out. He was glad to be alone again; he thought that he would walk awhile to settle himself before going home. Home had long since ceased to hold any charm for him. Home was where one slept, and ate, and changed one's clothes. But the heart—the very spirit of the home, which was properly held to reside in the control of its mistress—ah, that was not there! Had not been since before Sophia—

He was aware of a woman before him. No apparition could have been more distasteful. Damn the sex—!

"Good evening, sir."

39

They recognized each other at once. At once they drew back, each heart wrenched, each mind stunned into unspeakable mortification. By the glare of the street lamp each saw the other's face clear: and that bold, unmistakable look by which she had so often announced herself now flinched and fell. She turned away. She wanted to run, but she was weak, still, and badly stunned; she needed a moment to recover before she could move to get away.

And in that moment his hand shot out and clasped her arm.

"Look at me."

She would not. He shook her, lightly, but with a strong enough force to remind her of what she had already endured at the hands of his sex.

She shuddered; with great effort she lifted her head. She saw his face: he was very angry.

"What in God's name are you doing?"

She had begun to tremble violently. She felt that she could not speak.

"Answer me. What do you mean by this? Is this how you live?"

She nodded. She felt his painful grip on her arm, but she was glad of it now for if he had not held her, surely she would have fallen.

He closed his eyes for a moment but she did not see, for she had bowed her head again. For the second time that evening, in the space of only a few moments' time, he felt himself seized by an unaccustomed (and therefore frightening) force of emotion. No sorrow now, no mourning what might have been: but anger, positive burgeoning fury at the spectacle before him. It was inconceivable to him that anyone who had lived in his house, who had shared his food, his family, his very life, could fall to such a state. And if it were to become known among his peers that he had once been the protector of this—this—

"I ought to have you arrested," he said roughly. "You ought to be in prison for this. Accosting decent men—"

Two women approached, late arrivals for their supper. Bradshaw turned aside, averting his face, but the gesture was wasted on these two. They were tired, hungry, intent on sitting down to rest their legs and backs. They did not care who stood under the lamp post parlaying with a wretched example of what they themselves might become.

For a moment Bradshaw's grip loosened. With a violent wrench that startled them both, Sabra broke free. In an instant she was away and running.

He stood alone on the quiet night street. His hand still felt the solidity of her flesh and bone against his. Gone! He looked about him. Gone! Had he dreamed the dreadful encounter? Had his brain, overtaxed from the day's demands, manufactured for him that unhappy vision?

Slowly at first, and then with increasing rapidity, he began to walk back toward the mill yard where his carriage awaited him at the gate. He would not go home. No! He had no home, no place of refuge from the burdens of his life. No: he would go where he could find the company of men—decent, strong-minded, hard-working men like himself, untainted by the viciousness of the female character.

For the first time in memory, he put the whip to the horse's back as he moved away.

40

All that night Sabra walked the streets of the city. No one spoke to her; she was unaware of anyone passing by. How strange this landscape seemed! She might never have seen these deserted thoroughfares, these darkened shop windows, shuttered homes, empty meeting houses. She walked because she was walking. Like a machine set in notion she moved through the city; whatever power propelled her had not failed yet, and so, like the untended machine, she moved endlessly back and forth, back and forth.

She had misunderstood God's will. She had evaded the test with which He had confronted her, she had run away from the plague of vermin, had thought that she had been given a sign to go out into the streets when all the while, certainly, He had intended that she stay in Mary McCormic's hovel. And be devoured? Her flesh torn by their razor teeth? She did not know. How could she? She did not understand God. How could she? It was not her place to understand. God did not want understanding. He wanted obedience. But how? What was she to do? Why could He not send an intelligible message?

Very late into the night, she found herself at the entrance to a small graveyard tucked away between houses on a hilly street. She did not know where she was; she had never seen this place before. The gate was closed and locked but the bordering stone wall was low. She climbed over it. The place beckoned her; she wanted to walk among these ancient, ruined slates, she wanted to rest at the grave of someone long dead.

As she sank to her knees among the tombstones, she felt the presence of—who? She waited. The other would make itself known. She had only to let it come.

But of course—of course! It was Eldress Hannah. Relief flooded her soul. The tight iron bands of bitter defeat which crushed her spirit seemed suddenly lifted. The awful loneliness of her existence seemed suddenly dispelled. She heard Eldress speak: her mother's voice.

I am here, Sabra. I am always with you. Do not despair. Live as you can. And when you can live no more, leave that world and come to live with me for all time. There is no illness here, no death—all is light and pure, all is peace. Do not despair, for I await you.

At first light she arose and left the graveyard. She found her way back to Cork Street, to the Widow Scanlan's. Clara was still asleep, but the

Widow was up and about, shaking up those of her boarders who had to be out to work. As she explained later to Mary McCormic, she would have spoken to Sabra but for the odd expression on her face, the vacant look in her eyes. She greeted her, after all, but Sabra pretended not to see her. Privately the Widow had never understood Mary's loyalty to Sabra and her child, but it was none of her affair. She watched as Sabra, surprisingly strong, lifted up her sleeping child and carried her out. A sense of unease had overcome the Widow then, a sense that something was wrong, but by the time she thought to protest, or inquire, Sabra had gone. She had looked out the door, down the street, and had just caught a glimpse of the two of them, Clara walking now, turning the corner. But then one of her people had spoken to her, and she had fallen into an argument about the rent, and Sabra had gone out of her thoughts.

Easily, lightly, with a pace quickened by anticipation, Sabra walked with her child. Soon. Soon. The early sun glittered on the tall white cupolas of the mills, on the tall white spire of the First Baptist Church. The red-brick city looked fresh and clean under the bright blue sky: it might have been newly made in the night, and today its first day on earth.

She knew a place, not far, where the land sloped gently down to the edge of the Concord River, where the water fell sharply over jagged rocks into foaming whirlpools before flowing swiftly on to join the Merrimack a mile downstream. It was a relatively deserted place, a street of country cottages, away from the center of the city where she might be seen by the hordes of operatives just now being called out to their work.

She came to it: a wide, tree-bordered meadow between two cottages. She walked through the high dewy grass to the water's edge. She saw the rapids, the deep rocky pools. The water ran high and fast, fed by the thaw.

Their clothing would drag them down. They would sink fast, she would hold tight to the child.

I am coming.

She lifted Clara and held her close. She stood poised at the edge. She gathered up her courage. Already she could feel the shock of icy water on her skin.

Now.

"Wait!"

Small hands pulled her back; a thin, wraithlike body wrestled with her own. Wide eyes burned in a pale face. A voice came at her from a great distance.

She fell into darkness.

41

A soft bed; a warm room; hushed voices; the fragrance of an applewood fire and, closer, the bitter smell of ammoniac salts.

Sabra opened her eyes. She lay in a room of flowered wallpaper and ruffled curtains, of shining mahogany and cherrywood furniture. Sunshine streamed through sparkling windows. Her bed was narrow but soft, piled with silk and velvet quilts and tasseled pillows. She looked down at her arms lying on top of the bedcovers; she wore a fine white nightgown trimmed with lace at the wrists.

Two people were in the room with her, a man and a woman. They stood by the fireplace murmuring to each other, watching her. The man was a stranger. The woman was she who had pulled her back—Clara!

She sat up. They broke off their muted conversation and came at once to her side.

"Where is my little girl?"

"She is quite safe. She is in the kitchen with Mrs. Flaherty; she has had a good breakfast and dinner and now she is making friends with the kitten." The woman sat on the edge of the bed. Her face was kind, not at all pretty but bearing an expression of such sympathy and concern that her appearance was more pleasing than that of any beauty. Her hair was brown overlaid with gray; her eyes were gray, luminous, intelligent; her dress was black, plainly made except for v-shaped rows of silk braid running across the bosom. She wore a mourning brooch at her throat. She was perhaps forty-five years old.

The man advanced, took Sabra's hand, felt her forehead. His face was stern; he did not smile.

"Very well, Mrs. Wethertbee," he said after a moment. "She seems to be quite all right. No pain—no dizziness? Good. I shall look in again tomorrow. A glass of raspberry cordial at bedtime would do her nicely, I think. No, don't bother. I shall see myself out."

Having thus efficiently attended to his patient, he efficiently departed. Mrs. Wethertbee pushed up the pillows behind Sabra's back.

"There, now. Lie back and rest. Dr. Young said you need sleep and nourishment. In a week you will be fully recovered."

She smiled. Sabra obeyed. She could not quite realize what had happened. The last thing in her memory was the river's bank, the beckoning depths—and now, somehow, she had come to this room, which contained evidence of affluence and comfort such as she had almost forgotten existed.

"What time is it?" she said.

"Just past two o'clock. If you had not awakened within the hour, Dr. Young would have brought you round. He was convinced that you were all right, but of course he would have had to make sure. Would you like some tea, and a little bread and butter?"

"Yes." Sabra watched as Mrs. Wethertbee poured the steaming brew from a delicately flowered pot into a fragile cup. But when she tried to lift the cup to her mouth it seemed very heavy and she spilled a little, and so Mrs. Wethertbee held it for her.

"You must stay in bed for several days," said Mrs. Wethertbee. "You are not ill, but you are very weak."

Sabra took a slice of thin-cut buttered bread from the plate. A blast of cold April wind rattled the panes and sent a shower of sparks from the fire. "Why did you bring me here?" she said.

Mrs. Wethertbee laughed. "What was I to do? Let you throw yourself into the river? My dear, no! And then of course the moment I saw who you were I realized that God had indeed guided me to you."

Sabra frowned, looked again at the plain pale face. Had she perhaps begged from this woman?

"You do not remember me. Well, perhaps it is not so strange. You are Sabra Palfrey, are you not? You lived for a time some years ago with my brother Josiah Bradshaw."

The sound of the name was like a knife plunged into her heart. *My brother—?*

"I came for Thanksgiving dinner that year, with my husband and my—my infant daughter. I remember you. You had just come, you were perhaps sixteen. Josiah told me how your parents had died and how you had come down to Lowell all by yourself. I remember your mother, you know. We all grew up in Newburyport together. Josiah was very taken with her at one time, but she—well. That's past." Again she held the cup to Sabra's lips. After she put it down she was quiet for a moment. "I never learned what had become of you. We did not live here then, and I saw Josiah infrequently. I see him infrequently still, although we have been in Lowell these past three years. He said once that you had gone on the Corporation, that was all. But I recognized you immediately. You have changed very little, although you are quite thin, even thinner than you were then. No—don't speak. We have plenty of time to talk. At any rate, I awakened in the night, last night, and I could not get back to sleep. I am often troubled by insomnia, but last night was different, somehow. There seemed to be some reason to be awake, to be up and about, something I had to do. My husband was sleeping peacefully, I even went downstairs to see if perhaps Mrs. Flaherty had been taken ill.

Everything seemed in order, and I felt so terribly odd, wandering around the house at three in the morning like a somnambulent chatelaine making her rounds! But something called me, I didn't know what. Finally, as it began to grow light, I dressed and went out of doors. Perhaps, I thought, God wanted me to see the sunrise. I didn't know. I sat on the back porch, watching the river, watching the sky grow light, the sun rise—and then I saw you. You came down from the road through the meadow, leading the child. I did not recognize you immediately, of course. I saw only a woman and a child, obviously poor—forgive me, I do not mean to insult you—obviously not out for a casual stroll, obviously distraught, seeking what must have seemed a solution to her troubles—and instantly, hardly aware of what I did, I was on my feet running. I called but you did not hear me. You quite deliberately stepped to the edge of the bank. A moment more and you would have been lost. No one could have rescued you from those rapids—certainly not I. O, Sabra—"

Mrs. Wethertbee reached out and framed Sabra's face in her small hands. Her eyes were filled with tears; her lips trembled.

"Do not think, my dear, that I do not understand despair. Many times I have been distraught, even to the point of questioning God's will, God's love. We are some of us sorely tried in this life. Certainly I—well, this is not the time for my story. But I want you to know that I do understand. Life's burden sometimes seems insupportable, and then we are tempted to slough it off—to seek release in Death, and fly to the arms of the Lord. But that is wrong. Very wrong! It is God's judgment to take us when He will. We cannot make that decision for ourselves. Sometimes we cannot understand why He acts as He does, leaving the old and sick to live and taking the young—"

Her voice broke. She dropped her hands; she turned away. With great effort she composed herself and turned again to smile determinedly at Sabra.

"You would like to see your little girl. She is a darling. So bright! She was shy at first, of course, and concerned for you, but she has made herself completely at home. Finally she told us her name and I knew we were friends. I will fetch her up, and then you must sleep again."

If Sabra had in fact drowned and passed on to another life, she could not have awakened into surroundings more different from the horrors of the Acre. Here at the cottage at Wamesit Falls was a settled family: husband and wife. Here were a housekeeper, a pet kitten, a full larder, an ordered routine. Here was time for recreation, for reading and playing the piano; time for parties, for afternoon calls, for visits to the theater, for a leisurely supper at the end of the day's activity, before the evening's events began. Here were three meals every day, as regular as clockwork; here were warm fires and soft beds and ample clothing to ward off the bitter spring winds. This was not wealth like Josiah Bradshaw's wealth, much less like that of his employers, but it was Paradise compared to the Irish shantytown.

Mr. Wethertbee was employed as chief accountant at Whipple's Powder Works some distance upriver—a position which supported him and his wife well enough, but which, by the constant possibility of explosion, had left him in a highly nervous state. He suffered from a pronounced facial tic; he insisted upon absolute tranquillity in his home when he was present, since the slightest noise, suddenly occurring, startled him into a positive fit of trembling. He was in fact something of a martyr: he was convinced that he would meet his end within the confines of the powder works as had so many before him, since the nature of the business made frequent explosions, more or less fatal, an inevitable consequence of the manufacture. His predecessor had in fact been blown to bloody fragments not two weeks before Mr. Wethertbee had applied for the job—a fact which he did not discover at once, since they were anxious to hire a replacement. But they paid him a good salary —more than he could have got for similar work elsewhere—and he wanted the money in order to provide, after many years of uncertain income, a comfortable home for his wife.

Mr. Wethertbee loved his wife very much. His heart wept for her every time she bore a child and shortly buried it. Only one had survived beyond infancy, a girl who had lived to the age of three. He had feared, at that death, that his wife would die too. He had feared for her sanity, for her own desire to live. But she had survived, and in time she had learned to live with her grief, and even to use it, as artists will, in the compositions which she began to present to the public.

It was for this reason—to allow his wife to assuage her grief in her chosen way—that Mr. Wethertbee permitted her to indulge in what he called her scribbling. He had not at first approved. It was all very well for her to compose a clever couplet for a friend's autograph album, or to fill her own private notebooks, late at night, when her housekeeping duties were done. But to publish—to send out to magazines and newspapers those same verses, and in her own name! His name! That was a very different thing. Mr. Wethertbee thought at first that it was unladylike. He was aware of the growing fashion for female authors; he was aware that many women published, and certainly many of them must be as gently bred as his wife. And, too, the sight of her words in print seemed to give her such satisfaction, such a blessed release from the ever present sorrow, that he had neither the heart nor the courage to forbid her this whim.

To his surprise, she was paid for some of these efforts—not much, not enough to live on, but a little here and there. After that he disapproved less; he came, in time, to look forward to her appearance in the *Christian Register* or the *Ladies' Jewel Box.*

Further, he discovered that his wife was rapidly becoming a person, if not of great consequence, then at least of some small notice, in the literary world. People knew her name; they sent acknowledgments of her work. One day, beaming, she showed him a letter from William Cullen Bryant; a few months later came a note from Mrs. Sigourney, a female scribbler whose fame (and fortune) far surpassed her own.

Mrs. Wethertbee was not content only to publish and to correspond, however. She came in time to want a more immediate intercourse with people like herself: people of sensibility, of artistic aspiration, people whose lives encompassed more than the usual humdrum money-grubbing. To that end, with her removal to Lowell from the barbarities of Buffalo three years previous, she promptly began what had since become a Sunday institution at the Wethertbees' second only to attendance at Unitarian services. She called these occasions her "gatherings." "Gleanings" might have been a more appropriate term, for these festivities were by no means all-inclusive. Certain standards had to be met; certain literary or artistic credentials had to be owned, if not actually presented at the door. Frequently Mrs. Wethertbee managed to entice visiting celebrities of more or less renown. On one occasion Charlotte Cushman, in Lowell for a week's engagement at the Museum Theater, came by for half an hour. On another, Mrs. General Gaines, the celebrated she-lecturer, spent an entire evening.

These Sunday salons were the high point of Mrs. Wethertbee's week. She received her guests while she sat on a low-backed chair in the Empire style which had been fortuitously placed in the center of the parlor; around it were a number of low footstools upon which her admirers could perch as they engaged her in repartee. Whenever a lion was present, however, she surrendered this strategic position to the visitor and hovered gracefully close by his—or her—side. No one could flatter a noted visitor more adroitly than Julia Bradshaw Wethertbee, while at the same time contriving to keep some small portion of attention for herself as the instigator—the moving force—of these select occasions. She was a luminous moon to the succession of temporary suns; when they departed she assumed once again the central illuminating position. No one, not even the most celebrated visitor, was allowed to forget that it was the noted poetess Mrs. Julia Bradshaw Wethertbee who entertained him. Over the past three years she had accumulated quite a little bundle of thank-you notes from those strangers to the city who had endured her hospitality, and from time to time, when her correspondence (or rather theirs) languished, she took these letters from her desk and read them over again to reassure herself that she had indeed met these well-known folks, had entertained them, fed them, detained them under her roof for a little time; and they in turn had written to her. They had graciously acknowledged her existence.

Every Sunday evening at nine o'clock, when her guests had departed, Mrs. Wethertbee ascended to her bedroom and threw herself, exhausted and exhilarated, onto her bed. At first, seeing her in this condition, her husband had wondered aloud if such strenuous entertaining might not be too much for her delicate constitution to endure. She had thrown him a look of such horror—fear, and contempt, and disgust, all intertwined—that he had promptly retracted his words. Never again did he make such a blunder. Privately he continued to believe that she overextended herself at these parties; certainly most Mondays she seemed unwontedly out of touch, her eyes wandering, her thoughts astray. Her Monday behavior had in fact become so predictable that Mr. Wethertbee took to visiting the Middlesex Mechanics' Association Hall every Monday evening after his day's toil at the powder works. Tired as he was, he preferred to spend a few hours away from home rather than see his wife in such low spirits.

Still, despite their drain on her fragile resources, he could see that her Sunday gatherings made her happy. Therefore he permitted her to continue them. They were essentially harmless, he thought: essentially a diversion. Nothing important. Let her continue, then, and he would speak to Mrs. Flaherty about whipping up a daily mid-morning eggnog to strengthen Mrs. Wethertbee's constitution; he would entice her for a Sunday afternoon stroll before the guests arrived; he would urge her early to sleep as many nights as he could.

Mr. Wethertbee had a kind heart, a limited perception, and no imagination at all. He was perhaps not the ideal caretaker for a female such as his wife. Then again, she could have done worse; he was not, after all, an absolute Philistine. But because of his deficiencies (of which he was dimly, inarticulately aware) he failed to see the transformation in his wife during the late winter and early spring of 1848. The usual people were no longer enough. Occasional celebrities were no longer enough. She had to have, it seemed, someone special—someone new—every Sunday. Such specimens were not always available. Lowell was a thriving city, a natural stop on anyone's tour; but even Lowell did not get a lion a week.

Since Mrs. Wethertbee did not speak of her growing discontent, her husband failed to know of it. He was aware that she was somewhat restless; he noted her increasing fits of irritability, of melancholy; but he put these things down to her age, or to her occasional failure to get her most recent poem published in the journal of her choice. He did not understand that like the opium slave, Mrs. Wethertbee required ever increasing amounts of her chosen narcotic. To be denied her drug—her lions—was torture. And so, with the desperation born of an addictive need, Mrs. Wethertbee had begun to contrive ways of assuring herself at least one new personality each week. More often than not she was successful, but the effort took its toll; she became more nervous, more fatigued, more likely to snap at him. The thought of spending even one Sunday without the titillation of a new face had become unendurable to her. And so with pen and paper, with charm and grim determination, she stalked her prey.

As February stormed into March that year, and March melted into April, she discovered the most magnificent catch of all. And, discovering it, began to plot to bag it, to capture it live and exhibit it in her parlor.

She was sure that she would succeed. She was, she thought, invincible.

43

Sabra mended. Under the tender ministrations of Mrs. Wethertbee and Mrs. Flaherty her body strengthened and her spirit found calm. She stopped feeling surprise at what had seemed her miraculous rescue; she relaxed and let their solicitude envelop her. She watched Clara bloom. She sat on the porch in the sun. She ate her fill and rapidly gained fifteen pounds. She lived.

She even came to agree with Mrs. Wethertbee, who said that since she had endured so much, she was due for a change in fortune.

"After all," said that good lady, "it isn't as if you had purposely hurt anyone, is it? I mean, you always did the best you could in the circumstances."

They sat on the back lawn enjoying the afternoon air, watching that same river where, several weeks before, Sabra had so precipitously hovered. Clara sat near by, stroking the kitten into a paroxysm of purring. In the small garden, bees hummed about their work; myriad birds performed small concerti in the trees. Because the day was cloudy (but oppressively warm) Mrs. Wethertbee did not need to bother with a sunshade; Sabra would not have held one in any case, since she had not fully come back to middle-class womanhood. The women in the Acre did not use parasols to protect their complexions.

She met Mrs. Wethertbee's eyes and looked away. She had given out, from time to time, small recitations of her life's history since she had left the Bradshaws. But by no means had she told everything; by no means did Mrs. Wethertbee know the whole story. Sabra wondered, not for the first time, what she would say if she did. Sabra did not want to tell it all. Even so generous a heart as Mrs. Wethertbee's might harden if it heard the worst. It was not worth the risk. Wait a bit. Mend. Strengthen. See what you can do for yourself. Then, perhaps . . .

There was one point, however, of which she had to be sure. Ever since her first day there, when she had learned that Julia Wethertbee was Josiah Bradshaw's sister, she had worried about his influence over her, and whether he, learning who it was whom his sister harbored, would insist upon the guest's expulsion. Would he disown Mrs. Wethertbee if she defied him? Persuade the owners of Whipple's to discharge their chief accountant? Find some other means of pressure against a sister who took in a fallen woman? The problem had nagged increasingly at her mind. Now she determined to solve it.

"Have you seen Mr. Bradshaw recently?" she said.

Mrs. Wethertbee seemed surprised at the question. "No. I seldom see him. Why? Did you want to speak to him? You could send a note—"

"No. No, I didn't want to see him. I just wondered what he would say if he knew that I am here."

"I don't see why he should say anything," replied Mrs. Wethertbee with unaccustomed tartness. "We each of us live our separate lives. My affairs are no concern of his, nor his of mine, for that matter."

"I understand. But as I'm sure you know, he—he doesn't like me."

"He doesn't? Whyever not? Although I must tell you, since we seem to be sharing secrets, that he doesn't like me much, either." She giggled. "He thinks I'm unbearably frivolous. He sees no value whatsoever in any of the things important to me—literature, art, philosophy, music. He told me so, last Thanksgiving. He thinks that I am wasting my life. Although whatever else I should do with it I couldn't tell you, and I'm sure he couldn't either. I'm hardly a candidate for a place in the weaving room, am I? But why do you say he doesn't like you? I've never quite understood why you left his house in the first place. Did you displease him in some way? He is most easily displeased, as I'm sure we both know."

"I—yes," replied Sabra hesitantly. Here, surely, was one confession which could be made. And so, choosing her words carefully, she told of the visits to Mr. Hale, of Rachel's discontent, of her joy when the summons to action came at last, of the disastrous night ride transporting the forbidden cargo. She listened to her voice reciting the long-ago events. What an ignorant child had been that girl Sabra Palfrey! She watched Mrs. Wethertbee's expressive face change from interest to surprise to fascinated horror. Such a daring escapade was totally beyond the poetess' imagination, which dwelt in the safe realms of generalized high purpose rather than the dangerous paths of specific, direct action motivated by that same purpose. In Mrs. Wethertbee's canon, it was admirable in the extreme to hold worthy moral positions, and to expound them; it was not always in good taste to act upon them. She detested Mr. Garrison.

When Sabra stopped speaking, it took Mrs. Wethertbee a long moment to collect her shocked self in order to make a reply. Finally she willed her tense body to unbend as far as her corsets would permit. She reached out and clasped Sabra's hand and then, quite overcome, she embraced her.

"My dear child," she said softly. "So that was it! I must tell you that at the time, when I got Josiah's letter, I could not understand why Rachel had been sent away so abruptly. And Amalia's letter, following, did nothing to enlighten me. I thought somehow that Rachel must have had an unhappy affair of the heart, but they were so maddeningly vague that I hadn't the faintest idea of what really was happening. And then just a few months later, to be summoned to Sophia's funeral, you have no idea how tragic it was, but Josiah wouldn't let anyone speak about it, we all had to be as silent as Death itself the entire time, and I left afterward knowing very little more than I did when I arrived. I never understood it at all. And of course I've never dared question him about it—certainly not at his wedding to Margaret, and I was unable to attend poor Amalia's funeral, I had just given birth, and soon enough we had a funeral of our own to get through—" Her voice broke. She paused to collect herself. She continued: "I saw, that Thanksgiving when I met you, that you were much in awe of Rachel, even then, when you had been with them for only a few weeks. You sat in a corner and said very little, but I saw how you watched her. To be perfectly frank, my dear, I must tell you that even though she is my brother's child, I always thought that Rachel was much too forward. With her looks, and her background, she could have made a brilliant match. But she would have none of it. She was headstrong, she delighted in parading her erudition and so putting off any eligible young man. Mind, I think every woman should be well-read. But to speak of it in public—to insist that one is as learned as gentlemen—is totally unladylike. I can't think why they didn't restrain her. And now I see the consequences. Well!" She smiled. "You may be interested to know that Rachel has been for these past five years a teacher at a Female Seminary in New-York. I do not correspond with her. But Josiah has told me once or twice that she is well, and happy. She has not married."

Sabra digested this news. The daughter, erring, was the daughter still, helped, protected, hardly punished—rewarded, indeed, for Rachel had not liked Lowell, she must have been glad to escape, even in disgrace. Whereas she— No. She shook her head. No good would come of bitterness. They were what they were: some rich, some poor, some helped, some left to survive as they could.

She was unable to reply, however, because Mrs. Flaherty came just then to inform them that their tea was ready. As she collected Clara and the kitten she realized that she had not explicitly settled the question of Josiah's wrath; but she felt that for the moment at least, she was safe. As she followed Mrs. Wethertbee up to the house she heard the first faint warning rumble of distant thunder; a few drops of rain fell, making dark spots on her new brown poplin dress. She walked faster, hurrying toward shelter.

44

Every morning after breakfast Mrs. Wethertbee retired to her desk, which was in her bedroom, to write her poems and attend to her voluminous correspondence. For the past week—it was now late May—she had approached her labors with an especial urgency: there was much to be done, details to be attended to, commitments to be given and received. The other members of the household were aware that something important was about to happen (she having been unable to resist dropping a few tantalizing hints at the dinner table), but, knowing her sensitive temperament, her need to make her little surprises in her own good time, they did not press her. She would tell them—and everyone else—when she was ready. Meanwhile they must content themselves to wait.

While Mrs. Wethertbee worked at her desk every morning, Sabra had her own tasks to accomplish. If Mrs. Flaherty did not need her in the kitchen, she sewed a new wardrobe for Clara and herself, for Mrs. Wethertbee had presented her with cloth for dresses, petticoats, chemises—

even a new cloak. To have had these things made up at a dressmaker's would have been too great an expense, as well as too unhappy a reminder of her own failure; besides, as she slowly recuperated, she enjoyed the monotony of sitting quiet and sewing, on the porch perhaps if the day were fine, watching Clara play in the garden and knowing that at the appointed hour, without having to worry about it for a moment, dinner would be on the table and she and Clara could eat as much as they liked. More than a month after her arrival at Wamesit Cottage, she still felt a little shock of surprise every time she sat down to a meal: the abundant food still seemed a miracle.

She had not forgotten Mary McCormic. She thought of her quite often, in fact. She realized that her actions on that last night, that night when she had been attacked by the swarming rats, when she had offered herself to Bradshaw, had been impelled by her own desperate situation; but by those actions she had been unfair, even unkind, to Mary. Mary would have come back from the wake by midnight. Finding Sabra gone, she would not have worried at first, perhaps. And if she, too, had come upon the invaders, that event undoubtedly would have driven all other considerations from her mind. By the next morning, when Sabra still had not appeared, Mary would have gone to the Widow Scanlan's to see about Clara. She would have heard of Sabra's abrupt departure, taking her child away. And there the trail would have ended. Mary would of course have inquired about whether any bodies fished out of the canals might have been Sabra's. But the Acre's underground network of communication was not perfect; Sabra might have drowned and Mary not heard of it. And, not hearing, she must suppose that Sabra had simply gone away. But she would have been puzzled, hurt, that Sabra left no message. She would have felt betrayed by the girl whom she had helped so much as best she could. Sabra pictured her looking out the door of her shack, peering down the narrow noisome alley, waiting for news.

There was no question of returning to the Acre to let Mary know that she was all right—more than all right. Sabra felt that she could not have made that journey on pain of death. Still, it was only right that she communicate with Mary. She did not want to see her personally. The knowledge and significance of her rescue would have come between them like a wall: for Sabra had done what Mary could never do. She had escaped from the Acre. She had been taken back by people who were her own people: Americans, native-born, well-fed, well-clothed, accepted members of society. True, she could not work on the Corporation since she was blacklisted, but perhaps she could work at something else. A door had opened for her once again; it was a door which Mary would never even approach.

Sabra mentioned her concern one rainy night in May when she and Mrs. Wethertbee sat cozily before the fire in the poetess' bedroom.

"You should send her a note, of course," said Mrs. Wethertbee.

"She can't read."

"No—of course not." Mrs. Wethertbee smiled slightly to cover her faux pas. Despite Sabra's version of life among the Irish, she had in fact no idea of them at all. She had seen them, of course, working on the canal gangs, begging through the streets. But she had never known any immigrant from Ireland; her own devoted, dependable Mrs. Flaherty was second generation and, through long association, almost as American as the Wethertbees themselves. Her husband had died young; she had gone to Mr. Wethertbee's family in Portsmouth soon after. He had inherited her, so to speak, from his late mother. Mrs. Flaherty was as close to the Irish as Julia Bradshaw Wethertbee had ever come; she was not sure that she wanted to come any closer.

"Perhaps—could you send her a note and someone could read it to her?" she said. "Surely some of them can read. The priest, perhaps, could help her."

"They don't get on. She—she doesn't go to church, you see."

"Ah. Yes." Mrs. Wethertbee did not see at all. She had assumed that all Irish were devoted papists. Her mind these days was full of her newest and grandest coup; she had no energy to spare to solve the mysteries of the immigrant classes. "Well, you must do as you think best, Sabra. Certainly a note is one solution. I'm sure she could find someone to read it to her. Mr. Wethertbee will be happy to send a boy from the office to carry it down for you if you like."

"Yes," said Sabra. "Thank you. Probably that is what I will do. A note, telling her that I am well, not to worry—"

"What is it?" said Mrs. Wethertbee. "You don't look happy with your decision."

"I am. But I wish that I could help her, somehow."

"God helps those—"

"Yes, but it's so difficult. For them, I mean."

"They bring their distress upon themselves. I am positive that all this dreadful famine over there—in Ireland, I mean—is the result of their intemperance. They seem absolutely determined to inebriate themselves at every opportunity. That is why, when I made my donation to the Famine Relief, I gave my money to the Quakers. They have established admirable feeding stations, so I understand, and there is no danger that money given to them will contribute in any way to even a single Irishman's drunkenness."

"Yes," said Sabra. She thought of Patrick, as sober as Mr. Wethertbee himself; of Mary, who had a "drop" on only the most special—or sorrowful—occasions. But it was no good arguing; undeniably, Father Mathew had many souls to harvest wherever he preached Temperance among his countrymen.

In the end she printed out a note. The boy from Mr. Wethertbee's office, well tipped to allay his fears of enemy territory, carried it down to the Acre. There was no reply; Sabra had not expected one. The boy said he had delivered it to Mrs. McCormic in the flesh. She had to believe him or make the journey herself. She chose to believe him; but she resolved, as soon as she could, to find a way to send something along to Mary. Of course she had no money, not a cent. But perhaps she could make up a parcel and have that same boy carry it down: some food, and a length of cloth—yes. Surely Mrs. Wethertbee would let her do that much.

45

On the Fourth of July that year the poetess Wethertbee was invited to carry the standard for the Mechanics' Institute phalanx in the parade. Her constitution was not so delicate that she would forgo such an honor. She sent a gracious note accepting the invitation. She had now lived in Lowell for three years and more; it was about time, she thought, that she receive some major public acknowledgment. Carrying the Mechanics' banner would do as well as anything else. Lowell was not, after all, Boston; there was no literary establishment in Lowell save her own Sunday groups, and one could hardly announce one's triumphs—one's latest appearance in print, one's latest letter from some celebrated gentleman—in one's own home. Aside from these gatherings there was no place in the city where she could receive the recognition which she had come to consider, in all modesty, to be rightfully hers. Lowell did not know what a treasure it had in Julia Bradshaw Wethertbee. Well: she would show them. And later in the month she would show them again. There would be no doubt in anyone's mind, when Mrs. Wethertbee had done, that a person of consequence resided among them.

She smiled to herself. She began to consider an appropriate costume. She could hardly contain her great secret. She resolved to share it with a special few of her friends—and of course with her husband—after the festivities on the holiday.

The day dawned hot. By mid-morning the people of the city gasped and wilted as they lined the streets waiting for the parade. The sun blazed on women's pale bonnets and caused many of the men, gentlemen all, to remove their sweat-stained jackets. Clara, formerly jumping with excitement, had settled into a heat-stunned lethargy. Sabra mopped the child's perspiring face and looked for a seller of shaved ice.

At last it began: no more than a cloud of dust at first, the first faint reverberations of the drums. Then gradually appeared the marching rows of bodies; strains of military music played loud and clear. A platoon of mill girls in their Sunday best carrying banners of the several Corporations; a troop of boys and girls from the high school; the Jackson Militia stepping smartly in time; the Mechanics led by their standard-bearer, the frail poetess, her perspiring face lighted by her spirit shining through. She saw them waving, her husband and Sabra and small Clara; under the burden of the banner, she cast them a brilliant smile. Look at me! she seemed to say; see me!

This Fourth of July, in 1848, had a special significance far beyond the appearance of the poetess Wethertbee in the Lowell parade. Not many months previous, at the close of the Mexican War, the nation had gained a vast new territory in the southwest. Whether that enormous region would be slave or free was a question not to be thought of on this day of celebration; after the parade, patriotic orators neatly sidestepped the issue while uttering pompous platitudes about the wisdom of the Founding Fathers, the glory of military conquest.

In the late afternoon, Mrs. Wethertbee served salmon and green peas to her guests in her dining room; afterward she escorted them to the garden for lemonade. She felt an acute sense of anticlimax. Everyone was exhausted by the heat. The ladies hardly had strength to wave their palmetto-leaf fans. Conversation rose and fell with the breeze. Everyone said that it was really too hot to live. One of the gentlemen remarked that the signing of the Declaration of Independence should have been delayed until September; the rush to finish the business in July had shown, he said, a total disregard for the comfort of the posterity who must annually celebrate it.

The guests left early. By nine o'clock Mrs. Wethertbee was able to remove her corset and put on a comfortable dressing-gown. Stretched on her bed, a cool, wet cloth across her forehead, she summoned Sabra to her room. All in all, the day had been oddly disappointing; to march at the head of the Mechanics' phalanx had not been anything like the triumph she had anticipated. Ah, but wait! In less than two weeks' time—!

"I am going to tell you my secret," she announced. Her voice trembled with excitement; her eyes glowed with a passion that had nothing to do with ordinary human desires. "Sit by the window to catch the air. Is Clara asleep? Good. Now: can you guess what I have been planning all these weeks? Of course you can't. Listen to me, Sabra. This is more exciting than anything you can imagine."

No fire burns so hot as the fire of thwarted ambition; no pain burns so deep as the pain of being ignored. The poetess Wethertbee was as a woman possessed; the heat of the summer night was an Arctic blast compared to the heat of the flame of her ambitions.

"The announcement will be in all the papers next week," she said. "Of course there will be an immediate rush for tickets. I have saved a dozen for my best friends. You can be sure that I will be the most sought-after woman in Lowell."

From the distance they heard the faint pop! of exploding firecrackers. Closer by, the crickets in the garden sang their hypnotic song. The Concord River rushed by at the foot of the meadow. A faint breeze stirred the muslin curtains.

"Sabra, who is the most brilliant poet in America?" Mrs. Wethertbee laughed as she spoke; she was like a child unable to contain itself. "Who is the greatest genius? Mr. Emerson? Mr. Hawthorne? Mr. Longfellow?"

I must show a greater enthusiasm, thought Sabra; she deserves a better audience than this. "I don't—"

"That's right! None of them! Not a one of them can compare to him! He is unquestionably the greatest of them all."

Sabra was uncomfortably aware that her face was a blank. She had not the faintest idea of whom Mrs. Wethertbee spoke.

The poetess reached for a volume on the table beside her bed. She held it like an offering on her two hands outstretched. "Genius," she said. "Look: pure heavenly genius. Do not tell me that you have never heard of him!"

Sabra took the volume; she opened it and looked at the title page. *The Raven and Other Poems*. The author's name was unfamiliar. "No," she said. "I do not know him."

"But you must! You must know him! He is— No. Of course you do not know him. Even though he is so highly praised, he has as yet only a small circle of admirers. He is not yet as widely read as he will be one day. One day, when no one remembers so much as a line by Mr. Emerson, this man's works will still be read everywhere. And that, Sabra, is why his lecture here is so important. Yes! Here! He is coming in two weeks to speak! He will appear at a reception in this house—my house! He will be my guest! It was I who persuaded him to come! Yes—Julia Bradshaw Wethertbee! Some people think that I am an amateur—a dilettante. But he would not have accepted an invitation from a dilettante. He knows that I am one of the Muse's devotees. He has even complimented me on my work. Yes, indeed: we have had quite a little correspondence. And he will be here, Sabra, and I will be his hostess! And no one who has been unkind to me will receive an invitation to meet him! His visit will be the triumph of my life!"

She blinked away her tears of joy; she shuddered in the grip of her emotion. For the first time since the death of her first infant, twenty years before, she was glad—genuinely glad—that she had not died too.

46

In the years that followed the poet's visit to their city, the people of Lowell manufactured so many different versions of the occasion that some people, finally, did not believe that he had ever been there at all. One story had it that he got drunk, insulted Mrs. Wethertbee, and paid a fervent visit to her pretty young neighbor—not necessarily in that order; another, that he behaved like the Southern gentleman that he was, but that the code of the South was of course very different from the way decent people behaved in Yankeedom. Some people said that he had been charming; others, that he had offended everyone. Some people said that the young neighbor had thrown herself at his head; others, that Mrs. Wethertbee had prostrated herself at his feet. Even those who had actually attended Mrs. Wethertbee's reception for him told different stories, but all the variations contained one central kernel of truth: he had been enchanted by the neighbor, and Mrs. Wethertbee had lost her lion to someone else.

In time, it came not to matter what had in fact happened. People did not care, they had no taste for historical accuracy. Historical accuracy was dull. Titillation, embroidery, exaggeration—those were the thing!

The point was that once again someone famous had visited the city. He could be named, over and over again, in the roster of visitors; he could be bragged about, usurped—perhaps he would even give them a kind word or two to be quoted in the self-adulatory publications put out from time to time by the city's business leaders.

Had he lived permanently among them, they would not have looked at him twice unless he disgraced himself by staggering drunk in the streets; had he lived among them, he would have been tolerated as an eccentric: no more. They flocked to see him, to hear him lecture, because their betters elsewhere had praised him. More: he was an exotic, a curiosity every bit as strange as one of Mr. Barnum's freaks and fancies. Left to their own judgment, they preferred money to art, possessions to talent, the power to hire and fire rather than the power to evoke the evanescent presence of Beauty and Truth. If you had asked them, "What is Beauty?" they would have replied, "A column of figures showing profit." And as for Truth—well, Truth was an awkward thing, often as not, best left to the impractical; they had no time to consider it.

The one point upon which everyone agreed was that Mrs. Wethertbee no longer allowed the poet's name to be spoken in her presence.

47

In the autumn, Mrs. Wethertbee fell ill; by Christmas her husband despaired of her life. But she hung on, and as spring approached she seemed to improve. When the weather grew warm she sat with Sabra in the garden, her frail body wrapped in lap robes against the breeze; when autumn came she moved permanently indoors again, pale, indomitable, fighting hard to the end.

They did not tell her at once when the news came that her lion had died. They were afraid of the shock to her nerves; they waited for a time when she seemed stronger, they broached the subject delicately, with infinite tact. Mr. Wethertbee sat on one side of her bed, Sabra on the other.

She gazed at them from calm gray eyes; she gave no hint of grief.

"When?" she said.

"Six weeks ago. In early October."

"How?"

"He—he collapsed in the streets in Baltimore."

Mrs. Wethertbee nodded slightly; her face, lined with pain, bore no expression. "He was not a gentleman," she said. "But it doesn't matter. It doesn't matter at all."

That night, very late, she roused herself and sat up in her bed and demanded pen and paper. Even as they watched, she wrote an ode to the departed genius. She wrote smoothly, effortlessly, as if she had memorized what she had to say. Setting it down on paper was an act of willpower, not of literary composition.

"I want the world to remember that I was his friend, and he mine," she said. "That is all I ask. I am not a greedy woman."

Three days later she was dead. For fear of meeting Bradshaw, Sabra did not attend the funeral; she and Clara stayed in the kitchen with Mrs. Flaherty when Mrs. Wethertbee's friends came to call, but she need not have bothered for Bradshaw did not appear. The week after they put his wife into the ground, Mr. Wethertbee, bowed down with his sorrow, told Sabra that he could no longer bear to live in Wamesit Cottage, filled as it was with memories of his wife. He had decided to accept the offer of a position at the Custom House in Boston, he said. He was sure that she understood. Perhaps, if all went well, she might consider letting Clara come to live with him—?

No, said Sabra. She stays with me.

She went looking for work, and to her surprise she found it: carving designs into blocks of wood for embroidery stamps. She worked in the back room of a fancy-goods shop on Gorham Street; she and Clara boarded near by. When Clara turned six, in March of 1850, she began to go to school. She was a bright child; she learned easily.

As the weeks passed, and the months, Sabra found that she and Clara were surviving after all. She had not thought that they would. They had very little money; they had no one to help them. From time to time, berating herself for her weakness, she inquired at the post office; but there was never a letter for her. She did not expect one; she inquired only to confirm that expectation. Silas was gone. He would not return.

And yet: and yet—

Perhaps, said the traitorous voice in her mind. Perhaps, one day, when he has completed his mission in the world, he will come back and expect to find us waiting.

She tried to silence that voice, but she could not. Late at night, in the small quiet hours when she lay sleepless beside her child, the hope would come to her all over again, the fervent, life-giving faith: he will come back. Some day we will see him again.

And then one day as she sat at her worktable next to the window, she put down her tools and moved to raise the blind to get more light, and she saw that the blind was already as high as it could go, the outside shutters folded back, the whole expanse of glass free to admit the sun.

She looked again at the small, two-inch-square block of wood upon which she was carving an intricate design of leaves and flowers, every tiny petal, every vein of every leaf needing to be perfectly cut, one mistaken line and the entire piece needing to be discarded, the work begun all over again on a new block, its cost charged to her pay. The pattern wavered, the design was only a blur. She blinked and rubbed her eyes. The lines came clear for a moment and then blurred again.

Dear God, she thought. Am I losing my sight? How will we live if I go blind?

She passed a sleepless night; and the next day she had a visitor.

PART

V

1

By the spring of 1850 the Yankee mill girls—the pride of New England, the boast of the entrepreneurs—had almost disappeared from the factories, driven out by the intransigence of the Corporations in the matter of wages and hours. Their places had been taken by the onrushing Irish who were glad to get any work at all, even under such conditions. No Irishman, fresh from the horrors of County Tip, would cavil at such a thing as a thirteen-hour day and the certainty of damaged lungs. A Lowell factory was paradise compared to what he had left, a berth in an Acre cellar a welcome place when one's belly was full. The longing for green and open country, the dislike of the sour smells, the life regulated by tolling bells, the constant thronging of other hungry, unwashed bodies —all this was tolerable, all welcome, even, if it meant eating. Living. Surviving. And if, on a soft spring Sunday after Mass, one wandered to the banks of the great river and gazed across to the green shore and thought longingly of the home one had left—had been forced to leave—why, that, too, was bearable. The man who preferred death to exile generally got death. If one had the luck to survive the voyage, the rigors of the new land, the torture of becoming a kind of machine oneself, why, then, one had lived to fight another day. One could live to get revenge. The British or the Yankees: they were all the same stock, the same breed of cold, imperious, hard-grinding tyrant to an Irishman. What mattered if one starved in a ditch in County Clare or coughed away one's life-breath in the Lowell mills? Here in America, at least, one had another chance. And when the time came, when the hunger had gone from the old country, when Death had reaped his final harvest there—why then go back, and form a rising, and throw them off forever. And use the money earned from Yankees to do it.

And yet—O, but it was a hard thing! To long for the smell of a turf fire and to have one's nostrils assaulted by the reek of machine oil! To long for the feel of green grass under one's boots and to tread hard-packed dirt and echoing boardwalks! To be seized with the longing to walk over the fields of an evening to visit a friend a mile and more away, and to be cramped and confined to the misery of the shantytown!

Around them, beyond their knowledge, their destiny was being shaped by the hands and hearts of adamant men, and women too, North and South, who would not yield one to the other on the subject of sacred property, on the subject of states' rights, the expansion of the slave-owning territories.

The Irish cared nothing for the rising national debate. They cared to survive. Nothing more.

2

A German family came. Refugees of revolution, they had fled from Cologne to Zurich and thence to Paris, to London, to New-York, and finally to Boston. Unlike many of their countrymen they had not gone west. The charms of the wilderness prairie, so enticing to so many Germans, did not appeal to them. They wanted secure and comfortable civilization: shops, schools, the means at hand to earn their way. No plough, no harrow and reaper for this family; no isolation on the western plains, victims of drought and grasshoppers and lethal Indian raids.

They had arrived in New-York harbor in September of 1852 with tears of joy in their eyes, their warm and sentimental Teutonic souls overburdened with the knowledge that they need flee no more. But New-York had proved inhospitable: dirty, hog-ridden, rude and pushy people. It had no place for an emigrant music-master and his large family, nor for his full-grown son who had learned English so quickly in London that he served as their guide and interpreter. The Shakespeare Tavern thronged with their fellow Germans, all looking for work suitable to their university training; few of them found it.

To Boston, then, to a more genteel atmosphere. But Boston was cold. Spring never came; the weather turned from frost to suffocating heat in less than a week's time, but the reception which the Bostonians gave to this little band of newcomers never lost its chill. No one wanted a professor of music or the leader of an orchestra, no matter how expertly he sawed away at his fiddle. No one wanted, either, an enterprising young man trained in the latest Parisian techniques of the daguerreotype. If you wanted to have your shadow fixed in Boston, you went to the Messrs. Southworth & Hawes in Tremont Row; Boston needed no strangely accented newcomers in that line.

To Lowell, then, where Herr Professor Hartmann had learned of a Mr. Gage, the manager of a prosperous theater housed in the former, infamous Freewill Baptist Church, who needed a good musician to conduct a little orchestra. And—yes, certainly—Herr Professor would have ample time during the day to give instruction on the violin. There were many charming young ladies in the city who would welcome the opportunity to acquire some facility on that instrument, and as for the daguerreotypes —well, perhaps. Perhaps. Mr. Gage knew of a suite of rooms on East Merrimack Street, just by the Concord River, with a small skylight over the third floor which might work well as a studio; it was a convenient location, slightly elevated so as to be out of danger from any but the most severe flood. He would take them to see it.

"*Ja,*" said Adolph Hartmann; yes, this is as good a place as any. He had come on with Klaus, just the two of them, father and grown son, to negotiate with Gage and find a place to live. They had learned, finally, what all immigrants learned: no streets paved with gold, no warm welcome and precious few helping hands. One came with what one could carry; live by wits, look out for every opportunity, and be thankful for every skill, every bit of training acquired in the old world which could be turned to advantage in the new.

He took his violin, brought for Gage's edification, and stood in the empty front parlor of the apartment and ran his bow across the strings. The A was flat; he stopped, turned the key, and played the first measures of a Mozart sonata. Gage looked doubtful. Adolph caught his eye, stopped abruptly, and began to play "Lilly Dale"—a new song, very popular in Boston. Gage looked a little happier. Some of his friends had warned him against hiring a foreigner; foreigners were undependable, they were thievish, they were drunkards—but no, Gage had said, that's the Irish you're talking about. Germans are different. They are like us.

And so it was settled: Herr Professor Hartmann was to become the conductor of the Lowell Museum Theater's orchestra for six evenings out of every seven. During the run of certain performances, such as the *Tragedy of Macbeth,* scheduled to begin next week, he would lead the musicians in light selections before the play; during others, his presence would be required for the entire evening. For these efforts he would receive fifteen dollars a week and passes.

Adolph put by his violin and looked up at his son. A silent message passed between them: it is not exactly what we want, but it is a beginning. A means to survival. Good: let us be back to Boston, where Anna and the children await our news.

Two days later they returned bringing all the others. The next eldest to Klaus, who was twenty-six, was Jutta, eighteen; these two were Adolph's children by his first wife who had died nine years previous. He had then married Anna Schaffer, a woman fifteen years younger than himself, who had rapidly presented him with Ludwig, now seven; Wolfgang, six; Franz, five; Johannes, three; and the new-born Elisabetta, three months. The gap between Franz and Johannes occurred because during the entire year of 1848 Adolph was away from home plotting against King Friedrich Wilhelm IV. But he was done with plots and revolutions now, and so he confidently expected to increase his family at regular intervals here in the new land. The gap between Johannes and Elisabetta was less easily explained; some would have said, "God's will," but Adolph had renounced God years ago. First God, and now politics. To live was the watchword; let others enmesh themselves in affairs of government over which they could have no control. He had seen with some annoyance one day in Boston that Klaus was practicing his English on a copy of the *Liberator*, painstakingly writing out each unfamiliar word in the small notebook which he kept for that purpose.

Adolph had remonstrated, but in German, and so Klaus had smiled at him infuriatingly, patronizingly—impudent pup!—and had returned to his studies. They had all tried to keep to their agreement, made even before they left London, that in America they would speak only English among themselves. But it was a frustrating business. Anna had no time to study, busy as she was with the younger children; and Jutta, unlike Klaus, learned slowly and unwillingly. She hated English, she said; it made no sense. It was a harsh and awkward language—unmusical. She was homesick. She wanted to go back to Cologne. Even Paris and London were tolerable—but America! A raw, new country populated by buffoons and ruffians and all the refuse of Europe. And as for the native-born Americans! The men spat and swore, and the women simpered and swooned, and the lot of them not worth a pfennig compared to the good burghers of Cologne. Filthy cities bounded by wilderness—she was sure that they would all be attacked by savages even on Boston Common. They had been insane to come, she said; at least they could have stayed in London, where there was a large colony of fellow refugees, and where one could speak to those of like sympathies in a civilized tongue.

But Adolph—and Klaus, too—had known better. They had no future in London. London was treacherous, for there they could have eked out the rest of their days in their little circle of refugees, plotting revolution, talking—in German—arguing, impotent: like Karl Marx. Everyone knew that he would never accomplish anything despite his unflagging pen. No: he would have done better to come to America. He was a brilliant man, and despite his unfortunate personality he could no doubt have made his way into a new life, forgetting his vendetta with the men who tyrannized his native Germany, breaking once for all with Engels.

Engels had written an angry account of the condition of the working class in England (although the English had not read his book, for it had been published only in Germany); he should come here, thought Adolph grimly, and see England all over again.

Forget Marx and his nasty tongue and his convoluted dialectics, said Adolph. Forget them all. They were the past.

The family settled in. Adolph began to whip the orchestra into a semblance of harmony. He advertised for pupils and by Thanksgiving had acquired five, including a lank young pharmacist who aspired to the Beautiful and whose fingers clutched the violin and bow as if they were mortar and pestle. Klaus opened his modest studio and slowly, as his customers gossiped to their friends, built up a small trade. Anna was relieved to be done with searching for a home; she had no time to regret the past. Jutta wept for two weeks and then obtained a job as a folder in the printing establishment of Ayer's Almanac. It was a position for which one did not need to know good English, and it paid two dollars a week. Of this sum she gave half to Anna and kept half for herself, and every night she cried herself to sleep at the thought of a refined and cultivated young woman (for so she was), the daughter of a Professor of Music, fallen on times as hard as these, forced to labor like any common girl.

By Thanksgiving, too, it became apparent that if the little ones were to succeed in school—as they must—they needed more help in learning English than Klaus could give them. And Anna needed some assistance with the children and all the housework.

Adolph turned to the helpful Gage. Might there be someone—a nursemaid, a companion, call it what you like—who could help not only with the running of the household but also with the problems of the language? Who could speak with them all and correct their pronunciation, and read to them and hear them read in turn, and generally assist them in mastering this difficult tongue?

Gage bethought himself. He liked this intense, stocky man whose fringe of graying hair around his bald pate made him look like a tonsured monk. But surely no monk had such a moustache—or such an imperious temper! Gage did not mind Hartmann's temper; the man had produced a decent sound from the orchestra, and nothing mattered more than that. The musicians liked him, too: they respected his knowledge, they were pleased to play so well.

He would inquire, he said. A few years back, of course, there had been a swarm of bluestockings on the Corporations, many of whom would have been glad to exchange their place at a loom for that of tutor. A dollar a week and board—and instruction in German? Certainly there must be someone. Had Herr Professor noticed the large blonde lady who frequently sat fourth row center? She often wore a purple bonnet. She knew everyone in Lowell, it seemed, through her acquaintance with the late poetess Wethertbee. Despite her regular attendance at the theater, she was universally regarded as a good Christian woman. She was reputed to be most charitable. Undoubtedly she would know of some worthy female—

"*Kultiviert,*" said Adolph. "She must speak good." He grinned. "And not to mind a kindergarten, eh?"

3

In the crowded children's bedroom of the Hartmanns' apartment Sabra leaned close in to the small mirror to smooth her hair, badly mussed during the exuberant bedtime embraces which she had just endured. She saw a gray hair—two, three. Not gray but white. She stared at herself. You are thirty-one years old, she thought; your life has had some bad times—almost unendurable times. Her hazel eyes were clear and bright, her skin still fine and smooth. She had been pretty once; she was pretty still, if you discounted those silvering strands. Certainly Klaus had not been put off by them. She touched the cheap silver brooch at her throat. He had given it to her at Christmas; an embarrassing moment, at first, and then, because he was so kind, so courtly in the European way, not embarrassing at all. He was fond of her; that had been obvious from the moment they met. His eyes had followed her; he seemed constantly to be inventing excuses to speak to her. She realized that she had forgotten how comforting—how enjoyable—a man's admiration could be.

Behind her, in the big bed, she saw the four flaxen-haired moppets who lay watching her, their round blue eyes wide with admiration, their chubby red cheeks glowing on the spotless white pillowcases. They were in awe of the American Frau Blood—how kind she was, how patient!—and they refused to go to sleep until she had gone. Then, of course, they would not go to sleep either: they would giggle in the dark, and whisper to each other in their familiar mother-tongue which was forbidden during the day; inevitably they would begin a pillow-fight. Then Mutter would appear, or perhaps Klaus, and scold and spank and helplessly laugh at all their inability to express themselves, to give the full range of their feelings in English. Then they would beg Clara for a story. From her cot next to the wall she would perhaps oblige, and she would tell them a fairy tale by the wonderful Grimms, sounding so strange, so exotic in this new language; or perhaps a story about the Pilgrims, or General Washington: they were very fond of military tales. Sometimes she would fall asleep at the most exciting part, but the children, because they loved her almost as much as they loved her mother, would not awaken her; they would whisper a little longer among themselves, and then, despite their most strenuous efforts, one by one they would fall asleep.

Sabra crossed to Clara's cot, bent swiftly to embrace her, whispered a private "good night," and turned to the quartet in the big bed. Really, they looked like the little angels they were, she thought; and the baby, Elisabetta, just three months old, asleep in her basket in her mother's room, was the sweetest of all. Quickly she kissed each high, shining little forehead; she beamed at them as she pulled the down-filled comforter firmly under their chins.

"Sleep at once!" she commanded with mock ferocity. "If Klaus or your mother must come to quiet you, I will not take you to Fort Hill tomorrow."

"Yes, Tante Sabra," they warbled. Wolfgang could not suppress a grin. "You are wearing Klaus' present," he said. "That means you like him!"

"I like you all. Now to sleep!"

"Where are you going, Tante Sabra?"

"To see a friend. But I have sharp ears. If any one of you makes a noise I will know it."

"Your ears are not sharp. They are soft. And they are covered by your hair."

She heard Clara giggle. She was grateful to Wolfgang for amusing Clara, for loving her—"Good night!"

She opened the window the prescribed two inches—Adolph Hartmann was very strict about that—and, closing the door behind her, went into the dining room where the older members of the family were finishing their supper. In the absence of his father, Klaus sat at the head of the table opposite his step-mother. He was a handsome young man of twenty-six, the only one of them all to have inherited Adolph's dark hair. In the manner of his countrymen, he seemed the dashing hero of a romantic novel with his full moustache descending nearly to his chin, his soft felt Kossuth hat adorned with a feather in the band, his flowing short cape, his exotically accented English. As he strode down Merrimack Street of an evening, he seemed extraordinarily out of place; he belonged to a land of castles and old walled cities and an ancient aristocracy.

At his left sat his sister Jutta, who had only just arrived home from the Ayer printing establishment. Her plain face had settled into a sharply etched portrait of fatigue and discontent. Sabra pitied Jutta, but she found her impossible to like. Frau Hartmann sat opposite Klaus at the far end of the table, happiest now as always in the evening when another day had been survived without disaster, when she had seen her family fed, when she knew that her husband would return safe in a few hours' time, unthreatened by arrest, having earned a few precious dollars more by his work as the director of the theatrical orchestra. They all gazed admiringly at Sabra and greeted her with affection.

"Come, sit, have coffee before you go," said Frau Hartmann. She poured a fresh cup and motioned to an empty chair beside her. She was a sturdy blonde woman of thirty-five, once beautiful in the Nordic way, now attractive still, dressed in a blue bodice which brought out the fading color of her eyes. Her face showed the struggle which her life had been, but the past year in America had smoothed the lines drawn by fear and hunger and had stilled the restless blinking of her eyes. No longer did she see in every stranger an informer for the Prussian secret police; no longer did she give way to frightened tears if her husband returned a half-hour late from his work.

A short while later, Sabra took her bonnet and shawl and went out. Her destination was a storefront three buildings away, which had been in succession a milliner's shop, a stationer's, a confectioner's, and, for the past six months, the salon of a seeress who called herself Madame Jewel but whose real name (as she confided to Sabra) was Abby Smith. She had been on the Lawrence Corporation until an attack of consumption had so weakened her lungs that she had been forced to resign. She had always had, she said, a second sight; at the boarding house where she had lived she had often amused the girls with palm-reading and the analysis of tea leaves. The sensational success of the Fox sisters had encouraged her to try her luck, and so, after recuperating in her country home, she had returned to the city and rented the storefront where she now presided six evenings a week. Her talent was prophecy, although on several occasions she had accomplished an extremely effective communication with the Beyond.

The night was cold and clear; wind whipped at Sabra's dress and stung her eyes. She shuddered with memory rather than the cold: on such nights, once upon a time, she had prowled the streets like a foraging animal. The same stars were in the heavens then as now; the same river flowed endlessly to the sea; the same heart beat in her breast—and yet how her life had changed! She had been saved, been given hope, purpose, friends—and surely, surely all would come right. She had been rescued from the Acre; been given respite at Mrs. Wethertbee's; rescued again from the drudgery of stamp cutting, the danger to her sight averted. Her eyes no longer troubled her; she and her child were healthy and safe. The Hartmanns' optimism was contagious. To reinforce it, she had given her hand to Madame Jewel to read and had heard only favorable predictions: a new life, new friends, money. Ah, let it come true!

4

On the red velvet cloth covering the table was an astral lamp turned low. Madame Jewel, attired in black with a circlet of gold beads like a crown upon her head, sat with her client. Their faces were above the light so that Sabra saw only their hands, resting on the table. Madame Jewel did not speak when Sabra entered, but motioned her to an empty chair.

What Nature had omitted, Artifice had supplied in Madame Jewel's appearance. Born plain and four-square, she had disguised her features with a quantity of powder and rouge and charcoal pencil to her eyebrows. The result vaguely suggested the desired gypsy look without altogether eradicating the evidence of her Anglo-Saxon heritage. She looked sufficiently exotic for her purposes, however; her clients never saw her in full daylight, and had they passed her on Central Street of a morning on their way to market they would not have recognized her.

She folded her hands before her and closed her eyes in silent communion with her spiritual mentors. Although she insisted that all her clients remain anonymous, she frequently knew their names; perhaps some of them knew hers also. But this new one—arriving unannounced last Wednesday night with a demand for private consultation—was a mystery. She wore a sable cloak; from the narrow brim of her silk bonnet a heavy veil descended to her chin. Her apparent affluence had heartened Madame Jewel, whose ambition it was to acquire an exclusively wealthy clientele.

Madame Jewel cleared her throat and at that signal the woman stirred and leaned forward.

"Please," said Madame Jewel. Her voice was low and naturally husky, a fact which made no little contribution to her success. "Let me see your hands."

The woman fumbled as she removed her gloves; her hands trembled as she put them, palms up, on the red cloth. They were neither so soft nor so white as might have been expected, but her gold wedding band was wide and heavy, in keeping with the richness of her costume.

Madame Jewel studied the critical lines; after a moment she took the hands in her own.

"I thought—" The woman's voice was shrill and startlingly loud. "I understood that this was to be a private consultation."

"This is my good friend," said Madame Jewel soothingly. "Her spirit is highly attuned to my own. Frequently I ask her to be with me when I am to have a special audience. She is discreet: you need fear nothing."

The woman twitched her fingers, shrugged in what they took as a gesture of assent.

"Now tell me," said Madame Jewel. "Your problem is of the heart?"

"Yes. Well, no, not exactly—"

"Your husband—?"

"Yes."

Madame Jewel studied the hands; Sabra studied Madame Jewel. It could not be denied by the most severe skeptic—Klaus Hartmann, for example—that this woman possessed some power, some perception which enabled her to see, to sense more than most.

"There is a weakness," said Madame Jewel. She spoke more slowly now; her voice was hoarse and slightly slurred. "Or perhaps it is not a weakness. Perhaps it is a void, a lack, a place empty which should be filled. Is that correct?"

"Yes."

"So." Madame Jewel held the hands lightly, tenderly, oblivious to everything except what they told her. "This emptiness is the cause of the trouble."

"Yes."

"It is not your fault."

"No."

"But you suffer the consequences."

"Yes."

There was a long pause. Sabra heard nothing except the hissing lamp, an occasional carriage passing in the street. She saw nothing except the dim circle of light upon the red cloth, two pairs of hands, strangely disembodied, lying one in the other. She felt suddenly faint. She blinked and moved slightly in her chair. Despite the tight-closed door, she felt—what? Who had come?

"I see a separation. Yes. A parting. But it is very small, very far away. You are in darkness. You are—no, I cannot see where. I see only that you are in distress."

A pause. The woman's hands had begun to tremble again. Sabra watched their small involuntary movements.

"You will survive in good health," said Madame Jewel. "But I cannot see where you will be, or in what circumstances."

Sabra's eyes clung to the light. She felt the new presence in the room. Who had come? She strained to see, to hear. Madame Jewel spoke again, but Sabra did not understand the words. She heard her own voice instead, silent in her mind.

Come, she cried: speak to me and I will hear. She felt suddenly overpowered by her longing. Come: I wait for you, I have waited all the years. She felt her body shaken as if by fever; she heard Madame Jewel's voice go on, unintelligible still.

O God. O Silas. Come back to me.

And then it was gone as suddenly as it had come, and she sat once again an observer to the two women before her, her vision already only a troubled memory rapidly fading.

After a moment she thought: I was mistaken. It did not happen.

And in that instant she knew that it had. He had stood behind her; she had needed only to turn slightly in her chair to see him. If she had looked back toward the darkened corner of the room, he would have been there, waiting for her. She knew it as well as she knew her own presence now, waiting for Madame Jewel to finish.

Too late: he had come and now he was gone.

Madame Jewel withdrew her hands; she sat limp in her chair. Her client remained leaning over the table in an attitude of supplication; then she too relaxed somewhat and folded her hands in her lap. A shudder passed through the seeress' body. Her eyes focused upon their faces. She turned up the lamp. Still no one spoke.

"Is that all?" said the woman after a moment. Her face was still hidden by her veil, but her voice betrayed her annoyance.

"I can tell you only what I see," said Madame Jewel.

"But it was nothing—no help at all! I came for advice—"

"It is only the second time. If you could come back—"

"I must learn something that may help me." The woman's voice quavered. "I am in desperate need. I trusted you, I had been given to understand that you are an honest person."

"So I am. That is why you are disappointed, perhaps. I could tell you a great deal, a fiction manufactured especially for you, but I am not like some of the others."

The woman made no reply. She seemed to be studying Madame Jewel. Then she took several coins from her reticule and laid them on the table. She stood up; again she hesitated as if she would speak, but then, without a word, she turned and went out. Sabra felt the cold blast of air as she opened and shut the door. She turned an amused glance upon her friend.

"You will never get a clientele at that rate, Abby."

Miss Smith shrugged her heavy shoulders. Her painted face sagged; her eyes were puzzled. "What did I say?"

"That you saw her alone, dim, far away—"

The seeress shook her head. "Poor woman. So desperate. Like all of them."

"You thrive on desperation."

"Yes. Yes. And sometimes—sometimes I do help them. You know that I do."

Sabra leaned over and patted her friend's arm. "You do your best. And as you say, you are honest."

Madame Jewel put her hand over Sabra's. They sat quiet for a moment. Then: "What is wrong, Sabra?"

"Nothing."

"Yes. I feel it. Some trouble—something that worries you."

"No."

"Something is about to happen."

Sabra shook her head. She withdrew her hand. She did not want to know. She would deal with it when it came. Madame Jewel understood; she did not pursue her intuition.

"Come and have a cup of tea, then," she said, "and tell me about those little Dutchmen you take care of all day. I can't understand"—for here Madame Jewel's intuition failed her—"how you stay sane."

They gossiped for a long time; it was past ten when Sabra closed the door of the little storefront and hurried back to the Hartmanns'. She knew that everyone there would be asleep; a lamp would be burning for Adolph upon his return from the theater. Frau Hartmann, like her husband, was an advocate of physical fitness. An early bedtime was an indispensable part of it. She tolerated Sabra's occasional late nights because she understood that native Americans, like everyone else in the world, had not the German discipline in such matters; but she never failed to observe, the following morning, the shadows under Sabra's eyes or the slowness of her movements.

Sabra hurried up the stairs to the apartment. The lamp glowed on the parlor table, and in its light she saw that Klaus stood by the window. Had he been watching her as she hurried down the street? He turned as she came in, but instead of his accustomed smile, she saw that his face was somber. Even so, he was a beautiful young man—tall and well-made, a high brow, straight nose, full firm mouth, strongly angled cheekbones accented by his flowing moustache.

She unwound her shawl and dropped it on a side chair; she untied the strings of her bonnet and took it off. Still he did not speak, or move toward her, and his silence, his immobility, warned her more than any action could have done. Not for the first time, she wondered whether he had ever loved a woman, or whether any impressionable young girl had ever loved him. He was the type of young man who might break many a fragile feminine heart, for he was charming as well as handsome, and a glance of his long-lashed eyes would have been quite enough, she knew, to have turned her own head once upon a time. She was five years older than he, but even now, she thought, were I a different person, had I lived a different life, I might be weak enough, rash enough—

"And how is your friend Madame Jewel tonight?" he said at last.

"Very well. She has a new client who seems to have some money." She heard her voice: bright and cheerful, entirely impersonal.

"I am sure that Madame Jewel will be able to tell her how to spend it."

"Or save it, perhaps."

He came toward her into the stronger light. He looked tired and troubled. They heard a church bell toll the half-hour. Soon Adolph would be home from his evening's work. Frau Hartmann would get up, perhaps, as she often did, to fix him an egg or a cup of chocolate. She would listen to him as he related the evening's events, the actors' shortcomings, or, occasionally, someone's unexpectedly good performance.

Klaus spoke suddenly, startling her. "MacKenzie wants to leave."

She needed to think for a moment before she understood. Then she remembered: MacKenzie was Klaus' journalist friend, a dark and glowering Scot, an abolitionist as fervent as Garrison himself, whose political views were equally unpopular and whose newspaper, in consequence, had only a minuscule circulation. MacKenzie was sole proprietor of the *Morning Chronicle;* he owned it, wrote it, printed it, and distributed it. In his spare time he sold advertising space. It had been Klaus' dearest wish for some months past to help MacKenzie in his enterprise, and in fact he had written several items whose use of English had been astonishingly good. MacKenzie had not been able to afford to pay, but such matters were of small importance to two ardent fighters (as they saw themselves) in the cause of freedom.

"He is going to Kansas," continued Klaus. "It is important to settle the Kansas territory with Northerners, but it is important, too, to keep the *Chronicle* here. He will not go if he must give it up. But if I can run it for him, printing all the anti-slavery news—"

She felt a great tiredness descend upon her. She sank onto the sofa. Her fatigue seemed to spread from her brain through her body and down into her limbs. Had the tenement been in flames, she could not have risen to flee.

"Sabra? What is wrong?"

There had once been a foolhardy young woman who had wanted also to free the poor souls enslaved at the South; and an even more foolish girl who had consented to help her. Would this earnest young man like to hear their story, she wondered.

"Sabra, do not look so! I told you, I am not leaving, I will stay here." His face had come alive with joy. He sat beside her and clasped her hands; still entangled in her clinging net of memory, she was hardly aware of what he did.

The night had been dark—no moon, no stars—and the wind had blown like a fury, and the terrified passengers with whom she had shared the carriage had been hardly more frightened than she. Rachel had worn boys' clothes. And Rachel's father had taken his revenge for their transgressions.

"Sabra?"

She came back to him. She realized that he still held her hands, that he looked at her with concern, with—what? Affection? No: more than that.

"What is it, Sabra? You look—I don't know the word. Are you sad? Have I said something to make you sad?"

She contemplated him: such a beautiful young man. He radiated health, energy, intelligence—ah, why was he so taken with MacKenzie? Why could he not simply make his way in his adopted land as did so many others? Why agitate, why devote his life to a hopeless cause?

For it was hopeless to believe that the South would free the blacks, just as it was hopeless to believe that the North would allow the South to secede.

"No," she said at last. "No. I—I remembered something that I had forgotten, that is all. If Mr. MacKenzie wants to turn his newspaper over to you, and if you are happy, then I am happy for you."

"I can make a success of it, Sabra. I am sure that I can. MacKenzie is a fine man, but he has no business sense. He will do better in Kansas. But I can put out a newspaper that people will read—nothing dull, but simply printing the truth. And the truth must be told. This is a city that supports the Southern position. The other side is never heard. That is why MacKenzie came here. I must continue his work when he goes."

O God, she thought. Let him stop.

"I am sorry," he said; the light in his eyes dimmed. "You are not interested in politics. I thought—"

"I am tired," she said. "Only that."

"You are right, perhaps, not to care. No—I don't mean that. Everyone must care. There is no question more important. Except—"

Suddenly he raised her hands to his lips. She felt the soft warm pressure of his mouth upon her skin, the brush of his moustache—and then, before she could react and pull away, they heard Adolph's step upon the stairs. As he pushed open the door, he took them in with one swift and penetrating glance. "*Guten Abend,* children!" He put his hat and his violin case gently on the table and walked to the fire to warm himself.

Sabra stood up. "Let Anna sleep," she said. "I will fix your chocolate."

"*Nein*—no, I don't want it," said Adolph. "I had beer with Gage." He smiled at her. Like all his family, he was fond of her, and deeply grateful that she had stayed on to help them despite the fact that there were many weeks when her salary was not forthcoming. He had suspected for some time now that his eldest son was growing daily more devoted to her. He had wanted Klaus to marry a woman with some money. "Go to sleep," he said. "It is late. You also, Klaus. I will sit for a while and try to read." The newest issue of *The North American Review* lay on the table underneath the violin case. Every month, Adolph persevered until he had read it through; but each page was a hard contest between him and the English language, and he liked to be alone while he struggled. As his skill improved, he had been humiliated to discover that *The North American Review* disliked the recent German immigrants—the "forty-eighters" —as much as it disliked the far more numerous Irish. It disapproved of the Germans because they were "irreligious": they organized freethinker societies, they denounced the blue laws, they celebrated Thomas Paine's birthday. Not least, they wanted to drink beer in public on the Sabbath. On the other hand, it disapproved of the Irish because they were devout —but at the wrong altar. Adolph sighed. He would have to find another publication on which to practice: this one depressed him, it made him never want to read another word of English.

Sabra obeyed his order, glad that her uncomfortable interview with Klaus had been so abruptly ended. She looked in on the children before she retired to the room which she shared with Jutta. The four little Hartmanns lay scattered across the bed, covers kicked off, arms and legs entangled, Franz loudly sucking his thumb, Ludwig hanging off the edge. Gently she pulled them straight and drew the comforter up to their chins. Then she turned to Clara, who, alone on her cot, lay straight and still, hardly rumpling the quilt. In the dim light, Sabra could not see her daughter's expression; but she seems a happy enough child, she thought. If she were not, surely I would know as I watch her sleep. Surely she would cry out in her dreams, or grind her teeth, or toss and turn restlessly all the night.

O Clara, she thought, we are not badly off here. They are kind, and as generous as they can afford. God knows we have been worse off, you and I. She felt again the pressure of Klaus' lips on her hand. I must tell him, she thought; I must explain to him that I wait for Silas.

Klaus is beginning to love you, said the voice in her mind. He is a fine young man.

Be quiet. Let me think.

As she drifted into sleep a short time later it was not Klaus who invaded her dreams, but the tall, ungainly figure of the father of her child; and she dreamed all night, it seemed, unable to escape him, still bound to him: still waiting.

5

Clara loved all the Hartmanns, but she would have loved them more had they not all been so tightly packed into the small apartment. Many days, trying to find a quiet corner in which to finish her lessons, or weep over Mrs. Stowe's saga of Uncle Tom and Little Eva, she wished that her mother had never met Adolph Hartmann, had never agreed to live with his family. The winter just past had been the worst time: even the Hartmanns, sturdy and outdoor-minded as they were, ardent advocates of physical culture, fresh air, exercise—even they had finally given up in the face of the foul, damp New England cold, and had retreated indoors until the return of milder weather in the spring. All the cold months they had endured each other in their cramped quarters, tempers growing short, made frantic by confinement; now, as April and May advanced, they relaxed in the warm sun, they ran downstairs and out of doors to the banks of the Concord River flowing almost under their windows, they went gladly with Sabra as she shepherded them to the North Common, to Belvidere Hill, to Fort Hill. Jutta complained that she had only Sundays free to join them. Clara felt sorry for her. She was so obviously unhappy, so obviously homesick and lonely. But when Clara tried to talk to Jutta, she came up against the language, for Jutta refused to learn more than a minimum of English. She knew a few handy phrases, as a traveler might learn enough to get herself through a week's tour in a strange land, and her refusal to learn more implied that she would not stay; Clara was sure that of all the Hartmanns, Jutta was the one who would return to Germany.

Clara knew where Germany was, for Adolph had showed her a map of Europe, and had pointed out his native city. She would have liked to go there, for all she knew that the Hartmanns had had to flee. But now, safely away, they seemed to hold no rancor; they told her of the majestic course of the Rhine, which, they said, made the Merrimack seem a mere rivulet; they told her of the castles, and the terraced vineyards, and the great cathedrals—the greatest of all in their native city, Cologne; with tears in their eyes they reminisced about the warm-hearted people, the lebkuchen and sausages, the Christmas celebrations, the music.

Ah, the music! In the emptiness, the dislocation of their lives, it was music which brought courage to their hearts and peace to their troubled souls. Every Sunday evening Adolph would play to them, and Jutta and Frau Hartmann would sing lieder, and the children would sing kinderlieder. They could not believe that most Americans knew nothing of music—nothing, that is, of the only music worth hearing, which was that of the Bachs and Buxtehude, of Mozart and Beethoven and Haydn. In America, music meant "Yankee Doodle" and a parade march, or off-key hymns sung once or twice a week at church.

They had learned that this was a land of many sounds: the jingle of coins in the cash box, the clacking of railway carriages over miles of new-laid track, the peal of church bells and factory bells, the rumble and thump of machinery in the mills, the sharp tattoo of the drum as militia companies drilled, the harsh voices of men in angry, bitter political debate. And underneath it all, unheard save in the tenderest hearts, heard there to the exclusion of every other sound, was the agonized and never-ending cry welling up from the South—a cry of pain torn from the throats of black slaves to echo through the souls of white folk, and fester there, and never give peace.

As much as Clara enjoyed the musical evenings, she enjoyed more accompanying Adolph to the afternoon rehearsals at the theater. Often, afterward, he asked her opinion of the play. Invariably she liked it. At ten, she was too young to have developed any discrimination; she was enthralled simply by the costumes, the music, the ability of half a dozen quite ordinary-looking people to go up onto the stage of the shabby little theater and suddenly create a world far more enchanting than that in which she lived. Watching them, she forgot her life: the unmemorized table of eights, the unparsed sentences, the hours of sewing to make a new petticoat. Forgot, and entered that grand, make-believe place of sound and light and thrilling emotion.

The program changed weekly. The resident troupe was expanded—enhanced—by visitors as the occasion demanded. Adolph had ten men in his orchestra. He got an amazing amount of noise out of them, and he never failed to please the singers with his promptness on cue. One week in late May the company undertook a new drama of love lost and found, *The Bridegroom's Dilemma.* Clara, watching the rehearsal, had been unable to follow all the complications of the plot, but one strand of it had particularly struck her. This was the moment when the bride, performed enchantingly by the resident leading lady, Miss MacNaughton, had been confronted on the eve of her wedding by her long-lost father—a meeting which, occurring in the first act, had occasioned a number of heart-rending complications in the succeeding two.

Miss MacNaughton was thirty-five at the very least; her breath often smelled of whisky, and her voice often lapsed harshly into her native Scots burr; but in that moment of recognition she summoned up all her talent, such as it was, and, sublimely virginal, sublimely innocent, brought tears to the eyes of the hardened stagehands, the bored orchestra members—and certainly to Clara's eyes—as she confronted the paternal cad. Clara had been fascinated: would such a confrontation be the same, she wondered, in real life? Was that sobbing, shattered, repentant man a true representative of all missing fathers everywhere?

She had never questioned the absence of her own father. Many children, she knew, had only one parent. She remembered Mr. Wethertbee. He had been very kind, and she had cried when they had said good-by. But now, having seen the emotions produced onstage and off by the rehearsal of *The Bridegroom's Dilemma,* she began to brood about her situation, and to wonder if it was perhaps through some fault of her own that her father had never appeared, so to speak, in their own little drama.

She asked her mother about him. Sabra's face had remained calm as she explained: your father went away, she said, to do a very important work in the world. When he has done it, he will come back to us. They sat on the bank of the Concord River. It was a warm evening in the first week of June. On the main thoroughfares of the city, crowds of operatives thronged the shops; in the boarding houses, women finished their suppers and gossiped in the parlors. But the patrons of the shops were not so genteel now, in 1854, as they had been ten or twenty years previous; the inhabitants of the boarding houses were permanent boarders now, having no country homes to return to; and in the shops and in the parlors the careless laughter of young women was somewhat more raucous than it had been in years past, and their speech carried a distinctive brogue; and any young Yankee woman on a lonely upcountry farm who wanted to escape her solitary life would not think of coming to the factory towns, for to go to work in a textile factory, now, was to ruin one's reputation—to lose one's middle-class standing, and so throw away one's chance to marry well or even to marry at all.

Clara watched the dark water of the river flowing at her feet; if she lifted her eyes, she could see, beyond the spires and rooftops of the city, the salmon-colored western sky. She saw the evening star; she closed her eyes and concentrated all her thoughts down to the one fine point of her wish—her sudden longing. *Let him come. Please let him come back to us.*

She felt her mother's arm slip around her shoulders. She leaned her head against her mother's bosom; she heard the steady beating of the heart within. Although she had no memory of her father, she could not remember a time when her mother had not been with her. Her earliest recollections were confused and dark. She had a dim and fast-fading vision of endless walking, and her mother speaking to strangers, and a crowded, filthy alley where pigs and chickens rooted in the mud, and a pallet on a dirt floor in a fetid room. She did not know why she remembered these things, for they fitted with nothing else that she knew: the

Wethertbees', the rooming house where she and her mother had lived before coming to the Hartmanns'.

"Mama?"

"Yes, love."

"Where will we go when we leave Adolph and Frau Hartmann?"

"Are we leaving?"

"Won't we, some day?"

Sabra sighed; the child felt and understood the slight movement. "I suppose so," she said slowly. "But not for a long time." It was an inadequate answer, but she had no other to give.

Later, after they had walked home and Clara had gone to bed, Sabra sat in the parlor with Anna and sewed ruching on a new summer bodice for the child while she listened to Anna read aloud for pronunciation. Anna had an easy time of it, this night, for Sabra's thoughts were preoccupied with her daughter's questions. The wonder is, she thought, that she has not asked about him before. She is an intelligent child, she must have wondered about our situation many times. What would she say to him if he suddenly appeared? What would he say to her? Would she, Sabra, be able to go with him and live as his wife? What if he did not want her? What if he wanted only his child?

She uttered a small cry as suddenly she started, stabbing her finger. A drop of blood appeared, and then another. She sucked it clean, hardly aware of the small sting of pain.

He would not return—never. But if he did, he could return only to claim Clara. He could take her away. He had every legal right to do so. She could not prevent it. Dear God—surely he would not be so cruel.

But why not, said the voice in her mind. He has been cruel—monstrously selfish—all these years, leaving you alone to survive as you will. This new cruelty would be no surprise.

She realized that Anna had stopped reading, and was staring at her with concern. Sabra forced a smile to reassure her. "Go on," she said. "I have only just pricked my finger. Do go on. You are reading very well."

But she could not free herself of the new fears that Clara's questions had aroused. All during the next day, and the day after that, she worried and agonized and told herself over and over again that she had been a fool not to have considered this possibility—this threat of losing her child, one day, to a man who might turn up all of a sudden and vanish again just as quickly, taking Clara with him with the full approval of the law.

She said a new prayer, then: let him stay away, let him never come back.

And then one oppressively warm and humid morning her fear was for a time driven from her. As she walked home from the market-house, her large wicker basket heavy on her arm, she turned the Central Street corner and almost collided with a woman hurrying down Merrimack

Street. Sabra stopped to apologize; the woman, hardly pausing, glanced at her and muttered a word or two as she continued on her way.

She was a tall, plainly dressed woman perhaps a year or two older than Sabra; she moved with an air of purpose, an assurance of her place in the world, that one saw usually in men. Her face, swiftly glimpsed under the brim of her dark blue bonnet, was striking not so much for the handsome arrangement of its features, as for the firm set of the well-shaped mouth, the direct gaze of the deep-set eyes. Most women did not look so; most women would not have wanted to look so, for this was unquestionably a strong-minded female—a she-lecturer, perhaps, or, despite the fact that her skirts swept the boardwalk in thoroughly acceptable fashion, a disciple of the unlamented Bloomerite craze.

Sabra stood quite still. She watched the woman wait at the corner to cross. Surely I am not mistaken, she thought. She stared at the back of the bonnet, willing its wearer to turn to face her. She felt the perspiration trickle down her arms. All around her rose the noise of the traffic, the smell of horses and chemicals and soot which formed the particular odor of this bustling, thriving town. She was oblivious to everything except that commanding figure. Look at me, she thought. The traffic slowed; the small cluster of pedestrians scurried across. The woman was not among them. As if in response to Sabra's unseen stare, she turned back; and now her face was no longer so assured, her eyes were puzzled and wondering, her mouth half-open in astonishment. And—yes—great joy.

Still she hesitated; still she was not sure. She walked back. She paused. Sabra waited for her. She met her eyes. Then recognition flared between them, and with a half-choked cry the woman rushed to embrace her. Sabra allowed herself to be enfolded; she stood as still as a stone, she felt the years vanish as if by magic, and once again she was a poor child brought home on Josiah Bradshaw's whim, and Rachel stood in the lighted doorway to welcome her, and take her in, and use her as she saw fit.

6

"But of course you must let her come with me. She must see something of the world, she is not too young to begin. And to think that she is Silas Blood's daughter—why, Sabra, you know how dear Silas was to all of us, you cannot keep his child from me."

From a footstool at her mother's side, Clara watched the visitor cautiously and tried to understand, not what she said, for that was plain and forceful enough, but why. Why did this elegant, voluble, energetic woman want to take her away? Why did her mother say "No"? Why did they not let her speak for herself?—for several times she had tugged excitedly at her mother's skirts, only to be rebuffed, and she did not think that she could remain quiet much longer. To go away! To travel in the company of this fascinating stranger!

"Perhaps she is too young," said Klaus. He had come in late to meet the visitor, but he had seen the look of concern on Sabra's face, and because he was of all the Hartmanns the most fluent in English, he had caught at once the drift of the conversation. "Perhaps in a year or two?"

"New-York," said Adolph. He shook his head. "It was not a good place for us. For you—" He shrugged.

"O, but it is a good place," said Rachel quickly. She smile around at them, including them all in her reassurance. She was used to having people resist her ideas. At first. Generally she brought them around. Even the New York legislature, after three years of hearing her testimony in the matter of the divorce bill, was beginning to listen, to give in. Accustomed to facing such monumental obstacles to human happiness as the judiciary committee in Albany, she thought of this small assemblage as no impediment at all. "It is an interesting place—much more exciting than this, or even Boston."

"I cannot let her go," said Sabra. She heard the astonishment in her voice. How could anyone think that she would ever part with her child? "You are very kind to offer, Rachel, but—no. It is impossible." She reached down as if for reassurance and laid her hand on Clara's dark hair, as much to quiet her as to show affection. Although the child squirmed with excitement, Sabra had no intention of letting her join the discussion.

Sabra did not know whether to laugh or cry. How like Rachel Bradshaw, suddenly to appear after how many years—fifteen? was it possible?—and at once demand to have her way! She had always been so: strong-willed, determined, careless of other people's feelings. She had spoken briefly of her life, and, at greater length, of the issues to which she devoted it: abolition, temperance, women's suffrage, dress reform. She had long since given up her position as instructress at Mrs. Hallowell's Female Seminary; she had no time for it, she said, but then, laughing, she had confessed that Mrs. Hallowell had dismissed her. "She was outraged when I slipped out one night to hear Mr. Garrison. Many of her young ladies came from the border states, and of course it would not do for her to have an abolitionist on her staff."

She had come to Lowell to attend her sister Lydia's wedding, which was to be held three days hence. As she had confided privately to Sabra, she had been reluctant at first to return to her father's house: "He banished me like a heretic—which of course I was, and foolish and ignorant, too. Do you know, Sabra, that I made a complete ninny of myself at the first Women's Anti-Slavery Convention that I attended? I told Mrs. Kelley that in the space of a year—two at most—we would no longer be needed, for as soon as we told everyone how great a wrong slavery is, the slaves would be freed instantly. It needed only for us to speak and our wish would be granted. That was twelve—no, thirteen years ago. And since that time, public interest has almost completely died. We must thank Senator Douglas for reviving it. In his eagerness to get a railway terminus at Chicago, he has offered up the territory of Kansas like a piece of bloody meat to be fought over by a pack of wolves. I'd go to Kansas myself if I were a man. O, how I wish I could vote! They have no right—Sabra?"

For Sabra had stopped listening to the sense of the words; she heard the tone of the voice only: excited, passionate, buoyed up by boundless energy. It has been my fate, she thought, to fall among fanatics: Rachel, and Silas, and now Klaus with his anti-slavery newspaper. Yes, and Julia Wethertbee, too, was a fanatic in her way. And John Prince. Most certainly John Prince. They come and go; they catch me up as a leaf is caught in the whirlwind, and then they go on, they vanish and leave me here behind to live my life. A single human life means nothing to them. They are concerned with all humanity; they cannot be bothered with individuals. Finally, feeling the need to say something—anything—she ventured an opinion: "You look very well, Rachel. Your work agrees with you."

Rachel smiled. Many men would gladly have bought that smile, had they remained blessedly ignorant of what lay behind it. Although she was now middle-aged—thirty-four years old—Rachel Bradshaw bloomed like the girl Sabra once had known. Her pale skin was unlined, fresh and glowing with good health; her full lips were as red, her eyes as sparkling as those of the girl who had welcomed Sabra into the Bradshaw household. Sabra feared that she herself looked older than Rachel, although she was two years younger; but then, she thought bitterly, I have had a considerably more difficult life. She was aware that Rachel was speaking again, but she hardly heard. She sat limply in her chair and allowed great waves of anger and recrimination to wash over her and then recede, leaving her body weak and her mind alive with bitter memory.

And yet she could not hate this woman; no more could she hate the river in flood, or the winter storm which swept down from the north, burying all in its path. One did not hate a force of Nature; one simply tried to withstand it.

But she had no words to tell Rachel of her feelings. Rachel exhausted her. And she had been wise, she thought, to say nothing, for she needed all her strength now to deal with Rachel's demand to take Clara away.

The Hartmanns, once recovered from their initial astonishment at a specimen of American womanhood heretofore unknown to them, gave Sabra their support. They were pleased to welcome her friend, but they sensed some strain, some awkwardness between the two women. They did not ask; they trusted Sabra to tell them in good time. But in the matter of Clara's going away—*nein, nein,* she was much too young.

Rachel appealed to Adolph. "Persuade her for me. Tell her how wonderful it would be for the child."

"*Nein, Fräulein.*" He smiled at her, but his eyes never lost their cool appraisal. Of them all, he liked her least. He had known them in Europe, these fanatics. He had been surprised to find that they thrived equally well on American soil. This native-born American woman's devotion to the cause of abolition would only inflame Klaus' own. No: Adolph did not like her. And besides, he loved Clara like a child of his own. There would be no taking her away.

From Lydia's wedding party, Rachel brought for the children a piece of heavy, white cake bursting with orange peel and nuts, golden raisins and currants. This was to be her last visit, for on the next day she was to return to New-York—alone, as she finally understood, but with a promise to return. As she explained to Sabra, "I had not realized how old Father looks, how tired he is. I have not seen him for nearly all the years since I went away. Were it not for Lydia, I'd not have seen him yet. And I won't hesitate to tell you that that dreadful woman and I do not get on. I can't imagine why poor Aunt Amalia let him marry her. But there—we've forgotten and forgiven, Father and I, and I've promised to come back to visit him soon again."

They sat at the windows of the Hartmanns' parlor overlooking East Merrimack Street. The long June day had darkened into twilight; the strip of bright sky in the west faded rapidly as they watched. Adolph was at the theater; the children were asleep; Anna and Jutta had remained in the kitchen after clearing away the supper, a tactful withdrawal for which Anna would expect no thanks, but which Jutta would chalk up in her personal accounts as one more indignity suffered in this hated refuge. No one knew where Klaus had gone; late the previous night, when word had been received on the telegraph of the fighting in Boston, he had gone at once to his newspaper office; and then, that afternoon, a boy had come to them with the message that he himself had gone to Boston.

Rachel had arrived after supper brandishing an issue of the Boston *Transcript*. "There!" she said triumphantly. "They've put up a grand fight against the slavecatchers, and still poor Burns is taken back in chains to his master. His master!" Her eyes flashed; her slender fingers gripped the rolled-up paper as if it were a club. "Three men were killed," she said. "A little war, right by Faneuil Hall. They dragged Burns to the wharf between two lines of militia. The people fought to reach him; they did not let him go quietly. They know, now, that Mr. Garrison has spoken the truth all these years. Almost twenty years ago, a Boston mob tried to kill him. Now they attack the slavecatchers. We have made some progress, after all."

And Klaus had gone there. Anna's face was pinched with worry. Although Klaus was not her own son, she loved him for Adolph's sake. She had not understood all of Rachel's news: there was some trouble about a *Neger*, some fighting for reasons that she did not comprehend. She knew only that Klaus had gone to where the trouble was. She watched Adolph across the table. His shoulders sagged; his eyes were haunted—frightened as she had seen them on a night in Germany six years ago and more, when the secret police hunted him and he had fled only moments before they burst in to search the house for him. This stranger seated with them now seemed to think it a wonderful thing that Klaus had rushed to the fighting. Anna sighed. Politics! Where in the world could they live at peace?

Klaus and the fugitive Burns were far from Rachel's thoughts as she sat now with Sabra in the comfortable darkness of the Hartmann parlor. They had not troubled to light the lamp, and as the twilight deepened into night they had felt more greatly at ease with each other; their talk flowed in the dark, their memories flooded up around them. Each shielded from reading the other's face, they drew close together as once they had been. Rachel Bradshaw was an intelligent woman. When she troubled to lower her eyes from the events on the great stage of the world, she was quite capable of understanding the feelings of people close around her. She understood now that she owed to Sabra more, perhaps, than could ever be repaid; but she knew that now, this night, before she returned to her life, she needed to make at least the effort to set the accounts straight between them. Had they sat in the light, she might not have had the courage to speak; but the darkness had loosened her tongue, and almost as if she spoke to herself, she said:

"They never told me where you had gone. I asked to see you, that next day—I begged to be allowed to speak to you—but they would not permit it. They would not tell me what had become of you. I think that Father would have killed me, that day, if he conveniently could have done so. I know that I killed a part of him. He never understood me; he does not understand me now. But he is older now, and I think that he is very lonely. And so he is willing to see me again, even if neither of us can speak of what is in our hearts. O, my poor girl—"

Sabra heard the rustle of Rachel's dress as she turned suddenly in her chair. Through the open windows the night wind came to cool their perspiring faces, for they were swathed in layers of fabric from neck to ankle and they had suffered in the heat of the day. And now she understood that she had misjudged Rachel, for Rachel was not now concerned with the black slave, or the rumseller, or the intolerable condition of women; if only for this brief time, she was intently concerned with herself, and of the wrong she had done, and of how to rid her conscience of the weight of it: and so she turned in her chair, and her voice came halting and harsh, and "O, my poor girl," she choked; "O, Sabra, what have you suffered because of me? Please tell me about your life, tell me how you have lived all these years! Help me to believe that it has not been so very bad for you, for all that Silas went away, and I cannot understand why he did so, I cannot understand how a gentleman born and brought up as he was could simply abandon you—o, Sabra, tell me that I did not send you down into slavery for helping me to rescue that mother and child!"

The wind blew colder now. Sabra's face was wet with tears and the wind chilled them on her skin; and yet she did not move to wipe them away, she sat as still as if she had been cast under a spell. She allowed Rachel's words to fall upon the surface of her mind like tiny bright pebbles thrown onto the smooth and placid surface of a forest pool. The pebbles fell deep, far down to the thick mud silted on the bottom; their ripples soon faded, but they had fallen all the same. Some of them were instantly covered; some of them lay exposed.

They heard a sudden commotion from a distant street: a firebell and its attendant clamor, the clatter of horses' hooves, of the wagons bearing hoses, the shouts of men and boys suddenly materializing out of the darkness where all had been silence a moment before. They ignored the noise; they did not look out to see the rising glow in the sky; and yet the incident had recalled them to themselves, it had brought them back from their dangerous contemplation of the past. Sabra felt as though she herself, just then, had been rescued. She took her handkerchief from the cuff of her sleeve and wiped away her tears. Then she stood up, ignoring the pale shape of Rachel's upturned, importunate face; she struck a light to the oil lamp on the table. After a moment, when her eyes had adjusted to its brightness, she said, quite calmly: "We have survived, Clara and I. That is all that matters. How we have done so is not important."

"But it is!" said Rachel. "It is! I must know—you must tell me! How you have lived, and where, and with whom—you cannot shut me out, Sabra! You have not even told me how you and Silas came to marry!"

Sabra shook her head. "It does not matter." Rachel was baffled and not a little angry. She was accustomed to having her own way; she was something of a bully in that regard, she knew that people liked to talk about themselves; and yet she understood that it was to be her punishment, perhaps, not to know.

But if she could not know what had happened in the past, she could venture a guess about the future. She had eyes to see, she had—after all—a woman's heart sensitive to the emotions of those around her. And so as she took her leave she wished Sabra well, and did not bear a grudge against her for her reticence, and promised soon to return—as soon as her multitude of political activities would allow. She kissed Sabra's cheek as she whispered a parting thought: "He is a splendid young man, that Klaus Hartmann," she said. "Be kind to him, for he loves you very much."

7

In July of that year—the year before "bleeding Kansas"—the fanatic, Garrison, harangued the crowd at an Independence Day rally in Framingham, in bloody Massachusetts, and for the edification of his audience put to the flame various pieces of paper on which were printed the Constitution of the United States; the fugitive slave law; the decision of Commissioner Loring to return to the South the runaway, Burns; and Judge Curtis' charge to the grand jury which handed down indictments of those involved in Burns' attempted rescue. This performance at Framingham, commented the Democratic *Advertiser*, "was the act of a silly fool." Klaus Hartmann printed Garrison's speech entire. The following night he suffered a long, jagged cut on his forehead as a gang of roughnecks stoned and shattered the windows of his small office on Central Street. Some said that the roughnecks were Paddy Camp Landers; some said they were nativist Americans. Although the street had been filled with people, no witnesses came forth; inevitably, there were no arrests.

In the days that followed the attack, Adolph Hartmann learned to live again with the fear that he had thought to leave behind when he arrived in New-York harbor. He had learned, in Germany, the bitter lesson of defeat: live one's life, and do not try to challenge authority, for authority will crush you as if you were a cockroach under the heel of its boot. To challenge the state is to sign your death warrant—look at him, at Garrison, who lives with the threat of assassination, who sleeps in his clothes, ready to flee, with an armed bodyguard on watch. Is that what you want? Did I save us from the secret police, from imprisonment with Gottfried Kinkel in the fortress of Spandau, only to bring you safely here so that you may throw away your life on this side of the ocean instead of that?

For hours he shouted at his beloved son; he ranted, he raved, he forgot every word of English that he had so painfully learned. His voice hoarsened from the strain of his exhortations; his face grew haggard, his hands trembled so that he could not hold his bow, he could not exert pressure on the strings of his violin.

At last he gave up. Klaus was his son, after all. His soul was as beautiful as his face, it shone through his eyes to look upon an erring world. In their brief time in America, and most particularly in New England, Klaus had become as implacable as the native-born agitators against the great evil; like Garrison himself, he had determined to devote his life, if necessary, to eradicate the stain of chattel slavery from his adopted land.

You led me to it, he said to Adolph; you taught me in Germany all that I need to know here and now. We will win here as we could not win there. Amos A. Lawrence himself—the son of a textile manufacturer—has taken charge of the Emigrant Aid Society. They are sending out trains of people to settle in Kansas—Northerners who will hold the territory for the Northern side. They all carry Beecher's Bibles to shoot anyone who tries to stop them. I would go with them—

"*Niemals!*" cried Adolph: "Never!" He could hardly speak from exhaustion. His boy was breaking his heart; somehow he must learn to bear the pain. He wept, then; and his boy wept with him, and Adolph said no more. But every time now that he saw Klaus, he thought: this may be the last time. I saved him for this: to die for a hopeless cause. In his desperation, his fear for Klaus' safety, he looked around for help. His eye fell on Sabra. Klaus seemed fond of her. He had thought, in fact, that Klaus seemed more than that, but in recent weeks the new agitation over Kansas, over Anthony Burns, had distracted the young man's attention. Adolph had wanted Klaus to marry a woman with money; but now money seemed unimportant. Give him a wife and child—his own child—thought Adolph, and he will be more careful, he will not be so ready to put himself in danger. He was not sure whether Sabra's husband was alive or dead. He would ask her outright, he thought; he had, after all, a right to know. She had no money, but she had many virtues, not least of which was the fact that she was apolitical. He had watched her face as her Amazonian friend, Miss Bradshaw, had talked of her many interests. Klaus had been willing enough to listen, but Sabra had looked bored. More than bored: uncomfortable. Extremely unhappy. Good, thought Adolph. She does not like politics. She is like my Anna. If they would marry and have a child—*ja.* And she is still pretty, she is not so many years older than he, she is bright and kind and already we all love her, we do not want her to go away. If they marry, we will have her always. And Klaus, too.

As the summer passed, he plotted and schemed to throw the two of them together, as if he were a marriage broker, an arranger of other people's destinies—*ein Heiratsmacher*. He had little success. Klaus was increasingly busy at the newspaper, and when he was not at his cluttered little office, setting type in the glow of oil lamps because he had no money to repair the boarded-up windows, he was attending public meetings from Boston to Worcester, from Nashua to Taunton, trailing in Garrison's foaming wake, chronicling the course of the abolitionist crusade.

His daguerreotype studio gathered dust. Once in a while, on request, he took a portrait if the sitter could adjust his or her schedule to his own. But on most days the equipment lay unused, the skylight grew dim with accumulated sooty dirt dropping from the heavens. It did not matter now to Klaus whether the day was fine or dark; his present work could be accomplished in any weather, and in fact often the shadow of night was preferable to the glare of the sun, for with the growing furor over Kansas, and the South's increasing terror that its millions of dollars invested in human flesh would be lost to it—taken forcibly away—the chains on the black man wound ever tighter. And so the schedule of the Underground Railroad became increasingly crowded as the two sides, North and South, hardened their positions and began to sketch out their battle lines; and the national Congress, bereft of Webster's sophistries, rivaled Babel itself. And not squat Douglas nor passionate Sumner, not wily Seward nor intransigent Stevens could brake the juggernaut which sped them all to the coming confrontation—the inevitable, longed-for, lusted-for conflagration, the clash of armies, the call of bugles, the whine of bullets and the roar of cannon which brave men in Congress visit upon their hapless constituents.

Klaus' wound healed. The ugly red scab fell off; the bright pink tender skin beneath healed to a thin white line covered by the falling wave of his dark hair. When he had been a student at the University at Bonn, he had refused to fight duels, not from personal vanity, not through fear of being scarred, but because he had thought dueling a stupid pastime for all that every German student engaged in it. His fellows had borne the marks of slashes on their cheeks like badges of honor while his own face remained unmarred. Now, he thought with some amusement, they should see me now; his was not a clean, straight cut like a dueling scar, but it carried with it an infinitely greater significance.

8

On a warm evening in late August, Klaus and Sabra sat at a table in Sheppard's Park Gardens, nibbling at plates of raspberry ice, enjoying a little respite from their lives. This place, at the corner of Andover and Nesmith streets near the top of Belvidere Hill, was a horticultural fantasy where people could not only come to enjoy the lush plantings and, in the evenings, the fairyland effect of lanterns glowing among the shrubbery or hanging from the trees, but where they could also purchase many of the specimens from the adjoining nursery and take them home to their own gardens. From here, one had a panoramic view of the city below, which lay tucked into the great bend of the Merrimack as the beloved lies in the curve of her protector's embrace. Only moments ago, the sun had vanished in crimsoned splendor behind the purple hills to the north and west; its afterglow lingered in the sky, reflected in the shining opalescence of the ribbon of water. Sabra heard all around the rising laughter, the soft, happy conversation of people who took their ease at the end of the day; she savored the cold, sweet confection slipping down her throat; she allowed herself to forget for a moment that this pleasant interlude was the exception in her life, not the rule.

She gazed at the city as if it were a foreign place; like a child, she pretended that it was a place of fascination, of hope and promise. But even as she looked upon it, she heard, faint upon the breeze, the factory bells dismissing the operatives, and the vision of foreign fascination faded, once again, into the reality which she knew.

It had come to her with increasing certainty over the summer that she and Clara must get away. It was impossible for her to say what she wanted for her child, for she had not a full knowledge of what the world had to offer; but she knew more surely with every day that passed, that the full extent of the world's possibilities could be found only if one went to seek them. We must get away, she thought; somehow we must live someplace else. As soon as the Hartmanns' new baby comes and Anna is well again. She remembered, with a sharp twist of her heart, that once she had promised herself that she would stay in Lowell for only two years. Now she had lived here almost half her life. Clara must have a better chance. She will not go into the factory, thought Sabra. She had a brief vision of the noise, the choking dust, the endless strain of matching one's movements to the machines. No: never.

She had come out with Klaus, this evening, because Adolph had insisted upon it. At supper he had scolded them, lectured them on the evils of overwork. "You are tired. She is tired. Go and enjoy yourselves."

And so now they sat companionably together as the soft warm darkness descended, and they found themselves in that uncomfortable condition that exists between two people when what is unsaid is more important than what is said, when the mind gropes for the simplest, most commonplace phrase which, when it finally comes, is spoken clumsily, mispronounced, botched and halting so as to be almost unintelligible. Three times he had turned to her, his full heart's emotion shining in the light of his eyes, for he knew why his father had sent them out together. He did not mind. He accepted Adolph's order as tacit approval. But each time that he had thought that he must unburden his heart to her, she had deflected him with some remark about the weather, or the newspaper, or some equally impersonal thing. And so now at last there was nothing for him to do but take her hand, as he had done before, and put it to his lips, as he had done before, and so try to show her what he could not say.

She did not pull away; but her face, when he looked to see, was sad beyond all reason; and its sadness touched him in some secret place so that suddenly he had words to speak where he had had none before.

"Marry me," he said.

"I cannot."

"Why?"

"I am not free to marry."

"Why not?"

"My husband—" She choked on the word. How strange a word it was, how inappropriate for what Silas was to her.

"Is he alive?"

"I don't know."

"Marry me."

"Please—" Her tears broke her voice; she turned her head, she pulled her hand away. He said nothing more. Soon after, they walked home. The lamplighter had been negligent; the streets along their way were dark, pinpointed at great intervals by a single inadequate flame atop its post. In one of these stretches of sheltering darkness, they halted as if by mutual, unspoken consent. She was only human, after all, and weary and discouraged as Adolph had seen; and she had been alone all the years struggling to survive; and so now she came into his strong young arms, and put her face up to his, and only after their mouths had met and held did she feel the rise of passion in him, and in herself as well, so that at last, having gently entered the embrace, she had to pull herself forcibly away, shaken by long-forgotten, deeply buried feeling.

He could not let her go. "Marry me," he said.

"I cannot."

"You must. You must."

She shook her head at him in the darkness. "No," she said. "No. Forgive me." She pulled away; she walked rapidly onward. She was appalled at her stupidity. I should not have come out with him, she thought; I should have known that something of the sort would happen. She stumbled over the granite curbstone and was only just saved from falling by his hand gripping her elbow.

"Sabra—"

"No. No. We must get back." And in that instant she knew that it was so. Something was wrong, someone needed her—Clara, perhaps, or one of the Hartmann children suddenly taken ill. The certain knowledge of it grew on her with every step. She walked more quickly, she half-ran the last few yards to the building, she pounded up the narrow stairs as fast as her hampering skirts would allow.

Anna met them on the landing. Her face was haggard from the drain of pregnancy on her body; her eyes showed an alarm which had nothing to do with her physical condition.

"Where have you been?" she said, although she knew.

"What is it?" said Klaus, coming up behind. "What is wrong? Is Papa—"

"A man," said Anna. "A man has come." Her hands went automatically to her swelling abdomen, as if she would protect her unborn child from harm. She looked accusingly at Sabra. "For you," she said. "He says that it is very important. He has come two thousand miles, he said, and he would not come back tomorrow. Now, he said. Tonight."

9

He was perhaps forty-five years old: a lean, grizzled, ramshackle-looking man who wore a fringed leather jacket, doeskin trousers, and a stout pair of boots badly worn and scarred. On the table rested his broad-brimmed soft leather hat. He stood waiting for her as she shut the door on Klaus and Anna. For a moment she rested with her hands behind her, clinging to the door knob, waiting for her heart to subside, her trembling knees to support her again. *Silas,* she had thought in the instant before she entered the room; but she had been mistaken, and now she needed a moment to realize that fact before she could speak. This man was a stranger. She was struck by the expression on his weatherbeaten face: he was wary of her, for some reason, and yet oddly friendly, as if somehow he knew her already. His eyes gleamed at her from the expanse of seamed and wrinkled, sunburned skin which he presented to the world; below his prominent nose, the place where his mouth was curved up into a smile. He held out his hand. "Ma'am. Hiram Stringer."

She took his hand, harder than any she had ever touched; she released it quickly and motioned to him to sit down. He pulled a chair away from the table; she sat on the small sofa near the empty fireplace. In that moment of greeting she had caught his odor. He smelled the way she imagined a bear might smell, rising from his winter's sleep, before he plunged into a mountain stream to rid himself of the stench of hibernation.

"Kind of you to see me, ma'am." He cleared his throat. "I'll confess I had a time findin' you." His voice was harsh; each word came out separately, a little forced, as if he were not accustomed to speaking more than a word or two at a time. "Been goin' around town all day lookin' you up. Finally met a fella at the 'pothecary who set me on the right track. Course I never expected to find you here anyway. I'd been told to look with Mr. Brown in Harvard Village, but he's been gone two years an' more, they told me."

He paused, as if, having depleted his small stock of words, he needed to cast about for more. From the kitchen came a muffled crash: Anna, very nervous, dropping crockery. Sabra stared at him. He licked his lips; he blinked, wary of the impact of his words. Mr. Brown—!

"So then I came on here," he said. "Knowin' that your—that Mr. Blood came from here, as he told me, an' knowin' that this is a likely place for a woman to find work, I thought I'd try."

She could not reply—could not say a syllable. Her mind lurched from fact to fact, trying to make sense of his labored message; and yet, simultaneously, her thoughts leaped ahead. She knew what he would say, he did not need to go on. And yet: say it, say it, I have lived too long on hope, on faith. Now tell me the words that will end my hope, now give me back my life to live.

He pulled a small leather pouch from his jacket pocket. "There's two ingots here," he said, "worth fifty dollars."

He held it out to her but she ignored his gesture and so he put it on the table. He understood what she wanted; he tried very hard to find the right words to tell her. He had known that this mission would not be easy, but his admiration for his friend, his devotion to him, gave him strength.

"He would have wrote you a letter, but he was too sick. It came on real sudden. Cholera, it was—took most of the camp. He was spry an' healthy one day, an' the next he was near gone." He paused, grateful that she had not begun to cry. "When he saw how things were—when he saw that he was never goin' to get back east—he told me to come an' see you. He was waitin', y' know, to get enough to come back hisself. An' he would have. He would have. We hit a real rich claim an' there was just the four of us, we'd have made it all right. But then this damn Indian—excuse me—came wanderin' through an' took sick an' in a week they'd all gone down with it except me."

The apartment was quiet. No more sounds of breaking dishes from the kitchen; in their beds the children slept, strengthening their small bodies for the next day's struggle. O Clara, she thought. She stared at the man before her, but she saw far back in time: she saw, very vivid, the unhappy face of the young man in the orchard at Bountiful on a golden autumn afternoon, the young man who longed to make a better life, to take the world in his hands and give it a violent shake, to rearrange it to his idea of perfection. . . .

"So he told me to come an' see you. An' of course I wanted to do it for him, 'cause I thought the world an' all of him. I never understood much of what he was talkin' about mind you—'Collective Yewtopy,' he used to say, an' I confess I never did know what that was. But he was a real fine gentleman. Up in the mountains, along the North Fork of the Feather where we was, pannin' all day, talkin' half the night, y' get to know a man pretty good. Them as don't like to work hard gets out fast, and them as ain't as straight an' honest as they should be—well, they don't always get out, but sometimes they get put out. If you follow. An' Mr. Blood, one time, he caught a fellow goin' into my share an' he just took an' pitched him into the creek. An' the fellow naturally got upset, bein' treated like that. So Mr. Blood had to pacify him some more. An' he did it for me, y' understand, not for hisself. So naturally I 'preciated it. An that's when he started talkin' to me, after that fellow went away. At night we'd sit around the fire, an' it was always pretty cold, an' we'd build the fire up big an' we'd all talk about what we was goin' to do with our shares. An' the other fellows'd talk about all they was goin' to buy—land, an' horses, an' fancy clothes. One fellow was goin' to set up shop in San Francisco, and one was goin' to come back east an' buy a big house an' a fine carriage an' a real pretty lady. But Mr. Blood was different. He never talked about what he'd buy for hisself. He was goin' to try to set up that Yewtopy of his. O, he had some mighty fine ideas. It'd take a lot, he said, an' so he just kept workin'. But he never got more than enough to pay his way, until the last, an' then he got enough for these bits here. An' then he took sick."

He was breathing hard now, for he was afraid that the woman who sat across from him, her eyes fixed steady on his face, her hands clasped in her lap, did not understand him. As relieved as he was that she did not cry, still he would have liked some response—some acknowledgment of the heavy burden of news which he had come so far to bring. A pretty woman, he thought: a lady sure enough. Not in a class with her husband, but then few were. He had not expected to find her living with foreigners.

She had been so inexorably silent that when at last she spoke, he was startled.

"Did he—did he mention me at all?"

And then he was embarrassed at having left out so important a part of his message.

"O, yes, ma'am. Like I said, he told me to find you at Mr. Brown's. An' he said—how did he put it, now? I'd have wrote it down but I can't write, nor read neither—he said, 'Tell her to remember the dream.'"

There was an awkward silence. Then: "Nothing more?"

"No, ma'am."

"He did not mention the child?"

"No, ma'am. He never mentioned no child."

He was surprised to see a tight, bitter smile twist her mouth. "He—we—have a daughter. She is ten years old this past March."

He blinked. "Yes, ma'am."

He moved uncomfortably in his chair. Her tears, so long withheld, seemed about to come. He could not bear the sight of a woman weeping. He stood up, he held out his hand to her once again.

"He was a real good man, ma'am. An' I'm pleased to make your acquaintance."

She rose to shake his hand. I must thank him, she thought; he has come all across a continent to bring Silas' message. And the gold. Probably there was more, but no matter; what is here is worth more than I have ever had. And Silas did remember me, after all.

Through the open windows they heard the clatter of a horse and carriage in the street. Past curfew, she thought. She felt a sudden, shocking desire to laugh. Silas has overstayed his time. He will be dismissed. And then: No. Men had no curfew.

"You are very kind to have come," she said. "Please—will you have a cup of coffee? Or something to eat?" She smiled at him briefly, wanly; he was relieved that still she did not cry. As if to thank her for sparing him that embarrassment, he cast about for some last bit of intelligence to give to her before he went away. Silas Blood, dying, had been a hideous sight and of course he would spare her that, but something else, some last item—

"No, ma'am," he said. "Nothin' for me. I got a room at th' American House an' tomorrow I'll be goin' to see my sister in Montpelier. But I am glad I found you. He didn't suffer at the last near as much as I've seen some do. Believe me. He went real easy. Just a bit o' delirium. He was talkin' about 'Sabra'—that's you, course—an' then all of a sudden I knew he had the fever real bad because he made a mistake. He said 'Sophia.' I thought perhaps he had a—a sister, maybe. Or a—now, ma'am, you look real bad, you ought to sit down. Here—"

As he cursed himself for staying too long, for adding too many details to his sorrowful message, they heard the sound of footsteps on the stairs. Abruptly the door opened. Adolph came in, carrying his violin case; he stopped in surprise as he saw the stranger.

"Sabra? Where is Klaus?"

"I was just goin'—" began Stringer, but Adolph, after one swift glance, ignored him.

"What, Sabra?" In the next moment he was relieved to see Klaus standing in the doorway. Behind him stood Anna, bearing the tray with coffee urn and cups. They pressed Sabra to drink; she recoiled from the burning liquid and waved them away.

"No—no—I am all right. I am overtired, the heat—" She made an effort. She stood up and presented Stringer to the Hartmanns. The tension, the sudden alarm had passed. Finally Stringer was able to make his escape. Sabra accompanied him downstairs. As he stood on the doorstep he turned to her for a final word; they shook hands again. Then he went away; he disappeared along the darkened street, and the sound of his footsteps faded into silence.

She closed the door and shot the bolt and went upstairs. Adolph, Anna, and Klaus awaited her in the parlor. She saw that Klaus had taken up the leather pouch which Stringer had left; as she went in he put it down. She faced them, feeling the oppressive force of their concern for her, their curiosity about her visitor. How good they were, how kind—!

She wanted to run away.

"Bad news," said Adolph. "*Ja*. What is it?"

If I tell them, she thought, it will be true. But not unless I tell them.

Klaus put out his hands to her; he helped her to sit. He looked very worried—alarmed. Why, she wondered. Do I look so bad?

Anna sat beside her, her face drained of color; she was breathing hard. A difficult pregnancy.

"Don't talk about it unless you want to," said Klaus. "Perhaps you should not—perhaps you should rest—"

I must say it, she thought; I must, they have a right to know. "He came to tell me that my—my husband is dead." She got it out in a rush, afraid that if she hesitated longer she would not find the courage at all—not now, not tonight, not ever. "In the gold fields. Of cholera."

She bit her lips. I will not cry, she thought. She clasped her hands in the folds of her voluminous gray skirts. She knew that if she looked at their kindly, sympathetic faces, her tears would begin and then whenever would they cease?

They understood. "So we will talk in the morning," said Adolph. "To bed now." He nodded a warning to his wife and son. Anna obeyed him at once; as she rose to leave, she patted Sabra's arm reassuringly. Klaus hesitated. For the second time that evening he had worked himself up to a speech, and now, for the second time, he repressed it. He picked up the pouch once again and, as Sabra did not willingly take it, he lifted her hand and closed it around the leather. Despite his father's command he lingered for a moment, standing so close beside her that once again she felt the force of his presence, his warmth, his strength. Hardly moving, she could have leaned against him; his strong young body would have supported her; his arms would have enfolded her.

She did not move; and so with a whispered word which she did not comprehend, he too went out. And now Adolph, having been properly heeded by his family, awaited her obedience also.

"Go on," he said. He was sincerely alarmed at her appearance. "Sleep. It will be better tomorrow."

She obeyed him, then; but before she went to her own bed, she went to look at her sleeping child. Clara lay on her side, her dark hair tumbled across her face, nightcap on the floor. Sabra lifted a strand of hair, damp with perspiration, and stared at the child's face. And now she felt her tears, so long held back, come on at last. She sank onto Clara's cot as she felt the heavy pain of her heart drag her down; she felt the pain of all the long years, the heavy weight of fading hope, the sudden crushing blow that ended hope forever.

"Tell her to remember the dream," Silas had said.

And in the end he had called for Sophia. The visitor, trying to console, might as well have stabbed her through the heart. O Silas. I waited for you and you never came. And now it is too late.

Secretly, silently she wept. She lay desolate beside her child in the hot, still night and felt the sobs tear at her body as if they would wrench it apart, she felt her breath catch in her throat and choke her, she felt the tears scald her eyes, soaking the pillow to a sodden pile, draining her of strength, of life itself. All the world seemed one vast darkness; she thought never to see daylight again.

Alone in the parlor, Adolph took his violin from its case. He drew the bow across the strings; he called forth the first statement of the notes, high and pure and infinitely sweet, filled with the promise of a line of ecstatic sound unfolding in its inevitable progression. Long and short and long again; down and up and down again; a fine thin thread of melody intertwined with another, an unplayed, unheard line of counterpoint heard all the same; brief tension created and released; a sound that rose and fell back upon itself and rose again, ever sweeter, ever closer to perfection, soaring up to glory as it spun on and on into the silent night; a voice dead more than a century and yet living still as it would live for all time, speaking to him, the atheist, of the mysteries of God, of order in the face of chaos, eternal life triumphant over Death, the transcendence of the human spirit over time and place and untoward circumstance.

Lying beside her child, lost in the wilderness of her grief, her desolation, Sabra heard as he had intended her to hear; she understood that he played for her, that he spoke to her in this, his most eloquent language, offering hope, and life, and new promise through the beauty of the music. She heard, and she was comforted; and after a time her tears ceased and her body came to rest; and the darkness was no longer darkness but merely the time before the day. Her deep wound had begun to heal; and so she slept.

10

Winter came early that year. The autumn rains fell steadily day after day. At the beginning of November the temperature dropped and the rain turned to snow, transforming the city into a subject fit for the industrious draughtsmen and women employed by the Messrs. Currier & Ives.

In the weeks following Hiram Stringer's visit, Sabra taught herself to live with the knowledge that Silas was dead, and that all she had of him was a leather pouch holding two ingots of gold. I can never spend them, she thought; I must keep them always. I have nothing else

Except Clara. As the days passed she looked at her child with new eyes. She saw little enough of Silas in her save her coloring, for Clara's skin was darker than her own, and her straight, dark hair, thick and rather coarse, was Silas' hair all over again. For the first time, Sabra wondered about the Blood family tree: had an Algonquian slipped in somewhere back in the chaos of Colonial times?

But Clara's features were delicate—beautiful, even—and her slight build was her mother's, not the lanky, rawboned frame of Silas Blood. In temperament, too, she seemed very unlike him. She was a lovable child, friendly and bright, little given to the long, brooding silences, the fits of melancholy so frequently suffered by her father.

I must tell her, thought Sabra. I must show her the ingots, I must let her know that he remembered us. And—yes—I will lie to her, I will tell her that he asked for her before he died. She looked for her chance to speak. It seemed not to come. September passed, and then October, and still Clara did not know that her father had died. And as the urgency of the news faded, as her heart mended, Sabra continued to delay. I will wait until she asks again, she thought. She looked from the front windows of the apartment over the dreary landscape of rooftops, all gray in the relentless rain. She heard the noon bells ringing at the factories. For a moment she went back: the hot, noisy, lint-filled rooms, the crush down the narrow stairway, the shock of cold air in the lungs, the frantic run to the boarding house to wolf down the heavy meal, the race back to the workrooms so as not to be late, the constant pressure to produce more cloth.

Her mouth tightened as she remembered. Never, she thought: Clara will never go on the Corporations. I would rather see her dead than slaving in the mills.

Two weeks before Thanksgiving Anna gave birth to a girl. Adolph had summoned Dr. Greenhalge to attend her, a new man highly recommended by the manager of the theater. Although Anna survived her confinement, she had had a difficult, exhausting pregnancy. She had vomited day and night for months, the muscles supporting her bladder had given way, the veins in her legs had swollen like ropes under her skin, she had lost three teeth and a quantity of hair. Her face on the pillow looked like a death's-head, the eyes sunk deep into their sockets, the pallid skin stretched tight over her cheek-bones, her mouth gone slack. Sabra bent over her.

"Anna?"

"*Ja.*"

"Can you take the baby now? She needs to nurse."

"*Ja.*"

But Anna's arms were too weak; she could not hold her child. The baby's faint, mewling cry seemed an echo of her own exhaustion. She did not hear it. Delivered at last of her burden, she closed her eyes and drifted back into unconsciousness, oblivious to the new life which she had borne, clinging weakly to her own.

Dr. Greenhalge delivered himself of his professional opinion: she might live, she might not. Meanwhile he knew of a reliable wet-nurse who could take the baby and keep her alive. The woman was clean, free of disease, she had ample milk. He would send for her that very evening.

The children huddled in the parlor. They understood Adolph's fear—although not its cause—and they themselves were afraid, of what they did not know. Mutter was ill; Sabra was busy caring for her; Klaus was absent as usual but Jutta had not gone to her work, she hurried back and forth between kitchen and bedroom, stopping every now and then to look in on them and caution them, unnecessarily, to silence. They turned to Clara; they begged her to read to them. For once Clara was not interested in reading. She wanted to creep down the hall to the door of Anna's room; she wanted to eavesdrop, to hear what the adults said about Anna's condition. She knew that giving birth was women's affair;

men could not do it. She was nearly eleven. Very soon she would be a woman herself. She wanted to learn about babies and how they came, she wanted to know why Anna had cried out so loud and then all of a sudden fallen so terribly silent. Would Anna die because she had had a baby? She had had five children already and she had not died. Why was it different this time? Or perhaps it was not different; perhaps she had been ill like this with every one of them.

Clara shuddered. She was more frightened than any of the others. She never wanted to suffer so, she never wanted to have a baby and be so ill. Had her mother nearly died when she was born? Would her mother have another baby and die? Clara loved her mother very much. When she thought of her dying she felt sick. Ludwig reached out to her but she pushed him away. Ludwig was a boy. He could not understand. The littlest one, Elisabetta, had fallen asleep in the corner. Would Elisabetta die some day when she had a baby?

Clara felt her stomach turn over. Ignoring the whispered questions of the little boys, she stood up and tip-toed out of the parlor and down the hall. The door to Anna's room was closed, but just then someone opened it. She heard the baby's cry, like a cat's cry—a sick cat, she thought. Adolph and the doctor came out. They were talking; they did not notice her. The doctor, a large, heavy-set young man with gold-rimmed spectacles and several gold rings on his meaty hands, spoke in slow, solemn phrases: "weakened condition . . . difficulty in stopping the flow . . . must take nourishment . . . no reason to fear . . ." Neglecting to close the door, they proceeded to the landing. Clara crept inside the room. Her mother sat by the bed, attempting to spoon a fragrant broth into Anna's mouth. Jutta sat opposite, holding a little wrapped bundle from whence issued the strange-sounding cries. They did not notice her at first. Then Jutta turned and saw her.

"*Raus mit dir!*" she snapped: "Get out!"

Clara pretended not to understand. Sabra, intent on her task, ignored them until she realized that the interloper was her own child and not one of the Hartmanns. Then she paused; she looked from Clara to Jutta and back again to her daughter. It was natural for the child to be curious. She remembered that she, herself, had once lingered so in a house in some one or another of the mountain villages where she had spent her childhood. Her father had been preaching; the neighboring women had come in to attend the birth. She had longed to ask questions of them, but she had been too shy: why has this happened, and how, and will this poor woman live?

"Let her stay," she said to Jutta. And, to Clara: "Stand by the door—yes, close it—and don't talk, don't move. You may stay for five minutes only. No, I won't answer questions. Not now."

The next day, when the baby had gone to the wet-nurse and Anna seemed somewhat improved, she attempted to explain.

"Babies come only to married women," she said, "and it is entirely a natural thing."

"Ellen Adams' mother died having a baby," said Clara. "Ellen had to stay home from school to take care of her little brothers and sisters."

"People die every day," said Sabra. They sat on the parlor sofa drinking cocoa; the afternoon had darkened into early evening, but the cheerful fire in the hearth provided more than ample light. "People die from accidents, or illness—having a baby is nothing to fear."

"You are married," said Clara. "Will you have a baby?"

There it is, thought Sabra. Now I must speak. And still she dreaded it, still she searched for the right words. She said nothing; she tightened her arm around the child's shoulders. At once, sensing her mother's distress, Clara twisted out of the embrace and sat apart in an attitude of confrontation.

"Will you?" she said again.

"No."

"Will you, if—if he comes back?"

"No."

"Why not?"

"Because—" Say it, she thought. Get it out.

"Why not?" Clara's eyes were large in her small face. She had always understood that there was some difficulty—some irregularity—in her parents' arrangement of their lives, even beyond the obvious fact of her father's absence. She had never seen him, or not that she remembered; and now, all of a sudden, she understood that she never would.

"He died," said Sabra. The words seemed to echo in her ears, and so, to quiet them, she added: "In California. Months ago—years. He had gone to the gold diggings."

She watched to see a sign of grief from her child, but Clara remained calm, digesting what she had been told. So long I have dreaded telling her, thought Sabra, and she shows no emotion at all.

"So you are not married any longer," said Clara at last.

"No."

"And you will not have a baby and die."

"No. Certainly not."

Clara nodded, as if something had been settled in her mind. She looked away; she relaxed a little.

"Did he ever see me?" she said.

"When you were quite small."

"How old was I when he—when he went away?"

"About seven and a half months."

Clara was silent for a moment, staring at the fire, pondering the mysteries of adulthood. If he had loved her, he would have stayed; he had not stayed; therefore he had not loved her. Possibly, she thought, she had been a fussy baby, crying at all hours, annoying him. Or possibly he had wanted a boy.

Suddenly, in a rush of emotion, Sabra embraced her; and Clara forgot about her father in her happiness at being so loved by the only parent she knew. She hugged tight; she kissed her mother's thin cheek. Let children with fathers endure their beatings, their stern discipline and harsh voices, she thought. She and her mother were better off alone. They could survive without a man's support: they had done so all these years, had they not? And soon she herself would be able to earn a little money somehow.

Anna mended slowly. Because she was unable to oversee the usual elaborate preparations, the family celebrated a subdued Christmas. With Klaus and Jutta's help, Adolph decorated a small tree, and Sabra stuffed and roasted a fine, fat goose. On Christmas morning, the children found oranges and peppermints and new spinning tops in their stockings. But it was Anna who gave them the best present of all: she walked to the table and ate Christmas dinner with them. Adolph was beside himself with apprehension: she would tire herself, she should not attempt it, she must stay in bed, she would suffer a relapse. Sabra watched him as she smiled to herself. How he loved her! How bereft he would be if she had died! She caught Klaus' eye; she felt herself flush as she looked away. Since the night of Hiram Stringer's visit he had hardly spoken to her alone, and she understood that he was intentionally avoiding her. He waits for me to speak first, she thought. He had been busy day and night running the newspaper, working with the newly energized anti-slavery organizations. He seldom spoke of his work, for he knew that his father did not approve of any political action whatever. Leave politics alone, said Adolph; it only makes trouble. The Know-Nothings had recently swept the state elections. They were ignorant men, demagogues, united like rowdy adolescents in their love of secrecy, their hatred of all things foreign. To the Know-Nothings, Catholics were the great enemy; but all foreigners, including educated Germans, were suspect as well.

Later in the day, when Anna had returned to bed, they serenaded her from the parlor with the Christmas music she so loved to hear: *Stille Nacht,* and *Adeste Fideles,* and *O Tannenbaum.* And once again, as they sang, Sabra felt Klaus' stare; she could not endure it for more than a moment, she was forced to look away. When they had done singing, and the children had gone sleepily to their beds, she lingered purposely in the kitchen helping Jutta to clear away the remains of the dinner; but then Jutta, too, had retired. Adolph had gone to the theater; Klaus, she knew, was alone in the parlor. Presently he came along the hallway to the kitchen to find her.

"Come and sit with me," he said. "I am all alone, and lonely, too." He smiled at her; he held out his hand. How beautiful he is, she thought. And he knows it: no homely person would dare to make such an admission. But she did not want to sit with him. She was certain that he would begin again to speak to her of marriage, and she did not want to hear it. One day, she thought, he will catch me unawares and I will say yes, and then it will be worse than ever, for certainly I will never marry him and I would only have the agony of withdrawing my promise. Better never to give it in the first place.

On the other hand, she was not tired; if she went to bed she would not sleep, she would lie in the dark beside Jutta, waiting for the morning, aware of Klaus awake in the parlor, staring alone at the fire.

"Come," he said again, still smiling, refusing to be put off. "You worked all day, you work every day, very hard. Come and rest awhile. Would you like tea? I will bring it to you—I will be your servant." And he mocked a bow, cajoling her, charming her.

She gave in. Knowing what he would say, she allowed herself to be persuaded. Sooner or later, she thought, it had to come; better to have it done with.

They sat in the quiet room which only a short time before had rung with the songs of Christmas. The candles on the tree had been extinguished, but their warmth had brought out its tangy odor which, like the music, lingered in the air. Sabra drank the tea from the cup which he put into her hands, and after she had swallowed the last of it she began to relax a little. Klaus sat at her feet, his back resting against the leg of the chair; he looked not at her but at the fire, and so she did not see the somber expression which had come to his face as he sat in silence. And then, when finally he began to speak, it was not of their personal affairs but of state and national politics. Politics! She smothered her irritation; she disliked politics almost as much as Adolph did. For politeness' sake she tried to follow his explanations, but she could not understand; she was not familiar with the names, the places—what had Nicaragua to do with abolitionism?

"They make little wars now," he said, "while they wait for the great one. Every man in the South—and every woman, too—longs to fight us. They believe that they will win on the battlefield what they cannot win in Congress."

How ridiculous, she thought; surely he is mistaken. And yet it was true that tempers were short everywhere. Men used the slightest excuse to start small battles; hardly a week went by without a fresh report of a riot between Americans and Irish. Every city in the North saw such conflict, and there were battles with the slavecatchers, too, as they pursued their prey and met armed resistance from diehard abolitionists. And every city had its militia, drilling regularly, playing ferociously at war. It was not only the South, it seemed, that longed for battle.

"Would you join the Army?" she said.

His hands, which had been clasped loosely across his knees, suddenly tightened. She could see only the top of his head; his face was turned from her still.

"I would have to, I think," he said slowly, thinking it out, taking into account all that it meant. Men died in the Army, or were horribly wounded, or captured and held prisoner: and yet, "Yes," he said with more conviction, as if her question had helped him to resolve his doubts. "I would join. I fight the South now with words while MacKenzie fights in Kansas with his gun. But if war came to us here, then, yes, I would fight here."

"To free black men whom you have never seen?"

Suddenly he turned to her; and now it seemed that he, too, had had enough of politics. Before she realized what he did, he had knelt beside her. His arms went around her waist; as if he still did not want her to see his face, he put his head in her lap. He pressed close on her. She felt his warmth. Once again, as on the night of Hiram Stringer's visit, she felt her own emotion rise to meet his. Even through the several layers of her petticoats and the heavy stuff of her skirts, she felt his face against her.

And why not, she thought, weakening even as she had feared. Why not let him love me? I have had little enough love in my life. She touched his hair; she felt the back of his neck. As she did so, she had a sudden memory of Clara's anxious questions. "Will you have a baby and die, Mama?"

Dear God, she thought. What am I doing? She put her hands on his shoulders and pushed him roughly away so that he almost lost his balance and fell backward.

"What—"

"No," she said. Her voice was harsh, as cold as she could bear to make it. She saw the hurt in his eyes. Swiftly he recovered himself; he knelt on one knee before her, the classic pose, the maiden's dream. She hardened her heart against him, calling up all her reserves of strength, but he would not be put off.

"Marry me," he said.

She wanted to stand, but she had no strength; as if he feared that she would go, he put his hands on the arms of her chair to keep her.

"You have no reason now to refuse," he said. "Your—your husband is dead, you are legally free."

"No."

"*Why?*" His voice was low and urgent, frighteningly intense. "You know how I love you. I have loved you from the first."

"No." How could she make him understand?

"You must give me a reason."

How could she make him understand? She must try. He would learn to bear the hurt; we must all learn to live with our pain, she thought, and he will live with this.

"I do not like—no, that is not right. I fear—yes—I fear what you are, what you have become."

He stared at her, frowning a little, trying to understand. "What is that?" he said. "What am I?"

"You are—you have become—a political man. You work night and day for the anti-slavery cause."

He laughed: a short, harsh sound. "Yes? Go on."

"That is all. I fear you because of your devotion to them—to it."

He shook his head. "That is not a reason. It is an excuse."

She could not help but smile. How well he had learned his vocabulary! And how beautiful, how appealing he was, how she wished that she were young and free to take him, unburdened by the memories of her past! It was impossible; she could never explain to him the fear that came to her at the thought of his devotion to that cause—to any cause. She wanted only to live; what life remained to her must be hers alone, hers and Clara's. Not sacrificed to some grand ideal.

She began to speak. She told him the story of her life. First her father, then Rachel, then Silas Blood and John Prince—all of them working in their separate ways, all of them sacrificing their own brief time on earth for the sake of some future good. She spoke briefly, too, of Moses Trueworthy and his feckless dream, and without mentioning her mother she explained the rigid doctrines of the United Society which had driven two poor souls to desperation and death.

She did not tell him about her life in the Acre, for that time was not pertinent now; but she remembered it, and she wondered, now, how she had survived it. She had almost not survived it. She had had a second chance. She did not intend—so she explained to him—to make the same mistake again. She would not involve herself with causes, or movements, or schemes to better the world. That was work for others to do. For herself, for Clara, she asked only to live quietly, to have food and shelter and good health. The world would go on, regardless; she wanted no part in trying to change it.

At last she fell silent; and because she had spoken for so long, the silence seemed especially oppressive. She was not an eloquent person. What if still he did not understand?

And, indeed, it seemed that he did not. He took her hand; slowly, lovingly, he kissed it, over and over again. She let him.

"You have told me a great deal," he said, "and yet you have told me nothing. Nothing that you have said makes any difference. I am not like all those others. I will not desert you, I will not betray you." He put her hand back into her lap. "I understand now why you are afraid. But you must not be afraid. No—say nothing more. I will not ask you again to-night. Papa is coming now."

The next evening he asked her again to marry him, and again she refused; three days later, again; a week after that, again. She dreaded seeing him. Finally she appealed to Adolph. "I must leave you if he keeps on like this," she said.

"No! You must not leave—Anna loves you, she needs you, the children need you." He did not know who annoyed him more: his beloved, headstrong son, or this quiet, steadfast American woman who had helped them all to survive in this strange new land. Why was Klaus so intent on her? On the other hand, why did she continue to refuse him?

Adolph sighed. He looked out at the soot-darkened snow; he reached for his violin. He would play for a while; perhaps a solution would come with the music.

Sabra, seeking an answer to her dilemma, had somewhere else to turn for help.

11

Madame Jewel's voice came slowly, without expression, without timbre. "Heat and light," she said, "and cold and dark." It is hardly a living voice at all, thought Sabra. It comes from some place beyond living.

The small room was oppressively hot. Sabra had already undone the top two buttons of her bodice; not wanting to disrupt the seeress' concentration, she did not dare to move now to wipe the perspiration from her face. Still, despite her warmth, she felt herself trembling. She was very much afraid. She wished that she had not asked the seeress' help. And yet she needed help from someone; she needed direction, advice, some knowledge of what the future might hold. Others lived on faith, but she had very little faith left. She needed information.

Madame Jewel sat deep in trance. In the dim light of the single candle, Sabra saw the medium's wide, vacant eyes, her blank and rigid face. This woman was not a fraud, no matter how the Hartmanns mocked. She wished that Adolph had come with her; then he would see how sincere, how frighteningly real Madame Jewel's visions were.

She came as all the others had come, she thought, remembering the well-to-do woman in the heavy veil. But she remembered, too, the vision that she had had that night: the overpowering sense of Silas' presence. And not long after, the visit from Hiram Stringer announcing his death. She shuddered again. Too late now; she had to stay.

"And death. Death all around you in the dark. First a great crash—a falling down. Then death. Then heat and light, and death again. And cold and darkness, and death still with you." Now Madame Jewel herself began to tremble; she shook so violently with the terror of her vision that the table beneath her hands began to move back and forth upon its unsteady legs. Sabra reached out to hold the candle, but she could not look away from Madame Jewel's face. The seeress had begun to moan; then she whimpered for a moment, then moaned again. It was a low and long-drawn sound, occasioned by some insupportable pain. Still her eyes were wide and staring; still the blank face, all the more frightening because it did not reflect the anguished sounds coming from the painted mouth.

What does she see, thought Sabra. She battled with her fear, and for the moment she won. She had asked Miss Smith to try to see something of the future which would guide her in the matter of Klaus' demand that they marry. Miss Smith—Madame Jewel, rather—had gone quickly into trance; for some minutes she had sat quiet, wide-eyed and staring, until Sabra had feared that nothing at all would come forth, that she would be left to go as she had come, with no direction, no support for the decision that she had in fact already made. Then, quite suddenly, Madame Jewel had had her vision, and she had begun to speak. She continued to repeat the word: "Death." And: "Death" again.

Sabra could hardly keep from crying out to her: "Stop it! Come back, tell me nothing more!"

But it was dangerous to interrupt a medium in trance, she did not know why, and so she forced herself to be still. To wait for further revelations, something more pertinent, something that she could understand.

Madame Jewel sat immobile. Her violent trembling had stopped; she hardly seemed to breathe. There was no sound in the room. From outside, from the nighttime city, came the muffled noise of iron-rimmed wheels grating on cobblestoned streets, the clop-clop of horses' hooves, the faint peal of church bells tolling the hour, an occasional human cry or the bark of a dog. But inside Madame Jewel's storefront room, where the two women sat locked in concentration, there was no sound. Nothing. Not the wheeze of breath, the shuffle of feet, the slippery rustle of women's dresses as they shifted in their chairs. No sound: only silence.

And then Madame Jewel screamed.

Sabra started so violently that she knocked over the candle. Mercifully it went out. They sat in darkness. The echoing shriek hung in the air. Sabra's mind had gone blank at the sound; she could not think what to do. She could not move; she could not speak. She smelled the acrid odor of the velvet cloth singed by the flame. Her jaws ached from clenching her teeth. She sat frozen in her chair, stunned into immobility by the voice that was not Madame Jewel's voice, although it had issued from her throat. It had been the voice of one in agony—of a body stretched on the rack, of a martyr burning at the stake. Ordinary human concerns did not call forth such a noise.

Why? What had she seen?

An endless time elapsed. Sabra waited in the dark. If I hear that sound again, she thought, I will faint, my heart will stop, I will surely die summoned by that scream.

At last Madame Jewel came free of her spell. She moved; she coughed; she cleared her throat.

"Sabra? Are you there? Why is it dark?" And, hearing no reply, she said again: "Sabra?"

"I knocked over the candle."

"Mercy! Why didn't you say so? We might have gone up in flames!"

Sabra heard the seeress rise, she heard her footsteps as she walked across the room; then came the rasping sound of a match being struck.

"There! Hold the candle—so." Madame Jewel peered into her friend's eyes across the flame. Perspiration had melted her face paint as if it were dripping wax, so that she looked curiously indistinct. Hardly a person to ask for advice, thought Sabra. And yet—what had she seen?

"Well?" Madame Jewel set a kettle to boil on the small iron stove; she opened the door slightly to air the room. Then she sat again at the table and looked at Sabra expectantly. It was as if she waited to hear a particularly choice item of gossip. "What did I say?"

Does she really not know, thought Sabra. She looked away. If I do not tell her, she thought, it will be as if it never happened—as if she never spoke.

"Never mind," said Madame Jewel after a moment. She looked slightly embarrassed. "It isn't always true, you know—the things I see. I had a poor girl last month who said I told her about sickness and ruination, and then a week later she learned that her uncle had died and left her a fortune. That doesn't cancel out the sickness, of course—but at least now she can afford a doctor."

The kettle, boiling, emitted a fierce little shriek of its own. Madame Jewel rose heavily and went to prepare the tea. I suppose it tires her, thought Sabra, to have these travels back and forth in time. She watched the seeress with mingled wariness and affection. How strange, to be at the mercy of such a gift!

They settled down with their tea cups. Madame Jewel chatted easily of ordinary things until she saw that Sabra was at ease again, and then they said good night.

Sabra did not tell Klaus that she had visited Madame Jewel. She put the seeress' revelations out of her mind; in time she denied them altogether. It never happened, she thought; it was a bad dream.

Klaus stopped pursuing her, she did not know why. Politics, she thought: just as I said. He is more devoted to his newspaper than to me. But because she was uncomfortable in his presence, she avoided him when he was at home. She wanted no further assaults on her emotions. To her relief, he was seldom with them. He began absenting himself for days at a time; once she overheard him as he hurriedly threw out an explanation to Adolph: "We must get them across the river into New Hampshire," he said; "their master sent a man to capture them. We must take them tonight."

She stood listening in the parlor as she heard him clatter down the stairs. Once she, too, had been party to such a journey. She remembered her own terror, Rachel's mad exhilaration. And still they came, these wretched chattel seeking freedom; and still found friends to help them.

The winter wore on. Anna mended; the baby, whom they named Annalise, came home from the wet-nurse. Adolph received a raise in pay; in turn, he increased Sabra's wage to a dollar and a half a week. Clara began to go more frequently to the theater; once or twice Miss MacNaughton came to dinner. Sabra did not like her. She thought her coarse, unladylike—much too forward. "She is very nice to me, Mama," said Clara. "She lets me try on her costumes, she gives me her old paste jewels to play with."

"No," said Sabra; "I don't want you to take them." How tall the child was! Like a dark cloud over her thoughts hung the problem of what Clara was to do with herself—how she was to live when she finished her schooling. "I will be an actress like Miss MacNaughton, Mama," said Clara. "And people will come to see me, and applaud and laugh and cry—"

"Never," said Sabra. "Not while I live. It is not a respectable profession."

"What, then?" said Clara. "I can't sing like Jenny Lind, so Mr. Barnum wouldn't want to hire me. And I hate sewing. And I don't have the patience to teach. I know!" And her face brightened; her eyes saw great visions. "I will go to work for Miss Nightingale! That would be better even than the theater, because I'd be helping all the poor soldiers."

"Dear God," said Sabra. She looked aghast at her child. "I'd rather see you on the Corporation. No—that is not so. I would not."

She had a letter from Rachel:

> I am coming to visit Father. Look forward so much to seeing you again. How is Clara?

She might as well have asked again to have her, thought Sabra. But I cannot let the child go to her; I would miss her too much—and in truth I do not trust Rachel. She does as she pleases; she might harm Clara in some way. I cannot take the risk.

But I will ask her opinion, all the same: what can Clara do with herself? Rachel knows more of the world than I do. Perhaps she can advise me.

Dear God: Miss Nightingale!

12

"When?" said Patrick. "How many?"

He stood behind the counter at Codwell's grocery—his, now, since he had bought the old man out two years previous.

"Just now gone," said his brother Michael. "Fifteen anyway—from Boston, from the state house. They're investigatin' all the convents in the state, they said. Lady Superior ordered them out, but they wouldn't go. They was all over—cellar to attic. Lookin' for priests, they said. Man named Joe Hiss is at the head of it."

"The Smelling Committee," said Patrick. His eyes were cold, his thin face sobered with hate. "They were in Worcester and Roxbury last week." Know-Nothings from the legislature: haters of Catholics, of foreigners, of blacks—of everyone not Protestant native Americans. "Where are they now—still at th' Notre Dame?"

"Depot," said Michael. "It looked like a riot, the boys gatherin' by the church, so they left."

"Run down and make sure they all get on the train," said Patrick. "And come back and tell me."

One missing, Michael reported half an hour later. Hiss himself, he said: he took a woman to the Washington House.

Patrick grinned. "Got 'im," he said. "Got 'im, Michael m' boy! Now. Set someone to watch 'im."

The woman was a Mrs. Moody, alias Mrs. Patterson. She knew all the tricks of her trade. For a price, she was willing to perform them.

The hotel's walls were thin, the waiter's ears were sharp. When he reported Hiss' activities to Patrick the following morning, Patrick laughed outright despite his rage. "Got 'im again," he said. He thought for a moment. "Munson won't publish this" (his heart missed a beat and then resumed) "and neither will Freddie at the *Advert.*" But of course there was no question of where to take the story. Only one newspaper in Lowell would print such a tale. Klaus Hartmann, the editor's name was. Patrick hoped that he spoke so that a man could understand. The *Chronicle* was an anti-slavery paper, but no matter. Patrick had nothing but contempt for the abolitionists, but for his purposes now the *Chronicle* would do nicely. Hartmann was a foreigner. The Know-Nothings were Yankees. Therefore, in this instance, he and Hartmann were allies against the ruling class—descendants of the hated English.

That afternoon, during the slow time, he left his store in charge of his clerk—his next youngest brother after Michael—and proceeded down Central Street to the boarded-up office of the *Chronicle*.

To his annoyance, Hartmann hesitated; despite Patrick's promise to circulate the paper widely in the Acre, he would not at once commit himself to printing the story of Hiss' escapade.

"Who broke my windows last summer?" he said. "Was it Irish?"

"No, never," said Patrick. "We've enough trouble of our own, we needn't go lookin' for it."

Klaus was his father's son; he was briefly charmed by the music of his visitor's lilting speech.

"This is a nasty story," he said. "Someone won't like my printing it."

"True. But we'll help you out if they try to mob you again. I'll bring a dozen lads to stay with you, if you like. But we want this printed. We want it known what they're up to, what kind of scum they are."

"The Mayor is a Know-Nothing. And the Board of Aldermen. And the Governor, too, for that matter."

"Makes no difference. We have to get it out and around what they're doin'. They blame all the trouble on us—they grind us down, they won't give us jobs, they want to close off immigration when all Ireland's still starvin' an' the rackrent as bad as ever. Between English and Yankee there's little enough difference as makes no matter, but I'd say the Yankee has the edge on hate. They're good haters, Yankees. You'll find it out if you haven't already. An' they hate us worst of all—worse than anti-slavery men, worse than you folks from Germany or folks from Sweden or Norway, worse than other Catholics—French or Spanish—worse than anyone, they hate Irish. I don't know why, but they do. And o' course we hate them back."

Klaus gazed at the thin, pale face, the eyes hard, the thin mouth drawn tight. Such visible anger seemed strange, combined as it was with the lovely music of the talk.

"So you see why this must be printed," said Patrick. "And I'll make sure y' don't regret it."

Afterward, however, he did not get his lads in soon enough. Klaus was caught alone in his office. When the members of the Hibernian Relief

Committee arrived, he was hardly breathing, as near to death as a man can be and still live.

Who had attacked him? No one knew.

13

Clara understood that for all the rest of her life she would be haunted by the memory of the night they brought Klaus home to die. Three husky Irishmen carried him up the narrow stairway and laid him gently on his bed. Clara glimpsed his face as they passed down the hall; it was unrecognizable, a swelling pulp of bloody bruises. A deep cut had been opened under his left eye, both lips were split, his hair was matted with blood. His jacket and shirt were ripped half off his body.

At once her mother and Anna had begun to work over him, even as the three strangers got out their explanation. They had been sent to guard him, they said, but they had arrived too late. They had found him lying on the floor of his office. The place had been wrecked, files torn out, desk overturned, two chairs shattered against the wall. In the back room, the printing press had been smashed, fonts of type thrown on the floor, fresh supplies of newsprint ripped and scattered. They had not stopped to inventory the damage; they had brought him home directly.

Sabra paused for a moment, dripping cloth in hand, while she looked carefully at the three men. Their accents had taken her back for a moment to her time in the Acre. Had she known any of them when she lived with Mary McCormic? No. She did not recognize them. She said nothing more than thanks; if I ask them who sent them to Klaus, she thought, they will tell me a name that I do not want to hear.

They saw that they could do nothing to help, and so they went away filing down the narrow hall, clumping down the stairs in their heavy boots, slamming shut the outside door.

A dreadful silence settled over the apartment, broken only by Jutta's high-pitched sobs. Adolph was at the theater; the children, except for Clara, were asleep. Suddenly the summons came: "Clara!" She ran to Klaus' room, a tiny space hardly bigger than a closet. Her mother and Anna bent over the inert form stretched on the bed; she could not see its face. Sabra spoke as she worked. "Clara, do you think that you could run for Dr. Greenhalge? He lives on Chestnut Street, number seventeen. I know it's dark, but it's not so late—not nine o'clock. Run all the way, don't stop for anything and come back with him, not alone. Do you think you can do that?"

She did not look at Clara as she spoke, but the child heard the urgency in her voice.

"Yes," she said. There was an unpleasant smell in the room. She backed away, her stomach churning. "Yes," she said again. She was glad of something useful to do; she wanted to run, she wanted to feel cold air in her lungs, to escape her rising fear.

She flew like the wind through the darkened streets. She heard her lightly pounding footsteps, she heard a high faint ringing in her ears. It might have been the song of the demons pursuing her—the little devils of fear who drove her on, ever faster, until she arrived breathless on Greenhalge's doorstep, hardly able to yank the bell-pull. Hurry, she thought. She had begun to shiver. Running had warmed her; now she must stand still and wait. Her breath came in painful spasms. When at last the door was opened by Greenhalge himself, she could hardly gasp out her message. He understood her, however, and, telling her to wait, he shut the door while he fetched his satchel.

When they arrived at the Hartmanns', they found Sabra and Anna sitting helplessly by Klaus' bed. They had bathed away the blood and staunched the wounds with clean cloths; now they could only wait for Dr. Greenhalge's ministrations. Accustomed as he was to viewing trauma —he attended many operatives crushed and torn by the machines—he clucked his tongue in astonishment at the sight of Klaus' battered body. "How did this happen?" he said. They told him what little they knew. "Attempted murder," he said. "Have you notified the police?" They had not; nor had they been able to send for Adolph. "Never mind," he said, removing his coat and rolling up his shirt sleeves. "I'll need you here." He glanced up at Anna, whose life had hung in the balance not six months ago. These people were strong and healthy, they were well-fed, well brought up to physical fitness. Therefore, they had at least a chance to survive when illness or injury came. He would do all that he had been trained to do, and perhaps again his luck would hold. He set his fingers onto Klaus' jaw; they heard the first faint *click* as the bones snapped into place.

Klaus did not die. For many weeks he lay comatose, his life despaired of; from time to time he would come fully awake and speak lucidly, painfully, before relapsing again. He had not recognized his attackers, he said; they had said nothing to him beyond asking his name. Adolph, raging, had gone to the police and demanded that the culprits be arrested. You know who did this, he shouted; bring them in and charge them! The police were annoyed. We know nothing, they said. Probably your son provoked the attack and the men who hit him were simply defending themselves.

The police were Native Americans; they did not like foreigners. A new jail had recently been built: an elaborate stone castle, a turreted Gothic nightmare in the latest fashion. Within its forbidding walls was an experiment in criminal justice: separate quarters for male and female prisoners. This jail was packed full of lawbreakers from the moment it opened, and most of them were foreign-born. O yes: the police knew all about foreigners. Go away, they said to Adolph.

Through the spring and summer and into the fall, Klaus came slowly, agonizingly back to life. By midsummer he was able to sit up; in September he took his first few hesitant steps. All during his convalescence he had a private nurse. After the first days, when it seemed that he had a chance after all to stay alive, Clara had gone to him; thinking of Miss Nightingale, she had taken the cloth from Anna's hand and begun to bathe his face. As his periods of consciousness lengthened, she sat by him and occasionally read to him, or answered his few questions, or fetched his meals. She had been glad when school was done for the month's vacation in August, for then she could devote all her time to him. She felt that she had been given a special responsibility; was it not she who had fetched the doctor, and so saved him from the very first?

Sabra watched her daughter with mingled concern and admiration. Surely it was not right for an eleven-year-old child to spend her days watching by a sickbed? And yet she had to admit that she preferred Clara at home rather than running off to the dubious pleasures of the rehearsals at the theater. And certainly she, herself, would have been shy of tending Klaus, knowing his feelings for her. Probably, she thought, he would not have recovered so quickly had I been nursing him. My presence would have upset him, he would have suffered a relapse. A dozen times a day, she passed the door of Klaus' little room and saw Clara sitting there, as competent as any adult, reading to Klaus, or helping him to eat his meals, or even, once, writing down his thoughts as he dictated to her. When she inquired, Clara told her that she had been writing a letter for Klaus—a letter to MacKenzie in Kansas, telling him of the fate of his newspaper. Even Dr. Greenhalge, busy and distracted as he was, commented on Clara's devoted care. "He is fortunate to have so faithful an attendant," he said.

"When she grows up she can go to work in the hospital, eh?" said Adolph. He was not aware of having uttered a faux pas; relieved as he was at Klaus' recovery, he was merely trying to make a little pleasant conversation.

Dr. Greenhalge was appalled. "In public? Good heavens, man—would you ruin the girl for life? No decent woman goes to nurse in hospitals. Women belong at home. At home, their nursing duties are entirely appropriate. But to work at it for money—who would marry her after she had had such an experience?"

Although Sabra agreed with him, she did not like his rudeness to Adolph. She murmured a word or two about Miss Nightingale.

"Miss Nightingale is a freak of nature," said Dr. Greenhalge. "She ought to be permanently shut up in an asylum for the insane. I can assure you that if any female in my family behaved as she does, intruding on men's affairs—no modesty, no decency, no sense of woman's proper sphere—why, I would have that woman committed at once to the facilities at Worcester, and there she would stay for the rest of her life. Such behavior in a woman makes it obvious that she has lost her powers of reason."

Clara, on her way to the kitchen to make a cup of tea for her patient, had overheard this exchange. Her face showed no expression; it was a cipher that Sabra could not read.

During the first week of October, Rachel Bradshaw came to the city to visit her father. In due course she came to see her friend Sabra as well, and when she had heard the story of the attack on Klaus she was politely indignant but hardly deeply moved. "He did not impress me as being stupid," she said privately to Sabra. "He had an anti-slavery newspaper which he was building toward a good circulation—a terribly important weapon for us, believe me. And what did he do? He antagonized the Know-Nothings. He had no business to do that. In a city like this, a city so dependent on cotton, we need a good abolitionist paper. Now he has thrown it all away. I am sorry for him, but he should not have printed the attack on the Nativists. It was a tactical error. Some of them, after all, lean to the anti-slavery position."

They heard the downstairs door slam shut, small feet thudding up the stairs: Clara, home from school, rushing to her more important work. She looked in briefly to say hello; in a moment, seeing that Klaus was napping, she returned to have a cup of chocolate and a visit with her mother's guest. Rachel was delighted to see her; she inquired in some detail about the child's life, her progress at school. She has not given up, thought Sabra. But of course she had not: anyone would want such a child, bright and pretty, sweet-tempered and companionable—but she is mine, you will not get her.

After a moment with her thoughts she came back to them and realized that their conversation had taken a new turn, and that now Clara was questioning Rachel.

"Why, child, I don't know," said Rachel. She seemed oddly at a loss for words. "I haven't the faintest idea. One learns from experience, I suppose—which you certainly are doing here with Klaus. Of course nursing is not a respectable profession, but doctoring certainly is—for men. And of course there is no good reason why women should not become doctors as well, is there?" Her still-lovely face hardened for a moment. "No reason except man-made rules. Listen—I know a woman who is more active than I am in the women's cause. She still wears the Bloomer costume, I believe. She helped to organize the Women's Convention at New-York, and she has quite persuaded Mr. Garrison that the women's cause is equally as important as the slaves'. She puts him on the platform at every opportunity to speak for women, and he faithfully signs all her pronouncements. She may know of some way to help you. Of course no medical school here will accept female students, but perhaps abroad—perhaps in Paris, or Germany—yes. I seem to remember that someone mentioned a place in Bonn. And in the meantime, you have the perfect opportunity here to learn the language. Perhaps it is fate." She smiled at Clara, who sat open-mouthed at the sudden, unexpected vistas opened to her. Paris! Germany! She glanced at her mother, who was as astonished as herself. There has been enough tutoring of English here, thought Clara; now it is my turn to learn a new language.

"Of course," continued Rachel after a moment, "it would cost a good deal of money."

"I can work," said Clara eagerly, "I can go on the Corporation—"

"No!" said Sabra quickly. Rachel nodded agreement. "No, Clara. You need your schooling if you are to take advanced study, and besides, it would take you twenty years to save enough. No: stay with your lessons, for the time being at least, and your mother and I will put our heads together and see if we can find a solution."

Sabra felt as though the two of them, Rachel and Clara, had conspired against her. Suddenly, in not five minutes' time, Clara was to go to Germany to study nursing—or, worse, doctoring! It was wrong—very wrong of Rachel to put such notions into the child's head. Such a course of action was unthinkable. I will not receive a visit from Rachel again, she thought; she will never change, she will always be spouting some outlandish idea, ordering people's lives.

That evening, Clara confided her news to Klaus. Much to Sabra's annoyance, he approved. "She has a gift for it," he said. "Just as Papa has his gift for music. And we must follow where our talents lead us—*ja,* or we are always unhappy." His face, now almost fully healed, took on a wistful expression, and she knew his thoughts: where would his own abilities lead him, now that his life had so unexpectedly been given back?

Winter came on, bitter cold and snow and ice locking them once more within doors. Klaus paced back and forth through the apartment to strengthen his muscles and take his necessary exercise; he might slip and fall if he went outside, and then his recovery would have to begin all over again. He was glad to have some new task to which to apply himself, and so in addition to her regular lessons, Clara had an hour each evening of German grammar and pronunciation. She was very bright; she learned quickly. Adolph beamed at her. "She learns *aber schnell—*

very fast. *Ja,* she is young, her brain is strong." He paused, his long tweed cloak around his shoulders preparatory to leaving for his evening's work. The older members of the family, including Clara, sat in the parlor: warm and safe, adequately fed, surviving in spite of all—yes, in the face of enormous odds, he thought, they had achieved some small measure of peace and freedom. His realization of this fact came to him every now and again at unexpected moments, stunning him into small episodes of amazement, of gratitude. All that he needed in this world to make him happy was Klaus' recognition of the fact that politics—any politics—was a luxury that they could not afford. And certainly, after his narrow brush with death, Klaus would now agree. He could return to his daguerrean studio; he could make a living free from worry and fear. Eventually, perhaps, he would find a wife with money, since Sabra did not seem to want to marry him. And the children would grow up healthy and happy and make their own ways in life—yes. All was well. He called good night and went out.

The next day, as Sabra was ladling out bowls of ox-tail soup for the noon meal, a boy arrived at the downstairs door with a note for her. She stared at the fine copperplate script: "Mrs. Sabra Blood." According to the letterhead, it was from the offices of Blood, Robbins & Spring, Counselors at Law. His father's law firm. Why? What now? Silas was dead and gone, and his father had told her most cruelly, years ago, that he wanted nothing to do with Silas' putative wife and child. Then why this note? Open it—but she was afraid. She had done with the Bloods, father and son alike. Why could they not have done with her?

"Bad news?" asked Klaus.

"I don't know."

"Go on," he said. "Read it. You will imagine worse than the truth."

Cautiously, as if it contained an explosive charge, she broke the seal and unfolded the paper. And it was, after all, an innocuous enough message:

February 11

Madam:

Kindly be present in our chambers at two o'clock tomorrow afternoon, February 12, 1856.

Very sincerely yours,
John T. Spring

14

A bitter, breath-snatching wind tore at her cloak and bonnet as she picked her way along the frozen expanse of Merrimack Street. The sun shone bright but gave no warmth; the few pedestrians whom she passed walked in peculiar attitudes, hunched against the wind, hardly seeing where they went as they slid and slipped and staggered to their destinations. She had come to hate winter. One was never warm, no matter how many flannel petticoats one wore; each year she felt less able to withstand the long siege from October until late April. And yet she reminded herself that she was not so badly off. They have it worse in the Acre, she thought, or upcountry, when the coming of winter often means that a family on a farm sees no one except themselves until the thaw. Once she had spent a winter like that at Bountiful, waiting for the child who was Clara. As always when she thought of her daughter, she felt a small rush of joy. She forgot the wind and the treacherous walking, she forgot her dread of the interview awaiting her. She was sustained by her optimism until she approached the offices to which she had been summoned; then, like the coldest wind yet, her apprehension overcame her again.

Would he be there? Why had his associate sent for her, and not he himself? Was this the commencement of some legal proceeding? But what claim—? She stopped still, paralyzed at her thought. Clara. A woman behind her swerved to avoid a collision, but she did not notice. Clara. They would try to take her away. The old man wanted her, perhaps, or at least wanted her away from her mother. She remembered his bitter face, his voice harsh with outrage. I should go home, she thought; I should not see them. I will pretend that I never received the note. But after a moment's reflection she realized the pointlessness of that course: they had found her once, they could find her again. She had no way to avoid them except to leave the city, and she could not leave the city without prospect of employment—of a means to live elsewhere. And even then, she thought, they will find me wherever I go. I would have to flee to the ends of the earth, and still we would not be safe. Better to face them now and discover what they want of me. She walked on.

The gold-lettered glass announced to her that she was in the presence of Authority; the obsequious yet strangely insolent clerk announced by his attitude that she was in the presence of Authority; and the short, thin, canny man who received her announced before he ever said a word that most certainly she was in the presence of the most awesome Authority imaginable: the Authority of the Law, by whose codification and subsequent entanglements men tried to order their lives and the lives of those whom the Law decreed to be their inferiors: women, children, slaves, mental defectives, and all the criminal classes. The celebrated Englishman, Mr. Dickens, who was celebrated in Lowell because he had so nicely satisfied the vanity of its ruling class, had said that the Law was a Ass. Indeed: but the Law was also a labyrinth—a narrow, twisting, doubling-back, dead-end, formidable maze through which only the shrewdest counselor could lead his bewildered client. Such shrewdness gave to a man the Authority which informed the gentleman who welcomed Sabra now: Mr. Spring, as he introduced himself, casting his shrewd legal eye up and down her windblown person, smiling cannily at her as she settled herself in the proffered chair. To put her at her ease, he shrewdly remarked that it was a very cold day; since the firm of Blood, Robbins & Spring was primarily a Corporation firm, and therefore extremely conservative, he would not commit himself any further on the subject of the weather. He decided, shrewdly, to come directly to the point of her visit.

"You are Mrs. Sabra Blood," he said.

"Yes, sir."

"And you are the—ah—widow of Silas M. Blood."

"Yes." She had never known his middle name; she did not learn it now.

"The late son of our late partner, Enoch Blood. Ah—you did not know that he had died? Your—um—father-in-law. Yes: before the New Year. Very sudden, there's a mercy."

She stared at him, too surprised to simulate grief.

"Yes. Of course he never fully recovered from the shock of his son's death. And, if I may say so, from the manner in which he was given the news: a stranger appearing like an apparition, delivering his tragic message, and then disappearing again as suddenly as he had come. Of course Mr. Blood contacted the authorities in California and they confirmed the news. I understand that you were informed also—? Yes. Please accept my profoundest sympathies, however belated. Now. To our business." He smiled at her again in a shrewd and genial way. "It is my pleasure to inform you, madam, that you have been named as a beneficiary in Mr. Blood's will—the elder Mr. Blood, of course. He has left to you the sum of—ah—five hundred dollars. I have the draft here. You have only to present it to the Railroad Bank. Of course I would advise you to deposit the money there or in some other bank, since it is foolish to risk the loss of so large a sum." He peered at her as if he were not sure that she could be entrusted with such an amount.

She sat speechless before him, trying to understand, struggling to adjust her thoughts. She had been prepared to deal with antagonists; now she must accept, as gracefully as possible, evidence of—what? Friendship? Hardly. Remorse, she thought. He was trying to ensure his entrance into Heaven by giving me—and his granddaughter—this gift.

"How did you know where to find me?" she said at last.

"It is our business to know, madam." His small shrewd eyes gleamed at her. He was not an unkind man. Often his work gave him genuine distress—when he defended a Corporation, say, against an operative's suit for allegedly unpaid wages. Now, having an opportunity to give money rather than withhold it, he enjoyed a pleasant feeling of beneficence. "And if I may say so, you have my sincerest good wishes." He held out to her an envelope. She took it, glanced inside to see the draft. Five hundred dollars. From the street below came the sound of firebells. They were very close, the horses hauling the hose and ladder engines just under the window. Five hundred dollars. She had never imagined having such a sum. It seemed a fortune: freedom. She felt light-headed. Suddenly, she had no idea why, Madame Jewel's words came back to her: "Cold and darkness, and death." She wanted very much to laugh, but she restrained herself. I must tell her, she thought, to make unhappy predictions to all her clients so that they, too, will have good fortune.

In a pleasant haze of bewilderment she took her leave of Mr. Spring. When she reached the street the shock of cold air on her face brought her back somewhat to the practicalities of her life. "Deposit it," Mr. Spring had said; and, indeed, she knew that she should do so at once. The Railroad Bank was at the corner of Shattuck Street, in the direction opposite to the Hartmanns'. Go there, she thought, and see the money safely put away. But she wanted to show the precious slip of paper to all of them before she changed it into money and put it away. Tomorrow, she thought, will be time enough to visit the bank. She opened her reticule to reassure herself that in the space of the last few moments the envelope had not disappeared. Then, shutting the purse firmly and keeping a tight hold on it, she turned to retrace her steps down Merrimack Street toward home.

And now, for the first time in some minutes, she was aware of her surroundings—of the eternally busy street, the bustling shops, the life of the town going on around her.

Everything had stopped. All traffic—all the confusion of carts and carriages and stages and drays—had come to a halt, pulled over to the side. Through the narrow way now came yet another fire wagon, horses straining, bells ringing, red-faced volunteers clinging to its sides. She smelled the acrid smell of burning painted wood, of cloth and oil and—what? She could not identify it. Over the cerulean sky drifted a pall of smoke, and now, looking to see its source, she saw heavy black clouds of it billowing from the roof of a building perhaps a block away. Intermingled with the smoke were tall tongues of bright fire leaping up; even from where she stood she could hear the sharp *snap* of burning wood, the roar of the flames as they consumed it. People stood still to stare, pedestrians stopped, customers forgetting their errands, shopkeepers standing in doorways neglecting to tend their businesses. The shouts of the firemen counterpointed the harsh clanging of the warning bells; and now from a distance came the answering calls of the bells of other companies—more men, more hoses and engines responding to the alarm.

The burning building was on her side of the street; she could not be sure, but it seemed to be the building opposite Central Street, at the join of the T.

Dear God: the Museum Theater.

She could not see, and the crush of holding traffic and the oncoming firemen made it impossible to cross to get a clearer view. A shirtsleeved man stood in the doorway of Clements' Apothecary. "Which building is it?" she cried. He shrugged. "Dunno. Looks like the Museum, don't it?" Dear God. Adolph had gone to a rehearsal—

She pushed through the thickening crowd. Small boys darted in and out; a growing murmur of people's comments filled her ears. "It's the Museum Theater, for sure." "Them gas lights is dangerous. Ought not to allow 'em." "It'll take the whole block if they don't hustle." "Hi, boy, out of the street—let the horses through!"

Blacker and blacker came the clouds of smoke, obscuring the sky, choking off their breath; sparks and cinders rained down upon them; the heat of the blazing timber melted the snow to pools of water in the street. *Adolph—*

She pushed on until, confronted by a solid mass of people, she could go no farther. Up ahead, a line of constables blocked the way to give the firemen room to battle the conflagration. But the firemen could do nothing: already the roof had begun to collapse, and now as they watched, the steeple and then the wall beneath it crumpled and fell, releasing an enormous shower of sparks which, shooting up, was transformed into a rain of cinders.

Helplessly she watched, caught in the crush, unmindful of the small holes burned in her only cloak, her best bonnet. And for the second time that day, Madame Jewel's voice sounded in her head: "Heat and light," Madame Jewel had said. "Heat and light; and cold and dark. And death."

15

"*Ja,*" said Adolph, "I am here."

He held out his arms to embrace her, and he could not help but smile at the dazed expression on her soot-stained face.

She had thought that she would never get home. She had been trapped in the crowd for an endless time; at last she had turned and made her roundabout way through Shattuck Street, down Market to Central, down Central to Church—for hours, it seemed, she had walked in the cold as darkness fell and the night sky glowed like dawn as it reflected the blaze. The Museum Theater had gone, and both buildings adjacent, and the buildings in the rear. It was only as the wind died that the exhausted engine companies had been able to bring the fire under control. The whole block might have gone—the whole city, had the fire leap-frogged to the mills and set to work on baled cotton and oil-soaked wooden flooring.

Sabra had arrived at the apartment half-frozen, perishing with cold; and yet, she thought, better to walk the streets all night than face them with the news of Adolph's death. But of course they would know before she arrived; the theater was not three blocks from where they lived, they would have been aware of the fire from the beginning, they would have watched it, frantic to learn Adolph's fate. She must be with them; and so she pressed on, no longer even feeling her feet, pulling her cloak over her face for warmth, remembering all the while to keep safe her reticule and its precious slip of paper.

And when at last she stumbled up the stairs, Adolph was there to greet her. "*Ja,*" he said again. "We were worried about you. Where have you been?"

They crowded around her as if her life, and not Adolph's, had been in danger; they gave her hot tea, and a tub of hot water for her feet, and a seat by the fire while Jutta fetched her supper. At first, everyone talked at once, especially the children; little Annalise, sensing their excitement, toddled across the room to Sabra's knee and almost fell into the foot-bath. Then Adolph ordered them to silence, and Sabra told them of how, caught in the crowd, she had seen the fire, and of how she had made her way home dreading the news of Adolph's death.

"Almost," he said. He sat opposite her; and now for the first time she noticed that his right hand was shiny with beeswax, red and puffed—a bad burn. "It started backstage, in the wardrobe room, or in the scenery —I don't know. I was with the orchestra, going over the new score. All of a sudden we heard someone yell 'Fire!' I told my men to go out the front. I went behind, to the dressing rooms—*ja,* I know, I know." He caught Anna's accusing gaze. "I should have got out with the rest. But someone called, I had to see if she—" He stopped, wincing at the pain in his hand. "It was Miss MacNaughton. I knew her voice." Sabra felt Clara's hand heavy on her shoulder; she reached up to cover it with her own. In the clothes-press in the children's room were Miss MacNaughton's cast-off odds and ends: a torn lace shawl, a black silk petticoat, a frilled shirt-waist of a vaguely Elizabethan cut. In a box on the dresser were red glass ear-bobs and a battered brass crown. It had been many months since Clara had visited her friend. If Klaus had not needed her; if she had continued to watch the rehearsals; if she had been in Miss MacNaughton's dressing room that afternoon— As tall, as near grown as she was, Clara sank onto her mother's lap and buried her face in Sabra's neck. Sabra held her close. She felt the child's body shuddering with sobs. She looked questioningly at Adolph. "*Ja,*" he said softly. "She was caught. And Gage, too. The others got out in time. I couldn't get to her. I called to her, but behind the stage, where she was, it was all in flames in a minute. I couldn't get through. I was almost caught myself. The smoke, the heat—"

"No, Papa," said Klaus. "No more. The child doesn't want to hear it."

That night, Clara dreamed that she was trapped with Miss MacNaughton in the burning building. The actress had fainted; she lay heavy across Clara's legs and Clara could not move, could not escape the crackling, searing flames which licked and devoured the dry wooden structure all around them. On and on came the fire; the smoke blinded her, it choked her nearly to unconsciousness, but she was pinned to the floor, she could not move, she could not run, she would surely be roasted alive—

Sabra rushed in. The children in the big bed had awakened at Clara's screams; now Sabra reassured them, she ordered them back to sleep and mercifully they obeyed. She sat beside her own girl and they wept together, mourning the dead.

"If only she had died in some other way," sobbed Clara. "But to die in a fire— O, Mama, how horrible to burn to death! I can't bear it—can't bear to think of it. Adolph's hand pains him terribly and that isn't even a very bad burn. Think of burning to *death,* Mama—think of it!"

Klaus hovered in the doorway holding a glass. "Give her some wine—here, I have it for her," he said softly. Obediently Clara drank it, hardly noticing the unpleasant taste. Klaus and Sabra stayed with her until she slept again. Then they withdrew, leaving the door open; they sat in the kitchen, drinking hot chocolate, neither of them sleepy—wide awake at three in the morning. "I will listen for her," said Klaus. He was fully dressed; his long recovery, bedridden, had left him with a distaste for nightclothes or even for his bed. Often he spent the night in the parlor, reading, napping on the sofa, alert for the sounds of running feet, hard-breathing men come to attack him. So he knew about night terrors; he would keep watch over Clara, who had so devotedly watched over him these past months. He smiled at Sabra reassuringly. He is as beautiful as ever, she thought; he has healed without a scar. If one looked closely, one could see that his nose was ever so slightly crooked: only that, and the scar, hidden by the fall of his hair, from the first attack when they had broken all the windows of his office. They had not wanted to kill him that night; the cut on his forehead had been accidental. Dr. Greenhalge had shaved off the long moustache, and Klaus had not let it grow again. Clean-shaven, he looked younger, much less European—"foreign." "Finish your chocolate and go to bed," he said. "If she cries out again I will sit with her."

Clara slept peacefully until morning; but the next night, and the night after that, and the next—every night—she was caught in her nightmare again and she shrieked for rescue, until her pretty face became haggard as it had never been during all the long wearisome weeks when she attended Klaus' sickbed. Their roles were reversed now: he appointed himself her nurse, and since he could not give her a glass of wine every night for fear of making her ill, he brought her hot chocolate, or weak, milky tea, and sat by her bed and whispered stories to her in German.

The Museum Theater was no more: it would not be rebuilt by some new entrepreneur. There was no possibility of other employment for Adolph in the city; he had a few students, but their fees did not amount to more than three or four dollars a week. "Not enough, eh?" he said to Sabra, smiling bleakly. He suddenly felt his years. He was fifty-four: hardly a good age to begin all over again to make a life in the new country. He had hoped to stay in the east; he had not wanted to follow the majority of his countrymen into the wilds of the Western Territories. Now, it seemed, he had no choice. He had an acquaintance, a former Professor of History in Bonn who now operated a Biergarten in Milwaukee. He had written to Adolph some months ago at the time of Klaus' convalescence; he had urged the Hartmanns to join their own kind in the new state of Wisconsin. At the time, Adolph had thought that yes, perhaps—but not until Klaus recovered. Now they would go.

"Milwaukee?" said Sabra. The name meant nothing to her. She wanted to leave the city, yes—but for some civilized place. Certainly she did not want to follow the Hartmanns into the wilderness. "I have five hundred dollars," she said. "We can live on that for a long time, until you find a new position."

"*Ja*," said Adolph. "*Almosen*. Am I living on your charity now?"

"But I have lived—"

"You have earned your way. We will earn ours. Come west with us and see the Indians."

She looked from one face to another—Adolph, Anna, Jutta weeping softly, about to meet the dreaded savages at last, the children anxious not to lose their beloved Tante Sabra, but eager to go all the same, wanting the adventure. Clara sat with eyes downcast, her expression unreadable; this was her family, and how did one willingly separate? On the other hand, she was sure that one could not receive any kind of education, let alone a specialized one, in Milwaukee. Sabra looked last at Klaus. He met her glance, and she saw—with vast relief—that there was no longer love in his eyes, no hungry pleading, no begging her to love him in return. He hesitated for a moment and then slowly, deliberately, he shook his head.

Adolph understood. "So," he said, "you want to stay here so they can kill you?" His voice was tired and discouraged. He had lost his eldest son long ago, perhaps even before they came to America; only now did he fully realize his loss.

"Not here," said Klaus. "I will go wherever I am needed."

"By whom?" said Sabra; and as soon as she had spoken she knew the answer. By Mr. Garrison, of course. She wondered what kind of man he was, this Garrison, who long ago had cast a spell over Rachel Bradshaw so that she threw away her life—and Sabra's as well—to serve him; and who now, so many years later, still exercised so powerful an influence that a bright young man like Klaus Hartmann would for his sake give up everything, leave his family, travel wherever he was needed—even into the Valley of the Shadow of Death, she thought. Even there will he travel, he will risk his life again for Mr. Garrison.

Adolph wept, then; and they wept with him. Three days later the family began their journey. After seeing them off at the depot, Sabra paid another visit to Mr. Spring. She thought that he might help her to relocate in Boston. She knew no one there, she said. Did he have any advice for her?

He did: a likely property not half a mile from where they sat. You will not prosper in Boston, Mrs. Blood, he said; he smiled at her in a jolly way. But here in Lowell—yes! "My client's catastrophe shall be your good fortune. He wants very badly to sell a fine boarding house in Charles Street. He will take much less than it is worth. You will have ten rooms to rent for a good income, and a pleasant suite for yourself and your daughter. I could not give better advice to a member of my own family, were she in your position. The property will not be on the market very long at this price, I can assure you. It is a wise investment; there is no better place to put one's money than real estate in a rising market.

This city has not done growing yet. Property values must continue to go up. In a few years' time you can sell at a large profit."

And so she became the proprietress of a boarding house, subject to all the demands and difficulties peculiar to that occupation. She did not mind. It was a way to live as good as most, and better than many. She made friends with some of her neighbors, thus filling in part the void left by the departed Hartmanns; she managed the place well enough always to be fully rented; she and Clara had three meals a day and warm beds at night. For the time being, she asked no more. Clara could keep at her schooling; when she finished, they would decide what to do next.

16

Endlessly, inexorably, the river flowed down to the sea. Dam it, divert it, pollute it—still it flowed, life-giving, energy-giving, its power harnessed to turn the great wheels of the manufactories which lined its banks in Manchester and Nashua, in Lowell and its new spawn, Lawrence, in Haverhill and Amesbury and so on down to Newburyport. Had it been a river of gold it could not have more greatly enriched its depredators. Millions of dollars came to the capitalists who built the factories—millions multiplied as new factories went up, new hands were hired to make cloth, new tons of finished goods went through the offices of the selling agents at Boston to points east and west, all around the globe.

Once upon a time, the looms and spinning jennies clustered in red-brick palaces along the Merrimack's green banks had seemed a miracle. They seemed so, still, to many people—although not to the hordes of Yankee women who, having sampled the pleasures of factory life, had seen their minuscule wages cut down once too often, had had the machines speeded up beyond endurance year after year. Many, faced with the prospect of factory labor, chose prostitution instead: the brothels of Boston and New-York, so it was said, were filled with refugees from the factory towns. And although the entrepreneurs might have regretted the loss of a native-born work force—for who could brag about hiring an Irishman?—they did not miss the turnouts and petitions, the outside agitators who came to stir up trouble. The Irish wanted no part of strikes and combinations; they wanted only to earn their week's wage, small as it was, and to live free of apprehension about the next potato crop.

And so the factories continued to run, powered by the great river and now by steam as well; and the owners continued to take their dividends. It seemed that the world had an unending need for cotton yard goods, and for woolen as well; the Yankee entrepreneurs were only too happy to supply it. As the hands in each factory were pushed to the limit of their production, more factories were built.

In the mid-1840s, the newly founded Essex Company bought land ten miles downriver from Lowell. There its directors ordered the construction of a huge dam and a network of power canals. Then, in their time-tested fashion, they began to sell land and water privileges to their friends.

People in Lowell watched jealously as the new city began to rise on the river's banks. The entrepreneurs let it be known that this new place would be an industrial wonder, just as Lowell had been supposed to be a generation previous. Now the Lowell Experiment had not failed: certainly not. On the other hand, certain unforeseeable problems had arisen. The entrepreneurs had not thought that their native American female operatives would desert them. They had not imagined a catastrophe like the potato famine, which, in driving the Irish from their homeland, had sent a permanent factory population to the mill towns of New England, with all the attendant evils of that permanence. They had not even anticipated their own greed, which would seduce them to drive their operatives to the point of death in order to maintain the companies' profits.

In Lawrence, the entrepreneurs said, we will profit from our experience in Lowell. The factories will be larger, and they will be built in a solid wall along the river: we will not allow unproductive open spaces between them. Nor will we exhaust ourselves by making rules for the operatives' conduct. Most of them will be Irish in any case, so their morals are no concern of ours. Further, we will tolerate no nonsense like *The Lowell Offering*. Certainly we will tolerate no Ten-Hour nonsense, and in any case the Irish are not capable of organizing against us. The Lowell Experiment opened the door to large-scale manufacturing in America; now that factory work is an accepted thing—which it was not before the founding of Lowell—we need no longer concern ourselves about public opinion. Even if factory labor is as degraded here as it is in England, no one cares now. People grovel to us because we are rich: they do not concern themselves with how we got our fortunes.

At first, everything went according to plan. Once again the men owning land near the river were swindled by Corporation straws; gangs of Irish laborers were brought in to dig canals and lay foundations twice the length of those of the mills in Lowell; shares were sold as soon as they were offered. But in 1847, fifteen Irishmen were killed when a coffer dam collapsed; and in 1854 a bloody riot occurred between Irish and native Americans which, widely reported, gave the city a notoriety entirely unlooked-for by the entrepreneurs.

But the production of woolen and cotton cloth continued apace, and so the city's notoriety was soon overcome by its prosperity. Like Lowell, it gave enormous profits to its founders. They congratulated themselves; they kept on building. One of the new factories was the Pemberton Mill. The owners wanted the very best man available to Agent it. The name of Josiah Bradshaw was mentioned at a Corporate meeting in Boston: an experienced, capable man, twenty years and more at the Commonwealth in Lowell, a man with a firm control of his operatives, never sick a day. But after some discussion it was decided instead to give the job to a man named Chase, who was a nephew of one of the largest stockholders.

Although they did not know it—had no idea of it—Bradshaw would not have wanted to leave Lowell. In Lowell, he had a position whose duties formed the familiar pattern of his life. He knew all his overseers and second overseers and many of his hands; he knew every inch of his mill as well as he knew his own house (he thought of it as his mill, although he owned not a single share of stock); he knew every machine—every part of every machine—as if the iron and wood were living, breathing flesh. The Commonwealth Mill had been his private domain for so long that its daily routine fitted him as comfortably as an old slipper. He could rule it —Agent it—in his sleep, so well did he know it; he would not have wanted to go to a new place.

And yet he had his troubles like everyone else. After thirty years of hard use, the machinery was wearing out; and after the annual dividends were paid to the stockholders, there was no money left to replace it. Almost every day, it seemed, came from one or another of the workrooms a call for a mechanic. The mechanics, unlike the operatives, were still mostly native Americans and therefore clever and quick enough to suit any employer, but even a mechanical genius could not breathe life into a machine hopelessly worn out, used long past its time. They did the best they could: smart lads all, they tinkered and patched and invented new parts on the spot, and somehow the machinery was kept in service and the mill continued to produce to capacity. But it was a grave concern to him: operatives were dispensable—worthless, even, since there were so many of them; but a good power loom was beyond price.

The operatives, of course, were another problem, albeit of a lesser order. Like his brother Agents at the neighboring Hamilton and Appleton and Lawrence Corporations, Bradshaw had put his qualms and his fine feelings away for safe-keeping for some years now, and when the Yankee women had decamped, he had filled their places with hordes of Irish. But it was not the same, now, as it had been in the old days. The workrooms stank, now, from more than oil and starch; the sullen, ignorant faces which he saw each day were still an unpleasant shock after years of genteel Yankee girls; and the boarding-house matrons, long past their first brief protests at boarding Irish, were nonetheless still unhappy at being forced to do so. He seldom visited the Commonwealth's boarding houses; he disliked the matrons' barely concealed resentment.

He made it all right with Boston. Boston no longer cared about curfews and cleanliness, because a high moral tone in the city was no longer needed to attract new hands. Corporate responsibility for the boarding houses had become a nuisance in recent years, and Bradshaw had no doubt that in good time—when the price was right—they would be sold to individual owners and left to deteriorate even further.

And so he passed his lonely time, hardly speaking to his wife when he saw her, not needing to speak very much to his subordinate men at the mill: for they knew their jobs as well as he knew his, they needed little direction from him. In the evenings, after closing bell, he had for some years past fallen into the habit of dining out. Sometimes he visited his daughter Lydia at her new home on Wyman Street; more often he took his supper at the Merrimack House. Here he met a variety of people, all of them transient, with whom he could pass a pleasant couple of hours before making his way up Belvidere Hill. One evening, some time past, he made the acquaintance of a Mesmeric lecturer whose most casual conversation seemed extraordinarily intense; here was a man who could make you believe that day was night, that up was down—that wrong was right, even, so uncanny were his powers of persuasion. After they had conversed for some time, the man led Bradshaw upstairs to one of the rooms. The light was dim; Bradshaw could not see very clearly. He saw only that on the bed reclined a figure. He thought at first that it was a young girl with her hair cut short. But when he turned in surprise to his companion, he saw that the Mesmeric lecturer had vanished.

Had the child awaiting him on the bed that night been a girl, Bradshaw would very probably have left the room at once. At most he would have satisfied his lust on her and then departed as quickly as possible, never to return. But the child had not been a girl: and so he had stayed. Very soon—for he was a clever man—he had become exquisitely adept at this new indulgence, this undreamed-of ecstasy. And very soon, too, the site of his encounters was transferred to a small house on an alley off Moody Street: a safe house, run by an efficient and close-mouthed eunuch. Perhaps half a dozen boys lived there. A number of gentlemen visited them each evening. The boys were a miscellaneous lot; none of them spoke English more than a few words. One was a black from the illegal slave trade which had lately revived, one was some sort of Indian, the others white. Two of these were little Gaelic lads picked up on the docks of New-York or Liverpool by some enterprising shark. They all knew what was expected of them; they performed for their very lives, and grew infinitely adept. When one or another of them died from rough handling, he was quickly replaced; for the eunuch, in his way, ran an establishment as efficient as a Corporation mill.

Of course such indulgence was risky. It left a man open to blackmail. Bradshaw began to pay, in regular installments, during the summer of 1855. In the next two years he paid out close to a thousand dollars. He was a proud, intelligent man; he saw very well where his weakness led him, but he no longer cared. He had found pleasure at last—for which he would have paid the sum twice—three times over.

In the spring of 1857, one of the sharks who procured the boys made a serious error. He had strict instructions to bring the children in from other cities; no local boys were to be used. But an epidemic of pneumonia during the past winter had killed three boys; all the visiting gentlemen, some of whom came as far as thirty and forty miles, could not be accommodated. The shark waited for two weeks; and then, having received no new shipment nor any hope of one, he took a walk one night in the Acre.

It happened that on that same night, a group of Irishmen had attended a fund-raising meeting of the Hibernian Relief Society at the Widow Muldoon's. Several of them were just coming out into Cork Street when the shark made his catch. Patrick O'Haran, preoccupied by thoughts of conspiracy and armed revolt as his countrymen rose against the hated English rule, was not at first sure what he saw. By the time he realized, the shark had vanished around the corner with his prey. Motioning his comrades into a silent column, Patrick followed in the direction the man had taken; he saw him at a distance as they turned the same corner. The man was easily discernible as he hurried along under the street lamps, his small companion trotting at his side. Patrick and his friends tracked him to his destination. They waited half a block away. In perhaps forty-five minutes the man emerged from the house to which he had delivered the boy. He was a small man, he wore an oddly shaped hat, he walked with a distinctive gait. They nabbed him; they persuaded him to tell them what he had done with the child. In the end he was so frightened that he even told them the few names that he knew of the gentlemen who patronized the house.

In the morning he was found floating in the Northern Canal, his life garroted out of him by a piece of thick rope which had been stolen from the yard of the Lawrence Corporation some time during the night. Because the theft could not be proved, the watch was let off with a warning about sleeping on the job.

17

Clara put down the heavy bucket of soapy water and paused for a moment, bracing herself with one hand against the wall until she recovered her breath. She should have gone down to the back kitchen again to get clean water from the cauldron heating on the stove, but the thought of one flight down and two up, to the third floor where she now was, had defeated her. She was scrubbing only the halls and the stairs; the water that she had used for the second floor would do for the third. The water had slopped over, forming a dark pool around the bucket. She went back to fetch the mop; as she climbed the stairs again she lectured herself to keep up her spirits. Half an hour more, she thought. Then her mother would have returned from the market, and they could have a comfortable hour together peeling potatoes and drinking tea. And then perhaps she could read until supper; her English instructor at the high school, Miss Clarke, had loaned her the first volume of a new novel, highly recommended. "Have a handkerchief handy," Miss Clarke had said. "The death of the first Mrs. Dombey is simply excruciating."

So Clara attacked the floor with renewed vigor, buoyed by the thought of the unlooked-for treat of a new book, and wanting to tell her mother about the funny incident that morning when Alice Harvey had been called on to recite from *Paradise Lost,* and, having forgotten the passage in question, had simply improvised, hoping that Miss Clarke would not know the difference between her own verse and Milton's. Clara laughed out loud, now, even as she performed the hated task of scrubbing. Alice was a funny girl: no scholar, but a good, true friend.

"Can I share the joke, little lady?"

The mop handle clattered to the floor. She turned to see Mr. Slocum standing at the door of his room. She had not heard him open it, had not known that he was there. He was a second hand on the Appleton. He had boarded with them for nearly a year. During that time she had not said a dozen words to him. He was a tall, rawboned Vermonter whose eyes never quite met those of the person to whom he spoke. They did not meet hers, now. She stared at him, badly startled, as if she could make him vanish by focusing on the door frame behind him.

The house was quiet. It was mid-afternoon; everyone was at work. Why wasn't he? Never mind, she thought. She bent to pick up the mop. He shifted his tall body and leaned against the other side of the door frame. He grinned as he watched her. She turned so that she faced him as she spread the film of water over the floor and then wiped it up. She did not look at him again, and he said nothing more. He accepted her rebuff with surprising good humor. He simply stood and watched her as she worked, as she drew close to his room at the end of the hall.

"You didn't finish the third floor?" said Sabra later, as they sat together in the kitchen. "Whyever not?" I have no right to be annoyed, she thought; the girl works as hard as a hired girl here, and she keeps up with her schoolwork as well. Still: it was unlike Clara to leave a task undone. She had a positively Teutonic thoroughness, picked up, no doubt, from their time with the Hartmanns.

But when Clara explained to her, she struggled to keep her alarm from showing. Dear God! Mr. Slocum! She had never liked him. She had taken him on simply because she was desperate for boarders—had been, ever since the crash in '57. Half the mills in the city had shut down; shopkeepers had been ruined from the loss of the operatives' trade, the churches had made frantic appeals for food and fuel for distribution, the Reverend Horatio Wood, Minister at Large, had had no time to walk the streets searching for objects for his charity, since his offices were mobbed from morning till late night with the desperate unemployed.

Sabra resolved to speak to Slocum. At once. I will tell him—what? She paused by the door. Not to speak to Clara? Not to stare at her? But everyone stared at Clara, men and women too. She had always been a pretty child. Now, as she approached her fifteenth birthday, she was growing into a beautiful young woman. Even in an old smock, thought Sabra, even scrubbing floors, she was beautiful. It was not surprising that a man—any man—would make overtures. But you will not have her, thought Sabra. None of you. There was not a man in the city who was good enough for her girl.

Where, then?

Wearily she returned to the table where Clara sat, paring knife in hand, making her way through the mound of potatoes to be peeled. There was nothing that she could say to Slocum. He had not after all committed any offense, whatever might have been in his mind. But if it happens again, she thought, I will tell him to go. We will manage somehow. They say the Hamilton is to reopen. People will come back to the city to work. I will have a full house again.

For about a year after she had purchased the boarding house, she had thought that she had made a wise decision in following Mr. Spring's advice. But then as the effects of the financial panic began to be felt, and as she watched her boarders drift away, thrown out of work, forced to leave the city, she had felt the old fear once again, the desperate question—how to survive?—and she had berated herself for her stupidity in wasting her inheritance. I should have saved the money and left the city when I had the chance, she thought; I should have gone west with Adolph and the family; only now, when it is too late, do I understand my mistake in buying this house.

She knew nothing of business. Of course not: no woman did. But even the most astute businessmen in the country had been unhappily surprised when the panic struck in the summer of 1857. Suddenly a man's holdings, which he thought qualified him as a rich man, were worthless pieces of paper; suddenly men were ruined, families disgraced, factories closed, the effects of the crash felt all down the line to the operatives and those who lived on their trade. The Northern business interests demanded that Congress do something—anything!—to help; but Congress, so effectively dominated by the South, lowered the protective tariff instead and thus further ruined the Yankees by allowing imported goods to come in cheap. Now, in the spring of '59, prosperity seemed as far away as ever; but people kept their faith, they knew that something would happen soon to bring the good times back.

Clara's fifteenth birthday fell on a Saturday, and all of a sudden, at the last minute, it seemed that there could be a party for her, after all. Rachel Bradshaw called in two days previous. As usual her appearances were unexpected, unlooked-for. Rachel was a questionable influence on Clara, filling her head with new schemes, preposterous ideas—the idea of studying medicine, for example, which Clara mercifully seemed to have forgotten. On the other hand, Rachel was good company, always ready with an amusing story of her multifarious activities. We have not so many friends, thought Sabra, that we can ignore her when she comes.

Coincidentally, the next day, Sabra answered the door bell at four in the afternoon to find Klaus Hartmann standing on the step. She was genuinely glad to see him, and Clara, of course, was ecstatic; she could not have been more overjoyed had he been her brother. She ran into his great hug, she kissed him unabashedly on both cheeks. "Months!" she cried, laughing and yet close to tears. "For months you've not been to see us!" They led him into their small apartment on the first floor, they demanded that he stay for supper—a private supper, they said, after the boarders had been fed. And he could stay with them, sleep in one of the empty rooms. No need to go to a hotel.

And so Clara, the next night, had her birthday party, and the four of them drank her health in champagne (bought by Klaus) and admired her new paisley shawl (bought by Rachel), and ate a birthday cake baked by Sabra, who had scrimped a little money, too, for a shirtwaist trimmed in lace, which she had had made up by a poor dressmaker whose business, like everyone else's, had not yet recovered. They sat around the table and read the birthday letter from all the Hartmanns. The family was continuing to do well; they had settled in, Jutta was to be married, Adolph had more pupils than he could handle and a promising orchestra besides. They wished that Sabra and Clara would come out to them: the West was not nearly so bad as they had feared.

Hearing the voice of his father come strongly through the still uncertain English grammar, Klaus looked inquiringly at Sabra after Clara had stopped reading. "Would you go?" he said.

"I don't know. Possibly. I'd need to sell the house, of course, and I doubt that I could find a buyer now."

"Things will pick up," said Rachel confidently. "They always do."

"I'd be happy, right now, if they picked up only enough to rent all my rooms," said Sabra. She laughed a little, to show them that she did not intend to throw a pall over what was, after all, intended to be a happy occasion.

"Are you getting by?" said Rachel. "You aren't forced to go to your savings, are you?"

Sabra laughed again, more sharply and with less mirth. "My savings, as you call them, never really existed. I told you before: I spent almost every penny of the inheritance on this house. I still have the ingots, of course. Safe in the bank."

"There's a mercy," said Rachel; but already the distant look in her eye indicated that her thoughts had traveled on to problems of more general significance. She turned to Klaus; although they shared no liking for each other, they were after all soldiers in the same army—Mr. Garrison's army—and therefore, she thought, they should exchange information when they met.

"Have you news of Captain Brown?" she said. "He promises some definite action, but he will not say when. I met him some months ago. People say he is mad, but he is not. He made perfect sense to me."

They discussed Captain Brown for some minutes; and then Rachel, who once upon a time had been taught manners by her Aunt Amalia, seemed to remember that the evening was Clara's, and that it might be thoughtful to redirect the conversation to her. Such a pretty girl, with her dark hair and her delicate features and her good, quick mind. How she would have loved to take Clara away, to show her some of the possibilities of the world! Even for women, the world had possibilities in this spring of 1859; and undoubtedly, within a decade at most, the elective franchise could be secured for the female sex and all problems, everywhere, would be solved through women's intelligent use of the Ballot.

"Now, Clara," she said, "you must tell us about yourself. Neither Klaus nor I has seen you in half a year at least. You must make a birthday speech, and tell us how you are, and what your plans are now for the future, and everything equally interesting."

Her voice seemed a little too loud for the small sitting room where they sat; and when she stopped, the silence seemed a little too quiet. It was as if she had touched on some communal nerve. They had all three passed their youth; even Klaus, the youngest of them, was now thirty-two. But here before them, in the person of Clara, was youth and hope all over again; they looked at her with confident affection as they waited to hear her reply.

Now life is made up of strange coincidences; had Clara been presented with that request only a week previous, she would not have had an answer. But she had had a long and complicated conversation with her poetic friend, Alice Harvey, on Monday last as they walked home from the high school, and Alice had been extremely persuasive in her argument. And so now Clara had a prompt reply; she was relieved to break her news to her mother in the presence of others so that Sabra's reaction would not be too extreme.

She smiled at them, quite calm, quite decided, as if she were Queen Victoria herself issuing a royal edict.

"I will leave school at the end of the term," she said, "and go with Alice Harvey to work in Lawrence." She saw her mother's shocked expression, but she ignored it. "The Pemberton is hiring. Alice knows an overseer there. It's time I began to earn my way. It will be for a year or two only, three at the most. Just long enough to save up two or three hundred dollars."

She smiled at their shocked faces. She was not unpleased at the little sensation which she had made. The knowledge that soon she would be earning more than two dollars a week gave her a welcome sense of adulthood. My childhood is ending, she thought; and my life is about to begin.

18

In the late afternoon of Tuesday, January 10, 1860, Clara Blood stood at her looms on the first floor of the Pemberton Mill in the city of Lawrence and watched the heavy wooden shuttles slamming back and forth between the warp threads strung on the four looms which had been assigned to her. In a far corner of the weaving room, quite a distance away, she could see the overseer as he greeted the Agent, Mr. Chase, and Mr. Howe, the Treasurer of the Corporation. They were all three gesturing to each other, unable to speak in the deafening racket of the machines. Then they began to walk the central aisle of the weaving room; it was an enormous room, nearly three hundred feet long, eighty-five feet wide. It was twice the size of the rooms in the older mills in Lowell. Spaced throughout were the tall, thin cast-iron pillars which supported the thousands of tons of machinery in the four stories above; Clara almost collided with one of them now as she turned from loom to loom, watching the progress of the shuttles, monitoring the endless lengths of cloth.

She was an excellent weaver. Even Mr. Reynolds, the overseer, said so; and Mr. Reynolds was a strict man, a difficult man to please. She had begun in August in the spinning room. But after only a month, an apprentice place had fallen vacant in the weaving room, and Mr. Reynolds, impressed by the fact that Clara was a bright, literate American girl who learned easily and well, had taken her on in preference to a number of Irish applicants.

Mr. Chase and Mr. Howe, having made their progress through the weaving room, had disappeared into the upper floors. Reynolds had come back to confer with a girl whose production consistently lagged; because of such inefficiency, his bonus payments were less than they might have been. Around the walls and along metal pipes overhead, the gas lamps suddenly glowed with light; darkness still came early now, and "blowing-out"—the old-fashioned term still used, although sperm-oil lamps had no place in this modern facility—would not occur for another two months and more.

The factory building shuddered and thumped with the sound of its production. Like so many other factories, it had been idled by the panic of '57. A year ago it had been sold at auction to Mr. George Howe of Boston for $325,000—only a third of the cost of its construction in '53. The people of Lawrence had been overjoyed at the news, for many of them had been thrown out of work when the owners shut down during the panic. Now they would have wages again: the starving time was past. And fortunately the new owner, Mr. Howe, was an experienced man in the manufacture of cloth. He had large holdings in Manchester; he would retain the former Agent, Mr. Chase; he would make sure that everything went smoothly so that the factory would not close again. The jobs at the reopened Pemberton Mill would be steady jobs. Mr. Howe traveled up from Boston once a week to inspect, as he had done this day. Every operative in the mill knew him by sight. He was a concerned, conscientious man, eager to succeed in this enterprise which promised sustenance to his employees and untold riches to himself.

It was four forty-five P.M.

On Canal Street, just across the canal from the mill yard, a man whose name was never recorded walked by and looked up at the huge building humming with industry, now brightly illuminated by the hundreds of gas lamps. As he later reported, he was close enough to see the forms of the operatives through the tall windows; he could see them working in the lighted rooms. There were more than six hundred people in the building at that moment, most of them women; the exact number was never determined. He could see them very clearly: the entire wall was so cut up with windows from foundation to roof that it seemed like a wall of glass.

Four forty-six.

It was very cold: a cold, clear January twilight. The emerging stars in the iridescent sky paled next to the illuminated factory. A waxing moon hung low. The man did not linger by the canal; he hurried on to his destination.

Four forty-six and a half.

The man paused. He lived in this city; his ears were well accustomed to the sounds of the working machinery from within the red-brick walls.

Some new sound, just now, had intruded. He turned to look back at the giant structure of the Pemberton Mill, and then he blinked and shook his head and looked again. He could not believe what he saw.

The building had begun to fall. The southern end collapsed first, with a sound like the sound of a great heavy tree falling in the midst of a thick forest. Like a house made of cards, like the flimsiest jerry-built New-York tenement, within a space of fifteen seconds, with not a moment's warning, the entire mill from south to north collapsed with a sound like the rushing of the wind, like a puff of breath from the heavens. In no more time than it takes to tell, the Pemberton Mill was gone; in its place was an enormous heap of dusty rubble, a shattered baby-house stamped to pieces by some angry giant of a child-god suddenly moved to wrath.

It was four forty-seven P.M., Tuesday, January 10, 1860.

And it seemed that the end of the world had come at last.

19

Sabra stood at her new cast-iron stove inherited from a kindly neighbor and stirred at the big pan of mutton stew. It was about five-thirty, she thought, not long gone dark: the meat seemed tough, but supper need not be ready for some time yet. Stewing would soften it. Her boarders could not complain of her cooking; remembering the lessons learned years ago when she had boarded on the Corporations, she always tried to do her lodgers well. And, despite Clara's absence, she managed to keep the house clean. She had been able to hire a girl to come in two days a week; they would get along, she thought. Everything would be all right. She had a full house now—had had, since before Clara went to Lawrence in August. Business had picked up everywhere. Most of the factories were on full schedule again.

She replaced the cover on the pan and crossed to the wall of cupboards to take out the dishes for the evening meal. Eleven of everything, for she always ate supper with her boarders now. The heavy blue and white stoneware had served her well, she thought: best to buy the best in the beginning, and not constantly need to replace. And people noticed when you had nice things: they told their friends, you built up a good reputation.

She had gone with Clara to Lawrence to inspect the Pemberton's boarding houses. The system was the same as that in Lowell: an operative could board at any of the Corporation's houses which had a vacancy. Clara and her friend, Alice, had found two places at Number Eight. The landlady, a small, pleasant woman, had promised to look after the two girls as if they were her own. As she had confided to Sabra, it would be a pleasure to have two nice clean American girls in her house; she would see that the Irish boarders didn't bother them.

And so Sabra had been somewhat reassured. At least Clara had a decent place to live. And as for all her own repeated, heart-felt resolves never to allow her daughter to go on the Corporation—any Corporation—Well. She had chastised herself then; she did so now, six months later. But she could not after all forcibly restrain the girl. And certainly they needed the money. It would be, as Clara had said, for two or three years only. Make the best of it: wait for easier times.

As she laid the places at the long dining table, she heard the bells in St. Peter's Church, two blocks away, begin to toll the hour. She glanced at the Waltham clock on the wall: five forty-five. She had wound it only the day before; it was a good clock, not usually slow by more than five minutes. She set down the last two plates; she began to fold napkins. The bells still rang: seven, eight, nine . . . It was five forty-six. Perhaps the clock was running well, after all. Twelve, thirteen, fourteen . . .

She was alone in the house. The hired girl had gone; none of the boarders had returned from their day's work. Nineteen, twenty, twenty-one . . . She put the napkins down. After a moment she went to the front door and opened it and looked out. She saw nothing save the dark, deserted street; but she heard, now, the peals of other bells from other church steeples, she heard the higher pitch of clanging firebells. The night sky was dark. She saw no sign of flames. What was it? Even a major accident at one of the mills would not be announced by every church in the city—for the voices of the tolling bells had suddenly multiplied to form a great chorus of warning: all the city was alive with bells sounding the alarm.

Of what? What had happened?

She stood shivering in the open doorway of her house and listened and peered into the darkness, searching for someone passing by whom she could question. Save for the bells, the city seemed entirely normal. Then a man came running down the middle of the street where the thick cover of snow had melted to the cobblestones. She called to him.

"What is it? Why are the bells ringing?"

He kept on going as fast as he could; his shouted reply was lost in the sound of the bells. She caught only one word: "Lawrence!"

So it was a mill accident, after all. The Lawrence Corporation was adjacent to the Commonwealth. She was very cold. She turned and went inside and took her shawl from a peg in the hallway. Some poor girl with her scalp torn off by the teeth of the carding machine, perhaps, or a second hand mangled in the belts and shafting. She went back to the dining room, to her unfinished tasks. She glanced at the clock again: five minutes to six. Every bell in the city had been ringing for ten solid minutes. She heard them still: on and on they went, high and low, short and long, all mingling and pealing together into one great voice, from mill towers and church steeples, from every quarter of the city, a ragged, endless dirge signaling catastrophe: a terrible alarum.

For one poor operative? Or even two or three?

She heard shouting in the street, a sudden clatter of horses' hooves. There was a livery stable at the corner. Someone wanted a carriage to go somewhere very fast. The bells kept on ringing. Her body gave a sudden, involuntary shiver; her shawl did not warm her. She went to the door again; she saw the dark figures of men running toward the stable.

"What is it?" she called. "What happened?"

The sound of the bells filled the night. One of the men called back to her; and again only one word came clear: "Lawrence!"

Why did they need carriages to go to the Lawrence Corporation? They had only to run in the opposite direction and they would be at the Corporation gate in five minutes.

A woman's bulky figure came hurrying down the street. As she approached, Sabra saw that it was one of her tenants, Miss Lewis, a teacher at the Hamilton Corporation primary school. Miss Lewis was a calm, reticent person who kept to herself and never, as far as Sabra had seen, showed any emotion at all.

But now, as Miss Lewis came into the path of light shining from the open door, Sabra saw that the woman's face was distorted with fear. Frozen tears stained her wind-whipped cheeks, her bonnet was awry, she was breathing hard as she ran up the few steps to the door. Sabra backed away from her as she came in. The bells tolled and tolled, crying their warning. A dozen operatives at least must have been injured, thought Sabra; perhaps as many as twenty. She slammed the door on the sound, but still it came. Miss Lewis stood before her in the hall. She looked into the dining room to see if she were the first boarder home. She looked back to Sabra. Miss Lewis had always liked Clara. She had thought that the girl was foolish to leave the high school without a diploma, but of course she had kept her opinion to herself.

Now, confronting her landlady, Miss Lewis saw that Sabra did not yet know what had happened. I cannot tell her, she thought. I cannot; I have not the strength. She had hurried here to comfort, not to enlighten. She had been sure that by now Sabra would have heard the news. She had not thought to have to tell her herself. She prayed for divine help; she burst into tears.

Sabra had a strong sense of watching herself as she put out her arms and drew the weeping woman into her embrace.

"Tell me," she said. She heard her voice quite clearly over the sound of the bells. "It was at the Lawrence Corporation—?"

Miss Lewis lifted her blotched and anguished face from Sabra's shoulder. She shook her head. "No," she whispered. She wept beyond control. She felt that she would never recover from the horror of this moment, when she alone was fated to confront this unsuspecting woman with the unimaginable, inconceivable news of what had happened. Wild hysteria suddenly seized her. She wrenched free. "No! No! Not the Lawrence Corporation!" In the narrow hallway, in the endless tolling of the bells, in the extremity of her torment, she shouted out the news which soon would be flashed around the world. "No!" she shouted, very loud against the terrible sound of the bells. "In the city of Lawrence! A dreadful disaster! They sent word over the telegraph! Mrs. Blood—Mrs. Blood, listen to me!" Weeping and shuddering, hardly able to speak, poor Miss Lewis collapsed again onto Sabra's thin support, and then, summoning all her reserves of strength, she finished what she must say. "The Pemberton Mill, Mrs. Blood! You must go there at once! The Pemberton Mill has fallen to the ground, and six hundred people are trapped in the wreckage! Go—you must go! Run to the stable! For God's sake, go now! You must find Clara! Mrs. Blood! Mrs. Blood—!"

Miss Lewis stood alone, shuddering with fear and with the bitter night cold that blew mercilessly in upon her from the wide-open door of the house.

20

The carriage careened through the darkness, heavily overloaded, the horses straining every muscle to pull its weight. Ten people were packed inside. Two more had tried to bully their way on at the last moment, but the harassed livery man, fearing for his stock, had threatened them off at gunpoint. "I'll find another rig somewhere," he had shouted, "but I'll not kill the horses pulling this one!"

Sabra had been the last passenger allowed in. She had been given a place only because the owner knew her as a neighbor; he knew that her girl had gone on the Pemberton the previous summer. She had had no money for her fare, but there was no question of money. "Get in!" he had said; and so she sat now tightly wedged into the narrow space. This is not happening, she thought. I will awaken at any moment to find her on my doorstep, arriving for her Sunday visit. But she looked around at the other dark forms packed in close on her, she heard their muttered snatches of conversation, and she knew that she was not in a dream. She was awake here and now. There were two other women among the men, both with daughters who, like Clara, worked at the Pemberton. No one knew any more than Miss Lewis had known: the mill had collapsed. They might as well have said: the moon has collided with the earth; or, New England has broken off from the continent and fallen into the sea. Such things did not happen; the human brain could not comprehend them. The sun rose daily in the east, it set in the west, the earth turned on its axis, mill buildings stood where they were built. They did not fall to the ground. It was against the natural order that a factory building constructed by one of the leading Corporations would collapse like an Irishman's shanty.

Sabra closed her eyes. She saw Clara as she had seen her last, running down the steps on Sunday evening to meet Alice and catch the seven o'clock stage to Lawrence. Clara had been happy, healthy, pleased with herself for being able to withstand the rigors of her new life. Dear God, prayed Sabra; let her live. To keep from weeping, she concentrated on that single thought: let her live. Let her live. Let them all die, but let her live. We have survived all the years: let her live.

The carriage slowed; she heard the driver's warning call. As she peered out the window she saw that the road was thick with traffic, all of it going in the same direction, all the drivers frantic to reach the same destination. After a few moments they were forced to stop. From behind came shouts of "Move on! Make way!" And from ahead the answering cry: "No room! Turn around!" The driver climbed down from his seat; he came around and opened the door. "We can't get through. The horses will go down for sure. You'll have to walk."

They were too desperate to protest. They climbed down and began to fight their way through. Sabra had grabbed her cloak as she ran out of the house, but she had not stopped for her bonnet. The night was bitter cold; she pulled her shawl over her head and held her cloak closely around her shoulders and hurried on, following the crowd. They had stopped perhaps a quarter of a mile from the mill. As far back as she could see, the road leading into the city was clogged with stalled carriages and carts and wagons, their side lights flickering in the darkness like a thousand fireflies out of season; and the houses along the way, too, were brightly lit as if in preparation for some great event, and here and there a door was left thrown open—even as she had left her own, and her mutton stew simmering dry on the stove—their owners fled to the scene of the disaster. An enormous crowd made its way along the road past the useless vehicles. It was impossible to run; there were too many bodies blocking the way. A huge tide of humanity surged toward the city, and if a lone woman lost her footing in that crush, she would be trampled into the ground with no chance to survive, for everyone here was mad to get to the mill, no one would stop to help. They pushed and struggled to get ahead, and as they came near their muted, muttering voices swelled into a chorus of anguished cries directed at the towering mass of rubble across the canal. They came on; they could see it now, illuminated by a score of bonfires, a black misshapen mountain of brick and timber and twisted iron; and as it came into view they began to call to it, for it held within it the bodies of six hundred human beings, and so they cried the names of their loved ones trapped inside, they raced to the mountain and began to tear at it with their bare hands, they attacked it with all their strength, crying all the while to the poor wretches within.

And from the ruins they heard one answer, then another, and another, and they called to those still coming on: "Hurry! Hurry! They are alive! We can save them!" And they fell on the mountain with redoubled strength, they swarmed over it like ants, and they began to hope that somehow, somehow they would rescue all those trapped inside before they froze to death in the rapidly falling temperature.

Sabra halted at the end of the canal bridge and stared with unbelieving eyes at the scene before her: a pile of wreckage fifty feet high and more, hundreds of people crowded around it, over it, into it, their movements illuminated by the glare of huge bonfires whose crackling flames formed a sinister undertone to the frantic voices of the rescuers. It might have been a moment in Hell, she thought; it was the Devil's work, this night in Lawrence.

She pressed forward. She felt the heat of the flames. Her eyes strained to see into the darkness of the wreckage. She reached the first fallen timbers and bricks scattered on the filthy, hard-packed snow. A man running by collided with her; she staggered and then caught herself before she fell. She peered into the blackness of the fallen mill—a ruined building alive with cries for help. Fitful, flickering firelight played on the rubble. She could see evidence of living people: a beckoning arm, a leg, a white, panic-stricken face peering back at her from perhaps ten feet away, its body pinned by a fallen beam. Not Clara's face. She grabbed hold of the end of a splintered timber and tried to move it.

"Clara?" she called. She pushed and pulled at the wood. "Clara?" It would not give, not so much as an inch. "Clara?" She let go and tried another. "Clara?" It gave a little, but it threatened to let down a piece of flooring. She abandoned it. "Clara?" She began to toss aside a pile of bricks from which protruded a stockinged foot. "Clara?" The foot fell away; there was no leg attached to it. "Clara?" Where next? O God, where next? "Clara? Clara? *Clara?*"

21

By six o'clock that evening the news of the disaster had gone clattering over the telegraph from Lawrence to the office of the Associated Press in Boston, and as the word spread, journalists began to race to the railway station on Causeway Street to catch the late trains to the scene. As the message was telegraphed on to New-York, the editor of *Frank Leslie's Weekly* promptly dispatched three of his best artists; the *New-York Times* had a man in Lawrence that very night. By nine o'clock there were at least a dozen reporters among the hundreds—thousands—of spectators being held at bay by a line of constables.

Very quickly the work of rescue had become organized, and now small teams of men worked methodically at likely points all over the mountain of debris while distraught friends and families waited impatiently behind the police lines. As each new body was brought out—sometimes living, sometimes dead—it was carried past the crowd. By the light of the bonfires, people craned to see its face—sometimes recognizable, sometimes not; and if it lived and if it could speak it told its name so that the rescuers could call it out.

"Catherine Murphy!"

"Ellen Mahoney!"

"John O'Brien!"

"Mary Stevens!"

"Kathleen Carrigan!"

On they came, mangled and crushed, bones shattered, flesh torn away —but many of them lived despite their wounds, and so as the night drew on, the beginnings of optimism began to spread through the waiting crowd. Perhaps the worst damage had been done to the building, after all; perhaps almost everyone caught inside would be saved.

Each body carried out, living or dead, was taken to the City Hall by a little cortege of volunteers. A makeshift hospital had been set up in the main hall, the settees pushed away and piled in tiers along the walls. All through the night, the citizens of the town sent in mattresses, sheets and blankets, bandages, cordials, medicines; people came to volunteer to tend the wounded; doctors rushed in from all the surrounding towns and from as far away as Manchester and Boston. A large room down the hall served as the dead-room. Its floor was soon covered with mangled corpses, soon further mangled as people jostled through searching for their dead, turning over the bodies or parts of bodies, looking for a recognizable face. There were many more killed than had been thought: many, many more, at least thirty.

Still, there were known to have been at least six hundred people in the building when it collapsed, and by eleven o'clock there had not been a corpse brought in to the dead-room for more than an hour. All new arrivals at City Hall had been alive—many badly wounded, but alive all the same. Perhaps the worst was over.

At the site of the disaster, the teams of rescuers, well organized and working hard, had been heartened by the scores of voices calling to them from the wreckage. People were trapped, pinned by fallen pillars or machines or piles of brick; but, wounded as they were, they were alive still. With luck they would live, they would not freeze to death before they were rescued. Many of the weavers on the first floor had been saved because they threw themselves under their looms, whose high cast-iron arches served as buffers against the immense weight of the collapsing building above; they had two or three feet of space in which to breathe. Those who could crawl out had done so long since. The rest must wait. But they knew that every effort was being made to save them. They heard the shouts of the men crawling over the wreckage, and they shouted in reply. Leg caught, they yelled; arm caught, foot crushed—but we can breathe, we can live until you get us. But watch the sparks from the bonfires, for we are a pile of oil-soaked tinder! If the ruins catch fire we are done for! They heard the shouted debates of the teams of men outside: perhaps the best way to get to them is to chop through the flooring. The flooring had been stronger than the walls: it had fallen solid, four sections of it, like a stack of flapjacks. Those caught between the upper floors had been crushed to death, many of them; but the weavers on the first floor had had their looms to shelter them, and so, caught and injured as they were, they were not as badly mangled as those who had been above.

After a time, an operative caught deep inside the wreckage began to sing a hymn. Soon from every part of the mountain of rubble came the sound of voices lifted in song to God, a song of thanksgiving for having been spared untimely death. We can wait, they called; we will sing to keep our courage, and trust in you and the Lord for our rescue. The spectators waiting behind the barricades heard the familiar melodies drifting from the pile, and they understood: people are alive, they sing as they wait, we will see them soon again. A palpable wave of relief, of new hope, passed through the crowd. The constables on the guard line nodded confidently as they shared their bits of news, they hummed along as the crowd, too, began to sing: a thousand voices—many thousands, singing their faith in God's love, in His benevolence even in this, the most terrible night in memory. "Abide with Me," they sang, and "Rock of Ages," and "Nearer, My God, to Thee." Under the starry sky, on the banks of the great river, a hushed and quavering chorus drifted up to Heaven in praise of the Lord; the bonfires lighted up their faces, the music soothed away their fears. "Fairest Lord Jesus," they sang, "Thee will I cherish." But they did not sing loudly; they knew without being told that they must be soft, so that the men could hear the cries for help from the wreckage.

Shortly after eleven o'clock, two men working their way deep into the ruins heard a tapping noise perhaps fifteen feet ahead of them. The light from the bonfires did not penetrate so far in, and so the taller of the two carried an oil lantern. They were well away from the other men, deep into the base of the mountain. They needed to go carefully, testing each step before putting down full weight; at times the taller one needed to bend nearly in two, and more than once both of them had to crawl. Faintly, in the distance, they heard the sound of hymn-singing. They had come to search for bodies. But now they had heard a nearer noise, evidence of life. They paused; they called into the darkness ahead.

"Anyone there?"

No answer. They held their breath; they strained to hear.

"Hello?"

They listened again. Tap-tap. Tap-tap. For fifty feet above their heads, the mountain of what had been the Pemberton Mill creaked and quivered as teams of rescuers scrambled over it. Perhaps this noise was simply the sound of their activity. Tap-tap. Tap-tap. Ahead, they agreed; the sound came from the darkness directly in front of them.

"Where are you?" they called. "Can you tell us where you are?"

No answer. The smaller man, Thompson, made a moment's survey of their position; then he took the lantern and began to pick his way. He negotiated the twisted shape of a drawing frame; gingerly he stepped on a piece of splintered shafting to see whether it would hold his weight. It did. He proceeded. He held the lantern high in front of him and strained to see. He took a few more steps and paused again. There.

A face stared at him, barely visible in the lantern's tiny glow. He thought that it was a man's face. Where the torso should have been he saw a crumpled mass of wood and iron—the remains of a machine, he could not tell what. The arm nearest him protruded from underneath, and now he saw that the hand clutched a broken brick; the sound that they had heard had been the tapping of the brick on metal. Thompson saw that blood trickled from the operative's mouth; the eyes focused on his own.

"All right," he said. "We'll get you out. My partner's back a bit. If we can get on either side of you and lift up that load, can you slide out?"

With what seemed an enormous effort, the face nodded.

"Good. Hold fast now, you'll be out in no time. Seth! I've got someone here alive! Come in!"

He waited to hear the other's reply, and then he lifted his foot to find a safe place to put it down. A piece of leather belting caught at his ankle. He felt his balance go; instinctively he put out his hands to save himself

The lantern fell from his grasp. It rolled away from him under a broken cast-iron pillar lying horizontally about a foot above a stretch of solid flooring. He reached to get it back, but he was a fraction of a second too late. It had rolled beyond him, he could not touch it. And now he saw what must happen. The lantern had rolled to a pile of fluffy, oil-soaked cotton waste. He made a queer sound in his throat. Suddenly he could see quite clearly the operative whom he had meant to rescue. The man's face was illuminated by a soaring flame. The fire leaped up as if by magic. In another moment it had reached its victim. It licked at the oil-soaked wooden frame of the machine which crushed him down. His bloody face melted into a mask of horror; his eyes widened, begging for release, but still he made no sound. As Thompson backed away he saw the man lift his arm. The sleeve was on fire; the arm was a blazing torch. The fingers still held tightly to the brick.

Thompson could see everything now, for the blaze was as bright as the sun. He felt the heat of the flames burn his face. He pulled back. He yelled a warning. Then he turned and scrambled for his life.

22

At first it might have been the eye of God winking at them from the ruins. It was only a small patch at the beginning, only a little place burning, and surely a hose and force-pump could be brought up quickly to put it out.

Because of course it must be extinguished at once. Quickly! Sound the alarm! Get the engines in! These people are trapped here, they cannot move to save themselves!

The eye winked and was no longer an eye: it was a little bonfire now, which some fool had ignited in the wrong place. But still they could contain it. Hurry!

And once again in only a moment's time the blaze transformed itself, and it was no longer a bonfire but a conflagration. It roared up from the center of the mound of rubble; it forced back the swarm of rescuers as if they had been ants caught on a log in a blazing hearth-fire. Within five minutes the mountain was a sheet of flame. The fire leaped up from the depths, it raced over the full height of the ruins, and as it went it fed on tons of oily cotton waste, it devoured tons of wood soaked with machine drippings.

The hymn-singing quavered to an end. For a moment, people in the waiting crowd stood silent as they tried to understand what had happened. They could not believe what they saw. It was unthinkable that a fire, so long dreaded, so long delayed by the mercy of God, should begin now, so late, when the rescue was proceeding so swiftly, when everyone had begun to believe that all victims would be freed, at least alive if not uninjured, and when the long agony of waiting would be over at last.

They shuffled uneasily in their places; they began to murmur anxious questions back and forth: what is that light? Why have they a bonfire there? Has some further accident happened? And yet, for the moment, they remained calm. They did not panic.

An inhuman cry suddenly broke their silence. It did not come from them. It came from within the ruins. It was an animal's cry, torn from some primitive consciousness far beneath the ordinary range of human affairs.

And then they heard another, and another—a swelling chorus of the panicked voices of living human beings begging, shrieking for release.

And then suddenly the full horror of what they saw broke over them, and they panicked, too, and they rushed the police and broke through the lines and fell upon the burning mountain only to be driven back by the all-consuming fire.

They could see people burning to death before their eyes. They could smell the smell of roasting flesh. They heard the sharp *snap* of burning wood; they heard the awful sounds coming from the poor lost souls within. All their lives they had been warned about falling into Hell's eternal flames, and now here was Hell before them. They saw it, they heard it, they felt it, smelled its stench—and merciful Lord they could do nothing. Nothing.

As an animal caught in a leg-hold trap will chew off its paw to save itself, so now these poor operatives, without hope of rescue, began to do the same.

One girl who was unhurt except for two fingers which had been caught and crushed in the machinery, thus preventing her escape, now tore herself away and left the fingers behind.

A man whose foot was pinned by a fallen pillar begged the men outside to throw in an ax. They did so; and as they watched he hacked off his foot and crawled to safety not a yard ahead of the raging fire.

Another man, not so fortunate, whose lower torso and legs had been crushed by a section of flooring, found a small splinter of metal by his side. As the fire came on, he saw that he had no hope of being saved from slow and certain agonizing death. He plunged the sliver into his jugular and died before the flames reached him.

A woman whose hair was caught, who had waited cheerfully and patiently through the long hours of cold and darkness, urging the men to rescue people more badly off than she, now saw the flames sweep up all around her. She tried to pull the hair out of her scalp to save herself. People outside saw her do this; the flames illuminated her writhing, jerking body very clearly. But she could not get free; and before she burned to death, she went mad.

And where were the fire engines, the force-pumps and hoses?

In fact they were brought in very promptly. In ten minutes' time, a dozen streams of water played upon the inferno. Several of these came from hydrants at the adjacent Washington Mills, since the Pemberton's own water-works had been rendered useless by the crash.

But a man might as well try to piss on one of the bonfires, as try to play a hose on such a blaze. The water could not penetrate the oil-soaked wood, nor could they put it where it was needed most, in the center, in the deep interior of the mountain. They were powerless with their thin little streams. The fire raged unchecked by anything they could do to stop it. For thirty miles around, people saw the light in the sky: and those who knew of the disaster felt their hearts go cold with the knowledge of what that terrible glow must mean.

23

In the dead-room at the City Hall, the man in charge heard a shout in the corridor. Thinking to receive another corpse, he stepped outside to direct those who brought it in. But he saw no body, no group of half a dozen men carrying in a new victim. Instead, he saw a single frantic half-grown boy who had raced in to call his news. The boy stood alone in the corridor between the temporary hospital and the dead-room; he shouted out the words again: "Fire! Fire in the mill! People still trapped!"

In a moment he was joined by others running in from the scene, and they confirmed it: a fire had broken out, no one knew how, and now all hope was gone, for there was no way in the world to extricate those still pinned down by the wreckage.

The man in charge of the dead-room retreated to his charnel-house and steadied himself against the wall. He was a man with a strong stomach. He had not faltered once during all the long night when they had brought in the mangled, hideously broken bodies to lie on the floor so that people could come to identify them. He had volunteered for the job. Mayor Saunders had wanted to put a physician in charge, but the physician had argued, quite rightly, that he could be of no use in the dead-room, while in the temporary hospital he might save lives. So Samuel Fiske had volunteered. In the past hour or so, no fresh bodies had been brought in, and he had begun to think that perhaps none would be. He had said as much to the woman who had come in not five minutes ago.

Now he leaned against the wall and tried not to imagine what the boy's announcement had meant. The woman had heard it, too. She stared at him as if she expected him to deny it—as if he could assure her that it was not true. She was a thin, slightly built woman, with a frantic look to her like all the other women who had come through looking for their dead; some of them wept, some cried out, moaning prayers, calling to the loved ones whom they could not find. But this one was quiet. She had come earlier in the evening, and now she was back again: still one of the lucky ones, still left with hope, not finding whom she sought either among the corpses on the floor or in the hospital down the hall. She stood in the middle of the room; unlike him, she had no wall to lean against.

He looked away. He almost preferred hysteria to the silent anguish of the woman before him. In the corridor they heard many voices now, the thud of feet, all the sounds of fresh alarm as hundreds of people who had come to search for their wounded raced out again into the night, back to the fallen mill.

He heard her move; she looked right through him, she brushed past him and out into the corridor. He saw her begin to push through the mob rushing from the hospital room. Then he lost her. He shook his head. If her husband, or her sister, or whoever it was, had not been pulled out by now, there was no hope. His mouth dropped open as he thought about the scene at the mill. He looked for someone to talk to, but there was no one. The hall was empty; everyone had raced outside. He felt a need to share his feelings; there had not been such a disaster in memory—beyond memory. Nothing like this had ever happened in New England. He would tell his grandchildren about it, and they would tell their grandchildren. But just now, when he wanted to talk, he had no one; he was surrounded by dead bodies. He opened his mouth and began to speak; he heard his voice, and it comforted him. It assured him that among all these dead, he lived. He began to tell them the story of the disaster.

Sabra, coming out into the night, saw the ruddy sky and the glowing faces of the mob in the street before her. It was true, then: the mill had caught fire, the boy had shouted not rumor but appalling fact. The smell of the fire hung in the air; as far as she could see, all was alight with the dreadful glow from the burning pile.

For a moment she leaned heavily against the door as if she could not go a further step—did not want to, could not bear to. Then she allowed herself to be pushed down into the street. Thousands of people blocked the way. She could not move in that solid wall of humanity. Every face was turned toward the rising light; eyes wide, mouths open, wondering at it, trying to comprehend. Like flowers following the light of the sun, they turned their faces to the conflagration, awed by its might, by its inexorable progress. Those near the mill, behind the police lines, had briefly panicked and run in; but these people were blocks away, too far to see the writhing bodies, too far to hear the agonizing shrieks for rescue. They simply stood and stared at the terrible light in the sky and took the acrid smoke-filled air into their lungs and felt cold tears slide down their blanched faces.

O merciful Lord: why has this thing happened?

They were too appalled to move, to try to battle through. A thousand people stood frozen in that narrow way, struck dumb by the awesome evidence of God's wrath which had been revealed to them.

O merciful Lord: how have we offended Thee?

"Make way!"

They obeyed. Six men staggered through carrying a seventh. Their faces were black and bloody, their eyes wide with the horror of what they had seen. They lurched up the steps of the City Hall. Those who stood close saw that the body which they carried had no face; the face had been burned away, and the hands as well. Its clothing hung in charred shreds. They closed up behind as the men disappeared inside; they turned their faces toward the light once again. They shivered with more than the cold of the January night; they knew that they were spectators to God's anger, that for some unfathomable reason they had been chosen to see. They were humbled by that knowledge.

Sabra struggled through toward the mill. She did not need to shout, to shove; they were very quiet, almost reverential, and as they heard her steady voice—"Excuse me. Coming through. Excuse me, please"—they gave her space, they let her go past. Only as she came near the canal, and the burning mill beyond, did she begin to meet resistance; for here the crowd was more unruly, here the cries of the victims had been heard, the victims themselves had been seen as they were incinerated—and more than one woman had been immolated as she flung herself into the burning wreck in a vain attempt to rescue her child.

Even from across the canal, the heat from the blaze was enough to burn people's skin. The fire had shot straight up from the center of the ruins; now, burning on, it consumed the whole, spreading the length and width of it, unchecked by a dozen streams of water. There was here, in contrast to the City Hall, a bedlam of sound: the crackling, roaring fire; the shouts of the impotent rescuers; the shrieks of the victims; the answering cries of the crowd. No one voice could be distinguished in that riot of sound; no one cry for help could be answered. Those who had been trapped when the fire broke out were doomed to die in the onrushing flames; no power on earth could save them now.

She is not here, thought Sabra. She has been got out; if I go back now to the City Hall I will find her in the hospital. It was impossible that Clara would die in that conflagration. God could not be so cruel. Clara was alive.

She felt a hand clutch her arm. She turned to see a woman's frantic face, strangely red in the reflected light of the fire.

"Help me! Please help me! They didn't get her out—my sister, she hasn't come out!"

The woman began to pull her across the canal bridge. Given extraordinary strength by her fear, she pushed and shoved, dragging Sabra behind. When they were half across they heard a great shout from the far end of the fallen mill. They could not see what had happened. The woman pushed on. They got across. They stood within fifty feet of the fire, packed tight in the solid mass of living flesh. Another shout went up, and then another. The woman let go of Sabra's arm and pounded on the back of a tall man in front of them. "What happened?" she cried. "Can you see?" The man glanced around. "They raised some flooring down there. Can't tell yet if they got anyone out. Wait, here they come—they're bringin' out two—no, three. Watch out! They got 'em before the fire—look, just in time, too, the fire's gone right to the end. Make way!"

The crowd parted as easily as the quieter throng had done before; no names were called out, for these victims could not speak. People craned to see their faces. A man and two women. They seemed dead, or at least unconscious; they had no visible wounds, but a blow on the head or a crushed chest is not always immediately apparent. Seemingly unscathed, immobile, their eyes closed, they were borne on through the crowd, their features illuminated by the brilliant light of the fire. Who were they? To whom did they belong? Sabra saw them clearly as they were carried past.

A man and two women.

And one of the women was Clara.

24

The fire burned through the night. When dawn paled the sky with a softer light than the light of the searing flames, the people of Lawrence, and all the people who had flocked to Lawrence all night long, gazed in weary disbelief at the pile of blackened bricks and twisted metal which was all that remained of the Pemberton Mill. Smoke curled up from the ruins; the water from a few fire hoses, still wetting down the rubble, raised a hissing sound and clouds of steam as it fell upon the mass of wreckage which still retained an overwhelming heat. All that day the workmen searched the ruins for the dead. A few more were found and brought out, burned beyond recognition. As night fell, a drizzling rain turned to snow. On Thursday morning smoke still rose from the ruins where the water and the snow had not penetrated; the water congealed and turned to ice, encrusting the wreckage, transforming it into a weird and fantastical frozen palace from an old-world fairy tale. As the day wore on, the rapidly falling snow covered the ice and sifted down through the crevices of the ruins to weave a winding sheet over those dead still trapped inside.

On Friday morning the Pemberton Corporation brought in derricks to lift the fallen flooring and broken cast-iron pillars. Nearly one hundred men were employed at this work, most of them men who until the disaster had worked in the mill. Thus the Pemberton continued to provide employment to the citizens of Lawrence. For the next ten days, bodies were taken out and delivered to the dead-room at the City Hall. They were identified by a scrap of fabric still clinging to their charred flesh, or a ring on the bone of a skeletal hand. Thirteen of them were not identified at all; they were held for several weeks, and then, in early March, they were buried in a common grave in a lot purchased by the Corporation in Bellevue Cemetery.

As soon as the news of the disaster had been telegraphed to Boston and beyond, people had begun to send in money and supplies for relief. Amos A. Lawrence, the son and nephew of the Lawrence brothers who had founded the city, and who had died some years previous, promptly sent five thousand dollars by special messenger. The Pemberton Corporation took one of its boarding houses for a hospital; a doctor and staff were brought in from Boston. But in this case charity and cupidity ran head-on, for the wounded operatives refused to go there. Or perhaps they were prevented by their families, who were amassing an unexpected windfall from the benevolent visitors who prowled the streets of the city, looking for worthy objects for their charity. Naturally, the families received nothing if their injured relatives went away to the hospital; and so out of all the wounded hundreds, only eight could be persuaded to go to the hospital, and as it turned out, they were from out of town; they had no families in the city to care for them and receive the visitors' largesse. This generosity soon reached enormous amounts. Eventually the relief fund amounted to more than seventy thousand dollars, as well as tons of supplies; food, clothing, bandages, bedding—every imaginable thing was sent in.

There were those who took instead of giving. Had the pile of rubble been allowed to remain indefinitely, it would have been cleared away, at no cost to the Corporation, by the thousands of curiosity seekers who came to see it in the days immediately after the catastrophe. By train and stage and every available cart and wagon they came, and many hundreds walked. They took away with them a splinter of iron, or a broken brick or a lump of mortar—a small souvenir was all they wanted, for the fall of the Pemberton Mill was an international sensation. Everyone in the civilized world knew of it. People everywhere were horrified: what caused this dreadful disaster to occur? Who is responsible? The ministers of the city of Lawrence, ever mindful from whence their livings came, preached of the mysterious workings of Divine Providence. The *Times* of London, less dependent on the Boston capitalists, commented angrily that a careful and impartial investigation must be made at once.

This was done. While the ruins still smoldered, an inquest was called. On Thursday, January 12, Dr. William G. Lamb, coroner, and six jurors and a clerk assembled to hear evidence. What they heard made an interesting tale. People had had doubts about the Pemberton Mill, it turned out, since the day its construction began seven years before. The workmen had questioned the firmness of the foundation; the masons had questioned the quality of the bricks and mortar, the latter having been made with Vermont lime, which, as everyone knew, was not the best. The masons had questioned further the thinness of the walls. They were from Lowell; they had built many mills there, the finest mills in the world; and the walls of the Pemberton, they said, were not thick enough to withstand the weight of the thousands of tons of machinery which would be put into the building. They had been so concerned on this point that they had not even bothered to speak to the chief engineer (a West Point man: Captain Charles H. Bigelow); they had at their own expense taken the cars to Boston to put their fears directly to the Treasurer of the parent Corporation, the Essex. This man, J. Pickering Putnam, was a gentleman of the highest social standing. He assured the masons, the Tuttle brothers, that he would look again at the plans, but that he was sure that Captain Bigelow would not risk the project to save eight inches of brickwork all around. But the Tuttles were right: before so much as one power loom was brought in, twenty-two tons of iron plating had to be put into the walls to prevent them from buckling. This had been hushed up at the time—as much as twenty-two tons of anything can be hushed up—but from that moment, rumors had been widespread about the building's safety. People looked at the newly built walls and they saw only glass: an acre of windows, they said, and how will a building of glass hold all those tons of machinery?

But the most interesting testimony of all at the inquest centered on the cast-iron pillars used throughout the structure to hold up the successive layers of flooring. The pillars had been bought cheap by Putnam—cheaper than Bigelow could have got them. Because Putnam was his superior, Bigelow had used those pillars in the mill even after one of them broke before his eyes on the day they were delivered from the foundry in South Boston. The authorities tried now to find the owner of the foundry; wisely, he had disappeared.

So it came down to a question of time: time lost while new pillars were cast. And time was money; and the parent Corporation, the Essex, was in business to make money. To save time. To waste nothing. To finish building the mill so that the manufacture of millions of yards of cotton cloth could begin as quickly as possible.

And so Putnam and Bigelow and Bigelow's assistant, Benjamin Coolidge, had rationalized that broken pillar and convinced themselves that it was a freak. All the others must be sound. And besides: how did one test the strength of a cast-iron pillar? They did not know. And so they went ahead and used them, and now seven years later at a judicial proceeding which none of them could have imagined in his worst nightmares, they were being called to account—held responsible—while the real culprit, the man who made the pillars badly, had vanished. It was, they felt, entirely unfair. All during the proceedings, Putnam and Bigelow sparred back and forth, each in his gentlemanly way trying to shift the blame onto the well-tailored shoulders of the other. It was a real and deadly battle for survival, for if criminal negligence could be proved, a man would be ruined for life, fined, imprisoned—everything lost.

Back and forth they went, first one and then the other, for eleven days and nights, their testimony alternating with that of survivors, of witnesses, of men who had worked at the construction (including the conscientious Tuttles), of experts in the business of mill-building; and always the two of them were recalled, each wanting to make some further point in his own defense, wanting to cast some further guilt on his opponent.

There was one piece of evidence which never went into the record, although Putnam had written it down seven years previous when the mill was under construction. He had had a dream; and it had haunted him for days afterward until he had sought to deliver himself of its burden by writing about it in a letter to a friend. He had dreamed that the mill was built, and that all the operatives had been hired, the turbine wheel working well, the machinery in place. It was winter; there had been a heavy fall of snow. It lay two feet deep on the long expanse of the roof. And in his dream—how clearly he had seen it, how it plagued him!—the roof had been unable to withstand the weight. It had collapsed. He had seen it with agonized dreamer's eyes: had watched it fall, unable to turn away, unable to escape. Of course such a thing would never happen. It had been only a dream—a nightmare. He had awakened panting and frightened, sweating in the hot July night. He could not rid himself of that terrible sight, and so had written it to his friend. But the friend—a Boston capitalist unconnected with the Pemberton—was never called to testify, and so Putnam's premonition was not mentioned at the inquest.

The jury's verdict was withheld for weeks. When finally it was made public, around the time that the unidentified bodies were buried at Corporation expense, it was published obscurely, with little fanfare, with headlines in small type.

The jury found Captain Bigelow guilty of negligence, and it censured him. Nothing more.

In addition, a casualty list was made up. As near as could be reckoned, eighty-eight people had died; two hundred and seventy-five were injured.

Immediately work was begun on a new Pemberton Mill. Captain Bigelow was not employed on the project. He was taken on by a Corporation in New Bedford; soon he went into a decline, and a year or so later he died of what was rumored to be a broken heart.

In time the new mill was finished, and people went back to work in it, glad of wages once again. In more time still, the Massachusetts legislature passed laws that said that buildings had to be built safely.

In the meantime, Fort Sumter had been fired upon and the bloody struggle for the Union had begun. The world which had shuddered and wept to read of the fall of the Pemberton Mill now shuddered and wept to read of the cruel fratricide between North and South. By and large, the Tenth of January, eighteen-sixty, was forgotten. But in Massachusetts, and indeed in all New England, people remembered it still. For years—decades—afterward, a happy crowd around the dinner table would be thrown into appalled and anguished silence if someone pointed to one of their number and said, "She was in the fall of the Pemberton Mill." It was as if someone had said: "He was at Gettysburg"; or, in a later age: "He was at the Somme"; or: "Iwo Jima," or "Auschwitz," or "Nagasaki." The name conjured up unimaginable horror. To have survived such an experience marked a person for life. Inevitably came a sudden silence, a hushed and reverent moment of respect for what that one had suffered: for he or she had paid a visit to Hell and lived to speak of it, and such people were different from everyone else, they were forever set apart.

As the passing months and years mercifully softened the sharp and painful edges of their recollection, some of the survivors found that they were able to speak calmly, almost objectively, about their experiences on that awful night. Eventually they came to feel as if they were speaking of someone else: their hearts no longer burst with panic, their ears no longer rang with their own cries or those of victims less fortunate, their minds' eyes lost the vivid pictures which they had thought were etched there forever.

But most people caught in the collapse of the Pemberton Mill never fully recovered from the experience, even if they had received no physical injury at all; and these, the majority, were never able to speak more than a few words about the events which they had survived. Most of them were deeply troubled, oddly enough it seemed, by the fact that they had lived while others died. Why? Why had they been spared? They had not lived blameless lives, they had sinned and sinned again: why had they been spared, when that sweet child, Mary Garven, nearest thing to an angel on earth, had burned to death and no one could reach her to pull her out? Or little Peggy Connelly, or Terence Rafferty?

Faithfully they went to church; faithfully they prayed for revelation. Why did it happen? Why did we live and others die? Why there? Why then? Why didst Thou choose us? What aroused Thee to anger, O God, and how can we placate Thee?

Speak to us, O merciful Lord, speak to us in the dark night of our affliction, for Thine is the Kingdom, and the Power, and the Glory forever and ever. Amen.

25

Clara could not speak. Could not, would not—she lay on her bed, her eyes wide, unfocused, and she might have been six feet into the ground for all she knew of what went on around her. Perhaps she hears us after all, thought Sabra, perhaps she understands—but then why does she not speak to us, why does she not respond?

All through the winter and into the warmth of spring, Sabra tended faithfully to the silent, immobile figure which had been her daughter, and she kept her boarding house running, too, and insisted to herself that all would be well, that Clara would recover, that she needed time, and peace, and loving and constant attention.

They could not find any physical injury, not so much as a lump on her head: only a small bruise or two on her legs where she had been pinned by her loom. The high metal arch had protected her from worse harm. But still she had been trapped; had they not gotten her out when they did, she would surely have burned to death. That was the cause of her condition, said Dr. Spencer. Like most other doctors in Lowell, he had gone to Lawrence at the first news of the disaster; he had worked all through that night, and through the next day and night as well, and so he knew the victims' thoughts as well as their wounds. He had treated a man who had lain in the path of the fire and who like Clara had been rescued in the nick of time; but that man had been able to speak, afterward, and he had told Dr. Spencer of the horror of waiting for immolation. "Can you imagine," Dr. Spencer said to Sabra, "what she must have felt during those moments, when she did not know that they would get her out, when she thought that she must die, roasted alive? Instinctively her brain must have retreated from such knowledge; by denying everything around her, refusing to acknowledge what was happening, she was trying to prepare to die in the least painful way. The danger is over now, but for some reason her brain does not know that. We must find a way to tell her."

When the men had brought her out, only moments before the fire reached the place where she had been, she looked as if she had merely fainted. The men had carried her past, and Sabra, hardly believing her eyes, had cried out in recognition; and the crowd had urged her on, had pushed her with a hundred hands to follow the men who carried her child to the City Hall—but not to the dead-room, not to the morgue. They had felt a pulse. She is alive, they said; and Sabra, overjoyed, had gone with them as they pushed through the crowd, while behind them the ruins of the mill had been consumed by the flames which so nearly had consumed Clara as well. At the temporary hospital, there had been no free mattresses. The men put the new arrivals on the floor. A doctor hurried over; in his first cursory examination, he had determined that the other woman had suffered a broken leg, while the man had a crushed chest and, therefore, serious internal injuries. Clara seemed miraculously unharmed, he said to Sabra. He motioned toward the platform at the far end of the room, where tables had been set up for the distribution of medical supplies. You may go to get some smelling salts, he said; say that I sent you, it will be all right.

But smelling salts had done no good; Clara lay with her eyes closed in deep unconsciousness, and so she lay all night long as Sabra watched by her side, kneeling on the floor, Clara's head cradled in her lap and her shawl thrown over her for warmth. Eyes closed: as still as death. But she was alive. Sabra could feel her pulse, could see the vein throbbing in her throat. She looked quite calm, as if she had fallen asleep in that unlikely place, and would awake in the morning refreshed and ready to begin another day's work.

She did not awake. On the Wednesday—when the City Hall received its greatest crush of people searching for their loved ones—forty thousand by the best account—Sabra, still sitting on the floor with Clara's head in her lap, saw a familiar face: Alice Harvey's mother, whom she had met when the girls had gone on the Corporation. Mrs. Harvey had been frantic like all the others, for she had not found Alice, had had no news of her. She paused at Sabra's side; her voice shaking, her face drawn with fear, she knelt to look at Clara. She took her hand.

"What is it?" she said. "Has she not come around? We must wake her! She will know what happened to Alice!"

But Clara slept on; and so Mrs. Harvey had left them to resume her weary, heart-breaking rounds. But an hour later Sabra had been startled to see a man standing before her, inquiring if she were Mrs. Blood, announcing that he was taking a party back to Lowell and that Mrs. Harvey, hearing of it, had sent him to find her. Mrs. Harvey would stay in Lawrence until she found her daughter.

And so several volunteers to carry Clara to the wagon had been quickly recruited from the thousands clogging the way, and Sabra had taken her home.

For three days Clara lay unconscious on the narrow bed in the room that she shared with her mother. On the morning of the fourth, Sabra awoke before dawn, as she always did, and she struck a light to the candle by her bed and held it over to look at her child.

And then she started so badly that she almost dropped the candle, for in its dim and wavering light she saw that Clara's eyes were open. She has come back, she thought; O Clara—

"Clara?" She put the candle stand on the night table and swung her feet to the floor, she did not stop to take a shawl, she bent over Clara's inert form and sank on the bed beside her, trying to lift her into an embrace. "O Clara, we were so frightened, we thought you'd never wake up—"

Clara's body was limp. She seemed not to hear. She stared at the ceiling; after a moment she blinked, very slow.

"Clara?"

No answer; no indication of having heard. Sabra pulled back. What was the matter with the girl?

She had begun to shiver in the cold, which the small box stove did little to dispel. She reached for her clothing; she began to pull on her thick black stockings and then her petticoats and her dress. She needed to start breakfast, for all her people were employed and most of them needed to be on the job by seven at the latest. But how could she leave Clara, even for a moment, when the girl's eyes had opened at last and she needed to have someone watching constantly at her side to respond to her first words?

Miss Lewis, thought Sabra; and she hurried upstairs in the darkness, still buttoning her bodice. Miss Lewis did not need to be in her schoolroom until eight, by which time the hired girl would have arrived and Sabra could sit with Clara once more. She knocked softly at the door. Miss Lewis, fully dressed, answered at once.

"Clara has opened her eyes. She doesn't speak, she doesn't seem to hear, but I don't want to leave her while I get breakfast. Can you sit with her?"

Miss Lewis' equanimity had been shattered forever on the night of the disaster, and so now her reaction was voluble joy as she accompanied her landlady downstairs. Ever since Clara had come home, Miss Lewis had hoped to be called on for help—hence her completed toilette at five in the morning, for she had slept fully clothed—and now she entered the small bedroom as an acolyte might enter a shrine.

Clara had not moved, but her eyes were open still. "This is the beginning," said Sabra. "She is coming back. At any moment she will realize where she is, and I don't want her to be startled or frightened. Sit with her, Miss Lewis, and comfort her—I will bring you coffee, I will come at once if you need me, but I must feed the others."

That first morning, when it seemed that Clara had begun to revive, Sabra had been filled with a joy, a gladness such as she could not remember. She had never been so happy, it seemed, she hummed a tuneless song as she stoked up the fire, she trembled as she carried out the pies and the pots of jam and butter, she wiped away a happy tear as she fried the beefsteaks and skillfully turned hotcakes on the griddle.

But when the hired girl came, and Sabra was free to carry in a tray of breakfast to Miss Lewis, her joy faded once again as she looked at Clara's staring eyes. No: not staring. Wide open, looking at nothing. Or does she see what we cannot, thought Sabra. Has her gaze been caught forever by the sight of the fire coming to devour her?

Miss Lewis went away, then, and Sabra sat watching by her child. In time she came to feel that she had never done anything else. She could not remember what her life had been before. Day after day she sat: week after week. From time to time, Clara's eyes would close, as if in sleep; then they would open again, but not in consciousness, for she never said a word, she never responded or willingly moved. Sabra fed her: she spooned broth into Clara's mouth, and some of it dribbled out and some of it went down her throat. Sabra washed her, and sat her up in bed and laid her down again. Clara never resisted, she never cooperated, she simply let herself be handled and never gave so much as a twitch of a finger to show that she knew what went on around her.

"Talk to her," said Dr. Spencer. "Tell her, over and over again, that she is home, she is safe, she is not hurt."

Sabra obeyed him, although not without difficulty: the first time or two she was unable to say more than a few words before she choked on her tears.

"You must believe that she can hear you," said Dr. Spencer on his next visit.

"Can she?"

He shook his head. "I don't know." And then, seeing her expression, he added hastily: "Yes. Yes, of course she can hear you. The fact that she does not respond means only that she is still trapped—just as she was trapped in the mill, waiting for the fire. You must help her to get out."

He refrained from speaking false encouragement. On the other hand, he did not tell her of some he had seen, like Clara physically unharmed but with their minds destroyed. They raved, many of them; already he had had four of them committed to the lunatic asylum at Worcester. Driven mad by their fear—and who would not have been? Dr. Spencer shuddered, but so slightly that Sabra did not see it. Like those who had been imprisoned in the burning wreck, he would carry to his grave the horror of that night; for he had treated the survivors, and no one did such work unscathed. At least she is quiet, he thought; I need not grieve the mother more by committing her to bedlam.

Sabra sat by her child in the lengthening days of spring and talked until her voice grew hoarse and her mind could think of no new words to say; and then she took a drink of water and started all over again.

"Clara, you are home now. You are safe. They got you out in time, and now you are here with me. The winter is past. If you go outside now, you will see that the trees are green again, and the rose bush in the back is full of buds. Clara, we have had a letter from Adolph. He sends you all their love. Jutta is married now. She wants to come to see you. Would you like that? Klaus is coming up from Boston on Sunday. He will stay for dinner. Clara, look at me. You are here. You are safe. Look at me."

But Clara never answered. She sat like a figure at Madame Tussaud's; but she was so gaunt, so dead, that those clever wax imitations seemed far more sparked with life than she. And Sabra, who clung to hope because she had no firmer life-line, felt her grasp weaken and go slack. Hope was futile. Clara had been damned to this living death through some malicious whim of an inscrutable God. He had cast them out and turned His face against them.

"You must pray, Mrs. Blood," said Miss Lewis. "Come now and kneel with me. You do not need to go to church to ask God's love. Let us pray together, now, and beg God for her recovery."

She put a tentative hand on Sabra's arm. Instantly Sabra threw it off. "Damn God!" she cried. Miss Lewis pulled away; the horrified expression on her face goaded Sabra to cry out again. "Damn God!" Even in her anguish, her desolation, she paused to listen for the thunderbolt which would strike her down. It did not come. "He does not deserve my prayers! He has done this awful thing for no reason at all, He has as good as killed her, and you ask me to pray to Him! I will never pray to Him again!"

Day after day she sat by her child; and she wept all the nights; and she waited.

26

The people of Lowell, once past the initial horror of their reaction to the Pemberton disaster, agreed among themselves that if such a thing had to happen, it was lucky for them that it happened in Lawrence. Such a tragedy gave a place a bad name. The citizens of Lowell were well aware that visitors no longer trooped through the cotton factories, marveling at the benevolence of the entrepreneurs; the bloom had gone off the rose, and the mills on the banks of the Merrimack were no longer one of the wonders of the civilized world. But if they had fallen from the state of grace in which they had lived for the first quarter-century of the city's existence, at least (so they assured themselves) we are not yet like the English; we are not even like Lawrence, where mills collapse and crush the operatives to death.

No one knew exactly how many Lowell women had gone to Lawrence to work on the Pemberton. Except for two, all of them had been Irish, and the Irish were slippery: no one could keep a proper accounting of them. The two Americans, of course, were soon known throughout the city: Alice Harvey, who had died; and Clara Blood, who seemed to live. The people of Lowell would have made a heroine of Clara, had she been able to respond to them. As it was, they gossiped about her condition, which was poor, and about her prospects, which seemed poorer still; and a few of them, whether from curiosity or compassion, called to visit with her and see for themselves how she did. They brought small presents; they stood awkwardly before her, fumbling for some polite and cheerful thing to say, their sensibilities badly shocked by the sight of her haunted face, her listless, unresponding demeanor. They did not stay long; they paid their respects to her and then they went away, leaving behind a pot of plum jam, or a pretty embroidered pin-cushion, or a nicely framed view of some pleasant rural scene.

Sabra let them in. She hardly wanted her daughter to become a public spectacle, but surely, she thought, it cannot hurt to let them look in on her, and say a kind word or two. And perhaps one of them will move her to react—to speak, even to nod. So she welcomed them, the few who came; she was aware of their mixed motives, but she did not mind. If the sight of new people will help her, she thought, I will have the entire city parading through.

One of those who came was Patrick O'Haran. He appeared on the doorstep one cool and breezy August evening with a copy of *Godey's* under his arm and a bouquet of roses in his hand.

"Well, Sabra," he said, smiling in his practiced way, "I wanted to see how she's doin'."

She stared at him in disbelief. All these years, she thought, he has known where we live, how we live—he has always known everything that happened in this city, from the time he delivered for Codwell and came to gossip with me in the Bradshaws' kitchen. But that friendly, open boy had been a different person altogether from this self-possessed, hard-looking man. How old is he, she wondered. A year or two younger than I? Thirty-six or -seven, then. A man in the prime of life: not wealthy, perhaps, but as far above his beginnings as an Irishman could reasonably hope to get. He did not even look Irish any more. He wore a sober brown frock coat and a well-tied gray cravat, and his shoes were polished to a high shine with not a speck of Acre mud upon them.

He walked into the narrow hall and with one glance took in the circumstances of her life. In the dining room the boarders were finishing their supper. Through the open door to her apartment, he saw Clara sitting in a chair by the window. The room was in shadow; Clara had sat alone while Sabra served the meal, and the lamp had not yet been lit. Clara seemed never to care whether she sat in darkness or in light. Sabra had asked her, once, if she preferred a lamp at twilight; but the girl had made no reply and Sabra had not asked again.

Patrick paused, still holding his offerings. He looked closely at Sabra. "I hear she's not recoverin'," he said. "She wasn't hurt, but she had a kind of shock."

Even in her amazement at his having come, Sabra registered the sound of his voice, the lilting cadence which belied his sober, Yankeefied presence. That was the voice she remembered from the half-starved delivery boy: and, later, from the angry, bitter young man who told her of Biddy's ruin. He was kind to come to see us, she thought. She wondered if he had married after all. "Yes," she said. She motioned him in. "Dr. Spencer says that she can hear us, she can understand us, but she cannot break out to answer." She bent over her daughter and touched her shoulder. "Clara? Here is an old friend of mine. I knew him years ago when you were small, and even before you were born."

Patrick pulled up a straight chair and sat close in front of Clara so that he could look into her wasted face. If he was shocked or repelled by what he saw there, he gave no sign. He spoke to her quietly, in an unforced, friendly way; he did not gawk or stutter as some of her visitors did, unnerved by her unfocused, inward-turning stare.

Sabra lit the lamp on the center table. She needed to get back to her boarders, to clear away the dishes and wash up; but just for a moment she stood by the door of her small parlor and looked at the two figures sitting there, and she wondered at Patrick's ease, at the self-possession which allowed him so easily to confront the poor damaged soul before him. He talks to her as if they were old friends, she thought; she has not had a visitor who is so calm, who accepts so naturally what she is and does not let it anguish him to the point where he cannot speak. Perhaps she will understand. Perhaps he will be the one to break the bond which holds her. For a moment, just before she turned away, she allowed her heart to lift free from its heavy burden and soar to tentative hope. Speak to him, she urged. O Clara, speak!

Later, when she had done with her work, she put Clara to bed; then she sat with Patrick, breathing in the heavy fragrance of the roses, and tried to make the acquaintance, so to speak, of this new man. He was as thin as ever, his brown hair as carefully combed. But his face was lined now with years of worry and work, and his eyes held a coldness, a wary look of having seen too many unpleasant things, that contrasted oddly with his still-beguiling speech.

"I'm sorry, Sabra," he said. "It's hard, seein' her like that. They told me about it, but I couldn't believe it till I saw her myself. It was a terrible thing that happened. Terrible. Did you go there to fetch her? Annie Rourke's girl was killed that night, and she never found her for three days. They pulled her out in pieces."

I will never get free of that night, she thought; and I had not the worst of it. It was no wonder that Clara had—not lost her mind, no—but that she had retreated so far from the threat of death that she could not find her way back.

"Well," he said. "There's nothin' can bring them back, poor souls. I hear the Corporation's buildin' again. They'll get plenty of hands to work when they're ready to start up. Folks don't have any choice. Well. How're you doin' here, Sabra? I heard you were livin' with the Dutchman until he lost his place when the theater burned. Why didn't you go West when they left?"

I will not ask, she thought. I do not want to know. Klaus was nearly killed because he printed certain information. I do not want to know where he got it. "I wanted to earn my own way," she said. "I thought that I could do so here. I was not sure of it there."

He nodded; he looked around the room. Muslin curtains hung at the windows; an inexpensive Bigelow carpet covered the floor; the furniture was plain but decent, with a good cherry Windsor chair by the fire and a pretty pattern covering the small sofa.

"You own this place outright?"

"Yes."

He gave a grudging smile of admiration. "Old man kick off?"

"How did you—" They laughed together then; they began to feel at ease. Soon she found the words to ask him how he prospered. He shrugged and smiled.

"Well enough," he said. "Folks always need to eat, so groceries is a better business than ribbons and ruffles." Although he did not say so, he had spent little time at the store in late years. His younger brothers had taken over its management, leaving him free for—well, for more important work. Nor did he spend Sunday afternoons drilling with the Jackson Militia: such pastimes seemed child's play now. He had given himself over to a more demanding discipline. Like Klaus Hartmann, he had begun to travel, to meet and work with others who shared his dream. It, too, was a dream of freedom: not for four million black slaves, but for two millions of his own countrymen who starved and suffered under British rule.

Like that of many transplanted Irish, the logic of his growing hatred toward England was simple and direct. The sons of England—the Anglo-Saxon "native" Americans—hated Irish immigrants more than the English at home hated those Irish who had stayed. At least in London or Birmingham or Liverpool an Irish priest could walk the streets without fear of being beaten half to death. Here in America, many people rode priests out of town tarred and feathered on a rail: the latest such incident had happened only the previous month in Ellsworth, Maine. So one could not escape, it seemed: the new land held no hope of freedom from British oppression. And therefore (so the argument went, night after night in crowded, high-tempered meetings thick with the fog of conspiracy) the fight must be taken up again on Irish soil. The forty-eighters had failed there, as their brethren had failed on the Continent; their leaders fled to exile, imprisoned, murdered by British troops. Now a new rising must be planned, fed at first by arms and money from far-flung points around the world, and then in time—soon: very soon—brought home to make the revolution which would throw off forever the hated English rule.

Already he had personally collected over a thousand dollars for the cause. He had helped to build a network of sympathizers all over eastern Massachusetts. Like the labor organizers of an earlier day, he had traveled ceaselessly from town to factory town, to wherever there was an enclave of Irish. They were everywhere, those orphans of the famine: there was not a factory in New England, now, that did not run on Irish labor. But they were hardly assimilated; they felt too keenly the contempt and hatred of the ruling Anglo-Saxons. And so it needed only a clever speaker (and what Irishman was not?) to stir their feelings, to loosen their purse-strings for the secret plotters. Fenians, these men called themselves, after the legendary *Fianna,* the warriors of Fionn MacCumhaill. Patrick O'Haran was one of their most valuable men. They had promised him that soon—very soon, within the year, perhaps—he would be called back to Ireland. He had proved himself as a skilled organizer in America; when the time is right, they said, you will organize on Irish soil.

Already he had begun to make his plans to leave. His family was well provided for. His mother, widowed a second time, would be tended comfortably by his brothers' wives. Thanks to the income from the store, there was no shortage of money. When the time came, he would go. He wanted only to be given a few days' notice. Give me three or four days, he had said to the men in Boston who directed him. There's somethin' I must do before I leave. After that, I'm with you for good.

But he spoke of none of this to Sabra on that August evening, nor on any of the subsequent evenings when he returned. He was not a sentimental man, nor even a very kindly one. But he saw in Clara the living testimony to all that he had come to despise in the new land where once he had hoped to make his fortune and live happily ever after. Well: he had made enough, if not a fortune; but the happiness had eluded him. He had given up trying to understand why. He understood only that irreconcilable hatred lived on both sides, Yankee and Irish. It would not die in his lifetime. Meanwhile he had his work to do, and visiting this poor girl was part of it. She fed his hatred; she was a living victim of the enemy.

Sabra was glad of his visits. Not many people came, now: the summer passed and autumn drew on and the novelty of Clara's condition wore off. Miss Lewis was faithful, of course, and Klaus came three times from Boston. None of the Hartmanns traveled east, after all: Jutta was pregnant, and so they stayed in Wisconsin and sent monthly letters instead. Faithfully she read them aloud to Clara, but they struck no spark. Not even Rachel Bradshaw, whose visits had once been a matter of such interest, was able to awaken her. Rachel came especially to see Clara; she spent a half-hour with her, talking to her, holding her hands, and then she turned away in anguish, unable to bear any further sight of the child whose promised blooming had moved Rachel to ask to have her. "She is a living testament to their greed," she said; unlike Patrick O'Haran, she could not bear to contemplate that knowledge.

In the country at large, the fall of the Pemberton Mill receded into history. New items gripped the national attention. A presidential campaign took place; the Republican candidate was elected. Outraged, the Southern states began to secede from the Union, South Carolina led the way. The Northern manufacturers—the old "Cotton Whigs"—watched in rising alarm: if the South could not be placated, profits might fall or even stop altogether. Such an event was unthinkable. They conferred anxiously among themselves; they scrambled for cover in the face of the growing storm. At last they hit upon a plan: they would send a delegation, they said, to treat with the Southern firebrands and beg them to reconsider. Surely some solution might be worked out.

In April, 1861, William Appleton and a party of friends boarded the steamer *Nashville* in New-York harbor and cruised down the eastern seaboard to Charleston harbor. But he was too late. Even as the ship lay to off the bar beyond the harbor, Confederate troops attacked the federal installation at Fort Sumter, bombarding it from shore; and so without ever having had a chance to make peace, the Northern delegation turned and fled in the face of war.

27

Poor Bradshaw, people said. He looks very bad: has he been ill?

He was sixty-four years old. He had spent a lifetime supervising the manufacture of cotton cloth. Through bad times and good; through years of panic and years of full production; from the days of genteel Yankee girls through the times of labor unrest and into the present, when the Irish were everywhere and the Yankee girls a distant memory: for all those years he had ruled the Commonwealth Mill, and never a complaint had come from Boston. He had done his job well. No Corporation in Lowell had had profits equal to the Commonwealth's; its owners had made back their investments ten—twenty!—times over. They could not have done so without him. He had worked as faithfully as ever a man did. And so now, in the summer of 1861, he presented to the world a haggard face and a slowed walk and eyes that did not focus instantly upon you as once they had done. He was not ill: but he had worn himself out in his service to his employers.

They had proved to be singularly ungrateful. Ten days after the attack on Fort Sumter, when the new President had issued a call for volunteers and the supply of cotton had been seemingly shut off, a few key directors of the Corporation had ordered that production be stopped. Every textile factory in New England was frantic for raw cotton; and so we will sell the Commonwealth's supply at an exorbitant price, they said, and make a greater profit than if we manufactured cloth. We have a million pounds of it and more stored in the sheds. Sell it to Manchester and Lawrence, to Fall River and Chicopee! This so-called "war" will not last six months. We will bid on this summer's crop and by next January we will be back to full production. But now, this year, our greatest profit will come from selling our raw cotton, not manufacturing it.

When the directors' decision was announced to Bradshaw, he did something that he had never done before: he protested. He argued with his employers in Boston, he warned them not to make this fatal mistake. If you close down the works and dismiss the operatives, he said, we will lose all our skilled hands. They will go elsewhere to find work. Only the unskilled will stay. For ten years and more, my overseers have trained up these miserable Irish, taught them to follow directions, to have some sense of order and discipline and steady habits. Some of them are very good hands—not as good as the Americans, but reasonably dependable.

When you start up the mill next winter, you will have only the least skilled hands left to employ. It will take years to bring production up to the level we have now. Listen to me: keep the factory running!

They ignored him. He has Agented the Commonwealth for a long time, they said; too long, perhaps. He is an old man. Perhaps, when we start up again, we will need to have a new Agent in his place. Old Saunders' nephew is a charming gentleman, well liked by everyone. Perhaps he could be persuaded to take the job.

And so Bradshaw had been ignored, and he had given the order down the chain of command: everyone dismissed.

The great water wheel in the basement was stilled; the bells no longer tolled the daily schedule. The factory stood silent and deserted. Only a few stray mice and rats scuttled across the empty yard. Wind moaned around the red-brick corners of the buildings and whipped the weather vane—a gilded shuttle—atop the white-painted belfry; and now, with the machinery stopped, it seemed a very loud sound. Never since the first day that production began, in October, 1823, had the Commonwealth been so quiet; even on the Sabbath, there had always been a crew of mechanics in one building or another, fixing a broken mule spinner, realigning the shafting. But no one came now save two watchmen, one for the day shift and one for the night. They routinely walked their rounds, trying the locked doors; but most of the time they sat in the empty storage shed and slept. There was a better watchman than they on duty, most times: they did not need to be too careful.

They could see him through the small-paned windows of his office. He sat in a straight-backed chair; sometimes he stood at the windows staring out into the yard. They avoided him. They were not exactly afraid of him, but he had a strange look about him, like a man whose mind is elsewhere even as he nods and says good morning. Once in a while he would take the keys and walk across the yard and unlock the door to one of the buildings. They watched him as he went: a tall, stooped figure moving with unwonted slowness. They remembered the way in which he had walked formerly, with a long, purposeful stride, his face alert to all the complexities of his job. Now his face was closed and locked, even as the mill.

He did not know what to do with himself. Like the Corporation's directors in Boston, he had been kept on full salary, and so, unlike his hapless operatives, he did not need to look elsewhere for work to stay alive. But how was he to pass the time until the factory started up again? He paid a visit to the reading room at the Mechanics' Institute, but he was not interested in reading. He went to see his daughter Lydia on Sunday afternoons; he did not want to intrude upon her further. Besides, he did not like her husband. He thought to call upon his fellow Agents at the other Corporations in the city, but he no longer knew many of them. The men with whom he had dined at Matthew Munson's years ago had all gone away, or died. Their replacements, new, younger men, no longer gathered at the publisher's table. Munson's value to his Corporate masters now was in his role as a representative in the legislature: there, a few years previous, he had supervised the distribution of thousands of dollars in Corporation bribes given to key men to persuade them to vote against a Ten-Hour bill. But he himself no longer needed to be bribed with the presence of Corporation Agents at his dinner table, for he was safely their creature forever.

After the announcement of the Commonwealth's closing, the other factories in the city, all governed by interlocking directorates, had shut down as well. Nine Corporations closed: fifteen thousand operatives and more were dismissed. The Corporate directors in Boston gave no more thought to these poor creatures than they would have given to a swarm of flies brushed away from the carcass of a horse.

In the Acre, that summer, hard times came back with a vengeance. For many people it was the famine all over again, but here in their festering slum they did not even have a patch of earth to plant. The priests began to take up collections for the most destitute; anyone with anything extra —food, clothing, money—was soon shamed into giving more than he thought he could afford. Patrick O'Haran was a natural target. He came upon Father Crudden one broiling afternoon as he walked down Central Street; he had not been to Mass for a month, and he saw that the priest—a County Mayo man—was angry with him.

"Will y' be comin' to see us soon, *Mister* O'Haran, if it won't trouble you too much?"

They stood in the shade of the awning and squinted at each other in the reflected glare from the dusty street.

"Sure, Father. I'll be there on Sunday."

"*If* it won't trouble you. We don't want to interfere with your busy schedule, now do we? Not even to save you from the flames of Hell, now do we?" The priest turned away with an exaggerated gesture worthy of Junius Brutus Booth himself; then, as if he had just thought of a final word, he turned back. "And I'll tell you now, *Mister* O'Haran, that I'll expect a fine large contribution from you, food as well as money, for the relief fund. I know where you've been, I know who you collect money for. Murderers. But here and now we've people hungry. So stay at home now for a while, and help us here. There's no work for anyone—no hope of work. A lot of the lads will enlist, but even so. I'll send around to the store," he said, "and I'll tell your brothers you approved."

Patrick watched him go. Let him take what he wants, he thought. The store was no more concern of his. He had waited a long time for a certain message, and only yesterday it had come. And so when Father

Crudden gave his foodstuffs to the Acre's hungry, he, Patrick, would not be there to see. He would be away. Probably, as Father Crudden had warned, he was condemning his soul to Hell. He did not care. He no longer worried about the Church's Hell. If in the end he went there, he would have ample company. In the meantime, he was not content to spend his life behind the counter of a grocery store in Lowell; nor would he throw it away in the stupid war between Northern Anglo-Saxon and Southern Anglo-Saxon. Whichever side won, they were no friend to the Irish. No: he had more important—more exciting—work to do across the water.

And before he went away, one task here remained. Later that afternoon, he called at a tenement where lived a man named Finnerty; this man had a night job, he did not leave for it until a quarter to six. Patrick had plenty of time to explain what he needed.

The red-brick town baked in the midsummer sun. It seemed a town struck by plague—by sudden death. The sound of the working mills—the steady rumble and thump of machines—which had for so long formed an accustomed undertone to the town's activity was no longer heard; and now people were uneasily aware of the silence, even as new arrivals had once uncomfortably heard the noise. Some shops were boarded up already, their owners decamped to more profitable places; most of the Corporation boarding houses were as locked and empty as the mills; the water in the canals lay stagnant, a thick green slime already beginning to cloud the surface. The only bells heard now were church bells; the only machines, the looms of the Middlesex Mills, where the owner, Ben Butler, a new-minted general with good political connections, had got a contract for woolen uniforms for the Union Army.

Far away to the south, "Stonewall" Jackson had earned his soubriquet at the first Bull Run, and those Northerners who had been confident of an early end to the conflict were now forced to think again. Many Massachusetts boys were killed that day, some of them from Lowell; and so to the silence of the empty mills and deserted streets came the heavier silence of mourning in homes where Death had called.

28

Finnerty walked across the mill yard, his bull's-eye lantern shining faintly beside him as he went. He did not need it: he carried it because he had been told to carry it. A full moon sailed high over the black rooftops of the mill buildings which encircled the yard like the battlements of a castle. Finnerty had seen a castle once, in County Galway, and it had been as silent and deserted as these buildings were now. Despite the warmth of the summer night, despite the heat still rising from the hard-packed dirt under his boots, Finnerty shivered. Enough to give a man a proper fright, this place was now. He didn't like it. He thought that before the cold weather came, since he had no wife or child to hold him, he might enlist for the war and send the bounty pay over to his ma.

As the church bells struck ten, he approached the gate and silently slid back the wicket.

"He's in."

The man outside made no reply. As soon as Finnerty had opened the gate, he slipped inside. Finnerty locked up again behind him.

"Where?"

Finnerty pointed to a building across the yard. "Number Three." Black rectangles formed patterns on the ground; the moon shone bright enough to read a newspaper. Number Three was as dark as the others: a high facade of darkened windows. Through some of them could be seen moonlight shining in from the windows opposite, facing the river.

With Finnerty leading the way, the two men walked along the buildings instead of straight across the yard. When they reached the door of Number Three, Finnerty handed the lantern to his companion. Silently he produced a ring of keys; he inserted one of them into the lock and turned it. Metal grated on metal; the sound seemed loud enough to wake the dead. They listened, tensed to retreat. After a moment they breathed again. Cautiously the watch pushed open the door and stepped aside to let the other pass.

Inside, as the door closed silently behind him, Patrick stood at the foot of the narrow, curving stairway, his eyes adjusting to the deeper darkness, his ears listening for the sound that he needed to direct him. Through an open door he saw a long room filled with machines. Moonlight flooded through tall windows. He took a soundless step to the doorway; he looked into every corner of the room. Not here. Soundlessly he stepped back. He had never been inside this mill, or any other. He needed quickly to learn its arrangements. He began to climb the stairs.

In the fourth-floor weaving room, the Agent Bradshaw stood by a window on the river side. Although his face was turned to the glass he did not see the black-and-white landscape spread below him: the shallow water of the river glistening in the moonlight; the exposed rocks of the river bed lying like bleached bones; the dark line of the opposite shore; the lightened sky, here and there the pin-point of a star pale beside the brilliant circle riding high. Nor did he hear the silence all around him: the silence of stopped works, of shut-off production. In the workroom of his mind, he heard the familiar noise of the machines, the clash and clatter of the looms, back and forth, up and down, a mind-shattering din louder now than ever in life.

How many years in these buildings! How many thousands of lives in his control, even as he was controlled by Boston. Once upon a time he had seen the future bright before him: a beautiful, obedient wife; good employment; plenty of acquaintances to fill his house whenever he liked; the hope of a son to succeed him. Somehow things had gone wrong. He did not understand why. He had been unable to control every event in his life. Only in the factory, it seemed, had he ruled absolutely—and even there he had been confronted by unruly women, or slow-witted Irish, or outside agitators come to stir up trouble. But he had survived them all. And now, after so many years, his defeat had come from the only possible place: from above. From Boston. From a group of smart money men who knew nothing of running a factory. From a selfish, greedy, shortsighted cabal who neither knew nor cared about the long-range consequences of their actions.

He turned his face as if he listened to some new sound: or perhaps at last he was simply trying to escape the noise inside his head. He was a man in a dream; he could not wake. As vividly as in a dream, faces flashed across his mind's eye. They were faces from another time. He was content—glad, even—to see them. His life in recent years had been so lonely that he was grateful for even this shadowy company. Fascinated, he watched as they came and went: Sophia's face, and Amalia's, and Rachel's face when she had been eighteen. And another: the face of a servant-girl who had briefly given him his dearest wish. At the time, when the child had died, he had not thought that he could continue to live. It had been impossible for him to see the girl. His conscience had tormented him: you must go to her. She gave herself to you, and now you reject her.

I cannot. My grief is too great.

And what of hers? Do you not think that she is mad with grief? She has lost her child and you as well.

I cannot. I cannot see her ever again. I did her great harm and I have been punished for it.

Standing now at the tall window, he shook his head and felt his body shudder with the memory of his desolation. He put out his hand to steady himself. The inside of his cheek was raw where he had chewed it. His head cleared. He knew where he was. He looked down. A man would die if he jumped from such a height. Moved by a sudden impulse, he tugged at the sash. It did not give; the windows had been nailed shut since the day the factory was built.

The sound of the machines came up in his mind again like an orchestra on cue. Thus he did not hear the footstep at the door. He stood facing the river, listening, and so he did not hear the small sound as a moving foot accidentally hit the iron frame of a power loom.

Like the landscape outside, the weaving room was a study in black and white. The shapes of the machines standing silent in long rows formed an intricate and beautiful pattern, dark against the whitewashed walls. The two animate forms spoiled the design. One of them moved quickly now, while the other, leaning against the window, seemed at last to hear the warning footstep, and so now he moved in reaction; but he was a moment too late.

"Finnerty?" Bradshaw heard his voice come harsh and dry from his throat, just like any cotton operative's. He had hardly spoken to anyone for days; his voice was as rusty as an unused spinning jenny.

The intruder's face was in shadow; Bradshaw could not see who it was. But now the man moved in close, and the moonlight caught a gleam of metal flashing from his hand.

Bradshaw veered to the side as the man came at him. He knew that he could not turn his back and run, for he was old now, past running. In his confusion he did not yet understand that this was not his employee.

"Finnerty!"

He backed along the aisle between the windows and the first row of looms. The intruder's face was plain now as he came into the cold and brilliant light streaming from the windows. Not Finnerty. Bradshaw had no idea who. He saw the knife clenched tight in the hand. From the corner of his eye he saw that he had reached an intersecting aisle. Still facing, he turned on his heel and began to back down it, keeping his hands outstretched, lightly touching the machinery to balance himself. And as they moved into darkness, he heard his own voice again.

"Stop! Tell me what you want!"

He noted with satisfaction that he was not afraid. It was not a question of being brave: rather, he felt a curious sense of the inevitable, of acting out a play whose conclusion he already knew. Even as he moved he felt a sense of having overstayed his time.

Back, back—he felt his shoulder strike a pillar. Careful. He came to another main aisle: the central one which led directly to the stairway door. If he turned and ran, he might have a chance. It occurred to him that the stranger could have rushed him by now, had he wanted to. Instead he was taking his time. Why? Who was he? Why had he come here, why did he engage in this slow-moving game when in three steps he could have the knife home?

Bradshaw knew the ending, but he did not know his fellow player. Death, of course: Death come at last to find him. But in whose person?

"Get over by the light again, Mr. Bradshaw."

The sound of the quiet, steady voice frightened him terribly; the reply coming so long after his own words startled him more terribly still.

"Go on."

An Irishman. Probably one of the hands thrown out of work by the shutdown. He knew the end of the play, he knew that it was pointless to argue. Still: perhaps some arguing was called for. Death was not an unwelcome visitor, but like everyone else he must be made to work to reap his harvest. He edged past the intruder, back to the window aisle. Again he saw the flashing of the blade. Finnerty must be dead, he thought, or he would have come to help me. Finnerty was a loyal, trustworthy man, devoted to the Corporation. He would never betray it, no matter that the Corporation had betrayed him and all his kind.

He stopped with his back to the window and peered at the white face staring at him. It spoke again: "Go down on your knees."

The habits of a lifetime are not easily put by. Bradshaw was unaccustomed to hearing in such an accent any but subservient tones, and so now at last he bristled; he felt his long thin lips draw down to an expression of stern disapproval. He remained standing.

The intruder came close; his face was in full light now. Bradshaw stared at him.

"I said go down, damn you."

"No."

The man's face was tense, very angry, but completely in control. He held the knife in his right hand, its blade pointed at Bradshaw's stomach. Suddenly the hand moved and Bradshaw felt the tip of the blade pressing against his waistcoat. The intruder's face was not a hand's breadth from his own.

"You owe me two lives."

No stench of whiskey, no wavering of the eye, no tremor in the voice. The man was killing cold sober.

Why?

The left hand moved then; it went to the pocket of the rough and shapeless jacket that covered the man's thin shoulders. It pulled out something else that shone: a small golden disc like a miniature sun. The left hand held it high, while the right kept the knife pressing close.

"Your daughter's life, Mr. Bradshaw. You gave me this for saving it."

Bradshaw's eyes followed the gleaming coin. Again his memory reached back: Lydia had gone through the ice and a smart, quick lad had saved her. Bradshaw could not recall the boy's face. Was this he? The boy had been Irish, he remembered that well enough. Yes: he had gone to Codwell's to pay him. It had been a fair reward; he remembered that the lad had been very pleased.

He could think of nothing to say. Except—

Heavy clouds passed over the moon; the light dimmed. In the darkness the man's face was only a white blur. The coin no longer gleamed.

Bradshaw felt the moments of his life slipping away, although not a drop of his blood had yet escaped him.

Except—

"And the other?"

The blade penetrated with amazing speed. It went clean into him; it kept on going until it hit his spine.

"The girl you ruined."

Bradshaw sagged a little; he felt the other support him with his left hand, even as he twisted the blade with his right. They stood very close; they might have been lovers locked in an embrace.

He sagged again, more heavily now, more difficult to hold. He felt the pain of the wound; he heard a harsh sound which he knew to be his dying breath. The knife stayed in him, twisting, until the end.

Patrick left him where he lay, soaked in a pool of his blood; then he hurried downstairs in the dark. When he got out into the mill yard he whistled softly to his friend. There were no shadows now, no dark rectangles forming patterns on the ground: only a general blackness. Finnerty came on, bobbing his little lantern. He held it up to see Patrick's face; his own was apprehensive.

"Was he angry I let you in?"

"No. Not a bit." Patrick saw Finnerty's eyes travel down to where the knife, no longer shining, rested in his hand. Then Finnerty's eyes returned to meet his own. This time Patrick did not engage in dialogue: a swift thrust in and out and Finnerty lay dead on the ground, his bull's-eye clattering down beside him, the flame guttered out.

"Easier so, lad," whispered Patrick. "Easier so. Else they'd think you did his nibs, and they'd give you no end of trouble."

Toward morning, a light rain began to fall; and at six o'clock, when the day watch arrived, he came in to a steady downpour. He knew at once that there had been trouble, for the gate was unlocked. He stood in the pouring rain, staring down at poor Finnerty, and it was more than a minute or two before he saw that the door to Number Three stood partly open. He did not stop to investigate; he ran to fetch the police, and so it was they who came at last upon the body of the Agent Bradshaw.

They carried him out in the rain; they took him into his office and laid him on the couch. Already he was quite stiff. Certain robbery, they said: look at his hand. They tried without success to pry open his fingers, which were tightly curled around what looked to be an old-fashioned five-dollar gold-piece. Certain robbery, sure enough; it was not until late afternoon that someone pointed out the fallacy in their logic, and by that time they were so frustrated in their investigations that they simply rebuffed this new difficulty. Robbery, they said, and that's that.

As the days passed and the murderer remained at large, the police kept coming up against the fact that Patrick O'Haran, the owner of Codwell's West India Store, had not been seen in the city since the day before the murder. He traveled often, they knew, but never before had he been gone so long. Father Crudden had been one of the last to speak to him, and he kept his opinions to himself and gave the police only fragmentary facts. Patrick's family were not alarmed; he went to New-York to see a friend, they said. Look for him there.

Bradshaw was buried in the Lowell Cemetery, a green and peaceful Eden of marble statues and rolling hills and valleys and winding gravel paths. His widow, heavily swathed in mourning, said nothing to anyone; several weeks later she sold the large white house on Belvidere Hill to a physician with a quantity of offspring and went to live with her stepdaughter. It was not lost upon people that never once, from that time until her death five years later, did she visit her husband's grave. Shocking, people said; what a cold-blooded woman she is.

When the Commonwealth Mill started up production again, after the war, old Saunders' personable nephew was hired to Agent it. And before so much as a single bale of cotton was taken to the carding room, he ordered two second hands to sand the floor where it had been stained by his predecessor's blood. The second hands worked for an entire day, and then they reported that the stain had gone too deep: it could not be removed. And so a bucket of black paint was brought in, and the entire floor was painted over. And when it dried, the raw, new operatives flocked to their places to learn their jobs, and production, slow and halting, began again.

29

Two letters came for Sabra, brought from the post office by the faithful Miss Lewis on an oppressively warm and thundery afternoon in late August. Of all her tenants, Miss Lewis alone remained; all the others, discharged when the city closed down for the duration, had gone elsewhere to look for work. Soon, no doubt, Miss Lewis would go as well.

She opened the first letter: from Anna, not from Adolph. Thus she had not recognized the handwriting.

August 12, 1861

Dear Sabra,

Adolph asked me to write to you. He could not do it, but he wanted you to have the news.

Klaus was killed three weeks ago in Virginia. His father had a letter from the Captain. It was a bullet through the heart. He did not suffer. We bury him here.

If Clara can travel, will you come out to us?

With love from us all,
Anna

For a long time, Sabra sat in her small parlor listening to the thunder, the letter lying in her lap, her mind wandering free back to her memories of that brave, beautiful young man who once had loved her. But he had loved Mr. Garrison more. It had been better so. Had he been burdened with a wife and family, he would not have been free to work for—what? Freedom? Justice? Abstractions: meaningless sounds.

How did the death of one man ensure the freedom of another?

She did not understand war; nor the impulse to kill; nor the blood-lust running through the men and boys who marched to fight.

She heard the splattering rain; the air blew suddenly cool. She had no tears. She did not understand the need to kill: but the need to die—? Was that what Mr. Garrison inspired?

Klaus had come to her before he joined his regiment. He had looked touchingly young in his uniform of blue serge, and far too warm, perspiring in the unseasonable heat of the May afternoon. He had been excited, naturally enough: the light in his eyes reflected visions of a victory far away, and the timbre of his voice—familiar, comforting—was yet strange enough, anticipating the adventure to come, that more than once during his visit she had needed to remind herself that this was Klaus Hartmann before her, and not some impostor.

Too soon, before she was used to the sight of him, he had to go away. He put a small purse into her hands.

"My money," he said, smiling down at her. "Keep it for me until I come back. And if I do not—"

"No!" she cried, and silenced him with the reflexive gesture of her hands, the terror in her eyes. Dear God! There had been enough death, enough suffering and loss. He must not tempt Fate by speaking so.

"It is yours," he finished.

He held out his arms, then, and she entered their shelter for a moment and put her head on his chest and bit her lips to keep from crying. Dry-eyed, she had seen him off; and all that night she had wept, certain that she would not see him again. But at least I sent him away with no tears to burden him, she thought. That is women's function in a war: a facade of bravery, telling lies to their men.

And now she had no more tears for him when he was gone. She stared at the small, familiar room, remembering the sight of him sitting in the Windsor chair, the sound of his voice in the silence of her life.

Miss Lewis had gone upstairs. Toward evening she came down to help with supper and found Sabra still in her dream. Miss Lewis lit the lamp; she looked in on Clara and saw that she was asleep. Sabra seemed to rouse herself, then, and she took the second envelope lying on the table and opened it.

Dear Sabra,

Again, I apologize for stopping so briefly after Father's funeral. Much has happened since I returned to New-York. As you see from the return address, I am now in Washington. There is work to be done here. Will you come? Sell your house if you can, or leave it to Mr. Spring to attend to. You will starve there for want of boarders, but I can get you paid employment here in a government office. And by all means bring Clara. I have recently met a doctor here who says he can help her. Let me hear from you by return post.

Rachel

30

They stood at the Dutton Street depot, a trio of soberly clad females, two middle-aged, one young; the older two watched anxiously as the iron monster chuffed in and halted before them. It was the Nashua train: not theirs. They moved back, hustled aside by the guard: "Move away, missus, move away!"

A small commotion occurred within the train. Those who waited on the platform were aware of an unusual amount of delay in the disembarkation of the passengers who had taken tickets for Lowell.

At last a figure appeared at the door: an elegant lady of a certain age. She looked down at the waiting throng with an undisguised contempt. Directly over her green velvet shoulder could be seen the face of another lady, this one young, and beautiful in the ancient, aristocratic way as a piece of fine porcelain is beautiful, or a swan gliding on an artificial lake: hers was not an American look. And if in the gaze of this younger woman could be seen a distinct lack of enthusiasm for the heterogeneous crowd filling the platform, that was understandable, for this younger, so beautiful lady was the Princess Clotilde of Savoy, daughter of Victor Emmanuel II, King of Sardinia, now King of Italy. She blinked once, twice, as if to rouse herself; then, just before descending the narrow steps to the platform, she cast an unhappy glance to the man standing behind her, as if to say, "Must I really do this?"

Indeed she must. The lady-in-waiting went first, followed by the Princess, followed by the Prince: Jérôme Napoléon Bonaparte, nephew of Napoléon I and youngest son of Jérôme Bonaparte, recently dead, King of Westphalia long ago.

Since their names were not announced, the exact identity of these splendid ones was unknown to the crowd of ordinary Yankees. But it was obvious that personages of the very highest rank were progressing now toward the open barouche waiting in the street. A gentleman stood beside it: an American gentleman, a Lowell gentleman in fact, a gentleman with the highest connections to the manufacturing interests. It was his duty, this day, to escort the royal visitors through the city. He did not mind: there was little enough else to do now that the works had been shut down. The difficulty was that he had very little French, and the royal personages had even less English, so that communication was a chancy thing largely dependent on signs and grimaces.

The royal personages climbed into the barouche; the lady-in-waiting and their guide followed; and so they set off to tour the principal streets of the city.

The Prince's face was enigmatic: no one could have told what he was thinking. He had been forced to leave his beloved Paris because that fool, the duc d'Aumale, had taken amiss certain statements uttered by the Prince. A duel was threatened; the Prince had had to escape before it became necessary to fight it. But perhaps, he thought, he might benefit from such an excursion. He had consulted his friend Michel Chevalier, who twenty-five years ago had made the American tour and had written so eloquently of his experiences. Chevalier had recommended no American place so highly as Lowell. "*Incroyable,*" he said: "You will not believe the industry, the high moral tone, the beauty of the women." The Prince had looked forward to seeing such a Paradise.

Briskly they proceeded down Merrimack Street. It was ten o'clock in the morning. The boardwalks were deserted, the shops closed. Down John Street to the Boott Mill: a silent, empty shell. Around to the boarding houses on Kirk and Dutton streets: closed, boarded up, empty echoing rooms.

The Prince frowned. He was not amused at Chevalier's little joke. He muttered to himself. He cleared his throat and glanced at his wife. He was aware that in this silent, empty city, he and his party looked ridiculous: like latecomers to a fashionable ball which had been held the previous evening, which had gone on regardless of the Prince's absence.

Irritably he turned to his guide. *"Les femmes,"* he said. He could not remember the English. *"Ou sont tous les femmes—les belles?"*

The American gentleman, embarrassed, shrugged—a Gallic gesture—and spread his hands. In the cramped space of the open carriage, he tried to bow. "Thank you," he said. "Thank you, Highness. Driver—to the Falls!"

At the depot, the Boston train had arrived. Miss Lewis hovered anxiously. "Write to me," she said. "I will leave for my sister's this afternoon. Are you sure that you have her address?"

"I have it," said Sabra. She did not smile; but then again neither did she weep, and that, she thought, was a little triumph.

The carriage was crowded; people pressed in close on all sides. Miss Lewis embraced both of them and then fled to the safety of the platform. She waved and called good-by. The train pulled out and gathered speed. Sabra settled herself beside her child. No one seemed to notice Clara's unwonted stillness; they were all too absorbed in their own affairs. A number of young men in uniform were in the carriage; the sight of them, and the memory of Klaus, brought a painful spasm to Sabra's throat, a wrench to her closely held calm. She looked away; she stared at the passing countryside, green and gold in the bright September sun. Here and there a tree showed early scarlet. Soon winter would come again. The climate in Washington, no doubt, would be considerably milder. She relaxed a little, growing used to the unaccustomed sensation of being borne along at such an improbable speed, enjoying the rackety vibrations of the iron wheels on the tracks.

She had been looking out the window, enjoying herself. Automatically she glanced at Clara. What if she became upset—frightened—by this strange new experience? Underneath the brim of her bonnet, Clara's face was immobile: lovely and still, the eyes staring unseeing. No flicker of recognition showed.

The railway carriage rocked and swayed; the warning bell clanged the alarm as they sped through a crossing. Sabra reached out to take her daughter's hand, to reassure her, to comfort her.

Slowly, as if in sleep, Clara turned her face. Her eyes met her mother's. The train rattled on through the green country, away from the factory town by the great river, the place which had given them grudging shelter for so many long and weary years.

I am mistaken, thought Sabra. She did not move: it was only the carriage jolting her. But her eyes clung to Clara's face, her hands grasped Clara's limp and unresisting hands.

I am mistaken, she thought again. I am seeing wrong. Still she looked, hope leaping up, reason denying it, hope and love refusing to die.

She looked.

And in that moment, Clara looked back. Her mouth curved up; her eyes registered her mother's presence. Her smile was the smile of the shyest child at the party, the newest, youngest pupil in the class: it held within it not joy so much as the anticipation of joy, not confidence so much as the absence of fear.

It was the break of dawn: a new beginning, an end to the night.

It was a human face now.

It was Clara come back again.

The train hurtled on into the bright day.